BOOKS BY GEOFF MICKS

Inca

Zulu

Beginning

Middle

End

Copyright

Acknowledgments

This book is for Paulette Micks.

I plan to write many more, and in a way they will all be for her. My mother is my greatest supporter and my harshest critic. She is my foundation. I love you, Mom.

This book has been blessed with the encouragement, generosity, and assistance of a team of friends and well-wishers. I could not possibly name them all, but particular mention should go to Seana Dawson, Chris Bourque, and Matt Cimone, people who have known of this work since its earliest days. Thanks as well to Leigh Beadon: His fresh eyes and brilliant mind guided a red pen through a stack of paper five inches thick to catch inconsistencies and embarrassments and nonsensical drivel that had escaped me time and again.

I'm grateful to David Fugate, who did his best to open doors and make things happen. I also need to praise Desiree Finhert and Jeremy Britton, two firm friends who have always been in my corner. A special thank you as well to Jillian Warring-Bird: After reading my manuscript we met at a Peruvian restaurant where she presented me with a winning literary bingo card with squares like 'Flood Scene' and 'Laugh Out Loud Moment.' Thanks also to Meghan Kelly, whose approval means a great deal to me. Finally, I'd like to thank my father, Terry Micks, whose simple comment, "This... This is like a real book," is all I could have ever asked for.

There are hundreds of others, of course. From teachers and authors to friends and total strangers, those of you who have helped me in thought or word or deed, thank you.

Any errors you find in these pages are mine and mine alone. Some are deliberate after much hand-wringing, and the rest are not for want of trying.

Cheers!

MAP

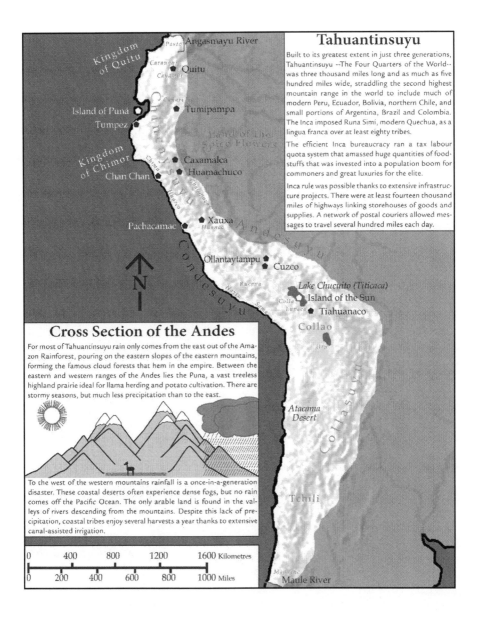

Tahuantinsuyu

Built to its greatest extent in just three generations, Tahuantinsuyu --The Four Quarters of the World-- was three thousand miles long and as much as five hundred miles wide, straddling the second highest mountain range in the world to include much of modern Peru, Ecuador, Bolivia, northern Chile, and small portions of Argentina, Brazil and Colombia. The Inca imposed Runa Simi, modern Quechua, as a lingua franca over at least eighty tribes.

The efficient Inca bureaucracy ran a tax labour quota system that amassed huge quantities of foodstuffs that was invested into a population boom for commoners and great luxuries for the elite.

Inca rule was possible thanks to extensive infrastructure projects. There were at least fourteen thousand miles of highways linking storehouses of goods and supplies. A network of postal couriers allowed messages to travel several hundred miles each day.

Cross Section of the Andes

For most of Tahuantinsuyu rain only comes from the east out of the Amazon Rainforest, pouring on the eastern slopes of the eastern mountains, forming the famous cloud forests that hem in the empire. Between the eastern and western ranges of the Andes lies the Puna, a vast treeless highland prairie ideal for llama herding and potato cultivation. There are stormy seasons, but much less precipitation than to the east.

To the west of the western mountains rainfall is a once-in-a-generation disaster. These coastal deserts often experience dense fogs, but no rain comes off the Pacific Ocean. The only arable land is found in the valleys of rivers descending from the mountains. Despite this lack of precipitation, coastal tribes enjoy several harvests a year thanks to extensive canal-assisted irrigation.

Please note there are glossaries of characters and terms at the end of the novel.

QUOTATIONS

"Explain your words so that I can understand them.

They are like a tangled skein.

You should put the threads in order for me."

-- Act 1, Scene I of the Quechua play Ollantay

"Tempus edax rerum."

Time, the devourer of all things.

-- Ovid

I am tired, Friar.

I am tired of you, and that shoddy brown robe you wear. I would not have given such an embarrassing rag to the poorest llama drover who ever worked my flocks.

I am tired of this thing we must do together before we have even begun. I used to savour a long and difficult task, but now I begrudge even the small annoyances of finding you parchment and ink. The scratching of your quill sets my teeth on edge. I would weep, but even a useless old man knows his tears will change nothing.

I begrudge the new reality that darkens the twilight of my life. I used to be able to guide the lives of millions of people with just a few balls of string, but now all I can do is sit here and speak to you in your clumsy tongue. My life's work is gone, and those squiggles you labour over shall produce my only lasting legacy.

I feel it in my bones. I am weary all the way down to the marrow. I ache where the monster of Time gnaws at me, swallowing my accomplishments, digesting all the people and places and things that I have ever loved. Time is relentless, unstoppable, and it devours all memory, some faster than others. When the monster voids its bowels, everything I care about vanishes into the emptiness and loneliness and stillness and silence that is to be forgotten forevermore.

I can see you don't understand, and your ignorance exhausts me. How can I make you see what I am trying to do? Speaking in Spanish is like trying to play the drum when all you have is a flute. It is a lover's language, and full of colourful obscenities, but it is not a proper medium for lofty discourse.

Do you know that the Inca chose a language that was not our own with which to rule our world? You call it Quechua, which is the name of an unimportant tribe of river people who live not too far from Cuzco. We call it Runa Simi, the Language of the People, and of all the tongues I have mastered I always marvel at Runa Simi's versatility, its capacity, its grace.

Take the word Pacha, Friar. Pacha means Time, Earth and Universe. You can tell which one a man means by the context, but it is always there in the back of your mind that Time and Earth and Universe are all one whole, inseparable from one another.

There is another word, Cuti, which means change, movement, alteration. A simple term, to be sure, but what happens when you put it together with a word that has three meanings that are the same thing seen from different angles? How do you translate Pachacuti, a thoroughly complex and beautiful word in my tongue, into your unimaginative language? Does it mean Earthquake? It does, but not always. Does it mean Change of Time? Yes, but what does that mean to you? It terrifies me, so I must find a better term than a mere Change of Time for Pachacuti.

Think of the world you know, Friar. Think of the reality of your life that wraps around you like a warm blanket. That is not the way things are. It is just the way things are right now. At any moment the world you know can stop, and a new and different world, unimaginable and unacceptable to you before, will begin. That is a Pachacuti. It is the end of one era and the beginning of another. It is the Apocalypse. One era ends and a new era begins. Do you see now?

One of our emperors even named himself Pachacuti so there would be no confusion: There was a time before him and a time after him, and during his reign the old world changed and a new world —the world that was divided into four quarters with each paying homage to the Inca— was born.

Your very presence here is because of a Pachacuti that clenches my heart and disturbs my dreams. My old eyes fog up with regrets sometimes, and when I try to blink them away I see flashes of what we were, and what we should have been long after my death. When I was a boy my people ruled. Today those few of us who survive bow to your kind, or we cower in the darkness of the hacha hacha, the cloying sticky jungles that are fit only for beasts and men prepared to act like beasts.

That was a Pachacuti. Our time is gone, and now I must spend my final days bitter and useless and defeated in your time. The world has changed, and not for the better. I am so tired of being helpless, of not being able to correct the great wrongs and injustices that have swept my world from Quitu to Tchili, from the never-ending ocean to the never-ending forest.

I have brought you here, Friar, to preserve some small part of all that I have lost. After a Pachacuti no one remembers what life was like before. What will the future remember of the past? Shaped stones, abandoned cities and dusty graves are no fit legacy for all that my people accomplished, but someday that will be all that remains unless I do something with the few days I have left to me.

It falls to me, or it will never be done. I am the only one left to do it. My kind ruled Tahuantinsuyu, an empire the size of which the world has never known. It was forged in the crucibles of war and diplomacy by grandfather, father, and son. I am related to all of them.

The first was Viracocha Inca, who took the name of our creator god as his own and then set out to earn such a title. The second was his son Pachacuti, a name whose implication I have already explained to you. He took the Imperial Red Fringe from his father's preferred son and defended Cuzco in its darkest hour, when Chanca invaders were about to reduce us to serfdom.

Pachacuti turned his victory into a war of expansion, pushing the edges of Tahuantinsuyu further than his father would have imagined possible before giving his armies to his son Topa Inca Yupanki. That grand old man stretched our Empire to almost its furthest extent, and all before your Christopher Columbus found his New World —though I can assure you this place is as ancient as the one on your side of the Never-Ending Ocean.

Viracocha Inca was my great-grandfather. Pachacuti was my great uncle, and he ordered my grandfather —his bastard half-brother— executed on a whim. I met Old Topa several times when I was a young man and spent my adult life serving his son and grandsons. There is no Inca of the Blood left alive better suited to tell you about Tahuantinsuyu.

I have seen more than seventy harvests come and go, and Time is stalking my last days. Am I to stay silent while your kind tells the story of my people? What do you Spaniards know about the Inca except that we had mountains of gold and big ears, and with us out of the way you can pillage across the rest of Tahuantinsuyu, the Land of the Four Quarters, just as you have done to Royal Cuzco?

Among the many duties I have performed for my people throughout my long life, I have done my best within the narrow window of my own experiences to record the great events of my land as they actually happened, and not as some would prefer them to be remembered, be they Spaniard or Inca—

You snort your disbelief, Friar? To quote one of your peers, 'Oh ye of little faith.' Just as you have your scribe's tools laid out before you, so

8

I hold in my hands threads that can speak of great victories and foul deeds, of love's triumphs and lust's treacheries. Your conviction that we were too stupid to record the world around us is still further proof that only a true Pacuyok, an Earplug Man, can tell our story.

From an empire of twelve million there may have been five or ten thousand with my special education. Building the empire took its toll on us, and the plague was worse. Both were as nothing compared to the War Between the Brothers, and you Spaniards killed most of the rest. Now there are so few like me that you have never heard of the Royal Quipu, the knotted strings that remember words instead of cold numbers. I have my story 'written' —though in the Language of the People the term is tied— across hundreds of thousands of knots, but who will be able to read my tangled skein after I'm gone?

It seems Time will swallow up the last of the capac quipucamayocs, the royal quipu masters, just as it has swallowed up Tahuantinsuyu. Perhaps one day the Language of the People will be replaced with Spanish. I shudder to think of a time when the hills around Cuzco forget the sound of Runa Simi echoing from their faces.

No, I must save some small part of the truth. I must take these knots of string and make them speak in Spanish. Even if no one is interested now, someday someone will look at the ruined cities of the Inca and wonder what glories and tragedies were played out in these places.

If I am to cheat Time I will have to do it in Spanish with the help of an educated Spaniard, but where was I to find one while hiding in this city, deep in the jungle? We have several of your countrymen living here, deserters from Almagro, but they're as illiterate in your writing as a Colla potato farmer would be with my royal quipus.

I think your God and my gods have conspired to help me, Friar. When our pickets said a Spanish priest was wandering in the hacha hacha I ordered them to spare you. I need you. I need you enough to let you live when all I want to do is burn you alive as you and yours have done to me and mine.

So we have each other's oaths, Friar. You shall write my story word for word as I read it from my quipus. Where my Spanish falters we shall use other translators to aid us, and we shall go back and forth through the story until my words are as lucid in your language as they are in mine. When I allow you to leave this place, you will make sure the manuscript is stored somewhere safe for the future to contemplate. One day someone will want to know what really happened, and my story will be found preserved within these pages.

In exchange for this task you will have the run of the city and permission to preach your Christian gospel every seventh day to whomsoever wishes to hear you. I will even sit in the front pew for every sermon.

Who knows? Clearly your God beat my gods, or you would not be here, and I would not be in this stinking, chittering, sweating jungle, and there would be no need to transfer a royal quipu from string to parchment, knot to ink. Perhaps you will convert me, but I warn you now I am a stubborn man, and old. I have walked a long road under a harsh sun to appear before you today. If you can change me now then you will be the finest son of Castile I have ever met, but considering the ilk of your countrymen that might be an easy feat.

Enough rambling, it is the blessing and curse of the elderly to be able to sit and talk all day, whether anyone wants to listen or not. Let us begin...

My father was not much of one to tell stories —he preferred to lecture and instruct— but I remember being a little boy, waking in terror at phantoms and ghouls who swirled through my dreams and seemed to lurk still in the quiet corners of my dark room. My father would show affection in the night that he would never have given in the light of day, cradling me in his strong arms and whispering stories that always began with Ñaupa Pacha, Once Upon a Time.

The story of my life will leave my father behind far too soon, and so much will be left unsaid. Thus I begin my tale as he would have wanted me to, and I beg you to write it in my own language as well as your Spanish so that a piece of him will be remembered.

Ñaupa Pacha, Once Upon a Time, there was a land called Tahuan-tinsuyu, the Four Quarters of the World, which was ruled by the Intip Churi, the Children of the Sun.

Just calling it the Four Quarters of the World does not convey how immense it was. At its highest zenith it was literally the entire known world, including areas only discovered as we conquered them.

Tahuantinsuyu was bigger and broader than the mind's eye can imag-ine, holding every trick of land and water that the most imaginative of gods could conjure. There were mountains so tall that their peaks punched through the roof of the sky, so that a man could suffocate at their tops. There were weed-choked swamps that reduce the ground to a perfect flatness all the way out to the horizon, so that a man born in that fetid place could not conceive of a slope, let alone a hill, and never dream of the sky-piercing mountain.

There were deserts so dry that not one green thing grew, and you dared not open your mouth for fear that the greedy air would snatch your life's moisture from your insides. There were jungles so wet that when it rained a man looked at the ground to create a hollow for his nose to draw air, otherwise he would splutter and drown where he stood.

All of this was Tahuantinsuyu, and all of it belongs to a single man, the Sapa Inca, the Only Inca, the Shepherd of the Sun, the Son of the Sun, the Emperor. It all belonged to him, this king of kings, the Impe-rial leader of the Imperial people, and everyone knew it.

Pomposity? Hubris? No! One need only look back before the Spanish Pachacuti to see the proof of it. In the most remote village of the snowy land of Tchili, or in the smallest mountain hamlet in the dark jungles beyond Quitu where the people had so little they paid their taxes in dead fleas and lice plucked from their own bodies, even there you would see that the Inca rule: Ask for a drink, beg a meal, and it would appear in an Inca beaker, on an Inca plate.

In the four quarters of the Empire there were eighty tribes, and before each one was firmly fixed into the State, before our legions had even left, a colony of settlers was imported from a land long loyal to the Sapa Inca; that colony's job would be to make the standard Inca pottery, the same made in all directions for a thousand topos, roughly the same distance as your Spanish leagues.

Every man, loyal or rebellious, needs to drink; he pours his drink from an Inca amphora into an Inca beaker before he puts it to his lips. When he eats, it is off an Inca plate. He will be reminded with each sip and every bite that he lives with the permission of the Children of the Sun, and if he wishes to do so in the future he must stay in their good graces.

That was the awesome power of the Sapa Inca, the Only Inca, the Emperor. Lands he would never see recognized him as the most important thing in their lives.

It was in such a world —though not yet extended to its highest glory— that I was born. By and large people born up in the mountains do not keep track of their birthdays or their exact ages, but my household never forgot that day. All the omens were bad, and all of them proved true.

While no one can speak with great authority on the moments of their birth, my coming into this world was unusual enough at the time that many people remembered it. What I am telling you now is drawn from the accounts of many who I respect, and I have spent a lifetime without hearing a single contrary version of the story.

I was to be my father's first legitimate child by his official wife, so he had summoned two fortunetellers to make their predictions for my future. The first was a kalparicoc, a diviner from the lungs of sacrificed animals. He killed a guinea pig and inflated its lung with a straw. The veins on the outside of the gory balloon foretold a life that would cause woe early and experience it often.

The next man was a spider augur, capable of answering only yes or no questions. My father asked if I would be a boy, and the man pulled away his pot to reveal a giant spider from the distant jungles with legs neatly splayed out, meaning yes. My father then asked if the kalparicoc's gloomy tidings were wrong. The pot was pulled back again to show the spider had shifted a hairy leg askew, meaning no.

My father tried to pay the two men for their time with bolts of red cotton, but their predictions had been so unpleasant that they declined payment. While I'm sure they did so in the hopes that their bad tidings would prove false, my father took their refusal as yet another bad omen. His life's work revolved around maintaining reciprocity, an equal exchange of goods for services. He retired to his counting room to work while he worried.

There was much to concern an expecting father, and he did not need the services of fortunetellers to know that my birth was poorly timed: I was born in the month of Ayamalca Raimi, just thirteen days before the shortest day of the year. By your calendar that would be June the Eighth of the year Fourteen-Seventy.

That is the worst time of year for a birth, because there are no crops in the ground. Tahuantinsuyu was surviving off its storehouses. Meanwhile, the cold and damp that herald the presence of Supay —our version of your Devil— crept into every room, threatening mother and baby alike with sicknesses while they are at their lowest ebb.

Worse still was the weather. Ayamalca Raimi is a month of storms that come off the never-ending forests of the east in rolling black thunderheads, sending rain and hail and snow one after the other to make even a walk across a courtyard a miserable affair. Such a storm was overhead all day and through most of that terrible night. The thunder god Illapa, crashing his fist against a great drum in the sky, caused such noise that twice my father came down to the kitchen to see if the servants were smashing the crockery.

Even the best efforts of the thunder god, though, paled beside those of my mother.

I have left the worst until last, and unfortunately the worst is my mother. She was unable to bear me with the quiet suffering of so many Inca women. I have been told that my mother's screams made the stone walls of my house tremble, but I think that is an invention of one of my nursemaids. My father's head was always turned by frail and fragile maidens, thin and graceful, like stately willow saplings beside a cold mountain brook. Not the sort of woman whose lungs could make stones quake, or the sort whose hips could easily pass a child.

Except for my own delivery I have never been present as a woman gave birth, but I know for most of my broad-hipped race the feat is no great effort. I have heard of many peasants who begin labour out in the fields, deliver, assure themselves that the baby is all right, and go back to work.

My father thought women with the figures necessary for such ease were too squat and ugly for a man who could have any woman in the world. My mother was of the Chacapoyas, the Cloud People who live on the mountain slopes just above the hacha hacha. Their women are pale and tall and slender even compared to you Spaniards.

She had been born far below my father's station and should never have been eligible to become his official wife, but he was so taken with her —and not just with her beauty but with her heart— that he gave generous gifts to her father until my maternal grandfather could buy his way into the highest ranks of his nation's nobility. Once the necessary station was established my father obtained special permission from the Emperor himself to marry the newly ennobled princess.

My father loved my mother in a way few men are lucky enough to find. She was bright and always cheerful, and she returned his affections without reservation. In all the years of my life I have never heard any-one, from family friends to our most vicious enemies, speak an unkind word against her memory. She had only one flaw, narrow hips, and I killed her for it.

When her screams stopped a midwife entered my father's counting room and told the great accountant, "You have a son!"

He allowed no smile to break his composed facade but continued moving his pebbles around his counting board by the light of a single rush torch. "And my wife? Is she still in pain? Can I see her?" He said.

"No lord, she is dead," was the reply.

I am told his hand froze over the board, and it trembled as he set down his stone. "That is unfortunate," was all he said.

Some might think my father's lack of reaction was truly heartless, and his enemies at Court certainly circulated the story far and wide with that interpretation applied, but I have always known how hard he took the news of my mother's death. I endured a tangible and constant reminder of his sorrow with me throughout my childhood, and until a decade ago there were many who could remember the penance I served for killing his beloved.

There is a tradition among mountain people to call a newborn simply Wawa, Baby, until it has lived long enough to live a good while longer. Only then is it given a childhood name. When I escaped my infancy without suffering any fatal disease I was named Waccha, Unfortunate, and every time my father called me to him he was reminding himself of what he had sacrificed for an heir.

My father was a Tocoyricoc, He Who Sees All, one of only four such men in all the world. He was in charge of making sure one quarter of the Realm ran smoothly, free from any corruption that cheated the Emperor of his taxes and the Emperor's subjects of the state services those taxes provided. In the pursuit of just government he answered only to the Sapa Inca, and he could order any man save one of the four great viceroys, each the absolute lord of one quarter of Tahuantinsuyu, to aid him in his task.

I spoke earlier of the length and breadth of Tahuantinsuyu, and how each tribe recognized the Inca as supreme. It was men like my father who made it so.

I said my father had enemies at Court, and he did; not from envy at his rank and station or jealousy at the special trust the Sapa Inca placed in him, but for the fear of his talent and his ruthless honesty. When my father found a guilty man that man was brought to justice, and for that reason a great number of my father's colleagues had to be honest men. He was very good at finding corruption.

My father's name was Tupac Capac, Royal Lord. He had others, seven or so, for it is the fashion among nobility to tack on adjectives like jewelry. Once people call you a thing, Just, Fair, Wise, generally the honorific is adapted into your name. Whatever his full name, his few equals called him Tupac, and his legions of subordinates called him Inca, Tocoyricoc, Lord, Sire, Sir, or, in my case, Father.

We lived in a great house just off one of the main streets of Royal Cuzco. From the narrow lane outside it was unremarkable, a solid wall of fitted masonry joining us to the houses of our clansmen to the left and right. We had neatly thatched eaves and a single doorway of massive teak decorated with an alpaca wool blanket dyed with the family's personal shade of yellow.

Our home was a compound, as all great houses are in Cuzco. We had eight buildings circling two courtyards, and the two buildings that linked the inner courtyard to the outer one were two stories tall with the counting room tower mounted on top of that.

My father's counting room was a marvel: In my school days I had many friends who mocked my home for only having eight buildings, for there were palaces in Cuzco that had a hundred, but only the houses of tocoyricocs had counting rooms, and the counting room's tower gave a magnificent view of the entire city.

This elevation was strictly for business, of course. The room had huge windows with thick silver frames, and the inside walls were of precisely fitted fieldstone speckled with sparkling chips of mica that were regularly whitewashed with lime from burned seashells. The end result was that from before sunrise to just after sunset and even on rainy days the whole room was brilliantly lit so my father could work.

The building is gone now, of course. Most of Cuzco is gone, but I can close my eyes and see that place still in my mind. I can remember my father's assistants waiting outside in the early morning, stomping their feet at the cold but making as little noise as possible lest they disturb my father's rest. After the household had made its dawn sacrifice of burned coca leaves —and not a moment before— our doorman would unbar the teak entrance. My father's underlings would come in with great mountains of jars in their arms, quietly fighting for position to be the last to admit their failures to the Tocoyricoc.

Inside each jar lay a quipu, a length of rope with strings descending from it, littered with knots. I am sure through my long life I have run more quipus through my hands than I have hairs on my head, for the knots record all manner of valuable information for those with the knowledge to tease the facts out of the skeins.

Among the quipucamayocs, the quipu masters, the strings brought to the house of He Who Sees All were called the problem quipus, because they recorded the inconsistencies in the records of the Empire as discovered by hundreds of accountants working in the Great Quipu Repository, the beating heart of the efficient Inca bureaucracy.

When my father was in Cuzco it was his job and special talent to look at the problem quipus. He could take an incompatible set of numbers that had baffled a dozen men before him, move backwards and forward through the ledgers and invoices and requisitions, and arrive at a solution.

16

The men would climb the ladders one by one to reach him in his counting room, and he would be waiting there, perched on a low stool carved from a single piece of mahogany to look like a man crouching in deep thought.

Up there he would stretch out the troublesome threads and run his fingers along the knots, the numbers lodging in his mind, faster than he could speak them aloud. Then he would turn to his counting board, a maze of boxes and compartments spread across the floor, littered with coloured stones. He would move the pebbles around, and to someone who did not know their pattern it seemed he would arrive at an answer by magic; then he would take some yarn from a basket behind him and tie the answer down, passing it to the man waiting at the top of the ladder. Each would scuttle off as fast as dignity would allow so that the next man and the next could climb the ladder, and so it would go for most of the day.

There were times where my father would snort with impatience, handing the quipu back to his assistant without even resorting to the counting board, barking the answer that he had seen while the knots were still tangled in the quipucamayoc's fist. He rightly took those errors as a waste of his time and an insult to all the hard training he had put into his subordinates.

When a really complicated problem arose he took it as a personal challenge; he would furrow his brow and set his face as hard as granite, staring at the knots and daring them to defy his mind. You could always tell when my father was stuck because he would call for akha, maize beer, and the mug would appear instantly from the kitchen two floors below. He would usually have the answer by the time he drained the cup, and the rare times he did not that would mean an audit. Only he audited within his quarter of Tahuantinsuyu, but he loathed admitting he was stumped.

"Huaman Paullu! Note: Fifteen bags of maize are missing from the Cusi Tampu in the Nazca province. The ledgers say ten bags were destroyed by rodents, but what kind of idiot tampu keeper doesn't notice mice eating ten bags of maize? Also, there's no mention of what happened to the other five bags. Next trip we audit that tampu, and his ledgers had better be clearer than the copy he sent us or we'll replace him with someone who can tie a two without making it look like a four!"

Behind him his faithful secretary would tie knots on a royal quipu, recording sounds instead of numbers. If there were four new strings on the audit list by the end of the day my father would be angry at his failure; meanwhile, hundreds of discrepancies had been corrected by his mind, the worst problems that had already defeated long days of bureaucratic scrutiny.

And that was the way of things. My father either solved the unsolvable or he would conduct an audit. Every year, sometimes twice a year, my father would leave Cuzco and follow the Royal Roads throughout Condesuyu, the western quarter of the Four Quarters of the World. He would stop at each inn and way station, each hamlet and village along his route between problems, making a long circle ending back at Cuzco where he balanced his archived account ledgers with the findings of his most recent trip. Doing this meant that every community in that entire quarter of the Empire was visited by He Who Sees All at least once every five years.

I spent my infancy and childhood in that man's shadow, and I have always marveled at my good fortune. My father was a driven man. He cared only for results and hard work.

As you would expect from one so devoted, my father led a quiet home life, shunning the outside. There was one group of visitors, though, that even a man as powerful as my shut-in father could not turn away: The Ocllo sisters.

There were three of them, all more than ten years his senior, and all married to the Emperor Topa Inca Yupanki. My father could not have denied them entry even if it were within his vast power to do so. They could make a river freeze over with their glare. They were my father's bane.

The eldest, Mama Ocllo, was actually Old Topa's official wife, his Coya, his Empress. Her two sisters, Chiqui Ocllo and Cari Ocllo, had been married on the Imperial whim of having the entire trio within the Emperor's harem. All three of them had long passed out of favour with the Sapa Inca and now contented themselves with using their considerable influence to bother quiet widowers like my father.

I can remember one visit in particular. They arrived without warning, as was their preference, and the leader of their bodyguard threw our doorman aside as he opened our teak portal. The guardsman stepped into the middle of our outer courtyard and announced the arrival of the Coya and her two sisters in his best parade ground voice; then he blew his conch-shell trumpet, rattling the teeth of every jaw in our compound.

My father descended from his counting room to join me, slightly dazed at the volume of the summons. Only when the entire household was turned out in the courtyard to greet them did the three preening women and their retinue come in from the street.

They were small, plump, and solid, and they looked around with unapologetic criticism on their faces as only the powerful can do. Our house was frugally decorated, as befitted the nation's greatest accountant. We did not have elaborate tapestries, jaguar skin rugs, gold idols or silver icons. We may have been the only house on the street without a garden or fish pond or aviary of jungle birds. The three of them read this as a lack of taste. They each sniffed their disdain several times to make sure it was noted before deigning to be greeted.

My father and I blew them a kiss and bowed, followed by our household. Mama Ocllo nodded her acceptance and then pinched my cheek hard enough to take it off. "Little Waccha gets taller every day, Tupac! He grows like a maize stalk."

"Skinny as one too," Chiqui Ocllo added, her tone implying she was bored already.

"Yes, well, your son Capac Huari was the same at his age, and he's filled out nicely," my father replied. In his place I would have smiled sweetly to add insult to injury. It was a well-known but unspoken fact that her husband was not Capac Huari's father. Chiqui Ocllo had cuckolded the short Emperor with Viceroy Hualpaya, the tall ruler of Andesuyu, the eastern quarter of Tahuantinsuyu. All Chiqui Ocllo could do was nod in agreement that her darling son had indeed been scrawny as a boy.

"When are you going to take little Waccha out on one of your inspections?" Mama Ocllo asked, patting my head as I would a llama, a dumb animal that did not know it was being talked about.

"He's young for that yet," my father replied.

"Nonsense! Do him good to get out of these walls and see the world. The sooner the better, if you ask me. It's not natural keeping a boy inside, especially in a house without a woman." The three of them each harrumphed their agreement and straightened their dazzling robes, as if to reassure everyone what women looked like.

"I have fifteen women living with us," my father sighed. I could tell from his tone that he was rehashing an argument that he knew he would not be allowed to win.

"And which one do you call mother, Waccha?" Mama Ocllo asked.

My father only rarely sought the solace of one of his concubines' arms, and without the clear signal from him none had stepped forward to be a mother to his only legitimate child. I opened my mouth, but my father beat me to it. "My domestic affairs are my business, good lady, and I will thank you to leave the raising of my son to me."

I had seen quipucamayocs recoil as if burned when my father took that tone with them, but Mama Ocllo just sniffed a little, as if he had merely singed a nose hair. "You need a proper wife, Tupac. You're too young to live alone."

"I think there's something to be said for a life of dedication, and if that leads to celibacy, so be it." That was another calculated shot, as all three of the Ocllo sisters were much neglected by an Emperor with a thousand wives. Everyone knew of Chiqui Ocllo's famous dalliance, but the other two were just whispered about, so far.

Our household suffered their company throughout the afternoon, and we were beginning to worry that they would stay for supper until Mama Ocllo delivered her ultimatum.

"Find a wife, or we will find one for you, Tupac. We don't like you living alone. At least a wife would have the courtesy to invite us to visit once in a while. Oh, and take young Waccha out on an inspection. If he doesn't look capable of taking over your position, Cari Ocllo has a friend whose son could use the opportunity."

My father gave his least sincere smile and saw the three old hags out. He then ordered the teak door barred and had our servants sweep the courtyard, as if by removing the dust on the flagstones they could rid the house of the memory of this latest invasion of his home.

He muttered to me as he climbed the ladder back to his counting room, "Cari Ocllo has a friend, does she? Wants his son to be Tocoyricoc one day? You had better be as smart as you seem, boy. When those three get an idea in their heads, they're like a dog with a bone..."

I lay awake all that night, wondering and worrying. As his only official son I had known from a young age that one day I might take my father's place as a tocoyricoc. Can you imagine how frightening that is to a little boy, to see your father work with all the benefits of an education that staggers you and know that it might one day fall to you to do the same? It gave me nightmares.

Within days of the Ocllo sisters' visit my father decided to go on an audit tour and to take me with him.

I had a number of older brothers, though none were official sons because my father had sired them with concubines instead of a wife, as he had me. Still, illegitimacy is not an insurmountable handicap —my father himself was a bastard of one of the Emperor Viracocha Inca's bastards— and so the two of my father's sons who were older than me and had shown some ability to think for themselves had each gone out with him on an inspection and returned in tears. He had told them flatly that they would not receive the patronage required from him to secure the education of He Who Sees All.

That might sound cruel coming from a father, but remember He Who Sees All is always looking for government waste, and there are few things more expensive than training a tocoyricoc.

All Inca sons can expect the standard four years at an Inca school, but a boy destined to become He Who Sees All will need much more. His schooling starts as soon as possible and continues on past the state school for another three, and throughout the entire time there are extra tutors and subjects and assignments and projects, and all the people involved in his training, including the student, will be fed and clothed and housed and feted at State expense.

You can put a legion of conscripts on the frontier for three months for what it costs to bring up a tocoyricoc-in-waiting, and so the selection of candidates is a serious business.

Whether it was Mama Ocllo's prompting or not, he took me, and he had high hopes as he offered up the sacrifice to Inti, the Sun, at the beginning of our journey. For my part I had done my best to seem the ideal candidate: Of all his children I spent by far the most time in his counting room with him, watching him work. I asked questions and was interested in the answers.

My father took pride in his job and position in life, and I think he sensed I was his last chance to pass the post on to one of his sons. If I should fail he would start going around to schools, asking for the top students of mathematics, quipus, and Runa Simi. He would pick the

21

best candidate for the good of the Empire, even if it meant leaving his boys to make their own way in the world.

I remember that inspection tour as one long lesson. Everywhere we went he lectured me in his crisp and exact manner of speaking. It was fascinating to see the world outside Cuzco and have all of its complexities explained by one of their foremost experts.

It wasn't just my father and I on our trip, of course. My father's retinue consisted of dozens of quipucamayocs carrying copies of ledgers and inventories for every community on my father's route. Then there were the interpreters for the few languages he did not speak. My father took a handful of soldiers for the rare cases where a show of force might be necessary, and a few parcel couriers who could run across rough country all day, if need be. He also had dozens of llamas and their drivers, loaded with beautiful gifts to give as rewards to the deserving.

Then there was his retinue of thirty men of the Rucana tribe dressed in identical blue livery: These were a mark of true prestige and power for they carried his litter, a vehicle whose use could only be granted by the Sapa Inca himself.

My father's one indulgence was his gherkin fetcher. The man's job was to work up and down the royal highway and off down the side roads, searching for gherkins.

The tiny vegetable, watery yet firm, was my father's absolute favourite. He ate handfuls of them at a time when it was seemly to do so. As a boy his odd love of them had inspired my grandfather to give him the childhood name of Gherkin, just as mine was Unfortunate, and so they were a part of who my father was. Many villages kept crops of gherkins just for his visits, a gesture of his popularity that did not escape my notice. Between these villages, meanwhile, he still had the craving, and so we had the gherkin fetcher.

As ungainly as all these people sound, my father moved fast, thanks in large part to the Capac Ñan, the Royal Road. Today the system is a shambles, but when the Inca ruled the royal roads were a network of transportation and communication stretching the length and breath of Tahuantinsuyu, tying together people separated by mountains and deserts and rivers and jungles into a unified whole.

The royal roads were not for the commoners, though they could use the road to go about their tax-paying duties provided they had a pass. Instead, the roads were for anyone on the Emperor's business.

Every night my father and his procession stopped at a tampu, a depot of storehouses with an inn that provided free food and lodgings. The tampus were spaced about a day's amble from each other, but my father often moved so quickly that our procession would skip the first tampu to eat and sleep at the second.

I have walked the royal roads many times since I was a boy, but I still think of the landmarks in Condesuyu as I saw them on that first journey I took with my father. There was the gorge of the Apurimac River that we crossed on a great rope suspension bridge, more than a hundred of my small boy's paces long. The river below moves so fast across an endless series of rapids that it was always roaring, and the steep sides of its canyon bounced the sound around to form untranslatable words and conversations, thus the Apurimac's name, the Speaking Lord.

I remember the rolling puna, and stepping off the swept and leveled road to feel the ichu grass against my calves. The puna is a treeless prairie between the two mountain ranges where llamas graze and potatoes grow, and where the wicked green eyes of pumas watched our fires in the night, hoping one of the tampu's llamas would venture out of the stone-walled corral.

I remember the coastal desert, where a heavy fog often settles on the ground, and you can smell the rain coming, teasing, taunting, but never delivering. Up and down the Empire from Quitu to the lands of Tchili rain comes only from the east, out of the great forests. The rain clouds climb the slopes of the eastern mountains until their weight lets them climb no more, so they dump their load of water to bob higher, up and over, perhaps dropping a little more rain between the eastern and western mountains.

By the time the clouds reach the coastal desert they can promise rain and flaunt their damp fog, but no rain will come. To grow crops on the coast of the never-ending ocean men have to live on the banks of the rivers that make their way down from the rainy mountains to the sea.

It was in such a community that I first saw the awesome power my father wielded as a tocoyricoc, the power of life and death. That coastal village tried to cheat the Emperor, the Empire, and themselves. He Who Sees All could not allow such deeds to go unpunished.

As a boy I thought the collection of huts and houses was large, but looking back on it now I remember the curaca, the headman, was a local with the rank of pachacamayoc, master of a hundred taxpaying families. That would make his village, perched on the arid land above the delta of a river valley, quite small in the grand scheme of things.

Throughout his tour my father had given me a running lesson on where we were, and this valley was no different. He looked down on me from his litter and said, "This village is part of the Sama tribe. It chose to join Tahuantinsuyu voluntarily, but that might have had something to do with the wars your great-uncle Pachacuti won up and down the coast from them. We have been good to them, and they have prospered under our rule. This village would not be a third this size without the Inca, for the river delta floods too often to make farming a safe and reliable source of food.

"The fields belonging to the Sapa Inca and the Sun grow cotton, which is then shipped to tampus throughout Condesuyu in exchange for their surpluses of maize and potatoes. Now if a flood destroys the personal plots of the people here, they have reserves grown by their neighbours up valley, ready and waiting for them."

He gestured with his staff of office to a bluff on the slope. After a month of touring with my father I easily recognized the round store-houses containing maize and the square ones holding potatoes, as well as all the other buildings and warehouses of a well-provisioned tampu.

"What is that smell, Father?" I asked, for the wind off the sea was coming across the fields and I smelled something stronger than the usual llama and human manure.

"Just offshore there are islands that have been the nesting place of sea-birds since Viracocha made the world," my father said. "Their guano is piled three times the height of a man in places, and all that digested fish makes perfect fertilizer. The village exports it to farms as far away as Xauxa in exchange for wool, potatoes, and quinoa. They also use a lot of it on their own fields."

Behind my father a group of quipucamayocs were decanting a storage amphora and pulling out the various quipu ledgers for the community below us. One of them noticed a black knot on the census quipu's crime thread.

"My lord?" The man called.

"Yes?" My father did not turn around on his litter.

"This is the village that killed a man for venturing out to the bird islands during the nesting season."

"Very well," my father said. He turned his face down to look at me, his stern expression from before difficult to maintain as he popped a gherkin between his straight white teeth. "There is a good chance you are going to see someone trying to swindle the Emperor. Watch the curaca's eyes. Only the best liars can control their eyes. Remember always that men do not need to be clever to be greedy, but they have to be exceedingly clever to get away with it."

My father brought his staff of office down onto the floor of the litter twice and the Rucana bearers smoothly increased their pace, jogging without jostling their burden. They were the best porters in the Empire, so much so that their tribe paid its taxes exclusively by carrying the Sapa Inca's favourites. Other tribes enviously called them, 'the Feet of the Inca.'

We descended the slope down to the tampu bluff to find the entire village turned out in their holiday dress. Taxpayers were issued two sets of clothes by the State when they marry: A set for working and a set for festivals. Many women supplemented their families' wardrobes with their looms, but when they did so it was usually to replace work clothes. The result was that older couples were often in drab, stained and patched holiday clothes, and the younger families often rubbed dust into their mantles so as not to shame their neighbours before He Who Sees All.

One young man in the front of the crowd stood out among them like a parrot among a flock of sparrows. He was dressed in a blazing red tunic with a flamboyant blue and yellow mantle over it, secured with a silver pin at the shoulder. His hems were decorated with copper discs, and the llama leather of his sandals was bleached white. His neck, wrists, and ankles hung with jewelry made from seashells. His smile was broad and blinding, like that of a man offering shoddy tribute. He blew a kiss when my father's litter stopped, and the villagers repeated the gesture.

My father got down from his litter with dignity and stood tall and proud, flanked by his retinue. Where the village curaca —he could be no other— used gaudy colours and chunky ornaments to set himself apart and above those he ruled, my father was the height of noble fashion.

His knee-length tunic was blue vicuna wool with a short red fringe. His mantle of office was dyed the bright yellow of jungle flowers, trimmed with gold plates and the multi-coloured feathers of hummingbirds. His ears, like all Inca men, were pierced and stretched by golden earplugs, but his oval ornaments were so heavy with seniority that the bottom of his lobe almost touched his shoulder.

"Curaca Taraque, it has been too long." My father rumbled the pleasantry.

"Yes, my lord. Five years since my village last had the pleasure," Taraque enthused.

My father looked up at the sun without squinting. It was two thirds of the way across the sky.

"We will stay the night. Inform the tampu staff."

"At once, my lord." Taraque pointed at a man in the crowd who took off at a run.

I was watching it all, alerted by my father's words without knowing what I was looking for. The crowd was tense, but they did not seem guilty. There was something wrong though, of that I was certain. I watched their eyes and every one of them was looking at Taraque.

"In five years your population has grown six percent. My congratulations to you, and to all your people," my father said. The village blew him a kiss of thanks.

"Your tax figures have been good. Everyone has done their share. Your women will be happy to know your cotton cloaks have been issued out to Huanca conscripts doing garrison duty in the jungles of Andesuyu, and the light cotton is much preferred to the wool they could have been given." The crowd seemed pleased at this.

"The bird guano you shipped up the valley has resulted in a bumper crop of tomatoes and chilies, a tenth of which will be sent to you. I have ordered a great chef from Rimac to come here three festivals from now to show you how to spice your fish stews with them." My father continued in this way, telling them where their taxes had gone and how they benefited real people. At last he came around to the matter of the criminal.

"I understand a man was punished for going to the bird islands during the nesting season." My father did not make it a question.

Taraque's eyes darted left and right, as if looking for escape. His smile grew broader. "Yes, my lord, a terrible thing. What if the birds had been too badly disturbed? We all know the story of the village that was disbanded because the birds did not come back to roost the next year."

"The man was caught in the act?"

"Yes, my lord."

"So where is the grave?"

"Grave? No, lord, he is still alive," the curaca said.

My father arched an eyebrow. "Present him."

The curaca raised an arm and a dejected looking wretch was brought out from the tampu office. His tunic was in tatters, and he was thin as a half-hearted scarecrow. The hollows under his eyes spoke of sleepless nights.

"Your name?" My father asked the man.

"Zambiza, my lord. Please don't hurt me!"

"You went to the islands and killed birds?" My father asked as if the man had said nothing but his name.

"Yes, my lord, but not for myself! My wife was pregnant, and she wanted a bird or two for the pot, and—"

My father interrupted him smoothly. "The laws are not made without reasons. Yes, your wife's craving would have been satisfied by your act, but what about the life of your child? How badly will future generations suffer when the birds move to a new nesting site because of your thoughtless actions?

"Without the guano on that island this village is not capable of trading its way to self-sufficiency. The clans will be split up and relocated. All that could happen if you spook the birds or someone follows your bad example."

My father was stern, but he spoke simply, as he would to a child. Zambiza was weeping now. "There is another law, a simple law that was also made for a reason. It says that any man who breaks a law must be punished, so all who know of his crime know it was a crime and that crime is punished. Is this your first offence, or your second?"

Through his sobs Zambiza choked out that it was his first. My father nodded, for it was rare for anyone to survive his first punishment, so rare that he had originally asked for the grave instead of the man.

"Then you shall be sentenced now. Hold him down."

Zambiza struggled, but there was not enough strength left in his thin body, and the men guarding him soon had him face down and spread eagled on the ground. From inside the tampu office two villagers laboured under the heavy weight of a round stone. A third appeared holding a short length of blood-red string.

"Zambiza, for the crime you have committed the first offence is punished by the Hiwaya, the dropping of a stone onto your back. If you should survive, know that you have paid your penalty and will return to your family without any further loss of station or privilege. The State shall do everything in its power to heal you, and you and yours shall be fed at public expense until you can again provide for yourself. Do you understand?"

My father enunciated each word, speaking in a slow calm voice so the man heard him through his whimpers. When Zambiza nodded as best he could with his face in the dust, my father nodded to the man with the string.

The string man positioned himself over the prone Zambiza. He took one end of the red thread in his left hand and placed it between Zambiza's shoulder blades. Holding it there, he pulled the other end taut with his right hand until the twine stood straight up and menacing, measuring the distance fairly for all the villagers to see. The two men with the stone moved into position on either side of the prisoner until the bottom of their rock just brushed the high end of the dark red string.

The string man moved aside so that the stone was now two cubits above the captive's back, no more or less, and with nothing in between. Zambiza stopped crying and my father nodded. "Take it like a man, son," he said.

With that they dropped the stone.

Men do survive the Hiwaya. I've seen it. If they can lift themselves off the ground a little, or are fat, or strong, or even just blessed by the gods, then they can survive. None take it easily, but those who live recover.

Zambiza was none of those things. The stone landed with a nauseating plunk, and his splintered ribs drove out through his skinny sides, soaking his threadbare clothes in a dead man's blood. When the stone men lifted the rock off Zambiza's corpse I could tell that the inside of his spine must have been touching the inside of his breastbone. His heart was crushed to a pulp.

A woman burst out of the crowd with a baby carrier strapped to her back. "Bastard!" She screamed, pummeling my father's chest with her small fists. "Inca bastard!"

He seized her wrists in his strong hands, and spoke over her head to the villagers. "I may be an Inca, woman, but your husband would still be dead whether you paid your taxes to your old rulers or your new ones. The Sama tribe punished killing a bird in nesting season with disemboweling. With the Hiwaya he had a chance. Your old laws would not have spared him."

She relaxed in his grip, surprised at his words. "Also, I did not hear you when Zambiza was still alive. Did you fear I would put you under the Hiwaya for your part in all this? Has is occurred to you that as a pregnant woman you could have asked for an extra meat ration from the tampu without threatening your husband's life?" The woman stayed mute, so my father spun her around and gave her a push back into the crowd. It parted for her but did not close again in acceptance.

My father looked at the baby strapped to her back. It was half a year old if it was a day. "Curaca Taraque, how long ago did the nesting season end?"

"Nine months ago, Tocoyricoc," the man said, his eyes shifting from the tocoyricoc to Zambiza's body.

My father held his hand palm flat over his shoulder, and one of his assistants had a quipu in it within moments. A cursory scan confirmed what he already knew. "I don't see the work Zambiza did between his conviction and now."

"But my lord Inca, the man was a criminal, he—"

My father cut Taraque off. "You kept him alive but put down in the ledgers that he was dead, and you've been working him at spear point every day since, haven't you?" My father almost whispered so the crowd would not hear. They murmured among themselves, trying to figure out what their betters were saying. A glance from my father stilled them. The curaca began to get indignant, but my father quieted him by pointing at the corpse.

"Look at his body. You starved him and strained him, now what did you have him do?" My father cast a critical eye over the scattered huts and buildings. "That's your house there, isn't it?" My father pointed to a rectangular compound on a bluff overlooking the mouth of the river.

"Yes, lord, you remember, you stayed there the last—"

"So what is that?" My father pointed up valley now to a little hollow on higher ground. The dip was filled with gnarled Huarango trees, but between their branches one could just make out a set of stone walls without a roof.

Taraque's eyes went wide for just a moment, but it was enough to show me his guilty conscious. My father began to walk towards the hollow, and when Taraque began protesting two of my father's warriors leveled their lances.

I looked at the crowd and knew they had all been waiting for this moment. The air was charged as it is before a thunderstorm. I followed my father, watching all. Taraque walked ahead of us, not saying a word.

The hollow was in a shady grove with a trickling stream descending from a spring above to the valley floor below. Inside we found a house complex that would not have been out of place in Royal Cuzco itself; twelve buildings around three courtyards, already half-paved in white limestone. The walls were incomplete, standing only shoulder high, but wooden roof beams that must have been hideously expensive on the coast where only unworkable Huarango trees grew lay piled and ready.

"Did the Sapa Inca send word requisitioning a summer residence?" My father asked Taraque, keeping his voice calm despite the appalling expense that must have been committed to a mansion that upon completion would indeed be a fit place for the Emperor to spend the night.

"You know he did not, my lord," Taraque replied. His broad grin was gone now, but his tone remained proud. I was impressed. He was doomed but still faced his end like a man.

"Why?" My father asked.

"Before my grandfather submitted to the Inca my family was the richest in this valley for as far as our traders went. The guano belongs to me. Now I see villages everywhere using it, and their extra crops send their people to the fairs on market days so that anyone can afford these," he gestured to his copper discs. "Or these," he rattled his seashell jewelry. "I wanted a home, a grand home for my descendants and I, so that we will never forget that once we were nobles."

"You are a noble, Taraque. Nothing the Inca can do to you will change that," my father said. Taraque smiled, this time with real pleasure. "Well," my father said, looking around. "Let me see if I can save you the trouble of confessing. You had Zambiza —who presumably has a raft of some kind— go out to the islands every day and fetch back loads

30

of guano that you stored..." My father trailed off, arching an eyebrow.

"In the courtyard of the house my family uses during the fishing season."

"Ah, of course, right next to the beach caravan route," my father said, as if this was a friendly conversation. "So you now have an inexhaustible supply of wealth that, presumably, every curaca up and down the coast would gladly send porters out to get."

"They purchased it in good faith, my Lord. Please don't punish them for buying illegal goods. I told them we had a surplus."

"And it's to their credit that they took advantage of that bargain. I'd noticed a rise in crop yield in the area. As the curacas reported their bumper crops instead of keeping their excess I shall not punish them." Taraque nodded his thanks. "But what about this?" My father gestured to the half-built palace.

Taraque shrugged his shoulders. "I traded the guano for the stone and wood, of course. What else is there?"

"Don't play coy, Taraque. Confess in full." My father waited, finally sighing. "Very well, I already know what happened. Zambiza was going to the island, and you certainly haven't imported any workers because no taxpayers in the surrounding communities have disappeared from my ledgers. That means the villagers are building this house for you. How did you get them to do it?"

"You've seen the ledgers. We have paid our taxes fairly for the last five years," Taraque said.

"Yes, I'm sure you would not be so foolish as to take the farmers out of the State fields, and you couldn't drag a man off his own plots during planting or harvesting. So they worked on their holidays... And how did you pay them?"

"Pay them?" Taraque said it as if the concept was foreign to him. My father laughed, and Taraque joined him.

"Nobles can expect many things, Taraque, but not free labour on a holiday. If they are doing something for you, you must give them something in return. That is how the world works. So what were you paying them?" Taraque remained silent. "Fine," my father said at last.

He turned on his heel and we all followed him back to the tampu where the crowd remained. He ordered the storeroom doors opened and commanded the strongest of the farmers to start removing bags of maize, potatoes, and quinoa at random. The sun was setting when they pulled out the first sandbag, buried in the middle of the pile. Only now did Taraque try to defend himself.

"My Lord, you know I would not steal from the State."

"You have stolen from it, and from your own people. You paid them with the Sapa Inca's food that he was saving for their time of need!" My father thundered.

"No, I was going to pay it back! We've had bumper crops two of the last five years. I've gone over my ledgers. I would have paid back every kernel of maize out of my personal surplus within fifteen years," Taraque said.

"Then what you should have done was save for fifteen years, then find a way to legally obtain the stone and wood, and then build your house after clearing it with you superiors," my father said. "Instead, you put this entire community at risk for a generation so you can build a third home? You paid them with their famine relief food? I have heard enough." The last statement cut through the air, sharp as the first blow of a bronze chisel on granite.

The crowd stilled. Taraque swallowed visibly. Even my father's retainers shifted. Here was the power of He Who Sees All. Corruption had been discovered and would be dealt with swiftly and ruthlessly, without appeal. In a moment this community would never be the same. A small pachacuti was in the making.

"Where are the chuncacamayocs?" Ten men filtered forward from the crowd, indistinguishable from the rest of the peasantry. Each of these men was the head of ten of the hundred taxpaying families of this community. "Those of you who speak Runa Simi well, step forward." Four men advanced further. "Look at their eyes, son." He said quietly to me before turning back to the four.

We watched them, and only one of the four watched us back. "You," my father pointed the man out. He stepped forward. "Nineteen farmers each work six days hauling guano in from the islands. How many tax days have they worked?"

The man kept his eyes open as he thought about it. "One hundred and fourteen, my Lord, but six days is longer than each man would normally work."

"It's only a test," my father said. "A man marries and has four sons and three daughters before the first son is married. How much land should he get when the fields are reallocated at the start of the planting season?"

"That's a lucky man to have so many children survive, my lord."

"Only a test. What is the answer?"

"One topo for the husband and wife; one for each of the sons and a half for each of the daughters. That's five and six and a half... Six and a half topos."

My father laid his hand palm flat behind him and two lengths of string, one yellow and the other green, were given to him. He offered the string to the chuncacamayoc. "Tie that down."

The man slowly tied one hundred and fourteen into the yellow string for days and six and a half into the green string for land. The knots were clumsy, but that would improve with time.

"What is your name?"

"Illaquita, my lord."

"Huaman Paullu, promote Illaquita from chuncacamayoc to pacha-camayoc of this community. Congratulations, Curaca Illaquita." My father walked over to Taraque and removed the silver pin from his shoulder. He gave it to Illaquita, who held it without swapping it for his own copper pin.

"What will my punishment be, my Lord?" Taraque asked.

My father turned to the crowd and spoke in a loud clear voice. "Your curaca put you at risk to benefit himself at the expense of the State. I cannot overlook this, despite the good conduct of his family in leading you all these years. However, this is Taraque's first offence, and though any crime against the State is a grievous one I shall not sentence him to death." There were murmurs from the crowd, but they were not angry.

"Taraque shall be demoted to a chuncacamayoc, if—" The word stopped the sighs of relief and the crowd tensed. "If he can survive the Hiwaya." The crowd breathed a subdued collective sigh. Taraque was a fine and proud nobleman, but he was neither strong nor fat nor lucky.

"Illaquita?" Taraque said. "Look after my wives?"

"Of course, my lord."

"I am no longer your lord."

"You will always be our lord, my lord. I will make sure your wives

33

are maintained in their noble status, and that you are buried with your favourite."

"Thank you," Taraque said, contented. He bit the collar of his tunic once to ward off bad luck, then he lay down on the ground without complaint, arms spread wide. The stone men and string man ran to the tampu office and returned with their burdens. My father repeated his short speech over the prostrate man, but this time he ended with, "Take it like a nobleman, Taraque. Make your father proud." The stone fell. Taraque did not survive.

"Illaquita?" My father murmured after the appropriate interval of respectful silence.

"My lord?"

"Call forward the heads of the households who were formerly under you." The nine farmers stepped forward. "Pick one to succeed you as chuncacamayoc." Illaquita picked a man who nodded his acknowledgement. All nine retired back into the crowd after Huaman Paullu had the name of the new man.

"Illaquita? As the stone and wood have already been obtained, I authorize you now to finish the construction of the palace. Name it Taraqip Cancha, Taraque's House, and bury him according to his custom under the biggest courtyard. It will be your official residence unless and until a high official should come through this valley in need of accommodation." My father put his hand behind him again, and the quipu authorizing the expense materialized there. His assistants were well trained.

"Also, I never want to see your villagers dirty their holiday garb again. If your older couples cannot find the time to make new festive wear, you will buy it out of your own surplus wealth. They will work harder for a generous lord. As there are so many old clothes at the moment, the Sapa Inca himself shall provide this time."

As soon as it was said it was done, and a storehouse of richly embroidered cotton was breached from which every man, woman, and child from a hundred families were given new clothes. The lavish Imperial gift barely dented the warehouse supply.

"I leave tomorrow, Illaquita. Show me and mine where we are to sleep tonight." My father and his entourage walked with Illaquita to Taraque's former house while the villagers sang a song of praise and contentment behind us. Two men were dead and a noble family line had ended, but the people sang because good government had prevailed.

We settled into three buildings, with my father, Huaman Paullu and I sharing a small room to ourselves. When Huaman Paullu began his snoring I turned to my father. I had a question. "Why did Taraque take it as such a compliment when you called him noble?"

"Because he understands," my father rumbled, pulling his alpaca blanket up to his chin.

"I don't. What does he understand?"

"That there is a difference between being a nobleman and being noble." My father closed his eyes, but I would not be dissuaded.

"What's the difference?" I have a characteristic that in an adult you would call unshakeable but in a child is derided as irrepressible. My father knew he would not sleep until I was satisfied.

"Anyone can be born into nobility, but where did that noble rank come from in the first place?" My father opened one eye to see if I could answer his question.

"The gods made some men noble when they made the world, and those men's children were noble in turn down to us," I said, thinking my answer was a good one. I had no formal schooling yet, but I had heard bards talk of the Good Ones, the first nobility who passed the traits down to us.

"Then how did Illaquita become a noble to his people today? Am I a god? I just elevated him into the low ranks of nobility." He opened the other eye and stared at me, trying to end my line of questioning. If I gave up without an answer I was not worth bringing up to follow in his footsteps. I could not back down in front of his stare.

"You are not a god," I said, unsure what else to say.

"There are two kinds of people in the world, Waccha." He sat up and leaned his back against the wall, warming himself for a lecture. "The vast majority of people take the world as it is. They say 'As!' 'It must be so!' and so it is, because they will do nothing to change their lot in life. A man who thinks of a way to better his situation or the situation of his people, that man is noble regardless of his rank. It is a state of mind, and that is why the Inca need to rule the world."

I did not follow the leap from one statement to the other. "Why is

35

that, Father?" Huaman Paullu snored beside me, oblivious of the wisdom the tocoyricoc was imparting.

"Because there was a time long, long ago when all a man needed was noble thought and he would rise to lead his community as the best man to do so, and all prospered. Those were the true Good Ones, Waccha. They were not god-made. They made themselves great by improving the lives of people who would not do it for themselves." I nodded, but my father was not done.

"But men are men, and they want the best for their sons, and so their sons became nobles with or without that noble way of thinking, and then there was the nobility as a rigid and hereditary caste. Generations passed and commoners toiled while nobles thought only of themselves."

His eyes flashed now with the fire of a religious zealot. "We Inca are different, Waccha. We all think in terms of change, of action, of altering the world around us. More than that, Inti has ordered us to build this Realm of ours. As we expand, we find others who think as we do, and we will elevate them as high as their capability will allow, something that would never happen without us. The vast majority of people will suffer what the universe gives them and call it fate, but those people who can make things better for the majority should be put in a position to do so. The Inca will make that possible."

"And Taraque, he was a noble?"

"He saw something in his way and instead of saying, 'It must be so!' he tried to change it. The problem is that it was the Inca way of governing in his way, and so we had to crush him." My father did not relish the words, but they were spoken as inevitably as the peasant whose crops are beaten down by hail will cry, 'As!'

"But he was a noble. Wasn't he supposed to lead?"

"Yes, but he had the responsibility to better the lives of his people. You and I, Waccha, we only work in the fields a couple of days a year as a token to the commoners. We eat off gold and silver plates. We wear fine clothes and have servants to do our cooking and cleaning. We get all this because we are Inca, but we are supposed to be getting it all so that we are free to make life better, safer, easier, for those under us.

"We rule a land where no one will ever starve, and no one fears his neighbour will kill him, a land free of crime and prostitution, a land where you can worship any god or goddess you want as long as you acknowledge that the Inca's god, Inti, conquered yours. We live in a land where the poor and old and sick and orphaned can survive even when they cannot support themselves.

"The Inca have made all this possible with our administration, our self-discipline, our foresight. Do you know why this village has five years' worth of food stored in the tampu above them?" He held up a hand with three fingers raised.

"Because one year in six they do not grow enough to eat, and without a reserve they would lose most of the new generation of children before they were old enough to become farmers." The first finger fell.

"Because if the neighbours they trade with today come to pillage them tomorrow, that food will feed the Inca army we send to mete out justice, and knowing that, their neighbours remain peaceful friends and allies." The second finger followed the first.

"Because a hundred things can go wrong in this world, and a full belly makes all of them bearable." He pointed the last finger at me and waited for me to look him in the eyes, to see how deadly serious he considered the matter. My father shifted his weight and brought his hands up in front of him as if he were holding a precious burden.

"Our system works, Waccha. Take the holiday clothes we distributed today: They were made by taxpayers, years and years of work went into making that fabric. Today that slow and steady accumulation was distributed to the people, and they will remember for the rest of their lives what it felt like to have that given to them.

"It was theirs already, or at least commoners just like them were the ones who made it, but by storing it up until it was truly needed it was worth so much more to them. It was special. It made their dull lives brighter, and they can take comfort in their finery where before they were ashamed at their lack."

I digested that for a moment, but one more thing still troubled me. "And why did you tell Taraque to make his father proud?"

My father put down his head and sighed so long and soft, so weary, that I thought he had fallen asleep. When he spoke again it was in a different voice. "I went to school with Taraque's father. We were friends."

"You killed your friend's son?"

"I made the system work," he said. "I taught Taraque when he came to school in Cuzco. I taught him his numbers and quipus. When his father died I came to this village, and we had a long talk; I told him the system comes first, and that there are no exceptions because the system does not work that way. He knew it."

We sat there for a long time, listening to Huaman Paullu snore. "Is it hard?"

"No," he shook his head. "It's fair. My job is the best in the world because it is all about right and wrong. Either something is helping the people or it is hurting them. I make sure the system works. That's my job. You can never play favourites, but you never have to, because there is only right and wrong, and you will know wrong when you see it. It will offend you. You will not be able to stand idle. The Inca have a plan for Tahuantinsuyu, and a Tocoyricoc makes sure the plan does not go awry."

I lay awake most of the night, my thoughts inspired by the purpose my father had found for his life. I decided as I fell asleep that I wanted that same responsibility for myself. I wanted to set things right and make people's lives better. I would impress my father and pass his tests. I would become He Who Sees All.

I'd wish you a good morning, Friar, but you're clearly not having one. Am I to guess from your expression that your first sermon was less than a complete success?

Don't take it so personally. You are in the last refuge of a beaten people, and it was your countrymen who beat us. Did you expect us all to request baptism the first day?

Do you know who flocks to a last refuge, Friar? Those who won't knuckle under and acknowledge that the world has changed. The Inca knew a thing or two about dealing with men like that, but I doubt our methods would work for you.

May I offer you one piece of advice as we begin today's work? Your first problem is mistaking your congregation for men without firm religious beliefs. Just because some of our deities are as hazy as morning mist, that does not mean we don't have faith in them. There is a single word, huaca, whose meaning you must learn to understand the people of Tahuantinsuyu.

You look less than impressed, but you will come to understand. From where the sun rises out of the never-ending forests to where it sets in the never-ending sea, all men recognize huacas. There are as many names for huacas as there are stars in the sky, and each is as good as the last as long as it's throaty and soft, whispering hidden promises and dreams and fears. That is what a huaca is, Friar. It is holiness incarnated.

A huaca is something different, separate, apart from the rest. It is every manifestation of beauty or ugliness, anything that inspires awe or fear or any other strong emotion that runs up and down your spine until the soles of your feet tingle and tell you, 'Here is the unusual.' A huaca is where power concentrates for men to see and honour. Huacas are the face and word and form and deeds of gods, Friar. Huacas are the palpable proof of divinity.

Illaquita's village had a huaca that was brought out to wish us well on our remaining journey. It was the bole of an huarango tree that must have been swept out into the ocean and washed ashore over and over, until the sand and wind and water scoured it clear and white as bone. The softer sections of the wood had disintegrated away to leave something approximating a human face with huge empty orbits that looked deep into your heart. My father plucked an eyelash and blew the idol a kiss as we walked away, and there was nothing foolish in paying reverence to something in which such power dwelled.

I told you we Inca knew how to handle the people we added to Tahuantinsuyu? It was through their huacas. However better we would make their lives in the long term, there were always people who could not accept the pachacuti of our rule over them, who wanted to keep fighting us.

Some we turned into mitmaks, the word literally means 'men moved elsewhere,' but I suppose you could call them colonists. We would move entire clans from rebellious tribes into a calm area of the Empire and resettle our own loyal subjects on the vacated lands. Sometimes, too, we heavily subsidized the newly conquered with food and clothes and women until they could see the advantage of Inca rulers. Whatever we did, though, we always pacified them through their huacas.

When we conquered a people we explained how our patron god, Inti, had defeated their gods, and we would build a sun temple on the highest point of land available so that everyone below could see his ascendancy.

Then we asked them what filled them with awe, and when they presented us with the idols of their gods we would fete and feast their huacas as we would our own, worshipping and praying and sacrificing to them with a fervour and generosity that no people could match. Then we brought the idols to Cuzco to honour their people's beliefs as our own.

Imagine what that means to a conquered people, to know the physical form of your god is in your conqueror's capital. Aside from the respect and honour your new rulers show your faith, which is flattering, there's also fear. We Inca held their gods hostage, Friar. Everyone knew the first thing we did upon word of a rebellion was to smash the offending tribe's idols into powder and throw the remains across a llama pasture. Threatening a man's gods is a good way to control him.

That said, our methods would not work for you, Friar. Your God is too jealous to share worshippers with others, as Inti was prepared to do, and you smash men's idols whether they are obedient to you or not.

I begin today's talk with an explanation of huacas because on the journey back to Cuzco I had my first true conversation with my father, not as a son but as a man, and we were discussing what was holy.

When the sun rose he told me it was huaca, and when it set and the stars came out each of those was huaca. Almost every stream we crossed and cave we passed was huaca. There are mountains throughout Chincaysuyu, and my father named each peak to me as a powerful huaca, worthy of my respect.

A thing does not need to be grand to be holy, Friar. Anything unique is a huaca, and the power of the huaca is proportionate to how strongly you react to it. Thus to walk by a field of maize and see twinned ears is to be in the presence of a huaca, but nowhere near as powerful a huaca as, say, the staff of office my father held, and that was as nothing to a single eyelash plucked from the Sapa Inca's face. Do you see?

The world around us is filled with magic, an invisible web of power whose threads can be pulled by men who know their secrets. My father acknowledged each one as a man would nod to an equal he passed on the road, but it seemed to me that he never seemed truly impressed. One day high in the western mountains I asked him, "Which huacas do you believe in, father?"

He looked down at me from his litter. "I believe in anything men find holy. To ignore divinity is folly."

I heard his warning tone, but I went ahead with an eight-year-old's recklessness. "Yes, but those are huacas that other men find holy. I can look at that mountain and see its power, but so can everyone else. Have you ever heard something or seen something that you knew was huaca without anyone telling you?"

My father's face softened for a moment. When he replied he spoke in Inca Simi, the private and personal language of the Inca since the ancient days and known only to us and the Kallawaya, a small tribe of medicine men who seemed to know every tongue spoken in the world. I realized my father was telling me something he did not want the Rucana litter bearers below him to know, a little piece of himself.

"There are three things I know to be huacas because I and I alone say so. The first is your mother's grave in the land of the Chacapoyas, three quarters of the way up a cliff and filled with more silver and gold than the curaca of the entire tribe owns. It is huaca because I say so."

We continued down the road for a while before he spoke again. "There is a lance with a serrated bronze head that hangs over our kitchen hearth. We have other weapons, but only that lance is special to me. My father gave it to me when I marched to my one war. It is my connection to him, the reminder that I was a favoured son, bastard or no."

At the time my father and I walked that road the Sapa Inca was a man named Topa Inca Yupanki, Honoured Royal Inca. Before he became Emperor he was his father's champion, leading the armies of the Inca in a long series of conquests. My grandfather was Tillca Yupanki, the most famous of Old Topa's generals. He marched across half the world with Topa, and in every village he seemed to sire a bastard, so that there were so many sons of the general that even his great name was not enough to secure them a good place in the rising Inca hierarchy.

Tillca had some legitimate sons by his official wife, but my father was not one of them. Instead, my father caught Tillca's eye from the multitude of his prodigy as a great thinker, and so the general made arrangements for the hideously expensive training necessary to secure his favourite bastard the position of a tocoyricoc.

My grandfather was put to death as one of the last spiteful acts of the Sapa Inca Pachacuti, Old Topa's predecessor and father. Pachacuti had been a great conqueror in his youth, but Topa outstripped all before him, conquering almost every nation ever heard of in Cuzco and many that were not. What was worse, my grandfather had insulted Pachacuti's Coya, and she bided her time until the Emperor was in a mood before seeking her revenge.

Pachacuti ordered my grandfather's death to remind Topa of his place and to please his wife. It was the petulant act of a proud old man whose power was slipping. Within months Pachacuti died too and Topa was the Emperor, and all my father had left was a lance to remind him that his father had loved him.

Again we continued in silence, but this time I grew impatient for I knew the final huaca would be something my father had saved to the end for a reason, something beyond my imagination. "What is the third thing, father?"

"The third is a secret, and it will remain a secret, do you understand me?" I said I did, and I do not think I am breaking that trust today. It is likely no one will read this account until after I am dead, and you, Friar, don't care about the faith of a dead man, so I am safe to tell the one thing that truly filled my father's heart with awe, not with familial love as had the first two, but true holy reverence: My father had been given a glimpse of the grand design of the universe as it was laid out by the Creator.

"You know the usno stand in Cuzco's Huacaypata?" My father began, naming the platform upon which the Sapa Inca's low stool sat high above the crowd on festivals. I said I did. "It has been carefully engineered so that at noon it casts no shadow to prove that it is especially favoured by Inti, the Sun, yes?"

"Yes, father," I replied, knowing he would not hold a mere stand to be his holy of holies.

"There is a place in this world where no special measures are taken to gain the Sun's favour. In the Kingdom of Quitu everything is so blessed. If you stand in Quitu at noon you have no shadow. None. Not only that, but if you go beyond Quitu, far into the jungles beyond the ken of our geographers, the Sun's shadow returns, but it points in the opposite direction from that cast on this side of Quitu."

He leaned back in his litter triumphant, as if he had proved his point beyond question. A long time stretched as I waited for him to go on. At last I said, "So?" He leaned down and cuffed me behind the ear at my impertinence.

"So don't you realize what that means? What that has to mean? When Viracocha made the world he made it with certain rules, and among those rules is which way a shadow falls, and the dividing place is not Cuzco! Whatever we are told by our priests and teachers, Cuzco is not the centre of the universe. Cuzco is the centre of Tahuantinsuyu, and all the quarters of the world meet there and all the roads lead there, but it is not the centre of the universe: Quitu is."

I was stunned at the thought that the gods could so favour a people who were not the Children of the Sun. "What can we do?" I blurted, thinking only that we must regain what we had lost, not realizing that we had never had it in the first place.

"Take Quitu, and hold it, and make it another Cuzco worthy of the first, and then expand Tahuantinsuyu as far beyond Quitu as it currently lies before it," my father murmured. Despite speaking Inca Simi he still leaned down from the litter and whispered to me, so that the Rucana bearers had to brace themselves against the uneven load. "It is already being done, Waccha. I have explained my discovery to Old Topa. We have taken much of the Kingdom of Quitu, and we will hold it in trust for the future."

He straightened in his chair, closing his eyes. "I will not live to see the Inca people migrate there, but I hope one day before I die that I will stand in the central square of Quitu and look down on the sunny ground to know it belongs to Inti's Chosen People."

He closed his eyes and smiled, and I knew in his mind he was there, seeing Inti bless him as he would in no other place in the universe. We continued our journey through the mountain peaks, quiet and subdued.

I suppose he was enjoying the conversation, even though he had nothing left to say, for he asked me a question that I knew did not interest him. "And what is it that you find holy, Waccha?" I could hear the condescension in his voice. He expected me to have a silly belief, a boy's belief, but I had a true huaca whose power was invisible to anyone but me. I reached into my coca bag and produced it.

It was a piece of braided grass rope as thick as my wrist but shorter than my hand, poorly made and fraying despite the fact that it had never been used. My father eyed it for a moment distastefully, and years later he admitted to me he had feared that I pulled out a girl's doll. He arched an eyebrow. "What is it?"

"This is made of grass from just outside Cuzco. I plucked it and twisted it myself, so wherever I go I have a piece of home with me." I did it on an impulse at the time, twisting the rope to see if I could, but I tucked it away in my coca bag and forgot about it. As I saw just one quarter of the vastness that now acknowledged the Inca as supreme I found myself reaching into the bag and holding onto the little piece of my home, the valley that had launched us out into the world but was always ready to welcome us back.

"That is a good huaca, Waccha." My father sounded impressed. "What will you do when you get home?"

"I'll burn it."

He arched his eyebrow again, and I think he enjoyed being surprised by me. His face split into a grin and he opened his coca bag to pull out two gherkins, one for me and one for him. "Why?"

"I'll be home. I won't need a little piece of it. I'll have the whole thing."

He almost choked on his gherkin, and when he had it down he tipped his head back and laughed and laughed, and he switched back to Runa Simi to repeat the story for his Rucana porters. When his mirth subsided he looked down on me fondly, but I had tucked the rope away for fear that I was being mocked. "You think like an Inca, Waccha. You think like the grandest Inca of them all... 'I'll have the whole thing.'" He started laughing again, slapping his hand on his thigh, which the Rucana mistook as a signal to increase speed. He lurched back at the unexpected surge, and then I was laughing and he was still laughing

44

and the Rucana joined in, and then the whole procession began, and our laughter echoed off the rock faces of the mountain pass so that the whole world shared our merriment.

I have ventured from Cuzco more times than I can count in my life, and every time I have taken a small length of rope with me, made from the local grass. I have one now, in fact, though the rope has dried and frayed and I fear I shall make no other. Cuzco is lost to me. I've asked to be buried with it when I die. But I tell you, Friar, and do not think me mad, when I rub that bit of rope between my fingers, even though it is an entirely different rope from the one I held as a boy high up in the mountains, I can still hear my father's echoing laughter. It makes me very happy, and very sad.

* * *

There are four royal highways that lead from Cuzco, one for each quarter of the Empire. The first goes to Collasuyu, the vast quarter of the Empire that stretches past Lake Chucuito, which you call Titicaca, all the way to the distant mountains of Tchili. Another goes to Andesuyu, the jungle quarter of the Empire that is much smaller than the other three, but is so rich and fierce and foreign that a man cannot claim to be well traveled until he has visited its forests. A third goes to Chincaysuyu, the Quarter that encloses the great subjugated peoples, the Chimu, the Chacapoyas, the Cañari, and the Quitu.

It was the fourth, the Condesuyu road that we were on, a great highway that led us back to Cuzco as sure as water running downhill. When my father and I spoke of our personal huacas we had left the coastal deserts and were negotiating the high passes of the western mountain, then we crossed the rolling puna, still traveling hard and fast. As we approached the eastern mountains, though, we began to slow down, as if my father realized that we were coming to the end of our journey and wished to extend it. You could almost hear my father's mind churning, calculating.

Was I to succeed him? My father was only middle-aged and could have sired more sons —bastards, as the idea of another official wife rankled— but he wanted to begin training now while he was in his prime rather than rush when time might be short. The closer we got to Cuzco, the slower we went, and it seemed that he found a reason to stop and teach me something new at almost every tampu we passed.

I remember one lesson in particular. I think it was the one that made up his mind. Even today it is a harsh blow to my idea of right and wrong. We were back on the Cuzco-side of the roaring Apurimac River, traveling through wild and rugged country ill-suited to cultivation but impressive in its beauty and grandeur.

Each tampu we passed was a garrisoned fortress, a throwback to the days when this had been one of the two invasion routes of the Inca's enemy, the Chanca, whose defeat had allowed Pachacuti to become Sapa Inca against the Emperor Viracocha's wishes. I remember watching bronze lances twinkle as they caught the sun's light over the battlements. It made Cuzco sleep better at night to know these rocky hills were defended.

My father had us stop for a whole day at one such fort, Pacaritampu, and I think in hindsight it took all his cunning to keep a sly look off his face. I thought nothing of it when my father let the Rucana porters scatter, stretching their arms and shoulders at the break before heading to the nearest akha house, which would provide them with as much as they cared to drink as they were the litter bearers of so distinguished a personage as my father.

The great accountant next sent his quipucamayocs to check the tampu's extensive collection of storehouses, warehouses, storage dumps, and silos. Then he released his gherkin fetcher to his usual task. Next he ordered his translators to interrogate travelers heading outwards from Cuzco as to the happenings in the great city. It was not until he threw his guard detail out into a ring around us with orders to let no one near that I realized he had rendered us quite alone.

"Do you know what this place is?" He gestured to the pitted and tumbled heap of rocks outside the walled tampu.

"This is the Inn of First Appearances," I said, repeating the name I had heard when my father ordered the stop and got everyone out of earshot.

"It is called that because this spot, right here, is where Manco Capac and his three brothers and four sisters emerged from their cave after the Great Flood and began their journey to find Cuzco, the land promised to them by Inti and Viracocha."

You can ask any tribe in this New World of yours, Friar, and regardless of which gods they worship they will all tell you that the world before this one was destroyed by a Great Flood, a deluge that wiped the earth clean, and that their people emerged from a cave

46

or a mountain top, put there by their own particular deity, to start again. We Inca emerged from our cave thanks to Inti, but he took his gift one step further and ordered us to conquer the world, beginning with Cuzco.

My jaw dropped to think I stood at the very spot, the beginning of my people's journey to greatness, and my father gave me a moment or two of reverence before a low rumble started in his throat that climbed higher and higher until finally it burst from between his lips as great gulps of barking laughter.

I looked at him, aghast that he would profane such a holy place with his outburst. This, where I was standing, was where our people began, a people who now ruled the known world. Standing there was like putting a hand on the cradle of the Emperor.

"I want you to remember this, Waccha. People will believe what you tell them, and the more they want to believe it, the more they will." He stopped laughing. "It's a fake, son. The whole thing is a lie."

I must have looked hurt, because he put a hand on my shoulder and sighed. "I'm sorry, but it is better you learn young so that you can get over the disillusion and see what a useful tool this is for governing people."

He kept his hand on my shoulder and started walking towards the rocks, waving his other hand at them grandly so that anyone observing us from out of earshot would think he was extolling the virtues of the holy place instead of revealing it as a fraud.

"This is a supreme act of statecraft, Waccha. One quarter of all the people who come to Cuzco take this road, and every one of them sees this place and knows this is where it all began, that the gods set us off on a divine quest to bring the light of civilization to the dark places of the world."

My father barked his laugh again. "That is the power of a story, Waccha. This place is no different from that hill over there or those boulders back there, but Pachacuti picked this spot and said it was the point of our origin, and it has been ever since. Everyone who remembers when this was just an ugly heap of rocks is long dead."

"So where is the real place, father?"

"Who knows? It has been forgotten, Waccha. Truth to tell, my belief is that there was no cave and no divine quest. It's all too neat and tidy."

I did not look up at him this time. I felt foolish and betrayed, and I did not want to also appear naive. "The whole story, Manco appeared here because the gods willed it, and they sent him out with a golden staff to find land so fertile the staff would sink and disappear into the ground and there he was to make his home, and that he would teach the ignorant all the civilized arts like masonry and agriculture and weaving... It sounds like our history was changed after the fact to make it more appealing."

"Who would do that, father?" I asked, malice in my voice. Changing the truth to a lie has always upset me.

"Who wouldn't? You would, I would, Sapa Incas, curacas, everyone if it suited their purpose."

"I wouldn't!" I said.

"I said the same thing when I was your age," my father smiled at me. "But you'll learn. You'll learn. You should know what really happened, but telling people that the gods are involved, Waccha, makes the gods get involved. Did Inti order us to conquer the world, or did we claim he said it so he helps us rather than be seen as ineffectual? I don't know. I only know what the story has been changed to."

"What does that mean, the story has been changed?" His story was like taking a purgative: It made me sick, but I was the better for it in the long run.

"I'm not sure, but I can guess: Down on the coast there are irrigation canals thirty topos long, and today you will hear that Sapa Inca Pachacuti made them, but they were there long before he conquered those people. There are graves out in the desert where the bodies are dressed in clothes as fine as those we wear today, yet the locals will tell you the cemeteries haven't been used in all memory. We didn't teach people how to weave.

"The Kingdom of Chimor's wise men will tell you that before the Great Flood an earlier world was destroyed by a Great Fire, and it is possible that another before that was destroyed by a Great Storm. Their knowledge goes back much further than ours, and they have ruins of old cities and temples that have been empty since Cuzco was a mudwalled village to prove it. I have seen them, Waccha. I have walked abandoned streets and climbed unused steps, and I tell you those cities have been empty for longer than the Inca have had our divine quest.

"On the far side of Lake Chucuito there are stone ruins called Tiahuanaco whose masonry must be the oldest in the world. The art of bringing stones together did not start in Cuzco, and even today we import our best masons from the Colla and Lupaca lands around Tiahuanaco. Doesn't that seem odd to you, if we invented masonry?" He let the question hang, but before I could try to defend our people's honour he began again.

"Then there's Inca Simi. If we are from this place," he gestured to the ugly rocks again, "Why do we speak a language so close to the Colla tongue? Why did we pick Runa Simi, a language from the Cuzco area, as our language of Empire while keeping our ancient foreign dialect a secret?"

"So what really happened?" I asked again, swayed by his arguments.

"I think Manco Capac was a sinchi, a war leader, whose clan was living somewhere too poor to support them, and I think he conquered the people of Cuzco just as the Chanca tried to do to us in my father's time, but that's not a very nice story, is it? Were we starving marauders who took what we wanted? No, much better to say Cuzco was meant for us, given to us by the gods, so we took it and everyone benefited and today the world has clothes and food and stone buildings because of us."

"I don't like that," I muttered, sullen at what I saw as a dirty trick played by the powerful who I was supposed to trust without question.

He smiled at me. "Think of how many people there are in this world, Waccha: There are the common taxpayers, the purics, over eleven million of them. Then there are the yanacona, the personal servants of the Inca, and no one knows how many of them there are because they don't appear on the census data. The leaders of the purics and the yanacona are curacas, and there are hundreds of thousands of them if you include all the ranks. The pacuyoks, the earplug men, the Incas and the Incas-by-privilege, we number maybe twenty thousand adult men. We want what's best for all those other millions, we really do, and we can do more for them than they can do for themselves. It is things like this that let us control those silent stupid masses."

"Why are you telling me this?" I asked him.

"Because you're upset by it, and I respect that. One day you will have to be a part of the lies too, but that doesn't mean you have to believe them. Do you know there was a Sapa Inca between Viracocha and Pachacuti? His name was Urcos, but he was too cowardly to fight off the Chanca so Pachacuti took over from him in a coup. You are one of a very few people who will remember Urcos, and by the time of your grandchildren he will be forgotten forever.

"Things are going to be lost in your lifetime, Waccha, unless you do something about it. I did my part, and my father before me, and now I want you to remember and pass it on to someone you trust to do the same."

My mind hesitated at the thought. "How can I do that?"

"You will learn to read and tie the royal quipus, and you will record the true events among the high circles and low places of the world." He said it as if the job was as good as done.

"It takes years to learn to do that."

"I will arrange it." Again, as good as done.

"Does that mean..."

"Yes," he said, and my heart leapt. "You will be my successor. None of my bastards have a thought in their head for anything but soldiering, and you are my only official son. It is you, or the position slips from my family. My other sons wouldn't do the job. They don't care about the truth. You can do it. You care about the people, and you know right from wrong. You aren't a fool." That was high praise from my father. "You will be a tocoyricoc."

And that was that. My father said it, and he never threatened to change his mind. He would make the next ten years of my life one long lesson, first on his own and then within the structured system of school, finally ending in an apprenticeship at his side.

I remember turning to face the pitted heap of rocks, no better than any that I had passed in all the hills and mountains I had climbed since leaving Cuzco. I must have smiled a dazzling smile, perhaps done a little dance, but I don't recall any of those things. I remember a gust of wind picked up and ruffled my hair, and I remember my father saying something I did not hear. It was snatched away by the zephyr.

He probably gave me the obligatory warning of what hard work it would be, or that I must not think I was being rewarded. My father always knew how to deflate a moment. When I dutifully asked him to repeat what he had said he must have misunderstood me, for he smiled and said the part that I had heard quite clearly the first time.

"You will be a tocoyricoc."

We stayed the rest of the day at the falsely named Inn of First Origins to celebrate. The Rucana porters got drunk; the translators returned with what gossip they had gathered; the warriors asked the tampu keeper for any broken pottery he had and took turns hurling sling stones at the shards, and the gherkin fetcher found a mighty haul at a condiment tampu down on the banks of the Cusipampa. My father shared them with me as we celebrated. It was a good day that ended with my first drink of unwatered akha while all of my father's retinue toasted his decision.

The next day we crested the ridge between the hills of Picchu and Puquin, and there, finally, we had a view of the Huatanay Valley, home to Royal Cuzco.

The valley of the Huatanay River is broad, with gently sloped hills peeling back in all directions, and everything in it was carefully arranged to lavish riches upon the richest city ever built: There were fields of maize and quinoa and potatoes in neat rectangles of green and russet and purple, and great flocks of llamas and alpacas grazed wherever land lay fallow. Where the slopes were too steep the terrain was shaped into step-like terraces filled with rich earth held in by walls of gray fieldstone.

There were storehouses everywhere, storehouses for everything the earth can grow or man can make: Clothing and pottery and weapons and tools, feathers and medicine and musical instruments and leather, fertilizer and precious metals and food. Oh, the food! There was enough to feed the entire valley of two hundred thousand people for ten years without a single new potato being grown.

You do not believe that the valley had two hundred thousand people, Friar? I assure you it did once, before all that my tale will tell transpired. Aside from the twenty thousand nobles in Cuzco itself, there were neat little hamlets of mud and stone evenly spaced throughout the valley filled with all the peoples of the world.

A portion of each new tribe added to the Empire was settled in the Huatanay valley as colonists. They were even placed in the valley as they were positioned in Tahuantinsuyu, so that people from the west lived on the west side of the valley, and distant tribes lived further from Cuzco than nearby ones. In this way Cuzco had access to every culture it commanded, as well as unlimited labour to build and to grow and to serve the Children of the Sun.

But it occurs to me I am speaking of the valley as if it were a plain, when its hills are just as important as its fields and villages: The hills to the immediate east and west of Cuzco had the sun posts that lined up with the rising and setting sun, keeping our calendar in perfect synch with the seasons. To our left as we stood on the Condesuyu Road was Puquin Hill, home of the Great Quipu Repository. This great building was the nexus of all Inca bureaucracy, and its four counting room towers saw thousands of quipus come in and out every day.

To our right was the distant windswept hill of Huanacauri, our war idol who was a brother of Manco Capac turned to stone. At his feet every Inca boy became a man, and no army marching into battle with Huanacauri had ever been defeated. In front of us squatted Sacsahuaman, Speckled Hawk Hill, where the fortress of Intihuasi had been under continuous construction by twenty thousand workers for fifteen years already and would continue to be built until the arrival of the Spaniards. It was a fortress designed to survive the end of the world.

The flanks of that hill were ravines cut by steady streams which ran out onto the plain, gently merging together to enclose a triangle of land, and there was Cuzco, the most beautiful city in the world.

Oh Cuzco, Royal Cuzco, the rich city, the holy city, the only city! It answered to all these and more. Any words I use will seem too grandiose when in fact they are so insufficient they border on paltry.

Cuzco. I do not know what it meant in the beginning, for it was the original name of the village occupied by Manco Capac in the name of Inti and the Intip Churi, but in Runa Simi it was interchangeable with the words centre, navel, focal point, for that is what we turned it into.

Do you know what it is to look at a place and know that your eyes have found the point upon which the whole world turns? That was Cuzco. Our city was as perfect as a people with absolute power could make it. Every stone in every wall was a work of art. Foreigners often fell to their knees in awe at their first sight of it, and today I hear the people remaining in the valley after all that has happened often sigh, even weep, at what they have lost.

The city was like a puma lying on its side, with the hill of Sacsahuaman for its head and the great temple of Coricancha on the point of land where the streams meet to form the Huatanay River itself forming its tail. There were two main roads running from Upper Cuzco to Lower Cuzco, informally called the Spine Road and the Belly Road. Crossing these avenues at pleasing perpendicular angles were the streets of the city, like ribs and haunches.

At the centre of the city, where the four great royal roads meet, was the Huacaypata, a holy plaza that was the beating heart of Cuzco, and by extension the world. I suppose in Spanish Huacaypata would mean Recreation Square, but the better translation would be the Place Where One Ceases to Work and Begins to Enjoy. It was two hundred paces by one hundred and fifty paces, covered in dazzling white sand brought all the way from the beaches of the never-ending sea and piled so thick that a man could dig half his height down before hitting the flagstones beneath.

Here my father's procession entered the city in silence, and everywhere we went pacuyoks and yanaconas blew my father a respectful kiss as he passed. When we reached our front door with its yellow blanket my father descended from his litter, picked me up onto his shoulders, and we entered our compound in triumph.

"My son will be Tocoyricoc!" He shouted, and the household cheered as if I had already performed a worthy feat. It was another good day. My father sacrificed to the household gods in thanks, and secretly threw a pinch of precious coca leaves into the kitchen's hearth fire as an offering to the serrated bronze lance hanging above. With the ancestors and the deities thus satisfied, I began my long education.

My training started with small jobs. The first of these saw me awaking each day before dawn and going out into the street to prioritize the quipucamayocs waiting there in the darkness by the severity of their problem.

For some time they resented taking their orders from a boy, but I was firm with them, and as I came to know the job they accepted that I was making a small difference in the efficiency of the process. Through this task I came to understand the different levels of clerical error, and I also learned the names of all my father's subordinates in Cuzco. It was a good first job, and little by little I came to understand the greatest accountants' art.

I ate my two simple meals just after dawn and just before sunset with my father in his counting room. As I have said, he was not a social man, so we usually worked through his meals. A compulsive counter, he made a game of keeping a tally of how many potatoes I ate in a given month, tracking my progress over the seasons to estimate when

I would experience my next growth spurt. My mother's Chacapoyan blood made me grow so often he could hardly guess wrong.

Every three or four days we would go to the Great Quipu Repository up on its hill. It was a distinctive looking building with huge trapezoidal windows facing east and west to give its chambers the maximum amount of light. We would stand outside and strip down to the bare minimum of polite dress before entering.

Bureaucracy is not an activity known to keep a man fit, but for all our administrative prowess we Inca were a warrior people. Every one of these quipucamayocs might be called upon to serve in the elite Inca legions or command a conscript legion made up of purics. We could not afford to let our accountants grow fat, and so the Great Quipu Repository's rule was that all quipucamayocs must work inside dressed in their breechcloths so that any lack of fitness could be spotted and chastened by the fellow's peers. It was an effective rule, for the accountants I saw were all thin and wiry looking, despite their sedentary occupations.

Huaman Paullu would walk my father up and down the rows of squatting quipucamayocs labouring over their counting boards and quipus, and my father would spot mistakes as they were being made without turning his head.

"Carry the two, Huaritico," he would say, the man blushing furiously. "What's five times nine, Taipi? I thought so," he'd say to another, and so it went.

Then he would inspect the archives, long deep shelves of jars, each holding quipus of priceless value. Some were hundreds of years old, recording data from when the Inca did not even control all of the Huatanay Valley. Others were royal quipus recording history, philosophy, astronomy, and the words of the Sapa Incas.

Without being told, I could feel the power emanating from the jars. This place was as much a huaca as any temple to Inti or talking oracle. There was tremendous knowledge here for any man with the mind to decipher it. One day I would have such a mind.

Towards the end of our inspections we would climb the tower reserved for my father's use. Sometimes we would take a summary quipu with us, sometimes not, but when we were up there we always poured a cup of akha out the window as an offering of thanks for the power entrusted in us, and gave a respectful prayer to Viracocha, the

Creator, to keep our fingers nimble, our eyes keen, and our minds sharp.

Sunset brought the end of the workday for the Great Quipu Repository, for no one would dare work by firelight. The building was the equivalent of one giant wool warehouse; the flammable dust swirling through the place from all the distressed yarn would have had the very air itself burn at the first lick of a flame. No, when the sun sank beyond the western hills on inspection days the quipucamayocs filed out and my father would throw a subdued party for them back at our place to reward them for their hard work.

It was a quiet way to grow up, and I loved those simple days, not realizing how quickly they would pass. I was ten years old when I was first thrown into the greater world, outside the closed ranks of my father's quipucamayocs. Once I was out it was years before I ceased pining to be let back into my previous cozy life where I knew all the players and the rules and could put no foot wrong without meaning to.

It started innocently enough with an invitation to a party. Not really an invitation for me, of course, because who did I know? The invitation was for my father, and I watched from one of the side rooms of the outer courtyard as the messenger arrived. His bright alpaca mantle was so extravagant he could have been mistaken for a huarangacamayoc, a master of one thousand tax-paying families, instead of an errand boy going door to door.

I knew my father would politely refuse. My father worked, slept, and ate his gherkins; that was all the fun I ever saw him have. It was not until he thanked the man and turned from the closed teak door to bellow for our servants to start airing out his finest clothes that I saw the red and blue threads the messenger had given him. The blue was an impressively deep shade, the official colour of the Socso Panaca. The red was even more powerful, the colour of the Sapa Inca himself. My father's presence was not just requested, it was demanded.

Even then I was not more than mildly interested. It was only when one of my father's concubines appeared at my side and began measuring me for a new tunic and mantle that I realized I was invited as well. My father entered the room to oversee the procedure.

"I'm going too?" I asked eagerly, raising my arms for her to find the measurement of my small chest.

"Yes, and don't say anything to disgrace yourself. That's the point of this little evening."

I frowned. My father was using the tone he saved for a stern reproof, but he did not seem angry at me. "Sorry?"

"The theme of the Socso Panaca's party is 'Tomorrow.' Every powerful pacuyok and curaca in Cuzco is supposed to bring his favourite child." I did not puff up at the compliment. I knew I was the favourite. "Everyone will be judging everyone else's choice. What a way to introduce the next generation to one another, to have each picked out and ranked by his parents as better or worse, and all a month before the next intake at the House of Learning."

I smiled, confident that I would be well-liked. My father was not so sure. He snapped at the woman measuring me to find something beyond sumptuous that was the right size for my tall and skinny frame, and he muttered that if he had been given more notice he would have had something made to order. It was only as he left that I realized he was worried. My mind flew to Mama Ocllo's suggestion that other men wanted their sons to become He Who Sees All.

The day of the party came, and I had never worn such rich clothes before. That is saying something, Friar, for my father's station required me to wear clothes every day that were finer than a puric would wear even on a holiday.

My little tunic was of interlocking red and white rectangles, and upon each white one was a smiling face embroidered in red stitching, while upon the red were faces of white. Each smiled in a different way, so that some smirked and others grinned, some looked pained and others seemed to be in mid-guffaw. Just by looking at it you could sense that the embroiderer was a woman of rare intelligence, the heart of her community. I wondered who she was and what special boon she had been given for going so far beyond her tax service quota.

A belt of silver-studded llama leather cinched my tunic at my waist, and I remember wearing sandals with matching silver studs decorating the lacings. The coca bag at my side was covered with silver scales. My mantle was my clan's yellow with short white tassels at the fringe, held together on my shoulder with a pin of heavy gold whose broad head was worked to reveal the face of Inti peeking over the horizon between two mountains. My hair had been specially cut short that day and plastered flat so that not a single strand could drift out of place. Every speck of skin on me was scrubbed clean until I seemed to glow.

When my father finally came out of his chamber I could not recall him ever looking so fine, and he always dressed well on his tours of Condesuyu. That night he wore the uniform of an Inca general, a rank my father did hold even if his education denied him the battlefield.

He boasted both the red and white tunic of bravery granted by a battlefield commander and a chest disc of undecorated gold that said he had commanded a unit that made the crucial difference in a battle. My father had only been to war once, but once was enough. Many career soldiers did not boast such a disc upon their retirement.

His mantle was also of the clan yellow, but where mine was of alpaca his was of cumpi vicuna, that softest and finest of wools that is spun so perfectly you Spanish liken it to your silk. His staff of office was polished with wax. A blue tassel hung from his shoulder, the deep blue of the Socso Panaca. We were ready to go.

The Spanish do not have panacas, so I should explain them: A panaca is like a clan, but it is the clan that honours a dead Sapa Inca. When an emperor dies his spirit goes to the Upper Universe and his body is mummified, becoming a huaca of tremendous power. That power is not just spiritual, either. Sapa Incas do not pass their wealth down to their heirs, only their rank. Panacas controlled all the wealth of their dead emperors' estates, the palaces and the villas and the flocks and the fields. To make them even more powerful, any noble could pledge to serve, giving the panacas constant influx of new members with each generation.

These cults gave members of the female nobility real influence, for women control the religious side of the panaca court, including translating the mummy's wishes into vocal commands. An ambitious woman could come to control a panaca, wielding more power than any other woman in the world except the Sapa Inca's Coya.

Now I would never speak ill of any panaca, but my father often did: They were collection points of malcontents and idle royals, scofflaws and layabouts. The women who joined a panaca often did so because of the sexual license permitted within the dead emperor's palace. The private parties were so wild that the music and sounds of drunken orgies filled the nighttime air of Cuzco.

You might wonder, Friar, why a panaca is not a house of quiet veneration? After all, its purpose is to honour the mummy of an emperor. Well, there is certainly worship, devoted worship, but there is also immense wealth and power, and panacas tended to attract a dangerous mix of ambitious nobodies and aristocratic scoundrels. All this, combined with the inescapable fact that a dead emperor is never going to run a disciplined household when his wishes must be interpreted by his panaca's members, leads to orgies and the feasts and the parties.

Knowing my father's views on both unnecessary fun and unnecessary expense, it must seem odd that he felt we had to go to the party. The Socso Panaca's one redeeming virtue in my father's eyes was that it was dedicated to Viracocha Inca, his grandfather, the man who led the Inca out of our valley and set us on the road to world domination. The mummy we would visit had our dried blood in its veins. From its now desiccated loins had sprung his father, my grandfather.

If my father was being invited to a party by the worshippers of dead Viracocha Inca, and the invitation was reinforced by the command of Viracocha's grandson, the Emperor Topa Inca Yupanki, my sovereign lord, great-uncle, and the best friend of my murdered grandfather, then my father would swallow his dislike for frivolity and attend.

The party was to start mid-afternoon, but my father had enough social acumen to know no one of importance arrived early. The sun was beginning to set when our honour guard arrived at our door, all dressed in the clan yellow. These pacuyoks were seasoned soldiers in their late twenties and early thirties, bastards of my father's brothers and cousins. Ten of them formed two lines to either side of the narrow street in front of our teak door, and when my father and I were enclosed within their ranks they began to march in step, the studs on the soles of their sandals ringing loud against the cobbles and echoing eerily among the stone walls.

My father did not need protection, of course, except that his station demanded an entourage of some kind. With the possible exception of kicking a stray dog out of the way there was nothing for them to do except walk us there and then walk us back. My father had considered taking his litter, but he knew the best of his Rucanas might be poached out from under him by other lords at the party. The men of our honour guard were blood relatives. No one would take these men away from the service of Tocoyricoc Tupac Capac.

We approached the Amauracancha, the Serpent Enclosure, as the Socso Panaca's palace was known, and my father's expression darkened as if he truly were entering a monster's lair. He put his hand around the back of my neck. "You are going to see bad behaviour in there, boy. Just remember I brought you up better than this." With that final warning we entered the largest of the panaca's courtyards.

It's funny to think what first impressed me as to the wealth of the Socso Panaca was not the gold platters or silver chalices, the legions of yanaconas or the dozen llamas rotating on spits: It was the fact that the torches had been lit long before sundown, and as we arrived still more were being fired up despite the cheery glow of sunset still visible in the sky. In my household as long as there was enough light to walk the even floors with confidence we did not need a flame's illumination for help, but then my father was frugal in all things.

Women circulated through the crowds with trays heavy with cups of akha, and my father's grinning honour guard lightened the women's loads before heading off to a smaller courtyard set aside for servants, escorts, and retainers.

The main courtyard of the Socso Panaca was big enough to fit our house inside it without touching any of the surrounding buildings; it was filled with dazzling white sand like the Huacaypata. Spilled drinks were easily dealt with by kicking fresh sand over the wet.

Drums and cymbals and flutes filled the space with their merry beat, and the revelers took their cue from that, mixing and mingling, each eager to see the chosen child of a friend or rival. The party's theme was a huge success.

I was stunned to see so many nobles, pacuyoks and curacas alike. Everyone was in their best dress, and these people were entitled to wear the best in the world. The colours exploding from the cottons and wools were as vivid as any jungle bird could boast.

My father wasted no time on casual banter. He looked neither right nor left as he led me towards the Emperor, his hand firmly on my shoulder so I could not fidget or flee. The far end of the great courtyard had been separated off from the rest by a translucent cotton screen behind which the Imperial Court could feast without inflicting the rest of the guests to the rigors of court protocol. Within the screen, however, we were in the presence of the Emperor himself. Great measures would be taken to show our respect.

In an anteroom —really just another cotton-walled partition— my father and I removed our sandals and placed small burdens on our backs. Those who stand in the presence of the Shepherd of the Sun must always remember how humble they are.

Upon entering the Imperial Presence your eyes are overwhelmed by the splendour of the gold and silver, the feathers and clothes, the jewels and furniture, but you cannot stop to look around. You approach, head bowed, never dreaming to look at the Emperor directly, then you stop, bow from the waist with arms stretched out in front with the palms open and facing down, then you make a kissing noise.

You remain there, in that awkward position, the weight on your back and your bare feet reminding you just what differences in status separate you from the most powerful man in the world until the Emperor acknowledges you. Only then can you straighten up and look around.

For this party the Imperial Court was roughing it, bringing only their most transportable luxuries. There were dancers and jesters and acrobats and jugglers and bards lining the walls, waiting respectfully for a moment when the Sapa Inca should order an amusement. There were four royal quipu masters in one corner, ready to tie down any proclamation. There were also hangers-on and flunkies jockeying for position. My father and I passed through this multitude to genuflect before the Emperor.

A stage of interlocking teak had been erected on the sand, and only the truly worthy could stand upon it. There were the four viceroys, of course, each in charge of one quarter of Tahuantinsuyu: Viceroy Mayta of Condesuyu, my father's only direct superior save for the Sapa Inca, stood at one end smiling at us; Viceroy Achachi Michi, one of the greatest military minds the Inca had ever produced, was reading a quipu and chewing on a wad of coca. He claimed he could not go campaigning anymore because his work as ruler of Chincaysuyu took too much of his time, but there were whispers in the halls of power that his back hurt, terribly, and that only the sweet relief of chewing coca allowed him to rise from his sleeping pallet in the morning.

Also on the dais the brothers Viceroy Hualpaya of Andesuyu and Viceroy Illyapa of Collasuyu stood engrossed in conversation with the three Ocllo sisters. Illyapa was emphasizing a point by waving his staff of office, on its end a chunk of black glass —the rarest of jewels— sparkled in the torchlight.

While I was conscious of everyone, there was no way to ignore the Sapa Inca. A smaller platform rose up from the stage almost to waist height, equipped with an elegant low wooden stool; upon this throne, called an usno, sat the Shepherd of the Sun, unquestioned Lord and Master of the Four Quarters of the World. Everyone had their body turned to face him. He was the centre of our universe.

Sapa Inca Topa Inca Yupanki must have been in his late sixties at the time, and his face bore every line one would expect from a man who had fought his way across the length and breadth of Tahuantinsuyu, married a thousand women, and established the stamp of our civilization on more than fifty reluctant tribes.

His golden earplugs were so big they brushed his shoulders. His headband encircled his brow five times, with the red fringe of vicuna wool marking his Imperial office dangling from golden tubes to cover his forehead. Tucked into his headband with a golden holder were two short feathers, a white one and a black one: These came from the Curiquinque bird, so rare that it is said that only one mating couple exist at any time.

Topa Inca Yupanki's attire put the rest of the nobility's garments to shame. His mantle was of woven bat fur, dyed bright yellow, and anyone who has ever seen how short the fur of a bat is can appreciate what that means: Tens of thousands of bats had been caught and shaved, then their fur, shorter and finer than eyelashes, was dyed and spun into threads. These were worked onto a loom whose warp and weft was so tight that hundreds of threads would go back and forth in the area covered by my thumb.

As if this embarrassing richness of human labour were not incredible enough, the mantle was decorated with blue and red hummingbird feathers —each smaller than a kernel of maize— that made up an elaborate geometric pattern.

In total the mantle must have been the work of dozens of weavers, dyers, hunters, and pluckers, and may have taken five years to go from concept to finished product. The Emperor never wore the same clothes in a given month, and unless he took it off and gave it to a favourite as a gift the mantle would only be kept in his wardrobe for a year before it was ceremonially burned as an offering to Inti.

As we waited there for him to acknowledge us my subtle inspection moved from the Emperor to the man standing closest to the usno. His heir, Titu Cusi Huallpa, also wore a royal fringe on his forehead, but where the Imperial fringe was red his chosen successor's was yellow. Titu Cusi Huallpa was a short broad-chested man, not yet in his twenties, with a kind-looking face marred only by his eyes, which were hard and black and seemed to miss nothing.

"You are welcome here, Tupac," the Emperor said at last. His voice was a dusty rattle, as if he had lived forever. He was old, yet timeless.

"Hello, Sire," my father said. "This is my son, Waccha." He pushed me forward and I genuflected again.

Old Topa looked me up and down, interested to see the boy whose birth had caused such a stir. "He is tall for his age," he said. I tried to stretch even taller in response to the praise; we Inca, like all mountain people, tend to be short and burly. I was already as tall as a short man thanks to my mother's Chacapoyan blood.

"I agree he is too tall," my father said, quick to make the Emperor's compliment a complaint to cool the hostility of the surrounding lords. "And skinny too. I hope he builds some muscles: It takes broad shoulders to carry the burdens of a tocoyricoc."

"My son has broad shoulders," Viceroy Achachi Michi said from around his mouthful of coca. I wondered if he was the friend of Cari Ocllo's who wanted his boy to succeed my father. "But I wouldn't trust him to add two to four. Leave administration to the smart ones." He flashed me a smile flecked with shredded green leaves. I decided then that I liked the general, a decision that would keep me in good stead throughout my life.

"Do you want to be tocoyricoc, son?" Topa asked me.

"Yes, Sire," I said, my heart jumping to be spoken to directly by the red-fringed Emperor.

"You wouldn't prefer to be a soldier? Your grandfather was my finest soldier." Topa smiled the smile of an old man reminiscing, then he perked up, as if at a sudden thought. "Isn't that right, Pilla-huaso?"

From the crowd of nobles behind the stage a strangely dressed man stepped forward. His tunic and mantle were of green cotton, and his headdress boasted a small emerald in the centre of his forehead. You could see that once he had carried himself with more pride, stepped with more swagger. "Of course, Sapa Inca," the man said in accented Runa Simi.

"Tell the boy who you were, and what his grandfather made you," Old Topa ordered.

"I was the highest sinchi of the Quitu armies, and with the death of

62

the last Scyri of the Kingdom of Quitu I am the most senior noble of the Cayambi tribe," the man said in a tone implying he spoke by rote. "Your grandfather, Tillca Yupanki, made me a hostage against my people's continued good behaviour. When—"

"If," Topa corrected him.

"If they revolt, I will be strangled and my body will be left for the crows."

The yellow-fringed heir Titu Cusi Huallpa smiled at that. "Come now, we can do better than that for you! A man of your station should only be eaten by condors, don't you think? Crows are for purics." His mother Mama Ocllo laughed, and when the Coya was amused, the Imperial Court dutifully joined in her merriment. Pilla-huaso did not. He stepped back to his appointed place, and I could see now it was a crowd of foreigners, some dignitaries and some hostages, none of whom would be allowed to speak unless spoken to. Such was the Sapa Inca's power.

"Is there anyone else back there you want to talk to?" Topa asked, noting my interest.

I should have said no and terminated the interview, but there was one so exotic looking that I could not contain myself. "Who is that with the face paint, Sire?" Several courtiers chuckled at my ignorance, but the man stepped forward. His face was painted in a complicated pattern of red and white, and the long silver ornament through his nose was complimented by a bulbous one dangling from his lip. "I am Minchancaman, the Great Chimu of the Kingdom of Chimor."

Every Intip Churi within earshot scowled to hear him speak: Here before me was the former ruler of the coastal empire that had been greater than our own. The Chimu's armies were so numerous that the Sapa Inca Pachacuti and Topa Inca Yupanki had both forbidden their generals to provoke a war with them. The general who sparked the conflict was beheaded for it, despite being the elder brother of the Viceroys Hualpaya and Illyapa.

Only a supreme and unwanted struggle won us our victory, but now the greatest of the Chimu stood here, a mere Imperial toy. He reminded me of one of those pots his tribe makes showing people performing all manner of unnatural sexual acts: intriguing, but provoking a vague sense of guilt.

"Would you like to tread on the enemy, Waccha?" Topa teased me. It was traditional for a battlefield commander to step on the neck of a surrendering foe to show his dominance, but I had not beaten Min-chan-caman. It had taken every Inca general, three hundred thousand men, and fourteen years to do that. Minchan-caman's face twisted, and Topa's amused smile disappeared. "You should be grateful to be alive, Great Chimu. You could be something much worse." Topa gestured to a corner of the curtained Imperial enclosure.

I looked over and my head snapped back to the Sapa Inca. Sitting there in the corner was the Emperor's personal runa tinya, man drum. A Colla rebel general had insulted Topa Inca Yupanki to such an extent that his corpse had been skinned and stuffed with a drum in his abdomen so that men could beat on his belly with sticks and hear the echoing boom come out of his mouth.

"I want to be a tocoyricoc, Sire," I said, wanting this interview to be over. The thought of more of our former foes being trotted out made me feel ashamed, as if they deserved better. All of our enemies had been offered peaceful amalgamation into Tahuantinsuyu, where they would have been retained at their appropriate rank and station. It was their own fault —their resistance to the inevitable— that had led them to this humiliation.

"Then do well in your studies, son, and the job is yours," he told me. I genuflected again, and my father reached out to lead me out of the Royal Presence.

"Don't you think it's time Tupac takes another wife?" Mama Ocllo asked her husband. My father's hand froze. All eyes turned from the Coya to the Sapa Inca and back.

"My mother often speaks of you, Tupac," Crown Prince Titu Cusi Huallpa said. "She seems to think you're lonely."

"And what do you think, my lord?" My father asked respectfully, for this man would be our emperor one day.

"I think my mother is not often wrong about these things." He gave Mama Ocllo an affectionate smile. "What would it hurt to indulge her?" Those hard eyes of his looked out from under the yellow fringe. He loved his mother as no one else in the world seemed to, and I think he suspected my father spurned marriage just to vex her.

"I do not refuse to displease her. I just know I will never be happy with another wife, at least not happier than I am with the concubines I already have," my father said.

"Well I think it makes all the difference in the world." The Coya adjusted her shawl like a preening bird.

Now it was the Sapa Inca's turn to speak. "I don't know. Having an official wife differs little from having a concubine except that the children are legitimate." Both Mama Ocllo and Chiqui Ocllo straightened a little at the reproof. The Viceroys Illyapa and Hualpaya gave looks of embarrassed sympathy to the Imperial women. Viceroy Achachi Michi spat his plug of coca into the sand and drew a new one from his bag. Viceroy Mayta just cleared his throat.

Old Topa ignored them all, turning back to my father. "You are dismissed, Tupac. I will see you tomorrow to review the Huanca levy figures."

"Yes, Sire." My father genuflected. When we were in the anteroom we removed our burdens and put our sandals back on.

Outside the party had picked up, thanks in no small part to the quiet distribution of the illegal liquor viñapu, much more potent than mere akha. The banquet portion of the evening was still well off, and so the nobles were toasting each other with wild abandon to pass the time.

I did not know exactly what to expect at a social event of this size, but I did notice that because of the theme few nobles had brought their daughters. Girls could not hold government or military rank and so would not be the heir to any of the invited guests' positions. Any girl in the courtyard that night stood out, for she must either be the jewel of her father's eye or a child of a sonless house. There was one girl, though, who would have attracted stares even in a parade of daughters.

Every boy remembers beautiful girls from his youth, but to recall their face and form from the lofty heights of adulthood is disappointing. So many girls are just that, girls, not women. For a full grown man to desire the fancies of his youth would be to admit to being the worst kind of pedophile. There was that one, though, who young and old could not tear their eyes from. I do not remember ever viewing her as a boy does a girl. Never. From the very first she was always a woman to me.

I learned later that she was twelve, two years older than I, but she had the body of a woman full-grown. True physical beauty cannot be captured by words, but I can describe some of its manifestations so you can picture a pale imitation of the wonder that walked that courtyard, absolutely aware of the effect she was having on all of us.

She had swelling hips that swung through an arc like a weight on a string, a movement so irresistible that men near turned to follow their gyrations. She had breasts so pert —despite their full roundness— that as a tall man looked down on her the mounds of her nipples poked straight up at him through her filmy gown.

Her face was as pale as the moon, and it did not hold a single straight line except for a perfectly proportioned nose. Truly, Friar, if you carved the face of the Madonna in the image of that girl you would have less trouble converting us to your faith. She walked through the crowd, her thin clothes clinging to her in all the right places. She turned her head from side to side in slow and graceful movements. She had a long neck without a line or crease on it, as if she always carried her chin high. She was looking for someone, or perhaps she was weighing the merits of those she passed. I wanted to talk to her, but I could not stray from my father's side. When he caught me trying it he put a hand on my shoulder.

"Where are you off to?" He asked. I did not have to answer his question. He followed the direction of my gaze, straight as the royal road through the coastal desert. He harrumphed. "Oh, it's her."

I tore my gaze from her to look up at my father in confusion and annoyance. His voice had held no reverence, no respect at all. If he knew anything about the girl across the courtyard he should share it with me, but he should do so in a tone fit for someone capable of squeezing my heart at fifty paces. "Who is she?"

He grabbed my other shoulder and spun me around to face him. It felt cold to be turned away from her radiance. "Her name is Atoc China, the Vixen, and she is husband-shopping." My mind panicked, for I was far too young to marry and the thought of losing her when I did not even have her yet struck me to the marrow. He shook me. "Don't you fall for her too, boy! Half of Cuzco is besotted with her, and the other half has already been turned down in their courtship."

He let go of me and I turned back to face her. I could not look away. He harrumphed again. "I don't know what everyone sees in her, frankly. Her face is pretty enough, and you could build a mountain-top temple on that chest, but just look at the difference between her hips and her waist! Put your hands around her and your palms are almost facing straight down."

He sounded disgusted, and for a moment I smiled at being able to so clearly read my father as a man. The Vixen's greatest physical asset was the exact opposite for his own personal recipe for attraction, and so of course he thought the world was mad.

"You said she was husband-shopping?" I asked, looking around for any man puffed up enough to have been selected.

"Yes. She needs to marry up if she's going to get anywhere in life. She's the daughter of an Inca-by-privilege. He's third generation, but he's still a nobody. His own daughter makes him dance to her tune. No, she'll need a powerful husband to do what she says she wants to do. As it is, her father and Old Topa have put her into Cuzco's House of Chosen Women until she picks her husband."

I wondered for a moment how any girl, however beautiful, could have persuaded her father and Emperor to allow her such a privilege. "What does she want to do?"

I suppose my father decided I was paying her far too much attention, for instead of answering he pulled me into a circle of old soldiers discussing the latest Andesuyu campaign against the jungle savages. The group shifted so that I could only keep an intermittent eye on the Vixen, and this seemed to satisfy my father.

Eventually I did tear my gaze from her, but it was her doing. The Vixen was looking long and hard at something, so I turned my head to see what had so caught her attention.

Once I spotted him there was no doubt what had arrested the Vixen. I was closer to him than she was, and he pulled my eye to him for a reason that had nothing to do with beauty. You could sense a palpable force around the boy. Something was going to happen.

He was tall and thin, making him stand out from the squat solid boys who were crowding him against a wall. He was taller even than I, and he used his height to glare down at the others, daring them to show a weakness he could use. His eyes were hard and black, their gaze sharp as obsidian flakes as he looked from boy to boy. His nose was a beak that threw shadows over a lipless mouth. He had a long, drawn face with cheek bones so high that he looked gaunt, as if he was starving. Of all the children I saw, only he looked like a man.

I watched as one of the boys began to taunt him. The tall boy lifted his arm to show bulging knotty biceps out of all proportion to his long thin arm. When I look back over the griefs and pains and regrets of my life, I laugh to think my first glimpse of Chalcuchima was of him flexing his muscles to intimidate a bully.

Pretending to be unimpressed —though I noted the laughing boy did not offer to compare his own strength— the gang leader gave the tall boy a shove. They began to argue, and the circle grew larger to allow the two to scuffle, but it would be no private battle. I could see already the other boys up on the balls of their feet, opening and closing their hands. They would rush him once the first blow landed.

I wonder now where their parents were, but I did not look around at the time and now I can only speculate that the children were nothing special and their parents had dismissed them to enjoy the party after the Imperial audience; whatever the reason, the boys were unsupervised and in a moment things would get ugly.

Instead of hitting the short bully and beginning the fight he could not win, the tall boy began saying something slowly. The gang's leader shook his head, speaking fast. I watched, stunned, as the tall boy stuck his hand into a nearby torch, his eyes locked on his challenger.

I imagine my face must have looked much like the shorter boy: Slack-jawed stupefaction replaced by dawning fear. The tall boy's condor-like face did not even twitch as his hand hovered in the flame. The discipline, the mental control of that act, stunned me.

At last —though thinking back it could not have been more than a few moments— the short boy slapped the hand free of the flames. The lipless one gave a joyless sneer to acknowledge his victory. The former bully looked at the ground, shamed at his defeat.

I heard a raised voice and saw a curaca swoop down on the short boy, yelling at the tall one. A woman emerged from a nearby crowd and pulled away the burned boy. Who was he? I decided to ask.

"Father, who is that?" I tugged at the sleeve of my father's tunic and pointed at the retreating mother and son.

"That's Capac Yupanqui's widow and the aucca's son, damned nerve bringing him before the Emperor. Viceroy Illyapa told her not to." I stared up at my father for a moment. Runa Simi has a number of words for traitor, and aucca is the worst of them: To call a man an aucca and be proven right is the man's death sentence, but to falsely accuse him gives the man the right to kill you without punishment.

"What's his name?" I asked.

"With that nose and those eyes? Mallku, Young Condor. Though his father's dying wish was that the boy's adult name should be Chalcuchima, and he was a powerful enough man that most people call his son that out of respect."

Now that I had shown interest in someone other than the Vixen my father relaxed his hand on my shoulder and I slipped out of the circle of old men. I headed straight for the girl, of course, but slowed when I saw her go to join Mallku.

He was not cradling his hand, despite the blisters already appearing on its palm. She picked it up and turned it over, as if to predict his future in the bubbles between the lines, a more accurate prediction than any of us could have imagined, but that was a lifetime away yet.

At last I gathered the nerve to approach her, but all of her attention was on Mallku's hand. He seemed totally uninterested by the obvious pain he was in, though he did shift his position to put more of his strong body between me and the Vixen, who was commiserating with him.

"Is he badly hurt?" I asked her. I should have asked him, of course, but he meant nothing to me, whereas she was fast becoming the thing I valued most in the world.

"Wasn't he brave?" She whispered, at last releasing Mallku's hand. The tall boy turned on me. He set his jaw until the muscles in his neck twitched, something I later learned meant he was deeply annoyed. He had succeeded in drawing the most desirable girl at the party to his side, and I was ruining his moment of triumph.

"I suppose he was, if making himself useless is bravery." He glowered at me with those dark eyes of his. "That is your right hand, isn't it?"

"I use my left hand for my sling and lance," Mallku said stiffly, not prepared to have another altercation but clearly uncomfortable with keeping his temper in check.

"What did the other boy say to you that provoked you to do a thing like that?" I could think of nothing that would make me burn myself.

"He was trying to pick a fight, but he had six other boys with him. I told him one on one I was stronger than any of them, and when they still didn't offer to even the odds I said I was braver than all six of them put together." Mallku held up his palm. "The trick is to know that you can take it longer than they can. Someone was going to stop me. The pain doesn't matter. It's a temporary thing."

I eyed the heat blisters. Nothing looked permanently damaged. "What was the fight about?"

"He insulted my father," he said. "My father conquered his people, long ago."

I don't know why I said it, but I asked, "Wasn't your father a traitor?"

Mallku puffed himself up, the resemblance to a strutting condor obvious. "My father was a great soldier, as I will be. He was killed by the Emperor for his success, and only his rivals dare say he betrayed his people."

I tried to sound reasonable, knowing I was dealing with a boy prepared to burn himself to prove a point. "My grandfather was also a general: Tillca Yupanki. He was executed on the order of Pachacuti, but no one calls him a traitor. What did your father do differently?"

"What is your name?" He grunted at me, his neck muscles clenching. He knew now that I was well-born: Tillca Yupanki had been a half-brother of the Sapa Inca Topa Inca Yupanki.

"Waccha. My father is Tocoyricoc Tupac Capac." I saw the Vixen fix her full attention on me, and I must have puffed up a little too. I felt a strong finger poke me in the chest, and I turned my head back to see Mallku almost purple with anger.

"My father has done more for Tahuantinsuyu than your father ever will, and I will do more than you ever will. The head of my clan is my uncle, Viceroy Illyapa! My sister is betrothed to the heir, Titu Cusi Huallpa! I have more Imperial blood in my veins than you, more military talent in my little finger, and I even have a manlier name than you, Unfortunate. Remember your place and respect your betters." His eyes darted over to the Vixen, but I had her full attention. I knew my family had impressed her, and all of Mallku's statements had not won her attention back to him.

I admit I was scared of him, for even at ten he was a scary man, but in front of the Vixen I could show no fear. I put on my most pompous airs. "I think I hear your mother calling you, Mallku."

"My name is Chalcuchima."

By sheer coincidence his mother did, in fact, notice her son on the brink of another fight, and she called him to her side in a tone that brooked no argument. He shot me one last look of disgust, a quick glance at the Vixen to see if she was going to say goodbye, which she was not, then he turned and stormed off.

Later I would think about the way he left and remember he clenched his hands into fists despite his blistered palm. A boy who could turn off pain: It sounds like a monster in a children's story, doesn't it Friar? He was real, though, all too real, and he was furious with me. He had won the Vixen's attention, and I had taken that prize from him. Knowing what I know now, I am surprised he did not try to throttle me on the spot. He could have done it, blisters or no.

I said I thought about all this later, and I mean just that. The Vixen was before me, and I could think of nothing else in her presence. However beautiful she may have been from a distance, all my preconceptions were washed away when I looked into the Vixen's eyes.

When the Vixen looked at me I could hear counting boards clicking and quipus being tied. She was always thinking, and her calculating brilliance shone through those two brown-irised portals to bathe me in attention.

"I am Atoc China," she said. A twitch of her thin eyebrows and a quirk of a smile from the corner of her beautiful lips implying she thought well of me.

"I know," I said, robbed of all intelligence by the mind her eyes revealed. I was overshadowed, dwarfed, and I was terrified she would know it. Her laugh was deep and rich, not the tinkling giggle of a little girl but the warm chuckle of a woman full-grown and worldly. She touched my arm and I felt as if I, too, had stuck it in a fire to earn her attention.

"Don't be shy, Waccha. I know all about you, though we've never met. I know how you got your name. I know that your father doesn't like me. I know that you're his hand-picked successor, which means you must be brilliant because Tupac Capac is too honest in his dealings to choose his son over a better candidate. You are destined for greatness, Waccha. Greatness..." She let the word trail off, and a silence grew between us that I was loathe to break.

At last I thought I had something worth saying. "My father tells me you have plans of your own, but he wouldn't tell me what they were."

Her eyes danced. One of her long fingers drifted down my arm to clasp my hand in hers, and her other arm waved all around her, taking in the party, the courtyard, the whole palace complex. "This, all this, will one day be mine, or something very much like it." She smiled, pulling those generous lips back to reveal perfect square white teeth, absolutely straight, as if a mason aligned them on the orders of the Emperor himself.

"For men the ranks of the world go Sapa Inca, Viceroy, Tocoyricoc, then down through the various governors and masters of taxpaying denominations." She spoke quickly, her words carefully rehearsed and often repeated. "But for women there are fewer positions, which means each has that much more power. The top position, of course, is Coya, but the man wearing the Yellow Fringe is already married, so for my generation the top spot is taken."

I had never heard a woman talk about power the way a man does, and like everything else about the Vixen I found it intoxicating. "You would have had trouble with that one, not being a full sister. Most coyas are blood relations of the emperors," I said. She nodded her head and shrugged. "So what is the next step down for women in power?"

"Having my own panaca," she said it with awe, and I knew just as my father longed to stand in the plaza of Quitu without a shadow, so the Vixen had revealed her dream to me.

"Your own panaca?" There was no disbelief in my tone. At that moment I felt this girl could do anything, but she removed her hand from mine and drew it to her chest.

"You don't think I can do it?" She asked sharply.

"Of course it's possible." Again, I did not intend to sound critical. I just did not want to pour my adoration at her feet for fear it would be unwelcome.

"You think it's my low birth, don't you? My family has been Inca-by-privilege for as long as the Inca have been raising purics up into the ranks of pacuyoks. Your own mother was a commoner elevated up to Inca-by-privilege by your father. If she can make that vaulting leap, I can make this smaller one. All I need is a powerful husband, and for one of the panacaships to free up—"

"Or for a new one to appear," I clamped my mouth shut, realizing I had just said that one day Old Topa would die. Men had died for less. She warmed to me now, adjusting her stance so all her weight was on one hip, the other titled up at an impossible coquettish angle. It was the most erotic thing I had ever seen, and I took a physical step back at the force of it.

"You and I will be going to the House of Learning together soon, you know. I have made arrangements to attend so my education will not be lacking when I do become leader of a panaca. You and I could become friends there..." There was a lingering promise that I could not decipher. I was too young, my upbringing too sheltered, but the Vixen knew exactly what she was talking about. A word never came out of the Vixen's mouth that was not calculated by that mind of hers.

"I..." I could not think of anything to say, and the conversation ended against my will as my father's hand settled once again upon my shoulder. I muttered something about seeing her in school, then I was dragged away to the understanding snickers of the fathers and sons around me.

* * *

If there is one ability mountain men have that never fails to impress you Spaniards, Friar, it is our capacity for drink. An Inca banquet had food and music, of course, but more than anything it is a drinking party, a competition of drink, a celebration of inebriation, of capacity and fortitude in the face of alcohol.

We sat together in our clans, facing across the courtyard at our rival families from the opposite end of Cuzco, and the akha never stopped flowing. The area between us was filled with jugglers and acrobats, actors performing their plays, bards telling the history of Viracocha Inca, whose mummy was now presented for the panaca's veneration. Colla Topa, the major-domo of the Socso Panaca, moved through the crowd dressed head to toe in the deep blue of his panaca, his big booming laugh reminding us all that we were here to enjoy ourselves.

And while we did enjoy ourselves, of course, our eyes never strayed too long from our vigil of the opposite clan, watching for the first signs that their steady consumption of akha would unman them before us.

As a boy I was not subject to the same punishing pace as my father, but I soon understood why viñapu was illegal: Akha makes your head grow fuzzy, like uncarded wool, but it was a slow fogginess that crept up on you. The young men who I saw sharing the flagons of viñapu at the beginning of the party were either snoring in the sand now, being mocked by friends and foes alike, or they were swaying violently, sitting in a quiet stupor, oblivious to the party around them. Akha is a challenge. Viñapu is a vice.

My father had locked eyes with the two viceroys sitting across from us, Hualpaya and Illyapa, and his beaker was never emptied before a panaca girl filled it for him. Their game was a friendly rivalry, in a way, for nothing was being wagered except pride, but they were members of our rival clan and so he drank for the family's honour. One by one his relatives and retainers succumbed, acting raucous or taking a woman off into one of the guest rooms, but still he sat on his stool, taking long pulls from his cup and making little conversation. I watched him and gradually so did everyone else wearing our clan's yellow. Tonight he was our champion.

"One more, Tupac," one of my uncles said.

"That's incredible, Uncle," a cousin slurred.

"Is that cup full of water?" Hualpaya finally called from across the courtyard. The drummers and flautists stopped. The silence stretched.

My father was grinning ear to ear, a sign of weakness, but he managed to sound sober when he asked in a polite tone, "Have you had enough?"

"Nowhere near," Illyapa answered for his brother, though he slurred his words.

"Well, shall we make this a real contest then?" A low cheer went up from the revelers, and I heard laughter from behind the Imperial curtain. "Sire, can we borrow your runa tinya?" My father raised his voice perhaps a little too far to be respectful, but the screen parted to show a group of guardsmen carrying out the Imperial man drum. At Colla Topa's booming commands, servants appeared from one of the courtyard's galleries with three high stools, one for each of the contestants.

The Inca, their high-ranking subjects, and the collected children all watched as the two viceroys and the tocoyricoc perched on their unnaturally high stools, their feet only just touching the ground. They were each given two beakers, one for each hand, and a yanacona with an amphora stood behind them ready to top off after each swallow.

"To the Sapa Inca!" My father began, raising one cup for the toast before draining it. The guardsmen began to beat the man drum slowly; the rumble from its belly coming out through its mouth to form a coughing laughter.

"To the Socso Panaca!" Hualpaya returned, and he and his brother drank.

It went on for a long time with the runa tinya speeding up and the crowd roaring their approval and encouragement. The toasts became hurried and silly, as both sides tried to keep pace with the drum.

"To the chosen women who warm your bed!" My father said, choking back a drunken laugh.

"To your cold pallet!" Illyapa returned. Hualpaya managed to strangle his chortle of glee at the retort.

"To Hualpaya's hiccough, there!" My father returned, lightning fast.

The challenge was not just one of putting the akha down, but of the quick and witty retort, the lack of emotion, the balance in staying on the stool. When you think that all three of them had been imbibing steadily since sundown, it really was amazing that they were able to play.

"To your wit!" Hualpaya toasted.

"To your lack of it." That got a roar out of the crowd. Even Illyapa laughed, and when he went to slap his brother on the back he missed and his stool shifted dangerously. Acknowledging defeat, he stood, gave a clumsy bow to his audience, drained the last of his akha to a smattering of applause, and then returned to his low stool to watch his brother defend the family honour.

"To your wife," Hualpaya said, trying to slow things down. The man drum continued its fast beat.

"To my wife," my father said, quaffing his cup like it was empty.

"To your future wife," Hualpaya smiled.

"To obeying the Emperor," my father returned.

"To..." Hualpaya trailed off, his head sagging.

"Well put." My father finished his last cup. Hualpaya sat on his stool, his head too heavy to bring his chin up. My father walked across the courtyard and wrapped him in a warm embrace. "Well done, cousin. Well done." Though they were from rival clans, the mention of their distant blood relation took all the sting out of the battle. The crowd roared its approval at the happy ending.

I do not know how the party finished, though from my experiences at future fetes I suspect it did not and many of the revelers just awoke in the sand, their cups still in their hands. My father, who was never really comfortable at parties, chose his moment of triumph to take his leave. He collected me and as many of his retainers as could still walk. He was quietly ill in a gutter half way home, but it was for the best. No one should drink that much.

He tucked me in that night, and he seemed almost sober as he did it. He made me change into a clean tunic as he laid down a couple of blankets onto a fresh pallet, stuffed with grass, then he made me lie down in the centre and wiggle around until I had a body-sized cavity.

He then put more blankets on top of me. I knew he would have a story for me, but I did not want one of his stories. I wanted to know what made Mallku's father an aucca. I asked him, and he swayed slightly as he sat down next to me.

"You remember the tale of how Pachacuti defeated the Chancas?" He asked. I nodded. The Chanca had come to conquer us when Viracocha Inca's fledgling Tahuantinsuyu began to rival their own confederacy, and such was their warrior spirit that Viracocha's chosen successor Urcos panicked and abandoned Cuzco, leaving a younger prince to win a miraculous victory over the Chanca on the field of Xaquixahuana. It was the battle that made the Inca Empire as it existed today possible.

My father frowned. "Well, you know how formidable a warrior people they were. For a time it was decided that once they were absorbed into Tahuantinsuyu the Chancas would pay their taxes exclusively in military service, just the way the Rucana tribe only give tribute as litter bearers and the Chumpivilcans serve exclusively as royal dancers."

I pictured a nation under perpetual arms, our bitterest rivals putting on their puma capes and vermillion war paint to die in our service. "You said for a time?"

"Mallku's father was named Capac Yupanki. He was a great general and a legitimate son of Viracocha Inca by his second Coya, making him a near equal of Sapa Inca Topa Inca Yupanki and far superior, by birth, of your grandfather. Capac Yupanki was ordered to take the rich valley of Xauxa in Huanca territory, former allies of the Chanca. He was also instructed to venture no closer to the Kingdom of Chimor on the coast, which at the time was as big as Tahuantinsuyu and much richer.

"His legion of Incas tried to storm the fortress of Xauxa and failed, and the next day the Chanca legion succeeded. The Chanca grew so hot-blooded that they had triumphed over their former allies in the service of their former enemies, succeeding where we had failed, that they picked up and marched into the jungle to the east, taking their women and children with them." I shuddered a little in my bed, imagining the Imperial fury that must have been waiting for Capac Yupanki upon his return to Cuzco.

"Embarrassed, Capac Yupanki did not come back from his campaign. Instead he attacked Caxamalca, an ally of the Kingdom of Chimor, against specific Imperial orders. He was trying to placate Sapa Inca

Pachacuti with fresh conquests, but the Chimu counterattacked in support of their friends and Capac Yupanki had to retreat, leaving five thousand pacuyoks defending the Caxamalca fortress with no hope of relief for more than two years.

"He lost us the Chanca. He dragged us into a war with the Chimu that he was specifically ordered not to start, a war that taxed us to the limit. He abandoned the flower of his troops to a siege and then marched back to Cuzco. It was a miraculous feat of arms that our warriors held out until they were relieved by Topa Inca and your grandfather," my father shook his head, remembering.

"For his crimes Capac Yupanki and his eldest son, Mallku's brother, were imprisoned for years then beheaded and their bodies thrown into the Sankihuasi, the Pit reserved for traitors. Capac Yupanki's full brothers, Viceroy Illyapa and Viceroy Hualpaya, adopted Capac Yupanki's infant son Mallku and declared that their brother had done no wrong. My father was the most vocal of his prosecutors, and so our clans have feuded ever since. There is rumour that the insult my father gave to Pachacuti's Coya was set up by those two viceroys, but I have no proof." He pulled himself up onto his feet, swaying as he did it.

"Do I have to go to school, Father?"

"Why would you even ask that?" He murmured, pulling the blanket up to my chin now as he prepared to leave.

"I'm afraid of Mallku," I admitted. Now that I was away from the distracting euphoria of the Vixen's presence, the thought that I had made an enemy like him frightened me as badly as any of my half-remembered nightmares.

My father stood over my pallet for a long time in silence, mulling over what to say. Finally he settled on, "You should be. From what I hear of him, you really should be." He kissed me on the forehead, ruffled my hair, patted my shoulder, and left my room.

I don't know whether he was trying to downplay my fears by agreeing with me, or whether he was setting me up for a challenge. Either way, I did not sleep well all that night.

Did you go to school very long to become a priest, Friar? Never mind. I have asked you not to write your own words except at the very end —if you wish— and so I should not countermand that order now and allow you to express yourself against my wishes. Let me just say that I have often heard Spaniards claim that we were a stupid people, without either steel or the wheel, but I doubt most of the illiterate conquistadores who pillaged my land would have prospered at the House of Learning.

Every Inca male and most of the nobility of our conquered provinces attended the House of Learning, and a few girls, like the Vixen, were also permitted to go. The standard curriculum lasted four years, but there was a great deal of variety as to what extra classes a student could sign up for.

The House of Learning was in the palace of the dead emperor Inca Roca. The whole complex has been rededicated to the task, and wise men knowledgeable in every aspect of the world walked its corridors, lecturing in its halls and courtyards. The Empire made a point of bringing in only the most brilliant men to teach.

Generals stopped in to give lectures and run war games. Bureaucrats from the Royal Quipu Repository rotated through, teaching a year at a time before they were eligible for promotion. Medicine men from the Kallawaya taught both their healing art and the many languages they had mastered. Priests taught religion, augury, divination, and astronomy. The official Inca historians told the authorized stories, only to pull aside promising students like me to whisper the true events that were too unsavoury to be official.

Every one of these teachers would add the honorific Yachapa, He Has Taught, to their full name, and for his occasional math lectures this was another of my father's many monikers.

School... I tell you Friar, my schooling was harder than any of my peers. I was enrolled in class from dawn until almost dusk, and after each session I had still more private teachers, so many teachers! I learned the Colla tongue from a disgraced lord of those people; Mochica, the language of the Chimu and the Cañari, from a retired caravan lord; Chibcha, the Quitu tongue, from a curaca of the Cayambi tribe brought to the Cuzco valley as a mitmak. I learned the art of oratory from an old wind bag who filibustered Viracocha Inca as a young man.

Before I started at the House of Learning I daydreamed about spending all my time there with the Vixen, while at the same time dreading Mallku. I need not have worried on either count. My father and I put together a course of study that kept me so busy I had only fleeting glimpses of either of them for months and months. I woke up, did my accounting chores, went to school, came home, did more classes, and slept. That was my life for most of my time at the House of Learning.

My early school days came to revolve around my father's math lessons. In my first year of schooling, two years before other boys would learn multiplication, I would report to my father's counting room. His rule was I would solve one math problem before I would be allowed to play, and if I did not have an answer for him by sundown I would work through the night.

He would sit on his stool with one of my sisters on his knee, and he would say, "Listen well: One hundred alpacas can produce thirty-five bags of fleece that can be spun into one month's tribute in cumpi cloth for Chiaquitinta, the curaca of Upper Tumipampa.

"If the flock loses one adult alpaca out of ten every year, and the seventy females in the flock each year produce one kid who may equally be male or female and take two years to breed and contribute wool, how many months of tribute can this one flock produce over the course of ten years? How much wool is left over? How many alpacas are in the flock after ten years? Do you have all that?" He would ask. "Good, because for each time I have to repeat it, you miss a meal. Round up or down as I have taught you, and assume any odd numbers for births and deaths affect the females."

To his highly trained mind this was a simple calculation, and he had the answer by the time he finished the question; meanwhile, I would labour over my counting board, moving my little chips of stone frantically back and forth with a hypnotic click, click, clicking. My siblings watched in fascination, for it seemed I moved the stones at random. Woe, as well, to whichever of my father's bastards moved a stone from its appointed place. I remember when my brother Ronpa did it I bodily threw him out of my room, knowing my father would not excuse the delay.

In the end it's a simple compound addition problem, and, like my father before me, I can now solve it in my head as fast as I can ask it: Thirty-six months of tribute with twenty-nine bags left over from the total of twelve hundred and eighty-nine bags, and the flock would consist of four hundred and sixty-nine females, four hundred and forty-six males, and eight hundred and thirty-four young.

Of course it's a nonsense question anyway because the birth and death rates are ridiculously arbitrary, as is the age at which young animals contribute to the community good. Also, why isn't anyone butchering the extra males for meat? It's also too simple, if you can believe it, because he did not make me factor in the size of the pasture involved, which would be finite and thereby limit the flock, plus the herders, weavers, and porters would all need to be compensated out of the State coffers.

You look less than impressed, Friar. You think it is a trick, perhaps? Or maybe just an example I already worked out? You have heard it said that in Tahuantinsuyu, a realm of twelve million people, not a single pair of sandals was ever unaccounted for. Who do you think kept track of such things? My father and I. Oh, we had our quipucamayocs and our ledger men and our accountants to help us, but my father and I had to be over and above such men, more talented in every way so that we could find any hint of impropriety.

As I said, this was only my first year of schooling, and it would be two years before my peers learned the counting quipus, but already I was expected to record the results of calculations in the strings, and even if I got the answer right but the knots wrong my father would ask still another question.

Most boys did not begin their formal education in quipus until their fourth and final year at school. The smart ones would take extra classes early, but it was by no means common. It was unheard of for a boy in his first year to take every quipu class offered, but that is what my father enrolled me in, and then he had extra classes on top of that scheduled for private tutors, including himself, after school each day.

It occurs to me I have spoken several times in passing of quipus, but now I shall be specific, Friar. There are two broad differences in quipus, the kind that record sounds and the kind that record numbers. It is not that simple, of course, though how I wished it had been as a boy. There are many styles of number quipus throughout Tahuantinsuyu. If I were to learn just the Cuzco style, that would only give me access to ledgers from a quarter of the Empire. There were regional variations in the

Collao, Chimor, and Quitu, to name just the major ones. Almost any tribe that had been large enough to keep track of their wealth had developed their own style of quipu accounting, and I learned all of them, as well as the art of picking up an unfamiliar quipu and puzzling out how it worked.

There are some common traits between all number quipus: They have a main cord with a clearly marked starting and ending point. From this cord dangle pendant cords, usually grouped together in a logical way rather than being strung at random, and from these pendant cords there can be further and further cords breaking away from them.

These strings are usually colour coded in some way to help the accountant remember what is being recorded, and the knots themselves are ones through nines in units of ten along the string, with blanks left for zeroes and placeholders. If a number became truly great, say, more than ten thousand, there were further knots to show the numbers multiplying beyond the ungainly thousands.

That is just the very broad idea, of course. For instance, some of the pendant strings are actually meant to be held up between thumb and forefinger above the main cord. Some quipus are meant to be held between the toes of one foot, pulled taut with one hand and read with the other, while others can be casually read held between two hands without actually feeling the knots.

I learned all of them, and, in truth, it was more the breadth of the variety of quipus than the actual art that I found difficult. The Colla quipus and the Chimu quipus, for instance, are almost identical in appearance but with almost all the rules reversed; many was the time I wondered how a Colla llama herder had afforded to slaughter three hundred and one prime breeding stock only to realize I was actually reading about a Chimu guinea pig butcher who was trying to requisition one hundred and three animals for slaughter.

No, looking back on it my complaints with the number quipus were merely the complaints of a young boy who wanted to be at play but was forced time and again into the company of wheezy old bureaucrats with long fingers callused from a lifetime of string work.

My real trouble was the Royal Quipus, those holy strings that record a man's thoughts and words and deeds.

I have told you, Friar, that these knots I hold in my hands right now record sounds, the sounds of the Runa Simi language. Do you know how many different sounds there are in that tongue? Six hundred and forty-eight.

Think about that, Friar. If you had to sit here with a bit of yarn and not move until you had created six hundred and forty-eight knots, what would some of those knots look like at the end? Huge hulking things that take far too long to tie and lack all elegance, aside from being impossible to untie afterwards.

Royal quipus take those six hundred and forty-eight sounds and replicate them in forty common knots and another eighty rare ones, each a word that uses different sounds from the Runa Simi language. Take the word Pachacamac, the coast's name for our creator god Viracocha. Pachacamac is one word, one simple and easily recognizable knot, but it is actually four sounds, Pa-one, cha-two, ca-three, mac-four. All one knot with four sounds that I can break up to show which sounds I wanted.

For instance, suppose I wanted to tie down only Pacha, Earth. I would tie the knot for Pachacamac and then tie two more knots, the numbers one and two. Pa-one-Cha-two. You see? And if I wanted to actually use the whole word Pachacamac I could do so without a following knot.

Elegant, simple, easy, fast, and still not enough, for a man does not speak forever in one tone of voice, does he? There is a rhythm, a beat of ups and downs. As I watch you write on your paper you stop one line and go down to the next. You punctuate to better make your words imitate what I have actually said. So too must the royal quipu master.

Royal quipus are so colourful that the undyed threads are the unusual ones, indicating some rare point of grammar, like a rhetorical question. If I want the words to be read quickly I tie them in red thread, slowly in blue. Other colours imply surprise, exclamation, enthusiasm, all the emotions that can be produced by the human voice. There are also ways to arrange the pendant cords to say where a sentence starts and stops, or to show two people speaking and make it obvious who said what and in which order.

It took me four long years to learn the whole system, and when I was proficient it was seen as such an event that my father summoned our clan together in the Huacaypata and sacrificed a hundred llamas, then threw a party with an enthusiasm I had never seen from him before.

But I'm getting ahead of myself. I should go back to the early years. I was walked to school each day by my father's door man and picked up afterwards by his gherkin fetcher. I was given no leave to play after their classes, and, to be honest, I did not have the time.

The other students fell into two broad categories: Ones destined for administration or bureaucracy, like me, and those destined for military service, like Mallku. It took most of the first year for me to really notice, but those two groups formed into cliques, and as the most outstanding individuals in the two groups Mallku and I came to the forefront whenever there was conflict.

Mallku's followers were the future legion officers, for he excelled in every military pursuit and leading by example is a fine way to inspire others. My own supporters were a mix of Mallku's enemies and a few boys who seemed to think the hard work I did as a tocoyricoc-in-training would somehow translate into a benefit for them. I had no time to cater to them, no time to make friends.

My one indulgence was to follow the Vixen with my eyes as she moved from lecture to lecture, and I must admit I signed up for classes on panaca ritual and augury that interested me for no other reason than because she was there.

No, it occurs to me that may have been my first reason for taking the class, but I must admit the teacher fascinated me: His name was Cusi Topa Yupanki, and even though he was only seven years older than me he was already acknowledged as being the finest living augur in Cuzco. Such was his passion for the divinatory arts that any bird or cloud would bring him to stop mid-sentence to scrutinize the hidden meaning.

One day after he dismissed his class I caught him looking up at two fledgling hawks circling overhead. He was smiling a distant smile, his mind far away.

"What do they tell you?" I asked.

"Do you have an enemy?" The Bird Man asked me. I told him I did not, but he just shook his head and pointed at the two young raptors above us. "They are so alike, maybe even from the same nest, but they are rivals. Only one of them will ever get the prey that they hunt, and then one will try to steal it from the other, and back and forth until they have grown old together."

I walked away, muttering under my breath that he was a strange one, but he was the best augur in Cuzco for a reason, Friar. He always seemed to know what was going on, and if you could tear him away from looking up long enough to tell you, you would be better off.

83

As I said, I did not see much of Mallku at school, but he was aware of me. He and I were the two stars of our age group, though because he reveled in it and I did not he seemed to feel slighted, even insulted. My attention towards the Vixen did not escape him either. He bided his time to confront me, but he would start us down a road together that would see us as old men before its end.

One day the gherkin fetcher was late in collecting me, but I was not angry. It was gherkin season and I was sure he was procuring a snack for my father. I was waiting in an outer courtyard, working on a word quipu my father had given me that morning. It was only as the noise level dropped away but the crowd grew thick that I realized I was the centre of earnest attention.

"What?" I said. There were easily fifty of them. Ten were future bureaucrats like me, the rest were Mallku's cronies. They had dummy lances and shields leaning against their shoulders, as they often did at the end of school. They would venture outside the city and play war games until supper. I had never gone with them, but I heard all about their mock victories the day after in the halls.

From the crowd emerged Mallku, a smile on his vulture face. I was not deceived. This was all too orchestrated for my liking.

"You never play with us. Are you too good for us?" Mallku's smile looked like a sneer. He couldn't help it. He had thin lips.

"Too busy," I replied, looking back down to my word quipu.

"With that bit of string?" His tone dripped sarcasm.

"Just because you haven't been allowed to learn how to read and tie the royal quipus doesn't make them worthless. I don't consider soldiering worthless, but I haven't been trained to do that." I tried to sound reasonable. I wanted no trouble from a boy who would take it too far.

"Pah! You haven't enrolled in the military courses because you could never be a soldier. Look at you! Twigs for limbs and an empty amphora for a chest. Spend more time with a lance and shield and less time with your twine and maybe you would have some muscle on those arms, eh stick boy?" He took the word quipu out of my hands. Other boys were gathering now. The courtyard seemed to be crowded with them, all with eyes ready to watch me being shamed.

"Give it back," I said, trying to sound firm.

"Give it back. Give it back," Mallku repeated in a falsetto.

"You couldn't understand a word of it. It is useless to you. I have to read it now because it is being returned to the Great Quipu Repository tonight." I dropped the name of the institution, hoping he would be afraid to damage or destroy state property, but he had other plans.

"Ah! Vixen my dear, Waccha and I were just discussing the value of royal quipus." I turned my head and, sure enough, the object of our mutual desire had entered the courtyard, a length of unknotted yarn between her fingers.

"I suppose you think them useless?" She said, and my heart skipped a beat at the thought that she would so openly side with me.

"No, far from it," Mallku protested. "I was merely arguing that Waccha here should spend less time with his string and more time with his sling, being a man."

"You spend all your time with your war toys, and it hasn't made you a man yet," I said, my tone too strident. I felt some of the boys flanking me slowly drift back, disassociating themselves with me.

Mallku smiled his lipless smile, running my word quipu through his fingers. "You can read this?"

"Yes, slowly, I'm still learning." I did not want him to try and make me demonstrate my skill. Royal quipus were not an easily mastered trick.

"If you can do it, so can I," Mallku announced. I looked over at the Vixen who was watching both of us, her eyes taking it all in and her mind reaching conclusions I did not like. If Mallku wanted a showdown with me in front of her, I would have to put him in his place. There was nothing else for it.

"You? You couldn't tie your own name!" Now this sounded good to my ears, but in truth I could not have been more foolish. I was learning to read royal quipus, but I had not yet learned to tie the knots. In truth, I could not have tied Chalcuchima's name. Also, Chalcuchima was a born military strategist: He knew all about reading an opponent and setting a simple ambush.

"Oh?" Mallku arched an eyebrow, and I felt a sinking feeling in my belly, for his condor face looked like he was suppressing a wave of triumph. "Vixen, my dear, would you kindly give me that string I asked you to bring?"

It was a set up, and I had walked right into it. She glided over to us, handed him the yarn, and without taking his eyes off me he tied the knots quickly and fluidly. He handed it to me and my heart sunk. Mall-One Ku-Two Chal-One Cu-Two Chi-Three Ma-Four. "Do you need me to fetch a teacher, or can you read that?" He asked.

"I can read it."

"And it says?"

"Your name." I would not call him Chalcuchima.

"Now Waccha," he wagged a finger at me, playfully. "Chusek over there could have told me I had tied my name, and he can't read a knot. What does it say?"

"These four knots say Mallku." I pointed at the top of the string.

"And the last eight?"

"The name you are to take as an adult."

"Which name is that?"

"You know which name."

"Remind me."

I twisted the string in my hand. "Give me back my royal quipu... Chalcuchima." He handed it back to me graciously, his lipless smile playing over our audience.

"Just out of curiousity, Waccha, can you tie down your own name?" I did so, slowly and carefully, never taking my eyes off the string as Mallku had done. Everyone noted the difference. The fact that Mallku had clearly interrogated a royal quipu master on the knots and practiced them at home for days escaped all of them except me, and possibly the Vixen. All they saw was their great Chalcuchima do easily that which I vaunted as being so difficult. He had beaten me, and he did it in front of her.

I brooded over the defeat for some time, and it was only after my shaming that I realized how few friends I had. Everyone made their excuses to distance themselves from me. I knew I would have to do something about it, but I could not fathom what. I was at school early and left school late, so my campaign for fellowship would have to be done in the halls and classrooms, but how could I win them over without licking their sandals or letting them walk all over me?

I should have known the Vixen had already worked it out. She approached me one day in a quiet corridor and pulled me aside into an alcove. It did not take much persuading. My heart was beating like a mason's stone hammer to receive such personal attention. Boys passed by too often to call our proximity private or intimate, but it still felt good to be so close to her.

"If you meet your father's expectations, one day you will be He Who Sees All?" She asked, toying with a spindle she had in her hands.

"I suppose so," I replied, my tongue feeling twice its normal size. I had to concentrate to not stumble as I spoke.

"No one else at school stands a chance at that."

She made it a statement, but I felt I had to confirm it. "Yes, that's true."

"And none will be a Sapa Inca, and none will be a viceroy."

"No..." I was not sure where she was going with this.

"One day you will be one of the most powerful men in the world, more powerful than any of these boys." I felt my mouth twitch into a smile at the thought but restrained myself. "Has it occurred to you that the friends and enemies you make here will be your allies and foes for the rest of your life?"

I shrugged, unsure what she wanted me to say. The gesture angered her. "You're a fool to be so distant to them. You will have tremendous power, but if every one of your colleagues works against you then you will achieve nothing at your post."

"You have a suggestion?" I asked, sure that this entire conversation had been carefully rehearsed by her ahead of time.

"You will be the greatest bureaucrat, so you need not worry too much with boys destined for the administration. They will be your subordinates, and the ones worth keeping will follow your orders whether you are their friend or not."

"Fine," I said, pleased to listen to her keen mind's labour.

"The same goes for officials: You will be the Emperor's watchdog. Allies are good, but if you have enemies among the provincial governors, city mayors, or masters of taxpayers, it is they who will have to worry about you, not the other way around."

"True," I said, not wanting to disagree with her. In truth I had already decided to be nicer both to my future subordinates and to my future resident officials. Friendly intercourse would make my job easier.

"What you need are friends among the officer corps—"

"I will not bow and scrape to Mallku," I interrupted her. I might have been besotted with her, but I had my pride.

"Is Chalcuchima the only young officer? Yes, he has the most promise, but more than half the boys here are destined for the legions."

I could find nothing against her logic. The army was as much a part of the Empire as the bureaucracy, and I had been prepared to throw the good potatoes out with the bad. I nodded and she smiled at me.

"I knew you'd see sense." She reached into her coca bag and handed me a small handkerchief of cumpi cloth, just clumsy enough in its weave to prove it was made by her own still-unpracticed hand. "There. That's for you." She smiled her perfect smile and walked away before I could thank her, and throughout the day whenever I fingered the cloth I seemed to float with the knowledge of her favour.

Over the next few days I noticed I was not the only boy grinning stupidly as he played with a small square of inexpert fine cloth. The Vixen had successfully marked every boy in our school whose ability earmarked him for greatness.

For some time I did not care to share what I thought was my own unique experience with so many others, but I soon realized what had happened: With the expertise of a general surveying green conscripts she had unerringly picked out who would prove worthy, then she had pulled each aside, told him of the flaws that she had observed and how she suggested he deal with it.

If the boy was too prideful to take her advice she cut her losses and he forever fell from her favour. If the boy showed himself receptive to her guidance, respectful of her intelligence and ravished by her beauty, then she gave him a token of her approval, nothing more.

It was perhaps a month after my conversation with her that I first spoke openly about it with another of her candidates. His name was Chusek, the son of a full-blooded Inca general of middling reputation. When I first saw him with a Vixen square, as the boys came to call them, I was surprised. His birth gave him no advantage over the other boys, nor did he seem a military genius.

Making his square even more unlikely, he never fawned over the Vixen, and he was one of the very few students or teachers who did not at least follow her flawless movements with their eyes. I found him actively seeking me out, always standing or sitting near me, waiting for me to be somewhere out of earshot of the other military boys.

88

He finally approached me one day as we moved from a math lesson to a religious class. He waved his Vixen square at me dismissively, a friendly, crooked smile on his face to disarm the dislike I had shown to the boys who gathered around Mallku.

"You know what this is, of course?"

"She's marked us," I said with a laugh, liking him.

"Cleverest girl I've ever met, and I've met my share." I would later learn that Chusek had eight sisters who all brought their friends to his father's house. Chusek was intimately familiar with a number of the girls, having slept with his first one at the age of eleven. He was twelve when he spoke to me of his Vixen square, and I think my young mind would have staggered to know this boy was so acquainted with the mysteries of the female body that he viewed the Vixen as just one among many possible conquests, more trouble and competition than she was worth and with none of the irresistible lures the rest of us experienced.

"First we realize we're special; then we notice a number of us were picked. We start paying attention to who, and the rest start noticing we're part of the group." He laughed, his crooked teeth oddly endearing.

"Why do you think you were picked?" I asked, curious what unique qualities Chusek possessed.

"Me? I'm different because she knows she can't control me with her looks." He laughed again to take the sting out of his implication that I was a slave to my lust.

"And what was her advice to you?" I asked. He eyed me wearily for a moment, and I thought perhaps I had been wrong about her advising boys on their future careers. "She told me I should try to befriend some of Mallku's friends," I added, hoping by confessing mine he would do the same.

Chusek seemed to weigh his next words carefully. "Chalcuchima? Would I be one of those friends?"

"She didn't specifically say Mallku's friends; she said the boys going into the legions."

Chusek nodded at my correction. He looked ahead and behind him to make sure none of the other students were paying attention to us. "She told me to be your friend."

I had also been looking around, and now I swung my face towards him too quickly to seem casual.

"Me?" I asked, too loud. A few boys looked my way, so I repeated it again, much softer. "Me?"

"Nowadays the Empire is just too big for a little general to climb to the top. The big campaigns get big armies led by big generals, the Sapa Inca, or the grey heads, or one day Chalcuchima if he's as good on the battlefield as he is in the war games."

He smiled his crooked smile at me, and I realized it made him look friendly, whereas when he smiled without his teeth he seemed solemn and perhaps a little gallant, which is a difficult impression for a boy to give. Perhaps that was one of the reasons he had come to the Vixen's notice.

I nodded, recognizing the logical statements that the Vixen made with such ease.

"And?" I prompted.

"And so I can't expect to ever lead an army, not a proper army on a proper war. There are too many men ahead of me. I can't be the commander, so unless I find a place for myself at his side I'll wind up like my father, transferred from garrison to garrison on quiet frontiers for his entire life, watching the years slip him by." Chusek made a face, but quickly brought his smile back in full force. "I need to be able to run a camp, read royal quipus, handle logistics, and all the other things someone like Chalcuchima will not have the time or knowledge to do."

"There's not a lot of glory in that," I said, not trying to dissuade him.

"There's not a lot of glory in my father's line of work either. He fought in two wars in his twenties, did well enough to get promoted to commanding a couple of border forts, and then faded away into obscurity. Just once he had a bit of excitement: A tribe came out of the jungle and ambushed a caravan. My father watched as one of the Sapa Inca's nephews brought in an army of twenty thousand to cross the frontier and burn them out. He's fifty now, and the only noteworthy thing he's ever done was a lifetime ago. I want better than that."

"So where do I come in?"

"My father sees me going no further than he has, and garrison commanders don't need royal quipus."

"But I do," I said.

"But you do."

"So she thinks I should tutor you?"

"It wouldn't be just a one way thing. There's a lot I could teach you too."

"Like what?"

"Like how to talk to people, how to behave, how to act... How to beat Mallku out for the Vixen."

It was the first time that I had heard one of the future officers call Chalcuchima Mallku, and at that moment I decided Chusek would be my friend. "Okay, then where would you like to start?"

"At the beginning."

And so it went that we both had another teacher, each other. I marched into my father's counting room and told him quite simply that I needed to spend more time playing with other boys my own age, and he agreed. I also told him I would be bringing a friend to some of my extra classes and he agreed to that too. As simple as that, Chusek became my first true friend.

He taught me how to use my sling, hurling stones at the rocks and bushes on the hills surrounding Cuzco. I taught him how to use a counting board. He taught me how to wrestle. I taught him how to speak Chibcha. In the end, though, it became less about learning and more about spending time together.

I remember once my father came out to collect us playing with our false weapons at the base of the Intihuasi fortress. On a bet, Mallku was holding off six of us at once with his buckler and padded practice mace, performing feats of agility and stamina every bit the equal to his strategic mind. Three of us, including me, held him at bay with our practice lances while three more, including Chusek, were trying to come at him from all directions with their maces.

Mallku seemed to be able to face every which way at once, his buckler always holding off the lances and his mace holding off the other three. The sweat flew from him, he huffed with each breath, and such was the obvious effort he was exerting that all the other boys on the practice field stopped to watch us.

Then my father appeared from the city's outskirts and called Chusek and I to him. I was tempted to linger, for no one could hold off six at once for long, but my father's tone was impatient and I brought up my lance and trotted out to him, followed with equal reluctance by Chusek.

I heard the thump-thump-thump-thump as Mallku brained each of our former allies with his practice mace. I heard his roar of satisfaction and the polite applause from the rest of the field. My ears burned, knowing I would have to honour my wager and call him Chalcuchima for the rest of the month, but I dutifully arrived at my father's side.

"He's a good one," my father said pleasantly, well aware of who he was complimenting and its effect on me.

"He cheats," Chusek laughed.

"How so?" My father asked.

"He can't do any of that leaping about. Only an acrobat can. Mallku's just so stubborn he can order his body to do anything for a little while, and then he puts up with the aches and pains for days after."

My father laughed too, and I somehow felt like I was the only person in the world who was scowling. "We would have beaten him just now, Father," I said.

"And would that have been an accomplishment to be proud of? Six beating one? Either way people would have cheered for Mallku, so isn't it better for him to be praised for winning?" I did not reply. "One day he will be an Inca general. Do you want him to remember beating six of his peers? Won't he be a better servant of the Empire knowing he can overcome odds like that?"

"There were only four when he won," I said stubbornly.

"Well then his imaginary army's slingers picked you two off and he finished the rest. Come along, I don't have all day to talk about young Chalcuchima." As it was meant to, my father calling Mallku by his adult name set my teeth on edge. I was quiet all the while we walked through Upper Cuzco, only growing curious as we passed our house in Lower Cuzco without turning down our lane. I had assumed we were going to be quizzed on quipus or given an accounting problem, but we were heading further and further into Lower Cuzco, so that we were rapidly running out of city in which to have a lesson.

"Where are we going?" Chusek finally asked.

"The Coricancha," my father rumbled. The two of us stopped for a moment, and he was walking at such a fast pace that we had to run to catch up.

"Are we allowed?" I asked in a hushed voice, as if there were Imperial informers hiding in the bare stone walls around us.

"Not usually, but I have to go there and I need a chaperone, so I

92

thought it would be something you boys would want to see," he said.

He was right, of course. The Coricancha, the Golden Enclosure, was the Holy of Holies of the Inca people, lavished with huacas that commoners could never see. Even when the walls were first erected we had used masons from the nobility to prevent purics from profaning the place. Only the Sapa Inca, the High Priest, and a small group of Chosen Women were allowed free access to the Coricancha.

"Why are you allowed in?" I asked. My father was a powerful man, but he did not hold any priesthoods that I knew about.

"It's that damned Mama Ocllo meddling again," my father harrumphed. "She's whispered to Topa Inca Yupanki that there's a chosen woman who serves in the Coricancha who would make a fine new wife for me, and apparently I'm not allowed to say no until I've seen her."

The idea of my father taking a new wife did not fluster me, but I was still put out at Mama Ocllo's matchmaking.

"And why are we the chaperones?" Chusek asked.

"Chosen women aren't Brides of Inti, but they're still supposed to be virgins when the Emperor doles them out. I need someone with me who can vouch that I haven't touched her, and I also want someone who won't report my conversation to Mama Ocllo. Besides, I thought you boys would like to see the place."

We certainly did. The Coricancha was the single finest building ever made. Each stone was a perfect, flawless block worked so precisely that you could not fit a splinter into any of the joints. The entire outside was ringed with a golden band as wide as my chest and as thick as my finger, so that as long as the sun shone so did the building.

That was all anybody knew for sure, other than that you always blew the building a kiss and plucked an eyelash in offering as you passed, and if you forgot you bit your collar to ward off the bad luck of disrespecting such a powerful huaca. The inside was pure conjecture, but it was supposed to hold the largest single collection of gold and silver in all of Tahuantinsuyu.

We reached the gate to see a long line of supplicants, each coming with an offering of some kind to give to the priests within in exchange for a few quickly mumbled prayers. The merest whisper inside the Coricancha was the equivalent of shouting your prayers from the mountaintops anywhere else. All the gods' ears were turned to that place.

Outside the line but seemingly guarding the door stood Viceroy Il-lyapa, high lord of Collasuyu. He nodded his recognition to my father, who nodded back.

"What can I do for you, sir?" My father asked.

"I thought you might need a chaperone," Illyapa said gruffly.

"No, thank you, I brought my son and his friend. They'll do well enough, and Mama Ocllo might not hear every word I say this way." Illyapa was Hualpaya's older brother, and Hualpaya's lover Chiqui Ocllo was Mama Ocllo's younger sister. We all knew anything Illyapa heard would be told to the Coya before the sun set.

"Well..." He seemed at a loss, finally reaching forward to tap me twice on the shoulder with his staff of office. The heavy black glass mounted on its end was his personal huaca, and so I supposed he meant the gesture to give me luck. I just remember the blows bruised me for days after. "Enjoy it in there, young man. It is the glory of our time. If my older brother had not pulled us into the war with the Chimu, half that gold would still be down on the coast." He gave a sharp whistle and his litter appeared from a side street, his blue liveried Rucana porters each blowing a kiss first to the Coricancha then to their lord, who bade us farewell with obvious reluctance.

"Shall we?" My father gestured with an open hand, a true showman. He might only have been inside a few times in his life, but he was pre-pared to act as if he owned the place. The priests guarding the gate let us in, and from that point on my eyes began to strain at the wonder of it.

The courtyard was flanked on all sides by the temples of our gods, but the courtyard itself was a temple, for in it dwelled the ideal of ev-erything, all fashioned from gold and silver. There was a garden of full grown maize with stalks and ears of silver and cobs of gold growing out of dirt that was sprinkled with gold dust. Next to it, growing out of silver pots, were golden flowers attended by gold and silver bees, butter-flies, and hummingbirds. There was a molle tree of silver with golden fruit, and in its shade slept silver llamas attended by a dozing shepherd of gold with silver clothing.

It was all done to life size and in such detail that you could see where the llama's coarse outer hair was accidentally parted in places to show the softer wool underneath. The whole tableau was surrounded by gold and silver fountains and benches decorated with inset emeralds and turquoise where a man could sit when the wonder proved too much for him.

"Can I help you, my Lord?" A chosen woman asked my father.

"I am looking for a girl named Kiske Sisa?"

"Inside the Coricancha-proper," she pointed to the largest of the temples facing the yard, and I shook my head to think that this garden with its heavenly metals did not yet warrant the name of the true Golden Enclosure. We walked across the yard and entered the home of the pantheon of our gods, and I felt like someone had kicked me in the stomach when I saw the interior.

I had assumed the compound was called the Golden Enclosure because its outer perimeter was lined with a golden band, but it was the inside of the main temple that was truly enclosed in gold, and not a band either. The walls were lined with plates of gold and silver, friezes and mosaics of golden pieces. The roof was lined with stars and lightning bolts of silver and gold. The far wall was decorated with representations of the equinoxes and rainbows and the most important stars in the sky, all of precious metals.

As your eyes lowered you saw the altar, upon which sat a golden egg to show the universe, flanked on either side by a giant golden disk to represent the Sun and an equally massive disk of silver for the moon. In niches set into the walls of the temple sat the mummies of the Emperors, each brought here by their panacas every morning to commune with the gods.

"Incredible," I whispered.

"She is pretty," my father admitted.

Only then did I look at the one figure who was not made of gold, silver, jewels, or priceless masonry. That said, I knew men would fight wars for her just as they would for any other treasure. She was a slip of a girl, just the kind my father liked, and yet she still seemed to have this invisible field of power around her, a living huaca.

My father had always said you can judge a person by their eyes, only the greatest liars in the world can control their eyes. This girl's eyes were like those of a fawn, big and black and helpless. She looked sad, not at anything or out of any personal injury, just sad. You wanted to wrap your arms around her and protect her from whatever made her eyes look like that. She was like a bird with a broken wing. You wanted to pick her up and cradle her.

"My Lord," the girl bowed low and blew him a respectful kiss.

"Get up, girl, get up," he said, stepping forward and bowing slightly himself in greeting. Chusek and I smirked to see my father so moved by a woman. "You are Kiske Sisa?" The girl said that she was, and they fell into a conversation, though it seemed my father did most of the talking. When he realized Chusek and I were still rooted to the spot just inside the door he laughed a little and took all three of us on a walking tour of the rest of the temples around the courtyard.

There was Inti's personal shrine, with a hole set high in the wall so that at noon the true Inti beamed down a bolt of sunlight onto his golden image. Within that gold-lined room stood all the representations and cult forms of the Intip Churi's personal patron. There was the sun disk Punchao, the Day, and Inti's mummy bundle, without a true body inside but just as much a huaca as any Emperor's mummy. There was a block of rock crystal the size of my head that was so clear you could see the hairs on your hand through it, while it's almost invisible interior facets could capture the sun's rays and make them swirl in panicked confusion, like a net catching a school of iridescent fish.

My father interrupted his talk with Kiske Sisa as we examined the crystal. "Would you excuse us for just a moment?" She acquiesced immediately, retreating to the far side of the shrine as fast as dignity would allow. The resemblance to a frightened mouse was uncanny.

When she was out of earshot he pulled us to him. "What do you think?" He asked in a low whisper.

"She's beautiful, father, but a little nervous—"

"Not her, boy. That's my decision, though I must admit Mama Ocllo seems to have done me a good turn for once in her life. No, I meant this place."

Chusek spoke for both of us. "This is incredible."

"I sent her away because I want to show you something she might not know, and she has probably been in this building every day for eight years or more." He took us each by the shoulder and steered us to a minor niche in the wall, unremarkably positioned and almost lost in the opulence. Its sole huaca was an ancient birdcage made of wooden withies, and inside sat a small bronze bird whose body was irregularly covered in a thick patina of verdigris.

"What is that doing in here?" I wrinkled my nose at it.

"When you think of the glories of this place I always want you to think of this one huaca, boys. Everything you see here started with that little thing in a simple wooden cage."

"What?" Chusek said, leaning in to examine the bird. It would have fit into the palm of his hand. If it was supposed to be a parrot or a hawk — it was difficult to say because of the crude workmanship and the heavy corrosion— then it was smaller than life size.

"That was the personal huaca of the real Manco Capac. That is the first and oldest idol to Inti that we know of."

To look at that clumsy statue and then the glories that had surpassed it was as humbling as any of the great works of art in that place, Friar. It reminded us that we, as Inca, were huaca ourselves. What other people had ever done so much for themselves, gone from such simple primitive beginnings to where we now stood?

We were veritable gods on Earth, and we had elevated the memory of the long dead Manco Capac to a suitable god-like originator. The truth was he had been a man poorer than young Chusek and I, were we to measure our few personal treasures against his. When my father felt he had made his point he called Kiske Sisa back, and we continued our tour.

Next door there was the temple of Mama Quilla, the moon goddess. Not one golden object was allowed in here, only silver, the colour of the moon, but each day at sunset her silver idol would be taken next door to her husband Inti to spend the night in his temple.

Next to those temples were shrines to Illapa, the god of storms, Saramama, goddess of the harvest, Mamacocha, goddess of the sea, and even a small altar to Urca Huari, the god of underground treasures. Appropriately enough, his altar was bare but my father assured me there was a hoard of silver, turquoise, and emeralds cached in the packed earth beneath it.

At last, opposite the Corincacha-proper, lay the small temple set aside for Viracocha, the Creator. The inside was bare, without a single golden ornament, except for a life-sized figure of an old man, all of gold, with a long silver beard and silver hair, and around his brow was wrapped a headband from which dangled a golden fringe. He carried a long stick of chonta wood in one golden hand, and his other was raised in greeting.

There is a legend that said Viracocha once walked the earth in just such a form, performing miracles before building a raft on the shore near the city of Tumpez and sailing off into the sea. Many years later the more credulous and fanatical of our religious figures would mistake the bearded Spaniards sailing to our shores as emissaries of Viracocha, but that is for later in my story.

"Why is his temple undecorated, father?" I asked.

"It doesn't have to be," he said, then caught himself about to say something indiscrete. "I'm so sorry, my dear. Would you excuse us again?" It was disconcerting how much her retreats looked like running, when in fact she moved at a pace so slow as to be obviously restrained. When she was outside he turned to us again. "I will tell you boys something in here, and I will tell it quietly. Illyapa and Saramama and the rest have no more power than we give them. Even Inti, the father of all our people who has put the Inca on the road to dominate the world, even he is not really worth worshipping." My father cast his eyes towards the ceiling, as if the roof might collapse upon him for speaking as he did.

"There is a higher power, the true power, and he is so great that the Inca do not encourage others to worship him. We call him Viracocha. The Colla and the Lupaca call him Kon-Tiki. The people on the coast call him Pachacamac. It doesn't matter what we call him, for he has no name, only titles. He is the Creator of everything, even of the other gods. Inti is our special friend, our mentor, and we thank him for his favour by making everyone in Tahuantinsuyu worship him, but if you ever really need something, you are an Inca: You beseech Viracocha. He makes time for an Inca's problems."

"So why not decorate the temple?" Chusek asked.

"Everything we offer to any god is really for him. No one but the Inca knows that, though. It is our secret. In public we sacrifice to Inti, or to Illapa, or to Saramama, but in our hearts we're offering it to Viracocha. We only make a temple for him in places that he has to be publicly venerated, and even then we do not decorate it as we do our sun temples, but every prayer is really for him. Don't forget it. He is not an enemy you want to make, but he is a powerful friend to win over."

My father called Kiske Sisa back to us, and we walked around the garden, admiring the sculptures again.

"How old are you?" he asked her.

"I am sixteen, my lord."

He frowned, and I think I knew what he was thinking. She was almost my age, and certainly too young to marry as a true partner. Marrying her now would be bringing another child into his home.

"How do you enjoy the House of Chosen Women?"

"It is my duty," she said too simply. Her eyes welled up with tears for a moment, and we all knew she hated the place.

"I will talk to the Sapa Inca and Mama Ocllo to see if we can't make your time there more pleasant."

"Forgive me, my lord, is this interview not to arrange a marriage?"

"It is, but I'm neither a young buck nor an old man. I don't need a little girl. Much better if we let you mature, grow up to the right age." Her frown was heartbreaking, but I could see some small flicker of relief in her eyes too. "I'll visit you often, so we are not strangers when the time comes." He smiled, then with a dexterous flip of the hand he made a cantut blossom appear from out of nowhere and offered it to her. "Until next time," he smiled again.

We left her in the courtyard, contemplating the flower, and we were out on the street before Chusek broke the silence. "You old honey dribbler, sir: 'Until next time,' " he mimicked the flick of the wrist and cupped an invisible bloom.

My father chuckled. "It is not easy to court a woman in front of your son." His step seemed lighter all the way home. As for Chusek and I, our heads seemed to be ringing from the wonders we had seen.

Our visit to the Coricancha was the talk of the school the next day, for no one else had been inside and most never would. Mallku saw the religious and the curious among his followers come to hear the story, and when his best friend Allallanka was among the defectors he put his foot down.

"What do you think you're doing?" He barked.

Allallanka was the son of Colla Topa, the Socso Panaca's major-domo. Were it not for the deep Socso Panaca blue of his headband, though, you would never have guessed it: Where Colla Topa was a jovial man, Allallanka's name, the Lizard, suited his temperament perfectly. Nothing seemed to visibly please or upset him. His face was a stone. He took one look at Mallku's puffed up chest and bunching neck muscles and said, "I'm hearing about the Coricancha."

"We're supposed to be doing weapons drill."

Allallanka was the biggest boy in the school, and his size made him gifted with the tools of war. He shrugged his broad shoulders. "It's an optional class that we're taking because we already know everything and we want to show off. I'll show up late."

"So what if his father took him to see a temple? What has he ever seen for himself?" Mallku huffed. He spoke as if Chusek and I were not there, and I was not prepared to let that pass.

"What do you mean, see for myself?"

"I mean have you ever had the courage to go somewhere you're not allowed to go?"

My mind flashed to the places Mallku might dare me to go: The Sanki-huasi, commonly known as the Pit, where traitors were thrown to die; the prison of sorcerers; the Imperial harem. While all of them were denied to me I would be able to visit any of them under the guise of running an errand for my father.

"Name the place, big man. As long as it's within walking distance of the city we can get there." I was a little too sure of myself, fresh off the high of visiting the Coricancha. Mallku might not have the special education of a capac quipucamayoc, but under no circumstances was he stupid. He had a plan, and like a fox to the duck pond he went straight at the opportunity to embarrass me.

"I just gave the Vixen something the other day. She's keeping it in her cell in the House of Chosen Women. Bring it to me tomorrow, or recite a long paean about how great I am in the House of Learning's main courtyard at noon for everyone to hear. I, of course, will sing one for you should you succeed." He leaned back and smiled. Chusek pulled a long breath in between his crooked teeth. Allallanka just looked at me, his face as unreadable as ever.

"You're on," I heard myself say. Inside I was despairing. Of course Mallku would have sent us to the House of Chosen Women. Of course he would. Men couldn't go in there on pain of death, and though we were not yet pacuyoks we had the equipment to qualify as men. Chusek had already bedded more women at fourteen than I would in my entire life. It was only after Allallanka and Mallku left for their class that Chusek rounded on me.

"How in Supay's name are you planning on getting into the House of Chosen Women? There's one door with a guard on it, and the few windows are all two floors up and too small to crawl through."

"When in trouble, ask Viracocha," I said, as if I had the slightest idea what I was talking about.

Far from Viracocha, my first stop was the Vixen, easily spotted as always by the crowd of admirers following her from class to class. "Oh, hello Waccha," her smile was so sweet that it had to be malicious. She already knew.

"You're not going to help me, are you?" I asked.

"I'm definitely going to help you, just as soon as you're in my cell." That brought out some hoots from the boys around her. She frowned for a moment. "And bring Chusek. We can't have nasty rumours floating around."

"I like to think I start those rather than stop them," he smiled his dashing crooked smile.

"Fine. I'll see you tonight then," I said. My next stop was closer to Viracocha, anyway. I went to Topa Cusi Yupanki, the junior priest who was fast becoming known as the best augur in history. He was at the Huacaypata, pouring a libation to the sun down the gold-lined gullet of the sacrificial altar.

"I've already heard," the Bird Man said.

"Has anybody not heard?" Chusek muttered.

"I will admit you two were among the last," he chuckled. A puco puco bird called, although it was well after noon. Topa Cusi Yupanki's head snapped around, identifying the errant bird perched on the thatch of the Emperor's palace. "I am supposed to help you," he concluded.

"The bird told you that?" Chusek asked. I elbowed him in the stomach.

"How do we get in?" I asked.

"Waccha, you can't enter without being challenged, but once you're in as long as you look busy and female, you won't be caught. Never stand idle, though. They hate that." He smiled his dreamy smile at me.

"You've been inside, haven't you?" Chusek asked, incredulous.

"It's not true that men aren't allowed inside," Topa Cusi Yupanki said seriously. "You can get in if you're dedicated to a celibate priesthood and escorted by enough Brides of Inti to keep you faithful."

"You aren't part of a celibate sect," I said.

"I was. I was called to a different faith."

"What faith?" Chusek asked.

"One where I can sleep with women." The Bird Man and Chusek exchanged their worldly smiles, leaving me in the dark.

"So how can I get in?" I asked.

"I haven't the slightest idea; just remember to look busy and female while you do it." He returned to his offering, leaving the two of us frowning out on the sand of the Huacaypata.

We walked to the House of Chosen Women, its solid walls of fitted ashlars forming an impenetrable barrier, two storeys high. There was only one door, and the guardsman, like everyone it seemed, had already been tipped off by Mallku. He ordered us to keep walking, and as I never thought he would allow us in anyway we kept moving.

"Okay, you're the one in the military classes. If this was a siege, how would you storm the place?"

"With two unarmed boys who aren't allowed to kill anyone? I wouldn't," he laughed.

"Seriously, think it through. One door, heavily guarded, let's consider it impenetrable. Windows are too small and unreachable. Where is this thing vulnerable?" We both craned our necks back to the steep thatch above.

"The roof," we said in unison. We looked at each other. "Ladder?" We said it together again.

"We couldn't set it up in the street," Chusek said.

I turned around to face the building across the street from the House of Chosen Women. It was the Amauracancha, the Serpent Enclosure, the palace of the Socso Panaca. "What about using the ladder as a bridge from their roof to the House of the Chosen Women's roof?" I paced off the distance between the walls. The street was eight paces wide.

"We'd need a man inside the panaca to get the ladder in and guard it at his end, and haul it back once we're across," Chusek said with more enthusiasm.

"Allallanka's father is Colla Topa. He can do anything he wants in that panaca," I said.

"Can you get us a siege ladder out of stores?"

I nodded. We stood in the street talking for sometime, putting the threads of our plan in order. By now the House of Learning was done

102

for the day and my father would be expecting me at home. We agreed to meet that evening after sunset, and I returned with the gherkin fetcher, dreading that somehow Mallku had let my father in on our wager, just as he had everyone else who might have been in a position to help me, but my father was blissfully unaware of his son's impending illegal activity.

The day's math problem was a difficult one and my mind would not stay focused, but when I had the answer after the third try my father grunted his approval and dismissed me for the evening. I put a length of requisition yarn in my coca bag as I left.

Chusek was admitted by my doorman, Allallanka in tow, and the three of us went to the tampu in the fortress of Intihuasi atop Sacsahuaman hill. Once there I produced the quipu I had made from the filched string, demanding the use of a siege ladder and two heavy bags of unspun wool. The tampucamayoc was no fool, seeing three boys about to do something unusual.

His doubtful expression was quickly soothed by my explanation that we were running a training exercise, carrying heavy weights up and down the ladder to simulate storming a citadel. As he walked down the rows of warehouses I saw him limp and suspected he himself was a discharged officer. It was my first lucky break of the day.

Carrying the ladder as innocently as possible, which is surprisingly difficult to do down narrow streets, we made our way back to the Amauracancha. The doorman was just as skeptical about the ladder as the tampucamayoc had been, but Allallanka silenced him with a quiet murmur about seeing an indiscretion at last month's party between the doorman and a married woman. We made our way unmolested throughout the panaca's palace, for while the sun had set there was no formal party planned for the evening so the panaca members were not using the courtyards and main corridors for their orgies.

"Ready?" Allallanka asked when we were in the courtyard of one of the buildings opposite the House of Chosen Women.

"No," Chusek said. I looked over at him, and he was smiling his dashing smile again. That expression meant only one thing, and I groaned. "Seriously, Waccha, we're going to need to look like women." He swaggered into the closest lit up building, and when he came out again he had two dresses and shawls.

"How did you get those?" I asked.

"And where are the girls to go with them?" Allallanka's face remained unmoved but his voice betrayed his interest.

"Oh, them?" Chusek laughed. "They're waiting for me."

He and I doffed our tunics and put on the dresses, wrapped the shawls around us, pinning them across the breast as women do. Then we took the heavy bags of unspun wool onto our backs with generously broad tumplines over our foreheads to conceal as much of our male haircuts as possible.

"How do we look?" I asked Allallanka.

"You must be the two ugliest chosen women I've ever seen. Too tall, too boney, flat chests, no hips, short hair, and Chusek has both crooked teeth and stubble."

Chusek looked over at me, hurt. It was true that he had an unusually heavy beard for our wispy-faced race, and it had been too long since he had last seen a razor or tweezers. "You look radiant," I assured him; then I bit my collar to ward off bad luck.

We scampered up onto the roof then hauled the ladder up after us. It was only on the steeply pitched thatch it sank in what we were trying to do, perform an executable offence. My belly dropped a little.

"Death or glory," Allallanka muttered, sensing my mood.

We put the ladder across the roofs, making sure it was firmly anchored in the House of Chosen Women's thatch before slowly crossing. I went first, feeling every little creak and groan in the wood while my eyes focused on the cobblestones below and the heavy bag of wool on my bag seemed to catch every gust of wind, throwing off my balance. When I was on the House of Chosen Women's roof I secured the end of the ladder and Chusek crossed with greater ease.

With some effort Allallanka hauled our bridge back over onto his roof, waved good luck to us, and was gone. Now we were on our own.

"Has it occurred to you that we have no way of getting down?" Chusek asked.

"That one I figured out for myself," I said, patting the heavy bundle of wool. We walked along the roofs of the House of Chosen Women, examining the courtyards below for one that was deserted. When we found a small flower garden we dangled our bundles of wool down to the ground with our tumplines so that the bags were together, then I jumped down. It hurt, but not as badly as if we had tried it without the

104

cushion. I repositioned the bags and Chusek joined me.

Redoing our tumplines and now looking like two low-ranking chosen women carrying heavy burdens, or so I hoped, we had a whispered argument over how we were going to find the Vixen's room. The House of Chosen Women in Cuzco was home to three thousand girls and women drawn from across the world. It was huge, and we had no idea where to go. In the end we decided we would just start walking.

The courtyard was ringed by a portico, and that portico led into a series of twisting turning corridors and hallways, dividing and segregating the compound. We passed a number of courtyards where women made akha or laboured on looms but nothing that looked like living quarters. After we had wandered the halls until we were quite sure we had taken every possible turn we returned to the small garden, which was unused during the evening.

"What do we do?" I asked.

"They've got to eat and sleep somewhere. We've just dropped into a work area," Chusek reasoned.

"Yes. I didn't see the way out onto the street either, so there's definitely a section we aren't getting into."

"There's got to be a way into it! The girls aren't climbing ladders to go to work."

So we took to following stray girls and women at a distance, taking the turns they took. It took a long time, for we had to stay far enough back not to attract attention. Gradually we worked out a section where three corridors met within the space of twenty paces before doubling back on themselves. Here was our problem. People went into that intersection but they were gone by the time we could follow them, and new people came out of that intersection who we had not seen before.

"This isn't good, Chusek. We've been outsmarted by a hallway," I whispered.

"Think it through," he hissed back. The intersection was well lit with torches and the stone walls were plastered over in a muted white colour. Floor-length tapestries lined the walls at intervals. Our investigation was made more difficult by the fact that we had to keep walking, and it was made exhausting by the very real weight of all that unspun wool. We must not be seen to be lost or idle, for that would raise questions. In truth we should not even be speaking, for this den of women was a strange place for male voices.

105

It was perhaps our twentieth pass through the intersection that we finally saw one of the tapestries peel back and a woman emerge through it. I was careful to conceal my shock. The tapestry was cunningly weighted at the bottom so that it dropped flush against the wall, concealing the passage beyond. We returned as soon as we could and peeled the heavy fabric back to reveal a narrow doorway, perhaps only a third the width of the tapestry and with a raised threshold so that no draft could penetrate. On the far side of the opening was the back of another weighted tapestry.

"Hey! In and out, you know the rule!" A woman scolded us as she rounded the corner. We ducked through the door and out the tapestry on the far side.

As a boy when I thought of the House of Chosen Women I pictured a pleasure garden of beautiful women, perhaps scantily dressed and giggly. The living quarters of the chosen women put that myth to rest. It was long hallways of tiny undecorated rooms without any covering on the doors. Each cell was furnished with nothing more than a simple straw pallet and a sooty torch. Women had to perform everything from brushing their hair to relieving themselves in full view of their neighbours. There was no laughter, and brides of Inti —women married to the Sun who would never escape these walls to have a husband and a family— wandered the halls, passing out stern disciplines to girls who violated the mysterious rules of this place. As near as I could see the girls either worked in big group projects weaving and making akha, or they sat alone in their cells, spinning thread or embroidering.

We wandered the entire ground floor before I remembered the Vixen had a window, meaning her cell would be on the upper floor. We were no sooner up a ladder then we were stopped by an elegant woman with a stern face. "You two! Where are you going with that wool?"

"Um, the Mother Superior asked us to distribute it?" I said in my most sincere falsetto, hoping desperately that in a compound of three thousand women and girls this was not the Mother Superior I was speaking to.

"Gods, what province are you two from? You must be the homeliest girls I've ever seen, and the stupidest! Wool is distributed at the beginning of the month!"

"I only do what I'm told," I said.

She leaned forward and slapped me across the face. "My title is 'My

Lady', and you do what you're told or I'll hit you again. Go about your business, and I'll go tell the Mother Superior that we have enough wool. Then I'm going to find you two and you'll go around with your empty bags and fill them up again."

"Thank you, My Lady," I murmured, casting my eyes down.

We wandered the halls again, stealing a glance into each room for the Vixen. For one heart-stopping moment I spotted Kiske Sisa walking our way, but she turned a corner before seeing us, and I imagine she would have looked right through us even if she had. Everyone here seemed to be either a stranger or an enemy to everyone else. The place breathed that special apathy that only women set against one another can produce.

At last, in the farthest corner of the compound from where we started our search, we found the Vixen in her room, working a backstrap loom and weaving one of her little cumpi squares.

"Excuse me," I said in my falsetto.

"You look ridiculous," she said without even turning her head. "Give me a moment." She unhooked herself from the loom and stepped out into the hallway. "Annas-Collque, Chimo-Urma, Samyukta, Toctollssica, Inguill, you know very well I have information on each and every one of you. Leave your rooms and don't come back until you've made yourself some potatoes."

Without a murmur of protest the cells around us emptied. I should have guessed that the Vixen would rule her hallway just as she ruled the schoolyard.

"Potatoes?" Chusek asked, taking off his tumpline.

"Put it back on. I can blackmail my neighbours, but I have nothing on the brides of Inti walking the halls." She waited until he complied before answering his question. "You won't be here that long, but Annas-Collque cries herself to sleep and it irritates me. As long as I'm getting her out of her room I might as well give myself enough time to go to bed in peace. The fires are out in the kitchens. It will take them forever to make some food."

"It's horrible here," I said.

"It's necessary for me to live here, but that doesn't mean I like it," she agreed.

"What's the rule involving the tapestry door?" I asked.

She looked blank for a moment. "Oh, of course, you had to go through a rape door."

"Rape door?"

"If the place was ever stormed, the main rooms, private rooms, and work rooms are all separated from each other by disguised doors. All the girls have to go through them as quickly as possible to limit the chances of anyone figuring out which are the doors and which are just wall decorations. Most houses of chosen women have them."

As interested as I was in this place every extra moment here was a moment where I could be caught. I had come here for a purpose. "I believe you have something for me?"

"Hmm? Oh, yes," she reached under her pallet and pulled out a thin plank of wood, about the size of her hand. On it was painted a figure dressed in a red and white checkered tunic holding a bouquet of flowers.

"What is that?" Chusek asked.

"That's Chalcuchima's way of telling me he loves me." We muffled our laughter, not wanting the unfamiliar sound to draw down the brides of Inti on us. "Oh, be nice. He really is quite a sweet boy."

"I think I'm going to be sick," I said, slipping the board into my wool bag. "How do we get out of here?"

We went through two more of the rape doors on our way out, which assured us that had we not asked we would have been lost in there until we were caught, for there was no way short of checking every tapestry to figure out which was which and no way to check without arousing suspicions. We went out through the single door into the street, telling the guardsman that our bags were being returned because they were delivered on the wrong day, wool came at the beginning of the month. He nodded and waved us out. We were too young, ugly and junior-ranking to require a formal escort.

We met Allallanka the next day at the House of Learning, and he had a big smile on his usually expressionless face. "So you got out alright?"

"Of course," Chusek said. "But that's not why you're smiling." Allallanka shook his head, unable to wipe the grin from his face. "So how were they?"

Only then did I remember the two naked women Chusek had left behind in the Amauracancha. Suddenly my adventure seemed paltry to the evening Allallanka must have had. My excitement came back, though, when Mallku entered the courtyard.

"Well?" He said with confidence. He had a gang behind him, ready to embarrass me. I pulled his painting out of my coca bag, and his face fell.

"Don't worry. I won't say what it means. I think your wager will be punishment enough."

He waited until noon, as agreed, and by then I had almost every student and teacher out in the courtyard to hear him sing my praises. No one knew the details of the bet, of course, but they all watched Mallku humiliate himself. He sang off key, but he did belabour my greatness and brilliance. In short it was a sweet song, and the Vixen smiled at me the whole time he bawled it out. It was a good day, Friar. It was a damned fine day.

I sometimes find myself thinking that we weren't really boys when we were at school, Friar. We were each so focused on what we would be for the rest of our lives that we forgot to live in the moment, have fun, get into trouble, break rules. Then I remember saying, "This isn't good, Chusek. We've been outsmarted by a hallway," and I smile.

You should always have an adventure when you're young, several if you are lucky, and when Mallku threw his head back and sang my praises it was the perfect finish to one of the happiest episodes of my life. There was no guilt, no complications, no headaches. It was good to have so little to worry about, Friar. Maybe that's what really separates boys from men, and why some people grow up faster than others.

Whatever the case, after that glorious afternoon the tentative group of people who had formed around me in the early days of school returned and redoubled, so that any who resented Mallku or had earned his displeasure befriended Chusek and I. Chusek remained one of Mallku's good friends, so he formed a bridge between our two camps and prevented further conflicts. Mallku and I spent long and happy months quietly going about our separate courses of study, so that graduation and the manhood ceremonies were approaching without incident.

The tying on of the breechcloth, the piercing of ears, and the taking of an adult name —the symbols that separate men from boys— are all done as part of the manhood ceremonies somewhere between a boy's fourteenth and sixteenth year. There are prayers and fasts and feasts, of course, but also feats of endurance and strength and manly virtue, concluded by a footrace among all the boys becoming men with the winners receiving special attention and fame, often for the rest of their lives.

It was the pleasant daydream of winning and the disturbing possibility that I might do very poorly that used to fill my head during the months where Mallku and I avoided each other.

That is, until the war game happened.

Friar, it is an old man's game to play what if, and my favourite hypothetical is what my life might have been like if attendance at the strategy classes was not mandatory for non-military students. Mallku and I had been rivals, certainly, but we were just childhood foes fighting over a girl neither of us could have. Such animosities are buried by time and distance, and Chusek was doing his best to give us both those healing commodities after the wager involving the House of the Chosen Women.

If Mallku and I had gone our separate ways, I suspect my life would now be unrecognizable to me. I would have loved different women, raised different children, performed different duties, impressed and offended different people. It all hinged upon a single sunny afternoon, and like so much in life I had no idea of the import of what was about to come. I was like a llama led to the slaughter who still concerns himself with a mouthful of grass on his way, totally oblivious to the futility of his actions.

The war game was Mallku's special domain. He was the finest student the school's generals had ever seen, and he reveled in it. He even had them call him General Chalcuchima when he played.

The war game was held in the largest courtyard of Inca Roca's palace. Heaps of earth and turf were brought in to create a miniature landscape, and carved blocks of wood the size of my head represented units of men. Two students commanded the wooden armies against each other, and victory was decided by the old warriors who gathered each day to watch.

There were more rules, I'm sure, and as I think about it some of them come back to me: It is the nature of our polyglot armies that a commander cannot give detailed orders once the battle has commenced, so both boys had to make their plans before the game began. Once a battle started they could only give short orders, and even those were delayed for a period of time that depended on how far the unit was from the commander's position on the imaginary battlefield.

When a boy won he would become the general of the wooden Inca army the next day, and each subsequent day after that until he was defeated. That way we students grew familiar with the idea of Inca invincibility, for the talented ones commanded the Inca side, working their way through the dross of the class quickly.

As I said, Mallku was a prodigy at the war game. He had a gift for the arts of war just as my father and I knew our quipus. It was his true calling. I honour his skill now, despite all the bad blood that was to flow between us. Mallku had the soldier's eye for terrain and for weak points in a formation of men, and he understood the limitations of battlefield communications to the point where he often gave his officers ten sets of contingency orders, each tailored to possible enemy actions.

He won his first game two months into our second year at school, routing the wooden Inca army facing him in what could only be called a total slaughter. He took his position the next day as commander of the Inca army and played for day after day for almost two years, defeating all challengers.

I was not enrolled in the school for military training, and my father tied me down with far too much extra work for me to volunteer to play. On the other hand I was an Inca, a high-born Child of the Sun, and so my attendance was mandatory. I used the time to practice my reading and tying word knots, and the war game courtyard was deathly silent until victory or defeat was declared, so it was well-suited for concentration.

The day came, though, when Chalcuchima had defeated each of the boys of his age who were enrolled for military training and his instructors suggested he go back to the beginning. He shook his head and pointed me out.

"I want to play against him." I was not looking at him at the time and was not aware I was the centre of attention until the boys sitting in front of me parted to allow the teachers to see who Mallku wanted.

"He's not enrolled..." One of them murmured.

"He's an Inca, isn't he? Great-grandson of Viracocha Inca? One day they might give him an army, and he'll have never even played at it before. Let him at least learn how to give orders," Mallku said reasonably. I knew he just wanted to trounce me in front of the Vixen, who sat under the shade of an awning with a perfect view of the model battlefield. He wanted to break our unspoken truce and take another try at humiliating me.

I shrugged when I realized I could not avoid it, deciding that the less I made of my loss the less he could make of it. I stood up and an officer took me by the arm, working my way through the crowd and out to my side of the war game field. I was placed opposite Mallku as one of the retired warriors pulled aside the sheet hiding this day's battlefield from us.

It was a rolling plain, obviously meant to represent the puna. There was an unwalled village to my left, made up of little wooden huts, and

112

two shallow dips of land in my centre. My right was flat and level all the way across to Mallku's left. I knew I would be on the defense, but the instructors had given me no advantage of fortress or heights to defend from.

I was careful not to protest only a fool would fight on his home ground without picking a defensible spot. The more I protested the more Mallku would claim I was an incompetent. I was an incompetent, I am still an incompetent when it comes to tactics and strategy and moving soldiers around a battlefield, but I am not a total fool; still, I would take my loss like a pacuyok.

"Today we shall play through a Colla uprising," the old general said. "The Colla in this province have refused to pay their taxes and have broken into the tampus to arm themselves. An Inca army has been dispatched –without any Colla units— to put down the revolt." I heard Mallku mutter something, for usually he put his doughty Colla warriors in his centre, protecting the small carved litter that represented his own person on the battlefield. The loss of them hurt, but he knew he would win either way. The instructor went on.

"The Colla number ten thousand experienced warriors in twenty units of five hundred men each. They are armed with the standard weapons. The Sapa Inca, in his wisdom, has given his general Chalcuchima fifty thousand soldiers in units of one thousand to put down this revolt. Two thousand are of jungle archers. Another two thousand are Cañari shock troops. The Sapa Inca has also provided Chalcuchima with a single legion of Inca to replace the untrustworthy Colla who usually make up his centre."

I swallowed but remained silent. The odds were realistic, even if the choice of battlefield was not. That did not mean they were fair: Chalcuchima outnumbered me five to one, and in his hands his five thousand special troops alone were probably the measure of my ten thousand.

"The generals will now give orders to their staff. We will begin the game upon their return." I was pulled by the elbow down to one end of the courtyard. Mallku was taken to the other.

The retired warriors around me were grumpy and impatient to return to their stools. They had seen far better tacticians than I fall to Mallku's careful plans, and they were already viewing the day's game as over. One of them asked me for my orders.

I sucked on my lower lip for a moment, looking at the rolling plain below. I had a really stupid idea, but it was a stupid game and I was the idiot playing it. No other student would try anything half so dumb, but I would be a tocoyricoc; I did not mind being thought a fool as a general. At least my tactics would be a novelty that might soften the later criticism.

"How does troop concealment work?" I asked, hoping it sounded like an intelligent question. It did not. I had just announced to them all that I did not understand the rules even after watching the games for two years. The old warrior grimaced.

"If your troops are out of line of sight from the wooden litter that marks Chalcuchima's position then we don't put your units on the battlefield until they are, but you have to tell us where you've put them in your mind. When any of his units do have line of sight on your hidden forces then, after the time it takes for them to send a messenger to Chalcuchima, we put that unit on the field."

"His name is Mallku."

"He will become Chalcu—"

"And I will become something other than Unfortunate, but I am Waccha for now, and he is Young Condor. For the short time I am your commander, he is Mallku." The old man stiffened a little, then smiled.

"You are your grandfather's grandson, boy. I served under him during the Chimu campaign. What are your orders?" He still did not sound enthusiastic about my chances.

"Do I have a wooden piece to represent my litter?"

"Yes."

"And I can only see what I can see from that point?"

"Yes, but the battlefield is almost completely open."

"What if I put my litter somewhere he can't see it, but I can see him?"

"That's not possible."

"Yes it is. This game is all about what could really be done and what would really happen, right?"

"Of course it is. That's why there're no dice. Experienced soldiers say whether a thing can be done and how it will turn out. That's to make it all as real as possible."

"So what if I put myself in one of the huts on my left? I could see his troops and mine without being in my centre, and he wouldn't see me, right?"

"No, he wouldn't see you, but if you aren't with your men it will take a long time for orders and information to go back and forth, and even rebels need a leader: If you're not with your men they'll run away."

"What if I was with them, in the huts?" I smiled.

"What?"

"Suppose I was actually a rebel leader out in Collasuyu. I have ten thousand men. What if I put five thousand of them on that little rise between the two dips in my centre, and put the other five thousand inside the village on my left, and I'm with the ones on the left. What would Mallku see?"

The old man thought about it for a moment. "I suppose he would see the five thousand on the rise, and that would be all."

"And I would be able to issue orders very quickly to the rest, because they would all be jammed into that village, right?"

"I suppose so."

"If you were Mallku, what would you do if you only saw half my army?" I thought I had a plan, but I wanted this veteran's opinion.

"I'd assume the other half was either in the dip behind the rise, the dip in front of the rise, or the village. Then I'd check the last two, the two I could check without engaging you, before I marched on your centre."

"But to do all that he'd have to change the orders he's giving right now, right?" I gestured down to the far end of the courtyard where Mallku was surrounded by his entourage. I wondered briefly if there was competition among the old men to support the winning boy.

"I suppose he would," the man said thoughtfully.

"Now, suppose I took one unit, five hundred men, and put them in the dip behind the rise in my centre. If I give them orders to march to their right and then march back into the dip like they were repositioning, would you put the piece on the field and take it back quickly, like it was a mistake?" I smiled again.

"Yes," he said, beginning to smile with me.

"And would you get angry at me if I shouted at you for giving away my surprise?"

"No."

"What if I wanted you to?" The man definitely smiled now. "Mallku is insufferable when he's winning, isn't he?"

"A real prick," the man grinned ear to ear. The other retired soldiers around me also began smiling. I gave them their orders and marched back to the centre. Mallku took three or four times as long, giving detailed instructions to his polyglot army before action was joined so they would know what to do no matter what. I could only hope he had not thought of my idea. I doubted it. Any real general would be crazy to do what I was about to do, but for me it was just a game. My only hope of victory was not caring if I won or lost and acting accordingly.

Mallku joined me at last and smiled sadly. "I'm sorry they made it so lopsided. I would have preferred for you to have a chance, but I'm sure you won't roll over for me." He said it as if he expected me to do just that.

"I'll do what I can, Mallku, but, as you said, it is lopsided." His smile disappeared.

"When we play, I am General Chalcuchima."

"Of course you are, Mallku."

Our respective staffs placed our pieces. Only half of my army was showing. Several of Mallku's officers cleared their throats, but one of my old men assured them I was playing by the rules with a scathing shushing.

Mallku's forces were drawn up as I expected. With five times the men Mallku had made a show of force, making his line three times as wide as mine while keeping it almost twice as thick. His jungle archers were out in front in a thin line of skirmishers. His Cañari were on his left, ready to take advantage of the flat ground. His Inca legion guarded his litter.

One of Mallku's officers stepped forward. "We are agreed that the size of this army, displayed this way, will demoralize the Colla rebels."

"Agreed," one of my officers said without consulting his peers.

"Where is the rest of Waccha's army?" Mallku asked his officers. The man who had served my grandfather in his youth stepped forward and put a five hundred-man piece down to the right of the dip behind my line of five thousand. I turned on him.

"What in Supay's name do you think you're doing?"

"Mistakes happen. The officer was eager and was repositioning his

116

men. He has been called back." The old man picked up the block and moved it back into the dip before removing it from the field.

I went on for some time, berating his incompetence. The man got angry, assuring me he had done the right thing. Several of the old men from both sides looked aghast that he had betrayed my hidden forces to General Chalcuchima, and one or two muttered about him trying to court favour with the promising boy. At last Mallku grew impatient with my temper tantrum.

"Calm down, Waccha. Accidents happen. He won't profit from it. I don't need favours to beat you, and I don't need incompetent crawlers on my staff." My old man looked as if he had been slapped. "Anyway, I figured you must have had your men in that depression behind your army. You wouldn't fill the dip in front of your position because then you would have to fall back uphill while I advanced, and you wouldn't use the village because without a wall it's totally indefensible. It's not a great place to put your reserves, but if you wanted to keep some forces back it's the best of your options. Good for you!" His condescension was palpable. I hoped very much that my plan would work. "Officers? Begin."

I watched in feigned consternation as the fifty wooden blocks of Mallku's army marched against me, each movement being announced and explained by one of his staff. The Cañari were making good time, doubling their pace and moving across flat ground, getting ready to flank me on the right.

I pulled the unit of five hundred out of hiding and put it at the end of my line of five thousand, facing perpendicular to the rest to anchor my right. I had issued the order as soon as I saw the disposition of Mallku's forces, but the Cañari were almost upon me by the time my officers decided the messenger had finally reached my men.

Mallku ignored the village; instead he wrapped his right around my left and halted his centre. Just before the Cañari attacked my line's right and his left hit my right my staff began placing my remaining nine units in the village, which now lay behind Mallku's litter.

At the sight of these nine the eleven Colla units atop the hill began advancing to their deaths down into the dip below them. The school boys watching the war game began howling until they were ordered to be silent. I snuck a glance at the Vixen to watch her fan herself with veiled interest.

117

"He can't do that!" Mallku hissed. My officers explained my orders to General Chalcuchima's staff, who admitted it could be done. "But the fifty-five hundred coming down that hill are now completely surrounded! They have no way out! What warrior would do that without his general sharing the danger with him? They have no way out!"

"They have a way out," I assured him.

Mallku began whipping out orders in short professional sentences, taking charge in a way that impressed me. It did not matter, though, for his officers would not bring them into effect until the appropriate time, and they assured him his messengers would have to take the long way around to his wings, as the shortest distance between his centre, right, and left were now occupied by more than half my army.

Mallku watched, jaw clenched and neck twitching, as my forty-five hundred outside and fifty-five hundred inside his encircling army made contact on the single wooden block representing the thousand-man legion of full-blooded Inca, Children of the Sun all, who guarded his personal litter. His staff pointed out that the units nearest Mallku would engage once they saw he was in trouble and my staff agreed, but that only evened the odds.

His left and right hung uselessly out on the rise I had vacated, confused by my actions and too disciplined to act without orders. Meanwhile, my imaginary men inside Mallku's ring knew the only way out was through, and my imaginary men outside had me leading them against General Chalcuchima's litter, urging them on to save their comrades and throw off the tyranny of the Inca.

Mallku's numbers would have won if the battle had been allowed to play itself through, but there was another officer present, Viceroy Achachi Michi, a man attached to neither staff and with no vested interest in the outcome. His job was to announce the random, the happenstance, and with great dignity he rose from his stool without so much as a grimace at his sore back and said, "Chalcuchima's litter has been overturned by the Colla rebels. His men have seen their general fall and have lost heart. It is the fortunes of war, but they are now fleeing the field in every direction. I declare this battle a victory for the rebels. Congratulations, Waccha."

I am sure Achachi Michi made the announcement for all the right reasons: Mallku had been undefeated for too long; my plan had been unorthodox; Mallku's centre truly had been pressed hard. Mallku did not care for any of those reasons. "You hated my father, and now you punish me with this? I outnumber him eight to one with his loses. His men on the inside are completely cut off and about to be annihilated!"

"No, they are not. They stand over your body. I'm sorry, son, but you have fallen," Achachi Michi said, putting a fresh wad of coca in his mouth.

Mallku kicked the wooden pieces on the piece of turf. The crowd began to murmur. I must have been smirking because he pushed his way free of his officer's hands and came up to stand nose to nose with me. "Do you have something to say?"

I opened my mouth, but he was not about to let me say anything, even though I meant to apologize and admit I would never be able to get fifty-five hundred men to march into certain death for me. "You couldn't have pulled that off in real life. You used the rules of the game and the biases of the judges against me. In real life you can't beat me."

My eyes drifted to the Vixen, who was smiling coyly at me. I felt warmth all the way down to my toes. Mallku saw it too, and backhanded me, provoking a murmur of discontent from everyone in the courtyard. "This is about pride, Waccha. Pride! I say I'll beat you in the manhood races. I'll eat your shit if I loose, but, so help me, when I win I will jam your face into a steaming pile of mine unless you admit right now you cheated at this game!"

I could not say that. It was a lie and a complete perversion of the ridiculous pride I felt at that moment, and he was asking me to do it in front of my friends, his clique, the old men, and the Vixen. "I don't have to cheat to beat the sons of traitors, and you should give up gambling because you're really bad at it," I said loftily. He backhanded me again and I felt the coppery tang of blood as he split my lip. One of the old men stepped forward to stop him from doing me further harm, but he threw off the interfering hands and stormed out of the courtyard.

Both Achachi Michi and the Vixen came over to congratulate me later, and I was surprised to hear the Vixen call the general, 'Uncle Michi.' The old man seemed to melt just a little under her kind attentions, but then didn't everyone? We walked together out into a smaller courtyard where he left us, and it was only when the hairs began to stand up on the back of my neck that I realized for the first time I was absolutely alone with her.

"You do know he'll hold you to that bet," she said.

"Well, I don't—"

"No, he meant it, and you and I both know what he can do when he puts his mind to it." I stood there, digesting the thought. A boy whose pride could overcome pain was a formidable opponent, and the gods knew Mallku was proud.

"I suppose you're right."

"And whichever one of you loses will be shamed in front of everyone," she said it carelessly, but those calculating eyes of hers were sending me a clear signal.

"That's right," I said. Her eyes flicked left and right, making sure that we were truly alone, then she reached out and pulled me to her.

When she kissed me time seemed to stop, and Inti shone so brightly his radiance passed through my eyelids, burning my mind. All that was as nothing, though, compared to the sensation of her hand seizing me between the legs.

I froze for an incredible moment, unable to shout the obligatory outrages for her tongue in my mouth. My loins became the center of my universe, the focus of all my attentions as she cupped my manhood. All too soon she let go, stopped kissing me, and stepped back. "I hope you win," she said as if she had done nothing at all. "You're better looking than Mallku."

The next day at the war game I commanded the Inca army and lost spectacularly to Allallanka, who managed to capture the wooden piece representing the idol of Huanacauri as my army fled the field. It was no salve to Chalcuchima's pride. He would not be allowed another turn before graduation and the manhood ceremonies.

Today, I can't even remember how I lost. The wager and the kiss took all my concentration, distracting me from things that were second nature to me now, like my counting board and ledger quipus. It was not long before my father realized something was bothering me, and a quick visit to the schoolmaster provided him with the answer.

He was waiting for me in his counting room, his hands on his hips. Before I was even up the ladder he asked, "You did what?" As if I had told him myself. When my father was angry his voice rumbled like far-off thunder; I could tell the storm of a lifetime was about to break over me.

I told the story in a rush: The rivalry, the argument, the girl and the bet. I could not lie to my father. He sat down on his stool, the stones on his counting board silent and still. I could not look him in the eye, and he refused to take his gaze from my face. I can close my eyes now and still remember the neatly thatched roof and the carefully joined masonry of his counting room that I studied at such length while I spoke. At last I was done.

"Do you think you can win?" He asked quietly. He knew the answer.

"No, father." I knew from experience that Chalcuchima had no pain threshold. He would run until his heart burst if he had to. When his will engaged, his body refused to disobey his mind.

"So you would have the son of a tocoyricoc eat the shit of the son of a traitor... For a girl?"

I could not tell what offended him more, the punishment, the prize, or the competitor. His tone drenched me in disbelief and disapproval. "Mallku will pick a pace and run it until he has won," I confirmed.

"You didn't choose your battleground. The terrain favours him. You are playing to his strength with your weakness."

"Yes, father."

"I cannot allow this."

"You would have me refuse to go through with the bet?" Even as I said it I wondered whether I was hoping or fearing he would.

"Of course not." I sagged a little with disappointment, which answered my question. "But I cannot allow you to lose."

"I don't see..." I trailed off, for my father did not make casual statements like that. I lowered my eyes to look at him, and I shuddered: His jaw was set, his brows calm. A decision had been made, and though I did not know what it was I knew I would not like it.

That afternoon my father ordered the household servants to pack my few possessions in a traveling bag. Only standing on the threshold of our door did my father reveal his plan: "When I wanted to make you a quipucamayoc I sent you to the math classes. When I wanted you to be able to speak Mochica I sent you to the language classes. Now I want you to win a race."

I stood there, a cool breeze blowing from down the narrow lane chilling my back. I waited. "So what do you do?" I asked. He did not answer aloud; instead he handed me a travel visa quipu. I look down at the knots and blanched. It was worse than I had feared.

121

I left Cuzco without fanfare or retinue, a boy who was almost a man traveling alone down the Andesuyu Royal Road, bound for the White Rock Chaski School. In my coca bag was another quipu, this one ordering the headmaster to return me in time for the manhood rituals but not to send me back at all if I was incapable of winning. I had been exiled to prosper or perish, and my father did not even say goodbye or wish me luck.

The chaskis were the specially trained sprinting couriers of the Imperial Post system. There were chaski post huts up and down every Royal Road, spaced about the distance a fit man could run at a full sprint without slowing down. Inside each hut two chaskis sat facing in opposite directions. When a chaski from the next post station appeared blowing his conch trumpet the sitting chaski facing that direction went out to collect a message and ran to pass it on to the next station. In this way a spoken message, quipu, or small parcel could make its way from the coast to Cuzco in three days, a feat I hear it takes your own postal carriers on horseback almost two weeks to duplicate.

Most chaskis are trained in their own communities. In rare cases, though, it is necessary to send the men to be trained in the art of running, and so the Sapa Inca Pachacuti established the Chaski Training School at the White Rock in Andesuyu. I have walked the length and breadth of the known world and I cannot think of a better place to sculpt the perfect runner.

Deep in the rolling hills of Andesuyu, where the eastern mountains begin to descend into the hacha hacha of the never-ending jungle, the local people worship a huaca they call the White Rock, an unusually bright boulder the size of a small palace firmly planted in the earth and shaped lovingly by the reverent hand of man to further make its holiness obvious to all who see it.

There is no way to tell how high above the ground the White Rock is, but even to a man from Cuzco the air seems thin and unsatisfactory. Around the White Rock there are a series of cliffs and steep slopes so that you can wake up in the morning in the humid lethargic air of the jungle and find yourself gasping for breath in the afternoon. That is just what they had us do.

There was a slope there called Beginner, but it was no easy incline to get new chaskis eased into their training. It was a hill designed to break men and leave their weak and trembling bodies exhausted at their defeat.

If I were to stand up straight I would find my toes on the same level as my ankle. This slope, the Beginner, continued at that grade from the altitude at which tomatoes will grow, hot and sticky with moisture and oppressive with the weight of air above you, all the way up to where quinoa will grow, that hardy mountain grain that flourishes even above the treeline. Despite a beautiful set of stairs, perfectly spaced and leveled to aid our climb, it seemed impossible to run the entire thing, but that was what they demanded of us.

My father had provided the proctor of the school with the special instruction that he was to show no favour for my rank, fear no punishment for my treatment, and turn out a runner capable of beating the best and fittest Inca in the manhood race. To this end, where other chaskis were allowed to collapse half way up the Beginner, I was forced to go all the way.

It was like putting hot coals on my chest, the pain of it. I started off at the base of the hill and four trained runners —big men with switches cut from saplings— would start yelling at me to get up the hill. Faster, faster, faster! They would swing at me, and if I was not really running they would make contact. My mind could not believe that these purics would have the temerity to strike an Inca. Mind you, I had no earplugs yet and perhaps they did not know. Whatever the case, I could not help myself but run my hardest at the bottom of the hill.

I was neither strong nor weak, but I could have been either and failed the Beginner. I would exhaust myself on the base of the hill and by the time I was getting up to the altitude at which maize would grow I would have happily collapsed, gasping, for a break. Not so. Now I staggered to a walk, but I could hear them behind me, coming up with their sticks, and I would gulp down lungful after lungful of air to fortify myself before breaking into a laboured jog.

As I climbed higher to where the purple blossoms of potato plants mocked my misery with their cheeriness my heart was racing ten times faster than my legs, and I staggered from step to step. It seemed as if black-winged birds passed before my eyes, blocking out the sun intermittently. Still I was chivvied along.

At the top of the hill, long after the other inductees had been allowed to collapse, I was a wreck. I could barely put one foot in front of the other. The air was so thin and lacking in nourishment that I was never satisfied. I swayed and staggered, and the sound of the wind in my ears seemed ridiculously loud when it had so little force. I fainted and awoke back at the bottom of the hill, having been carried there by my instructors. I wept in frustration. That went on for fifteen days, every day, up the hill, faint, wake up at the bottom.

The flesh melted off my bones. I had always thought of myself as slender, but now I saw where the softness I had taken for normalcy was actually padding, layers of fat hiding a lean and sinewy form. I was well fed, especially with meat and beans, which seemed to help build muscles, but I could not keep on the weight. I'm not sure whether it was repetition in the task or the weight loss, but it became easier and easier to climb that hill. By the fourteenth day I managed to run all the way to the maize before walking, but I still collapsed at the top.

I wanted to be back in Cuzco with Chusek and Allallanka and the Vixen. Even Mallku was a known quantity to me. This place stank of failure, and at times I knew I would lose my bet, that I would shame myself in front of everyone. When intelligent men do foolish things it is their curse to be smart enough to recognize their stupidity, and I was the stupidest man in Tahuantinsuyu. Like Mallku, I had promised to do something I knew I could not do. The difference was that he always somehow managed to do it, whereas I did not have his strength of will.

One night as I awoke at the bottom of the hill with hot tears of frustration running down my face I heard my instructors shouting at a new group of inductees outside. I had listened to their verbal assaults my entire time there, and it had blended into a dull background haze, an accompaniment to my pain and misery, but this time I was lying idle, unable to move even a single aching muscle, and so I focused on their words.

"This is the Beginner because by the time you are done this hill you have learned the only thing a beginner ever knows: Pick one pace, run it all the way, and in the end you will have a reserve of energy that you can use at the moment of your choosing. Run through the pain and it doesn't hurt on the other side. Breathe, but don't swallow air! Breathe the same way all the time, regularly, as if you were standing still. Breathe deep and enjoy each breath before taking the next one. One foot in front of the other, but swing your legs from the hip and let the weight of your foot move your leg in front of you. One pace! One!"

You could see why I had ignored it before. It was a bombardment of advice, none of which seemed to relieve the suffering. You had to gasp.

You had to strain. You had to run quickly at the bottom or they would hit you. I lay there, waiting for sleep to come, but it would not.

I remembered once, days earlier, when only three of my tormentors shouted me forward. The fourth was at the bottom of the hill tending to some administrative work. With tired backward glances I watched him run —run— up the Beginner. He joined the other three halfway up the hill, and then continue with them up to where I had slowed to a stop. I was standing next to a potato field, and he ran all the way up to me. He looked winded, but I was ready to faint and I had been walking since the maize.

If these men could do it, then so could I. They must all have been in my position at one time, but now they ran the Beginner every day. Oh, they stopped all the time, but that was so their students could get far enough ahead to slow down and stop. At that point the instructors always overtook the trainees before their unauthorized breaks could grant anyone relief.

The next day I tried something new. When they shouted and screamed at me to run I broke into a slow jog, little more than a walking pace. Their sticks touched my back two or three times, but when I did not accelerate they did not chase me. I put one foot in front of the other, using the momentum of my last step to drive the next forward. I made a game of inhaling until I could inhale no more before exhaling. I never ran fast, but I was running uphill.

I quickly overtook all the other trainees who had sprinted ahead of me. They could never sustain that pace. At my jog, slower and less satisfying, I passed all of them. I was still running at the potato field, and now I felt the pressure. I could no longer breathe deep. It hurt, but I ran through the pain, and on the other side my dull ache was just a fact that I could live with, and so I kept running.

At first I thought the instructors were not yelling at me because I had not stopped for a break, but when I looked back I saw that they were running after me just as they always had. The difference was now I was moving at the same speed; they could not overtake me. For the first time I managed to run all the way to the terraced quinoa fields, and after running that far I thought, why not all the way to the top? I was exhausted when I finally stopped, but there was no more hill in front of me. I had done it.

When the four reached the summit they were all smiles. "Congratulations," one of them said. I must have grinned too hard through my fatigue, for his next words were harsh. "You're now a beginner."

The Beginner was just that, a beginner's slope. Day by day they had me run different courses now, zigzagging switchback roads up the face of a cliff, treacherous downhill running where the desire to increase speed and blow your pacing is almost irresistible; paths that forced you to run through unbridged streams, something a chaski would never be asked to do. At night they would make me swim laps in a pond, first ten, then fifty, then a hundred. When I fell exhausted onto my pallet at night they would have me exercise my arms with stone weights, telling me to keep my heart pumping. They told me the school once had a trainee who had relaxed at the end of the day and his heart had given out at the sudden reduction in workload.

I took to running everywhere of my own free will. I would not walk to the latrine, I would run. I ran to the mess hall. I ran to the exercise yard. After the first month they gave me a day off so I ran up the Beginner, smiling at the struggling recruits I passed, and then once I reached the top I turned and ran back down it again at a pace only slightly increased from that which I had used to climb it.

Here was the difference, Friar! I felt like a winner, and my body became what I needed it to be. I would sleep soundly at night and dream of the Vixen's kiss, my mind playing with the memory so that it stretched out and lasted until the dawn. I never thought of Mallku at all.

But the White Rock was a chaski school, and there is more to being a chaski than just running. I began to carry parcels, and often they were ridiculously proportioned and weighted to throw off my pacing. I learned to blow into a conch trumpet while running at a full sprint. I learned to memorize messages of up to three hundred words perfectly upon only one hearing while running. I learned to run barefoot or in sandals. I learned to throw a sling without stopping. I learned to run in the middle of the night by torchlight, which is harder than it sounds for you have to run at a pace that will not burn out your torch while always keeping an eye out for shadows ahead that speak of obstacles in your path. Even an unexpected pebble underfoot in the night can throw you off your step.

I was at the White Rock Chaski School for three months, and I took as much pride in graduating from its program as I did from learning to read word quipus. No mere home-trained chaski had reached the peak of excellence forced upon me, and at our graduation ceremony the proctor told us we would never run so hard again in our lives.

We were each presented with a multicoloured sling to be worn as a headband: White for the white rock, green for the hacha hacha we awoke in each morning, gray for the bare-topped mountains we arrived at by the afternoon, and black for the nights spent running. I have mine still, though it is so worn from sweat and wind and rain that it is a mere wisp of material.

I ran home. Days and days of steady running, my few possessions held on my back with a tumpline on my forehead. Each chaski I passed blew me a kiss of congratulation at the mark of triumph I wore across my brow.

I passed coca plantations and forested valleys whose steep hills trapped the clouds, making a blanket of white that lay heavy on the forest, provoking the most thick and lush flowers imaginable to bloom. I crossed rivers and chasms by swinging suspension bridge, all the while examining the complicated rope-work involved in their construction. I ran so fast I would pass five or six tampus a day, each one set up to be a day's journey from their fellows for a man at a walking pace. I was home within days of my father receiving notice of my graduation.

I was proud. He was shocked.

I stood in the doorway, one hand on the yellow blanket and the other raised in greeting. The household had assembled in the courtyard to welcome me home, but they all had that vacant smile of surprise you wear when you don't know what other expression is appropriate. It was my father, descending from his counting room, who finally took a step backwards at my appearance. "You look like a totally different person!"

I was ushered in, of course, and a bath was run and food prepared and stories exchanged: My favourite bastard brother Ronpa, less than a year younger than I and nowhere near as annoying as our older brothers, had won a position in the Imperial Guard when he was done school; our laundress was pregnant with our doorman's first child; Huaman Paullu had finished building his new house outside of town near the Great Quipu Repository.

All the time the news was being told to me they were staring at me. At last I could stand it no longer. "Well, get me a mirror then, if it's so shocking." One of my cousins was up and running as if he had been waiting for the order since I arrived. He returned in moments with a silver mirror the size of a dinner platter. Looking at me from its surface was a stranger.

There is a period where children become men faster than seems possible, and my time at the White Rock had made a man of me. I already said that I had grown lean, but now I saw my build was not that of a wiry boy but of a sinewy man. I did not have Mallku's unnatural strength, but I did have the well-proportioned limbs of a tall man full-grown. My face had matured too, the fleshiness had melted away to show a strong chin, high cheek bones, and a large proud nose. If I had earplugs it would have been impossible to guess that I was only fifteen.

"This is going to be good," I said. My family seemed to find that funny, and we spent the rest of the night drinking and laughing and telling stories.

I returned to school the next day as if nothing had happened. I was so far ahead of the classes that I returned to the lectures having missed nothing. The few girls at the school, including the Vixen, had a hard time not staring at me in varying degrees of concealed admiration. Even Mallku grunted something about looking forward to a challenge, which was the closest he had ever come to complimenting me voluntarily. I walked proud.

Things were different for another reason too, of course. We were all about to graduate, to finish school and participate in the manhood ceremonies. As the great day approached we were required to perform rituals and duties after class to focus us.

I won't bore you, Friar, with all the details of the puberty rites, for the build up to the actual ceremony lasts more than a month and mostly includes either making our parents comfortable by making them akha to drink and mats to sit on, or making ourselves uncomfortable by fasting and exercising to harden our bodies.

The day of the race finally came, though, and we slept out in a field so that we were all together outside to sing Inti's praises when the sun came up. We worked our sleep-stiffened muscles with a few practice skirmishes, then we followed the priest Topa Cusi Yupanki and the yellow-fringed Titu Cusi Huallpa to the windy top of Huanacauri Hill.

This was the place, the start of the footrace that would settle my wager. I looked over at Mallku, but he was focused on the ceremony before us.

Upon the altar of the Inca's personal war idol Huanacauri, a brother of our founder Manco Capac who had been turned to stone, the sacrifice was made: A falcon had its neck broken; a vicuna had a needle driven through the back of its head; a fox was strangled; a hummingbird's skull was crushed; a serpent was decapitated, and a toad was cut in half. Each animal was supposed to give strength, speed, and cunning to the runners.

I adjusted my sandal straps and flexed my shoulders and back, working out the kinks. Mallku made his way through the crowd to stand next to me, frowning.

"Father sent you off to Chaski school, did he?"

"Yes, he did." I smiled at him. Beside me Chusek was careful not to grin.

"You better hope you're as good as you're pretending, or you'll never live it down," Mallku added.

"I could give you the same advice." The sun seemed to shine just for me that day. My moment had come.

The race would take us down Huanacauri Hill, across a rolling plain, and then up to the base of Sacsahuaman Hill. To our left the Emperor and his Court had seats carved into the rock of the mountainside, cheering us on, and some of the runners would be stupid enough to break their concentration, look over and wave. They had no focus. They did not want to win the way Mallku and I did.

At the end of the race women of our own age were waiting for us, among them the Vixen. That was the only person Mallku and I wanted to impress. It would be a good race. I was ready.

"Good luck to you all," Titu Cusi Huallpa, the Sapa Inca's heir, called out.

"May Inti shine upon you," Topa Cusi Yupanki added with an impressive oratorical sweep of the hands. For once there wasn't a single bird in the sky to distract him.

The race began to the sound of a conch trumpet, and we were running down a slope. I began my steady pace and smiled as scores of my former classmates surged ahead of me, some even wasting their breath to whoop their triumph at pulling ahead. The race was long, and they thought that the first hundred steps was victory. I thought for a moment that this would be easier than I had hoped. Even Mallku used the downhill slope to build speed that would only cost him later.

I ran my steady pace, breathing easily and feeling no strain as one by one the runners ahead of me began to slow and flag, falling out of the lead to trail behind me as best they could. Some lost their footing and tripped, others began to weave as they tried to keep running with spent lungs.

Gradually it came down to just the two of us out in front, with Mallku running ten strides ahead of me. I could tell from the muscles and veins standing up in his neck that he was running on pride now, ignoring his body's protests. It was like his hand in the fire, or holding off six of us at skirmishing practice, or lifting a classmate over his head: It was his mind giving his body orders and not allowing it to disobey his will. His pace was steady but his breathing was laboured. I could see the sweat trickling down out of his hair.

I was comfortable, running in a natural stride that I could have kept up all day. That said, Mallku was in front of me, and I had to do something about that before the race was over. I dipped into my reserve. As soon as I came up from behind him and entered his peripheral vision he put on a burst of speed that no man could maintain, stretching his lead out to ten paces again.

I ran a little harder, and he did it again. I ran harder still, and still he found the energy to increase his lope to a sprint until he was safely ahead of me. I was impressed at his fortitude and whispered a thanks to Viracocha that my father had sent me to the chaski school, for otherwise I would be in the middle of the pack far behind me, no match for this paragon of stubborn pride. As it was, I turned on the talent and used my reserves of stamina, running up beside him as if he had been standing still.

"Damn you," he huffed out as he exhaled, increasing his pace. I kept by his side.

"Relax and breathe regularly," I advised him. I was having trouble speaking normally, but I could see that he was beyond help. He could not have taken my advice if he tried, for at this point any change in his running tempo would have made him cramp up. Ahead of us, at the base of Sacsahuaman Hill, we could make out the line of chosen women waiting with akha to greet us. "Well, shall we make a race of it then?" I asked. I increased my pace. He stayed with me.

Friar, I do not know how he stayed with me, but he did. I ran as fast as I could go and he stayed right there, at my shoulder. I began to feel a deep burning in my chest, a roaring in my ears. My legs felt heavy and my tunic became soaked with sweat, but still I ran and he was right beside me. It got to the point where I could do no more. I was sprinting without thought of pacing. My chaski training was no longer a consideration. Now I just had to open a space between us before we reached the finish line.

The ground seemed to fly beneath us, bunches of ichu grass and loose piles of rock, a tumbled down llama corral that we both vaulted. The wind in my ears began to block out the sound of his breathing beside me. We were running so fast that the front of me felt cool even as my back burned. I felt one of my thigh muscles begin to bunch and knot up, but I ran through it.

There is a second wind, a burst of energy that lies on the side of an imaginary wall in a runner's mind. I thought I had already used it, but in fact it was there waiting for me fifty paces from the finish line. There was a moment of clarity and then I felt the cool wash of relief rain down upon me as I realized that my body had now gathered itself with new determination for a final effort that I could make and he could not.

I increased my pace again, moving so fast that the grass around me seemed to blur. Behind me I heard a choking noise and knew that it was Mallku. I crossed the finish line first to the sound of cheering, and when I looked behind me I saw that Mallku had fallen into the grass, gulping in great mouthfuls of air, choking and retching and weeping.

The two of us had run a race by ourselves and the next fastest runner was still two hundred paces out. "Come on, Mallku!" I shouted. He lay in the grass. "Come on!" I ordered him. He was done. Without the power of pride to propel him he was down.

I ran back onto the course as fast as I had run off it, lifting him to his feet with a strength I did not suspect I still had. "Up!" I said. He shook his head. "Second is still better than third." I whispered in his ear as he leaned against me, all of the muscles in his legs trembling and spasming, shaking him like a leaf in a storm. "They're coming, Chalcuchima, the men who will hold it over you for the rest of your life."

I do not know what made me call him Chalcuchima. He glanced behind us to see Chusek blowing hard, pumping his arms and legs as he broke into a sprint that would pass us in mere moments. Mallku shoved me away and began to move at a fast stagger, beating Chusek to the finish line by a single stride. He collapsed again on the far side, massaging his legs and gasping again, but there were no tears this time. I loped across the finish line again before the fifth runner was across.

The race ended, and we all went to bathe in a sacred spring to wash off the sweat and dust of our exertions, then we were presented with weapons and shields by our relatives and lead all the way back to the starting line at Huanacauri where the Emperor waited for us.

We were each given breechcloths, with the fastest ten men donning white ones and the slowest ten marked by shameful black ones. Then, one by one, we went with our families to kneel before the Sapa Inca and the war idol of Huanacauri. My father had his hand on my shoulder, his look of pride washing over me as cool and refreshing as the water in the spring I had just left.

The Emperor had his needle ready, waiting only for my father to give me my adult name. Usually the title had been privately discussed before hand, perhaps even negotiated on, but my father had kept quiet, even rebuffing me when I tried to bring it up.

"Well?" Topa asked.

"I was torn between two choices, depending on how he did in the races," Tupac said, drawing the moment out.

"I have a lot of men to stab here, Tupac Capac. What have you decided upon?"

"My son's name shall be Haylli Yupanki, so that he will never forget this day." I was grinning with unrestrainable pleasure even as the lancet pierced my lobes. Haylli Yupanki means Unforgettable Victory, and I knew that the common usage would come to be Haylli, Victory. For the rest of my life I would have a name of triumph and honour. No one at the ceremonies today would ever forget my race or how my name came to be.

The Emperor inserted the small golden tubes into my bleeding ears that would be replaced by larger and larger tubes until I was ready for golden earplugs, then he patted me on the head, congratulated me as Haylli Yupanki, and I stepped back from the usno to allow Mallku to become Chalcuchima. Viceroy Illyapa stood in for Mallku's father as senior male of the family.

I would have preferred to watch my other former classmates undergo their ceremonies than do what I knew was about to happen, but Chalcuchima would have none of that. I looked around for my father to

132

intervene, but he had pulled Viceroy Illyapa off into a very business-like conversation. Chalcuchima grabbed me by the elbow and dragged me out of sight of everyone.

We stood there, blood dripping from the tubes in our ears. "Thank you," he muttered. I was unsure I heard him, but I did not ask him to repeat it. "Now drop your breechcloth and let's get this over with."

"We don't have—"

"It was a bet. You had better believe I would have made you live up to it if our positions were reversed."

If I had lost I have no doubt he would have made me eat his shit in front of my father, but I did not lose and I was not that malicious. I will spare you the details of my defecation, Friar, but I will say he took the smallest pinch of it, put it into a generous wad of coca, and put it in his mouth. We did not speak the rest of the day, and we never spoke of what he ate again.

Cuzco celebrated that night, with every clan and household cheering the adulthood of at least one of their sons. My father's yanacona had prepared a feast in my honour, as well as little presents to show me that they were not acting merely as servants but as friends. The cooks made me a new coca bag. Our doorman made me a buckler of deer hide. Our laundress made me a new counting board, and I politely did not say it had the wrong number of compartments. I used it for years with a cup off to one side to hold the remainder stones.

As pleasant as it was, there was a better party waiting for me, and my father would never have dreamed of either keeping me from it or going with me. As soon as it was tactful he broke up our private celebration and prepared himself for bed, leaving instructions with our doorman to sleep by his teak responsibility in case I came home before dawn. I thanked my household and was out the door, heading for the Imperial banquet that my father would have hated but that the Vixen would love.

She was there, of course, in her finest dress and with cantut flowers in her hair. She had one arm around me as soon as I was within reach, claiming me, and we walked in an artificial hole in the crowd as everyone stepped back to make space for the combination of the winner of the manhood race and the most beautiful young woman in Cuzco.

Like a Sapa Inca and his Coya, it seemed everyone in the room came and played court to us. My friend Chusek, now with the proud adult

133

name of Kiskis, introduced me to six of his different girls, each cooing their admiration of me and giving the Vixen dirty looks, which of course were totally wasted on her; my Vixen was so far beyond these girls I smiled in both amusement and embarrassment at the silent womanly war acting out between them.

Allallanka, now with the absolutely appropriate title of Rumiñaui, Stone Eye, nodded to me severely. His breechcloth was just the standard colour as he had failed to distinguish himself in the races, but his headband was the deep blue of his father's Socso Panaca so I complimented him on the bold contrast as I gave him a commiserating pat on the shoulder. Then the Vixen whispered something in his ear that almost made him smile.

"What was that?" I asked.

"I told him two of my friends thought him handsome, and where he might find them," she winked at me.

I tell you, Friar, I had the hardest time imaginable trying to get her alone. She had no trouble at all. She just pulled me down a corridor, took a series of turns I would never have considered, and we were in a small bedroom.

"Congratulations," she murmured, running her hand from the nape of my neck, down around to my collar bone, then slowly down by chest and belly to rest with one finger inside the strings of my new breechcloth. Her eyes said she was not kidding, and I wasn't going to argue. I had the breechcloth off in less time than it takes to tell you, and then she looked me up and down as if she were choosing which shawl to wear. Fit as I was, I began to worry. "Very nice," she finally decided.

She withdrew her silver pin and let her gown fall off of her, and I was surprised to see a thin cord around her narrow waist. She undid it to reveal a beautifully sheathed dagger in the small of her back. I arched an eyebrow.

"Just in case," she murmured. She always was a practical girl, my Vixen.

With the dagger joining the pool of clothes around her feet I now saw what I had strained my mind to imagine since I first saw her five years earlier. She was nude, and she let me stand there admiring her just as I had let her, except that she knew that she would not be found lacking.

I discovered just how carefully she had planned this evening the mo-

134

ment we were on the sleeping pallet, for she had somehow arranged for this room to have vicuna duvets stuffed with goose down. It was like lying on a cloud. She kissed me as she had the day I made the bet, but this time she was on top of me and we had no clothes on, and after that the kiss went on and on and we did things that make an old man smile and a Spaniard stop writing.

It is my story, Friar, and we will continue despite your protests.

We had the room undisturbed all that night, and we made love more times than I can count in more ways than I could have imagined. The Vixen had never been with a man before, as was required of a Virgin of the Sun who lived in the House of Chosen Women, but my brilliant Vixen had long known that to use her body to its full effect she would need to know everything there was to know about the physical act of love. Often I had seen her chatting with old crones or going to Chimu pottery classes, but somehow it had never occurred to me until that night what my gorgeous Vixen had been learning. I appreciated it though.

She cupped and fondled and rocked and rode, kissed and cuddled and sucked and spanked. She nibbled and nipped and bit as her passions rose. I was not a statue in all this either, of course, and I quickly learned what made her gasp and groan, moan and shudder, made her cry out for more or beg me to stop. That night would have been enough for my entire life, but of course it would only be the first of many.

I was a man, Friar, a pacuyok with an adult name, an important position in the bureaucracy, and a beautiful woman to bed. I was full and complete, grown up. I was Haylli Yupanki, and insecure Waccha was gone, like the lump of clay that is moulded into the handsome pot.

I would go home each day, a smile on my face that was unmistakable to men of the world passing me on the street. I always had to compose myself carefully before entering my father's house, for only he was oblivious to my euphoria.

Months passed, and of course I could not see her every day, or even every few days. Now that I was out of the House of Learning my father accelerated my education —if that was possible— so that I worked double shifts in the Great Quipu Repository, took long trips into Condesuyu on abbreviated inspections, practiced half a dozen languages with native speakers, and learned how scores of trades worked so that I could better regulate their input and output of goods and materials.

What free time I had I divided three ways: First, I loved being a to-coyricoc-in-waiting, so I would often set myself pet projects and side tasks that I could not perform during my father's schedule, but I could proceed with on my rare afternoon off. For instance, I collated tribute data from the Rimac valley to see how much of the Sapa Inca's offerings to the Pachacamac temple were being recouped.

Second, I ran each morning, doing laps around Cuzco or running up mountains when I was away from the capital. I loved to run, and I loved to feel strong and healthy. My father never forbade me to do it. Once I caught him frowning at what he perceived as a waste of time, so I took to getting up earlier and running before the dawn.

Third, of course, was the Vixen. It was good to be young with that woman, Friar. It really was. Sometimes after we were done we would hold each other and she would tell me all her ambitions, how she wanted to be an opinion maker, a trend setter, a confidante of the powerful, a problem solver, a lobbyist for just causes. She could do all of it if only she was the power behind a panaca.

A few months before my seventeenth birthday I said, "When we get married—" and she was astraddle me before I could finish my thought. She made love with a vigour beyond all experience or imagination, so that when we lay together afterwards, utterly spent, I could not even lift my head.

"You were saying?" She purred.

I had no idea what she was talking about. I felt like there were bronze weights attached to my mind, pulling me down into sleep. "I don't remember," I confessed. She reached over slowly and pinched my nipple, hard.

"Let's get married now," she said. "We're young, but with the Emperor and our parents' permission we can do it. I want to get out of the House of Chosen Women. The girls in there just count the days until their fates are decided for them. It's depressing." She didn't sound depressed. She sounded satisfied, but I knew my proactive Vixen would do all in her power to start herself down the path to her panaca. Besides, I had been in the House of Chosen Women; I would not have wanted to continue living there either.

For my part marriage did not scare me. I was young, yes, but Topa Inca Yupanki had married Mama Ocllo at sixteen. The Vixen would be my wife, and together we would rise through the ranks of the aristocracy. I was not scared of marriage at all. I was scared of my father. "You know who's not going to like this?"

"You ask him," as tired as we were she somehow found the strength for her hand to wander down below my waist. "Let's make this official."

I staggered home that night, totally spent. I collapsed in bed and slept so soundly I missed my morning run, waking only to the last faint calls of the puco puco birds announcing the end of dawn. My father was up in his counting room, and I climbed the ladder with tired legs.

"Late night?" He asked, handing me a quipu that I ran through my fingers without conscious thought.

"Fifty-seven," I said.

"Don't tell me. Tie it down," he ordered. I did so.

"Father—"

"Have you seen the Atacama tribute figures? I know they live in a desert, but we're getting nothing out of them." He gestured to a basket full of tangled quipus. I almost recoiled at the sloppy organization in my father's holy of holies.

"What are we doing with this stuff? The Atacama is in Collasuyu, not Condesuyu."

"Viceroy Illyapa's tocoyricoc is sick. I'm helping."

"Is he so sick his staff can't store quipus properly?" I asked, pulling out a ball of strings that might be five or six separate ledgers.

"I don't know, just fix it."

We worked like that for most of the morning until I finally blurted it out. "Father, I want to marry Atoc China."

"You what?" He thundered at me with the same ferocity he had used when he had sent me to the Chaski School. He dropped his quipu to the floor and put his hands on his knees.

"I want to marry the Vixen."

"You are too young—"

"There is precedence."

"She has no noble blood—"

"Neither did my mother!" I knew I had crossed a line there. My father and I rarely spoke of my mother, and never with raised voices, and never negatively, and never to interrupt him twice in as many sentences.

"This girl is not like your mother, Haylli. Your mother wanted nothing in this world other than for her loved ones to be happy. This girl

137

wants to become powerful, and if you could not do that for her she wouldn't even know your name."

"You're wrong."

"I'm right, and you know it. Now go tell her that I've said no, and that I'll make sure a direct appeal to the Sapa Inca will also end in a no. Tell her to move on to the next name on her list and leave my son to the governing of Condesuyu."

I reared back at that one, enraged beyond all measure to have my father take such a casual tone with me or the Vixen or our future. "I will not!"

"You will, right now, and I will make you a promise in exchange." I turned my head, unwilling to ask him to go on. "I could yell at you, threaten you, but Haylli I am right about this girl, and I know you are smart enough to figure that out given time. So I will suggest this: When you reach normal marriageable age you can marry whoever you want, including the Vixen, without needing your father's permission.

"Go tell her that you cannot marry her now, but that you can marry her if she's willing to wait a few years. If it is a true love match, she will be willing to wait, and I will respect her for that. If she's just marrying you to advance herself in life you'll know it."

I left my father's counting room and made my way to the House of the Chosen Women. The Vixen and I had a routine: I lobbed a pebble through the window of her room and a short while later she appeared at the front door. I nodded to the guardsman, who nodded to me and went around the corner to relieve himself in the alley's gutter. The Vixen was out the door and in my arms, and we were both away before he was back. The guardsman was Kiskis, the adult name of my school friend Chusek, and after what we had gone through as boys to get in and out of the House of Chosen Women he was prepared to let the Vixen come and go if I asked it of him. I suspect he had a girl or two in there of his own.

We went in silence down to a secluded spot at the base of Sacsahuaman, a small vegetable patch that was out of sight of anyone. I spread out a blanket and we had a picnic, but before I could find the words to tell her what my father had ordered me to say she leaned over and kissed me in that way, and all thoughts of speaking left my mind.

I have often thought that making love to the Vixen was like wrestling with a puma. She raked me with her nails, bit my chest with her teeth.

138

Her body was in constant writhing motion, and she moaned and cried and screamed with such ferocity that I often stopped to make sure she was not in pain, only to be pummeled by her tiny fists and urged on, 'Faster!' 'Harder!' 'Don't stop!'

There was no mistaking when she was spent, for she would sag with exhaustion, muscles she had no control over would flex and tremble, and then she would lie still beside me, breathing softly and running her fingers up and down my heaving chest.

We lay on that blanket, watching the hawks circle overhead, and when the moment had passed and passed again I rolled over, propping my head up with one arm. "I can't marry you right now. My father is against it, and he says he will intervene if we go to the Emperor. He says we can marry when we're of legal age, but he says you will not be satisfied with—"

"Of course I won't be satisfied with that!" Things went bad quickly after that.

The Vixen in a rage was also like a puma, but a puma with the last finger's length of her tail cut off, all hissing and spitting and searching for vengeance. She raked my chest with her nails, drawing blood, then slapped me full across the face. Deciding this was not enough she got up and walked away from me, taking the most direct route through the streets to my home. I followed her at a safe distance, unsure what else I could do.

My father's door man opened our teak defenses for the crucial heart-beat it took her to shove the door into his face and march imperiously past him. There was none of the alluring sway of her hips now; her eyes must have been burning like two cinders, though she never looked back at me as I followed in her wake. My father's servants quailed before her and parted as if she had invisible guards shoving them aside to make a path.

When she reached the ladder up to my father's counting room the climb did nothing to humble her: She took each rung firmly and pulled herself up, barely using her feet. She was unstoppable. I was at the base of the ladder when she reached the top, and I was surprised not to hear a volcanic explosion of anger. In my mind I saw the bronze dagger she kept tucked into the small of her back and imagined my father's blood dripping down the ladder above me. I hauled myself up to stop my imagination from becoming reality.

I could not have been more stunned if she really had killed him. She sat there on a stool, facing him as an equal, speaking coolly and calmly. There was no trace of anger anymore. My head popped up through the hole in the floor and my father flicked his wrist, bidding me to wait against one wall while he talked with his uninvited guest. I was flabbergasted.

"Your son has taken my virtue," she said as a statement of fact.

"Yes," my father returned evenly.

"If I am not to marry him then my future husband, whoever that may be, will know that I am not a virgin."

"Explain to me why that is my son's concern?" Neither of them were using my name. I knew I was out of my depth.

"It is a problem because, for educational purposes only, I am a Virgin of the Sun. Until I am released from that station I am a virgin or I am guilty of adultery against Inti, and the punishment for that is death either by hanging by my own hair or being buried alive."

"Explain to me why that is my son's concern?" My father said in exactly the same tone he had used before. I opened my mouth to explain that I was concerned for the Vixen, deeply concerned, but he silenced me with another flick of his wrist.

"If I am revealed a wanton, I will not be mute about who I was wanton with. Making a cuckold of Inti will see Haylli buried alive with me." I stood in horror at what she had threatened me with. Where was the love between us? I did not want her to die, of course not! I wanted to marry her, but she had just said if she was dying she was taking me with her.

"My son will deny it, of course," My father replied, as if bored.

"Then I shall insist, and back my assertions with the testimony of various young officers from the Imperial legions: Chalcuchima, Kiskis, Rumiñaui, do I need to go on? Enough of them will support me. Your son was the leader of a school clique; that means he had enemies."

My father leaned back on his stool. "Your life is threatened and so you threaten my son's life. What do you propose?"

"Let us marry." My heart leapt to know she still wanted to marry me.

"No," my father said, dashing my hopes.

"Let us marry!" She demanded. "It's for the best. You know what I want to do with my life. I am wasting my time in that House of Chosen

Women. I won't join a panaca as an unmarried woman. I'd spend years polishing silver and making akha. Mothers have all the power. If I wed your son now, I'll be the youngest married woman to ever dedicate herself to a panaca. Waiting as long as you propose will give me no advantage whatsoever. If you don't object to our marriage in a few years, why not now when it will be of real benefit?"

"Do you know what you forgot to mention?" She did not respond. "How does any of that benefit my son? This marriage is all about you. If you do marry Haylli, how many children will you have? However many it takes to rise through the panaca's ranks. Where will you live? Wherever you have to in order to give you the advantage. And when you neglect my son for your work, will he be allowed the comfort of another woman? Of course not, because that would make you look weak. You will lead my son around like a puppy on a string for the rest of his life if I allow this marriage, and he'll be the fool who lets you because of the power you have over him."

She didn't even blink at my father's statement. "Suppose I am pregnant?" She had once put off my own fears of that with the promise she was taking a barbasco root contraceptive.

"Are you?" His tone never changed, and I was infuriated to be left silent. I opened my mouth again, but this time he turned to me. "Do not speak a word." He turned back to the Vixen, and it finally dawned on me that my father was locked in a duel, a battle of wills, and that he considered the Vixen his equal in the struggle. A compromise was about to be struck, and my father was fighting to make it as favourable for my future as possible. "I asked you if you are pregnant."

"I could be."

"But are you?"

"I won't know for sure for some time. I could have been impregnated this very day. Your son chose to dally with me one last time before breaking his news of your decision to me." My father cast me a baleful look and I blushed with shame. I had just cost him maneuvering room with my lust.

"So you are not certain if you are pregnant or not?"

"If I am pregnant people will know Inti had nothing to do with it. I will not keep the father's name a secret."

"If you are pregnant you will notify me and I will have it confirmed by someone I trust to be discrete. At that point we will discuss a quick marriage before you begin to show."

I almost cried out. My clever little Vixen had thought of a way for us to be together. I would bed her every day if I had to. My mind wandered for a moment to that delicious prospect, and I was feeling the stirrings of enthusiasm in my breechcloth when my father dashed my hopes again. "You will know if you are pregnant within two months. I will take Haylli away on an inspection during that time so there will be no further opportunities for that state of affairs to arise. Upon my return I am due to marry Kiske Sisa. We can call it a double wedding without too much fuss. Agreed?"

"And if I am not pregnant?"

My father shifted on his stool. "What do you want?"

"If I am not to marry your son then I will wed someone else. That someone else is going to expect a condition I no longer have."

"I am sure you can play the amateur. I am sure you can fake a little blood on your bridal gown the next morning." My father was talking about the Vixen sleeping with another man as if I was not even in the room. My pulse beat louder in my ears as all the blood rushed to my head.

"You know there's more to it than that. You are a man of the world. I am a young woman. You have access to certain resources..." She let her voice trail off, and I knew she had already cut her losses in her mind. She and I would not marry unless it was unavoidable, now she was just insuring her success with the next man on her list. I imagined Chalcuchima where I had been only a short time ago. I felt my eyes begin to burn with tears of shame and despair.

"You mean can I obtain for you a woman who can provide you with buckthorn ointment to tighten you and a pigeon fed with special seeds so its eggs have thin shells and red yokes to imitate certain..." I saw her relax ever so slightly as my father said he knew what she needed. "As you say, I am a man of the world, and I had my own indiscretions as a young man." He was prepared to warm a little now that he knew her price.

"I would have been a fine addition to your family," she said in a tone that sealed their bargain.

"No. My son would have been a fine addition to your designs, but you would have brought us nothing that my son could not obtain from a less conniving woman."

142

She flashed him her coyest smile, the one that forced a man to smile back and liquefied his loins all at the same time. "A conniving woman I may be, but I doubt a woman of less ambition can summon up the ferocity I gave to your son." I remembered her nails raking my back earlier in pleasure, just as they had later raked my chest in rage. She was flirting with my father in front of me. I felt my heart break.

My father smiled indulgently. "That is a good try, and please don't be offended if I refuse to take the bait. You have already proven yourself to be far more trouble than you could possibly justify, and you're even younger than Kiske Sisa, a woman who I've been waiting years to marry. Good day to you. We shall talk again in two months." She rose with frosty dignity and descended the ladder in silence. She had never so much as looked at me in the whole time since I told her my father's ruling.

We remained in the counting room in silence for a long time, he on his stool and I leaning against the wall for support. At last, he turned his head. "She was worth it, Haylli. Don't regret the mistakes of your youth. You'll treasure them later." He smiled a little and descended the ladder, leaving me alone to digest the morning's events.

Friar, there is a feeling every man gets from time to time around his father, the feeling of a chastised little boy. I was a pacuyok, a royal quipu master, one of the best chaskis in Tahuantinsuyu, a tocoyricoc-in-waiting who had bedded the most desirable woman in a city where every maiden is beautiful; still, I felt about eight years old.

He was angry with me, of course. When a normally quiet man makes a point of not speaking to you for days at a time you can sense his disappointment. We left Cuzco as a gentle dusting of snow fell, and by the time we were up into the mountain passes the weather was as miserable as I felt.

As penance for provoking this early inspection and making us travel through winter storms my father banished me from the side of his litter, sending me to the back of his procession to work as a llama drover between our stops. The purics there were kind to me, accepting me easily, I think, both because my father was a decent man, and because as a graduate of the White Rock Chaski School common men saw that I worked hard right along side them without the opulence and rewards that so many other Incas demanded as their due.

While my father meant it as a punishment, I think my time with them was well-spent. I learned a lot from those drovers, for just as my father loved his knots and numbers and order, so too did those men adore their llamas. The animals were their world, and rightly so; put simply, the highlands would be almost unlivable without them. A llama is the most useful and least demanding creature Viracocha ever made.

If you kill a llama before the age of three it gives you meat. Throughout its life it gives you coarse wool, good enough for bags and ropes. Its dung burns as clean and hot as wood, and is in much greater supply up in the treeless puna. It will eat almost anything you care to give it, but if you drive it up into the mountains where there is no fodder it can go several days without food or water.

The llama loves heights and the cold, and will sometimes take the rockiest path simply to revel in its nimble feet. It can carry almost as much weight as a man on its back, and will go the distance of one tampu to another every day without complaint. They are creatures of habit, eating only while the sun shines and chewing their cud only at night.

Even the animal's faults are strengths: A simple obstacle like a rope is enough to prevent them from moving forward, so two men can easily gather up an entire flock simply by holding two ends of a cord and walking towards a corral.

Just like men, llamas have pride and won't take abuse. When they are unhappy you know it. They spit long jets of saliva when offended, and when they are tired they lay down and would sooner die than shift until they are rested. Because of this, my father's headlong pace demanded we frequently rotate and swap our tired llamas for fresh ones, so that I came to know each buck and ewe in our caravan.

The finest of them had bells and copper discs dangling from their ears and necks, and sometimes they seemed to enjoy these decorations as much as any vain woman. You really can think of a llama as a person, perhaps a simpleton, but a knowable individual. If you have spent any time with llamas you get to know their minds, and as long as you obey their few limits you have willing friends.

Twenty of us drovers moved a flock of four hundred. Our caravan was bearing salt over the mountain passes to the Rucana tribe, who lacked it. Occasionally we encountered caravans going the other way, coming up from the coast or from the Rucana lands, and you would imagine that at night when we stayed at the same tampus it would become confusing: Our beasts mixing and mingling with others, and one llama does look very much like another. To make identification easy we pierced the ears of our llamas and decorated them with coloured yarn. My father's llamas all had the clan's yellow dangling from their lobes, making them easy to pick out of a corral.

Two or three times a day I was sent up to the front to make a report on the status of our flock, and my father would be sitting in his litter, silent and aloof. I would look over at my friend the gherkin fetcher, who would shrug helplessly. He was with us out of long habit, but he could do nothing to lighten my father's mood: It was the wrong time of year for gherkins, another inconvenience brought on by this early trip. My father took to scowling whenever I was within line of sight, something I took to being as little as possible as the trip stretched on.

We delivered the salt and my father left more than half of them there with one of his country estates. With the caravan so greatly diminished he could no longer maintain the pretext of needing me to help drive the flock, so I returned to his side, and as we went down the torturous passes of the western mountains, coast-bound, he finally unbent enough to make some small talk.

"Lonely out here."

It was a weak conversation starter, considering he was being carried on a litter by thirty Rucana porters and he was surrounded by more than a hundred retainers, but I took it greedily.

"Yes, it is," and as I said it I felt it. The mountains around us loomed large and timeless, and we were surrounded by them on all sides. There were no houses, no people, just the scattered llamas in distant meadows and the silent condors circling on their wide pinions above us.

We talked about nothing important throughout the day, but I was glad his anger had passed. That night in the tampu we slept in the same room, waiting until Huaman Paullu had fallen asleep and then making fun of his snoring, as we had done for years.

As we made our way down into the coastal valleys I began to look forward to our stops, as I had before our disagreement. Time and distance had made the Vixen less important, and I could see my father trying to take some of the sting out of his decision by showing me special attention, even letting me do most of the talking at our routine stops. One day when we were on the broad coastal road, flanked on either side by high retaining walls and molle trees, he leaned down from his litter. "I've never taken you to see Pachacamac, have I?"

We both knew he had not. I nonchalantly agreed with him, my heart pounding. The people of the coast are as varied as those of the mountains, but as a generalization they were all called Yungas, meaning Hot Lands, and the thing that tied them all together was Pachacamac, the Yungas' name for Viracocha, the Creator.

Such was the power of his oracle on the coast that the valley that was his home was called Rimac, Speaker, and when the Inca gained control of the area we had been reluctant to move his idol to Cuzco for fear of the religious revolts it would spark, choosing instead to build a temple to Inti and a House of Chosen Women in the Rimac Valley as a sign of the new order of things.

"Let's go," my father said, bringing his staff of office down on the floorboards of his litter. The Rucana broke into a trot without lurching their load, and the whole procession had to jog to keep up.

146

It was only a day's detour, but I reveled in it. I had been to the coast many times, Friar. I had seen the seabirds and smelled the salt air, watched in fascination as the rising and setting of the sun changed the directions of the prevailing wind. None of that was new. As for the Rimac River, which was new to me, it was like any other, a ribbon of green descending from the mountains to the sea, slashing across the barren desert and bringing life to the wasteland.

No, my rising excitement was with what was to come, and as we got closer I saw the first signs of what made this valley special: The long lines of pilgrims on the road, each having begged his Inca overlords to give a travel permit to consult the oracle; the oversized tampus bursting with goods that belonged to a foreign god, not the Sapa Inca or Inti; the look of awe in the eyes of the Yungas as they neared their holiest place.

Perched on the sterile land above the Rimac River delta was a series of towns, cemeteries, and temples, each larger than the last, each closer to Pachacamac's idol. Normally supplicants had to wait for months, performing purifying rituals and supplicating offerings, but Pachacamac's oracle had long favoured the Inca —a wise move on its part— and my father was in a hurry. We performed the bare minimum of the rites and walked past the long line of pilgrims. When a junior priest began to protest our lack of preparation my father casually mentioned he could conduct a full audit while he waited the appropriate amount of time. The high priest descended like a stooping hawk, furiously shushing his assistant and leading us up the hill to Pachacamac's home.

It was not much, really: A mountain-top cave with a narrow mouth, a small dirt-floored chamber, an altar containing an ancient piece of wood as tall as a man, carved long ago to show a gaping mouth that seemed to be shrieking; never the less, you could feel the holiness, Friar. The huaca of this place was palpable, so that every breath of air seemed to be the breath of the gods, and the hairs on the back of your necks stood straight up. Even the soles of my feet seemed to tingle on the floor beneath them, as if the ground was vibrating ever so slightly.

There is power in the ancient places of the world. For thousands of years the mighty had climbed this hill to ask for advice from the gods. Every day sacrifices were made here, offerings left, prayers and supplications surrounded by incense and song. The Coricancha could not boast such sustained devotion. Nowhere could. It was the oldest temple in the world.

Before there was metal, before there were llamas, before the Great Flood and the Great Fire and the Great Storm, this place had always been huaca. It did not need gold or silver. It was decorated with awe, something so spectacular even the blind could perceive it.

My father took his sandals off and put a burden on his back, as if addressing the Emperor. I did the same. We entered the cave without daring to look directly at the shrieking idol. We genuflected, blowing a kiss and plucking a hair from both our eyebrows and our eyelashes. The cave, which had seemed so small from the outside, swallowed us up. There was no light inside, and the small opening behind us failed to light all the dark corners of the room. I could hear whispering, but in no language that I knew. It could have been acolytes or it could have been spirits. I could feel the power of the huaca all around us.

"Great Pachacamac Kon-Tiki Viracocha, Creator, Ancient Foundation, Lord and Master, hear your Inca's question."

A long whistle, like steam in a panpipe, came from deep within the idol's shrieking mouth. From behind us the words, "I hear," were spoken. I turned my head but there was no one there.

"Most high and mighty lord, he of many names, I seek an oracle for my son." I shuddered, surprised and awed and shocked all at once that my father had not discussed this with me beforehand. This was the most powerful oracle in the world. I had assumed we were here to do reverence, perhaps offer a token sacrifice for the honour of my seeing him. Actually asking a question would cost my frugal father great flocks from his personal holdings.

"I listen and I speak," the disembodied whistle hissed.

"Noblest, Eldest, Greatest, Finest, my son wishes to marry, but I do not approve. What should my son do? What is the path his life must take?"

I shuddered again, but this time in real fear. Pachacamac's oracle was always right, and now my future was to be laid bare in front of me. I clenched my hands.

For a long time it was just the shrill scream, without words or form. We stood there, hunched under our burdens, and I looked over to see my father sweating. Behind us there was a rumble, like someone rolling boulders down the side of the hill. The ground beneath our feet actually trembled this time. I was sure of it.

"Haylli Yupanki has a long life in front of him, and much will happen." The idol screamed. I covered my ears at the volume, for it seemed the voice was inside my head. "That which he loves will disappoint, and one that he hates will redeem until he loves him. Know now is not the time to marry, but the time is soon!" My heart jumped, seeing perhaps divine favour in my marriage plans.

"Haylli Yupanki, aptly named Waccha, expect your first wife within two years. Your father shall not know her. Expect your first child soon after. Your father shall not see it. Expect your first son many years after that. Your first wife shall not bear him, but your father will know the mother. You will never bring your children here, but you will bring a boy you call your son. You will have many children who are not your own. They will do things that make you weep, and they will cost you more than you would ever pay." I shook my head, unsure what I was hearing but sure that I did not want to hear it.

"Haylli Yupanki," the shriek was a whisper in my ear now, and I looked over to see my father furrow his brows, straining to hear. "One day you will tell a story. Please say that I was powerful."

With that a cloud of smoke rose up from the idol's mouth and a priest dressed all in white appeared at the mouth of the cave, casting a long shadow on the floor. "Pachacamac has spoken, lords. I hope he answered your question."

My father and I spent most of the day in unusual idleness, sitting in the akha house of Pachacamac's finest tampu, puzzling out the prophecy.

"Your first wife in two years, but I shall not know her. That's the end of the Vixen," he said. I know that was all he had expected Pachacamac to say, putting the holy stamp of approval on my father's own harsh ruling. "I'm not sure I like the idea of you marrying someone I don't know, though. Your taste in women leaves something to be desired." He smiled at his weak attempt at levity and took a long pull on his akha.

I doubted his interpretation. I felt he did not truly know the Vixen as I did. I was sure that was what Pachacamac had meant. In two years I would be old enough to marry whomsoever I wanted, regardless of my father's opinion. I was sure the Creator had just promised the Vixen would wait for me. "What do you think he meant by my not seeing your first child?" He asked.

"I suppose she'll die young, while you're off on an inspection," I surmised, looking at the bottom of my empty cup. Children die. That's why we call them Wawa until we think they'll live. I still did not like to linger on the idea. As unpleasant as the whole prophecy had been, the part that really worried me was the whispered request at the end.

I asked my father if he had heard it, but he shook his head. "Don't tell me what was said to you. If Pachacamac had wanted me to know, I'd have heard it."

I tell you, Friar, it shook me to hear the Creator ask a favour of me, to say 'please.' How great could he be if he had to ask me to say he was powerful? He had said it in the past tense, too. 'Please say that I was powerful.' Would Pachacamac Kon-Tiki Viracocha one day fall from power? Would he do it within my lifetime? It scared me, unsettled my stomach.

Can you trust the prophecy of a god whose power can run out? Or did the prophecy mean something else? Suppose I was telling the story to my children, who I was never to bring to the idol, and I would have to convince them of his power without letting them experience it as my father had for me. Could that be it?

And what about my first wife not bearing my first son? I could not imagine the Vixen letting me take other wives willingly, so did this mean I would have to defy her for an heir? I quailed at the thought, remembering her fury when my father had refused us his permission. Also, was it important that the idol had said 'first son' instead of bastard? If my first wife, my legitimate wife, was not the mother of my son then he was illegitimate, but I was considered my father's 'first son' despite my older half-brothers because I was the son of his first wife.

My father and I puzzled over the clues and eventually gave up. I will say this, Friar: Every one of those predictions came true, and not one of them happened as I thought it would happen. You can tell me all about your saviour being whipped and nailed to two pieces of wood in a land I've never heard of. I have proof of my gods, though I wish to my gods that I did not.

We returned home by a route we had never taken before, cutting up to Tarma in Chincaysuyu to visit one of my father's old students. Tarma is a beautiful city in the mountains where the boys guarding the maize fields from the crows waved to us with their slings, calling out 'Moche! Moche!' —their name for Inti— to acknowledge us.

Taking the Chincaysuyu road home was a very different experience from our usual route because apparently the tocoyricoc of this quarter of the Empire was given to surprise snap inspections. As my father's distinctive litter wound its way down the flanks of mountains into the valleys, the villagers would sing paeans of praise to him, just as they did in Condesuyu, but their songs were placatory, more like prayers that he would not swoop down and punish them for their laxity.

They also took to sending runners ahead of us, warning others of our coming. We did spot checks to make sure there were no discrepancies, but it seemed Chincaysuyu's tocoyricoc different methods still worked: The tax system was as tight as the skin on a drumhead. We found no problems at all, at least not until almost the end of our journey.

I have often implied that my father had an intimate knowledge of strings, but I do not think I have pressed the point enough. You could put a hundred threads in front of him and he could arrange them unerringly youngest to oldest or by the experience of the spinner, their past uses, how they were stored, sometimes even where their fibre was grown. It was the kind of awe-inspiring ability that cannot be taught, only acquired after decades of painstaking work with countless quipus.

It was no surprise, then, when we came to the great tampu of Tarawari, guardian of the Chincaysuyu trunk road into Cuzco, that he immediately saw that something was amiss.

Despite all my years of careful schooling I just did not have the depth of experience necessary to quickly see why he stiffened in something very akin to fear. He stood mute, an inventory quipu stretched between his two hands with its pendant cords dangling beneath, dancing as his hands trembled. At last I saw it too and gasped.

The Tarawari tampu is situated within a day's march of Cuzco on one of only four roads leading to the capital, just on the Cuzco-side of a bridge that crosses the chasm of the Apurimac River valley. Any army marching out of Cuzco along this road has to stop there for an extended period of time while it crosses the Apurimac, and so Tarawari's storehouses were provisioned with everything an army would need, even those rare armies that numbered in the hundreds of thousands.

It was one of the largest and busiest tampus in the world, and, if the strings were to be believed, someone had withdrawn enough arms and armour to equip an entire legion.

That in itself was nothing unusual. It probably happened twice a month or so as warriors came through Tarawari to serve their taxes as conscript soldiers. No, my father's hands trembled because the weapons were off the inventory list without being put on the distributed list. Someone had tried to make the weapons disappear from existence.

Worse still, it was no accident on the clerk's part, for the proper knots had been untied by a clumsy unpracticed hand. No quipucamayoc would be so careless as to twist and tangle and fray the threads as someone had done here while struggling to undo their records. The attempted fraud was so inadequate that my father's expert eye could read the knots as if they were still there.

We immediately called for the tampucamayoc to see if it was merely someone tampering with the ledgers, but the equipment was missing from the armoury warehouses. The tampucamayoc remembered a company of a hundred warriors coming through and drawing arms, but he had not been included in the transaction and his apprentice clerk was quite sure he had tied the knots honestly.

A quick interrogation of the rest of the tampu staff produced a day guard who remembered seeing a young chaski mitmak named Puma leaving the quipu office unescorted by any of the staff. Chaskis came and went all the time, and the day guard would have thought nothing of it if the man had not looked so guilty upon emerging. The guard said he had checked the man's coca bag to make sure nothing was being pilfered. My father nodded his thanks and doubled the guard's akha ration. When the guard finished thanking him and backing out of the Tocoyricoc's presence my father turned back to his quipucamayocs and I.

"Fine. This Puma untied the quipus to conceal the theft, but no one man could move a thousand spears, shields, quilted cotton cuirasses, and chonta wood helmets by himself. It must have been the conscripts. Who was their officer?" My father asked the tampu clerk.

"Chalcuchima, my Lord," the quipucamayoc said. My stomach dropped. Things were happening too fast, and I had the ridiculous feeling that something was wrong. Not with the crime per se, but something was wrong with everything that seemed to be unfolding. I could not put words to my suspicions, though. I did not know what I feared.

My father nodded, I suppose because he had already assumed the worst: Some rebellious high-born pacuyoks, apparently including Chalcuchima, were going to try to rest power from the Sapa Inca. "A coup, fine, but a thousand men won't defeat the Emperor's ten thousand—"

"My Lord," the tampucamayoc interrupted. "Word came to me this morning that the Sapa Inca —may Inti forever shine upon him— is not in Cuzco. He has gone to Pacaritampu to honour the local manhood ceremonies there. He would have taken his guards with him."

"Then I have no time to lose," My father cut the air with his hand, stopping any who would break his concentration with advice at this point. "Send to Cuzco: Tocoyricoc Tupac Capac has discovered a coup in progress. A legion is arming to march on Cuzco in the Emperor's absence. Order an emergency muster. All men loyal to either myself or my father Tilca Yupanki's memory are to march on Cuzco and draw arms with my authorization from the Intihuasi tampu in the fortress on Sacsahuaman hill. We will hold Cuzco until the Emperor's return."

The chaskis were moving as soon as my father was done, each carrying the red string of a man on the Emperor's business along with the yellow thread of the tocoyricoc and another of our own house yellow.

My father and I armed ourselves from the Tarawari tampu and left all but the warriors in our party behind as we took off under a forced march for Cuzco. We jogged over hills and through valleys, knowing we might have less than a day's head start on Chalcuchima, whose hundred, burdened with equipment for ten times their number, had been seen disappearing down a side road, presumably to arm the rest of his legion.

Yes, there was a cloud over Chalcuchima because of his father's execution, but something still seemed wrong to me. He had a promising career ahead of him with a number of generals willing to vouch as to his talent for war. There was no sense to a coup, especially when two of the four viceroys were his uncles. He was going to overthrow the government? Where was his provocation?

Chalcuchima had always been a gambler, but he always assumed he would win. Our people have dice, just as yours do, Friar, but our die is not a cube: It is a flattened pyramid with the narrow top numbered as one and the broad bottom labeled as a twenty. Chalcuchima seemed to be rolling a hundred dice and expecting them all to come up twenty, that's how insane the odds were against him. For a moment I thought that the spurned Vixen had gone to him, said she would marry him if he did it, but even that should not have made him risk all. It was an unsatisfactory theory and I knew in my belly something was wrong.

We entered Cuzco to find the streets emptied ahead of us by hastily armed warriors, each wearing some item of cloth dyed yellow, identifying them as our men. Every earplug man was there, and every conscript in the area willing to serve had drawn their weapons. My father installed himself in the tallest tower of the fortress atop Sacsahuaman and waited for the assault.

It never came.

Instead, two days later, I awoke to find the axe edge of a halberd a handbreadth above my throat. The man wielding the weapon wore the red and white checkers of extreme bravery, and his headband labeled him as an Imperial guardsman.

With all the cunning and stealth of a fox who knew every way in and out of his den, the Sapa Inca Topa Inca Yupanki and his ten crack guard legions had made their way back into Cuzco, evading or overwhelming our pickets. My father and I were summoned to an immediate audience, flanked at all times by a retinue of heavily armed guardsmen.

We entered the Imperial Presence, barefoot and with burdens on our shoulders, but those small weights seemed to become as heavy as the world when we saw who else was with the Emperor: All fours viceroys, the other three tocoyricocs, and —most shocking of all— Chalcuchima, dressed and armed like a guardsman, standing in the Emperor's presence without any sign of being under suspicion of wrongdoing.

The Sapa Inca wasted no time. "Explain yourself, Tupac."

"Shepherd of the Sun, I—"

"Aucca! You dare speak!" Viceroy Illyapa shouted my father down, waving his staff of office in my father's face. The black glass atop the stick made it look sickeningly like a mace.

"You dare call me aucca?" My father roared back, taking a step towards the lord of Collasuyu. A dozen halberds lifted off the flagstones, ready to spit him if he came any closer to the Emperor's usno. He stopped.

"Sire," Illyapa said to the Sapa Inca. "His guilt is obvious! We have the testimony of the Tarawari tampucamayoc that he sent out word to collect and arm an army of his followers; he marched on Cuzco in your absence, occupied your fortress, and prepared to defend the capital against all comers."

The blood drained from my face as I realized what Topa Inca Yupanki was thinking: We were the auccas, not Chalcuchima. I looked at my former school rival, expecting to see triumph and joy at this position he had put us in. The dismay in his eyes was as surprising as anything else

I had seen this entire confusing morning. He had no more expected us to be traitors than we ourselves had. A shiver ran down my spine. Bad things were about to happen here.

"That's not true," my father said with great dignity.

"What's not true?" Viceroy Achachi Michi asked sadly, stepping forward to stand beside Illyapa. My heart sank to think the general with the bad back who I had always liked was convinced of our guilt too. "The part where you pretended to discover a discrepancy? The part where you used the threat of a coup to fill the city with your followers? The part where you planted an assassin among the royal entourage at the manhood ceremonies at Pacaritampu—"

"What?" My father and I said it in unison with such genuine horror that I think we convinced Achachi Michi at least of our innocence. I was genuflecting on the ground, arms wide in homage to the Emperor, aghast at the very thought of regicide.

Viceroy Hualpaya stepped forward to stand next to Michi Achachi and his brother Illyapa. "Tell your son to get up, Tupac. Keeping him in the dark to make his shock genuine isn't convincing. We caught your man alive."

My father took a step back in shock, which I'm sure everyone in the room took as proof of his guilt except me. The final viceroy, Mayta, also stepped forward now, leading a man by the elbow. His rich dress labeled him as a Lupaca of high rank, but he had clearly been badly beaten: There was a purple bruise over one eye and a weakness in his step that became swaying when he came to a halt. His skin was yellow tinged, though from what I could not guess.

"Say it again, in front of the Emperor this time," Illyapa barked at the man.

"And I will have what I asked for?" The man asked. A guardsman smashed the butt of his halberd into the man's belly, dropping him to the floor. Two more grabbed him by the arms and hauled him back to his feet.

"You will have all that I promised you: Your body shall be buried at home by your relatives; your sons who are proven innocent shall be spared; all of it," Illyapa said to the man, softer this time.

The Lupaca lord tugged at the hem of his tunic, aware now of the august company in which he found himself. "My name is Mamani. I am the heir to the Lupaca usno of Collao, not that such an usno exists now that my land lies under the Inca's sway." The nearest guardsman raised his halberd again at the man's impertinence, but a wave of the Emperor's hand let the comment stand. "I was to kill Topa Inca Yupanki during the naming ceremony at Pacaritampu and proclaim that the Sapa Inca Tupac Capac had already claimed the Red Fringe at Cuzco."

"And what were you to be paid for this service?" Illyapa asked.

"If I survived I was to become viceroy of Collasuyu. If I died I was to have one of my sons so elevated."

The room remained silent for a long time. At last Topa Inca Yupanki flicked his wrist and the two guardsmen holding Mamani up dragged him away to his death. "Well?" Hualpaya demanded of my father and I.

"Well, what?" My father rumbled. "You all know that one of two things has happened: Either I am an aucca, or one of you has gone to great lengths to make it look as if I am. Only those of us in this room have the power to do all that has happened here."

"Who?" Viceroy Achachi Michi asked.

"I don't know."

"Why would someone do this to you?"

"We all have enemies."

"None of my enemies would launch a nearly successful coup on my behalf," Viceroy Mayta muttered.

My father dropped to one knee, his head bowed. "Sire, may I speak?"

"Speak," The Emperor said flatly.

"I have served you since you put in my first earplugs. I have gone to war with you. Your father and mine were brothers. Ask any who know me and they will say I have never so much as killed a llama for my supper if it was not in your own best interest. I have lived to serve you and your people. The evidence against me is great, but isn't that in itself suspicious? You know me. Would I not have been more careful to cover my tracks? If I seriously wanted the Red Fringe, would you have found it so easy to get back into Cuzco? My men were all told to watch out for a thousand men approaching down the Quitu road, not ten thousand from the Condesuyu—"

"Quitu." Topa's single quiet word silenced my father.

"Sapa Inca?"

156

"It was your dream —your lust for shadowlessness— that triggered that war. Harder even than the war against the Chimor. We have been exhausted by it, and we still haven't won it over completely. You have left a burden for myself and my son with that campaign..." Old Topa trailed off, shaking his head. The room waited in respectful silence for the Emperor to come back to the point. "I will not condemn you for Quitu, but I will condemn you for this, Tupac. It was the act of a mad man—"

"Sire," There were gasps at my father's temerity in interrupting the Sapa Inca. "I am no mad man! You have known me my whole life. Am I capable of such treachery after the favour you have shown me?"

We waited for the Emperor to speak, knowing our lives rested with his decision.

"I cannot allow this to go unchallenged, Tupac," he said. My stomach dropped. "But you are right. Something is wrong here. There is something I do not understand."

"Sire, we have a witness who is testifying, knowing full well he is going to be executed either way. We have hundreds of men wearing Tupac's clan yellow in custody, all of whom were bearing arms against us this morning. He is guilty," Viceroy Mayta said.

Topa clearly did not know what to do. He was torn between his love for my father and his Imperial right. At last he shook his head with regret.

"I wish my heir was here. I know Tupac Capac too well to be dispassionate: Very well, a trial by ordeal, then. Were he truly a traitor I would put him in the Sankihuasi to die a terrible death. I cannot believe he is guilty, nor can I believe he is truly innocent, therefore I decree that Tocoyricoc Tupac Capac and his son Haylli Yupanki be placed in the Sankihuasi from noon of today until noon of tomorrow. Should they survive one night, they are innocent. Should they die, they have suffered their punishment. Let it be so."

I did not watch the Imperial secretaries tie down the decree. The Sankihuasi, more commonly called the Pit, was the most horrible place in Tahuantinsuyu. It was reserved for only the worst criminals; built as close as the Imperial architects could come to mimic our version of the Lower Universe, what you, Friar, would call Hell.

Just outside Cuzco there were a series of natural caverns deepened and expanded and sealed by teams of labourers. The walls and ceilings had been lined with jagged flints and obsidian shards. The only light was provided by a single opening in the roof of the uppermost corridor. Trap doors and sliding walls allowed the pits keepers to keep the darkness filled with all manner of monsters: Snakes and spiders and pumas, bears and rats and jaguars. They never cleaned out the bones of man or beast, just left them there to rot, to terrify traitors in their last moments before they contributed to the Pit's collection of skeletons.

A man put into the pit had no food, no light, and only what water he could find pooled on the floor, stagnant rain water mixed with the blood and urine of previous occupants. It was preferable to go mad and dash your skull open against the flint walls than starve to death alone in the dark, but even that luxury might not be left to you if the beasts found you first. There could be no worse place.

There was a single moment of silence before the guards grabbed us by the arms and dragged us away. As we left the Imperial Presence I saw now that the corridors were filled with bystanders. Everyone knew we were going to the Sankihuasi.

"Only for a day! We'll be out tomorrow!" I called. A guardsman slammed the butt of his mace against my jaw.

We were led out of town, a crowd following us at a distance, respectful of the heavily armed guardsmen. At the temple beside the Pit they finally stopped, and we looked down into the maw, the hole, filled only with blackness.

"Be here tomorrow and we will lower a rope for you. If not, the Sankihuasi will be your tomb." With that the guardsmen pushed me in.

The drop was three times the height of a man, but I landed well, bending my knees and rolling to absorb the impact. Even so, the corridor directly under the hole in the roof wasn't wide enough to let me roll away the impact; I smacked my shoulder into the flint-lined walls, tearing it open so that blood poured down my arm and began to puddle over my hand and onto the floor. Before I could even feel the pain I saw my father drop and I rushed to grab him, to keep him from hitting the walls too. I managed it, but he landed badly, twisting his knee and tearing the skin off his elbow on the hard flagstones.

"What can we do, father?" I asked.

"We stay right here. This is the only spot with light, and it's where we have to be tomorrow at noon. There's nothing to be gained by moving."

For just a moment I wondered if he had actually done this thing, had kept it secret from me. He was smart enough, and secretive enough, but why would he do it? My father had no more love of power than any other man, and a great deal less than some. I banished my suspicion as unworthy. We had more pressing concerns at that moment.

The floor beneath the hole in the ceiling was only illuminated to a distance of five or six paces out from where we had fallen. The walls were lined with black obsidian and grey flint, continuing off into the darkness in both directions. In the shadows just before the pitch black began I could see a rib cage. "Staying here didn't do that man any good," I murmured.

"He wasn't going to be let out. We are." My father said it with such confidence that I knew it was forced.

He tore his vicuna mantle and made a clumsy bandage for my shoulder. Then we sat there, back to back, watching the shaft of light from above shift as the sun passed its zenith and began to set. We sat in silence, wishing the day and night to end uneventfully with us both still sitting there. I was thirsty, but I did not fancy looking around for something to drink down here. I longed for the next day, for the new sun's zenith that would release us.

A hissing noise from above broke the spell in the late afternoon, and we looked up to see Kiskis's head silhouetted against the sky. "I asked the guards to look the other way so I could talk to you," he said quickly. "The Sankihuasicamayocs just put a puma in through a trap door on the far end. It hasn't eaten in three days."

My father cursed quietly. Three days was long enough to make the beast hungry without weakening it at all. We were unarmed and smelled of blood. "How big is this place?" My father asked. Kiskis's father had helped with the Pit's construction.

"There are three levels, each about the size of your house," Kiskis told him. Then something long and thin dropped from above, bounced once off the flagstones and lay still. It was my father's serrated bronze lance, the one that hung over our kitchen hearth. "Here. Take care. I'll see you both tomorrow."

"Thank you!" I shouted up, but he was gone.

My father had the lance in both hands, looking at his face reflected in the burnished blade. It was the width of three fingers and the blade was the length of my hand from the heel of my palm to the tips of my

159

fingers. It was serrated down one side and sharpened down the other to an edge that could take the hairs off the back of his arm. The point was sharp enough to punch through a triple thickness of llama neck leather. I felt better already, seeing the sunlight dance off its deadly beauty.

"I'll hold onto this, Haylli. Go down to that man and see if there are any long bones you can use as a club." I would have loved to argue, but instead I did as I was told and returned with a femur. The ball joint at one end looked just like a mace we had at home. I would much rather Kiskis had brought us that too. Touching this bone reminded me that men died down here, and when they did they stayed to rot away.

Now that we were armed and threatened by a puma we could not bring ourselves to sit. We stood and talked back and forth in low voices about nothing, hoping the sound would frighten the animal away. We had the rest of the day, all night, and half of another day, and the cat only had an area three times the size of our house to avoid us. We couldn't be that lucky. It would find us, and it would be hungry.

Twilight descended, and I could feel my pulse begin to race. What if the cat came upon us in the darkness? I shouldn't have had the thought, for the gods are cruel in their favours sometimes. The puma found us right then, as the sun was still throwing a feeble light down the hole in the ceiling above.

It came out of the darkness, just entering the difference between true black and the deepest shadows: Two green orbs, seemingly disembodied. My father was ready. Before I could do more than gasp he had his lance grounded, point towards the beast. It did him no good.

With a howl that seized me with panic the puma leapt upon my father's lance, flicking out with its forepaws to smack him mighty blows on both shoulders. The claws tore his flesh, and that he could have born, but the force of the cat pouncing upon the spear sent him backwards into the flint-lined wall. The sound of his impact haunts my dreams.

The old lance had shattered at the haft with the head buried in the cat's body. Cat and spear dropped at his feet. My father remained standing, and I was amazed at his control until I realized he was stuck to the wall, frozen in shock at the unimaginable sensation running up and down his back. The cruel stones had pierced him in a hundred places.

I cried out and leapt to his side, pulling him from the wall and cradling him in my arms. His blood bathed me and the dead cat beneath us. I kept calling to him, over and over, rocking him back and forth.

At last he opened his eyes and smiled at me, and I laughed in relief to think that maybe it wasn't so bad. He opened his mouth and said to me, "I didn't do it, Haylli. If I had done it, I would have succeeded." He sighed deeply and seemed about to fall asleep. I shook him again, and he looked past me to the hole in the roof and the last touch of sunlight still peeking over the rim. "I should have liked to have stood in Quitu just once, to have no shadow..." And with that my father closed his eyes and never opened them again.

I don't know how long I wept, Friar. When I stopped I was in total darkness. The sun had set, and father's and the puma's blood had dried on me, pasting the three of us together. I felt like I was burning up while they had both cooled to the temperature of the flagstones beneath me. The horror overcame me, and I tore myself free of their sticky bond, racing blindly down the corridor, several times brushing against the stones, cutting open my arms and hands.

I don't know how long I ran, nor how far I went once I staggered to a walk, then a crawl. I remember tripping over the skeleton of a snake because I ran from it too. At some point I dropped onto the flagstones and curled into a ball, not caring that I was in a puddle, nor that I was bleeding all over.

I lay there until I cried myself out, then I fell into a stupor that might have been sleep except that I had my eyes open all the time. I had descended at least one level, possibly all the way to the bottom. It was pitch black and silent as the grave it was. I was alone and in pain. I knew what it felt like to be dead.

I would never have come out of there —for I had no idea when it would be noon nor how to find my way back— had it not been for Kiskis. When he looked down the hole to see my father and the puma locked there in death he demanded the guardsmen descend with torches to search for me.

I do not think I wanted to be saved, Friar. My father was dead, disgraced forever, and I was just a lost little boy, bleeding alone in the dark. They pulled me out, though. They carried me bodily from that hole in the ground, and all the while they cooed to me and calmed me and reassured my thrashing form. I only let them take me from that place because I knew the truth, knew I had to set things right.

I had to prove it had all been a mistake. Only vindication would make it like it had never happened. My father was no aucca, and though he had died a traitor's death I could make it all better, I could make it as it was before, if only I could prove we were set up. I had to do it. I swore I would. I just had no idea how to go about it.

* * *

I emerged from the Pit in a daze to see a smaller circle of people waiting for me than had watched me descend. Before it was the curious and the cruel, those who took pleasure in the misery of others. Now there were friends and family: My father's doorman, Huaman Paullu, my favourite bastard brother Ronpa, my father's household servants. I did not hear Kiskis' words of commiseration. I hardly noticed the sound of an official declaring my exoneration through ordeal. I did not feel someone put my father's torn mantle around me, nor another sponge the dried blood from my body.

My mind was working too fast to take in what was going on around me. I would act now, immediately, to clear my father's name. The sun would not set on the disgraced corpse of my father. No man would call him aucca. His death was nothing to do with the gods ascertaining his guilt. It was murder, calculated and unfeeling.

The only people with the power to do this to him were his colleagues in the upper echelons of the Inca nobility, so it was also treachery and betrayal. Looking beyond the horror and grief that had entered my life, the Empire had been deprived of its greatest tocoyricoc. Who knew what other deeds and goals my new enemies desired at the expense of good government? It was treason!

Their actions would see them in the Pit with no hope of respite. They would go in there, into that nightmare beneath my feet, and their bones would decorate the darkness until they moldered away to nothing.

I had two names: Chalcuchima and Puma, the chaski mitmak who changed the tampu records. Chalcuchima would not help me unless I was able to force him to, so I would have to find this colonist, wherever he may be. There were probably tens of thousands of Pumas in Tahuantinsuyu, for it is a common name among all people except those who dwell in the hacha hacha. Still, how many Pumas had received chaski training? How many had been issued travel vouchers for an individual to cross the Tarawari bridge on their way to their new colonist duties?

Those were just the sort of questions that the Inca bureaucracy would be able to answer for me. My list would narrow. I would beg Topa to summon the man back to Cuzco this very day. Wherever he had gone he would come back, and he would say who had put him up to tampering with the quipus. Then, with Chalcuchima to verify the plot—

—Yes, Friar, perhaps I was deranged at my father's death, but I was thinking so fast when I emerged, battered and bloodied and bruised from that cursed hole in the ground, that it seemed as if the world slowed down.

I sent the household servants home, then with Ronpa and Huaman Paullu in tow I walked cross country, avoiding the busy streets of central Cuzco to cut through the suburbs to the west of the river. The Great Quipu Repository sat upon its spur the entire time, watching my approach silently, its great windows seeming to beckon me forth to justice. Hundreds of quipucamayocs would help me sort through the data. They would all want to vindicate my father.

The sky above me was lead grey, and as I arrived at the steps leading up to the door I remember feeling the first physical sensation to penetrate my concentration: I was taking off all my clothes except my loincloth, as was the Repository's custom, and I was chilled as I felt the first misting of rain raise cold bumps all over my battered flesh.

I was overcome for a moment with the idea that my father's body was directly under the hole, that he would be rained on. I clung to Ronpa for a moment, weak at the knees, then I handed him my mantle as if that had been my intention the whole time and bade him wait outside for me. Ronpa was only a little younger than me, but he had not yet done his manhood ceremonies and therefore he was mine to order about.

I did not worry about him standing there in the rain: If I went to the White Rock Chaski School to toughen me, Ronpa could get wet for a while. The thought of the White Rock Chaski School set my mind off again, for it occurred to me if this Puma was a mitmak he might have attended the school first before beginning his immigration. I went inside out of the mist that was fast becoming a drizzle. Huaman Paullu opened the door for me and added his own sympathy to the invisible weight on my shoulders.

I had barely spoken since the Pit had released me from its dark embrace, but now I said in a rush to my father's faithful secretary, "He did not do this thing, but I know how to find out who did." Huaman Paullu ordered all work stopped and the efforts of every quipucamayoc in the repository put at my disposal.

We went backwards and forwards through the census data looking for chaski requisitions, mitmak allocations, school enrolments, conscript duty registrations under the name Puma. We came up with hundreds of false leads but slowly a picture came together that made sense.

The Puma I sought was four years my senior. He was born outside the town of Caxamalca and demonstrated an aptitude for sprinting that had been noted when he was ten by the household inspector of the region. Caxamalca had a full compliment of chaskis, but Puma's excellence as a runner was noted again by his drill master during a garrison service to the gold smelting furnaces in the passes overlooking his valley.

A requisition was put into central mitmak processing almost a year ago bemoaning the lack of trained chaskis on the Maule River frontier of Tchili. Half-conquered some time ago, the area suffered from a high rate of defection as Mapuche men fled into the unconquered areas still ruled by their people. By a stroke of good fortune for the Empire the household inspector of Caxamalca had been promoted to head of Mitmak allocation and he remembered young Puma.

Normally mitmaks are sent as a whole clan at a time rather than individuals, but the Mapuche only needed chaskis, not the calming influence of a new population. A single mitmak of an age to have been trained as a chaski but not yet married was required. Puma was exactly the right age, but he had not been formally trained. The bureaucrat sent Puma to the White Rock Chaski School then returned him to Caxamalca to have a month's tax-free leave to spend with his family before shipping out to the Mapuche frontier.

I rocked back on my heels as it all became clear to me: Puma was as far from Cuzco as he could be and still be within the Empire. It would take even the redoubtable chaski network eight days to reach that distant point, with eight more days for an acknowledgement to come back. Then I would have to await Puma to arrive at his post and be sent back. It would be months before I could talk to him.

Still, I had said the sun would not set on my father's body while it was still labeled that of a traitor. I would start now, cast doubt on his conviction, and then gather what other facts I could while waiting for my star witness to arrive under guard. I thanked Huaman Paullu for his help and the help of his staff and left.

The drizzle had stopped, but I felt no relief. As if the day had not been cruel enough already, my stomach dropped again as I looked down the steps to see a group of people clustered around a prone figure. It was Ronpa.

I rushed down the stairs to my bastard brother to find a palm-sized dent in his temple. Someone had hit him with a slingstone. It was only as I moved my hand down to his breast to feel for a heartbeat that I realized he had put my mantle on to hold off the chill. We were of the same build, roughly the same face, and though I was taller, with the mantle on he would resemble me. He had no earplugs, but mine were still small at the time. I looked around through the legs of the people hemming me in and I saw my brother's killers.

In a crowd it would have been impossible, for the three of them were so unremarkable that they had obviously been chosen for their lack of distinguishing features. They were of average height, average build, with boring unmemorable faces and clothes that gave no indication of their rank or clan. Only two things set them apart: They were looking at the crowd of people without moving to help, and one of them had a hastily retied headband about his head.

Like most mountain people, his headband doubled as a sling, and a slung stone had been the murder weapon. We locked eyes through the legs, and I saw the man open his mouth to curse. He twitched his head to his two comrades and they began coming towards me without menace, as if they had at last decided to join the onlookers over the corpse.

I was up and running before I had decided to move. My chaski training kicked in, and I ran all the way home without breaking a sweat, barely feeling my fatigued muscles groan or the cuts on my arms and shoulders break open and then rescab. People were trying to kill me. I would have no time to clear my father's name. I would die that very day.

I told you that my brain was working faster, but perhaps it was my survival instinct, the animal cunning of a hunted beast. I could sense danger on the wind. I knew that my foes had beaters out, that a net was closing. Someone else knew that my father was innocent: The guilty man or men. I was not safe here in Cuzco.

I made it inside my father's house and ordered the door barred. I needed a moment to think. What could I do? Whoever had done this to my father had resources at his disposal that I could not imagine. I would have to leave Cuzco, but to flee would make me look guilty, despite my exoneration. Still, I had to go or be murdered before I could start.

If I wanted to see another dawn I had to leave that day, before those hunting me could close every exit and guard every road. I could not travel under my own name and authority, either, for then my assassins would follow me, or send word by the chaski network to have fresh killers lie in wait for me. I would never be safe until whoever was responsible for my father's death was brought to justice.

I called my household together and told them everything, save only where I planned to go and what I planned to do. I tied down a quipu professing my innocence, gathered a few supplies, and then had my relatives lift me up onto the roof of the building on the opposite side of our compound from our door. I scampered over the roof and dropped down into the empty street below and started walking. I hoped any surveillance of my home would be focused on our door, supposedly the only way in and out.

I swapped my gold earplugs for the wooden ones of a Chimu artisan, and I forged travel orders claiming to be a chaski mitmak, just like the man I sought: Puma, sent to distant Tchili. If I could not stay in Cuzco and wait for him to come to me, I would go to him. I would have my answers. My father's name would be cleared.

I took the Collasuyu Road without thinking of what I would pass until it was there on my right, the Sankihuasi, the Pit where my father's body would be left to rot. I took a cautious look around and then detoured towards the opening I had emerged from earlier that afternoon. A single soldier stood guard to keep away the curious, but he was just a conscript doing tax service, not a guardsman with the political savvy to recognize the disguised son of a disgraced tocoyricoc. I relieved his boredom with a few moments of friendly conversation. Finally I said, "I want to go down there."

"You what?" He eyed me as if I were deranged. I suppose I must have sounded it.

"You have a rope ladder? I want to use it."

"Why in the gods'—"

I had a thread out of my coca bag and was tying knots while still making eye contact with him; I think the ease with which I did this made the guard trust that I had the authority to ask anything of him. My words sweetened that impression, too. "If you take this quipu to any tampu in the Cuzco region for the next month it will entitle you to all the akha you can drink."

He looked at the thread in my hand, his mind working over the proposition. "Will I get in trouble?"

"You're job is to keep away the idle and the curious. I'm neither. I'm family to that dead man down there. If I can't bring his body up, I can at least pay it some small respect." I could see him hesitate. I made two more knots. "That's two months of unlimited akha. Any more than that and the tampucamayoc will start asking questions."

The guard disappeared into his post and reappeared with a rope ladder that he secured to two stone bosses built at the lip of the opening. "I'll give it to you when I come back up," I said, descending the ladder into the gloom.

My father was where he had fallen, locked together with the puma's body and drenched in rain water. I grabbed him under the arms and dragged his stiff form around a corner.

"Father," I whispered to his body. "I can't get you out of this hole right now, but over here you will be out of the rain and the snow until I can, then I'll bury you properly." It occurred to me I could offer my father very little, and he could offer me even less. I returned to the ladder, and then on a sudden urge I reached down into the cat's body and pulled out the lancehead. The spear had been so old that its haft had shattered, but the lancehead and the tang were still whole and sharp. I returned to my father's body and cut a lock of his hair, wrapping it around the tang. I now had a huaca of my dead father, just as the lance itself had been the huaca of his dead father.

I climbed out of the Pit and gave the man his string, smiling for the first time in days at the sight of him trying to wipe the dried gore off of it. When I was safely away I made my rope of Cuzco grass, took the lancehead out of my coca bag, and made an oath. I blew a kiss at the sun hidden behind the clouds and took a handful of dirt in my other hand. I would have my answers and my father's killers would be punished. I made my pact with the gods, the lancehead, and his memory. We would have justice. I could do no less for him, because I could do no more.

My father was dead, Friar. He was the most important thing in my life and he was gone. I would never again see him bite into a gherkin or work his counting board. He would never again have a cup of akha with me, or join me in teasing Huaman Paullu about his snoring. He was gone, and it took me a long time to pull that knot tight in my head.

My world was miserable without him. My arms and shoulders hurt from their cuts and bruises. The only good thing was that all my miseries had quite driven the Vixen from my mind, but what consolation was that, Friar? It just proved again how right my father had always been.

I missed him so much. I miss him now, and it's been more than fifty years. He was everything I aspired to be, and he was a better man than I became.

All I had was my promise to him, and so I walked towards Tchili under a cloud of despair. What can I tell you about the journey? I don't know. My memories are disjointed, my thoughts wandered. I just put one foot in front of the other without paying much attention. The topos dropped away beneath me, broken and measured by the chaski huts and the tampus. I could not even tell you if I made good time, something I normally prided myself on. I was dazed and confused by the rapid change in my fortunes.

I would learn later that as I walked towards the Maule River a terrible slaughter was taking place behind me in and around Cuzco. With my father proven guilty by ordeal and my own flight, the Sapa Inca decided our occupation of the fortress on Sacsahuaman hill had been a true coup attempt; he purged my father's followers ruthlessly, sparing only a few of my bastard brothers, too far away or stupid to be a threat, and Tupac Capac's most talented bureaucrats, like Huaman Paullu.

Of the army my father had called up from the Condesuyu populace that loved him so, many of the curacas were killed and the purics were reduced to the yanacona class. Hundreds died and thousands suffered, and we were all innocent of wrongdoing. It was an unavoidable travesty of justice, as unstoppable and uncaring as a landslide.

I just walked south, though there was no such word in Runa Simi. We have West and East, for that is where the Sun rises and sets, but North and South? No. We had 'towards Quitu' for north and 'into the Collao' for south, but I was to go beyond the Collao to a place my great-grandfather Viracocha Inca had never heard of, to distant Tchili, land of snow and mountain.

When I bothered to put words to my actions I thought of my trip as away from Cuzco, and the law aided that impression for it is the custom of Tahuantinsuyu that when two men of equal station meet upon the royal road the one heading towards Cuzco steps out of the way of the man from Cuzco, because anyone leaving Cuzco is assumed to be on the more pressing business.

I could not tell you what was going on around me as I walked through the Collao. I traveled those lands several other times and marveled at the true starkness of the land, where maize will not grow and men erect stone towers as mausoleums to their dead lords, but my first journey through their lands formed few permanent memories.

I do remember passing a most disturbing tree. A thick bole with long low limbs made it unusual, but what made it disturbing was its unlikely fruit: Two women had hung themselves from a low branch by their own long hair. I had heard of the custom, practiced by devout wives on the death of their husbands, but I had never seen it before. Both of the women were young, and though their blue bloated faces had stolen their beauty I knew they would have found other husbands, had other families. They threw that away to join their departed loved ones in the afterlife. It was the coward's way out. I walked out of sight of the tree as quickly as I could. I had seen enough of death.

I also remember passing fields spread out for the production of chuno, the miracle food of the mountains. The potato harvest was in, and now the crop was thrown onto the ground, doused with water, and a series of days of frost, sun heat, and crushing by barefooted farmers squeezed every drop of moisture from the powdered potato, creating chuno, a dry meal that could be stored for years. A handful of the stuff when added to boiling water could sustain a man for a day. Normally, I would have stopped to watch and ask questions, but I was no longer a tocoyricoc-in-training. The chuno production would have made my father smile. I put my head down to walk faster past the work.

My trip was miserable, Friar, and made worse by the weather. The people of Collasuyu divide their season into the Green Time and the

169

Ice Time, and the frosts so necessary for the chuno signaled the end of the pleasant Green Time and the beginning of Ice Time.

The Collao is famous for its winds, and they have to be experienced to be believed. The most freakish zephyrs even receive names: There was the phuku that comes up out of the eastern mountains and cuts across the puna in gusts so forceful they can lift a man off the ground. When there is snow on the ground it blows it up into a blizzard. Locals say the phuku penetrates the body to a depth where the sun cannot reach. I don't know about that, but I learned you cannot spit in disgust of the foul weather for it spits back at you with a gobbet that very much resembles your own.

Worse still are the fearsome tutukas wayra, which are phukus caught in natural wind tunnels like ravines. So channeled, the wind bellows, pushing against any obstacle so that it can rip stones off cliff faces and even dislocate a speaking man's jaw. Gravel blown by a roaring tutukas wayra has been known to kill men. On some of the stormiest days the tampus would not allow me to travel through mountain passes and narrow valleys for fear the winds would harm me.

I hated those days of forced idleness, for the Colla would tell me their stories again and again, as if I were a deaf man who must puzzle out their meaning by reading their lips with repetition being a boon to my understanding. They believe that Hail, Ice and Wind are three brothers too lazy to work their fields, but I can tell you there is nothing lazy about those three elements: They froze me to the bone when they were not pummeling me with their icy pellets.

I would spend the nights in the tampus, miserable and alone, and then continue on the next day, always towards Tchili, the unknown. Perhaps it was my mood, but I came to hate the tampus of Collasuyu. The local people speak in falsetto whenever they want something, so I was surrounded by high pitched voices of weary travelers seeking food and shelter. All superiors are mother and father, regardless of relationship, and all seniors are grandfather and grandmother, regardless of relationship, so everywhere I went it seemed to be a family reunion and I was the only one on the outside looking in. I often cried myself to sleep, but I was always careful to do it with silent tears in the dark, lest I wake someone or call attention to myself.

As the cold weather worsened the old began to die, and the Colla and Lupaca tribes have mourning down to a fine art, wailing by the side of the road morning, noon, and night so that all the travelers know of their grief. In my middle years I came to love that open land and its solemn people, but what few memories I have of my time as a fugitive there are bad ones, enough of the Collao.

I kept walking south, and gradually the country changed around me, growing even harsher and less habitable. Now there were mountains of sheer bare rock, as sterile on their slopes as they were on their bleak and snowy peaks. The only sign of life here was the road and its frequent chaski huts and less frequent tampus. The food here was all brought in by llama caravan, for the soil was too thin to grow even the hardy crops of quinoa and cold-weather potatoes.

Beyond those frigid peaks lay a great desert, the Atacama, different in every way from the deserts of the coast. If there is a drier place in the world it would make me wonder what the local people did to so offend their gods. The tampu at the outskirts of that barren place provides every traveler with two water skins and a warning: 'If you have not arrived at the next tampu in the time it takes you to finish your first water skin, use the second to come back to us. Otherwise you will surely die.' It was true. Out there, where the road is marked only by heaps of stones within sight of one another to orient the traveler as to his destination, the sun beats down on you and the sand cakes itself to your sweat, and you long for water as no man should ever want.

Without discipline you would drink your first skin before the tampu you were leaving was over the horizon. Many times I saw the skeletons of careless travelers by the side of the road, their bones scoured clean by the blowing sand.

Beyond the Atacama Desert come forested switchback ridges running east to west instead of the long north-south mountains ranges that hem in the broad puna. Each of these sharp hills seems a rampart to stop the southbound traveler. Were it not for the gold and tin and copper that trickles northward from distant lands, Topa Inca Yupanki would never have ventured so far south with his legions of conquest.

At last, on an insignificant river called the Maule, no different from the ones north and south of it, the great conqueror grew tired and bored of those hills and the dark pine forests. He erected markers claiming the place to be the end of the world, leaving the people there, the Mapuche, half-conquered, living on either side of the Maule. Legend said there was a broad rich valley beyond the hills, but Topa was tired and returned to Cuzco. It was there, not far from the Maule, that I came to the end of my long southward journey.

It was such an abrupt transition from the going to the arriving that I looked around me, as if awaking from a dream. The hills here were less high, less aggressive, patchily forested and otherwise pleasant. They grew maize on the low slopes, potatoes on the high, and llamas wandered higher still where quinoa grew haphazardly in fields still unterraced by the recent Inca conquerors.

The people here, the Mapuche, were a tribe divided. Their young men left to try their fortunes south of the Maule in land where they still ruled, leaving a disproportionate number of women and old men here in Inca territory to live in subjugation.

There were fortresses with wooden palisades on the prominent peaks along the road, manned by mitmak militia who farmed outside the walls by day but slept in the comfort and safety of their forts at night. They were an occupying force to prevent Mapuche uprisings or raids from south of the Maule, but it was hoped, in time, that their habits of obedience to the Inca would rub off on the locals. It might take generations, but at the time we thought Tahuantinsuyu would be eternal. We thought we had the time.

It was at such a fort, little different from the four or five I had passed before, that I was stopped and questioned and told I had arrived at my service post. Here, or more specifically in the Mapuche settlement scattered across the mountainside, lived the chaski mitmak Puma whom I had forged orders to partner up with at his chaski.

I was brought into the fort and presented to the local Inca administrator, a man named Tiso Yuncailo. I looked him up and down with concealed interest, for he was in a position that could mean one of two things: Either he was a man of great ability but low birth who was sent out to the frontier to make a name for himself, or he was a man of middling family and little ability dispatched to the edge of the world to hold the position of authority he was entitled to in a place where he could be quietly forgotten. It took me only his first words to know that he was the latter.

"I am an Inca, mitmak. Do you know what that means? It means I am your better, your lord, appointed by Inti to rule you. If you give me your absolute obedience you will live well here. Do you understand?"

"Yes, lord," I said as humbly as I could, broadening my accent to sound

172

like a puric. Inside I was thinking that it was men such as these that my father had always despised, the self-important bureaucrat whose pomposity inspired his underlings to cheat on their taxes. Men were basically honest until they were given motivation to stray. Officials like Tiso Yuncailo were the blighted potatoes that could ruin entire storehouses.

"What is your name?"

"Cusi Chala," I said, naming myself Joy Coast and hoping that sounded like a suitable moniker for a Chimu puric. I knew dozens of noble titles from the Kingdom of Chimor, but I had no frame of reference for their commoner names. Hopefully Tiso Yuncailo did not either.

"You are a Chimu?" He gestured to the wooden earplugs I wore. "Then you have had no weapons training?" There was a law forbidding the Chimu people to train to serve in the citizen militia for fear they would rise up against their Inca masters.

"No, lord."

"Then you will not live here in the fort. These are military mitmaks. You will live out there with the Mapuche," he waved his hand beyond the palisade, as if anyone living outside the walls were not his concern. This man was not the military governor of this province. He was administrator of a thousand tax-paying families spread across twenty or so small settlements. He should be out there living among them, or at least show more of an interest in their lives and livelihoods. "As it is, I'm glad you've shown up. So many of these boys leave that it's tough to recruit local chaskis. Your quipu says they want you with chaski mitmak number twelve. I believe his name is Puma. You may start now."

"Right now, my lord?" I allowed a note of incredulity to creep into my voice. I did not know where I was to sleep. I had not eaten yet today. I was going straight to work?

"Yes, immediately. I order you to go." He stood there, imperious, and I was careful not to look insolent or indulgent of his self-importance.

"Yes, lord." I left the fort and followed the road, asking at a chaski hut how many posts down would I find Puma. I walked on, coming to the right hut before noon.

He wore the same headband as I, the white, gray, black, and green of the White Rock graduate, and we broke into grins immediately, clasping each other's hands and then embracing when that gesture was not enough. We had not yet spoken a word to each other, but we were already friends.

"My name is Puma," he said. He was a likeable man. I could tell by sheer instinct that he had meant my family no harm when he untied the quipus at Tarawari.

He was shorter than I, and broader, a typical mountain man with a big chest that granted lung power and sinewy legs to make up for their shortness. He wore an ugly brown cloak of llama wool, oily and itchy and undyed. A man dressed like that would not have been fit to muck out the llama corrals in Cuzco, but out here on the edge of the world he was absolutely appropriate.

I spent that first shift with him as I would many others, sitting on a stool with my back to him. He looked one way down the road and I the other. We talked but little, for as far as he knew we had the rest of our lives to converse and there was no sense in wasting all our anecdotes at once. We whittled: Puma had a fine set of bronze chisels. We made stools, like the ones we sat on, and bowls and spoons and idols, and all manner of useful things.

Throughout the day our whittling was punctuated by the distant conch trumpet, summoning us out to meet the oncoming chaskis. I would come to learn my stretch of the road such that I could run it unerringly with my eyes closed, and in my dreams I run it still, knowing each slight curve of the road, even where rain and wind will drive pebbles onto the path and where trees drop their leaves and needles and nuts.

Originally I had meant to question him harshly about Tarawari and leave, perhaps that very day, but it was so soothing to be in that little shack, no more than three walls and a high steep roof, watching the road, whittling and speaking in long low conversations about things that mattered not.

I had come down here in such a hurry, my thoughts going in a thousand different directions at once, that to sit there and calm down felt good for my soul. Tahuantinsuyu was built upon people knowing their place, obeying the authority above them, and here I found that for the first time since my father's death. That first day I just relaxed and did my job, and the sun reached its zenith and fell without any discomfort entering my world. I was at peace. I smiled as the sun sank over the horizon, never imagining that what Puma was about to say would change my life forever after.

"That was a good day, but our shift ends at sunset. Here comes our relief. Why don't you go take a bath, and then afterwards I'll meet you at

174

the chieftain's homestead?" There might have been a knowing smile on his face, perhaps not. By the time I had the freedom to tie down my recollections of my time in Tchili my memory had grown hazy. That said, I think he knew what I was going to discover down there by the water. I had already decided Puma had no malice in his heart, but I learned to love him for the direction he set my feet upon that day.

I walked away from the post, dusty from my travels and now sweaty from my running, intent only on washing up in the little pond fed by a mountain stream that he had described to me. I followed a beaten path through a stand of trees to come to a broad meadow, and so intent was I upon my task that I was halfway across that grassy expanse before I looked up to see that I was not alone.

She danced among the fireflies. That's the only way to describe it. Let your mind wander and there she is, surrounded by swirling specks of honey warm light. Her smile lit the early night, her pale skin standing out clear as day against the dark meadow behind her. There wasn't a stitch of clothing on her, and she didn't care. She danced among the fireflies, and it warms my heart to know such peace and innocence existed at one time in the world.

If I were a Christian, Friar, I would call her an angel, for to see this girl was to know what angels must look like. She was short and slender, without the flamboyant curves of the Vixen but still a well-proportioned woman. Her face was the vision of kindness: A small sharp nose over thin lips, with laugh lines around her mouth and dimples that begged you to hold her face in your hands and marvel at the glory of mankind to produce such a woman. I was mesmerized.

When she finally noticed me standing there, rooted to the spot where I first saw her, she modestly covered herself with her hands. She seemed bashful without any resentment or accusation as to my presence there.

"I don't know you," she said with a small frown that asked me to forgive her for the lapse. In a community this small a stranger should have frightened her, especially as she stood naked in a meadow. I did not.

"I'm the new chaski mitmak, Cusi Chala," I said, tearing my eyes away from what her hands were barely concealing to look at her face. She nodded as if the name made all her discomfort fall away.

"My name is Koonek," she said. She was my age, perhaps a little younger, and I knew in that instant that were I to leave this place tomorrow and never return I would always carry the memory of a girl named Koonek with me, wherever I went.

We stood there for a moment, I trying to think of how to give her some privacy without embarrassing either of us, and she staring at me kindly, as if waiting for further casual conversation. "Have you come down here for a bath?" She tilted her head towards the pond behind her. The gesture was poetry in motion, pure elegance, her long neck turning and rearing back, tipping her chest up and stretching her already taut belly. I almost groaned. "You can go ahead and jump in. I suppose I shouldn't be modest and ask for you to wait for me to leave before you start." She spoke as if we were old friends.

At the moment the only thing keeping my manhood from running parallel to the ground was the restricting tension of my breechcloth: I did not think it wise to disrobe within sight of this woman. I told her, "I was going to wash up before meeting the village headman, but I think I might go there now, instead."

I turned to leave her, but she surprised me. "Oh, I'll take you to him. He's my father." She pointed to a homestead on a nearby hill, inadvertently exposing one pert breast for my inspection. Reluctantly I followed her outstretched arm to the distant glow of a hearth through the hall's small door. When I turned back she was slipping a dress over her head. I felt a mix of relief and regret.

"That's kind of you," I said. "Do you always..." I trailed off, unsure by her demeanour if she even saw anything unusual in what I had caught her doing. Perhaps it was a Mapuche custom, though I think if a tribe frequently let their women dance naked and alone that was the sort of thing the tutors and wise men of my school would have told me about.

"Oh, I don't like to put my clothes on when I'm wet. I end up smelling of wet wool, which is worse than I smelled before I bathed. Besides, everyone knows I dance out here after a bath —my mother approves— and so the villagers give me my privacy." There was something in the way she mentioned her mother that didn't sound quite right. Were she a dove the mention of her mother would have been like that last hesitant coo before the bird roosts to let a passing thunderhead speak with its fiery tongue.

I could not let it pass, even though I knew she would prefer not to explain. "Who is your mother, and why would she approve of you dancing out here?"

"You don't know Mama?" She asked, almost stunned. I realized that this girl, daughter of the village curaca, probably had never been out of sight of her home on the hill. Her world could be walked across in a day.

"No," I smiled. "I've only just arrived, and I'm from a long way away. It would take you months to walk to where I'm from. I don't know anyone here yet except you and Puma and Tiso Yuncailo."

Another cloud seemed to pass over her face at the mention of the Inca, but I thought nothing of it and within a moment she was talking again. "Oh, I'm sorry. It's just that everyone around here knows her. She's our clan's shaman, you see? She wants me to follow in her footsteps, but I don't..." She paused a moment, chewing on her bottom lip. "I can't see what she sees, do you know what I mean?

"When she was a girl she used to dance on a tree stump, and she could tell how good the coming harvest would be by the vibrations the Earth Mother sent up from the ground into her feet. She likes me out here after my bath because she thinks I'm communicating with the spirits, but I just like the feel of the grass and flowers against my calves and to not smell of wet wool when I come home." She blushed again.

"Well..." I said, embarrassed at her total honesty with a stranger. "Why don't you come and introduce me to your father?"

I followed her up to the curaca's homestead, hanging on her every word. She was little more than a girl, with a girl's perceptions of the world, but everything she said seemed so important to her that I could not help but listen, captivated, at how the tampu construction was going, or to the latest feats of her neighbours' mischievous guinea pigs. When we finally arrived at the distant light I was regretting that we had to stop.

Her father lived in a hall surrounded by outbuildings with a llama corral around back and a line of moderately rich clothes hanging dry on a line.

She entered without calling out an introduction, and the hall enveloped me in a warmth of family camaraderie that overwhelmed my senses. It was impossible not to feel loved here. A little girl fetched me a stool and a little boy took my cloak. A cup of akha was in my hand before I was sitting down, and they were all talking to me as if they had known me for years. We were friends within moments.

Her father's name was Antalongo, though the longo was his title, meaning headman. He had the proud bearing of a king, but here in his home he had the look of a hardworking peasant who was not afraid to get dirt under his nails when he worked his fields.

Her father and I talked late into the night, splitting a couple of flagons of akha between us and growing warm and friendly for our trouble. Antalongo had been a leader of his people since he was a boy, and his wife, whom he called a witch without any scorn in the term, had only added to his influence.

As if on cue his wife appeared in the door, and I was surprised at the reception that greeted her. Where I had been greeted with noise and joy, she was welcomed with respectful silence. She set her basket down against the wall, ruffled the hair of one of her young sons, and sat down at a vacant stool by the hearth.

She was short and thin, and in her youth you could see there had been beauty in her face, a hard beauty. She looked me square in the eye and said, "You're not all that you seem to be." A silence stretched. I waited for someone to introduce me, but the whole house was waiting for this witch to speak again. "You will sleep here tonight and go out tomorrow with Puma. I invited him to come by."

With that she scooped some stew from the pot into a bowl and retreated into the far corner of the lodge. The bowl was returned empty by one of her children, and when next I looked over she was asleep on a pallet.

The hall seemed to warm again as she slept, and when Puma appeared in the door he was greeted just as I had been, except a little quieter for fear of waking the witch. The children went to bed one by one, until it was just the three men still awake, speaking of the world in the way that men do when they drink.

Antalongo confessed to me that he and his people hated the Inca just as much as the Mapuche who had fled south of the Maule River, but what were they to do? They were tied to their farms, and there wasn't enough arable land outside the Inca's borders to accommodate all of them. Besides, where could his village go that the Inca could not follow, and each time the Children of the Sun reconquered his kin it would be another generation of boys slain and women taken off to be chosen women.

I agreed with him up and down, citing the example of the Kingdom of Chimor, which he had vaguely heard of. Puma filled in, "Your people have it easy compared to the Chimu, Anta. The Chimu were the richest people in the world, and now they are the poorest. You never had anything worth stealing."

"Oh no?" The old man spat into the hearth's coals, the sizzle emphasizing his displeasure. "That Inca overseer wants to marry my daughter. The next time that marriage inspector of theirs comes through, there goes my daughter!" At this I sat up, for I had met the incompetent royal scion out here, and the idea of sweet Koonek in Tiso Yuncailo's bed rubbed my unsuspecting heart raw.

"You're a chief. Aren't there boys lined up at your door for her?" I asked.

"Who would want to anger the Inca? And, of those, who would my wife accept? She doesn't have much patience for fools." He rubbed his jaw to show he thought himself in the same category as the would-be suitors.

"What did she mean when she said I'm not all that I seem?" I asked, afraid that I knew exactly what she meant.

"I have no idea," he sympathized. "But if she didn't like you she would have found a way to get you out of this house in a way that would make sure you did not come back."

"Let's turn in, Cusi. We're on duty at dawn," Puma suggested.

"Do you live here?" I asked.

"No. I've got my own place down the hill, but most people here spend the odd night with Antalongo. I figured this would be a good time for me to do the same." Puma and Antalongo were chuckling together.

"Did I miss something?"

"My wife has a temper," Puma whispered, glancing over at Koonek's sleeping mother to make it clear that his wife was not the only one.

"And do you sometimes spend the night with Puma's family, Anta?" I asked.

"No, but sometimes I spend the night outside with the firewood." We laughed together, drained our cups, and went to the pallets that had been set up for us. The next dawn saw Puma and I in our chaski hut again, whittling.

And that's how my days went for more days than I bothered to count. I worked fifteen-day shifts as a chaski and then fifteen days as a labourer, but as I did not have any fields of my own I lent a hand to Puma and Antalongo and my community, making a lot of friends in the process. I dug ditches, hauled chuno bags, cleared fields, planted trees. Eventually I built myself a rickety shack halfway between Antalongo's hall and my chaski post, but I spent most nights at the curaca's place. I enjoyed his company, and I enjoyed being near Koonek.

I remember building a retaining wall on the side of a hill, stone by stone, and then filling the far side of the wall with earth. The satisfaction I found in watching it grow a little, day by day out of my own sweat, was overwhelming. It was the work of a month, and it was thirsty work; four or five times a day Koonek would come by with water for me, just because she knew I would need a drink.

I remember burning the dead grass of a llama pasture to turn it over into a potato field for next season, and when the wind changed I was covered head to toe in soot. She spotted me on my way home, and without asking she took my mantle and tunic from my hut in my absence and washed all the ashes out of them.

It wasn't just me, of course. She did favours like that for everyone, for it was just Koonek's way to try and make everyone happy. The only time I did not see a smile on her face was when her mother was near, and I suspect it was because her mother was difficult to please and did not like people smiling for no reason.

Gradually it dawned on me that I loved the girl. I don't mean I loved her as I had lusted after the Vixen. Koonek was just a wonderful person, and I was happy to be near her. Not that I didn't want there to be more, for I was a young man in his prime in love with a woman, but she was unattainable to me in that way. Between her mother and Tiso Yuncailo there was just no way I would ever expect to bed her, even though the Mapuche did not hold chastity before marriage in the same esteem as the Inca.

It just seemed to me that the best parts of my day were when she was around, and if the time between her visits stretched on my work became harder, less rewarding.

I remember the day that I finally decided it was love that I was feeling. I was running my road, my fist full of accounting quipus. I asked myself why it had taken me so long to use the word 'love' to describe the feeling when it seemed so obvious, and I missed my stride and took a tumble as I realized I had not thought of the Vixen in a month.

I had been in love before, with the Vixen, but there was something so warm and comfortable about being in love with Koonek. With the Vixen love was a hunger, a craving to be answered. Loving the Vixen was like loving a falcon: You do it because of her beauty and her brilliance and her pride. It was as different as night and day. There was nothing soft about the Vixen and there was nothing hard about Koonek.

I never heard Koonek say a harsh word about anything; I never saw her bear a grudge. If I was complaining about something she would agree with me while still trying to justify whatever I felt was wrong. She gave everyone the benefit of the doubt and never thought people were capable of wrong. She disliked no one except for her mother, but even then I think she was just afraid of disappointing her. She did not have an angry bone in her body, nor one capable of thinking ill of anything. She was flawlessly good.

I lived there for long months, trapped in a happy place and distracted from my purpose by the good things that came unbidden into my life. As time passed I think Koonek came to feel something for me too, or perhaps it was a mutual and spontaneous thing. She visited me more often, even spending her rare idle time with me. I remember once she came to me in tears because her mother had reprimanded her for something, and when she put her arms around me I wanted to protect her from the world, and she could feel that.

It was the most casual and unspoken courtship I have ever heard of, but it slowly became known throughout our community —without any real incidents or events to spark it off— that Koonek and I were a couple, a pair, a matched set. All this without even so much as a kiss, and certainly no possibility of marriage.

Even a man as unconnected with the Mapuche as Tiso Yuncailo eventually came to realize that I was a threat to his ambition of wedding Koonek. The marriage inspector still had not set the date for his next arrival among the Mapuche, and day by day it was growing more difficult to find Koonek without me by her side. He decided to take matters into his own hands, and he did it in the incompetent manner I had come to expect from him.

I was in my chaski hut, whittling and listening to the thunder of a coming storm. Such is Runa Simi's eloquence, Friar, that we even have a word for the fast moving cloud rack preceding the tempest: Acapana. Those clouds were almost overhead when Tiso Yuncailo arrived with a couple of soldiers, as if he were merely inspecting all the chaski huts in his territory, something he had never done before in all the time I had lived there.

He stood there, waiting for me to say something, but I had already greeted him with a blown kiss and I was perfectly content to sit there whittling the rest of the day. Puma pressed his back into mine for support; he knew what the Inca was there for too.

"You aren't afraid of the thunder?" Tiso Yuncailo asked me at last, breaking the silence.

"No, should I be, lord?" I asked, continuing to whittle.

"Oh, yes. You are from the coast. You should never have heard rain and storm." His eyes were narrow as slits, probing me, but I could read him even without looking at him. He was suspicious of me, but he was grasping to find something improper.

"My lord, I attended the White Rock Chaski School, which is much closer to the hacha hacha than here, and then I walked across the world to get here. I may have been born on the coast, but I have seen thunderstorms many times since. I find them peaceful."

"Peaceful? Rain is a destroyer to the Chimu," he recited word for word a teacher at the House of Learning.

"Yes, because it only happens once in a lifetime on the coast, and it destroys everything," I replied, still whittling. "But up here there is no irrigation as we have down in the desert. Here the rain is life. Besides," I flicked another woodchip off the idol I was making, "To us, the sun is a destroyer too, and the rain hides the sun." I had often teased my father about Inti's vulnerability to the rain. Knowing the truth about Viracocha really makes one wonder how anyone can worship the sun.

Yuncailo stiffened, as he was meant to. "I don't think you are a Chimu at all," he muttered to me.

"Oh?" I said, unsure if I had gone too far.

"You are too... Smart."

"Our empire was as big as yours at one point. That takes some small intelligence."

"No, it's something else... You know things, you see things..." He furrowed his brow.

"May I speak, my lord?"

"Yes," he said, glad to have a moment to think.

"You are an administrator sent out here to keep the local population passive. You have no military rank, is this so?"

"It is so," he said.

"Yet you live in the fort surrounded by mitmaks. Do you know what this tells the people here? It lets them know you are afraid." He stiffened again. "Then you demand the chief's daughter as your wife, when an inspector has already come through this village and spared her from being a chosen woman–"

"She is ten times the beauty of any of the girls we took out of here."

"Yes, but why would the inspector —your superior in rank— leave her? Because the chief and his witch weren't willing to part with her, and the inspector did not want to alienate the one friendly clan in these hills. His good work wasn't noticed as a kindness, but it prevented an uprising."

"Your point?"

"Take her as a wife the next time the marriage inspector comes through here and the Mapuche will rise against you. You do not win these people over by marrying into them. If you want to do that, live among them. Set up a home out here in the fields. No one will kill you in your sleep. The Imperial legions would butcher every man, woman, and child if they did. Give Antalongo and his wife a gift to reward them from their loyalty, and leave Koonek's future in her parents' hands."

"This is why you are too clever, Cusi. You think like an Inca."

"And you dress like one, my lord." I heard the clarion call of a conch trumpet. I set down my woodwork, reached behind me to thump Puma on the back to let him know I was leaving, and took off at a run, leaving Tiso Yuncailo to frown at my swiftly receding form.

Koonek's mother heard about my conversation with the Inca, and that night she knocked on the doorpost of my simple shack. I knew it was her because I did not even have a blanket covering my door, so far had I fallen into simple happiness from the palaces of my childhood.

"Come out here," she bid me. I threw a handful of small potatoes into my pot of boiling water, added a pinch of ground peppers from a gourd, and came out to her while my dinner cooked. "You intend to marry my daughter?" She asked.

"I would like to," I admitted. "But it's an impossibility, and I accept that."

She looked up at me with a penetrating gaze. "Who are you?" She asked.

I remained impassive. Smiling would be the wrong reaction; so would confessing in full, obviously. She knew nothing, but she sensed something. After a moment I decided on a course of action. "I am that rarity: A good man coming at a good time to do a good thing for your family."

She harrumphed at me and turned to look at the meager potato patch I had planted just outside my door. "Why did you grow these, if this Inca State of theirs will feed you until you have a family?"

"Because I can. Why should the State support me entirely when I have two hands and free time?"

She harrumphed again. "Koonek is a difficult child."

This time I did smile, but her back was turned to me so I could do it without fear. "I think you're a difficult mother. Koonek's just fine. She's just not you."

She turned back to me, but my smile was gone at the first sign of her swivel. "You're more than you seem," she sounded frustrated.

"But you do like me." I did not make it a question.

She looked up at me, clearly upset with herself at some perceived failing. "Yes," she finally admitted. "Though I think I would like any man who would keep her out of the arms of an Inca."

"Why do you hate them so much?" I asked.

"We were fine without them!" She barked.

"You're better with them."

She stepped right up to me, tipping her head way back to look me in the eye, her chin almost touching my collarbone. "That remains to be seen!"

"No," I said firmly. "This is the seventieth tribe attached to Tahuantinsuyu, and within a generation or two, each of the sixty-nine before you have experienced population growth unprecedented in their remembered history. Crime and intertribal violence has fallen away to almost nothing. You will never be hungry or without shelter or clothing or—"

"That shouldn't be for them to provide for us! We should do that for ourselves."

I shook my head. "It is part of their process of making the world a better place. You cannot have an area of poverty on the edge of an area of plenty. It destabilizes things." I pointed towards Cuzco. "If the Inca had stopped ten valleys over from here and built their roads and tampus, the people there would have prospered while you did not, and soon enough you would have suffered: A hard winter, a drought, a landslide, a fire, a plague.

"Would you not then have tried to take things from your rich neighbours? Would you starve when you did not have to? The Inca cannot allow raiders to come against their taxpayers, and securing the borders of Tahuantinsuyu means pushing them out forever. As they expand, new people become taxpayers and receive all the benefits that that brings." It occurred to me as I spoke that I could not have sounded more like an Inca if I were caught haranguing an Imperial legion, but the damage was done.

"Cusi Chala," she said, looking up at me. "What right do the Inca have to make us work when we do not want to? To take our best daughters from us? To live in luxury while we do not?"

I pretended to think about it for a moment. "They will tell you it is because their god Inti gave them the task, but I think something different." I watched as she took a step back to judge me better. "I think the real reason is because they came up with the idea first, and they make it work: Keeping the system running is their task, not labouring in a field or driving llamas. As it is their system and their place in it is so different from everyone else's, yes, they are entitled to a few privileges, just as we purics are entitled to grumble about it behind the pacuyoks' backs."

We stood there for a while, looking at each other, then I heard the hiss as my pot boiled over into the fire and I rushed back inside to save what I could of my stew. When I had the pot off the flames the light from the door was blocked as she stood on my threshold. "I disagree with you, Cusi Chala, but I respect that you feel strongly enough about it for you to say it. No one on this mountain would speak to me as you just did, as a grandfather to a child."

I opened my mouth to deny that I was lecturing her, but she held up her hand imperiously and I fell silent. "To keep Koonek away from the Inca, you have my blessing to marry her. The inspector will be coming in two months. Pray to whatever gods you worship that she can marry you, because I hate the Inca enough for what they have done to my people that I will place a terrible curse on my daughter if she weds one: She will die alone and unhappy if she marries an Inca, Cusi Chala."

She stood in my doorway, threatening her own daughter with something we both know would torment Koonek, and I hated her for it. "Pray she doesn't marry an Inca. It will have a bad end."

She turned to go, but thought better of it and turned back to me for one last word: "I still say you are more than you seem." With that she left me to my ruined stew.

The two months passed swiftly, and word came down the chaski network that the marriage inspector was approaching. I felt a weight in the pit of my stomach: I was now of marriageable age, or at least I looked it, and I had faked my age on my Chimu identification so as to make it plausible for me to be a chaski mitmak.

Koonek was also old enough to wed according to the customs of her people. I should have had faith in the official, for the marriage inspector was chosen for his character: He made decisions that would make happy or unhappy homes for taxpayers, but this was a problem I did not see how he could resolve.

I met Koonek in her meadow at sunset the day before the inspector's arrival, and I made a joke about arriving too late for the show. She laughed her tinkling laughter and tilted her head to one side, still smiling.

I said to her, "You know what happens tomorrow?"

She shook her head. "No one does."

"Not even your mother?"

"She knows what she doesn't want to happen," Koonek said with a laugh. It was the closest thing she could say to snubbing her mother, and I reached out and hugged her for her bravery.

"However this works, Koonek, I want you to know that you have always made me very happy." I looked her in the eyes and she looked into mine, and I did not want that moment to end.

"You make me very happy too, Cusi. If it was my choice I would want us to be happy together for the rest of our lives." She leaned into me and I cursed myself for my height: If I were shorter I could have kissed her, but she did not tilt her head up; instead she nuzzled my neck and I held her close, and when we were done we separated and where she had pressed against me felt cold. "I will see you tomorrow," she said formally, then she turned and ran to her father's hall.

I made my way to my rickety shack to find Puma there with three big flasks of viñapu.

"Your wife threw you out again?" I asked.

"Tonight I threw myself out," he said, pouring the illegal liquor. "Now for the friendly word of encouragement: This marriage inspector isn't the same one who gave me my wife, so maybe he's a smart man." We drank from the same cup, in the Mapuche tradition. "How's that for positive thinking?"

186

"About as lousy as your marriage," I smiled, feeling the warmth in my belly.

"Okay, so here's the truth: You can't do a damned thing about tomorrow, but you can get really drunk with me tonight." And we did.

The next day all the unmarried men and women within walking distance congregated in front of Tiso Yuncailo's fort to blow a kiss of greeting at the Inca who would decide the rest of their conjugal lives.

He was a short, round man dressed in elegant vicuna robes of white and blue. His staff of office was appropriately carved to show a man with one arm around his woman. His golden earplugs bore the image of the sun and a moon, the married heavenly bodies of Inti and Mama Quilla. He looked intelligent and caring. I hoped he was.

The marriage inspector lined us up in two rows leading up to the gates of the fort, men on one side of the road, women on the other. We faced across from each other, carefully positioning ourselves to be as close to our sweethearts as possible in case the inspector did not know his business and just paired us off with our opposite number. Koonek stood off to one side by herself. Antalongo and Tiso Yuncailo flanked the inspector on either shoulder.

"This village has been harmonious, and that deserves special favour," the inspector said. "Any previously arranged pairs, step into the road and hold hands." Most of the men and women stepped forward to embrace one another before dutifully holding hands. "Go perform your ceremonies with the Sapa Inca's blessing." He bade them go with a dutiful swipe of his hand. The couples departed, married in the eyes of the Emperor and soon to be married by tribal custom.

The remainder, three men including myself, two girls, and Koonek, remained facing one another. The inspector asked each of us our name, frowning slightly in concentration. He paired up the two men with the two girls, and left Koonek and I standing alone.

"Well, Cusi Chala, you have me in something of a tough position," he said, eying Koonek kindly but with appreciation. "Tiso Yuncailo has explained this situation to me."

"Yes, Excellency," I said.

"I was also the inspector who spared her from the Houses of the Chosen Women during the conquest, did you know that?"

"No, Excellency."

He smiled at me, and I could see in his face that it was this sort of administrator, fair-minded and caring for the people under him, that made Tahuantinsuyu strong. If he chose to marry Koonek off to Tiso Yuncailo I would respect his judgment.

"Let me say that whichever of you gets her, there is a loss. If you get her, Tiso loses respect in the whole community. An Inca beaten out by a chaski?" He made it sound unthinkable. "But if he gets her and you don't, you remain an untaxable minor, doing chaski duties without growing food for yourself or producing children who will in turn pay taxes of their own one day.

"It will be three years or more before I return. You will be an unmarried bachelor for three years? Eating from the Emperor's granaries and potato silos? Letting the best years of your fatherhood slip past you?" We stood there, the breeze ruffling our headdresses. "What would you advise?" His eyes were shrewd.

"Your Excellency, it is not for me to suggest things to my betters—"

"That's not what Tiso tells me, but I am willing to allow you the pleasantry of saying it. Now, you want to marry this girl?" He pointed square at Koonek, who smiled her kind smile at me.

"Yes," I said, meaning it.

"Then the gods have gifted you with a swift mind to match your swift legs, and you have had nothing but time in your chaski hut to think of a solution to this problem. How do I prevent an uprising without embarrassing Tiso here?" It was just the five of us there, Tiso, the inspector, Antalongo, Koonek and myself, but I think we were all stunned at what the inspector had just asked.

I had not, in fact, been thinking how to solve the conundrum, and my temples still pounded with the hangover from the night before, but the answer still came to me as if god-sent. I will not bore you with false modesty, Friar. I am one of the best administrators Tahuantinsuyu has ever known.

"The issue is that Tiso demands to marry the best local girl, your Excellency, but you already demonstrated that Koonek was not even eligible to be a Chosen Woman. Give my lord Tiso Yuncailo two or three of the chosen women taken from this clan during the subjugation. He is marrying the very best of the local women, not just one but several, each of whom proved more worthy than Koonek to father the children of the Children of the Sun."

A bee buzzed by my face, but I did not flinch. The inspector nodded his head. "It is as you said, Tiso. This Cusi Chala should have been born Cusi Orco," he said, renaming me from Joy Coast to Joy Mountain, implying I should have been an Inca. I was careful to look humble at such a lofty compliment. "It shall be as you said." He smiled at me. I smiled back. I looked at Koonek and Antalongo, and we were all smiling. All except Tiso, who at least was not scowling. Being given a trio of beauties takes some of the sting out of wounded pride.

I embraced my wife right there in the road before remembering the huge favour that had been granted to me. I blew a kiss of thanks to the marriage inspector, and when this felt insufficient I stared into the sun and said, "I swear by Inti I will be worthy of this, your Excellency. I swear by my gods and all gods that I will earn this." He waved his hand, dismissing us, and Koonek and I were away before anyone could change their minds.

* * *

The Mapuche wedding ceremony was a prolonged thing before the Inca came, with haggling over bride price, feasts and prayers, then finally a mock abduction where the husband-to-be snatched up his bride and ran with her over his shoulder away from her family. Under the Inca it was much abbreviated: I promised Antalongo the first kid of the llamas the State would issue me as a married man, and I said goodbye to Koonek's mother. Now that I was husband to her daughter we were not supposed to speak again, a most fortuitous rule given how unpleasant she was.

I took Koonek to my shack that night to the encouraging jeers of Puma and some of our other friends. "Start a fire! Start a fire!" They shouted to us. The Mapuche word for woman is domo, which also means hearth. The word for man is wentru, which also means fire drill. A charming double entendre, don't you think, Friar?

Making love to Koonek was different from the Vixen in every particular. With the Vixen the act was pure carnal lust; pleasure was fought for, and the end of the struggle left us spent and exhausted. With my darling Koonek love was about slow and pleasant discovery, without haste or exertion. We would spend the whole night moving across one another with hands and lips until we had found every place which made us sigh or smile or laugh.

I tell you truly I might have been the most fortunate young man in the world to have experienced two such women before my twentieth year, for I had the energy to compete with the first and the ability to go without sleep to enjoy the second. There is no way to quantifiably say one was better than the other, but I will say this: Koonek never left me wanting, nor I her, and more often than not we lay in each other's arms, still awake, when the dawn birds told us the new day had come. I have never been so happy since, nor do I expect to be before I die and join her in the Upper Universe.

The whole community came together to build us a proper home, with even the soldiers from the fort coming down to take the stones out of my field and build a llama corral with them. We sang as we worked, interlacing the wooden withies for the walls, smearing them with mud, sweeping and pounding the floor within, setting the roof poles, thatching. We were done in two days, and I have never been more comfortable in any palace than I was that first night alone with my wife at the far end of the world.

My neighbours helped me plant my fields, as well. I was allotted a small field of maize down at the base of our mountain and a larger potato patch just outside our door. The men and I worked the earth with our footplows while the women broke up any clods of dirt with practiced swings of long-handled wooden hammers.

Boys and girls too young to do heavy work planted the seeds and chose which songs to sing as we worked. We often sang Haylli, the victory song of harvest, even though it was out of season. I bawled out the lyrics with the rest, careful always to stumble over a word here or there, for they do not have the song in Chimor so far as I know, and I was always careful not to seem too much of a mountain man.

And so it went, and we were happy. I took my turn with Puma in the chaski hut, fifteen days on, fifteen days off, and I worked my fields and my neighbours' fields. I sheared llamas and alpacas in high summer, and always I returned to Koonek's loving arms at night to hear what she had done that day, or what she had heard while fetching water, or what she was going to weave next. Then one day I came back from the fields, wiped the sweat from my brow with a damp cloth, sat down to dinner, and my wife told me the news, "We are to have a baby."

Gods, Friar, it was good to be alive and young with that woman by my side. It occurred to me that I could be truly happy there. Many months had passed since my arrival, but I still had not wrung a name from Puma, and now I found I did not want to. What was my quest going to bring me? Death, probably.

Here I had a loving wife, a baby on the way, jobs I took pride in, a community I liked, a field to work. I was as prosperous as my new found station in life would let me be. Even if I could win back all that I had lost in Cuzco, I would not have my father. My school friends were scattered across the Empire now. My enemies at Court must be powerful indeed. What would I be returning to?

I would lie awake at night, Koonek's arm draped across my chest, and I would think about it. During the day the weight of the grass rope and bronze lancehead in my coca bag seemed to drag me down like an anchor. I felt them to be heavy burdens.

Why did my father need vengeance? My grandfather had received no vengeance for his unjust execution, and I was sure he slept soundly beneath the ground and lived contented in the heavens. Whoever had killed my father would prosper, yes, but the monster of Time finds us all one day. Was I not entitled to the peace and happiness and love I had found here at the ends of the Earth? Would it be so hard to let it go and be free?

I was up late one night watching a fire. I was clearing some brush from the edge of my lowest field and had lit a tall bonfire too late in the day. Now I watched it burn alone to make sure no stray sparks would venture into the maize field behind me. I had my coca bag with me, and my hand strayed inside to rest on the grass rope of Cuzco. Home. Huaca.

These fibres were from my place. It was a little chunk of the home I no longer wanted. I took it from the bag, turning it over and over, noticing the fraying at one end. I reached down and took a handful of dirt from my field: My field, mine, my own ground issued to me by the master of one hundred tax-paying families, who was also the father to my wife and future grandfather of my child.

From this ground I would bring up the food to feed myself, my wife, and still have surplus to go into government storage. Upon this ground my children would be born, and under it they would be buried. This handful of dirt was so much holier than a chuck of useless rope from a place I would never see again. I threw it into the fire before I knew I had decided to do it, and I blinked away the tears as the fire took it, shriveled and twisted it. The rope was gone, and so was my desire for Cuzco.

Next I brought out the lancehead, the tang still wrapped in my father's hair under a protective binding of leather. Whereas the rope was my huaca of Home, this was the huaca of my quest. This was my father's burden, my promise that I would find him justice.

It was heavy in my hand and heavier in my heart, and I knew I could not throw it into the flames as I had the rope, for when the fire cooled there would still be a bronze lump in there to shame me. I got down on my knees and scraped a hole in my field. When it was deep enough to swallow my elbows I put the lance inside my coca bag and dropped the bag into the hole.

I put dirt into the hole one handful at a time, and then I found a large flat rock to mark the site where my father's quest was buried. I stayed up late into the evening, rocking back and forth, alone with my thoughts as the fire burned down to cinders. When at last I walked back to my hut and the arms of my wife I seemed to be floating. There was no weight holding me down anymore.

* * *

It came down the chaski network with the special blood red thread of Imperial security: A notification of a manhunt for an Inca fugitive, the son of the aucca Tupac Capac. The description was rather flattering but the rest of the message was ominous. He was to be apprehended alive along with any accomplices, accessories and co-conspirators. They would all be returned to Cuzco in cages, there to be sent into the Pit and never removed.

I passed the message on down the line, as I had been trained. There was no possibility of stopping it here, for updates would continue to come and Puma might run out and get those. I thought throughout the day about what to do and knew I had no choice.

Sooner or later someone would order all administrators to send in a census count for taxpayers of my age group, and the sudden unauthorized appearance of a Chimu chaski would be black threaded for the special notice of a tocoyricoc at the Great Quipu Repository. With a manhunt on the way it would not be disregarded as a welcome boon of an additional taxpayer. Elite guardsmen led by Inca officers loyal to the Sapa Inca would come to investigate. Where they mentioned accomplices, accessories and co-conspirators they meant anyone who had sheltered and helped me, so I would be sent to the Pit along with Koonek, and possibly her parents and Puma. Tiso Yuncailo would laugh at me as I was dispatched.

I sat silently throughout the day, and Puma did not disturb me, as was his custom. I was rocked to the core to think this life that I had found and embraced was to be torn from me by the unfinished business of my previous existence. I wished there was some way I could tell my anonymous foes that I would be no harm; that I was prepared to grow old here and die here without bothering them, but I could not.

It occurred to me that this manhunt, starting as it did so long after my flight from Cuzco, could only mean whoever had betrayed the Emperor was afraid of me. Why not let me go, otherwise? It was not Imperial justice that sought me. Imperial justice had ruled me innocent after a trial by ordeal. Someone had convinced the Emperor that an educated Inca on the loose was a threat to his throne, and that was why Imperial security was after me. Whoever had convinced the Emperor of that was the same man who had set my father up for death.

I had made a promise to my father to find this man and punish him, and I had selfishly buried that promise at the edge of my field. Now this man was pulling the strings again to destroy another part of my world, and it was all because I had decided not to act, to be happy with what I had and what I had found out here among the Mapuche. I would not make that mistake again.

I went home at the end of the day, no faster or slower than I had any other day. Koonek knew, though. As soon as I was within sight she knew that something was wrong. I sat her down on a cushion across from me, handling her as gently as if she were due, when she wasn't even showing yet.

"You love me?"

"Of course."

"You love me for who I am, not for what I am?"

She smiled indulgently, as if she had already forgiven me and now was ready to take the sting out of my apology. "You are a good person, Cusi. I love you. What's wrong?" She said it as if she could fix it.

"My name is not Cusi Chala." She furrowed her brow a little, as if this was a game and she was supposed to guess my true identity. "My name is Haylli Yupanki. I am an Inca, an Inca of far nobler blood than Tiso Yuncailo."

My wife did not gasp. She did not frown. She did not show any kind of surprise or disgust or horror or anger at my news. She just tilted her head, bird-like, asking, "So why are you here? Why are you working in the dirt and running on the road? Why aren't you living in a palace?"

I licked my lips. "My father was one of the most powerful men in Tahuantinsuyu, but he was murdered. I came down here because Puma knows who is responsible, but I met you, and bringing my father's killer to justice didn't seem important anymore." I waited for her to get angry at me for my lies, but she never did. She sat there, waiting for me to continue. "I thought I could stay here forever, but I can't. A royal quipu has just come down the chaski network—"

"You can read quipus?"

"Better than any man you have ever known." She looked a little proud of me, and I laughed with relief and snatched her up in my arms that she could still take pleasure in my abilities, be it whittling or ruling the world. "The quipu says they are going to start looking for me again. Whoever did this will not let me stay in one place." I let her go to look her in the eye. "I must go. If they find me here they will kill us all. I will find out who did this to my father, who is hunting me, and when I do I will send for you, you and our baby."

At last she looked frightened. "We wouldn't live here?"

"No, but would you want to? If you could live anywhere in the world, would you want to live within walking distance of your mother?"

The smile on her face was dazzling as the sun. "Oh, oh that would be so wonderful... But what am I to tell everyone? If I say I married an Inca, my mother will be very angry with me. And I can't lie to Mama. I can't." The fear in her voice was like a layer of ice on my heart, but I held her close to me and I could feel her relax.

"Just say I have committed a crime against the Inca, and I am on the run. That's not a lie. Tell her I've left to protect you all. That's not a lie either. Say if I'm not back within the year, you are to marry someone else, but I have a plan. None of that is a lie, and it will keep you safe. No one will touch a woman whose husband has defied the Inca, not here." I ran my fingers through her long hair, drinking in the smell of her. Behind me I could feel the last of the sun's rays sink away. Darkness had fallen.

194

"I love you, but I have to go. I will send for you as soon as I can." I held her hand and looked into her eye, and my brave Koonek looked back at me without tears.

"I love you, Cusi... Haylli. You are a good man, and a good husband, and if you say this is the right thing to do, I believe you." She smiled just a little, mischief on her mind. "I will get Mama to pray for your success. She has never prayed to help an Inca before."

I kissed her long and hard, snatched up a few possessions, and left. I looked back only once; Koonek was standing outside the door, a shawl wrapped around her shoulders.

My first stop was Puma's homestead, and he came out his door with a smile on his face and a pot in his hand. I had caught him cleaning up after dinner.

"What can I do for you, Cusi?"

"You can tell me which Inca bastard had you untie the quipus at the Tarawari Tampu." If I had tried to brain him with a mace he could not have looked more surprised. The pot fell from his hand and shattered on a stone. The sound of broken crockery set off the shrill voice of his wife from inside, but he silenced her with a short and uncharacteristic bark, grabbed me by the elbow, and pulled me away from his door.

"How do you know about that? No one knows about that!"

"It was part of a plot to kill a good man. I am that man's son."

His jaw fell open for just a moment, then he shook his head at me, wryly. "I knew. Somehow I knew you were just too damned smart to be a runner—"

"I graduated from the chaski school. I'm also an Inca, great-grandson to Viracocha Inca himself. I'm smart enough to know you didn't untie the quipu to murder my father, but I need to know who had you do it."

He swallowed once then nodded. "It was a pacuyok," he said, eyeing my wooden earplugs with a new interest. "Tall, with the face of a vulture and the neck of a bear, Chalcuchima was his name."

"Why did you do it?"

"He gave me a quipu doubling my allotment of akha for the whole trip down here, and the softest cloak you ever felt. You know the one I mean, the one that holds off the rain?"

"Go get it," I said, an uneasy feeling stirring in my breast.

195

He was gone and back in a moment, the plain brown foul weather cloak I had often seen him wear held in both hands and a curious look on his face. I ran my hand over the outside, feeling the waxy fleece of badly carded coarse llama hair. It was rough under my fingers, unpleasant, itchy. I had often wondered why he wore such an uncomfortable thing just to stay dry when an Alpaca wool cloak was warm even while wet and at least had the ability to take an attractive dye. I turned the cloak over and ran my hand over the inside, jerking my hand out as if I had stuck it into red hot coals.

The inside lining of the cloak, invisible from the outside, was of fine vicuna cumpi. Perhaps two thousand threads crossing back and forth in the space occupied by the end of my thumb. It was Inca cloth, high grade Inca cloth. A small convent of chosen women might take two months to produce such a lining. I saw now why my friend Puma had done such a foolish thing: In Tahuantinsuyu high-grade cloth meant more to my people than gold does to the Spaniards. Lesser men would have committed conscious murder for such a garment.

"What? What is it?" He asked, uneasy. He must have always suspected something was not right about the cloak, for in all our time in the hut he had never revealed to me its secret.

"If you are caught with this they will kill you, Puma. It's the Hiwaya for a commoner to own vicuna, and for you to own cumpi vicuna—"

"Cumpi vicuna?" He sounded awed, tentatively reaching inside to feel the lining again. My friend had probably never touched common grade vicuna. He must have felt like he was wearing the clothing of the gods when Chalcuchima first slipped the cloak over his shoulders.

"Puma, listen to me. I have to go." He looked at me with wide eyes, his hand still inside his cloak. "The man who gave you this is not the man in charge. He is not powerful enough. Do you know who he took his orders from?" It would have to be someone as powerful as my father to acquire this garment, but I had known since before going into the Pit that we had been set up by one of the most powerful men in the land.

"No, Cusi, I don't know."

"Tell no one of that cloak, Puma, and if soldiers come to arrest you, either you or your wife have to throw it on the fire. Do you understand me? Chalcuchima gave you that as both a bribe and as an execution order. When I know who he took his orders from I'll need you to bear witness for me, but until then Chalcuchima need only confirm that you've been wearing cumpi vicuna and they will kill you." I turned to go, but he called me back.

"Cusi, I'm sorry about your father. I thought the pacuyok was just committing a little fraud... He said I could get into the tampu office without suspicion and he couldn't, and if I just untied such and such a set of knots he would make it worth my while. I didn't know anyone would get hurt..."

"Hide that cloak, Puma. It's worth ten times more than the spears and shields Chalcuchima stole to trick my father into marching on Cuzco. It was meant to kill you, but I'll do my very best to make sure it kills the man who tricked us both."

"Cusi, you're an Inca?"

"Yes, I am Haylli Yupanki."

"Then go with Inti, Haylli."

I flashed him my very best smile. "Inti's just the god we let you rabble worship. He's more like our brother than our god. We worship Viracocha, but don't tell anyone. It's a big secret."

He grinned back at me, and then we embraced as only good friends truly can. He thumped me on the back hard, holding me tight. "I'm glad to have known you, Cusi."

"Look after Koonek. I'll send for her within the year."

"I will. Good luck."

"Take care."

I never saw my friend Puma again, though when it was still within my power to do so I checked up on him from time to time. He had a family, and lived his days as an obedient taxpayer of Tahuantinsuyu. As near as I can tell he survived our troubled times in relative peace. I envy him that.

I made one more stop on my way out of the clan's holdings. I stopped at my lowest field, the maize stalks turned under now. I found the flat rock that marked the spot of my father's burden and dug up the lance-head. The leather thong had begun to rot, but beneath it his hair was still dry and clean, wrapped round the tang. I replaced the leather with some cord I kept in my satchel to tie reluctant bean stalks onto their climbing poles, then I took up my promise of revenge, put it in my bag, and marched towards Cuzco.

197

With an Imperial manhunt on I should have been more careful, Friar. The officers sent out to the fringes of the Empire are all trying to make a name for themselves so they can return in glory to the centre of civilization. Without a war brewing, capturing me was the greatest prize available to them. I knew that, Friar, but knowing wasn't enough. I was almost caught on my second day.

My ears were hidden under the headdress of the Olmo people, a length of cotton over the top of my head and under my jaw. I had to travel thus, for the hunting parties were looking for a pacuyok, and even the wooden earplugs of a Chimu artisan would have been unsafe now that a mitmak chaski named Cusi Chala had deserted from his post.

My forged travel documents said I was being sent to a market two days away to buy replacement conch trumpets. It would have been more than enough for any tampu keeper's satisfaction, but I was a fool to think a soldier would bother looking at my knotted strings.

I was awakened in the dark by a violent shaking, hauled out of bed and barely given time to refasten my headdress before being hustled out into the tampu's courtyard. All the guests were assembled, and we were surrounded by conscript soldiers with lances at the ready.

"There is a fugitive from the Sapa Inca's justice. We are here to make sure he is not at this tampu!" From the tampu office emerged their officer, and my stomach dropped to see that it was Rumiñaui, my old friend whose childhood name had been Allallanka. His gave us the look that had earned him his adult moniker, Stone Eye. "This will be quickly done and you can then return to bed. I happen to know the fugitive on sight." There were some mutters of relief at that, for none of the sleepy guests wanted to be falsely accused.

Rumiñaui walked down the line of us, pausing at each to take a hard look at the groggy face, then examining the height and the ears. I watched and waited as he passed the men between us, and when he finally was before me all I could do was look into his eyes, the eyes of a falcon, remorseless and cruel. I could not tell what he was thinking. I shook my head. For two or three heartbeats he stood before me, then he went on to the next man.

At the end of the line he said, "I will interrogate five of you at random to see if you have seen any suspicious travelers. If you are not selected, go to bed." He pointed out four men and me. I stood in the courtyard, surrounded by a score of guards, as each of the others was brought into the tampu office and questioned. When it was my turn I took a seat on the stool provided for me, and Rumiñaui ordered his men to wait outside.

The tampu office had only a blanket for a door and generous windows, so he spoke in a low voice. "Haylli, you get one chance to tell me why I don't turn you in for the promotion that catching you will get me."

"I'm innocent; you know I'm innocent, and if you let me go I'll be able to prove it."

He leaned back on his stool, pushing the deep blue headband of the Socso Panaca up into his hair as he thought. His face was unreadable. He asked questions in a loud voice about my travel itinerary and what I may have noticed since leaving my village. He leaned forward again and whispered, "How can you prove it? You're an outlaw!"

"I can make any travel orders I want."

"That's why I'm supposed to catch you! With two balls of coloured yarn you could take anything out of any tampu in Tahuantinsuyu, Haylli! You could arm a whole tribe for an uprising. You could send mitmaks back to their homelands! Put in a set of golden earplugs and have the appropriate knots and you can do anything you want out here."

"All I'm doing is traveling, collecting evidence. If my father and I were traitors we would have put up a fight when we held the Intihuasi fortress on Sacsahuaman, right?"

He leaned back again, returning to his line of questioning about my conch shell purchasing errand. It was unnerving that his face held no expression. When he had finished his latest interrogation he whispered again, "So where are you going now?"

"Where should I go?" I asked, sensing a suggestion.

"You know Mamani, that Lupaca lord who confessed against you? He was executed, and they buried him in a stone tower not far from Tiahuanaco. If he gave false testimony against you there must have been a reason, something he was willing to die for."

I nodded. Puma knew enough for me to pressure Chalcuchima, but I would need hard facts about the conspiracy to pull a confession out of my schoolyard foe.

"You'll let me go?"

He looked me up and down, then nodded. "If your father was a traitor, he certainly would have picked a better assassin than Mamani. I was at the manhood ceremonies at Pacaritampu, Haylli. Mamani looked sick as a dog that got into the rat poison, and when he did lunge at the Sapa Inca he tried to knock over a guardsman twice his size, then he let go of his dagger on the first order to do so. It was like he wanted to fail, wanted to be caught alive."

He leaned back on the stool and said in a loud voice, "If you see anything suspicious, report it. We have patrols at your destination, and working up the next two side roads. Have a safe trip."

"Thank you, sir," I replied, then I went back to bed and somehow managed to sleep.

The journey into the Collao was no less arduous than the journey down to Tchili, but this time I did not feel adrift. Whenever the road in front of me was empty of curious eyes I ran, sometimes going past two or even three tampus in a day until the population density increased and I could no longer run without arousing suspicions.

The former kingdom of the Lupaca had held the southwestern shores of Lake Chucuito, and Rumiñaui's hint that Mamani's mausoleum was near Tiahuanaco was enough to narrow my search down to manageable levels. I changed my disguise and my travel documents every few days, and after half a month quartering the cold lake's coast I found the stone tower of Mamani's tomb, coincidentally enough during a ceremony in his honour.

His family was dressed in black, with the women covering their faces in soot and wailing their grief. Burly young men pried the stone blocks out of the doorway to the clan's tower. The inside was littered with bones, some ancient and some recent. The tower had been built before history began, and all the generations of this family since that time were interred within.

As the most recently dead, Mamani was given the dignity of a stretcher to keep his body intact for the series of celebrations following his death. The body, dehydrated by the cold and only slightly decomposed, was pulled from the tower and onto a low altar. Around his neck there was a rope to strangle his spirit if it tried to chase down any of his living relatives.

There was something wrong, though. I would not have noticed it were

200

it not for all the funerals I had before, but the hymns they sang to his memory were not sad. They were songs of gratitude. His family was thanking him for some great accomplishment. It did not strike me as the celebration of a man executed for failed regicide.

"Who was he?" I asked a group of the bereaved, as if I were just a curious bystander.

"He was the leader of our clan, the rightful curaca of the Lupaca," one of his wives wailed. I doubted her. The Inca usually kept the local rulers in place. The Lupaca were a mighty people who had warred with the Colla for total control of the Collao before we conquered them both. The sprawling royal family of the Lupacas must have had at least one line of pretenders, and I imagine Mamani's true claim to power was as the head of one of those families.

"How did he die?" I asked another wailing woman.

"Murdered, murdered by the Inca!"

"Damn them!" I consoled her. "For what?"

Between her sobs, which were for show so long after her husband's demise, she smiled at me. "Oh, that doesn't matter. What matters is that he tricked them. He tricked the Inca into doing right by us. He died for the family."

I felt a flush of excitement but limited myself to a sympathetic uncomprehending smile in return. "What do you mean? He's dead. How good a trick could it have been?"

She looked coy, pulling me closer to her. "He was dying anyway, and he sold his life to an Inca lord. In exchange my son was adopted into an Inca household. We will rule the Lupaca again someday."

"Which lord?" I asked too quickly. She looked at me sharply, suspecting now that I was more than a passing stranger. I was asking a lot of questions out of mere curiosity. Within moments I was flanked by the same hulking masons who had opened Mamani's tomb.

"Who are you?" She asked.

"I am Cusi Chala, a Chimu mitmak on his way to work at Tupiza," I said, naming a distant site of metal working.

"Let's see your pass!" One of the men grunted.

"Can you read it?" I asked, taking it out of my coca bag and handing it to them.

He looked at the threads for a while and nodded. "I can understand some of it. I was in the army that conquered the Kingdom of Chimor."

"You did a good job of it," I murmured. The masons chuckled. The quipu did identify me as Cusi Chala, and I did have my wooden earplugs in, but I doubt the man understood the significance of either of them.

"How many royal compounds are there in Chan Chan?" He asked, so he must have traveled to the Kingdom of Chimor at some point.

"Nine. One for each Great Chimu going all the way back to Taycanamo, the founder who came out of the sea. They won't let Minchancaman's son build a new one, though. He has to rule from the palace of Fempellec." He quizzed me a little further on a few rudimentary words in Mochica, mostly the crude words a soldier would use to find a woman, and when he was satisfied I knew more about the Chimu then he did he nodded to the widow I had questioned so tactlessly.

"Don't ask questions next time, or we will wall you up inside the tomb with Mamani," she threatened, turning back to the funeral anniversary. A woman was pouring a libation of akha into Mamani's open mouth and another was pulling a reluctant llama up to stand beside the litter.

I watched the preceding for some time before falling in beside the mason who had questioned me. We made polite small talk, for he had nothing to do until he had to replace the stone blocks, ending the ceremony. He knew nothing about Mamani's deal, or nothing he was willing to tell me, anyway. He wasn't even family.

He was from this clan's traditional opposite kin, and that launched him into a tirade against the Inca. Every puric has something negative to say about the people who keep him fed and clothed and safe and prosperous. People without education have no way of judging pros versus cons.

This mason also had a personal grudge, aside from politics. It is the Lupaca custom to arrange marriage between the rival clans, and he had been betrothed as a young man to a girl who grew to be so beautiful that the Inca village inspector had taken her away as a chosen woman. I expressed my sympathies, of course, but his next words made my interest genuine.

"By the gods, but Kiske Sisa was a beautiful girl."

My heart pounding, I took a moment to make sure my voice had not changed at the mention of my father's former fiancée. "Did she know Mamani?" I gestured to the open mausoleum.

He nodded his head with passion, attracting a few reprimanding looks from Mamani's bereaved. He spoke in a low voice after their censure, "I forgot to say, she was his daughter! I would have been marrying a Lupaca princess! I'd be running a quarry with those kinds of connections."

"What happened to her, do you know?"

"They sent her up to Cuzco, but it's recently come back down the chaski gossip network—" I smiled at this, for as a chaski I, too, had passed on almost as much unofficial news as official. "That she didn't become one of the chosen women who gets to marry. They've sent her to the House of Chosen Women on the Island of the Sun to learn to be a Bride of Inti. What a waste!"

He spat his disgust into the dust. He received a vicious glare from the Lupaca priest for his profanity, and the mason held out his callused palms in a gesture of apology. I drifted away from him, and when the funeral was done I resumed my journey north.

Kiske Sisa, my father's betrothed, was Mamani's daughter? That was too much of a coincidence to go unremarked; if Mamani really had been dying, his daughter might have known about that, might have told someone in power that she could obtain a reliable witness who would not mind dying to prove the veracity of his statements —given the right price. It did not sit right with me, though. Kiske Sisa was a quiet, nervous girl, not a cold-blooded conspirator. I had to talk to her, to see how she worked into this, if she worked into it at all.

I forged a requisition for priest's clothing, and by the time I arrived on the shores of Lake Chucuito I felt ready to pose as a special envoy of the Sapa Inca, charged with traveling to the convent on the Island of the Sun to interrogate Kiske Sisa on any knowledge she might have on the failed coup of Tocoyricoc Tupac Capac or the plans and whereabouts of his outlaw son Haylli Yupanki.

I had the red thread of the Emperor that would demand unquestioned obedience from the Mother Superior; I could tie up a royal quipu with an exhaustive explanation and authorization of my presence; I could wear my golden earplugs, and I was so intimately acquainted with all the details of the so-called failed coup that I could easily pass as an expert investigator on the subject.

As the sun set I bedded down in one of the largest tampus I had seen in all of Collasuyu. Here was an inn worthy of the Sapa Inca himself, for this is where he stayed while visiting the Island of the Sun. Such a busy place saw priests come and go every day, and I joined the other guests without incident. I was ready.

The next day I sacrificed a state-provided guinea pig to the success of my mission, blew a kiss to the rising sun, and ran my fingers down the bronze dagger in my coca bag. "Watch over me," I murmured. I bit my collar to ward off bad luck as I boarded the ferry.

Lake Chucuito —or Titicaca as you Spaniards have taken to calling it— is frigid. You can feel the cold even through the totora reed deck of the boat. I dipped my hand into the water and drank a mouthful, asking the lake's permission to cross. My bones ached at the chill of it, and I looked with new appreciation at the gnarled fingers of the local fishermen on the shore as they tied their fishing lures, made gaudy with geranium petals.

A gentle breeze filled our sail, and the ferryman punted us out of the shallows and onto the lake itself. I arrived on the Island of the Sun midmorning. I do not know the truth of it, but it is said this is where the Sun first emerged as Viracocha made the world, and where it last touched the Earth before vaulting into the heavens. I do know the sun-soaked rock was warm under my feet, and I drew courage from that.

The House of the Chosen Women dominated the shore, and I marched up to its single gate with all the confidence and swagger I could muster, very much aware that I was being judged with every step I took by the guards at the entrance.

"Please inform the Mother Superior that Topa Maila, special envoy to the Emperor Topa Inca Yupanki, wishes to speak with her," I said. The soldier did not look at me. Guarding a House of Chosen Women was not a post for conscripts: This man was a professional, with a professional's discipline.

I produced the Sapa Inca's red thread from my coca bag and dangled it before the guard's face with an air of confidence mixed with impudence. If the Emperor had sent me, no mere guard would ignore me. I watched as his eyes crossed to focus on the colour of the thread. He still did not look at me, but spoke. "We have had no warning."

"My mission wouldn't be helped by an advanced warning."

"And what is your mission..." The man finally deigned to look at me. "Sir?"

"The Sapa Inca's instructions to me are not your concern. My instructions to you are."

"I am only doing my duty, sir." The sir came faster this time.

"Your duty is to obey the orders of a man bearing the red thread of Topa Inca Yupanki." The man lifted his halberd in salute, nodded to the guard to his left, and disappeared inside. I did not have to wait long before a slip of a girl opened the door and waved me in.

The anteroom I entered was open to the sky; the flagstones were the lead colour of the cliffs around the lake. The walls were of a pale stone that had been further scrubbed and painted with lime to become a dazzling white. The young girl disappeared without gesturing for me to follow her, and I was left standing there, careful not to appear uncertain. At last my isolation was ended by the arrival of a woman who could only be the mother superior.

In her day she must have been the sort of beauty who stopped a man's heart. She had long white hair, undistorted by any wave or wisp. Her limbs were clean and delicately proportioned, and her every move spoke of an unconscious grace. Her clothes were as fine as anything the Emperor would wear. Her face was high-cheeked, straight-nosed, generously lipped, and wrinkled in all the right places.

"Good day to you," she bobbed her head for a moment in an acknowledgement of my presence that was polite enough for any lord but unpretentious enough to have been given to a peasant. This woman was the ruler of her little world; she knew I had no real power, even if I was from the Sapa Inca.

"And to you, Mother Superior." I dipped my head too, but found I could not help but make the bow deeper than her own had been. She nodded once to herself, as if I had confirmed the natural order of things.

"You come from my brother?" She asked. I did not know whether the Emperor was her actual brother, or if the Mother Superior of this influential convent was always considered the Emperor's sister, or whether, as a bride of the Sun, she considered herself family to the Son of the Sun. A priest and a special envoy would have known these things; I did not, so I faked it.

"I am here on the orders of the Sapa Inca," I said in a tone that could have been either a confirmation or a mild disagreement of her statement.

She arched one thin and elegant eyebrow. "And your orders?"

"I am here to interrogate a young chosen woman in your keep, Kiske Sisa, to learn anything she has to add to our knowledge of the attempted coup of Tupac Capac and the whereabouts of his fugitive son, Haylli Yupanki." I stood there for a long while, waiting for her to speak. She remained motionless. At last she shook her head.

"I have specific orders involving that woman, Topa Maila, and one of them is that she speak to no official."

That surprised me. Who would have issued such an order? I produced my red thread. "You would disobey Topa Inca Yupanki?"

"I am not a door guard to be dazzled by a bauble. I accept your authority to question the girl; I am merely curious why a viceroy would order her to speak to no one while the Emperor sends an interrogator. Is there intrigue in Cuzco these days?"

"Isn't there always?" I gave a ghost of a smile, hoping I was playing the convincing court insider.

"I suppose so." She turned so gracefully that her back was towards me before I could bring my eyes away from the shifting folds of her clothing. I followed her through a maze of passages, courtyards, and buildings, finally arriving at a large high-walled square with reflective pools and benches spaced evenly from one end to the other.

"Of course you will want privacy, and of course you must be supervised. I have no deaf attendants to chaperone you, so I trust this plaza will afford you the freedom you need to question the girl?" She made it sound like a question, but I knew there was no possibility of getting Kiske Sisa into a room alone.

"Of course," I agreed, putting the best face on things.

The Mother Superior walked out of the courtyard, her business with me concluded. I went over to one of the pools and looked down to see lake fish swimming by my toes. I did not see or hear Kiske Sisa's approach, only the clearing of her throat as she announced her presence.

I had worried about this moment: Kiske Sisa knew me, or at least she had known me. I had met her at least ten times as a boy when my father visited her. If she called out my name in recognition now I was surrounded by trained soldiers in a fortress on an island in the middle of a lake so cold I would not be able to swim fifty paces, let alone to the mainland. My freedom depended on her reaction.

I turned to her, my face solemn, and she did not recognize me. The years between boy and man had made a stranger of me. She was as beautiful as the first day I saw her at the Coricancha, still with that air of fragility that so enhanced her. She looked like a strong breeze would blow her over, and her huge and luminous eyes still beseeched protection, begging you to wrap your arms around her and keep her safe from the storm. I almost hugged her; instead I said, "You are Kiske Sisa, formerly betrothed to the dead renegade Tupac Capac?" She said she was. "I am here on behalf—"

"Is it time?" She interrupted me. Her tone was frustrated and impatient, perhaps even angry.

I remained silent for a moment, trying to think what she could mean. I had never heard her speak like this before. At last I decided there was no way I could learn more without playing along. "The time is drawing near."

She shuddered with anticipation. "So you are actually here on behalf of our mutual master?" She toyed with the hem of her shawl, not looking at my face. Who was her master, now that she was a Bride of Inti? The Sapa Inca?

"I am," I said, feeling the ground drop out from under me in this conversation. Kiske Sisa had always been so quiet, so timid, and for the first time I suspected there was something dark behind her pretty face.

"He gave me a test, a test to make sure that the man he sent to me was the right one. Did he..." She hesitated, still not looking at my face, "Did he tell you of the test?"

My stomach lurched, for I most certainly did not know the test. "Of course I know," I said.

"I am to ask you about the stone at the top of his staff of office." In my mind I saw a hundred nobles with staffs of office and dropped away all who had no such decoration. There were still too many to guess, but it was not the Sapa Inca. "Do you know the stone?"

Something in her husky voice gave me the clue. "It is not really a stone," I said, sure that if it was really a stone I could say I was speaking of its huaca-like property.

"Yes, exactly," she said in a rush. "Not a stone at first, but god-made. He was given it on his naming day, and on that day he named the new-found stone too. What did he name it?"

She had never impressed me with her intelligence as a boy, and her question did nothing to change my opinion. If you are administering a test you do not give hints, Friar, but she was so overcome with the thought of being on the inside of a secret that she delighted in giving me a glimpse at what she held. I could think of only one stone that was god-made and named on the day that its owner became a man.

"It is called Kakakacay, Thunder, for it is the glass formed from vaporized beach sand where a thunderbolt touched the ground." At last she looked up at my face and I saw not one flicker of recognition, only fevered desire.

"When will my lord come for me?" She asked.

My mind rebelled at the question. She was in here for life. She was a permanent Bride of the Inti, no mere Chosen Woman being held in a convent until the Emperor could give her as a gift to some worthy noble. She had been promised to my father, and now she was tainted by his treason just as I was. Why would anyone come for her, let alone Viceroy Illyapa, ruler of Collasuyu?

"The time is not yet here. I have come to let you know he has not forgotten his promises."

She shuddered with what looked very much like ecstasy, and I suppose it was only her lack of attention that kept her from seeing the dismay that must have played across my features. Her movement was sexual; I could read the word 'delicious' in the tremor. What was going on here?

"Tell him I cannot bear it here." She gripped my arm, her nails digging into me, her big eyes looking into my own for the first time. "This wasn't the plan! I'm not supposed to be here at all, and then he told me it would only be for a little while. This place is horrible!"

"Tell me everything," I said, hoping she would tell me more about the plan. She disappointed me.

"The sisters and Mother Superior watch me like hawks. I cannot move without their eyes upon me. It has been two years since I have known a man..." Her look became sly, and my flesh crawled at the starving desire I saw on her features. Beautiful or not, I had become a piece of meat dangled before a starving person. "Is there no way that you could take your master's place for a day? I promise he will never find out."

I removed my arm with great dignity. "That is quite impossible." Her desire masked my feelings from her. What did this mean? Kiske Sisa and Viceroy Illyapa? How had this happened?

"Tell me his new plan," she demanded, stamping her small foot. If she felt snubbed I could not sense it.

I saw my opening, "His plan cannot come into being until the capture and execution of Haylli Yupanki—"

I was stunned as she spat upon the flagstones. I looked at the gobbet of spit by my foot, overcome with the urge to backhand this woman. She did not notice. She was too busy hissing at me. "He's had two years to find that boy. Two years! He must be dead. Must be! Fell down a canyon or slipped on some ice or eaten by a puma. I pray every night that his corpse will wash up on a river bank somewhere, so that I can be free of this place."

She ran her hands down her body, pulling her gown tight against her small breasts so that for a moment her nipples stood high and proud, pointing right at my own despite the great difference in our heights. "I want to go back to the real world, where I can enjoy life as a woman, and not as a sexless lump of clay! You tell your master the boy of my dead fiancé should not stand in the way of our happiness."

"He asks me if you know where he might have gone—"

"I told your master two years ago to kill him when he went to the Great Quipu Repository, and he botched that! I have been shut in here for two years, and now he expects me to be able to help him?" She was shrieking at me in a whisper, shaking with fury. I felt it was only the hidden eyes upon us, staring out from the dark doorways surrounding the courtyard that kept her from having a screaming fit. "Just find the boy and kill him. He is the last obstacle, is he not?"

"What else could there be?" I asked rhetorically. She did not take it that way.

"Mama Ocllo, of course! By the gods you are dense! It's her fault I'm here. Tupac Capac was her fault too, with his boring quipus and boring morals. Wouldn't lay a finger on me. Not one finger." I was very glad to hear it. My flesh crawled at the thought of my father touching this witch in the guise of a helpless waif.

"How should our master deal with her?" I asked.

"I am not the second-most powerful man in the world. He is. Let him figure it out, but tell him to get me out of here! I cannot stand it." She began to weep, but I made no move to touch her. My desire to protect her was gone.

"I will tell him," I told the crying Bride of Inti. I turned on my heel and walked out of the courtyard. The idea of speaking to her any further made me want to vomit, and I knew if I stayed longer it would only be a matter of time before my self-control was lost. By the end of the day I was back on the mainland.

I had talked to Kiske Sisa, but I still did not know just how it all came together. I could not go to Chalcuchima with the few strands of the plot I had so far: He would twist them and turn them and I would never untangle the truth from the lies he wove. I needed to find out what connected Mama Ocllo, Viceroy Illyapa, Kiske Sisa, and my father. I would have to go into the puma's den. I would follow the royal road all the way to Cuzco.

* * *

Good morning, Friar. I am sorry to have kept you. It seems your conquistadores are trying to find us here in the hacha hacha. I have just dispatched two legions of jungle archers into the high passes to make things difficult for them. Where did we leave off? Ah, yes, thank you.

I made it to the Cuzco valley using half a dozen false identities, but I did not feel confident passing for a stranger in the city itself. Instead, I knocked my sandaled foot on the door of Huaman Paullu's country villa, hoping his doorman was smart enough to recognize me but stupid enough to forget I was an Imperial fugitive. He opened the door a crack but did not recognize me.

"State your business," he said.

"I have a problem quipu from the repository. I know it's after hours, but the boys are stumped," I said, hoping Huaman Paullu still worked at the Great Quipu Repository. Topa Inca Yupanki had spared him in the purge because of his education; surely that meant he had allowed him to continue working?

"It's late. The master is in his counting room, though. I'll—"

"Just let me in, Zope," I said, using the man's childhood name. When the doorman blinked in surprise I pushed the door into his face. My father's lancehead was at his throat in moments. "I'm an old friend of Huaman Paullu; he'll want to see me."

I was up into the counting room before the doorman could decide what to do, and the sound of his master's greeting finally sent him back to his post at the door.

"Where have you been?" Huaman Paullu said, gesturing for me to sit on a stool while pouring me a beaker of akha.

"I've been in the Collao and beyond, Huaman Paullu. I've done well, but I need more to clear my father's name."

A shadow passed over Huaman Paullu's face. "What can I do to help?"

"Get me into the Great Quipu Repository."

"For how long? Everyone knows you in there, Haylli, and there are a lot of the young ones with an eye to the future who would turn you in."

"They'd betray my father's memory?" I asked, surprised.

"The purge went deep, Haylli. Most of the ones loyal enough to keep the rest in line are dead or yanacona. I have a tough time getting the junior quipucamayocs to do their job, because I share Tupac Capac's disgrace."

"He didn't do it, Huaman Paullu."

"Of course he didn't, but at this point you can't make things as they were. It's become Imperial history that your father led a rebellion and the Emperor put it down."

My heart sank a little to know that the royal bards would have been given an official lay to sing; that news of my father's treachery was being sung on holidays throughout Tahuantinsuyu. Even total vindication would never remove the stain from his name.

"I don't care," I lied. "It will be enough to bring the real traitor to justice."

"Who is the real traitor? Why did he do it?"

"It has something to do with Chalcuchima, Viceroy Illyapa, Mama Ocllo, and Kiske Sisa. Other than that, I need time in the archives."

Huaman Paullu bit his lower lip for a moment in indecision, finally nodding his head. "For your father I will help you, but if you are caught—"

"Don't even ask, sir. Of course I got in on my own."

He nodded, relieved. Huaman Paullu had always been a little too timid. It was why he was such a good secretary and such a poor choice for tocoyricoc. I would protect him, if it came to it. My father would have wanted that.

We went to the Great Quipu Repository the next morning. I was dressed as a simple puric carrying jars of quipus. Huaman Paullu left me

211

to put each pot in its place, and as the sun rose higher, one by one, he moved the quipucamayocs around me out of the archives on separate tasks and chores until I was quite alone.

I went over the Imperial decrees and figures concerning military and mitmak allocations for Collasuyu. I found very little of use. It was only as I went into the chosen women census data that I realized all the knots I had been reading were tied by the same hand.

I know it sounds silly to you, Friar, for surely a knot is a knot, but when you have a complex system like the royal quipus and the ledger quipus, patterns of personal preference emerge. Some quipucamayocs pull some knots tighter than others, or leave more space or use extra thread while they work. From midmorning to mid-afternoon I had examining documents all tied down by a single official.

"Huaman Paullu?" I called. He appeared so quickly I knew he had been standing nervously nearby all day. "These are all done by the same quipucamayoc. Who?"

There were no signatures, and I had not been in the Great Quipu Repository in the years that the quipus were recorded. Huaman Paullu had, and with some concentration he came up with it. "Mama Ocllo's secretary."

The order sending Kiske Sisa to the Island of the Sun was tied down by Mama Ocllo's secretary. So was most of Collasuyu's high-level clerical work.

"Has he been made a tocoyricoc or a governor?"

"No."

"Then why is Viceroy Illyapa letting Mama Ocllo—" I stopped.

"What?" Huaman Paullu asked.

"I've got enough to go to Chalcuchima," I said. "Where can I find him?"

Chalcuchima had done well for himself during my time in Tchili, becoming commander of a legion supervising the looting of Chan Chan, the former capital of the Kingdom of Chimor. Conquered when I was still called Wawa, the city was still being stripped of art, treasures, and the artisans to produce future spoils.

The whole descent from the eastern mountains to the coast I was passing llama caravans going the other way, all taking riches to the highlands: Conch shells destined to be trumpets for officers and chaskis, as well as cheap ceramic copies of the conch shells worked by master Chimu potters for use in lower positions; the red and white mullu shells, so prized for jewelry that the Chimu were paid for them in precious coca; cotton bales, destined for highland looms; bags of chilies and spices to flavour a million mountain stews; sardine heads to fertilize puna fields.

The Yungas were rich beyond imagining, but that is why it was inevitable that the mountain men would conquer them: Such riches made people soft, decadent, sinful. I have lived as a lord and as a commoner, as an implement of Imperial justice and as a fugitive, but I have never thought myself decadent. The Yungas were decadent.

The people in the Hot Lands practiced every sexual exploit, reveling in things like sodomy and multiple partners, even replicating such acts in their pottery. I remember stopping at one tampu where akha was being served out of a jug whose top was decorated by a sculpture of a man riding a little girl as she slept between her two parents. I asked for an Inca amphora.

What goes on between a man and a woman is their own business, but the Chimu enjoy much more than is normal or healthy for people. They have cults to homosexuality, bestiality, and incest. Quite aside from offending me as a man, such things offend me as a tocoyricoc, for how many new taxpayers were ever produced by four men sharing a ten-year-old girl?

The Inca outlawed it all, of course, but it was so rampant we could not punish everyone, and so we could not eradicate it. We had to turn a blind eye. As for me, I was always careful to rebuff any friendly advances and to sleep quite separate and alone in the tampus. I escaped their infection, but I can still think back to some of the things I heard in the night and shudder.

I digress, and I am sorry, Friar. Perhaps I am just an old man who wants to shake his head and cluck his tongue at a people with morals looser than the warp and weft of a fishnet, or perhaps I just remember my horror at realizing I had been impersonating a Chimu all that time on the run without any real understanding of what image the well-traveled man would have about me based on that claim.

For all their excesses, the Kingdom of Chimor had been rich, though, fabulously rich. Down there in the coastal desert they had controlled all the river valleys between the oracle of Pachacamac and the city of

213

Tumpez. They channeled the rivers into aqueducts and canals, turning the desert into a garden that could get three or four harvests a year on most crops, and two a year for maize.

They had an inexhaustible supply of salt and cotton, and their coastal llamas, while not as vigorous as our mountain ones, were still capable of doing their transportation and providing them with greasy wool for sackcloth and rope. They could even graze their llamas out in the desert whenever the sea fogs made that practical, leaving them still more arable land for more crops.

All this bounty made them richer by far than the Inca: They had traded in gold and silver and tin and copper, emeralds, turquoise and conch shells and tropical birds, alpaca wool and chuno, all at advantageous rates to them. They gave military protection to the mountain tribes on the heights above them, which secured their water supply, and they built fortresses and long walls in the deserts to hold their coastal flanks secure.

Our war to beat them was a long and hard one, and when it was over we forbade them arms, a third of Tahuantinsuyu's population unable to provide for the state militia for fear of how difficult it would be to put down a revolt. Meanwhile, their land was so rich that all this time later they were still being looted, aside from their standard tax service.

Once into the former Kingdom of Chimor itself I put the gold discs of an Inca into my ears. My clothes were not sumptuous, and I did not walk with the degree of arrogance necessary to confirm I held office. I went unquestioned, and when I arrived in Chan Chan itself I was directed to a palace my schoolyard rival had requisitioned for himself.

I should stop and say that it was unavoidable to live in a palace in Chan Chan: That was all there was. Where Cuzco was hemmed in by the gulleys to either side, Chan Chan sprawled across a plain so that everything was built bigger and broader. There were palaces that could have fit Cuzco's Huacaypata inside of them. Purics did not live outside the city, as they did in Cuzco. The Chimu purics had their own wings within the palaces, villages within palaces within cities.

And the palaces had an exotic and opulent style, too. Even a panaca compound in Royal Cuzco, when viewed from the outside, was a building of somber stone and neat thatch. In Chan Chan every wall was a riot of painted colour, and the roofs —which would never see a drop of rain— were of stretched cotton to provide shade, so that at night every lit room made the canopy above glow in beautiful soft tones, like moonlight reflected in a thousand ponds. Chan Chan was so opulent that it was unavoidable that Chalcuchima would have a palace while staying there.

I did not want to be recognized by anyone, and so I went straight into the private quarters, eventually finding the one set aside for Chalcuchima himself. I waited in his suite with my bronze dagger on my lap, confident I would not need it. I had rehearsed my argument to him during my trip to Chan Chan, and now I waited in the dark for him to enter, which he did with the changing of the night guard.

He was even taller than I remembered, even more muscular, and I watched his dark form light the torches in their wall sconces before turning to see me sitting in the far corner on my stool. His composure impressed me. If our places were reversed I would have been a shaking mess of blubbering nerves to discover a man with such good reason to kill me in my dark room with a blade.

"Hello, Waccha," he said, taking his last torch and putting it in the sconce next to his sleeping pallet.

"Hello Mallku," I said. "Have you missed me?"

"With every search party so far, Waccha. We all assumed you had fled into the Collao, but I used to train my new conscripts by having them do manhunts for you. Have you just arrived, or did we fail to find you?"

"I've just arrived."

He grabbed another stool and sat across from me. "From where?"

"From Tchili, and the Island of the Sun, and Cuzco. I know how it happened. I know you were involved in more than you thought you were. I may even know more than you do. Here's what I'm willing—"

"Why don't I summon the night watch?" He asked me.

"Because at this point I can prove that I am an innocent man, and that my father was too, and I have the luxury of deciding whether the Sapa Inca needs to order your death." I watched him chew the inside of his cheek, thinking. His lipless mouth pursed.

"If you had all the facts you would not need me, and you would not have come all this way just to spare me," he decided at last.

"I know who did it, and I have witnesses and records that will attest to it. What I want is the confirmation of the motivation. I will trade your testimony for your life—"

215

"You know I've married the Vixen, don't you?" He tilted his head towards his pallet, though of course as a legion commander on his first active duty he had left his wife in Cuzco. I smiled for the first time now, amazed that his barbed arrow, which would have been so well chosen before I met Koonek, now flew so wide of the mark.

"Congratulations. I've married too, and we're expecting our first shortly."

A cloud passed over his face at this news, but he resumed his composed façade. "You have been busy down there in Tchili..."

"It's a big area, Mallku. Get the idea of investigating all the pregnant women out of your head." We laughed together without humour. "I know Mamani provided false testimony to elevate his son into the upper Inca nobility. I know about Kiske Sisa and Viceroy Illyapa. I know about the chaski with the vicuna cumpi cloak you had untie the knots. I have the entire plot." In fact I had little more than the names, but that's not what I wanted Chalcuchima to believe.

"My sister married Titu Cusi Huallpa, as well. I'm going to be the brother-in-law of an Emperor. Did you know that?" I did not reply, and so he stopped trying to divert me. "Well, it seems as if you have quite a lot already, Waccha. Where do you need me again?"

"I don't want to see the Vixen as a widow."

"Well, I thank you for your misplaced concern. I know my wife would miss me a great deal more than she missed you: We were betrothed within days of you running out of Cuzco like a whipped dog. She didn't give you much of a mourning period at all. Still, I don't need to worry about it either way. I think your wife will wind up being the widow, and with a baby to take care of too."

"Let's put the pleasantries to one side, Mallku, and speak as men do: Your uncle Illyapa was the head of your family. You could not refuse him. The Emperor will see that. Something you don't know is that this plot was forced upon him by Mama Ocllo." I could see by the small twitch of his thin-lipped mouth that he had known something about that, a good deal more than I did, probably. My gamble was paying off. "Now tell me why he ordered you to take the weapons."

"Well, Waccha, if we are speaking as men do, he told me that we were trying to disgrace your father, have him drop down in the bureaucracy. I did not know that Tupac Capac would be charged with treason. I am sorry."

216

"I don't want an apology. I want justice."

He leaned back on his stool, his hands on his knees, thinking. He sat there for a long time, the torch light throwing strange shadows across his condor face. With a final twitch of his neck, he decided. "I did not know it then, but I have figured it out since, you understand?"

"Yes."

"And when you go before the Emperor you will ask for him to spare me the death sentence?"

"You didn't do anything worthy of execution. The Hiwaya, yes, but I will ask for an amnesty for you."

"Your oath on it?"

"By Inti, Viracocha, and my father's memory."

"My family was used by the Coya almost as badly as yours, Waccha," he said. I could have pointed out that my family had shrunk considerably since this whole sorry episode began, but I held my peace as my old foe worked up his nerve.

Chalcuchima breathed out through his mouth for a long time, the muscles in his neck gradually unbunching, then he nodded. "Alright, grab some string and take down my confession."

Yes, Friar, he told me everything he knew about the conspiracy against my father and its aftermath, holding nothing back. There are many things I could call Chalcuchima, but he was never a liar. I think also that he wanted to tell it. He was like a man drunk on viñapu who would feel better after throwing up than he ever would by keeping it down. He confessed in full, and I tied it all down and read it back to him until we were both satisfied, much as you and I are doing now.

When we were done and I had what I needed I leaned back on my stool in relief, amazed at how much I had gained in this interview. My father would be vindicated by the strings in my two hands. I could feel it.

Getting back to Cuzco, though, would not be easy, for I had no sooner finished my work and begun to relax when he asked me, "So how exactly were you planning on escaping?"

I looked up at him, Friar, and I admitted I had not given it any serious thought yet.

"Well, correct me if I'm wrong, you're still a fugitive, which means I don't get into any trouble at all if my people catch you and kill you before that royal quipu in your hand comes to Court. Am I wrong?"

"You're not wrong..."

"Well, you have a dagger and I don't, so I suppose I can let you out of the room." Never turning my back on him I left his chamber, then I broke into a jog to open as much distance between us as I could. It was just as well, for before I was even down the corridor I heard a conch trumpet summoning the palace guards to a full alert. I barked a couple of orders at some of the sleepier looking conscripts and tried to look like I was on urgent business. I was challenged at the gates to the palace compound, but I only waved my royal quipu, as if it explained everything, and the illiterate guards let me pass.

As soon as I was out of their sight I began to run again, and I was out of Chan Chan before the chaski huts lit their warning fires, sending word up and down the network that something ominous had happened. Every soldier between Cuzco and Chan Chan would now stand ready, waiting for the explaining quipu, and I had no way to stay ahead of the alert. I turned south, into my father's old stomping grounds of Condesuyu. I did not have the spare breath to curse, nor the spare saliva to spit.

Of course Chalcuchima would hedge his bets by trying to capture me, and he was smart enough to know I would change my identity. I could not stay in any tampu, nor use the roads after dark when the traffic became conspicuous. As I left the former Kingdom of Chimor I entered areas familiar to me, and I was able to run across the desert at night, snatching sleep between the dunes until the sun came out to burn every inch of exposed skin. Many times I woke to see the condors circling above me, sure that I had become lost and was about to die.

I went south for days and days, passing the great wall running east to west through the desert that the Chimu's subjugated peoples had built to hold off the Inca assaults, never thinking that my grandfather would do an end run from the North while Topa Yupanki held the heights.

Only when I was quite sure Chalcuchima's authority could never stir up the garrisons so far from Chan Chan did I enter a lonely tampu on a spur of the Royal Coast Road with an improbable story about being a hydrological surveyor inspecting the route for a potential irrigation canal right through the heart of the desert.

The tampucamayoc dared to look suspicious, so I showed him my impressively credentials —all in string, of course— and demanded he draw me a bath. My Imperial bearing drove him to obedience, and I spent a day and a night recovering in that carefully chosen tampu, so isolated that it received no other visitors during my stay. The chaskis dutifully passed on messages from Chan Chan, but there was no garrison here to receive military orders. On the morning of the second day I ordered the tampu to provide me with a water skin, a three legged cooking pot, and a bag of chuno, then I set off back into the desert, heading east this time, east towards Cuzco.

The deserts of the coast give way to foothills, still barren but at least not featureless, then to rising hills, then to true mountains, thickly forested and craggy. When I was ten days out of the tampu with no signs of pursuit I abandoned my roadless wanderings, popped in a couple of wooden earplugs, and joined one of the ubiquitous llama caravans as it negotiated the high mountain passes.

The pass guards were vigilant, inspecting the face of each man, but though I had a proud bearing and a large nose those were not exactly rare. I think they were more looking for a solitary man, perhaps one with a bag full of knotted strings. I was a simple Chimu llama herder, moving with a group who were happy to have an experienced drover like myself lending a hand; my quipus were in my breechcloth for safe keeping. The soldiers did not have the time or the inclination to strip search every man on the road, and nothing less would have revealed my identity from the multitude.

Up and up and over the snowy mountain passes I went, marveling as I always did at the way our smiths harnessed the high winds up there to feed the blast ovens extracting gold and copper from ores. It was hard work bringing the fuel and stone up to these heights, but the winds could whip the fire up to a heat unobtainable below, making the mountain men the best smelters in the world.

I descended from the rock and snow down into the green highlands of the Huanca, whose capital of Xauxa was the destination of my caravan. I found some small pleasure among the other caravaners, passing the time joking about every dog we saw: The Huanca have an unnatural fascination with their dogs, eating their meat and making their trumpets out of dog skulls. We speculated on the future of every mutt and mongrel we passed on the road.

When the caravan unloaded I slipped out of the city's tampu that night and traveled further east, up and over the eastern mountain passes with my golden earplugs in my lobes. Here, now, I was traveling through lands intimately familiar with my father and myself, but despite the purges among my father's loyal subjects no one turned me in, and many men who had been reduced to yanaconas actually took me into their now simple homes to save me the trouble of making up some official business to sleep in a tampu. The reward on my head must have been a considerable temptation for them, but I slept soundly and awoke each morning to a bowl of stew and a beaker of akha, the best available to these unnobled nobles. They were good men and women, all.

The closer I got to Cuzco, the more troubled my thoughts became. Up until now I was safe in my anonymity, or being helped by contacts that had fallen under the same misfortune as me. How was I to enter Royal Cuzco itself? With the alert Chalcuchima had put out the already guarded roads would be on the lookout for almost anyone approaching Cuzco on a thin pretext, especially with earplugs of any kind. What's worse, I would be interrogated by bureaucrats who could read quipus as well as I, robbing me of my greatest tool as a fugitive. I needed a pretense so solid it would be unquestioned.

Only two days journey out from Cuzco I crossed the Apurimac River on a great swinging suspension bridge. As a lover of knots I have always been fascinated by these complicated constructions of rope, and I looked with admiration at the fresh lashings holding this one together. When I was across I complimented the Cuzco-side bridge keeper on the good state of repair, and he took the praise to heart, extolling to me how his tribe paid their taxes exclusively in bridge work, repair, maintenance, and supervision. As he spoke I saw the answer to my problem.

"I'm a labour service investigator," I said. "I have been dispatched by Crown Prince Titu Cusi Huallpa to find exemplary work like this for a study we're conducting. I want four of your experts prepared to travel with me to Cuzco tomorrow." The heir had sent my father and I on an errand like that once, and I presumed he still had the interest.

The man fell all over himself at the honour of his tribe's contribution to Tahuantinsuyu being brought to the attention of the future Sapa Inca, and the next day I left with four bridge experts and a perfect excuse to travel as far into Cuzco as I needed to go.

We were interrogated six times on the road, but each time my quipus proved I was who I said I was, and I had four excited men to swear up and down as to our mission. At last we crested the final ridge and saw all Cuzco stretched out below us. Two of the bridge builders had never seen it before, and they were both silent and solemn at the beauty and power of it.

I led them down the Condesuyu road, past the Great Quipu Repository, past Huaman Paullu's villa, through the suburbs and past the guard stations, until finally we reached a tampu for commoners from the western quarter of Tahuantinsuyu to stay in. "Remain here until I send for you. It will take some time to make the appointment," I said.

Originally I had planned to abandon them as I had all my other subterfuges, but they were so obviously moved at the thought of their work being recognized that I decided after my vindication that they would get their Imperial audience.

"Here is a quipu authorizing you to draw rations from this tampu for up to two months. I don't expect it to take that long, but I have other duties to attend to, and I may not see you for some time." They nodded their heads, convinced that I must be a busy man. When I was sure they

221

were settled in I walked into Royal Cuzco for the first time in what felt like a lifetime.

The streets seemed narrower, the walls more solid, the crowds more silent. With every step my feet seemed to tingle with the holiness of the place and my ears burned with embarrassment at being in the city under false pretenses.

I was also disappointed that no one looked at me twice. Had I been away so long, grown so unfamiliar? Had anyone even missed me? I had won the manhood footrace for my year; that should have made me a lifelong celebrity no matter who my father was or what I did later in life. Being an Imperial fugitive wasn't enough excitement for them? Well, things were about to get more exciting.

I walked across the white sands of the Huacaypata and up to the door of the Sapa Inca Topa Inca Yupanki's city palace. I had walked the length of Tahuantinsuyu in the pursuit of justice, and I felt dizzy at the thought that it all ended here, just a short walk from my old home. I drew myself up to my full height and demanded an audience with the Emperor. The suspicious look the guard gave me would have made me quail if self-composure wasn't all-important to my survival. In all my time on the run no guard had ever given me such close scrutiny. I saw him take in my golden earplugs, my presentable but clearly worn clothes, even perhaps my dirty feet.

At last he grunted a question, "Been away long?"

I looked at him with equal scrutiny, but he was a stranger to me, one of the new Cañari soldiers the heir was slowly putting into the Imperial Guard. "Yes, why?"

"I'm curious, sir, how a man with the authority to request an Imperial audience doesn't know the Emperor is in the Yucay Valley."

That was indeed a problem. Surely were I any kind of official I would have known of the Emperor's current location through the chaski network. "I've come down from the mountains. I was on an errand, and I haven't been keeping up with the posts. I—" But the guardsmen reached out and seized me by the collar, dragging me off the street and into the foyer as if I weighed nothing. Two guardsmen waited within, their maces raised and ready to smite me.

"You are Haylli Yupanki!" He barked at me, and the sound of my own name after so long made me flinch. He nodded to one of his compatriots, who stepped forward.

222

"On your lives, I have information of a plot against the Emperor! If he's out of Cuzco you will take me to whoever he left in charge of the capital!" The mace-wielder froze. He was another Cañari, and I knew he was cursing the ignorance of his people, new as they were to court politics. I started babbling names, Hualpaya, Illyapa, Kiske Sisa, Mamani, Mama Ocllo, Chalcuchima, and I could see the guardsmen wavering around me. "If not the Emperor, then the heir, take me to the heir!" I ordered.

They frisked me and found my dagger, which they confiscated. "You be careful with that. Don't lose it. It's a huaca." My audacity seemed to impress them. I'm sure most guardsmen are used to their prisoners begging for their lives, not giving orders. Never the less, the hand on my collar never slackened as I was physically dragged through the halls, an impressive feat of strength considering my size.

I was shoved down onto my knees in the presence of a man wearing the yellow fringe. It was Titu Cusi Huallpa, the baby-faced crown prince with the hard eyes. He set down his quipu and frowned at me. No one spoke. I just looked at that youthful face taking me in but not placing me.

"I know you," he said at last. "How do I know you?"

The guardsman opened his mouth, but I beat him to it. "My name is Haylli Yupanki. I am the son of the Tocoyricoc Tupac Capac. I was proven innocent through a trial by ordeal in the Sankihuasi. I have been investigating a conspiracy for the last—"

"I remember you now!" He boomed. "How dare you run all over Tahuantinsuyu under false pretenses! Do you know how upset you've made my mother? Haylli this! Haylli that! It's been years now of her ranting about your gross irresponsibility! What in Supay's name did you think you were doing?"

I held my peace about Coya Mama Ocllo, for I knew the Crown Prince had always had a special place in his heart for his mother. "I have proof of the plot that set my family up on false treason charges. I fled assassins myself, which is why I could not conduct my investigation officially."

He paced across the room in three powerful strides and hauled me up, looking me in the eye with the appraising stare of a woman inspecting a cracked pot, deciding if she can still use it.

"The plot was against you and your father?" He said, his voice a low rumble.

"My father was going to find out something that would result in death sentences for the conspirators."

He grunted, letting me go and pacing back to his quipu. He picked it up and ran the knots between his fingers, frowning harder. He ran the knots through his fingers again and again. I watched the knots move. He was struggling over a difficult series.

"Earthquake, Sire. An earthquake triggered a landslide blocking the pass. It's being cleared out, but the work will take months. It says the alternative route will take fifteen extra days at the least, Sire. What do you need all those Kallawaya remedy keepers for?"

He looked up sharply, furrowing his brows and scowling so ferociously he no longer looked youthful. "My father is dying."

For anyone else to have said it would have been treason, but that was the burden of being the heir, admitting that the Sapa Inca would one day die.

"Surely he has half a legion of Kallawayas already, my lord?" I asked, respectfully lowering my eyes.

"And none of them can cure him. I sent for thirty more, the thirty who have been keeping Chiaquitinta alive." I nodded my understanding. The governor of Upper Tumipampa was well over ninety. Old Topa wasn't dying of a disease, he was just old. There was no cure for old age.

"Titu Cusi Huallpa—"

"They call me Huayna Capac, now," he corrected me. I nodded my understanding. His contemporaries had always called him Young Lord as a nickname, and now that the day of his giving up the yellow fringe for the red one was coming people were making the nickname the title of their next Sapa Inca. Silence stretched between us. "You could read those knots from across the room?" He asked at last.

"Pachacuti was a difficult one to figure without the context, but I could see the knots for mountain pass, which meant it had to be a landslide. The rest was simple." I shrugged; my father would have been able to read the knots just by the way the prince's fingertips moved over them, so I saw nothing amazing in my performance. The man looked impressed at my own small ability, however.

"My father has retired to the Yucay Valley to rest," he said. "We'll go there, and you will tell him what you have found. We'll let him decide what to do with you."

I sagged for a moment, disappointed that my ordeal was not yet over but relieved at least that I was not to be summarily executed. He smiled at me for a moment. "You've been on the run all this time, but you've still managed to conduct a successful investigation?"

"Yes, sire," I sighed, exhausted at the mere thought of what I had done.

"I suspect my mother might be wrong about you, Haylli." For Huayna Capac that was high praise indeed.

* * *

When the Yellow Fringe moved hundreds went with him, and so it took Huayna Capac until the next day to arrange for our travel to the Yucay valley, even though it was only the next valley over to the east. As we left Cuzco a full legion of guardsmen marched ahead of us and our rear guard was made up of enough bureaucrats, administrators, courtiers, and officials to run Tahuantinsuyu from the road-side if need be. It was not enough protection for my comfort, though, for as we were crossing the Bone River to leave Cuzco-proper the litter of Viceroy Hualpaya intercepted us at the centre of our column by way of the Spine Road. He was ringed by a large retinue of his clansmen, including Capac Huari, the illegitimate son he had sired on Chiqui Ocllo who for appearances sake was considered a member of the Imperial family.

"Titu Cusi Huallpa, what is the meaning of this?" Viceroy Hualpaya didn't seem to notice me, but was it possible he did not know of my presence and the threat I posed to his family? I also noticed he did not address the heir as Huayna Capac.

"Is there some problem with a son visiting his father when he is... resting?" Huayna Capac asked.

"The Court belongs in Cuzco," Hualpaya said.

"The Court belongs with the Sapa Inca, and the Sapa Inca is in the Yucay. The Court was left with his son, and now his son is going to the Yucay." Huayna Capac shrugged with a magnificent gesture of indifference. I sensed the struggle for dominance between the two powerful men.

I watched Capac Huari turn and whisper something to his unacknowledged father, who leaned down from his litter to hear the words. He straightened again and smoothed an invisible fold from his mantle as he spoke. "My own duties in Cuzco are done for the moment, and I have one or two matters that would benefit from the Sapa Inca's mind. I would also like to see my brother, who is attending on your father during his... rest."

Huayna Capac nodded. "Very well. Men of our station can do as they see fit. You can act as our rearguard. My party is marching now."

Hualpaya concealed his fury at the heir's casual orders. The viceroy had only the clothes on his back and the litter under him. He gave the crown prince a stiff nod and whispered a few quick commands to some of his retinue, who broke into a run for Hualpaya's villa at the foot of Sacsahuaman hill.

I felt a strong breeze blowing against my back, the winds of change, of a coming pachacuti. Huayna Capac's star was rising; Topa Inca Yupanki was growing old, and my testimony was about to shatter the established government of Tahuantinsuyu. I shivered for a moment as those imaginary winds chilled me with their portents.

With a wave of the heir's hand, Huayna Capac's column began to march again down the Andesuyu Road towards the Yucay Valley. "I suppose he's wrapped up in this too?" The Crown Prince murmured from his litter. I opened my mouth to speak, but he waved me to silence. "Never mind. I do not want to hear it until my father does."

We marched towards Pus Cliff and the Pillars of the World, the colourful names for the bluffs that hedged in the northeast of the Huatanay Valley. Despite our crawling pace we were up and over before darkness fell, and we lodged in a tampu overlooking the Yucay valley as the sun began to set on paradise.

The Yucay, Friar, is the single loveliest place in the world except perhaps for the Kingdom of Quitu. Right next to Cuzco it is somehow warmer, lusher, more vibrant. Every crop in Tahuantinsuyu can grow in the Yucay, and so we grow delicacies like fresh tomatoes and chilies to supply the palaces there. The palaces, Friar...

A valley that lovely just a day or two's journey from Cuzco was almost entirely occupied by palaces, palaces for the Sapa Inca, for the viceroys, for most high officials, for the panacas. Each of these temples to leisure was perched on the uncultivatable land high up the side of one of the steep hills hemming in the valley. Each had a breathtaking view, enhanced by the playful hillside terracing which threw strange shadows at sunrise and sunset. It was on such a sunset that I contemplated my impending Imperial audience.

I found myself unable to stand still, moving aimlessly this way and that. Huayna Capac noted my discomfort and diverted himself from his unnecessary supervision of our procession's unpacking to order me some small comforts.

First I was provided with a stool by a fire, then a mug of akha was put in my hand and two amphorae were set behind me. I looked at the liquor for a moment, wondering if I was to be poisoned the day before my vindication.

The tampucamayoc was courtly enough to know my fears and took a large pull from the mug in my hand before topping off from both of the waiting amphorae and drinking again. We nodded our mutual satisfaction, and I was left to contemplate the fire until after the sun had set, then a figure appeared beside me and threw down a stool.

"May I join you?" I looked up at the tall figure of Topa Cusi Yupanki in his priestly garb and dumbly nodded for him to sit. Mercifully, there were no birds to be seen to slow his progress to the stool. My friend had always had the habit of putting augury before all else. "How are you?" He asked. "Never mind. I know how you are."

"How have you been?" I asked. I had heard nothing of him while I was away.

He looked into the flames for a moment, watching the llama dung glow. "Things go well for me, Haylli. I'm the favourite augur of the Crown Prince." I made some pleasant noises at this. One day Topa Cusi Yupanki could be High Priest if he stayed in Huayna Capac's favour. "I am not sitting here purely as a social visit, Haylli."

I shifted on my stool, unsure what he meant. "Oh?"

"There was a disturbing rumour going around when your father took you away for that last inspection," he murmured, not moving his lips and never taking his eyes off the fire.

"Oh?" I said again, sure he was talking about my bedding the Vixen but unsure what he was getting at.

"Your father was a good man, Haylli, and I would do what I can to help you clear his name. Tomorrow you will need the gods support, Haylli. You must have done many things before and during your time as a fugitive to upset them. Perhaps there are some things you wish to confess?"

I looked up from the fire at him, but he continued to look into the flames. "You are a Straw Man?" I asked.

"I am many things, Haylli," he murmured.

It is a Colla practice —but one all mountain men believe in to some extent— that there is a way to free a man's soul from evil influences at the moment of his choosing. Normally the ritual is only done upon a man's deathbed, for it loses its power through repetition, but as I might be sentenced to death during my audience with the Emperor I was intrigued. "We don't have a river up here," I said. There was a well at the tampu, but the ritual needed a strong current.

"The fire will do just as well," he said.

"We don't have any—" But he interrupted me by pulling a fistful of straw from his coca bag and handing it to me.

"Tell me all of it, Haylli. Every bad thing you've ever said or done."

And I held the straw in my hand and I did, Friar. I began as a child stealing food from the kitchen between mealtimes and I worked forward, sneaking into the House of Chosen Women to visit the Vixen, sleeping with the Vixen, taking up and abandoning a holy oath to avenge my father, all the crimes I had committed against the State while seeking justice. When I was up to the present he looked up from the fire for the first time. "Is that all?"

"I thought something terrible once—"

"Thoughts do not count against you," he said.

"This one might," I whispered to him. We had been speaking in low voices and moving our lips as little as possible, but of all my misdeeds against the laws and the gods, this one worried me the most.

"Tell it with the rest, then."

"I went to see Pachacamac," I said, seeing the Bird Man perk up at that all-powerful oracle's name. "And he asked me to one day say he was powerful. He even said please." I watched the augur frown. "Ever since then, Topa, I've doubted whether the gods will be powerful forever, and I've wondered when the change will be and what will cause it."

He took my fist in his hands, moved it over the fire, muttered an incantation whose words were too arcane for me to follow, then he let go and I released the straw. Normally the confessor releases the straw that have absorbed all his sins into a fast flowing stream to be diffused and

228

carried out of sight, but Topa Cusi Yupanki was right: The fire did just as well. My sins burned away.

"You are absolved before the gods and the ancestors, Haylli. As for Viracocha, just make sure one day that you act on his behalf. Then you will have done all that can be expected of you."

He left me, and after I was done my akha I left the fire too. On my way to the dormitory I passed Capac Huari leaning against a wall. I had never had too much to do with the supposedly illegitimate prince, and so I nodded to him in a distant way. He gestured with his chin to the dim fire I had abandoned.

"Confessing, eh?"

"Yes," I said.

"I don't know what this is all about, but my uncle doesn't like it." Hualpaya was almost certainly the man's father, but uncle was a better title for the man who sires a child by an Emperor's wife. I remained silent, wishing only to go to bed. Capac Huari decided to continue. "If you are sentenced to death, my uncle says I'll be the executioner. I have nothing against you. I'll make it quick."

It sounds strange, Friar, but his words comforted me. I thanked him and went to roll up in my blanket among the other bureaucrats. I felt easier than I had in a long time, and I slept the peace of a man content.

We awoke the next day to see the full glory of the Yucay stretched out below us, including the work gangs —twenty thousand strong— cutting, shaping, dragging, and positioning enormous blocks of red stone in the construction of the nearby fortress-palace of Ollantaytampu, designed to be as impregnable and important in the Yucay as the Intihuasi on Sacsahuaman was above Cuzco.

I admired the boulders, cut from a quarry on one hill, dragged across the valley floor, then up a steep road to be set into the walls. None of the men were on duty more than three months out of the year, eating and drinking at State-expense all the while, and while they were here their neighbours back home were tending their fields for them.

This was the Inca administration at work. It was beautiful and inspiring, and I felt a smile spread across my face that I could not resist. I wanted my job back, wanted to make that system work again. As soon as the column had shook itself into movement I advanced as far forward as I could manage, wanting to be among the first to arrive at Old Topa's villa of Chinchero.

We were there by mid-afternoon, but nothing at the Imperial Court of an old and ailing Sapa Inca moves quickly. There was the unpacking of the procession and the explanations as to our presence, and it was decided I would not appear before the Emperor until the morning. As calm and content as I had been that morning I was a wreck that evening, fearing a dagger while I slept. I stayed up all night with a few of my father's old quipucamayocs, drinking and trying to calm down while only getting more tense.

The lack of sleep and the steady consumption of akha left my mind dull for the most important interview of my life, so I dunked my head into a cistern as dawn broke over the eastern hills. Water ran down from my headband the whole time the guardsmen escorted me through a maze of passages, then checked me for weapons, gave me my burden, removed my sandals, and escorted me into the Imperial Presence for the first time since I was sent to the Pit.

Old Topa reclined on a sleeping pallet, a sign of how weak he had become, but the Court was not a dark room to die in: It was a roofed patio overlooking the valley, a sight made glorious with the early light, and diaphanous curtains of translucent vicuna stirred gently in the breeze. His pallet was raised up to shoulder level, and he was propped up on one elbow with a series of pillows so that his eyes were above my own.

Flanking his high bed were the viceroys Achachi Michi, Hualpaya, and Illyapa, the heir Huayna Capac, and the Ocllo sisters. There were no accountants, no courtiers, no other witnesses of any kind save the guardsmen who lined the walls. I would testify before an audience that would not spawn ugly rumours. I genuflected and blew the Shepherd of the Sun a kiss.

"Why did you leave us?" His voice was a whispered rattle. He did not sound hostile, but for him my disappearance was not the great catastrophe it had been for the people I was about to accuse.

"Sapa Inca, I am sure you know of the death of my brother Ronpa while I was in the Great Quipu Repository. His murder was meant for me. Staying in Cuzco for even the time it would have taken to obtain your permission to launch my investigation would have seen me dead."

His head slowly turned to his viceroys. I had the distinct impression that he had not heard anything about the dead boy on the steps of the heart of the Inca administration. "Very well then, you have come back."

I almost sagged with relief. With those words the Sapa Inca had forgiven me for my desertion. His next words were less cheering. "My son tells me you have a story to tell me."

I hid my desire to frown. 'Story' was not the word I would have preferred. "Yes, Sire," I said, deciding I would let the facts speak for themselves. "My story is filled with characters you know well doing things you had no idea about. They arranged the death of my father to keep those actions secret."

Viceroy Illyapa coughed gently into one hand. Old Topa turned to the man who ruled a quarter of the world in his name. "Yes?"

"Sire, I renew my objections to listening to a man who lived as a fugitive from Imperial justice for years, falsifying documents and traveling the length and breadth of Tahuantinsuyu without permission. Who knows what he'll say to try to save himself? His wild accusations should be handled by an administrative tribunal, not yourself."

"So that I can be judged by the men I mean to accuse, aucca?" I said. The room seemed to cool despite the cheery sunlight. I had thrown out the word, and now I must prove its veracity or die. No one moved for a long moment.

"Speak," the Sapa Inca demanded of me.

"My story begins when you were a young man, Sire. You married Mama Ocllo as your first wife, suspecting one day she would be your Coya when you were Sapa Inca. It was a good match, made for the right reasons of family and power, but it was not a love-match, Majesty." Mama Ocllo stirred at this, but no one in the room was prepared to disagree with what they all knew to be true.

"You married hundreds of women after her, and as the years passed she grew bored and restless among your many wives. This Coya of yours had absolute power in so many ways that she felt she could do anything she wished, and generally that was true." She scowled at me, for I spoke without reverence. It was about to get much worse. I directed all my attention to the Sapa Inca and braced myself for what I next had to say.

"I do not know if she actually took Viceroy Illyapa as her lover or not, Sire, but they certainly had a romantic relationship of some kind, even if only of the mind." It was the most delicate way I could think to put it, but it still provoked a storm of protest from all the powerful men and women in the room, save only Old Topa, who waved them all to silence.

231

Huayna Capac, the man who had made this audience possible for me, glared at me as if I were a poisonous frog swimming in his stew.

I continued, my pulse beating in my ears, speaking more from the rote I had prepared during my long months of travel than from any real thought of the moment. "She was an old and neglected woman by then, and he was a man who could have anyone but her, and so a misplaced passion developed between them. I do not know how long it went on, or what happened, but I do know that Illyapa did not plan to devote himself to her completely and forever, Sire—"

I was not deterred by the blur of movement in the corner of my eye, but I did stop when Viceroy Achachi Michi hurled his staff of office to my left. One of Mama Ocllo's sisters was screaming and the guardsmen around me were all in motion. Only then did I turn to see a guardsman sprawled out on the floor with a violent gash on his temple from Achachi Michi's well-placed blow. Six more guardsmen were pinning down the injured man's dazed form.

I recognized my attacker's face for its very lack of memorable features: It was one of the killers who had slain Ronpa. The man was dragged from the Imperial audience, the room in an uproar. I could hear Illyapa's voice over the others saying, "Sire, if the guardsmen have been compromised I think we should end today's business and conduct a full—"

"Excuse me, Sire!" I bellowed with the best volume I could get out of a chaski's lungs. The babble dropped away abruptly. "That's twice someone has tried to murder me before I could speak to you. How long do you think I'll last if we adjourn for the day?"

I did not see the Emperor's hand signal, but guardsmen moved in closer to surround Hualpaya and Illyapa. Achachi Michi gave me a nod of encouragement and put a plug of coca into his mouth, apparently ready to enjoy the show. The other two viceroys maintained their frosty dignity.

"I'm sorry, Sire. Where was I?"

"My wife wasn't able to hold Illyapa's attention anymore than she could hold mine." His dry laugh was music to my ears. He was too old and jaded to care about his elderly wife's dalliances. It was the worst kept secret in Cuzco that Viceroy Hualpaya had sired Capac Huari on Chiqui Ocllo, so was it such a stretch of the imagination to believe Hualpaya's brother might have had an intimate relationship with Chiqui Ocllo's sister?

Mama Ocllo clearly wanted the Court to think it was, for she glared at her husband with barely restrained fury. He was the one man in the world who could speak as if she did not matter. I was glad to have her attention diverted from me.

"Thank you, Sire. Yes, Illyapa decided he wanted a new plaything, and at some point he saw Kiske Sisa, a beautiful young Lupaca princess who had been taken from her people as a chosen woman to live in Cuzco. Sire, I think it's common knowledge that if a pacuyok and a chosen woman want to become intimate, walls and guards can only do so much to keep them apart—"

"You would certainly know," Illyapa interrupted me. "Didn't you become 'intimate' with Atoc China, despite her status as a chosen woman? Sire, must we listen to this?"

It was a much better attack than the guardsman, but this one I had expected. "Both Atoc China and her husband —your nephew Chalcuchima— will swear she went to her marriage bed a virgin." I did not point out that that was thanks to the preparations of an old crone my father had introduced the Vixen to before our ill-fated inspection. "And even if there were any improprieties, the Vixen was never going to be married off as an Imperial gift who must remain perfect, as Kiske Sisa was, aucca."

I turned back to the Emperor. "Illyapa and Kiske Sisa began a secret relationship. When Mama Ocllo learned he wanted Kiske Sisa as one of his concubines she panicked. Mama Ocllo is old enough to be Kiske Sisa's grandmother, and she knew Illyapa was replacing her."

The Empress decided she could contain herself no longer. "I will have you made into a drum for this! This is the most insulting story I have ever—"

"Oh, shut up and be still, woman!" The Emperor barked, provoking a coughing fit, and for a few moments he hacked into a vicuna cumpi handkerchief as the whole Court watched the Coya open and close her mouth like a fish pulled from the water. When Old Topa had restored himself he waved the cloth at me and said in with a rasp, "Get on with it. What does this have to do with your father?"

I was as stunned as anyone at how the Emperor had just spoken to his wife, but I had to press on while I had the opportunity. "It has everything to do with my father, Sire. Cast your mind back and tell me who suggested that Kiske Sisa should marry Tocoyricoc Tupac Capac?"

I did not wait for an answer. Everyone knew it had been Mama Ocllo. "Without consulting Illyapa, your wife betrothed Kiske Sisa to my father, a widower of high rank with an appreciation for women of Kiske's build. He was a perfect husband for Kiske Sisa, and he was too powerful a man for Illyapa to cross. The Coya was sure she had just ended all her problems. But the solution to her problems brought about my father's murder!"

I pointed at the viceroy of Collasuyu. "Illyapa had already deflowered Kiske Sisa in anticipation of her becoming his concubine. He never imagined Mama Ocllo would get involved. Now he finds he's besmirched a Virgin of the Sun who's about to marry my father, a man honest and worldly enough to know that someone has cuckolded Inti and religious enough to make it public knowledge. To save his own life Illyapa had to kill Tupac before Tupac could marry Kiske."

We all stood there, waiting to see whether the Sapa Inca would accept such a motive. "But what about the coup attempt? What about the assassin and the missing weapons?"

"The weapons were taken by Viceroy Illyapa's nephew, Chalcuchima, and hidden in a cave until after my father was dead and I was a fugitive. I have Chalcuchima's full testimony with me, obtained on the promise that I would beg you to pardon him."

I saw Viceroy Illyapa stiffen at this, but the guardsmen kept him still.

"As for the Lupaca assassin Mamani, he was dying anyway. Do you remember how yellow his skin was, Majesty? How unhealthy he looked? He was not long for this world, probably something to do with his liver, and he knew it."

It was Hualpaya's turn to interrupt me. "And how would my brother have known this Mamani? Known him well enough to know he was dying? Known him well enough to convince him to die before his time for the sake of a conspiracy?"

"Why my Lord Hualpaya, I'm surprised you have to ask!" I laughed, and the viceroy of Andesuyu blinked at my levity. "Mamani was Kiske Sisa's father. She would have told Illyapa about her father's health, and then a bargain was struck: Mamani accuses my father and goes to his death knowing that his daughter's children will be the progeny of one viceroy and that his eldest son would be adopted into the household of another viceroy and groomed for a senior administrative post. You are raising Mamani's heir as your own son!"

Viceroy Achachi Michi spit out his coca, and the Emperor smiled at me as if I had just done something truly remarkable. The Sapa Inca's approval made me bold, and I began to pace across the patio, building momentum in my voice with each footfall. "Send to the House of Chosen Women on the Island of the Sun, Sire! Order them to examine Kiske Sisa and they will find she is no virgin!

"If you call Chalcuchima, the chaski mitmak Puma, Kiske Sisa, or the household of Mamani to an Imperial audience you will have testimony of Viceroy Illyapa's guilt." I pointed at the viceroy of Collasuyu again. "That man killed my father, Sire, an innocent man."

Topa looked bemused; Achachi Michi thoughtful; Hualpaya pensive. Illyapa and all three Ocllo sisters glared at me as if they could make me burst into flames with their eyes. We all waited for the bedridden Emperor to break the silence.

"Speak," Old Topa said at last.

Hualpaya was the first to assume the Emperor was talking to him. "Sire, I knew nothing of a plot to kill Tupac Capac. My brother asked me to adopt an orphaned Lupaca noble. That is all." And just like that Hualpaya abandoned his brother.

Viceroy Illyapa sighed. "I am guilty, Sire. Do not call for the witnesses. I had to choose between killing Tupac and killing Kiske." He looked at me, his eyes full of tears. "Your father didn't deserve his end, but I couldn't bring myself to kill that beautiful girl. I'm sorry. It was him or her, and I chose her. I confess."

"No!" Mama Ocllo cried, pushing aside the guardsmen and rushing to Illyapa's side. "Topa, don't you do this! This is a good man! He has remained loyal to you, even after what you did to his brother Capac Yupanki. He—"

I took the extraordinary step of shouting down the most powerful woman in the world.

"Of course she wants Illyapa alive, Sire! He is her puppet!"

"What?" Half the Court demanded. Illyapa just lowered his head. At that moment I felt sorry for my father's killer: He would go to his death with all his secret shames brought out for public display.

"Your Majesty, aren't you curious why Kiske Sisa is on the Island of the Sun instead of back at the Coricancha, waiting for you to assign her a new husband? Did you order her sent there? No, it was Mama Ocllo's secretary who transferred Kiske to the Island of the Sun and elevated her from a Virgin of the Sun to a full Bride of Inti, chaste for life. Mama Ocllo's secretary isn't supposed to have that kind of authority, but he issued the order.

"In fact, Mama Ocllo's secretary has been doing most of Viceroy Illyapa's work, transferring wealth and officials as the Coya sees fit. Try to remember who wanted an Imperial manhunt to be pursued against me: Was it your viceroy or your wife? I'd be willing to bet even when Illyapa speaks to you, your Coya is always in the room. Mama Ocllo has been running Collasuyu since my father's death, and the only way I can imagine that happening is if your dear Coya, spurned by her lover, is blackmailing him."

"My Coya is running a quarter of Tahuantinsuyu?" For the first time the Sapa Inca looked surprised by what I had told him. Everything else was palace intrigue gone too far, but here the strings that controlled his empire were being pulled by another, by a wife he did not like. The Coya was supposed to be the most powerful woman in the world, but Mama Ocllo had also become the second-most powerful person in the world without the Sapa Inca's knowledge. With a trembling hand he pointed at his Empress, "We will discuss this later."

"Why wait?" She demanded. "What do you want me to say? Collasuyu has been running smoothly under my control. Tax revenues are up. There have been no revolts—"

"We will discuss this later!" He barked, a new fit of coughing overtaking him. He held his handkerchief to his mouth and waved her away with his other hand. When she did not move two guardsmen stepped forward to stand on either side of her, gently driving her from the Royal Presence. She caught sight of my wide-eyed stare and began to spit like a jungle cat, "This is your fault! You couldn't leave well enough alone! You had to bring this all up!" She continued all the way down the corridor, her words growing indistinct but no less vocal.

Huayna Capac rose to follow his mother, but Topa held out his free hand to stop him for a moment. "Whatever your mother says, Haylli Yupanki has done us a great service today. He has exposed dishonest men and women in my midst at great risk to himself. From now on I grant him the right of free speech in the presence of the Sapa Inca. I would suggest you give him the same when your time comes. It will be soon."

The whole Court froze for a moment in shock to hear the Emperor mention his coming death. His heir nodded, smiled once at me, weakly, and left the Royal Presence to try calming his mother.

With my long task done I began to shake all over, my knees almost too weak to stand. Old Topa smiled down from his pallet at me. "Someone get him a stool." I was allowed the privilege of sitting during a royal audience. "I never believed your father was guilty, Haylli, but I had no way of knowing for sure." Illyapa and Hualpaya still stood silent beside the pallet, and my exhausted mind did not quite understand what was going on. Were they not going to be punished?

"What can I do to thank you?" The Emperor asked me.

"I want to be a tocoyricoc again." Some part of my mind was still working, but I felt like an observer, watching myself speak.

"Done. You are your father's successor."

I seemed to speak without thinking. "I married a Mapuche woman down on the Maule River, Sire, a love-match, and there's a baby on the way."

"Congratulations."

"I would ask you to confirm the marriage and elevate my wife and child to Incas-by-privilege."

"Done."

"Those of my father's followers who remain alive, I would like them taken out of the yanacona class and reinstated to their positions."

Old Topa mulled on this for a moment, aware that returning all those men to their old jobs would then push out the people he had appointed to replace them. At last he nodded, "Done."

"Chalcuchima told me much that I would not have figured out on my own. He would have me ask that he be spared the death sentence he should receive for pilfering weapons and being involved in treason against the State."

The Emperor tilted his head slightly, as if evaluating me at a different angle. "Do you forgive him for the role he played in killing your father?"

"Never," I said a little too fast. I remembered my promise. "But I swore to ask for his pardon, and I would not be here without him. Besides, Illyapa is the head of Chalcuchima's clan. Chalcuchima could not refuse him."

"Then I do spare him, but I remove him from command of his legion. Anything else?"

"Yes, Sire," I smiled now, remembering another promise I had made, though less weighty. "Huayna Capac has to meet with some bridge builders in Cuzco." A few of the guardsmen joined me in smiling, feeling the tension leaving the room even while Illyapa still stood there next to the pallet, contemplating his fate. I explained my final request to the Court and the Sapa Inca chuckled with me at the bridge keepers' excitement.

The two remaining Ocllo sisters looked at us as if we were all deranged, for in a single audience I had overturned the established order of the Royal Court built up over decades and now the Emperor and I were laughing together as men do at the end of a drinking party. It was relief, I think, and exhaustion, and the tears streamed down my face. I don't think anyone could tell, though. My hair was still wet from the cistern I had soaked myself in an eternity ago.

"What about me, Sire?" Illyapa asked after the Emperor and I had fallen into silence, I on my stool, not yet dismissed, and he on his pallet, not yet finished the morning's Imperial edicts.

The Sapa Inca smiled at him, the tone of command returning to his dusty voice. "You, my old friend, will be buried alive for besmirching a chosen woman and being stupid enough to be caught. This boy in front of us has almost certainly gotten away with it. If you were to live only a little while longer you could have learned from him."

The Emperor flicked his wrist and Illyapa walked out of the Imperial Presence with dignity, flanked on either side by the ubiquitous guardsmen. I never saw him again. His brother stirred now, aware that he would not get to say a goodbye. "And me, Sire?" Hualpaya asked.

"You are not your brother, and he was head of your clan. You had to follow his orders. I do not blame you for his actions, just as I did not blame you for your eldest brother Capac Yupanki's mistakes. You will remain at your post, but that adopted Lupaca son of yours will go into the Pit and none of your sons will be allowed to succeed you." The Viceroy bowed his way out of the throne room. The two remaining Ocllo sisters made their excuses too and left, leaving just the guardsmen, Achachi Michi, the Emperor, and myself in the throne room.

"You should have seen Capac Yupanki, Illyapa, and Hualpaya when they were boys," the Sapa Inca murmured. I'm not sure who he was speaking to, or if he was just speaking aloud. "They were terrors. They could do anything they wanted and get away with it, and they knew it. I thought when I executed Capac Yupanki for disobeying me his brothers had learned their lesson, but I was wrong. Now Illyapa is going to die, and I am going to die, and Hualpaya is going to be left ruling Tahuantinsuyu with my son?" He shook his head, as if trying to shake a terrible vision from his mind's eye.

He looked Achachi Michi in the eye, then me, making sure were knew he was talking to us this time. "Watch Hualpaya, watch him for my son." We both nodded. "Good, now get out."

With those words a pachacuti happened: Achachi Michi and I were now the most trusted administrators in the world. We left, and I got Achachi Michi to put me in a guarded room where I slept all day, all night, and most of the next day too.

When I awoke Illyapa was underground, Mamani's son was in the Pit, and the chaskis were running south with two messages, one for Koonek on the Maule River, the other for the House of the Chosen Women on the Island of the Sun. The later would arrive too late, though. Somehow word had already reached Kiske Sisa of her lover's fall from power. The Mother Superior found Kiske in her room. She had hung herself from the rafters with her own hair.

Refreshed and reinstated, I returned to Cuzco at my usual jog to be met joyously by my household servants, my few remaining family, and Huaman Paullu. I threw a party of homecoming at which we were all equals —I brought in other yanaconas to serve my household servants— and then I emptied our house from top to bottom of the clutter accumulated by the family who had occupied it during my absence.

A message arrived from the Mapuche province saying that Koonek would not have to wait to travel because of the baby, which cheered me immensely, for by my count she should have been almost due, and then I would have had to wait a few months for the baby to be fit enough to travel.

I set about making a nursery out of the ground floor of one of our buildings looking into the inner courtyard, and though it would still take more than two months for them to arrive I had fresh flowers and herbs placed within each day to infuse the place with their scent.

There was only one thing left to do before Koonek arrived. I took a few retainers with me to the Sankihuasi, sacrificed a llama, then I lit a torch and descended into the Pit to collect the dry bones of my father. There were other bodies down there, fresh ones, but my father lay where I had dragged him, every scrap of flesh pulled from his skeleton. I wrapped each bone in a loose cotton weave before placing them all in a shroud. On a whim I took the puma's skull too. The cat no more deserved to rot in the Pit than my father did. I had the whole package hauled up through the hole in the ceiling, then I climbed out too and ordered all my men to relieve themselves into the pit that had caused me such grief.

I took my father's remains home and made a mummy bundle, as the Yungas do on the coast. It was a great egg-shaped thing of layers and layers of cotton with small huacas of gold and silver and coloured stones worked in between the folds. Every day I would sacrifice to it and increase its girth a little more. I even had ten life-sized silver gherkins made and placed near his mouth.

When I was satisfied that the bones would come to no harm through their protective cocoon I put the bundle in the alcove of my household gods with the jars of my father's and my grandfather's memoirs at the mummy's feet. I made offerings and sacrifices to my father's mummy every day that I was home for as long as I lived in Cuzco, and I often talked to him about my day and my problems.

Time passed, and when the advanced warnings I requested arrived I had all my kin who survived the purges join me on the Collasuyu road to greet my wife. We were dressed in the clan yellow, each of us wearing our best golden earplugs. I had drums and flutes and trumpets ready, and we would march into Cuzco with her in a spontaneous triumph to let everyone know that the Tocoyricoc's wife had arrived. Kiskis arranged to have the day off, and he appeared in full guardsmen ceremonial dress to welcome my wife to the Imperial City.

When my darling Koonek appeared with her small retinue of State-appointed porters I silenced the musicians and rushed to her: She was thin as a stick, pale as an ice sheet, and she was swaying as if each step were an effort she did not want to take.

I did not see a baby anywhere, Friar, and though I know infant mortality rates are always high, somehow the thought was a dagger in my heart that my child was dead without my ever seeing it. I grabbed her up in my arms and spun her around, hoping my greeting would bring some colour to her face. Instead, she started crying, talking too fast for me to catch it. I snapped a reprimand to one of the porters that he had allowed a woman in my wife's condition to walk, and I summoned my litter.

My family showed uncharacteristic understanding and followed us out of earshot, all thoughts of festivities out of their heads as I brought Koonek home. The banquet I had prepared in her honour was rescheduled, and I had her in bed with a bowl of stew as soon as I could shoo the last of my relatives out.

"What's wrong? Are you sick?" I asked her when we finally had a moment's peace.

"Oh, Haylli, when word came that you had sent for me Tiso Yuncailo read it aloud on market day. My clan found out that you were an Inca, and that I had known about it. My mother cursed me! She said I'm dead to her; that I must never come back to shame her; that the gods of our people will stalk me forever; that—"

I held her tight and let her cry again into my shoulder. I could see her terror and knew that for the two months that she had walked to Cuzco to be with me the fear of her mother's words had gnawed at her. All I wanted to ask her about was the baby, but I knew I must not. I must be strong now while she was weak, and I must drive this curse out of her head. When she was all cried out I ran my fingers through her hair.

"Don't worry, my love. I'll prove it to you. I'll prove to you that you're safe, and that you need never fear your mother again." I shushed her and cuddled her and spoon-fed her the stew, and I sat beside her until she fell asleep that night. I, however, could not sleep. I lay awake all night trying to think of a way to make good on my promise.

The next morning I was ready: First I dressed her in the richest clothes she had ever seen, telling her that she would wear this as everyday wear for the rest of her life. Then I led her on an inspection of the house, avoiding only the unnecessary nursery. I told her with each room and every servant that all this was now hers; that she ruled here as the Sapa Inca ruled Tahuantinsuyu. Then we ate breakfast, and when she was done I asked her to put on something suitable for going to a temple. She perked up at this, for so far I had done nothing to break her mother's curse.

"Where are we going?" She asked, wide-eyed with anticipation. I pressed my finger to her lips and bade her get ready.

We took my litter, she riding while I walked beside her. An honour guard of twenty yellow-clad soldiers proceeded ahead and behind us all the way down to the Coricancha.

"Normally only the Sapa Inca and the High Priest can go in, but exceptions can be made, especially for you," I gave her my most dazzling smile and helped her descend from the litter.

At the entrance to the Golden Enclosure I had a few muffled, vicious words with the priest manning the gate. I took my wife for a tour of the grounds every bit as overwhelming as the one my father had taken Kiskis and I on as boys. Only when she seemed dizzy at the wealth and power and holiness of the place did we leave, but that was not the end of my plan.

I next took her to the temple of the Mapuche, a fine and sturdy building with all the trappings necessary to honour her gods, but pitiful after seeing the magnificence of the Golden Enclosure. Inside I showed her the idols of her people, captured in war by Old Topa and brought here as hostages against her people's good behavior.

There was the boulder idol of Nanémapun, master of the land; in the next alcove stood the carved wooden image of Nanéchen, master of men. Pillan, the Mapuche incarnation of Supay, was represented only by an altar. Meulen, the whirlwind god of kindness and Epuñamuñ the war god were both small bronze figures set on impressive wooden plinths. She walked among them reverently, knowing they were her people's most holy relics but without ever having seen them before: They were all taken by the Inca before she was born.

"The gods your mother has asked to curse you are all in this room, Koonek," I said. I saw her shudder. "What does that tell you? Is this Mapuche territory? No. The Inca beat the Mapuche and brought your gods here. They are worshipped or not at the whim of the Inca. Do you think if they had any power over the Inca they would have allowed that to happen?"

She thought about. "No," she said at last.

"Well, I tell you the Sapa Inca has made you an Inca, so these gods hold no power over you. And I'll tell you this too," I said, raising my voice so it echoed throughout the Mapuche hall. "If any of these gods trouble you in the future I will have their idols ground into powder and thrown onto a llama pasture."

The threat hung long in the air; she took my hand and we walked

242

home together, our retainers dismissed. That night in bed she clung to me, and I could tell something still troubled her. I thought I knew what it was. "The baby was not your mother's fault." She shuddered again. "Babies die, Koonek. We both know that. That's why we don't give them names." I could feel her tears on my shoulder. "What is it?" I asked.

"She said I wouldn't have any more," she whispered.

I rolled over to hold her with both my arms. "Then we'll just have to prove her wrong, won't we?" That night I held her, but within days we began to live together as man and wife again, and within the year she told me she was pregnant.

We never spoke of her mother's curses again, and I never learned whether my first child had been a boy or a girl, or whether it was miscarried, stillborn, or died of a childhood ailment. My ignorance is my punishment for abandoning my family at the far end of the world. I wish it was the heaviest burden I have carried in my life.

* * *

Koonek and I were happy together, Friar, though it took my wife a long while to shake off her melancholy and enjoy the wonders her new position in life brought her. Like my father I was not given to largesse when it came to household expenses, but it was within my power to draw almost anything from the Imperial stores, so I gave Koonek the means to decorate our compound as she saw fit.

She did not want the flamboyant gold niche frames and jaguar-skin rugs. She chose simple and practical things like floor to ceiling tapestries that deadened the echoes of footfalls and warmed the room on cold days, and potted plants, a veritable forest of shrubbery and herbs and flowers to fill our courtyards with the smell of growing things.

I remember how delighted she was, her hands on her growing belly, when I sent to her homeland to bring back saplings of her native pines, though she understood they would never be able to grow to their true size in the harsher climate of Cuzco.

When my daughter was born I descended from my counting room to hold her in my hands, and I looked down at that wrinkled face, still wet from birth, and knew I wanted no more from existence. Here she was, the combination of my wife and I. She was the piece of me that would pass onto eternity through her own children. I fell in love with my little girl in that moment, and I distracted the servants by sending them hurrying for towels and akha and a stool and my sandals so that none would see the tears as I wept at the strength of my joy.

The three of us lived calm and quiet lives after my recent adventures, and every day I would return from the Great Quipu Repository to Koonek's kiss and a quiet conversation about what she had done that day. We mountain people do not like to show too much affection to our infants for fear of making them soft, but I admit I snuck into little Wawa's nursery at least twice a day to leave her a bouquet of flowers or herbs, or a beautiful feather dangling from a string above her head.

About twice a week Koonek and I threw a small but lavish dinner party, for my wife was fascinated by the thought that any food, no matter how rare, could be obtained for our guests. I remember once she had oysters brought in by the chaski network all the way from the coast, still alive in pots of salt water. We steamed them and ate them before our stew to the general delight of our guests, Kiskis and three of his wives. Our meal was interrupted, though, when a herald going door to door down my narrow street informed us that the Sapa Inca Topa Inca Yupanki had gone to join his ancestors in the Upper Universe. Old Topa was dead.

Kiskis and I looked at each other and downed our mugs of akha. Kiskis's first wife began wailing her grief, joined by the other two, and when Koonek realized she was to follow their example she too began to cry, and from all over Cuzco you could hear the sound of grieving women.

I went to Old Topa's Cuzco palace along with the rest of the upper ranks of the Inca nobility to hear his will read. We were all dressed in black garments of mourning, except for me: As tocoyricoc I was required to wear my yellow mantle, though the tassel hanging from my shoulder had been changed to a respectful black. I stood next to Kiskis. Chalcuchima was also there, despite his demotion. He was the high-born brother-in-law of the heir apparent. He would hear the will just like the rest of us.

Wills have always fascinated me as a royal quipu master, for of all our legal documents only wills are considered so sacrosanct that rather than tie them into string that can be undone they are whittled into sticks in the Cañari custom: The notches in the wood correspond roughly to the knots of a string, but these wooden knots are impossible to adjust after death.

Antarqui, Old Topa's High Priest, stood in the vacant throne room with the wooden will. He cleared his throat once, and began. "Our Sovereign is dead, but I can think of no better words to express his life than those his father, the Sapa Inca Pachacuti, said upon his deathbed:

"I have grown like a flower in the garden, until now;

I have given order and reason in this life and world.

Until my strength was depleted,

and now I am returned to Earth."

There were murmurs of sympathy from the men in the room. Personally, Friar, I have heard a dozen versions of the death poem and I thought they were all bad, but I digress from Old Topa's last testament.

"Now, on to business: Titu Cusi Huallpa is to take up the Red Fringe," Antarqui said. This was met with growls of approval. "However," the word silenced the crowd. "In his wisdom, the Sapa Inca asks his loyal subjects Viceroy Achachi Michi and Viceroy Hualpaya to act as regents to his son, to show him the way and help him become the monarch his father would want him to be." All eyes silently shifted to the youthful yellow-fringed crown prince.

"Topa's estates are to be put into a panaca to be known as the Capac Panaca," the high priest went on at some length about the formation of the new panaca, listing which of Topa's sons would be responsible for which palaces and estates. I listened with half an ear, for while this institution being born would come to be an important part of the State, I knew that the present organization would only last until a woman had bent the panaca to her will. Part of me wondered if that would be the Vixen, or if she would try to wrest an older panaca from some other woman's clutches.

"Old Topa—" The High Priest caught himself too late using the affectionate but disrespectful nickname. "Our Sovereign will be mummified and kept in royal state by that panaca, and he shall be called upon whenever his son needs his council."

Another moment of respectful silence passed. "Now, what you've all been waiting for." The High Priest took a deep breath, and we all leaned in, knowing what was to come: The last testament of a Sapa Inca included a list of wars to be won. In that moment we were not the refined Intip Churi of Royal Cuzco: We were a tribe of warriors whose dead sinchi was about to reveal the comings wars of conquest.

"The—"

The heavy mahogany of the throne room door was thrown wide to admit the wild-eyed Mama Ocllo, covered in black sackcloth, wailing her bereavement.

"Mother!" The Crown Prince stepped out of the front rank of nobles to grab her. She was inconsolable, as was appropriate for a Coya whose Sapa Inca had passed, but at that moment! One did not need to be an augur of Topa Cusi Yupanki's abilities to read the signs. Huayna Capac would not be the conqueror his father was, not as long as his mother lived anyway. The High Priest did not bother to read Old Topa's instructions to us. The spell was broken.

Over the next month Tahuantinsuyu grieved the passing of a great man. Altars ran with torrents of llama blood; the air fogged with the smoke of burned coca; akha was consumed in such quantities that the quipucamayocs had to double the nation's consumption quota for maize.

Most disturbing to you, Friar, each of the eighty provinces of Tahuantinsuyu took two youths, perfect in every way, led them up to the highest mountain, stupefied them with cold and liquor, and then strangled them. They were our messengers, our ambassadors to the gods, each sent to ask Viracocha and Inti to greet Topa Inca Yupanki as a brother and join him in watching over his people here on Earth. It was a weighty responsibility, and one of great honour, and I know men who volunteer their children for the sacrifice. I applaud their dedication, but I cannot emulate it. I am not pious enough.

While the Empire mourned, the Crown Prince underwent the lengthy coronation process of fasting and ceremony to become the Sapa Inca Huayna Capac. Meanwhile, Viceroy Achachi Michi and I did our best to keep our new Emperor safe from the most obvious threat to his Imperial usno, Viceroy Hualpaya.

Topa Inca Yupanki's will had made Hualpaya a regent to his son so that he would always be at court under our ever watchful eyes. I built a network of informants throughout Hualpaya's administrative bureaucracy, but the news they gave me was troublingly wholesome.

Achachi Michi and I would meet every few days to compare what our surveillance had produced, but to all extents and purposes Viceroy Hualpaya went smiling through his day, working hard to govern the people entrusted to him on the behalf of Huayna Capac. It did not make sense.

Two of Hualpaya's brothers were dead by Imperial decree, and his son would not succeed him to his post. One of the most powerful men in Tahuantinsuyu was to live under a cloud of suspicion and shame for the rest of his short life. Why was he so calm and well-behaved?

The only thing Achachi Michi and I had to talk about was how much time Hualpaya spent with his 'nephew' Capac Huari, but then at least that prince still had some political future ahead of him; perhaps Hualpaya was drawing some comfort from that.

More than a month into Huayna Capac's reign I hurried to meet Achachi Michi up on the battlements of the Intihuasi fortress overlooking Cuzco. It was a bright clear day, and he smiled at me with teeth flecked with shredded coca. "You look like you have something to say."

"I do, though it might be nothing." I looked down at Cuzco.

"Okay. Most of these meetings have been about nothing."

"Some weapons have gone missing from a nearby warehouse. It could be a clerical error, but if it is I haven't figured it out yet."

"How many weapons are we talking about?"

"Enough for a couple hundred guardsmen."

"Do you think Hualpaya would try anything with so few men? His clan can summon up fifty thousand soldiers if he can get out of Cuzco."

"Just as well Old Topa stuck him here as a babysitter," I laughed to take some of the sting out of my words. Achachi Michi was also a regent over Huayna Capac. Until Hualpaya's threat was found or proven false, the old general was stuck in the capital too. "In truth I think we might be looking too hard for a coup. Hualpaya heads a powerful family, true, but maybe he's content to live out the rest of his days as a viceroy without following his brothers' path." I gestured down at Hualpaya's compound below Intihuasi's walls. "He's given no reason to—"

"What is going on down there?" Achachi Michi muttered, squinting now at a small courtyard deep inside Hualpaya's city estate. I strained my eyes too, and I could make out lances and halberds catching the sun, a lot of them.

"Could he be trying something right now?" I asked, seeing a young man with the golden chest disc of a war hero addressing a crowd of soldiers.

"Well that's not him," the old general said.

"That's Prince Capac Huari!" I exclaimed, the pieces falling together in my mind: Capac Huari was a popular figure, free from Hualpaya's disgrace. If Huayna Capac should be struck down in a palace coup, Capac Huari could rally a lot of people to his standard. Viceroy Hualpaya was going to try to put the Red Fringe on his illegitimate son, and his descendants would become a new line of Sapa Incas. It would be a sweet revenge on the family that had killed his brothers.

"We're closer to Huayna Capac than he is," the Viceroy said. The idea that the coup could begin fast enough for that to be a factor was only just occurring to me. "You go and warn the Emperor. I'll rally as much of the garrison of this fort as I can and follow you."

I took off at my chaski run, tearing through the great gate of the fortress and down the hill, running through the sacred cornfield that was tended by the Sapa Inca and his own family because going around might take too much time.

Given the right of free speech, I did not have to explain myself to the Emperor's doorman, but I admit he protested my running past him at full speed, bounding through courtyards and anterooms before realizing the Sapa Inca was keeping court on the upper floor today.

I launched myself up the stairs three at a time and burst into the throne room to see Huayna Capac at his ease, off his usno and looking out the window at the gardens and Cuzco below. He turned to me, frowning to see my direct gaze and the lack of burden on my shoulders.

"Haylli Yupanki, what is the meaning of this?"

"Majesty, there is a plot to kill you!" I said it too fast, though I wonder now how one would say it right. However it is done, his eyes narrowed as he considered whether it was I who would murder him under the guise of warning him. At the word 'kill' his guardsmen brought their halberds up to point at me, and the quipucamayocs and court retainers snatched up their staffs of office, all capable of doubling as maces and clubs during a palace coup.

"Speak," he commanded, turning from the window to give me his full attention. The red fringe of a Sapa Inca seemed to suit him then, giving that single plain order.

"Hualpaya is moving against you with Capac Huari and perhaps a hundred—" But I was interrupted by the clash of arms from two floors below us. Half of his guards and retainers ran out of the door behind

248

me to join the fray. The rest eyed me wearily, ready to protect the Sapa Inca at all costs.

"What shall I do?" Huayna Capac was calm under pressure. I approached him slowly, my hands open to show I had no weapon.

"Majesty, Viceroy Achachi Michi is coming to relieve us, but we did not think Hualpaya could move this soon. We need to get you out of this palace."

"The exit is on the ground floor, and that's where Hualpaya and Capac Huari are," he said. "Someone give me a weapon." A mace was offered to him slowly by a courtier. The guardsmen tensed the whole time the weapon was being extended. This was going to be difficult for me.

"Majesty, if you die, they have won. I can't allow you to be in this room, fighting with us."

He arched an eyebrow, instantly turning his youthful face into the stern but amused continence of the supreme power on Earth. "And just what are you proposing?"

Behind me I could hear the Sapa Inca's loyal soldiers falling back into the throne room under the press of Hualpaya's forces coming up the stairs. I flicked my eyes to left and right to see the closest of his guards look to the door.

And with that I reached out with my hand, bringing it gently to rest on the Sapa Inca's sacred breast, then I pushed him backwards through the window with all of my strength. His ankle caught on the sill, and my stomach dropped as I watched him tumble towards the ground.

"Defend him!" I shouted to his guardsmen before they could decide to kill me. I stole one quick glance out the window to see the Emperor on his back in a flowerbed, holding his knee in obvious pain and glaring up at my audacity. Numb at what I had done, I felt myself waving to him, then my mind returned to reality as the room descend into madness behind me.

I spun around and ordered the guardsmen to put our backs to the window. Hualpaya and Capac Huari's men rushed us, a wave of reckless nobles at their backs. There was a clash of halberds and the dull thunking rumble of clubs and maces falling on bucklers and bones. I worked my way back and forth behind the line of guardsmen, extorting them to hold the traitors away from the window.

One by one the Emperor's loyal guardsmen fell until there were only seven, shoulder to shoulder in a semicircle, protecting the window with their lives, their halberds dripping with gore. I snatched up a fallen lance and took my place among them, silently cursing Achachi Michi's tardiness for bringing it to this.

They rushed us, and I fought as a man does when he knows it is the last thing he will ever do, so he must do it well. The lance was tipped like my father's, and its needle point was perfect for going at a foe's face, eyes, and neck. Shoulder to shoulder like that we were invincible, and when the melee fell back from us I watched as the traitors began untying their headbands to use as slings. None of us had shields; we would be smashed like a line of crockery sitting on top of a corral fence, mere sling practice for the Inca before us.

"For Sapa Inca Huayna Capac!" I surprised myself by shouting a war cry and rushing forward, followed in a heartbeat by the surviving guardsmen. Our enemies had their hands busy with their slings, so few could resist our charge with their own weapons. Several ran from the throne room.

It was a last hurrah, of course, eight charging fifty. It was only as I saw those who had run from the room return that I felt a surge of hope: They were not coming back because they had found their courage; they were backing into the room in fear of a larger force outside. Achachi Michi had come.

We killed most of them, saving only Capac Huari, Hualpaya, and the few who were injured before the reinforcements arrived. When it was done I ran back to the window to see the Sapa Inca in the garden below, sitting up and holding his twisted knee, watching the window to see who would prevail, whether he would live or die.

"You pushed me out of a window, Haylli!" He called up to me.

"Yes, Sire!" I shouted down. I tried to hide my anxiety.

"Who would believe you would push me out of a window?" And then my Emperor tipped his head back and laughed, as if I had told the most wonderful joke he had ever heard.

I was glad I was leaning against the window sill, for I was weak-kneed with relief.

I was always one of Huayna Capac's favourites after that day.

The next two years were good to me, Friar. My wife and I would sleep with Wawa's cradle between us in the night. My work was satisfying too, for with the rise of a new Sapa Inca after the long reign of Topa Inca Yupanki I was allowed to reform some of the outdated and inefficient regulations in the bureaucracy.

I drew up new standardized uses for all one hundred and nine dyes available to us, and I completed a brand new census of every taxpayer of Tahuantinsuyu. I made my inspections twice a year, auditing the tampus and villages and introducing myself to the curacas who had served my father all those years. My fingers grew so nimble with the strings that I took to braiding Koonek's hair in the dark as we lay in bed. She was always pleased with the results the next morning when she combed it out.

We attended the panaca parties and the Imperial festivals, and I arranged for Koonek to have the most glorious clothes imaginable, including one with thousands of gold scales sewn into the weave so that she looked like a goddess when the sun set. Perhaps my eyes were too filled with love for a true comparison, but it always seemed to me that my Koonek was lovelier than the Vixen at those parties. I don't know. I just know we were happy.

To add to my good mood, Mama Ocllo was dying. She blamed me for all the misfortunes and reversals of her life, and the fact that she could not get her son to side against me was the final proof that her influence at Court was over. I prayed privately for her to die. I think only her malice was keeping her alive. Her husband was dead. Viceroy Illyapa was dead. Even her sisters were dead, executed for their part in Hualpaya's failed coup.

My old school friend, stony-faced Rumiñaui was part of her guard detail, and he told me day by day she seemed to shrink and wizen, and one day she did not rise from her pallet in the morning. She was too weak to stand. I felt bad for Huayna Capac, of course, and I dutifully added my public prayers to that of the entire nation that Viracocha would grant Mama Ocllo more time on this Earth with her loving son. Huayna Capac had put off all his wars and royal duties that might take him outside Cuzco since his coronation, such was his love for his mother.

The idea of her imminent death distressed him so that he brought in the finest medicine men from the Kallawaya, renowned for their healing abilities. The nation's chaski system was put at their disposal so they could obtain whatever remedy they needed, but there was no cure for a bitter old woman running out of life.

She took to talking to herself, sometimes cackling and shouting with joy, as if a phantom jester were entertaining her. Then she would have flashes of lucidity and call for wise men and bards to come to her bedside, questioning them about distant lands and foreign peoples. I waited for her to die. She did not do it soon enough.

One day I was in Great Quipu Repository supervising a new shelving arrangement for the census data when an Imperial messenger arrived, ordering me to come at once to Huayna Capac's Court. I arrived, barefoot and burdened, blowing him a kiss and bowing as custom dictated.

"My mother has had a dream," the Sapa Inca said in a rush. My heart sank; I knew by sheer instinct that I would not like this vision.

"Oh, Sire?"

"She was on her deathbed," he paused at the word, finding it unpalatable, "and then she saw you and Chalcuchima venturing deep into the hacha hacha to the Napo River. You obtained the spice flower there, and the vanilla orchid, and you returned with the live plants through the Chacapoyan lands, over the mountains, and returning to her bedside. Her medicine men made a drink of the flowers you brought, and when she drank it she became a young and healthy woman again." He leaned back on his usno, his hands on his knees and a broad smile on his face.

"Sire, that is—"

"Incredible, I know!" Huayna Capac's enthusiasm knew no bounds. "I talked to her Kallawaya medicine men, and they have assured me that they have heard of such a potion."

I did not point out that they all feared execution upon the death of the Emperor's mother, and that they would say anything to pass the blame onto someone else. "Sire, I am a tocoyricoc—"

"I temporarily relieve you of all your duties until you and Chalcuchima have returned."

My stomach dropped to be so casually demoted. "Sire, it would take an army to reach the Napo River."

Indeed, Friar, Pachacuti and Topa Inca Yupanki had both lost armies trying to get nowhere near as deep into the hacha hacha as the Napo River. The jungle is no place for highland warriors.

The people who live in the never-ending forests are more animals than men, and they knew every step of the hacha hacha's vastness as a jungle cat knows his hunting ground. Arrows and lances flew out of the foliage to impale our soldiers. Then there were the snakes and the jaguars and the piranhas. I wanted to avoid the hacha hacha as I feared the Pit: It was a place where men were sent to die.

Now I knew why Mama Ocllo had been asking about foreign lands while laughing to herself. She was concocting the worst place known to man to send me to die on a fool's errand. I had to get out of it.

"She saw no army in her dream," he said to me.

"I am just supposed to walk into the jungle and walk out again with potted plants?" I asked, hoping he would see how ridiculous that sounded.

"You will take the Urupampa River as far into the hacha hacha as you dare. Our best wise men say that the Urupampa must meet the Napo somewhere. If you find it does not, get off the river and walk towards Quitu until you find it," the Emperor made it sound easy.

"Sire, why don't we just send a curaca from the Cañari province to ask their jungle trading partners among the Jivaro headhunters to obtain the spice? That would be faster. I can have the chaskis send a message today—"

"My mother saw you go; she saw you take the Urupampa River there, and she saw you carry it back personally. You can't even give the flowers to the chaskis once you return to Tahuantinsuyu. It's you, or the vision will prove false," Huayna Capac said. I looked around the room for help, but there were no high-ranking Inca lords present.

"The trip you're talking about would take months, Sire. What if, Inti forbid, your mother should be gone before I return?"

"I will not hold you responsible for the acts of Supay, but you and Chalcuchima will make every effort to hurry."

"Well, at least let me take Kiskis and Rumiñaui. I will need help, if only to carry the flowers back." I said it before I realized it was a statement accepting that I was going. The fear of going into the hacha hacha alone with Chalcuchima had me grasping at straws. Mama Ocllo was not counting on the terrain, the climate, the beasts, and the people to kill me: Chalcuchima would have instructions to murder me too.

The Sapa Inca chewed his lip for a moment before nodding. "Very well, Kiskis and Rumiñaui may go."

"How much time do I have?"

"She is dying, Haylli," he murmured.

"Majesty, I do not know the way. A few days in the Great Quipu Repository to go over the wise men's stories of the lands beyond Andesuyu; some time to send word to the Chacapoyan and Cañari tampus to prepare for our arrival on the return trip..." I just wanted her to die before I could go, and he sensed that.

"No. You will leave today." As good a relationship as he and I had, I heard the subtle tone, hard as granite, of the Imperial decree. To confirm it I saw his secretaries tying it down along one wall. Just by following the movement of their hands I could see them tie 'Haylli Yupanki will leave today.'

I bowed and accepted my fate, backing out of the room, My Imperial audience concluded, I rushed home to tell Koonek before she heard it through the city's gossip network. As usual, bad news traveled faster than the swiftest messenger.

"She's trying to kill you?" My Koonek trembled, holding back the tears.

"She's a powerless old woman who is about to die. She can't hurt me," I assured her, holding my darling wife close and stroking her hair.

"But you'll be leaving Tahuantinsuyu! You'll be going into the hacha hacha where no one can help you!" She began to cry.

"I'm going to pick some flowers, then I'm going to come home. That's all I'm going to do," I assured her. "But you're going to have to do something for me while I am away, alright? Take care of Wawa, and the house, and sacrifice every day for my safe return." I kissed her then, but I do not remember what it felt like. I wish I had paid more attention. "When I come back we're going to give her a childhood name, and I'm going to let you pick it. You have all the time that I'm away to decide."

When my doorman ushered my three traveling companions into my courtyard I was ready. I was no stranger to long trips, and I had everything I needed: A brown hooded alpaca cloak, an undyed cotton tunic, a breechcloth, my sandals, a sling wrapped around my headband, a coca bag filled with string, my father's lancehead, now rehafted as a dagger, and a mace. In a bag I intended to carry with a tumpline I had a cooking pot, a wooden cup, a change of clothes and an extra pair of sandals, a ceramic trumpet that I hoped would be less valuable than a conch shell in the eyes of the savages, and a fire drill.

The three officers were armed for a last stand, lances and shields and chonta-wood helmets, axes and clubs, darts and javelin-throwers. Their coca bags rattled with sling stones. Their tunics were the martial red and white boxes of bravery. I smiled at them. "Strip."

"What?" Chalcuchima spoke as if I had asked him to circumcise himself.

"Strip. You're not wearing those clothes, and you're certainly not taking half that weaponry." It took a long time to bully the soldiers into my way of thinking, but eventually I had them all dressed and fitted out with a kit bag like mine.

"I still think we should have our tunics. How will they know we're Inca?" Rumiñaui muttered.

"The earplugs will be enough of a give away," I assured him. "We don't want to have anything worth killing us for. Are we ready?" They nodded. "Let's go."

Koonek stood in the courtyard as we left, and stepped out into the street to watch until we rounded the corner. I waved goodbye, but I did not want to kiss her in front of Chalcuchima. That is what life is made of, Friar: Wasted opportunities.

We stayed that night at the tampu between Cuzco and the Yucay valley. The next day we were on the banks of the Urupampa, watching the placid waters go by and knowing we would come to hate this river. "Well?" Rumiñaui asked.

"We make a raft," I said with more confidence than I felt. "We travel by day and pull onto sandbars at night. We only get off the boat to cook. We only talk to the savages to ask directions to the land of the spice flowers."

The spice flower, which I am told tastes like what you Spaniards call cinnamon, was a rare and exotic commodity. My hope was that tribesman friendly enough to talk to us would know enough about trade to direct us to where the spice flower came from.

"And at what point do we say this whole thing is stupid and give up?" Kiskis asked.

"When we think we're going to fail," Chalcuchima said.

"I think that now," Rumiñaui and I said in unison. The four of us chuckled in that humourless way men do when they contemplate an unknown and ignoble fate, then we ordered the tampu staff to build us a raft.

We loaded it with pots of chuno and bundles of bronze axeheads to trade with the locals, then we pushed off the bank.

Our raft was a platform of fifteen buoyant logs lashed together side by each with a piece of flattened bamboo shoved down between the middle logs to keep it moving straight. We had paddles and poles, but usually we did not need them. The strength of the current as the river descended from the mountains to the forest kept us going.

The first few days while we were still in Tahuantinsuyu were not so bad. This was Andesuyu, the thin section of the hacha hacha that Viracocha, Pachacuti, and Topa Inca Yupanki had managed to conquer and amalgamate into our Realm.

On the mountains to either side of us perched royal palaces and tampus to store tax service for the local populations, and on our third day we passed the white granite peak of Macchu Picchu, Grandfather Mountain, whose beautiful city housed Andesuyu's largest House of Chosen Women. Kiskis made a string of dirty jokes as we drifted by, and our laughter bounced off the rock walls of the gorge to make our trip seem a happy affair, a joy ride. The rapids put a stop to that.

Think how high the mountains are above the ocean, Friar, and realize that the mountains descend almost that far into the forest. It's not a steady slope. The river wound down the face of the Eastern Mountains, interrupted by twists and turns of broken rocks that rise up from the furious waters, ready to dash our fragile raft to pieces.

The four of us worked paddle and pole from dawn to dusk to keep that from happening, but many was the time one or more of us would go into the water as the deck heaved under us, and we hauled ourselves back up in terror, aware of the stingrays that could paralyze a man for days; the eels whose bodies could shock a man senseless; the caimans who could snap off a hand or a foot given a chance; the piranhas who were drawn to blood in the water like pumas came to the bleat of newborn llamas.

256

Even when the water was calm we did not trust it. We beached our boat and went deep into the woods to relieve ourselves of our bodily functions. This might seem silly, Friar, were it not that the most hated of all animals lives in the waters of the hacha hacha, the carnero. I do not know if it is a fish, a lizard, or an insect. I just thank the gods I never saw one.

This beast, Friar, is drawn to the entry of urine into water, and it swims so fast that it can climb up the arc of a peeing man and enter his penis. Once inside, though, the thing panics and deploys spiny barbs that are supposed to ward off predators. When that happens there is no way to remove it, and a man must cut off his privates or he will die. We all were careful to piss on dry land, I assure you.

As we moved further and further into the hacha hacha we began to use my ceramic conch trumpet, blowing a mournful bray periodically to let the locals know we came in peace. Chalcuchima complained that we let half the jungle know where we were, but I would rather have everyone be aware of us rather than try to sneak past and have even one savage become offended at our subterfuge. The river was so narrow in places that a man could shoot an arrow from one bank to the other, and the idea of a whole tribe lining the shore having sport with us made my blood run cold.

We went for days and days into areas where our most well-traveled wise men knew of only third hand. We met two men fishing with barbed arrows as long as the men were tall, and through a smattering of half a dozen languages I knew, plus repeated mispronunciations of Napo River, both men pointed downstream. We punted on before it occurred to the fishermen that their bows could make short work of all four of us on the raft.

I have often referred to Supay, our version of your Devil, but rarely have I said why people try to placate him so: Supay has a sense of humour, but the joke is always on his victims. He waited until we were further into the jungles than any mountain man has ever been before, and only then did he send us our first true storm. It was very nearly the death of us.

In the jungle the storm starts long before the rain: The hacha hacha falls silent, as if holding its breath. The macaws and monkeys stop their squawking; the unexplained snapping and thrashing from the brush falls silent; even the branches and leaves cease to sway and rustle. Everything just waits, waits for the rain.

When the first drop fell I thought one of my companions had thrown a stone into the river, so isolated and powerful was its impact on the surface of the water. As the ripples spread out, a second and third drop fell, and then the Thunder God Illapa smashed his amphora and the deluge began in a great waterfall from the leaden sky with such force that it seemed to dissolve the sopping earth beneath it.

It had rained before, almost every day in fact, but nothing like this. We had already pulled over to the shore to cook our evening meal, but now we clung together beneath the trees on the river bank as the sky roared and thundered throughout the late afternoon, and as dusk fell early with the heavy clouds still above us I could just make out the river had risen and our boat was working itself loose from the shore.

"After it!" I shouted, but the storm snatched away my words, wrapping them in thick layers of water-soaked cotton so they could make no impact on my friends. Only Chalcuchima took my meaning and followed me down to the water's edge.

I reached out to grab the raft while it was still only a pace or two from the bank, but as I swung out over the water I saw where the rising river had undercut the sandy bank upon which my weight was now committed. I just had time to think better of my position and begin to throw myself backwards when Chalcuchima joined me. We collided, and like the expected twist in a panaca farce the bank disappeared beneath us, dropping us both into the brown and surging water below.

My head broke the surface, and back on the now receded shore I saw Kiskis and Rumiñaui discovering too late that our boat was drifting away. They called something to me, but I could not hear them.

I turned in a circle, but I could not see Chalcuchima. I had learned to swim at the Chaski school, but many mountain men did not. I dove under the water, moving my arms in wide sweeps to my side and kicking like a frog, trying to make contact with him. I came to the surface again and again, taking a gulp of air each time before diving back down.

On my fourth trip I found him, and that fleeting contact became a bolt of pain, as if some monster had seized me. Chalcuchima's grip was strong enough to crack a walnut. I barely made it back to the surface with his weight dragging me down, and when I did he climbed me like a cliff face, using every handhold and toehold he could find to haul himself up for air. His gasp was the first thing I had heard over the sound of the storm in a long time, a deep explosive grunt so close to my water-clogged ears that I felt nauseous.

Unsatisfied with the temporary nature of his spot above the water he tried to gain a better position by pushing down on both of my unsuspected shoulders. I went down with my mouth open and my nostrils flared, and the cloying muddy river went into every hole in my head, so that I panicked and spluttered, lashing out with my elbow into his groin. Through the water I could hear his outrage, for my head was close to his stomach and his groan came from deep in his chest. He let go of my shoulders and I bobbed back to the surface with the help of a powerful kick.

"I can't swim!" He shouted over the rain, his eyes looked into mine with a panic I had never seen before. Chalcuchima did not fear death as normal men do, but drowning left him almost helpless with terror. Only the luckiest of saves on my part had kept him from going under forever.

"I know!" I shouted back. He reached for me again, but I grabbed his arm and spun him around in the water so that my chest was against his back. I relaxed, and we were buoyant, and though he was on top of me both of our faces were clear of the water, upturned into the pouring rain. When he realized my intention he stopped struggling and we lay there in the water, drifting and recovering our strength.

I could not look around while in that position, but I knew our plight: The boat was long gone, and in my rescue efforts to save Chalcuchima I had swum well away from Kiskis and Rumiñaui on the shore. The current, swollen by the still raging storm, was pulling us ever further from them, and very soon the early dusk would become the total darkness of true night, disturbed only by the flashes of lightning.

If we did not find a shore, any shore, dawn would see us as two waterlogged corpses washed up on the river's edge for tomorrow's sun to bloat. With a shudder I realized I did not even know what carrion bird or scavenging rodent would pick my bones clean. How far I was from my mountain home where my childhood's condors and foxes would have done the service! I hated the hacha hacha. I missed Koonek, and I did not want to die.

The river swept us on, and it was pitch dark when my head smacked into a thick floating tree limb. "Grab on!" I ordered Chalcuchima. The branch did not submerge under our combined weight. It would keep us from drowning, but we were still in the river. "Now kick!" I shouted.

259

"Where?" He called back.

"Anywhere! We have to get to land!" It was a sad plan, for in the darkness we had no idea where to go, plus the leaves of our floating limb created a powerful drag on one end so half of our efforts went into lazy circling; still, we had to make land. We kicked through the darkness, and fit though I was my body ached by the time the jagged edge of our limb scraped the river bottom. "Let's go!"

We released the limb and Chalcuchima promptly went under. Our limb must have been an impressive length: Its one end extended down into the water deeper that the height of a man. I reached under and grabbed Chalcuchima by the back of the neck and hauled him up with the kind of superhuman strength I had seen Chalcuchima perform in extreme moments. I felt very close to him then, holding his head out of the water and feeling my arm burn as a warning of the pain I would endure later.

I swam towards the shore, dragging Chalcuchima behind me, and in the dark I went face first into a vertical bank, the stony composition of which split the skin above my eyebrow and drenched my face in blood. I still have the scar. Do you see it, Friar?

Stunned, I reached out with my free hand and felt upwards: The top of the bank was out of reach. We would have to swim further. I shouted instructions to him, including a few choice obscenities and questions about his manhood to fire his determination, then we began to move, he in a clumsy dog paddle and I with the inefficiency of a tired man whose one arm refused to move and whose strength flowed out of him through an open head wound that filled his gasping mouth with the taste of copper. I do not know how far we swam, only that it seemed like forever.

At last we found a place where we could pull ourselves up onto the bank with the help of a tree branch, though the branch had thorns and we both cut our hands open in the struggle. Unwilling to risk the shore falling out under us again, we staggered into the jungle. The rain continued to beat down on our trembling bodies. Only when I could walk no more did we lie down together and fall asleep in each other's arms, clinging to one another as the only familiar thing in a world gone mad.

I awoke the next day, uncomfortable for so many reasons. First, the humidity: The rain had stopped and the sun appeared so viciously that every puddle and pool that lacked the depth to resist the heat had evaporated, making the air oppressive with its stickiness. I was bathed in sweat, just as one is in the moments after making love to a woman on a warm evening. Following that thought to its inevitable daydream led to my next complaint: I was still clinging to Chalcuchima.

I rolled away from him with alacrity, setting off a whole new chain of sensations. The arm I had used to haul him up was so knotted I feared it would never work again. My palms and knuckles were cut with those tiny sliver-like lacerations that hurt out of all proportion to their injury, so that any movement of my hands was unbearable. I shook my head and regretted that too, for I had a pounding headache, and when I touched my temple I could feel the clotted gash above my eye.

"At least I'm alive," I muttered.

The sound of my voice awoke Chalcuchima, and he was on his feet so fast I wondered for a moment if I had only imagined our clammy unconscious embrace. He had the soldier's knack for becoming instantly alert. He shook himself all over like a wet dog, though we were both as dry as we were going to get in the muggy air.

"What a disgusting day," he declared with feeling. I could only nod my agreement. "What do we still have with us?" He was all business.

We took an inventory: We had both kicked off our sandals in the river, though we had our breechcloths and I still had my coca bag, somehow, with my bronze dagger, a useless chunk of Cuzco rope, and a few tangled and wet quipus. We had both lost our earplugs. We had no other clothes except our headbands, and fortunately these doubled as slings.

To summarize, Friar, we had nothing except loincloths, two slings, a single dagger, and few bits of string with which to face the hostile world. We were Inca, Children of the Sun. We could have done it with less, though I don't know how.

"What's the plan?" Chalcuchima asked, as if I knew.

"We should look for Kiskis and Rumiñaui. We're the ones who are lost, so if we find them they'll know where we all are." He nodded. "The problem is that we don't know which side of the river we're on, or whether they'll come looking for us, and we can't exactly walk through the forest calling their names unless we want our heads to be shrunk down to decorate some savage's lodge pole."

We both thought of that prospect for a moment. Chalcuchima spoke first. "Let's get started, then?" He helped me to my feet, his hands injured just as much as mine from last night's thorns. Several of our scabs burst as he hauled me up, and our blood mingled as if we had taken some sacred oath.

"Did you ever think you'd see that?" He asked, bemused.

"No," I confessed.

"Haylli," he said, and I think it was the first time he called me Haylli. "Thank you for yesterday."

We found our way to the river, which was still running high and fast. A glance at the floating detritus told us which way was upstream and which was down, and from this we concluded that we had landed on the same side of the river as we had last seen Kiskis and Rumiñaui, though we had no idea how far we had come downstream of them. We began to walk.

The first day was hard, but by the second morning my arm had forgiven me to the point of stiffness rather than spasm. Chalcuchima killed a monkey with his sling, and I skinned it and cleaned it with my knife, and we made a fire with two sticks, cooking the thing's stringy arms and legs, pulling the meager flesh from it bones like the starving men we were.

It was funny, Friar, but it was like we had never been in the hacha hacha until after the storm. I don't know. Somehow, I suppose, being on the river meant you always had the sky above you, whereas even walking beside the river that was never true in the jungle. Everything was so... Green.

Green isn't enough of a word, really. Green is a word mountain men have for the colour of growing things, but things grow in the hacha hacha every possible type of green, and all the hues between those possibilities, and every possible combination of light and shadow falling upon those shades. Vibrant greens and morose greens, deep and shallow, bold and cautious, I closed my eyes, but somehow I knew the green was still there, on all sides of me, as well as above me through three different tree canopies before reaching the sky that every mountain man should be able to see at all times when out of doors.

Then there were the noises. Everything in the hacha hacha moves, Friar, and in the moving it will squeal and squawk, bark and snap and sigh. Worse still is when the noises stop, because then the rain came again. Gods, how I hate the rain.

We made our miserable camp that night in a downpour, and as suddenly as it had started it stopped, as if some celestial engineer had diverted the flow of his aqueduct. Every drop of rain I had experienced in the hacha hacha, from morning mist to drizzle to raging thunderstorm, worked under a different set of rules from the mountain rain. It was infuriating.

We crawled out of our wet clothes and went naked into the undergrowth, looking for anything dry with which to rebuild our fire. When we managed that we lay on either side of it with our clothes propped up on sticks to dry. A long uncomfortable silence stretched between us.

"I admit that I was sent here to kill you." He was stretched out by the fire in such a casual pose that we might as well have been having the friendliest of conversations.

My guts froze, aware of the knotty muscles across from me and how quickly I could feel his hands around my throat. Then I corrected myself, remembering he had a walking stick that could double as a mace whereas I had my father's lancehead dagger tucked into my waistband. It wouldn't come to strangling, if it came to it. I surprised myself with the composure in my voice when I asked, "And why haven't you? We haven't seen Kiskis or Rumiñaui for days now. How easy would it be for you to kill me and tell them I died a hundred other ways?"

"Very easy," he said, using a stick to poke a piece of wood deeper into the fire.

"So?" I asked, bracing myself to jump up and run into the darkness.

"So what?" He put down the stick and looked me in the eye.

"So why don't you want me dead?" I asked, realizing only as I said it that it was true.

He sat up and rearranged his tunic on its drying sticks. "I've been asking myself the same thing since we reached the hacha hacha, and I think there are a few reasons... First, I am tired of being the puppet of coyas and viceroys. Doing their bidding last time did me no favours. This time will be no better."

I nodded, but he was not finished.

"Second, why do I hate you? For the Vixen? She's my wife now. For the race? A foolish wager I should have retracted as soon as you accepted. I made it knowing you could not win, forgetting the resources at your father's disposal. I chose my battlefield poorly."

"Is there a third thing?" I asked, sure that there was but unsure I wanted to hear it.

"Yes, and this is the one I have trouble convincing myself of, so don't you mock me..." He waited for me to shake my head in promise. "It has occurred to me that we are images in the mirror, and that's too close a thing to throw away." He waited for me to say something, anything to break the spell, but I was not that foolish.

"Think about it: We are both sons of fathers killed for a treason we feel they did not commit. We have both displayed natural god-given aptitudes for our fathers' trades and will take their place. We both love the same woman, and both have had her for a time. We are linked."

Again he paused, but I sensed the trap and remained silent. "Don't mistake this revelation for friendship. There is too much between us to be friends. I am only saying in you I have found an equal, different, utterly outside my ken, but equal. If we can't be friends then we still do not need the hot-blooded hate of enemies. Maybe we can agree to be merely rivals, goading each other with our own accomplishments to better the other."

I was quiet for a long while, watching the fire. I knew that if I agreed to this now I would survive the night, but if I asked a few questions I would know the rules of this new game between us and might have peace for the rest of my life.

"And what of our fathers? You know my feelings about your father's actions with the Chanca and the Chimu and the garrison at Caxamalca."

"You weren't there. Neither was your father, the man who gave you your opinion. Besides, you only speak of such things when we are fighting. I propose we leave our fathers behind us."

"And the Vixen?"

"What about my wife?"

"She was mine, and now she's yours."

"That's the way it will stay," for the first time I heard the warning rumble in his voice, saw those neck muscles of his twitch in anger as he set his jaw.

"I did not mean to say otherwise. I have Koonek. I have all I want. What I'm asking is do you hold it against me that I had the Vixen first?"

"Do you hold it against me that I have her now?"

"No," I said.

"Then no," he sounded so reasonable.

"And what about your career? You lost your legion because of me."

"I got that legion from my Uncle in exchange for setting up your father. I tried to take the easy path and I fell. I'll climb back up and take the hard road. It's the punishment for my part in Tupac Capac's death."

It was more than I ever would have hoped for. "Then I think we have peace, rival."

"We have peace, rival."

We both spat into the flames and listened to the sizzle, and then we rolled over to sleep.

I lay there, listening to his regular breathing, but I had a question that I could not imagine having a better time to ask. "Chalcuchima?" I called him by his adult name, something I suppose I would have to get used to. He grunted. "Why do you love Atoc China?" I rolled over to see him looking at me from the far side of the fire. "I mean, when I was a boy I suppose I was just drawn to her. That's her gift—"

"Quiet," he interrupted me. "I'm thinking about it," he murmured. We lay there for a while, then he sat up and threw more wood into the fire. "When my father was executed, my Uncle Illyapa held a very quiet memorial dinner party for him. We couldn't say it was in his honour, of course, because my father was executed for treason, and so no one was allowed to talk about him." He stabbed the fire with his stick, absently.

"She was there," he said, smiling now at something in the flames. "It was before she was a chosen woman, before she was any kind of woman at all, Haylli. She was a girl, six years old, maybe? Pretty for her age, of course, but not irresistible in the way she would become."

I sat up. It seemed disrespectful to lie down while Chalcuchima spoke of this. "Her family was invited because her father had served on my father's staff. Otherwise her whole clan were nobodies, third-generation Incas-by-privilege at the funeral of one of the noblest Intip Churi ever born. I had no idea who she was, but she knew I was the dead man's son, and she knew I was under strict orders to act like it was a simple dinner party." He stabbed at the fire again, absently.

"She walked up to me and gave me a hug, that child-like kind of hug that means nothing but you remember forever, and as she held me she whispered in my ear, 'He was a great man, and one day you will make

265

him proud.'" He smiled again. "It was the only thing anyone said to me about my father all night, but it was enough."

He looked up from the fire for the first time, and his smile was infectious. I started smiling too. "Did you ever wonder how she got her sweet deal, a chosen woman for educational purposes only, free to marry whoever she wanted?"

"I thought her father asked Old Topa to—"

"Her father was a military bureaucrat attached to my father's staff. Do you think he could ask a favour of the Emperor? Old Topa would have taken one look at the girl and taken her into his own household, and whatever she and her father wanted for her, they would have been forced to be flattered at the Emperor's decision."

"So how?"

"Me," he tapped his chest with his free hand. "I did it. Nine years old, and my Uncle Illyapa says I can have anything I want as a gift for being his favourite nephew, and I said I wanted that girl to be given all the support our family could muster. He offered me a villa in the Yucay, but I turned him down. I think it was his plan all along to give me an estate so I could support myself when the time came, but I refused any kind of property from him.

"Finally he agreed, and my two uncles kept her clear of the regular chosen women selection process four times, a process that would have taken her in an instant. Then they put her in the House of Chosen Women under a special dispensation. It was the only strings I ever had them pull for me as the son of their dead brother."

I leaned back from the fire and thought about it. "I'm sorry," I said.

"For what?"

"I've been as much of a problem in your life as you've been in mine." The fire popped in front of us.

"Yeah, you really have." He smiled his thin-lipped smile at me. "You were a pain in my ass for years."

"Well, what are rivals for?" I said, hoping our truce was still in effect.

"What are rivals for?" He agreed. We lay back down, and this time we fell asleep without further conversation.

* * *

266

The next day we found Kiskis and Rumiñaui on the bank of a minor stream. Our raft had been dashed to pieces where the stream emptied into the river, but much of our cargo had either sunk in the shallows by the wreckage or floated in their sealed pots to be snarled in tree roots sticking out from the undercut bank.

The two of them had fished some of the trade axeheads out of the water, hafted them, and set to making a new raft out of a nearby stand of balsas. We had no rope, so I twisted some out of split bamboo. Chalcuchima went hunting with his sling, and we ate well of monkey and bird, even decorating our punting poles with the feathers.

Two days later we were back on the river as if the storm had never happened, though in a way, everything was different. Kiskis was the one who pulled me aside first, asking why Chalcuchima and I weren't fighting. I had no sooner told him when Rumiñaui came over to ask if the crazy story he had just heard from Chalcuchima about a truce was true. The tension drained out of our journey, now that we were all comfortable together.

Ten days later our river joined another of equal girth, and we pulled up onto the bank of this new stream to try to learn its name. We blew our conch trumpet repeatedly throughout the day and lit smoky fires. It was around dusk that men appeared out of the hacha hacha around us, as silent as death and just as ominous.

We had some of our salvaged trade goods spread out on the ground below us, and I greeted the men with arms spread wide open. "Napo River?" I asked.

The jungle men were short and sinewy. Their bows were taller than they were; their arrows were tipped with serrated bone, mankillers.

"Napo River? Napu River? Nupu River?" I tried over and over, trying to guess how the locals might pronounce the name, if indeed this was the Napo. At last I got one of them to nod. "Good!" I said, perhaps a little too forcefully. One of them twitched his bowstring in surprise. I made a calming gesture with my open hands and began more gently. "Now take a look at the trade goods, good, and take us to your leader. Headman? Curaca? Chief? Sinchi?" The archer who had twitched earlier moved again at the word Sinchi. "That's right. Take us to your Sinchi."

They conversed among themselves in a language I had no hope of following. It was hunter-speak, an abbreviated form of a language I could not guess at. Their decision reached, the first archer gestured for us to follow. The four of us packed our trade goods onto tumplines and followed the hunters into the forest.

There was no mistaking the Spice Lands once you were into the depths of the forest, for the tall trees were covered in the dark brown flowers, and they smelled so rich on the tree that I wondered if you would even be able to smell your leavings when you relieved yourself. Everywhere we saw the spice flowers, but it wasn't until we came to a Supay's Garden that we saw the vanilla orchid.

A Supay's Garden is any area of the jungle that seems to have been cultivated, cleared of trees, weeded, pruned, watered, all without the hand of man. The clearing we passed through while following the archers was the very definition of such a place, and a shudder ran down my spine at the power of such a huaca. We could see the flowers there, each one heavy with seed pods, but there was not one blossom outside the careful confines of the clearing.

It was the shrieking parakeets that alerted me that this must be a sizable encampment: Our wise men had heard tales of villages guarded by birds trained to call out when two-legged visitors approached. I imagine it's a simple matter of feeding the birds whenever you return to camp; that said, training birds implies a long-term camp and a large population. I was right on both counts.

The savages had not cleared the forest, choosing instead to build their rude huts and lodges where they could fit between the trees. They wore almost nothing, but much decorative body paint, and their children ran after us squealing their delight at the strangers. I looked at the different doorways as we passed, but I saw no human heads. I took that as a good sign.

We were led deep into the centre of the village where a crowd had gathered, and there we saw the man our archer guides had brought us to speak with. We have no word for barbarian in Runa Simi, Friar. I suppose our closest is mana apuyoc, which means, "Men without a leader." Such is what we called the men who dwell in the hacha hacha, but that is false. This tribe had a leader, a thin old man with a heron's leg bone through his nose, wild grey hair decorated with macaw feathers, and painted nipples. He sat upon a tree stump, surrounded by his jungle splendour, judging us.

I tried Runa Simi, then Mochica and Chibcha. Finally I tried the most rustic dialects I could conjure, which did get his attention. He knew a few words, enough to hash out a communication between us. He gestured for us to wait, firing off a string of words that sounded like someone dropping round stones down a hollow log. One of his tribe's women appeared before us with gold dust wrapped up in a piece of tattered cotton. Her breasts were exposed.

"Is he offering us the gold or the girl?" Rumiñaui asked, tugging on his blue headband, surprisingly embarrassed for a panaca boy.

"Probably both," was Chalcuchima's opinion.

"He can keep the girl," Kiskis said. Even by his standards, she was not a beauty.

"He can keep the gold too," I said. "We'll be getting that anyway, one day. We're the only market for it. You see any gold ornaments on these people? They must pan the dust and trade it to the Jivaros, who trade it to the Cañaris, who give it to us. That lump of gold flakes will be one of your earplugs in twenty years." They all looked impressed at my grasp of economics, as if I were not one of the world's foremost experts on the subject. I told the chief by word and gesture that we did not want his gold; we wanted the spice flower and the vanilla orchid.

We haggled for a long time on the spice flower, and the old man clearly enjoyed the negotiating more than whatever we eventually would give him. He rocked back and forth on his stump, by turns angry and happy, aggressive and conciliatory. When he was done I had all the spice flower blossoms I wanted for a pittance, and he leaned back on his stump smugly, as if the trade goods I brought meant anything to me besides additional weight on my return trip.

The vanilla orchid was harder, and as we entered into the negotiations I could see the archers around us tighten their grips on their bow staves and lean in, muttering things to their chief. He became agitated, finally slumping on his stump, exhausted at the ordeal.

"What was that?" Chalcuchima asked.

"The garden is sacred to his people. The orchids must stay," I said.

"We're allowed to take the spice flower," Rumiñaui said reasonably.

Reason had nothing to do with it, but the chief had tried to give me an explanation for that. "The blossom comes off a tree, and though the blossoms go, the trees stay. The orchid can only be found in that garden. Whenever his people see it anywhere else they burn it. It is only for their garden and must never leave."

"We could extract the vanilla here..." Kiskis trailed off.

"And it will evaporate or spill or leak by the time we're halfway home," Chalcuchima finished Kiskis's sentence.

"Offer him everything we've got, everything. I don't want to be carrying any of it back with us anyway," Rumiñaui said. I offered the chief everything down to Kiskis' and Rumiñaui's earplugs. The only thing I did not offer was my father's dagger, for fear the grey-haired man would take it and send us away empty-handed.

When nothing would persuade him I made our excuses and we were led back to our raft at the river's edge to make camp for the night. "Why aren't we staying with them?" Kiskis asked.

"Thought better of the girl, did you?" Chalcuchima asked.

"It has been a long trip," Kiskis muttered.

"If we stay with them we can't steal the orchids tonight. That chief will negotiate with us for days because he enjoys it so much, but his people won't let him give the flowers away. We can't go back to Huayna Capac without them, so we'll take them."

"How?" Rumiñaui asked.

So the three military men and the tocoyricoc put their heads together to work out a foolproof plan to steal a tribe's holy flowers. Gods, Friar, men are stupid when they're young, especially the smart ones.

We were ready by nightfall, but we waited until the absolute dead of night to make sure any savages detailed to watch us would have grown bored and returned to their village or slept out in the hacha hacha. Who knows how mana apuyoc live?

High above us, beyond the tops of the trees, a red star shone. I have asked Topa Cusi Yupanki about it, for he knows all things to do with the heavens, and the Bird Man assured me you can see the red star in the mountains too, but it is lost among the myriad other stars. Down in the hacha hacha the air is so thick most of those little stars grow fainter, and that is why the red star dominates. Whatever it is, being born under that red star warps the minds of the jungle men, makes them lust for human flesh. I wished I still had my mantle so I could bite its hem. I felt unlucky that night.

"Are we ready?" I whispered. The three heads nodded. We had made

270

a footplow out of a formidable stick, hardening the end by fire. We also had the pots that had been holding our trade goods. A false trail had been broken that ended at the river, so that pursuers would think we were escaping by raft. We were as ready as we were going to be.

We crept through the forest as silent as the jungle cats we all feared. Supay's garden was bathed in the light of the stars and crescent moon, unearthly in its cold beauty.

By gesture we broke into our separate tasks, finding the orchids that were small and strong enough to transplant, pulling the soil from their roots, lifting them out and putting them in the pots, filling the pots with rich soil. We worked slowly and quietly, but whenever Kiskis was idle he tapped his hand on the footplow, displaying his nervous impatience to us all.

When we were almost done, Kiskis was standing idle again, and for some reason he took it into his head to stand watch, looking towards the savages' encampment, as if he would be able to see their jungle archers in time to do anything about it in that dim light. Realizing his limited vision but attributing it to a poor vantage point he began climbing one of the trees edging the garden, and while doing so his weight swayed the top of the tree enough to disturb the roosting birds.

Two or three jungle denizens took off in much-troubled flapping, but that was hardly a concern to us. No, our problem was that the tree was home to some of the camp's guard parakeets, and their whistle calls of 'Feed me! Feed me! You're not feeding me yet!' in their singsong language was worse than pounding on a man drum. Almost immediately we heard shouting from the camp.

"Time to go!" Chalcuchima said, taking charge.

We ran through the forest to our campsite, kicking our raft off the shore to drift downriver as it would, then doubling back into the woods. If luck was on our side the savages would see that no one was attacking their village and go to sleep, but we were not lucky. Shouts of outrage came from the direction of Supay's garden, and soon torches were lit, appearing to us like fireflies dancing through the jungle behind us.

We ran west into the hacha hacha, carrying only our weapons and flower pots. We ran through the night and most of the next day, and when we finally stopped to rest in the afternoon we could hear the search parties in the jungle behind us, so we stumbled forward again.

"I guess the raft didn't work," Kiskis said.

271

"The whole plan didn't work," Rumiñaui huffed.

"We have the plants," I said, trying to sound optimistic.

"And how far are we going to be able to take them?" Chalcuchima dared to ask. It was the truth, though. We were four; they were hundreds. We had no food; they knew how to live off the jungle. We were heading towards our mountain homeland now, which meant all the rivers were running against us. We would have to travel on foot, which meant we would have to stop to eat and sleep. Our searchers would be able to stagger out their rests so that some of them were always closing the distance on us.

"You're the military genius, Chalcuchima. What miracle can you perform for us?" I said.

"There are four of us, and we might as well be unarmed for all the good slings are going to do against those arrows," he said. The four of us slowed to a walk, each rubbing out some cramp or stretching a tired muscle.

"Could we start a fire?" Kiskis asked.

"This jungle is too wet to start a big enough fire in the time we have between them and us," Rumiñaui said.

"What's that?" I pointed through a rare break in the canopy to show three thin tendrils of smoke rising up out of the jungle ahead of us. We broke into a run again, and soon the noises of our pursuers dropped away behind us as we tore through the underbrush.

The smoke had seemed closer than it was, another trick of the damnable hacha hacha, and we were exhausted by the time we reached a ridge overlooking the village.

They were a worse sort than those we were fleeing, for shrunken heads and full-sized skulls festooned every post and pole of the village. On the other hand, perhaps they were just more flamboyant in their decorations: I hadn't seen proof yet that the mana apuyoc chasing us were not also headhunters.

"Are you boys ready for that miracle?" Chalcuchima asked, his hands on his knees as he pulled in deep lungfuls of air.

"Them?" I asked. "I think I prefer the people who already want to kill us."

"Sure," Chalcuchima straightened up. "But the truth is we don't like either of them, so let's get them to fight our battles for us."

272

It was a dumb plan whose one distinguishing attribute was that it was the only one we had except to run until we were caught.

We began by walking back towards our pursuers, marshalling our strength but closing the distance. We needed to surprise them, for them to come across us before they were expecting us. It almost went the opposite way, for we stumbled across the first of their archers at the base of our ridge.

Their skirmishers looked at us wide-eyed for a moment, and we used that moment to turn and run back towards the headhunters' village, calling out at the top of our lungs whatever sounds were most easily formed by men running for their lives and zigzagging crazily all over the side of a hill, avoiding the long arrows whipping through the foliage behind us.

We crested the ridge and dropped down the far side as fast as we could, sliding on our backsides when that was faster than a controlled descent.

Chalcuchima's plan relied on confusion, and we had to move as fast as possible to make it work. Behind us we could hear the whooping of the orchid tribe's archers, baying like dogs at the scent of their prey.

I was moving too fast through the undergrowth to get much sense of what was going on in the headhunters' village, but there was definitely commotion; the place seemed to buzz like a beehive. The four of us broke through the jungle on the outskirts of the village and kept running, waving our hands both to show we were unarmed and gesturing that we were being pursued. We must have looked ridiculous, loaded down with flower pots, covered in dirt, waving and screaming and running. At the same time, we did not look as threatening as the jungle archers behind us.

We did not stop running, nor lurching our direction back and forth at random. We just made our way through the village as quickly as possible. Women and children shrieked in alarm and men bellowed their outrage, but as they were snatching up their bows to kill us, a great many more intruders, our pursuers, emerged from the jungle.

I only snatched glimpses, but the orchid tribe's archers stood there, blinking in the sunlight, and then they realized they had launched an assault on their neighbouring tribe's village. The first arrow flew, and it was returned by one of the headhunters, and then the whole area descended into shouting and war whooping and volleys of silent arrows as men from both tribes charged one another.

Kiskis, Rumiñaui, Chalcuchima and I ran out the far side of the village and into the jungle, and we did not stop putting one foot in front of the other until nightfall. I do not know how the battle ended, or if either side ever sent out search parties to find us. We never encountered either of them again, and intertribal warfare is so rampant in the hacha hacha no word of the battle ever reached our Cañari trading posts.

We walked through the jungle, always west, towards the mountains and the setting sun. It rained every day, and the puddles steamed for the rest of the day, making the air unbearably thick with moisture. Our clothes rotted off us until we salvaged the merest rags in order to give us some semblance of modesty.

Our slings lost all strength, and one by one they stretched out and flew apart as we hunted. I carried my coca bag in my hand because the shoulder strap's wool had mildewed until I no longer trusted it to stay attached to me. We replaced the tumplines holding our flower pots with maguey fibers several times. The flowers loved the climate. We did not.

We meant to head towards the Cañari territories, but somehow we miscalculated in our wanderings, for our first contact with Tahuantinsuyu was a tomb cut into a cliff face as only the Chacapoyas do. The Chacapoyas, the Cloud People, for the first time I understood the name: This jungle was halfway up the side of the eastern mountains now, and the clouds off the never-ending forest came to rest here in thick blankets which would cover valleys while leaving hilltops clear, always swirling, sometimes revealing, mostly concealing. This land was filled with magic.

We saw no people for days after that solitary tomb, and it was that more than anything that drove home just how uncivilized Andesuyu, the Eastern Quarter of our Realm, really was. We were back in lands that gave at least some allegiance to the Inca; undoubtedly there were roads and tampus somewhere nearby, but we could walk for a month and not find one because the hacha hacha was so thick!

That night we made a fire and hung our rags to dry.

"They're your people, Haylli. Where are they?" Rumiñaui's face was as expressionless as ever, but his tone implied I knew exactly where to find the Chacapoyas.

"I've never been here before. I've met maybe thirty or forty of them in my life," I said.

"Why do we even have this province? What's it good for?" Kiskis asked.

274

"You're joking, right?" I said. The three of them looked at me with blank expressions. "Okay, for starters, all this country can grow coca leaves, and that's true of maybe three provinces of the eighty that make up Tahuantinsuyu." They still looked less than impressed. "It also has gold, both locally collected and traded from the savages out in the ha-cha hacha." Still nothing. "Okay then, how about the fact that they're a buffer between the mountains and the jungle archers; they have ri-diculously good looking women, and every one of their men is a born soldier?" That got their attention.

"Good looking women?" Kiskis's crooked smile was lit up by our fire.

"Born soldiers?" Chalcuchima murmured.

"You flatter us," a strange voice said, the first strange voice we had heard since running through the headhunters' village. We were on our feet with our axes up, but we were night-blind from looking into the fire. With only four of us we had long abandoned the normal marching discipline of posting a sentry.

"And you are?" I tried to sound nonchalant.

"I am Ozcoc, the tampucamayoc of Urpi Tampu. Can I ask why you lords are camping down here when there are beds for you at the top of the hill?" He stepped out of the forest with his hands open and a friendly smile on his face.

"You're serious?" Kiskis asked, smiling again.

"We can't see a thing in this jungle," Chalcuchima said by way of ex-cuse.

We followed the tampucamayoc up the hill, no more than six or seven hundred paces, to a modest tampu that looked like a palace after our long trip. I ordered fresh clothes, food, akha, and a place to sleep to be prepared. Though Ozcoc gave the necessary orders, the staff did not go about their business with the usual speed. I pulled him aside.

"What is going on here?"

"My lord?"

"I am a tocoyricoc on detached duty," I said, forgetting what effect that would have on a tampucamayoc. He dropped to his knees and began babbling apologies and excuses, and it took me a long time to soothe him and pull him up off the ground for me to question him. "I want to know why the staff is so…"

"They will be punished!" He promised.

"I didn't say that. I said... Something's wrong here. Tell me what it is."

His eyes looked both ways, as if checking to make sure the walls of his tampu office had not grown ears. "Sire, I am a loyal puric, but many of my people..."

He did not need to say more. The Chacapoyas had never been conquered: Old Topa won a couple of minor skirmishes and then paid their tribal chiefs huge sums of cloth to join their territories to Tahuantinsuyu.

In the years since we had built them roads and storehouses and provided them with goods they might not otherwise see, but every year we took more of their men away as soldiers and more of their women away as chosen women, and there were purics now who were boys when the deal was struck who felt their chiefs had sold their futures out from under them. There could be a rebellion brewing.

"Alright," I said. "My people and I rest here for tonight, then we have to make the best speed possible back to Cuzco—"

"Sire, the mountain passes are closed from the cold season's storms, and there's no road through the jungle."

I chewed on this for a moment. The Chacapoyas clung to the eastern side of the eastern mountains, but there was no province of Tahuantinsuyu between them and Cuzco on this side of the range. We would have no access to tampus or any other help. "We'll go through the passes, up and over into Huanca territory, then take the Royal Mountain Road all the way to Cuzco."

None of his protestations could change my mind, but I should have listened to him. One of the Chacapoyas legitimate complaints was that they were cut off from the rest of Tahuantinsuyu for a quarter of the year by poor weather in the treacherous mountain passes.

We followed the road, stopping at each tampu, shoring up our strength and nurturing our orchids against the increasingly cold nights. At the last tampu before the passes the tampucamayoc begged us not to go. I took what provisions I thought was necessary and went anyway.

Climbing those mountains out of season may have been among the stupidest thing I have ever done. We were alone and unaided, disconnected from the tampu system and the chaski network, blinded by snow, frozen by winds. The mountains seemed to swallow us in a white nightmare.

276

Our tropical plants were wrapped in translucent cloth to protect them from the worst of the elements. As for us, we were wrapped in wet wool, our eyes slitted, just putting one muffled foot in front of the other, often sinking up to our knees in snow. For a time Chalcuchima made a show of his strength by breaking trail, but when no one took notice he fell back and we began a steady rotation in miserable silence. Up there, where even the llama herders don't venture out of season, the road is just piles of stones called apacheta strung out within sight of one another.

Each apacheta is a huaca marking the nexus of bad spirits that overcome travelers at this altitude. They have been built up over centuries, for the pile is made up of gifts from passing travelers. The poor offered stones. Wealthy men left cloth or a pair of sandals at the apacheta. As for us, we were chewing five times our number's worth of coca, and we took to spitting our wads onto the rocks to appease Supay's minions. No one suffered soroche, the mountain sickness, so it must have worked.

When we crested the western mountains and descended into the highlands of Huanca territory, half the plants were dead and the rest sickly. Rumiñaui lost two toes to frost bite, and we left him at Xauxa to recover. We worked our way down the road as fast as we could, using our red thread to procure hammock-porters so that we could travel as we slept. Nothing must suggest to Huayna Capac that we dallied on our way home, not after we had actually succeeded in Mama Ocllo's ridiculous quest.

The three of us arrived at Huayna Capac's Cuzco palace, much battered and wearied by our travels, to find the Court dressed in the black of mourning. Mama Ocllo was six days' dead. Our ordeal had been for nothing.

We entered the Imperial Presence, burdened and barefoot, and when we saw the tears streaming down our Emperor's face I fell to my knees to show my sympathy for his grief. Behind me I could hear my two remaining companions blowing their plucked eyelashes at him.

"She's gone," he said, as if the sun would not rise tomorrow.

"Majesty, I'm sorry. We came as fast—"

"Of course you did, Haylli. Of course you did." He said. I felt a great weight lift my shoulders, so that I shifted to make sure my ceremonial burden had not come off.

"What shall we do with the plants?" Kiskis asked.

"They were never going to work, were they?" Huayna Capac smiled through his tears.

"No," I said.

"No," the Emperor repeated.

Chalcuchima snorted back a strangled laugh, and I looked at him out of the corner of my eye. His thick shoulders were shaking as he tried to hold in his mirth, and when it was obvious that he wasn't fooling anyone he started to laugh aloud.

I waited for the world to fall down upon us, but Chalcuchima's guffaws were contagious, and the Emperor joined his brother-in-law in laughing long and hard. On cue the whole Court felt the levity of the moment, the absurdity of sending four Inca of the Blood out into the unknown in search of eternal youth.

When the moment had passed Chalcuchima wiped a tear from his high cheekbone and rubbed it between his fingers. "Burn them," Chalcuchima suggested. "Burn the plants. Sacrifice them to her memory. She'll live forever now. She might as well have the cure she wanted."

Huayna Capac nodded, blowing his nose on a cumpi handkerchief. One of the palace torches was used to start a sacrificial bonfire on the flagstones, and when it was roaring the three of us each hurled our pots into it, watched the plants twist and char. The Emperor had stopped crying by the time the last orchid was on the pyre.

"Sacrifice a llama, too," I suggested, seeing the impromptu scene's cathartic effect on him.

Topa Cusi Yupanki led in a young brown buck, fed it a handful of precious coca leaves, and said the dedication prayers. The skin of a llama's throat is so thick it is the best leather for sandals, so the Bird Man buried a bronze needle into the back of the beast's head, killing it without a sound.

"Check the omens, sire," Chalcuchima suggested. Huayna Capac nodded, and Topa Cusi Yupanki opened the llama's abdomen. I have little training in augury, but even I could see the buck's liver was dark and healthy.

"The signs are favourable, Sire. The intestines speak of happiness, and the organs suggest gratitude. Mama Ocllo accepts your sacrifice and tells you not to grieve for her too long. She is watching over you," Topa Cusi Yupanki said.

"Thank you," the Emperor said, leaning back on his usno. "Well then, let's reward you all, shall we?" He signaled a secretary to step forward to tie down the authorizations for the Imperial boons.

"For Rumiñaui..." The Emperor let his voice trail off, and I could feel my heart begin to pound at the thought we would be able to pick our rewards.

"Sire, could I suggest you let him command a garrison on the Huanahuari frontier?" Kiskis asked, naming a hostile border bloody enough to win our eight-toed friend glory, but minor enough to keep the Emperor from taking personal command of the army. It was a career-advancing move. The Emperor nodded and his secretary tied down the orders.

"And for you Kiskis?"

"As you know, Sire, I'm a lonely man," several courtiers chuckled. Kiskis had six wives so far. "Could I have a couple of chosen women to keep me company, and a small puna estate to support them?" Again, the Imperial nod made it as good as done.

"And Chalcuchima, what would you like?"

"My wife," my rival said, emphasizing he had only one, "Wants to lead a panaca one day, Sire."

"I can't make that promise. The households of my ancestors run their own affairs."

"Could I beg you to support her bid when she makes it?"

"That is what you want in reward for your journey?"

Chalcuchima looked at me with his thin-lipped smile. "There were some other benefits of the trip, Sire. This I ask for my wife."

"Then I will do even more for you. She has not joined a specific panaca yet, has she?" Huayna Capac knew she had not. Everyone watched the Vixen, even if she was a married woman.

"No, Sire."

"Then tell her to join my father's Capac Panaca. I will donate a flock of a thousand alpacas to them at the same time. They will take the hint." The Emperor turned to me and smiled. "And you, Haylli? My mother may not have liked you, but I do. How can I thank you for doing this thing for her without a word of complaint?"

279

I felt like I was on fire, basking in such Imperial pleasure. "Sire, I have a wonderful wife and a wonderful position. I am content."

"Don't make an Emperor beg, Haylli," he said.

"If I must ask a favour, Majesty, could I be made tocoyricoc of Chincaysuyu and have its tocoyricoc put in my current position of Condesuyu?"

The whole Court paused, trying to figure out why I would ask for such a thing. The Emperor was the only one allowed to ask the question, and after teasing me with his silence he finally asked why.

"Sire, Condesuyu was my father's work. I want my own. I want to work with curacas who haven't known me since before I had a breechcloth. I want to administer the building up of the city of Tumipampa, the integration of the Chacapoyas, the gold workings of Caxamalca." My fingers began to twitch at the thought of the quipu work ahead of me.

The Sapa Inca rose from his usno and walked up to me, putting one hand on my shoulder in a sign of favour unprecedented in all my experience at Court. My shoulder went numb at his touch. I heard one of the chosen women attending us gasp. "Haylli," he said to me. "You are the greatest administrator in Tahuantinsuyu. I have never heard a man ask for more work as a reward for unpleasant work. If I had a hundred of you Tahuantinsuyu would run as smoothly as a chaski on a flat, paved road."

He looked around the Court at the lackeys and hangers-on that surrounded him, and he raised his voice, as if we were not all focused on every word to come from his mouth already. "Tocoyricoc Haylli Yupanki, Capac Quipucamayoc and friend, Chincaysuyu is your new post, and when you go there you will stay in palaces I will have built for you in Tumipampa, Quitu, and Tumpez. When you are on your leisure you can stay in a villa I will give you in the Yucay valley. For these estates I give you five thousand topos, five hundred alpacas, and a hundred yanaconas."

The Court froze for a moment at the Imperial largesse. I knew Sapa Inca Topa Inca Yupanki had confiscated that much and more when he seized my father's assets, but all that was the property of his panaca now. Huayna Capac had just given me an incredible portion of his still small personal estate.

"Sire, I must protest your generosity. I'm a tocoyricoc. I see the State quipus. I know—"

The Emperor laughed and took his hand from my shoulder to wave it around the room. "Then I will just have to conquer new peoples to increase my wealth, won't I?" The soldiers present, including my two companions, shifted at this. It was often said that Mama Ocllo kept Huayna Capac in Cuzco. Now we had proof. With her passing our glory days of new conquests would return.

"Now go home and make some more children with that pretty wife of yours to fill all the homes I just gave you." Though the Emperor's mood was much better than when we entered, the rest of the Court seemed to grow somber at what he had just said to me.

We bowed and scraped our way out of the Imperial Presence, each pleased by what we had seen: Huayna Capac was coming out from under his mother's shadow, and we were his favourites. Our fathers' generation had passed, and we would be the new Imperial leaders. It was overwhelming.

We made plans to get together at Kiskis's for a proper party that evening, then we went our separate ways to go home and tell our families all that had transpired.

As I left the Huacaypata, a wave of fatigue washed over me. I walked down the narrow road, my feet feeling like lead weights. The journey was over. I had never been so bone weary, truly bone weary, as I was at that moment. All I wanted to do was enter my home, wrap one arm around Koonek, kiss Wawa on her beautiful forehead, and fall asleep.

It had rained while we were in the Imperial Presence and the lane smelled of wet thatch and puddles on cobblestones. A servant girl from a neighbour's house was coming towards me, her arms piled heavy with laundry fresh from the bleachers. She saw me over her burden and I smiled at her, glad for the familiar face and the sign that I was so close to home.

The girl went as white as the clothes she was carrying, and I watched in dismay as she dropped her load and ran away from me. If I had been Supay himself with a legion of minions behind me I could not have made her run faster. I looked over my shoulder to make sure such a spectacle was not behind me, then tried to shrug off the incident. I stepped over her dirtied washings and made my way down the remainder of the street to my family compound.

The cloth of my clan's yellow had been removed from my door, leaving the bare teak to greet me. "I hope we gave it to a more reliable girl to wash," I muttered, thumping on the door with the heel of my hand.

My doorman opened up and then flung wide the teak barrier, not in greeting but in shock. The same fear was plastered on his face as upon the girl in the road, and I knew at that moment something terrible had happened. "What? What is it?" I demanded.

"You are dead, my lord!" The man called out, sinking to his knees.

"Get up! You can see I'm not," I smiled, glad that it was such a minor mix up. I grabbed the man under the arms and went to heave him up jovially, but he was as dead a weight as a sack of potatoes, and he kept shaking his head back and forth in horror.

"No, lord, no. Word came from the palace! From Mama Ocllo's personal body servant! You are frozen dead in the mountains west of Chacapoyas—"

"Almost, but not quite," I smiled down at him, shaking him so he could see that truly it was I, back from the dead. I could understand they had all been frightened, but here I was, fine, and Mama Ocllo would never trouble us again. "Go get Koonek. Bring her to me. Let her know I am not dead—"

The mention of my wife tore a cry of anguish from the kneeling man's throat, and now it was my turn to shake my head in dismay at his tidings.

"No, lord! Mama Ocllo's servant said that you were dead, and that her son had refused to grant your widow Inca-by-privilege status. Koonek was ordered to return immediately to her village among the Mapuche..."

I pictured the terror my wife had for her mother and knew there was no time to lose: I would send a message by chaski. She could be half way there now, dreading every footfall. I must save her.

"How long ago did she leave? I'll send word. I'll fetch her back."

"Lord, the Lady Koonek wouldn't go back. She kept saying her mother had cursed her."

"Well if she's still here, bring her to me!" I was getting angry at him, kneeling there, telling me one thing and then another.

"Lord, she went across the street and left your daughter with the neighbours, and then she went—"

"Yes? Where did she go? Out with it, man!"

"She went up to your counting room and hanged herself from the rafters with her own hair."

Gods, Friar, I can close my eyes and still imagine it: My Love, her long hair wrapped around her throat and then thrown over one of the mahogany beams. She is hanging there forever, behind my eyes, spinning; her face is blue. She looks so sad and lost. I never actually saw it, but I see it every day.

How could she leave me, Friar? How could she leave me and our daughter all alone like that? If I did not love her so much I would hate her for what she did, but I can't. I can't do anything but cry.

I'm sorry. We're going to have to stop for the day. I'm sorry. Please leave me alone.

Leave me alone with this for a while.

I am sorry about yesterday, Friar. I could not continue, not like that. I was not reading my history. I was speaking from the heart, and my heart is raw when I think about that. Leave it on the page, though. We will not edit that out. For my father's memory I gave you his most private belief and dying words, which I have told no one else; for Koonek's memory let the future know I still cry like a child when I think of that afternoon.

I have never gotten over that moment. I stood there in the doorway until I realized I was standing, then I fell to my knees. When that became impossible too I lay on the ground. The world seemed to spin. When my doorman tried to pick me up I hit him, hard, and he left me there.

Men in their grief can do strange things, Friar. I used my power to have the house my grandfather built and my father loved torn down, stone by stone. I ordered a labour gang to take the dressed and cleaned blocks out of Cuzco and drop them into a mountain stream. I wanted nothing to do with the place that had been her end. I never walked down that narrow lane again.

I was a house guest of Kiskis for a time, then of the Socso Panaca, then I took to sharing Huaman Paullu's small villa. Without a home, my father's last surviving bastards left. I was as alone as I had been when I was on the run, save only for little Wawa and a nursemaid I found for her.

I think now that I understand why Koonek did it. I'll never forgive her, but I understand. There was no fire in Koonek's heart. No strength. No resistance. Koonek was a flower in the breeze, and if that breeze gusted too hard she was bowled over.

She could not go back to her mother, for she feared that woman as she feared no man or beast. She couldn't stay, and she couldn't go, so she stopped. She handed Wawa to an Inca to look after, knowing the Inca would do all in his power to preserve an orphan of a former tocoyricoc, and she fled this world rather than face its cruelty. I once told you that woman was flawlessly good, Friar, but I was wrong. A woman without bad in her cannot cope with a world without good. I have never found a more grievous flaw in anyone. My Koonek was a coward, afraid of life.

So I lived in Huaman Paullu's home for more than a year, throwing myself into my work to bury my grief. I spent most of the day in the highest counting room of the Great Quipu Repository, physically separated from the world I shunned by a vertical drop as deep as ten men standing upon one another's shoulders. Up there the icy wind seemed to blow the pain away, and I focused all my attention upon the knots that ran through my cold, trembling fingers. The other tocoyricocs proctored my work and reported to Huayna Capac that there had never been such a single-minded devotion in the history of our calling. I was a driven man.

At night I would descend from my lonely tower and return to Huaman Paullu's house. There I would take the last stew out of the cooling pot in the kitchen, eat without thought or enjoyment, then cradle my Wawa to sleep, whispering sad stories to her and chuckling at the unknowing faces she would make at the end.

My little Wawa had her mother's smile, and a delighted gurgle that was all her own. In a dark room lit only by a single torch, her peaceful face could cheer me up as no friend could.

And that was how I spent my days in my period of mourning. There is no set period for widowers as there is for widows, for most men have many wives and most of those were acquired out of politics or a need for progeny or for the running of an orderly household, not love. Still, my mourning went on a good deal longer than society would accept, and one by one my friends tried to bring me back to reality.

Kiskis came by one night with his dashing smile and took me out to a panaca party. He got me blind drunk and draped a willing woman on my arm. She lured me to some dark alcove and began to undress before my booze-battered mind realized what was happening and rebelled at the thought of betraying my dead wife's memory.

I would like to tell you I left with dignity, but I fear I raised my voice and called the woman wanton titles that may or may not have been true. Kiskis kept his distance for months before returning to Huaman Paullu's house to ask if we were still friends. Of course we were, I said. By then, others had tried the same. I could not very well disown all my associates for wanting what was best for me.

Even Chalcuchima came to me, a surprise despite our truce. He climbed up to my high counting room with a crudely tied royal quipu. "I need a hand reading this," he said.

Furrowing my brows, I took the cords from him and read their knots: 'Your wife is dead, and nothing will bring her back. Be a man, accept that, and move on.' I balled it up and tossed it out of a window.

"It took me all morning to tie that down."

"I am in no mood for jokes."

"You haven't been in the mood for jokes in a long time."

"Leave me alone," I asked.

He pulled a stool from the rafters above and sat down heavily. "No, I'm not going to do that, Haylli. Normally I'm happy when you're miserable, but not this time. I just can't help thinking that if our roles were reversed and I had lost the Vixen, you would be doing something to help me. If I can't enjoy your pain, I might as well try to ease it, right?"

I looked at him as if he were speaking an unintelligible language. "What are you saying to me?"

"I'm saying I want to help. It's been too long since I've seen you out with people. You're going to come to one of my Vixen's panaca parties, and we're going to find you a lovely young somebody, and—"

"Thank you, really, but Kiskis has already tried—"

"Kiskis couldn't get you a good-looking girl if you put him in a House of Chosen Women: He's not fussy enough. I never spent much time with your wife, but I think I've got your type figured out—"

"Chalcuchima," I interrupted.

"Yes?"

"Is this you being nice?"

"Yes."

"I appreciate the effort, but another woman is not going to fix the problem. Would another woman replace the Vixen for you?"

He sat on his stool for a moment, his lipless mouth pursing as he considered whether or not he could get away with lying to me. "No," he admitted.

"Then thank you, but I will have to come to terms with this on my own." My rival left me alone, but I must admit when I had the room to myself I enjoyed a rare smile at his taking the time out to see me.

And he did not stop there, either. He went to Huayna Capac with a suggestion of how to snap me out of my depression. The Sapa Inca did

286

not regret my long hours of diligent work that I was giving to the State, but he agreed with Chalcuchima that I could not do it forever, that I was burning myself out. He summoned me to the Court and I arrived, barefoot and burdened by a small weight.

"Look at me, Haylli," he ordered. Honoured, I looked at his youthful face, and his hard eyes softened at my pained expression. "Tell me what I can do to help."

"More time, Sire. Time softens the blow."

"It has been a year and more, Haylli. More time is just more time to brood. You need to fill your days with new experiences to make the old ones fade away."

"I beg you, Sire, do not give me another wife," I said, remembering Kiske Sisa and the misery a State-imposed wife could bring.

"No," the man said, smiling with the pleasure of Chalcuchima's idea. "I'm going to give you a new job."

I felt a sharp pain in my chest. "Surely, Sire, you mean an extra job?"

"Yes," he agreed quickly, perhaps suspecting the fright he had given me. Huayna Capac and I were always close. "My brother-in-law Chalcuchima came to visit his sister, my concubine Palla Coca. He pointed out that now that my family is getting bigger I should think of how my children will be educated. Your name came instantly to both our minds.

"I have asked every wise man in the land, and they have all agreed there is not an Inca of the Blood with the same breadth of knowledge as you. I appoint you Royal Tutor to my sons. You will give them their languages and numbers and turn each one to the task that seems to suit them best. Do you accept this station?"

My mind flew to the responsibilities set before me, for Huayna Capac was producing sons at a truly Imperial rate. Also, he was beginning a tour of his Realm and would take me with him in his retinue, tearing me from the sanctuary I had found in my tall tower. And yet I felt it, a warmth of enthusiasm for such a task.

Imagine, Friar, to shape and sculpt the coming generation of princes, perhaps even to become the special confidant of the next Sapa Inca. What a mark I could make on history! What tales I could tell my grandchildren! "Sire, it would be the honour of my life to accept."

He smiled his Imperial smile at me, kind and thoughtful without losing any of its regal distance. "You will make arrangements for the chaski network to forward all of your quipu work to you, wherever you go. And you will move out of Huaman Paullu's house and into my entourage. I shall make an appointment for you with the Royal Architect and when we return from the inspection of our land you will have a new house built somewhere between the Huacaypata and the Great Quipu Repository."

Lining the walls on either side of us, Royal Quipu Masters tied down the knots that ended the period of mourning for my lost Koonek. I still missed her, I miss her today, but I would no longer be allowed to sulk in my self-indulgent grief, nor would I have the time to do so if I wanted. I was the Royal Tutor.

* * *

I built my new house as a suburban villa halfway between Cuzco and the Great Quipu Repository. The occupants of the Yanahuara mitmak hamlet under my new compound's foundations were elevated to my personal yanacona, my household servants, and they considered this such a jump in status that they threw a party for me out of their own savings, a small fiesta I enjoyed just as much for its sincerity as any Imperial gala offered to me.

It was very much like my father's old city house, except with all the room afforded in the country I made it bigger, with room in the courtyards for gardens and a reflective pool, parrot aviaries and a flowering tree where my daughter could keep a monkey when she got older. She was old enough now to have a childhood name, and so I called her Pariwana, Flamingo, because I could always get her to stop crying by dangling a flamingo feather in front of her eyes.

My counting room was unnecessarily higher than the tower of my father's old house. It was positively a spire. From its sliver-framed windows I could see both sets of sun pillars, Sacsahuaman, Cuzco, the distant snowy peak of Mount Vilcañota, the Great Quipu Repository and the Huatanay River stretching out all the way to Lake Muina. My guests often wondered how I got any work done with such a view. I sometimes wonder too.

A counting room is supposed to be an accountant's refuge, his sanctuary, his safe place, but some of the worst things that have ever happened to me happened in counting rooms. I was to have one more cruel experience atop a stone tower, and I suppose it is at about this point in my story that I must divulge it.

I was sitting in my counting room, watching the sun set as thunder-heads rolled towards me, when the Vixen came to visit, bringing an amphora of akha with her. I waited for her to pull up a stool and pour the drinks before I asked her to what I owed the pleasure of her company.

"I came to talk."

"That much I figured for myself," I smiled, enjoying looking her in the eye and seeing that mind of hers working. "Are we going to talk about Chalcuchima?"

Her husband had just returned to Cuzco after pacifying the Chacapoyas. He was to participate in a triumphal procession the next morning.

"I am sorry about your wife," she said, ignoring my reference to her husband.

"Don't bait me," I said, my smile disappearing. "She's been dead a long time, and you never came while I was grieving." I was harsh with her. I sensed her intent by the way she carried herself. I was not going to like any conversation she wanted to have where mentioning her husband was a bad idea.

"That would have been appropriate? Your lover consoling you while your dead wife is still settling in her grave?"

"Former lover," I corrected her. "And it's not inappropriate now?"

"You've finished mourning."

"And you've finished waiting." I downed my cup with a hard swallow. "So explain your visit to me." Outside thunder rumbled in the heavens, neatly mirroring my mood.

"I—"

"That's what I thought." Her eyes flashed that Vixen-esque rage at me, and I felt myself stir in spite of myself.

"Don't you dare interrupt me," she barked.

"Don't you dare suggest to me what I think you're here to suggest to me." I didn't say it as forcefully as I had meant to, and even as I chastised myself I saw her pounce on the perceived weakness.

"You haven't taken another wife. Not even a concubine. It's been more than a year—"

"I am not going to start with another man's wife, and I am certainly not going to start with Chalcuchima's wife!"

289

"I thought he was always Mallku to you."

"We have a truce."

"He told me," she leaned back, tilting her chest up. I could not bring myself to look away, for to turn my head would have been just as obvious as gawking would have been. "But I suspect your peaceful rivalry won't last long."

"It will last a lot longer when you leave. Kindly do so now." I gestured to the ladder. She did not move.

"I will tell you straight out, Haylli, I am prepared to ask the Sapa Inca's permissions to divorce Chalcuchima."

"What? Why?" I was stunned. A flash of lightning lit up the counting room, further dazzling me. I was still blinking as she explained.

"I need a baby, Haylli. I need a child to climb any higher in the panaca. I'm already held back as a late entry married to an officer demoted by Old Topa. Without a child I will never succeed! All the panaca leaders have to be mothers. I should have had a baby years ago, but Chalcuchima can't do it. You have a daughter. You can."

"What do you mean he can't do it? Can't do what? I've seen him with tampu girls on the road. I assure you he can."

"None of them ever got pregnant by him. I've checked. Neither have I." My jaw dropped. I knew it was physically possible, of course. There were llamas who could ride the ewes all day without producing a kid, but for Chalcuchima to be such a man?

"That's not grounds for divorce," I spluttered.

"If a man can divorce a woman for bareness, a woman can do the same. Besides, he'll agree to any terms I want to keep that reason out of the Imperial Court." That was for certain. With a father and two uncles declared aucca, Chalcuchima was clawing his way out of disgrace with his fingernails worn down to the quick. The last thing he needed was snickering about his virility among the Inca nobility.

"You have to be the most cold, calculating witch of a woman I have ever met!" I shouted at her, rising from my stool and throwing my empty cup against a wall, shattering it. "It's always about you and your damned panaca! Even when we were children! You used me, and when I was no further use you threw me aside. Now you're doing the same to Chalcuchima! Where is the love?" I don't know why I said the last part; perhaps I was remembering my father's warning about the Vixen in another counting room a long time ago. I certainly never meant for her to answer the question.

"I am not your wife, but you did love me. You loved me first, before her. I loved you before Chalcuchima. Is it so wrong for us to do it again?" I looked down at her, stunned by her tone. The Vixen, brave and bold and brash and brilliant, spoke like a meek and lonely woman. I softened my gaze; then she slipped her tunic off one shoulder.

I frowned and shook my head, but I did not stop her as she slipped the other shoulder off and stood up from her stool, leaving her clothes in a pile of fabric around her ankles.

The years had been kind to her, Friar, probably because she had borne no children and used her body as a weapon, maintaining it just as a soldier maintains his equipment. I shook my head again, and she stepped out of the pool of her clothes, closing the distance on me. I put my hands up in front of me to ward her off, and her breasts filled them unbidden. I pulled them away as if burned, stepping backwards until I found myself pressed against the wall. With no escape she was there, nuzzling my neck.

"This stops now," I said without conviction. The thunder rolled and rolled outside. The storm was coming.

"I've already sent a message to Chalcuchima telling him everything," she whispered, her hands undoing my breechcloth. "Your truce is over whether you like it or not, so you might as well enjoy it."

I shuddered once, feeling her hands on me, her breasts against my ribs, the warmth of her exhaling into my collar bone. Outside it began to rain, hard and fast and unrelenting. The storm was so ferocious it made the flames in the counting room flicker. I will not tell you what a force of will it took me to croak out, "What did you say?"

"I said—" But in that moment where she was thinking how to word her seduction I was free. I gave her a gentle push, and I had my breechcloth up off the floor and was descending the ladder before she realized I was leaving. At the bottom of the ladder I put the breechcloth back on, and I ran out into the courtyard.

I could see her leaning naked out one of the counting room windows, shouting down to me, but the rain stole her words away. I was out the front door and running towards Cuzco before I realized she was telling me that I would be back, and I was halfway to Chalcuchima's place before I decided she was right.

291

I don't quite know what I planned to tell my rival. How do you say, 'I don't plan to bed your wife, but would you please collect her naked from my home without being mad at me?' I never had the opportunity to try. Before I could reach his house I found Chalcuchima on the street, slowly walking towards me.

We were both soaked to the skin. The water poured down out of his hair and over his headband to hide his tears. He said something, but it was snatched away by the rain falling on the stone and thatch around us.

"What?" I bellowed.

Then he hit me, Friar. He struck me in the jaw with all of his anguish. I was lifted off my feet at the force of it, and I landed on the cobbles in a heap. He took two long strides to my prone form and kick me in the ribs, once, twice, three times. Each blow felt like the Hiwaya stone falling on me. My ribs gave in. I couldn't breathe. I couldn't resist. I would be beaten to death there in the rain for his wife's decision.

He stood above me, his shoulders heaving as he sobbed. I waited for the next kick, but it did not come. He swayed over me, my life at his feet, lightning and darkness above his head. He tilted his head back and roared, beating his chest and tearing his tunic with hands twisted into claws. His lips moved, but I still could not hear him over the downpour.

My moan was involuntary, but as soon as my lungs could take in air the noise escaped from my throat of its own volition. He looked down at me as if he had forgotten I was there; then he leaned down and hauled me up by my collar. I could not stand, but he was strong enough to hold my limp form eye to eye with him.

The last thing I wanted to do was look at him, but he shook me until my head flopped over to him. He leaned forward, his mouth by my ear. "It's true?" He whispered. There was no hope in his question.

I nodded, sure my world was about to end.

"Is she happy?" I could not speak. I could not explain. I could only nod again. The Vixen had played with her men like pieces in a board game. Whatever either of us wanted, she would have her way. Neither of us were free to make our own moves.

He dropped me back down to the hard stones of the road and walked away from me, the rain and dark swallowing him up before I could summon the strength to call him back, to apologize, to make it right between us. In that moment I knew he loved his Vixen as I loved my Koonek. She chose me over him, and he loved her too much to stand in her way.

Every breath was like a dagger stabbing me, but after an eternity of pain I regained my feet and staggered home. The Vixen was waiting for me at the door. All of my servants were hiding in their rooms. She put my arm around her neck and helped me to the kitchen. I sat next to the hearth as she stood over me, waiting for me to speak.

"Get out," I muttered around my swollen jaw, but all the strength has been beaten out of me.

For a moment her hand went to the pin of her shawl, but she took in my broken ribs and battered face and knew lust was beyond me. She decided to speak to me plainly. "You know I won't do that, but I will make you this promise." I hurt too much to do anything but listen.

"Your father was afraid I would lead you around like a puppy on a string, Haylli, but that's not going to happen. I am going to marry you, but you will not have to help me get my panaca. All I want from you is a son, and for you to be the best tocoyricoc in the world. That will be enough to give me the advantage I need, and it's not so much to ask, is it? You cannot undo what I have done. This is our future, and it's not so bad."

I know I should not have married her, Friar, but in some things I am not a strong man. My father would have left her without a husband to support her quest for a panaca, but I could not. When I said earlier that my father was a better man than I became, this is what I meant: My father had known right from wrong and he always did what was right. I knew what I should have done, but I was too weak. I took the easy path and married the Vixen. It brought me little happiness though, Friar, and I draw some comfort from that.

I want to be clear that I was never proud of myself for it, but I did marry the Vixen. I had a tough time looking my peers in the eye, but they all knew that I was not the home wrecker in this situation; in time I was forgiven by my community.

Not by Chalcuchima, though. The general applied for garrison duties in Tumpez as soon as he was done his parade. I did not see him again for years, and when I did we were enemies again, worse so than we had ever been at school. When the Vixen left him, what little kindness and gentle inclinations Chalcuchima possessed were burned out of his soul. His heart turned to stone that night in the rain.

Oh, how we Inca were to suffer because of it.

* * *

Friar, up until this point my story has been my own, my life in the empire the Inca created for ourselves upon the sweat and blood of those we ruled. I spent long nights tying down my memoirs in those days, never doubting that it would be read by my children and my children's children in a world not so very different from the one I lived in.

I was wrong, of course. So wrong that it makes my hands tremble and my eyes water to read the knots tied in a simpler time by a carefree Haylli, one who bemoaned his personal trials and hardships without conceiving that those tiny discomforts could be so totally dwarfed and eclipsed by what was to come.

From this point on my story has been heavily revised by my tired old hands to describe and explain the decline and fall of Tahuantinsuyu. Twelve million taxpayers were supposed to live out their lives in peace and plenty for all time, and that future came tumbling down like a loose fieldstone wall in an earthquake. I doubt today there are five million men, women and children up in the mountains above us. I am sure they go hungry. I am sure they do not know what the future holds for them. The world of Tahuantinsuyu is gone forever.

How did it happen? How did it happen so quickly? How did it happen while I watched, without being able to stop it? You would say it was the Spaniards, and you are not totally wrong, Friar, but the rot set in much earlier. Cracks appeared in the foundations of our Empire when I was a man in my prime, though they were too faint to see at the time. I think our problems began with the children that I would raise to adulthood.

My grandfather's generation built Tahuantinsuyu as I have described it to you after they defeated the Chanca. My father's generation grew up in a world of change, so that they were raised to strive, to overcome, to succeed. My generation, the best of us, were brought up in a manner our hard-working ancestors would have approved of, and we tried to maintain and improve our Empire just as a shepherd watches over his flock for the continued prosperity of his family.

Our children, Friar, the very children I had hoped would read my knots in a world as safe and secure as the one I occupied, it was somehow they who let us down. With hindsight I can see that I did not impart the values to them that I took as second nature. They did not care about the things that should have mattered most.

I raised those who were to follow me with all the advantages the Children of the Sun at the zenith of our high noon could lavish on our progeny, and though I cannot tell you where we went wrong, somehow my generation was too soft, too lenient, too understanding or forgiving of their young pride and selfishness. The fault was ours, and more specifically mine. I was Royal Tutor, and so to me was entrusted the proper upbringing of those who would one day rule Tahuantinsuyu.

How was I to know the babies I held in my arms would grow into beasts who would tear great chunks out of the living, twitching flesh of my Empire? That it would be my education that would sharpen their young fangs as I favoured some over others, creating rivalries for which millions would suffer and die?

It occurs to me that I am getting ahead of myself, Friar, for surely you now expect me to tell you stories of Prince Atauhuallpa and Prince Huascar scratching and biting each other in the corridors and courtyards of the Imperial harem? Yes, I have gone too far too fast, and so I would remind you that I had many children enter my life at this time. Some would grow to become my favourite people in the world. Some would break my heart. Some would fill me with a murderous rage. All but two are now dead.

The point is that I knew none of this at the time. They were babies, cute and fat and vulnerable infants, and you rarely see anything but hope and optimism when you look down into a cradle. I never doubted that they would grow into real people, but who would ever dream that a child will lead to the destruction of your very way of life?

That is where I want to resume my life's story, Friar. Whatever they were to become, they were just children to me then, and when I think of the prime of my life, the fifteen years or so when I was neither young nor old, I somehow always label it the time of children.

I had Pariwana, of course. Oh, how I loved my little girl at every age. As an infant I would bring her up to my counting room and we would chat happily about anything and everything, pausing only for me to snap stern reproofs at the quipucamayocs who came and went.

As a toddler I would sit her on my lap and tell her stories about her mother's homeland, about Puma and Antalongo and the fields and roads, never about her grandmother. As a girl I would take her for walks through the streets of Cuzco, introducing her to my friends as if she was a full-grown courtly lady. How she loved that.

I remember with a clenched fist and pounding heart the day the Canchacamayoc, the House Inspector, came to visit us when my little girl was six. The Canchacamayoc's job was to make sure people lived hygienic lives, stored and cooked their food properly, kept their dishes clean, their hearths empty of ashes, their bedding fresh. His other job was to examine female children to decide if they should become Chosen Women.

The idea of losing my daughter to that joyless building where she would weave and brew until she was married to either Inti or an ally of the Sapa Inca kept me up nights. It really did.

The Canchacamayoc entered our home and did a quick inspection, for he knew I was no ignorant puric who might not know how to keep a clean house, and he knew the Vixen would not have allowed it if I tried. When he had done the bare minimum of a pointless task he turned to me. "Let's come to the point, lord. Your daughter is such a perfect candidate for the House of Chosen Women that if I don't put her in there people will question my impartiality."

"You aren't impartial. I trained you. We are friends."

"Lord, you know I can't play favourites. If I were a hunocamayoc stealing coca you would drop a stone on my back in a heartbeat. Don't assume my job is any less important."

"How would you like a nice job collecting the Pasto lice tax for the rest of your days?"

"Threatening a royal official—"

"I was asking a simple question. Perhaps it's your dream assignment? It can be arranged for your clear devotion to duty."

Pariwana walked between us and offered the inspector a beautiful lily, plucked from our garden. "You look angry, Lord," she said in my Koonek's voice. "This is for you."

He looked at the flower and smiled. He straightened his face with some difficulty when he looked up at me. "All right, my quota is full anyway, but you might consider putting her in a House of Chosen Women anyway like they did for your wife. You're going to have boys beating a path to your door in a few years, lord."

I thought of my youthful escapades in the House of Chosen Women. "I would rather be responsible for my daughter here, where I can keep a fatherly eye on her."

"It's just as well. A girl that perfect would probably have been set aside and sacrificed to Viracocha one day," the man said. His job was a hard one. He brought a great deal of misery to people, collecting a tax that meant so much when it was taken away and so much when it was given as a state gift, but never returned to the family, never. He left, and I picked my Pariwana up onto my shoulders and took her for a triumphant parade through our home.

But I spoke of a time for children, and, though I would talk to you forever about my little girl if I could, I can never escape the fact that the Vixen had acquired me as a shepherd finds a stud llama for his flock. She was pregnant almost as soon as we married, but it was a stillbirth. Encouraged that she could conceive at all she came at me constantly, so that I could get no work done in my house, and my counting room became dusty at my absence. She miscarried twice, but both early enough that she had not grown overly hopeful.

She took to visiting me at the Great Quipu Repository for the purposes of procreation, so that I had to abandon my counting room there too and work in different houses every day, routing work to me through a complicated series of messengers and dead drops. She would not take no for an answer, and it was the only way I could govern.

Finally when my daughter was seven the Vixen and I had a son. She was overjoyed that our first successful child was a boy, and that he had ten fingers and ten toes and smiled when she touched his nose. It had taken two husbands and four pregnancies, but she had what she felt she needed to gain her panaca. Thinking about it now, I don't think she ever came at me for sex again. She was satisfied.

While I could not match the Vixen's devotion to producing another child —I already had my perfect daughter, after all— I must admit I hungered for the moment where I would first hold little Wawa in my big hands, just as I had when Pariwana was born. When the Vixen delivered I was at a tampu just outside of Cuzco, and I returned to the shouts of, "You have a son! You have a son!"

I rushed into my home, overwhelmed at the thought that now I would have an heir, a potential successor to all that I had accomplished, a boy who would one day become a man who would serve his Empire well. I reached the birthing room, my palms held up, and said, "Let me hold him."

The midwives froze, looking to the Vixen for permission. I was not upset at having my paternal authority so blatantly questioned, for this more than any time was a moment for women. Only when she nodded, looking a little strained by the effort of delivery, was the wailing bundle produced and put into my hands.

I took a deep breath and looked down at him. I remember pausing to take another breath, as if somehow I had missed the moment and needed to summon it back. I felt nothing. Oh, Friar, what a terrible omen for a father, to hold his son with less affection than he would a puppy? Where Pariwana as a baby left me weeping with love and delight, this puling pink lump of squirming flesh left me so unmoved that I made the conscious decision to be polite —polite!— to my wife.

"Congratulations," I muttered, handing the infant back to one of the hovering nursemaids. My wife nodded again, one of the midwives dabbing her brow with a damp vicuna cloth. I left the room as soon as I could; I never told her what I had felt, or failed to feel, upon first meeting my son.

When Wawa survived his infancy the Vixen asked that I name him Anka, Eagle. She said she had seen our son watch such a bird circle high overhead, but I believe she just wanted him to have a manly name as a boy; still, I gave him his first hair cut and named him Anka. It made her happy.

She loved that boy the way I loved Pariwana, but whereas I could dote on Pariwana without fear of making her soft, the Vixen loved Anka too much, held him too tight. She coddled him.

I wanted to like my son. What father doesn't want to like his boy? The trouble, I think, was that I was always working when he was little. I was not always there, as the Vixen was. I became a visitor in my own home, even if I was there for half a year at a time. I just could not bring my son up as I would have wanted.

When I was a boy I used to watch my father perform his duties, and I wanted Anka to do the same with me. How better to bring up a great accountant than to put string into his little fists as soon as he could speak? Anka was bored to tears the few times I forced him to come into my counting room during the day, and at night he used to amuse himself by climbing up there in my absence and untying and tangling State documents. I began storing my quipus up in the rafters, out of the reach of his little hands, but I could not avoid the thought that at some level my boy hated my work.

I tried other things, too, taking him out to see Chuno production, or masons working their stone, or alpacas being sheared, but this also bored him, and he had a ready escape in his mother. Whenever he saw me coming towards him with a pair of child-sized sandals, all he had to do was say, "I want to spend time with Mama," and she would sweep him up in her arms and carry him around the house, singing and laughing. How could I compete with that?

By the time he was old enough to have conversations, his mother had made him into someone I found unlikable. She never told him he was wrong, so he had to win every argument, and every one of our talks became an argument.

I remember once when he was seven or eight I decided to make a real effort to play with him, the way his mother did. He was always saying he would be a great general like Uncle Michi; he loved Achachi Michi. So I carved him a set of wooden soldiers. I really enjoyed that. It reminded me of the long hours Puma and I spent in our chaski hut, carving and chatting. I painted the figures too, red and white for the Imperial guard, green for the Cañari, deep red for the savages. I gave them to him as a spontaneous present.

He did not thank me, but his mother did, so I could not make an issue of it. I had him set them up in our courtyard, and I played a war game with him. He refused to let me say whether or not his strategies would work, and I agreed that if I were to be his opponent I really couldn't be impartial. I brought in General Achachi Michi, my son's hero, to referee our war game.

I told the viceroy before he came over, "My son is eight and thinks he's destined to be a great military strategist. If you want to give him some of your experiences, feel free. Also, I'm a man and he's my boy and you're his hero, so I'm going to let him win." I did not add that I was afraid he would cry if he lost in front of Achachi Michi.

So the general came over and sat on a stool and watched my son fumble his way through the war game. I am no great genius at military tactics and strategy, but I knew enough to have beaten my son at several points throughout the game. I didn't. I waited patiently as he sent his men in dribs and drabs into places they couldn't possibly fight their way out of. I did nothing to lure him in, and when he was in I refused to wrap his flanks, envelop him, and wipe him out. I should have, but instead I played a very defensive game, and my son took this as proof that what he was doing was working.

I had forgotten about Achachi Michi's back.

The general had sat on his stool for half the afternoon watching my son's stupid attacks go unpunished. He had forgotten to charge his coca bag that morning, and his old battle injury was hurting him. His irritation that I was allowing such a boy to win grew and grew as the time passed, and he finally blurted out, "In the name of Inti, Haylli, just take his damned flanks and call it a day."

My son was not the smartest boy, but he understood at once that I had been toying with him in front of 'Uncle Michi.' He lifted his chin and looked me square in the eyes, letting his anger pour over me. Without looking down at our map he pushed all his reserves after his latest assault.

"You can't do that," I told him.

"I'm the general. I can do anything," he sulked.

"You just heard your Uncle Michi say I can take your flanks there. You're throwing good men after bad."

"You won't take my flanks."

"Why won't I?"

"Because you're letting me win."

"I can't let you win if you attack me there."

"That's why I'm doing it." He pushed all his forces right into the trap that I had worked so hard all day not to spring.

I sighed and moved my warriors around his flanks. "I have to, Anka. Your enemy won't always be your father."

Achachi Michi began explaining what was happening on our battle-field: Anka's troops were surrounded on all sides, and many of my men were fighting downhill, pushing his forces back against one another so they had no room to maneuver and fight. Anka heard it all, grinding his teeth and glaring at me. All I could do was shrug. When the old general said the slaughter was over and that Anka had lost, my son began shaking his head.

"No, I didn't lose. The whole battle wasn't right from the beginning. If he had done that to my first probes I wouldn't have sent my main thrust in, but he didn't because he didn't want me to look bad in front of you, Uncle Michi."

"I am not your uncle," the viceroy said. It was a cruel thing to say to a sore loser. Achachi Michi allowed the Vixen to call him uncle despite the lack of blood relation, but now he was refusing the same to her angry son. "And there's no reason why your opponent might not have held back, hoping you'd be stupid enough to send your main thrust in there. There isn't a worse spot on the battlefield to launch that attack, but you didn't see that." Achachi Michi got up, rubbing the small of his back.

"I could go into the kitchen right now, bring out the woman who washes your dishes, and she could have told you that was a bad place to assault. You say it's your father's fault? He's been doing everything short of taking a nap all afternoon to keep from trouncing you, and he's not a military man. I am, and I am insulted that you are even thinking of becoming a battlefield commander. These war games are good tests, and I will tell you right now you fail. You can't read terrain, you can't keep calm under pressure, and you don't care about your men—"

Anka had taken all that he was going to take. "I'll show you how much I care about my stupid men!" He crushed his toys under his sandaled feet, snapping their lances and bows. Unsatisfied he jumped up and down on them, stamping down until my gift to him was destroyed. I sat perfectly still on my stool while this happened, unwilling to hit my son in front of Achachi Michi. Anka must have thought I was mocking him, because he ran up and pushed me off my seat. I was on my feet and reaching for him in moments, but he finally realized what a scene he was making and he ran off crying, looking for his mother.

The viceroy and I stood there looking down on the ruins of the game. "I'm sorry," he said. "That was not my place. I was just tired of sitting. My back is acting up again."

"I'm sorry too," I said.

I walked him to the door. He turned once we were outside. "Your boy starts school in a few years?" I nodded. "I'll stop teaching when he goes there. I wouldn't want to embarrass him in his military classes. He'll have a lot to learn, and he might as well hear it from someone he wants to listen to." Achachi Michi walked down the road, and I was tempted to go with him. I knew what kind of reception my wife would have waiting for me back in the house, and it would only get worse when I told her I would have to beat Anka for striking me.

But enough of my children for now, Friar; they were only minor players in the fall of the Intip Churi. As Royal Tutor I was responsible for the education of the royal menagerie, as my assistants and I liked to call our pack of princes. Huayna Capac would have over a hundred children in my care at one point or another, but there are three young Royals who entered my life at this point in my story who I should single out for special mention.

There was Ninan, who would later become Ninan Cuyuchi, Huayna Capac's eldest and best son. He was two years older than my daughter. Now there was a boy to be proud of: He listened when older and wiser men spoke, but when they were finished he would ask the most piercing questions, stripping pretentious wise men of their airs like opening a door will take the stuffiness out of a room. He picked up royal quipus as if he had been playing with string in the womb. I often joked with his father that it was a shame he was to become Sapa Inca because he would be such a loss to the tocoyricocs. I slept well at night knowing the Yellow Fringe of the heir would one day rest on his forehead.

The next prince who stands out in my mind is a less pleasant memory: Tito, Chalcuchima's nephew who later became Atauhuallpa. Yes, Friar, that Atauhuallpa. Let me tell you he was a royal bastard in more ways than one. I remember when he was first presented to me as a newborn babe: He was screaming a piercing wail that set my teeth on edge, and when he came within range of me he let loose a high stream of urine that drenched my face and collar. Within moments of the first splash his wails turned to unnaturally deep belly laughs of joy, and I think that came to define our lives together.

Tito was seven years younger than my Pariwana, the same age as Anka, and I think he used the trials of his infancy as a means to torment me. Potty training should not have been my concern as Royal Tutor, but his mother, Palla Coca, who was a kind lady —even if she was Chalcuchima's sister— beseeched my help. I could not refuse her.

He would not relieve himself into a pot, nor would he do so in a private place, and more often than not he would take great handfuls of his leavings and hurl it at his attendants. I used a switch on the soles of his feet many times in the months it took to train him, and in the end I think he just grew bored with his sport and agreed to behave. I believe he had known from the very beginning what was expected of him and refused to do it.

When he was learning Runa Simi he would argue over the pronunciation of difficult words, saying they should be different. He would then invent his own term and use it instead of the actual word, sometimes for months, so that his small retinue had to learn his new vocabulary in order to understand him. Once I found one of his words slip outside of the palace into common slang and I had to go to Huayna Capac with a heavy burden upon my shoulders to beg an Imperial decree outlawing its use.

Another place where Tito rubbed me raw was in the matter of my daughter. Being seven years older than him, she was always his highest pinnacle of beauty as he grew up, and he would follow her like a hungry puma, often sneaking down corridors to snatch a glimpse of her. I remember once he worked himself up into high dudgeon over something at a mere six years old and ordered me —ordered me— to attach my daughter to his household as his personal concubine.

There is a law that a noble's feet could not be beaten more than ten times in the course of every disciplining action, but Atauhuallpa's retinue looked the other way while I beat him ten times for each word in his sentence, then I put him on one meal a day for a month and forbade him to play outside.

He hated me, for I was a stern master. I hated him, but in my own way I respected him, for he was defying a power he knew he could not overcome, and he took his punishments like a man without ever viewing them as a deterrent to his next attack on me, my beliefs, or my training regimen for him. He had an insufferable smile, an insolent smirk that he used whenever he knew he would have to obey me, a grin that made it seem as if he was choosing to indulge me with his compliance. He was a brat.

When Tito was born Huayna Capac began an extensive inspection of the Collasuyu quarter. He took fifty thousand soldiers and at least that many bureaucrats, visiting every village in the Collao and the coast, even sending detachments down to the Mapuche land. I had him elevate Antalongo up to master of ten thousand families as an unspoken thank you. To my understanding he served the Sapa Inca loyally all the days of his life from that point on.

Huayna did not stop having children while he was down there, though, and in the third year of his tour, on the shores of Lake Chucuito, his concubine-sister Rahua Ocllo gave birth to another prince you may have heard of, Friar, for that little Wawa would one day be named Huascar, though we often called him Hummingbird.

I have never had the gift of the second sight, but I tell you when little three-year-old Tito asked to see his father's newest son only to spit on the child's face while he lay defenseless in his cradle, a tremble ran down my spine. I forget what punishment I gave Tito for that latest outrage, but it was nowhere near enough considering the animosity he would bear that boy for the rest of his life. Between the two of them they would tear the fabric of our world apart, and I would be powerless to gather up the loose threads and weave them back together.

Years passed, Friar, and you wonder where the time went. The best days of my life seemed to fly by in a blur, more happy than unhappy. Few things really punctuated the time, stood out from the rest. Huayna Capac went off and resubjugated the Chacapoyas —my mother's people— but I did not go with the army, and I somehow missed the triumphant parade of his homecoming.

Huaman Paullu, my father's old secretary, died, and I placed his mummy bundle with my father's, as he would have wanted. I put a half-tied royal quipu in his hand. It began, 'Once upon a time I was Huaman Paullu Yachapa, Capac Quipucamayoc, secretary and friend to Tahuantinsuyu's greatest tocoyricocs.'

I sit here and debate with myself what to tell you Friar, and I have decided that is unfair. If this is to be the story of my life I cannot pick and choose what to say. There was one brief encounter that my mind likes to linger on, and it falls into this part of my life.

I am that unusual Inca in that when offered as many wives as I cared to have I took only one. I suppose there are those who would point out that when I had the Vixen to sleep with and I already had a son and a daughter, who else would be able to tempt me? I will tell you a secret, Friar. There was one.

Huayna Capac had loved his mother, Mama Ocllo, so much that when he was done his period of mourning he ordered a golden idol of her to be made and established in a temple at Tumipampa. He granted it oracular powers, a priesthood, and a woman, a Cañari chosen woman dressed in his mother's favourite shade of green who would forever be known as Mama Ocllo's Voice, her interlocutor between supplicants and the Upper Universe.

I do not know what attracted me to the woman, or perhaps I should say I have several complimentary theories: First, the Vixen was punishing me with two months of abstinence, for what I cannot remember. Second, I knew wherever Mama Ocllo's spirit was, though I suspected it was more likely to be with Supay in the Lower Universe than with Viracocha in the Upper Universe, nothing would make her angrier than my bedding her official representative on Earth. Mostly, though, I think I was sad for her.

This woman, while no great beauty, had an air of calm and grace and intelligence about her. Not the self-serving brilliance of my Vixen, but the soft observant genius of someone who notices and understands things but has the discipline not to talk about it. This woman, who I have suspected I could have been happy with if she had not been chosen by Huayna Capac, was ordered to renounce her former identity and speak on behalf of an old hag she had never known and whom everyone except the Emperor had hated.

I met her at Court, of course. She was being regaled by the Emperor with stories about his mother. We were all waiting for the idol to be cast, at which time Mama Ocllo's Voice would never be allowed to leave its side, even sleeping at the base of the altar in Tumipampa. I devoured her with my eyes, my appreciation obvious to her but to no one else. As I said, she was observant.

When the Emperor had finished telling her how his mother had taught him to tie his sandals he was interrupted by a hunocamayoc on official business. She excused herself, and so did I, and we were in a side room making love without a word spoken. It was different from both Koonek and the Vixen, but I hold that memory just as precious as I do the other two.

It was her first time, and I was gentle. She cried at the end for a while, and held me with her finger on my lips to silence any attempt to interrupt the moment. When she was finished she said, "Thank you," the only words she spoke directly to me all that day. I went home that night, my head and heart in turmoil.

When I returned to Court the next day, I was still unsure whether I would apologize to her in private or publicly beg the Emperor to choose another so I could take her as my second wife. I never got to make the decision. The idol was finished early, and she was sent with it to Tumipampa. I would not see her green-clad form again for years, and by then she would be a high priestess to an important Imperial cult, sacrosanct. It occurs to me that I never knew her Cañari name.

It was shortly after this that Anka turned eight, and when the Vixen asked me to take him on my next inspection I agreed far more readily than I meant to, for I dreaded his failure. I would have to tell his mother that the future she thought of as Anka's birthright would go to another. To make matters worse, he did not want to go. He slowed our packing as much as he could, and when the day of our departure finally dawned I had to drag him out of bed by one ankle.

The surprise dissident in all this was the Vixen. She wanted him to become a tocoyricoc, of course, but she ran after us down the road to wipe some invisible grime off his face. I knew the truth: She did not want him to go out into the world.

We were barely out of sight of Cuzco before he started complaining that his feet hurt, and it was only after I pointed out that soldiers marched from tampu to tampu every day that he found enough pride to be silent about it. He still thought of himself as a military legend in the making.

He was a dismal choice to succeed me as He Who Sees All. He had no interest in the work or the people, saw no beauty in the complex system of roads and storehouses that were the sinews of our Empire. He regarded the whole trip as a waste of time, and because of that it was. His only delight was watching the Hiwaya stone fall, so that he accused honest men of terrible crimes just to see me punish them. I never indulged him in his bloodlust, and after one incident in which I ordered him to be silent in front of a thousand purics he stopped speaking to me for the rest of our inspection. It was a relief, really.

I did my rounds faster than I had ever done before or since, eager to finish and get him back to his mother. She ran out to greet him upon our return, holding him tight and laughing with relief. He was the biggest mother's boy I ever saw. I used to laugh at his ambition to be a soldier: I couldn't get the picture of the Vixen following behind him wiping dirt off his face out of my head.

That night after he had gone to bed I sat down with an amphora of akha, poured two mugs, and told my wife flat out, "He's not going to be my successor."

If I had slapped her she would not have looked more surprised. "Why not?"

"Because he wants to be a soldier." It was easier than saying he would be the worst administrator in the world.

"Well I don't want him to be a soldier," she said, making a face.

"Well I don't want him to be a soldier either," I agreed. I did not point out that I thought he would be terrible at that too.

"Well what can I do?" She looked around, at a total loss. My brilliant Vixen had a blind spot for her son's shortcomings. She had never imagined me refusing to make him my successor.

"You can't do anything. I don't think he'd even be willing to try to be a tocoyricoc. He's not interested, and we can't make him be interested."

She tugged at the hem of her dress pensively, but in the end I convinced her that I was right. I painted a rosy picture for her: After he was finished school I would pull strings to get him assigned to the Imperial guard. He would live and work in Cuzco, and she would be able to see him all the time. Much better than a tocoyricoc who had to travel all over the world. We drank the amphora dry and went to bed, where she cried in her sleep at the disappointment of it all.

The next day I went to the school, asking the teachers who would be the best candidate to succeed me. One name kept coming up, a boy named Cayo. I sat in on a math lecture, but the boy never raised his hand. Afterwards I asked the teacher why he had wasted my time; he handed me the boy's quipus. Cayo had gotten every answer right. He would answer anything asked of him, I was told, but he never spoke up on his own.

I went home that night and asked the Vixen what she would have thought of a boy in school who got every answer right but did not participate in class, and she surprised me when she said, "It would remind me of you."

"What do you mean?" I asked.

"You never spoke up in class because you knew it all already, and you didn't want to aggravate things with students who did not pick things up as fast as you did." I would never have made that connection on my own, but I took a fancy to it as soon as she said it.

I hope I have given the impression that my marriage to the Vixen was a passionless affair. She took advantage of my rank to rise to power, and in return I had a beautiful woman to sleep with when she was willing. At the same time, having a mind as sharp as the Vixen's at my disposal brought a few moments sheer pleasure to be in the company of someone that intelligent. I laughed and kissed her on the mouth, surprising her so much that she did not even have time to make it a lingering affair, as was her nature. I gave Cayo a chance, and to this day I am grateful to her that I did.

The next day I went back to the school and pulled young Cayo out of class. We sat on stools in the courtyard, and I decided to play a game with him, making him speak first. Do you know what that boy did, Friar? He spent the afternoon looking me up and down, to the point where he could have told me how many freckles I had on my arms or point out the hairs on my jaw that needed a visit from the bronze tweezers. The shadows were growing long before I finally broke the spell.

"You keep your own counsel, don't you Cayo?"

"Yes, my lord," he said politely, as if he had not been eyeballing me for most of the day.

"You can call me Haylli, Cayo."

"Alright, Haylli." I had never seen such self-composure in a boy, and I wondered whether he had a Vixen in his life, a girl in his class who had spotted him out as the boy who would go the distance. I hoped not.

"How would you like to be a tocoyricoc?" I had never meant to say it like that. I had meant to have a lengthy interview, but I could just tell that this boy was special. That afternoon of silence was all the interview I needed. This was a man in a boy's body, a quiet and thoughtful and mature man, an old man. Cayo was twelve that afternoon, but he had the soul of a man twice my age.

"I think I'm too old, Haylli. You took your son out with you when he was eight. If he had measured up you would have started at once, given him extra classes when he began school at ten, and after he graduated at fourteen you still would have apprenticed him for years. I'm four years older than your son. I'm half-way through school, and I've only taken the extra classes my father has been able to justify for me."

I leaned back on my stool, impressed with his candour but disturbed that he knew so much about my boy. "You have thought a lot about this?"

"I've had an afternoon sitting here, Haylli." He smiled at me, a shy smile that I could tell was rarely seen.

"How do you know how old my son is?"

"I have some small ambition to rise high in the administration, Haylli. When you think big from the beginning you have a long time to get there. I know how old all the tocoyricocs' likely successors are. I also know that your son doesn't measure up, because otherwise we wouldn't be having this talk."

I smiled at him. "I like you."

"I wish we had met each other four years ago, sir, but I promise you will never have a harder worker or a more diligent student than I if you pick me as your successor."

And he was right.

309

That very day we went to Cayo's home. His father was a middling bureaucrat for the Intihuasi tampu. He was so pleased for his son that he offered to let me adopt him, but I preferred total control over his schooling and it was given to me without hesitation.

Royal quipus, accounting theory, languages, politics, trade patterns, Cayo drank them up like pouring water into the sands of the Atacama Desert. The boy had no spare time by choice: When his teachers were done with him and I was done with him he would go to the Great Quipu Repository and watch the quipucamayocs work. Within a few days they were giving him his own tasks to do. I never got a problem quipu from him. He always figured it out for himself.

I took him on an inspection tour, and he had a natural flair for spotting the cheats. He was quiet and observant, but others saw his unperturbed manner as shy and withdrawn, leading them to get careless in front of him. Yes, Cayo could find the villains almost as well as I could, but he did not want to see them punished.

I did not think anything of it at the beginning of our tour, but Cayo closed his eyes whenever the Hiwaya stone fell. When I noticed his eyes were never open I tried to rationalize it away: He was young; it is a hard thing for anyone to watch; not wanting to see it did not mean he objected. Then one day in the coastal desert he did object. I was passing sentence over four prostitutes and the man who was their pimp when Cayo begged for their pardon in front of my quipucamayocs, the village curaca, the common purics, and the accused.

I looked down at him in surprise. "What did you say?"

"I said don't do this. Let them go!" He was pulling at my arm, tears running down his usually calm face.

"These people were selling their bodies to get out of their tax duties, Cayo. No one can be permitted to do that, and certainly not in a way that tears families apart, spreads disease, and brings shame, fear, hate and disgrace into a community."

"And how does dropping a rock on their backs set things right? Isn't it a crime to kill five people?"

I was not prepared to debate the point with him while criminals lay in the dust waiting for their punishment and a village stood in the hot sun waiting to see justice done. I ordered the Hiwaya stone dropped five times. Cayo threw up in a ditch.

I had a problem, Friar. A tocoyricoc cannot be afraid of violence in the pursuit of just administration. If Cayo's heart proved too soft for the job, he could never be allowed to follow in my footsteps. I had to make my young protégé understand, so I took a detour off my route between audits to that most freakish of regions, an area occupied by a tribe that never cheated on its taxes. They would never dream of defying the Inca.

I have your interest, Friar? I am glad. The territory of the Huarcos was a valley in the coastal desert whose single claim to fame was their fortress. When Topa Inca Yupanki was working his way down the coast, accepting surrender after surrender thanks to his recent conquest of the Kingdom of Chimor, the Huarcos alone stood defiant.

The fortress was impregnable, with cliffs dropping down to the sea on three sides and unscalable ramparts on the landward-side. Starving it did not seem likely either, for it boasted two springs and a series of storehouses to rival any tampu in Tahuantinsuyu. They laughed at our emperor from their walls, and he sat there for what seemed like an eternity as his highland legions fell to the lowland diseases and summer heat, unable to storm it no matter what he did.

I took Cayo to the Huarco fortress, the original adobe redone now in proper Inca masonry and with even greater storehouses, enough to feed five thousand warriors for twenty years, armed with enough javelins to hold the walls for a decade without wanting for weaponry. The warriors inside were crack troops, career soldiers who made up the single strongest Imperial garrison anywhere on the coast, all for this unremarkable valley.

We climbed the tallest tower of the fort with the sea breeze ruffling our hair, drowning out the call of the gulls. Alone up on the ramparts I told him the story of the Huarcos. "This land is worthless, Cayo Topa. I get more maize out of my small villa in the Yucay valley than this entire tribe gives to the State. Strategically this fortress is in the middle of nowhere, but it cost us a fortune to rebuild. As for the people—" I gestured down to their houses, built in the river valley below with extra wide doorways and windows so the garrison could see if they were meeting in secret. "If we rule them for a thousand years they will not be worth a thousandth the expenditure we went through to subdue them."

"What did we do?" Cayo Topa asked.

"This fortress insulted Topa Inca Yupanki, and he was not a man to bear an insult lightly, Cayo. It was intolerable, a single tiny tribe, smaller in number even than the pure-blooded Inca, facing down the might of Tahuantinsuyu with such confidence that they did not even bite their collars? Old Topa could not leave them be. He brought in new soldiers, and then new ones again when the first replacements fell ill. Knowing that the siege would last for years, he built a city, a New Cuzco over there." I pointed to a canyon off in the desert. "It's all there, the palaces, the courtyards, Huacaypata, the House of Chosen Women, built by the Huarcos who could not fit into the fortress until they died of exhaustion, and then finished by his regular taxpayers.

"It was an extravagant waste, of course. Think what could have been built by that labour instead of a New Cuzco? This whole valley could be terraced and irrigated by new aqueducts with the taxpayer labour spent on a second capital, but Topa Inca Yupanki was making a point, and the Sapa Inca ran Tahuantinsuyu from that canyon for two years, shipping in food and drink to a population of twenty thousand, sitting out there in the desert, waiting for the Huarco in this fort to die.

"Every day he would throw a party for one of the legions at the base of the walls, serving them akha and whole llamas cooked on spits, fresh fruits and vegetables, mountains of potatoes and maize. Then he would call up to the Huarco that their warrior spirit impressed him, that he wanted them to serve in his army, that all they had to do was surrender and they would receive his favour."

Cayo strained his eyes, looking at the canyon I had pointed out, but there was not one whiff of cooking smoke, no sign of chaski huts or pedestrian traffic. There was nothing except a well-swept road.

"Well, after four years from the start of the siege the Huarco were starving; they were even out of slingstones with which to kill seabirds. There wasn't a pebble left within these walls. Their people were almost skeletons when they finally walked out of this fort. We never did take it, and we are the greatest besiegers in history. They had nothing to offer, no gold or silver, no cloth or food, even as labourers they could pay no tribute. They were in such poor health that they could not work."

I paused, letting Cayo picture them. When my father had told me this story I had felt a hundred different things, wondering where the story would go. I could not now deny that same mental game to my future successor.

"So what did he do?" Cayo asked at last.

"Topa Inca Yupanki called them into New Cuzco, and they marveled,

312

for there is no city on the coast as grand as the temporary capital he built while waiting for them to surrender. They stood before him, nine thousand of them, and he said, 'You agree to render unto me any tribute that I ask in the service of Tahuantinsuyu, the Inca, and Inti?' They promised, saying that they now knew the power of the Sapa Inca and that they were his to do with as he pleased."

I let the moment stretch, then turned and gestured over the ramparts to the beach, far below. Cayo Topa looked over, and I thought I saw him gag. I looked over too, but I had grown accustomed to the idea of thousands of skeletons littering the pebbled shore.

"Topa Inca Yupanki was not a cruel man, Cayo Topa, but he said that the single greatest tribute the Huarco could render after their incredible siege was to demonstrate that resistance was futile; that when it became a matter of pride the Inca will grind anyone into the dust.

"He took nine out of every ten adults and had them thrown from the battlements to that beach below, and he sent the rest down into the valley to grow crops without Imperial subsidies. Many starved, for they had eaten their seed corn during the siege. This impregnable fort will belong to the Inca as long as there is a Tahuantinsuyu, and as long as there is a Tahuantinsuyu the whole coastal desert will remember what Topa Inca Yupanki did to the Huarco; know that there is no point holding out against the Inca, for the longer they do, the harder they will suffer.

"The Inca did not suffer at all. Our army lived in New Cuzco, and ate and drank and enjoyed women. It was a holiday, more fun than the garrison duties they are doing now. And when the Huarco surrendered and their survivors accepted our yoke, Topa Inca Yupanki walked out of New Cuzco and forbade anyone to live there again. It had served its purpose, and now it lies abandoned in the desert, one of the greatest cities in the world was built and abandoned within four years, just to prove a point."

Cayo Topa really looked like he was going to be sick, and I took him by the shoulders and leaned him over the parapet, forcing him to see the shore of bones, the empty orbits of the countless skulls glaring up at us.

"Look at them!" I ordered. "This is good government. This is Tahuantinsuyu! This single act, this single slaughter, has prevented a score of rebellions and a thousand tax cheats. They all would have died anyway if we had succeeded in storming the fort, but by doing this to them the Sapa Inca made their deaths so memorable that even though conquering the tribe will never pay dividends, the style in which it was done keeps forty Yunga tribes restive. This is just one big Hiwaya, Cayo!"

"Is that what this is about?" He huffed, pulling himself back from the parapet. "If I wanted to be a butcher I would have gone for the military courses."

"Administrators do not kill for pleasure. We kill so that everyone knows the system works and they will have to work with the system. This!" I gestured to the beach. "And that!" I pointed out to the abandoned city. "Are an administrative example of the power of Tahuantinsuyu. It allows fifteen thousand warriors in three garrisons to keep the peace in a third of our Realm!"

I saw him blink at that thought, and I had another one for him. "Let's say eight thousand people died here. How many more would have died if these eight thousand had lived, and we had put down ten tax revolts between then and now?"

He swayed for a moment, shaken. I had another one. "That city out there that no one is allowed to live in, do you wonder why the road leading to it is still swept? Because every dignitary coming up and down the Coastal Highway sneaks into the city to marvel at the idea that we dedicated that kind of effort to such a minor problem. How likely is that chief to go home and tell his people the Inca will just let them go if they revolt?" I dropped my arms to the side and spoke in a calm voice.

"This is statecraft, Cayo. This is showmanship! This impresses the masses with one display of punishment so that we don't have to make the small ones over and over without anybody noticing. Our people don't understand things like group benefits and net increases; they understand whether they are happy or sad, and as long as we make the lesson simple they understand they will be happier with us as their lords than with us as their enemies. Once they accept that, then we can make the right decisions for them —decisions inside a worldview they don't understand."

The wind picked up again, snapping our clothes. When it died down Cayo Topa had a thoughtful look on his face. "And what about the Huarco? How are we helping them as their rulers?"

"The Huarco never cheat on their taxes. They wouldn't dare. That means they have one of the most efficient ratios between work and rewards. We'll go down to that village, Cayo, and we'll see laughing children and smiling mothers and hard-working fathers, and if we come back in a generation we'll see the same thing, but there will be more of them, more than there ever would have been if we had never come.

"No one starves, as they used to do before they were conquered. No one goes to war, which the gods know they did often enough before they were conquered. Their storehouses are packed with surplus cloth and food and medicine. They have important duties to fill their days, powerful gods to worship, and children to dote on. They have peace and plenty, and if they have to put up with an Inca garrison that doesn't trust them, that is their punishment for the defiance of their fathers. I can live with that, and so can they." I held my hands out to either side of me, offering him everything that mattered to me in the whole world if he would just understand me.

"Let's go look at that village," he said at last.

After that day he still closed his eyes when the Hiwaya stone fell, but he understood why it was being done. That was all I ever asked from him.

Because we were so near, there was one more detour I made from our planned route. We descended into the Rimac valley and climbed up to the temple of Pachacamac, brushing aside the protesting acolytes, for who would dare lay a restraining hand on a tocoyricoc? The high priest was hustled out of his office to greet me, and after promising him a hundred llamas he agreed that I could take Cayo in to see the god as long as I did not ask for a prophecy. That suited me. I had had my fill of prophecies.

We performed a few purification rituals, removed our sandals, assumed our burdens, and we entered that small cave, just as I had remembered it, but different somehow. Maybe it was because I was a middle-aged man. The oracle that I received at my father's side was half-completed. My father was dead. My beloved Koonek was dead. I had little more to fear from the talking idol then that the rest of his prophecy would come true. I felt something in my belly as I genuflected. Slowly it occurred to me that it was angry bile.

There was no screech of steam this time. Instead there was a reverberating echo, like a drumbeat coming down a long brass pipe. Still the disembodied voice seemed to dance around us, an invisible spectre with an audible presence. "Yes?" the god asked before I could speak.

"You said I was to come back one day with a boy that I was prepared to call a son," I said, putting one arm around the trembling Cayo.

"Yes?" The voice of Pachacamac was impatient.

"I obey my god," I said, perhaps in a tone less awe-inspired than I should have used. To my ears it sounded stern, even reproofing. I saw Cayo wince.

"Why do you not fear me?" The voice whispered in my ear.

"Because of what I am to say one day," I replied. It had troubled me all the intervening years, but it was only now —standing there again— that I could feel my anger.

"Say it!" The whisper demanded.

"You are powerful," I replied.

"No..." The whisper hissed slowly, as if in pain. "I said to say I was powerful. Do not twist the words of your Creator."

"Your words are twisted enough," I spat. "My father shall not know my first wife? You could have said he would die. I might have been able to save him! My first wife will not bear my first son? You could have said she would die! You could have said it!" I took the burden from my back and dropped it to the floor with a hollow thump. It would have been the work of a single conversation to keep my Koonek from killing herself: Five or six words warning her not to trust Mama Ocllo's messengers. Viracocha denied me that.

"You dare—" The voice boomed.

"I am He Who Sees All! If I wish it I can have your idol cast down and this mountain upon which it sits leveled and thrown into the sea! It would take ten years and a hundred thousand men with footplows and buckets, but I can do it! I have that power!" I shouted, pointing at the god's open shrieking mouth. Cayo seemed to shrink away from me, trying to disappear in the shadows. The booming echo went on for a long time without speaking.

As I threatened my god, I realized why I was so different from the rest of my people: From the day I was born the gods had said I was to suffer, and I had. I had nothing to fear from powers that already wished me ill. I was to live a long life, they had all said so. If I was already to suffer then I could make them suffer too, without fear.

At last the voice spoke again. "You could not save your father. You could not save your wife. It was their fate to die. 'As!' It must be so."

316

Beside me I heard Cayo whisper, "As!"

I rounded on him, "Be silent, boy."

"Yes..." The idol whispered to me. "You think you have nothing to fear from me? Nothing left to dread for your disrespect? I make this prophecy, Haylli Yupanki: You will love this boy as you love no other. You will come to lean on him in your frail dotage. One day he will not be there. That is your punishment for what you have said today."

I laughed at the idol. "Twisted words, Viracocha! One day he will not be there? And I'm supposed to think that he will die, and dread that for the rest of my life? You never speak so simply! Your prophecies are as tangled as a quipu caught by the wind! One day he will not be there to lean on could just as easily mean one day I'll be an old man getting up from a stool and he will not be there to help me."

The rumble increased in volume and the ground underfoot trembled, but I did not care if Viracocha was angry with me. I was angry with him. "I'm not coming back here ever again. You have seen the boy I will call my son. He will never come back here either. That is my prophecy to you." I took the shaking boy's hand and led him down the steps. The priests and acolytes I passed were all weeping, but I did not care.

* * *

When we returned to Cuzco my quiet home was hosting a party of a size I had never seen before, made more disturbing by the fact that I knew nothing about it.

"This is why I should send a warning ahead of me," I muttered to Cayo as I descended from my litter at my front door, which stood wide open and unguarded. The clan yellow on the door had been overlaid with the deep brown of the Capac Panaca. Through the door, too, I could see scores of people, all wearing brown, all laughing and talking and drinking. I dismissed my procession, some entering the party to join the festivities and others leaving, then I took Cayo by the shoulder for moral support and dove into the den of iniquity that my quiet home had become.

I didn't know anyone. I should be more accurate: I recognized almost everyone, but I did not know anyone well enough to look like a fool in my own home by asking them, 'What is the meaning of this?' Instead, I worked my way through the crowd, ignoring the cries of pleasure coming from side rooms. In the innermost courtyard I saw the Vixen holding court, Pariwana beside her, both dressed in rich brown vicuna

317

cumpi. As calmly as I could manage I made my way over to her. She planted a chaste kiss on my cheek, never once making eye contact with me. While she was close I whispered, "What in the name of Inti are all these people doing in my house?"

"Paying reverence to the new leader of the Capac Panaca," she murmured back, then she turned from me and gestured to the mummy bundle of the Sapa Inca Topa Inca Yupanki seated on an usno in the shade against one wall, flanked by a dozen maidens waving fans and holding dishes of food and mugs of akha for the dead Emperor if he chose to partake of them. His man drum stood beside him, laughing a merry beat through its open mouth as a midget beat on its belly with drumsticks as long as he was tall.

"Congratulations," I muttered to the back of her head.

"I thought you would have been back days ago. What were you doing in the Rimac Valley? It threw your whole schedule off." She swung back to me, the smile on her face belying her reprimanding tone.

"Praying for your success," I lied.

"You are sweet," she said in a voice so honeyed I knew she knew I was lying. "Now stop looking so gloomy. I know the timing is bad, and that you're tired and sore from all the travel, but just be happy for me."

"I am," I protested. "And may I present Cayo to you, the next Tocoyricoc of Chincaysuyu?" I pushed my protégé forward.

At that moment a wave of brown-clad officials, including Achachi Michi and the mayor of Lower Cuzco, began crowding around us, and the Vixen turned from me to them, accepting each of their congratulations with that gorgeous smile of hers, making self-deprecating remarks that produced gales of laughter. Cayo stood there, an uncertain expression on his face. From the Vixen's far side Pariwana saw him and went behind her step-mother to speak to us.

"Congratulations, Cayo," she said, giving him a hug to add some warmth to her words. She then reached up and kissed me on the cheek. "And welcome home, Father. Mama really didn't mean to upset you with the party. She delayed it as long as she could, but she was beginning to worry she would offend the people who supported her bid."

"What exactly has she done?" Cayo asked. "I thought the woman who controlled the panaca was an unofficial position. She makes it seem like she was chosen by popular election."

Pariwana smiled at him. "You're right in saying it's all hidden politics, but she's just won the official post that marks her victory: She's been made chief personal aide to the mummy. That means she has the unlimited ability to translate Topa Inca Yupanki's spiritual wishes into temporal commands. She's been working her entire life to earn that post. Forgive her if she seems a little distracted." She took Cayo by the arm and led him away from the Vixen. I stood there, looking at my wife's back for a moment, then I too drifted away.

The party had divided itself into our three courtyards, each decorated with brown banners and bunting and tapestries that my wife had scrounged up from the gods knew where: The outermost courtyard was for the low dignitaries and officials; the innermost courtyard where I left my wife played host to the most powerful, and the small side courtyard with our garden had been taken over by the children, including Anka and his friends and many of my older Imperial students. I decided as I was unneeded in the other two courtyards I might as well watch the kids, and so I had a servant fetch me an amphora of akha and a stool, and I sat down in the shade of one of my trees, watching the boys run amok.

Kiskis had enough daughters to set up his own House of Chosen Women, but he only had one son, whom he had named Llakato, Snail. Just as I thought Anka had been misnamed, so too was Llakato's moniker almost a joke, for that child was fast as a stick swinging through the air, and just as loud and painful when he hit someone. He was fooling around with Tito and Ninan, playing a rough game whose objective seemed to be running up to unsuspecting boys, snatching off their headbands, and then tossing them over a high branch of one of my trees.

Their game led to a number of crying boys, but I did not see fit to intervene. Boys should not cry. It was unmanly. Swooping in to save them would only encourage them to be soft. What I did take exception to was when they began tormenting young Prince Huascar.

First they took his headband, Tito distracting his half-brother while Llakato ran in from behind, snatching it and tossing it to Ninan, who threw it high up into the tree. Then when the cold Hummingbird showed no sign of upset they began pushing him. Huascar was much younger than them, perhaps five or six to their eight or nine, and so I stood up from my stool, set down my mug, and went over to them.

"What's this all about?" I asked, as if I had not seen the entire thing.

"Nothing, sir," Huascar said bravely. I gave him a pat on the head, but he showed no sign of appreciating my gesture.

"We were just playing," Ninan said from beneath the tree. He was mature enough to look abashed.

"Well why don't you play at climbing up there and getting down all those headbands and apologizing to the boys you've been picking on?" I suggested. Ninan nodded once, eyed the branches above for a moment, and then launched himself up it, climbing as fast and sure as a monkey. He was a good boy at heart.

"Now you," I said, turning to Kiskis's son, Llakato. "What would your father say about picking on someone smaller than you?"

Tito beat me to it. "He'd probably say it was a good way to guarantee you would win!"

"Speak when spoken to," I ordered, not taking my eyes from young Llakato. "You and my son are friends?" I asked.

"Yes," he said sullenly.

"Yes what?"

"Yes, sir."

"Go find him for me," I ordered. The boy flashed a quick smile to Tito and ran off. I turned to Huayna Capac's eldest bastard. "I suppose you're going to say the game wasn't your idea?"

"We weren't doing anything wrong," he muttered.

"No. Boys play, and they play rough, and that's fine," I agreed. He looked up at me in some small confusion. I rarely said anything Tito wanted to hear. "What's not fine is that you're always picking on your brother Huascar. He's younger than you, and he can't beat you at anything because of it, but one day you will both be important men in Tahuantinsuyu and you're going to have to work—"

"I don't think I'll have to work with him at all," he gave me that insolent smile of his. "Ninan's going to be the heir. Even you say so. Ninan likes me just fine. Nobody likes sour-faced Hummingbird."

"That doesn't mean you can pick on him." I silently cursed myself for not disagreeing with the boy on the whole premise. Huascar was still within hearing range of us. Tito's smile grew broader at my slip, then his face fell as if I had produced the most scathing retort.

I followed his gaze to see Cayo and Pariwana coming into the courtyard, whispering to each other and sharing a private joke. I thought I had an idea. "Cayo? Come here a moment, will you?" My new successor dutifully trotted over. "Could you explain to young Tito what he is likely to look forward to, career-wise, as an Imperial prince?"

Cayo frowned at me, but I nodded once to him to urge him on. My protégé looked Tito in the eye and began in a dry tone, "You have no high position in the line of succession, so you will have no court duties. You are just a member of the nobility with access to the Sapa Inca. That means you can choose a career in the administration or in the military, possibly both, but it will depend on your own success or failure to advance." Cayo looked up at me, unsure if he was saying what I wanted him to say.

"And what about Prince Huascar?" I asked.

"Prince Hummingbird is the son of Rahua Ocllo, who became Huayna Capac's second Coya upon the death of Ninan's mother. He is illegitimate, but he is higher in the order of succession than Tito because his mother was later made legitimate. That said, he too will only be offered a military or administrative post based on his own abilities."

"So, over all, Huascar is more likely to hold high rank than Tito?" I asked.

"They're both young too make that estimate yet, but the odds are in Huascar's favour, sir."

"Thank you, Cayo. Now go enjoy my daughter's company." He gave me a shy smile, nodded once to Tito, then went back to Pariwana. I watched Tito's expression and knew I had just made Cayo an enemy, but I suppose that was inevitable: Cayo would become my shadow; he should be disliked by the people who dislike me.

"So you see now why you should be nicer to Huascar?"

"Because your perfect little apprentice suggests it?" Tito looked me straight in the eye now, that insolent smile of his creeping across his face. "I'll take his advice when I'm asking how to tie the knots on all of your death sentences." He was laughing now.

"You do have big ideas, don't you?" I laughed too at the very thought of it.

"The biggest," he agreed.

"Well, I think that's the product of a tired mind. I'll get your caretaker to put you to bed." He looked up: The western sky was aglow with the sinking sun.

"It's still light out."

"Not by the time you get home."

"Does anyone else have to go?" He looked around the courtyard at the other princes and noble boys.

"No one else is acting up."

"But I don't want to go to bed!"

"Oh, yes you do. I can tell. You can barely keep your eyes open," I said in my most condescending voice, raising a hand to wave over one of Prince Tito's keepers.

"I hate you!" He barked. "I hate you, and I hate your stupid know-it-all boyfriend!" He cast a desperate glance past me to see Cayo and my daughter talking again.

"Well, good night to you too, my Prince, and the next time you're invited to a party at my house, you graciously decline. Do you understand me?" His yanacona took him away, and I smiled the whole time he looked back over his shoulder at me.

Aside from Tito, whose opinion meant nothing to me, everyone seemed to like Cayo. Even the Vixen befriended him in the months to come. She always liked people as intelligent as she was, but with Cayo she would develop that rare friendship of hers where she did not want anything from him except his company and an occasional conversation. Cayo never treated her as anything less than an intellectual, and many times I would leave the house to attend to some minor errand only to return to find them discussing the mullu shell trade or the tin mining labour rotation.

If it is possible to say there is one thing that made me like him even more, it was how he treated Pariwana. My daughter had grown into a quiet beauty, like her mother, but with all the benefits of Inca education and a household that was always alive with conversation. Most boys her age tried to impress her, to win her attention with feats of strength or endurance. It always made me smile to remember Chalcuchima and I running until our hearts nearly burst to impress the Vixen, but such acts did not move my daughter. Pariwana, I suspect, wanted a man like her father. I was long past my running days.

Now Cayo was neither strong nor weak, tall nor short, but he was brilliant. It did not take him long to realize where every other boy failed, he could succeed by being unfailingly attentive. If my daughter entered our counting room and there were no extra stools she would have Cayo's seat, but he did it in such a way that it did not seem like crawling. He always included her in the conversation, always asked her opinion. Three sentences with Cayo impressed her more than any of the young idiots at school beating each other half to death with practice maces. I could see the day coming when I could propose the two of them marry, and they would live long and happily together.

Despite the fact that Pariwana was three years older than Cayo, I think his maturity made it so that she never felt it was an issue. She took to taking long walks with him in the fields, although I may have glanced out my counting room window often enough to know she always stayed within sight of the house and never even held his hand. They were just children, I thought, conveniently forgetting that Pariwana had just recently taken the adult name Pariwana Cumpi for her fine weaving, and that at her age the Vixen was in my father's counting room threatening to have me buried alive.

Years passed, and when young Cayo got his breechcloth and earplugs he took the name Cayo Topa, to honour Old Topa and the Capac Panaca. He began coming with me to the school as a teaching assistant instead of a student, which became awkward when Anka entered our classes.

It was my easiest class, of course, basic quipus. Anka would never read royal quipus and probably would never touch an accounting quipu once he was done school, but it was part of the minimum mandatory curriculum, so there he was. He whispered and snickered in class with his friend Llakato. When Tito joined the class too the three became a gang, all planning military careers, all expecting to never use quipus, all disrespectful of knowledge that they thought would be useless to them. It irked me.

To make matters worse, true to his word General Achachi Michi had taken a sabbatical for the duration of Anka's schooling, and so Huayna Capac pulled scarlet strings to bring in the finest living tactician to teach his princes their war classes. Chalcuchima was recalled from his Tumpez garrison by Imperial proclamation, and he was less than pleased to learn that in his absence I had been made Head of the House of Learning in addition to Royal Tutor. He had to report to me each day on the progress of his students, including my son.

"Waccha, your boy's a joke," he would say to me, as if I did not already know. In truth I think Anka could have been exceptional and Chalcuchima would have criticized him with the same fervour: Anka was the son he could not give the Vixen; his very existence twisted at Chalcuchima's soul.

"He'll never be a commander, but he can work a lance and a sling as well as anyone else," I said.

"I'm not here to teach arrow fodder."

"Fine, don't. I can't recall old General Achachi Michi ever teaching me anything. I'll never be a battlefield commander either."

"He's part of the military crowd, Waccha. He's taking all the courses."

"I won't refuse an Inca of the Blood the right to take the war classes just because he fails them."

Unable to get under my skin through insulting my son, Chalcuchima took the opposite approach: Tito, Llakato, and Anka became Chalcuchima's special favourites. Tito I could understand for, without a son of his own, his nephew was the closest thing Chalcuchima had to blood in the next generation. Even Llakato was a good boy at heart, if a bit disrespectful to his father and I. Anka, though, Chalcuchima doted on just to irritate me.

Just as in my school days, a military clique began to form, closeted and unfriendly to the future administrators and bureaucrats who made up the bulk of my own classes. I remember the time Cayo and I entered a courtyard to see Chalcuchima standing to one side as Llakato, Anka, and Tito separated off two of my most promising students, pushing them and taunting them. Rather than break it up myself, I went to Chalcuchima and ordered him to stop it.

"Five llamas says not one of your string boys steps up to save their friends, Waccha," was all he said to me. He always was a gambler.

"There's nothing wrong with a future working with quipus you thickheaded—"

"Lords," Cayo interrupted us. "Either we stop this now or we let it play out. Whatever we do, one of these groups of students is going to think less of us."

The circle had gotten bigger as the sounds of a fight drew other boys out of the corridors and into the courtyard for a better view. One of the two boys being picked on shoved back, knocking Anka off-balance.

The string boys —as Chalcuchima dubbed them— cheered.

"You're on, Mallku," I muttered, taking some small satisfaction in seeing him stiffen at his childhood name, his neck clenching. I rarely called him anything at all to keep from making the choice of being petty or not, but if he was going to have me gambling against my own son, I was going to make him suffer for it.

Cayo, Chalcuchima, and I watched from against the wall as the fight developed. Tito, encouraged by the fact that no one was trying to stop him, gestured more of his followers into the skirmish and formed a battle line. The two who had been picked out were quickly swamped with blows, but the crowd had grown too big to stand idle now, and the rest of my students leapt to the defense. I smiled just a little, and then Cayo and I went in and broke it up.

Chalcuchima waited until I had delivered the ten disciplinary blows to the soles of Anka's feet before stepping up and saying, "You boys cost me five llamas," and just like that he became my son's idol.

Anka, Tito, and Llakato would follow Chalcuchima from class to class like unweaned puppies following their bitch, and Chalcuchima reveled in it whenever I was within earshot, having my son run errands like a common servant and then praising his every little effort, intentionally ruining whatever manly pride my son might have developed as a full-blooded Inca. An Intip Churi does not need praise to know he is great. A pacuyok knows he has a god-given purpose in life. Anka needed to be congratulated if he managed to fetch salt from a storehouse without getting it wet.

As much as I disliked Llakato and Tito, at least they had pride. I began sending them off with my son on special missions, overnight trips to the Yucay valley or to the nearby town of Muina, hoping that they would teach Anka a little self-respect, but then he would come home to his mother to tell her all about it, and she would roar her outrage over every little adventure they had found along the way, chastising me for ever letting a twelve-year-old or a thirteen-year-old do this or that. Apparently she forgot my breaking into a House of Chosen Women at roughly the same age, which is strange when you remember that she was there at the time.

I remember once he came back with a dog bite on his leg and an improbable story of heroism, and I was all set to scoop him up and laud his feat when she let out a shriek to see her baby injured and swaddled him up in cumpi bandages. By the time I could pry him away from her he was convinced he had done wrong —apologetic to the point of tears for causing me worry— and refused to tell me what had really happened.

It was Cayo Topa, wise beyond his years Cayo, who came out with it one day as we were working through our mitmak allocation quipus, "You know Anka's a lost cause. right?"

"I suppose," I said stubbornly. I did not like to lose, but I saw no way to win.

"You know I like your wife, but he'll be a man next year, and she treats him like he's still not old enough to walk and talk; even if he were that age she'd be making him soft." I nodded my agreement. Most families kept their babies in a crib and never removed them except for changing. The minimum of physical contact and attention was supposed to make the infant mentally tough and self-reliant. Anka was neither of those things, and it galled me that there were toddlers superior to my boy. I almost wished his station in life would allow him to be a potter or a fresco painter. He had the sensitive temperament of an artist.

"Then there's Chalcuchima, who would rather spite you than make that boy into a soldier," Cayo pulled a knot so tight it was undoable, and I took his meaning. Anka was unchangeable now.

"Then there're his friends—"

"I get it."

"Let him go," my friend advised. I nodded, and I meant it. Anka was my son, and whatever he needed from me he would get, but from that day forward I never tried to make him into the son I wanted him to be. I had failed him at least as much as he had failed me.

Cayo Topa and I worked long into the night by torchlight, not because of a deadline or because we were buried under the work, but because we loved it. We loved the sound of the counting stones on the board, loved the feel of the wool and cotton and cabuya and grass threads, loved finding the solution to a problem, loved knowing that we made Tahuantinsuyu work. The moon had risen high, throwing a silver light over us both, when Cayo finally spoke again.

"You know I enrolled in poetry classes," he said.

I had, and wondered at it. I made a noise in my throat, my mind concentrating on a series of numbers, trying to find a pattern, totally missing the import of what my protégé was building towards.

"I'm not very good at poetry," he confessed. "It's always comparing a woman to a flower, or to a stream, or to the wind and the stars..."

That throat noise again. How uncomfortable I must have been making him. I don't think I ever apologized to him for my lack of attention.

"The thing is, Haylli —Lord—" That got my attention, for Cayo Topa almost never called me a lord. "Well, I want to marry your daughter." He said it as if it were a surprise to me, or as if I might slap him. My smile must have been like a reprieve from the Hiwaya.

He was young for it, of course, but I had been too when I wanted to marry the Vixen. "Of course, son, of course! Ask her, and if she—"

"I've already asked her."

A distant alarm call sounded in my brain, like those guard parakeets shrieking in the hacha hacha where we stole the spice flowers. "Am I expecting a grandchild?" I tried to make it sound like a joke, but he blushed so hard as he stammered to assure me I was not that I knew he was already bedding my daughter.

It took all my self-control to keep my protective paternal instincts in check, for I loved this boy almost as much as I loved my little girl; even if I thought of Pariwana Cumpi as my little Wawa more often than as a woman-grown I still must accept the fact that daughters do grow up, and that I could not ask for a better husband for her. At last I reached out and patted him on the shoulder. "Well, then, congratulations. Let's drink to the happy couple!"

He reached for the amphora of akha we had been draining slowly all day, but I shook my head and looked theatrically out of both sets of windows before putting my finger to my lips and pulling the lid off a wicker basket behind my stool. There, buried beneath a pile of string, lay a bottle of illegal viñapu. We broached it and got roaringly drunk. By the time the bottle was done we did not feel confident enough to descend the ladder, and so we slept on the counting room floor until the puco puco birds and the warmth of the dawn sunlight woke us to the pounding in our heads.

We did the wedding in grand style, not like the marriage inspector ceremony I had enjoyed with Koonek or the quiet private ceremony I had with the Vixen. I asked Huayna Capac himself to place my daughter's hand in Cayo Topa's, and then my son-in-law placed woolen slippers on Pariwana's feet to symbolize her virgin status, though I cannot say for certain that this was for mere appearance's sake: A father can dream. All I know is that we avoided the grass slippers of a woman known to have had intercourse before the marriage, as I had given the Vixen for the understandable reason of her prior marriage.

Normally everyone in Cuzco was married on the same day, but I obtained special permission for my daughter's wedding to be five days earlier so that everyone could attend. My entire clan came, and my staff from the Great Quipu Repository, and all of my Imperial princes, as well as Kiskis and Rumiñaui and my other school friends. Even Chalcuchima appeared, though he spent most of the party talking with his nephew Tito and left as soon as was polite.

As the father of the bride I got impressively drunk, for I could not refuse to drink with any guest and half of Cuzco chose to attend. I remember going through the better part of an amphora of akha with Kiskis and his son Llakato alone. The manhood ceremonies were approaching, and Llakato, Anka, and Tito would all be competing in the race.

"So have you picked a name yet?" I asked my friend.

Kiskis frowned. "My son's still right here, Haylli."

"Is he?" I said, swinging my drunken head over to look at the boy, who had his father's crooked grin plastered all over his face to see the head of the House of Learning so far gone. "Well tell me anyway. I'm trying to think of a name for my son, and I could use some inspiration."

"Well then my choice isn't going to help you," Kiskis laughed. "Besides, you can't tell me you're getting to name Anka. You didn't get to name him as a child. There's no way your wife will let you name him as an adult."

Llakato laughed too now, not yet accustomed to the large quantities of akha Inca men consume. "I imagine it will be something like Tito's," he said.

Kiskis and I both looked at the boy in surprise. "You know what the Sapa Inca is going to name Tito?" His father asked him. I waited too, for that would be news to me as well.

Llakato knew he had our attention, so he looked left and right, drawing out the tension. "Tito's been dropping hints to his father since he began training for the race, and the Emperor's promised if he does well he will be named... Atauhuallpa."

I laughed, and in a moment Kiskis joined me. "Triumphant Turkey Cock!" I crowed. "If ever there was a suited name!" We were all laughing, and I puffed up my chest and began to strut around in a very unsteady impression of the bird in question. I lost my balance and caught Kiskis around the neck. "Where is the pompous little..." I hiccoughed, and Kiskis flagged down a yanacona to fetch me a bucket in case I should become sick.

"I'll go get him," Llakato volunteered, no doubt wanting to show off the drunken schoolmaster to his friend.

I waved him away and then with exaggerated caution whispered in my friend's ear, "So what's his name going to be?"

The crooked smile was back. "Huaypalcon."

"What in Supay's name is Huaypalcon?" I asked, swaying.

"My first command was at a border fort named Huaypalcon," my friend boasted.

"How inspiring, poor kid." I hiccoughed again. We both laughed. Tito appeared before me, absolutely sober. "Why aren't you drinking?" I asked.

"I think you're doing enough for both of us, sir."

I turned to Kiskis. "I should get drunk more often. He called me sir!"

"I'd call you an ass, but I wouldn't want you to try and hit me in your condition," Tito said. Llakato and Kiskis both sucked in their breaths at that, watching my reaction.

I eyed the manling up and down. He had grown into a solid adult, with a body every bit as stubborn as his pride. He wanted me to hit him so he could hit me back. I could see it by the way he was up on the balls of his feet, the way his arms were tensed at his side to block a blow. He was not a little boy anymore that I could discipline. He was a man, even without the formality of a name, and that meant I would have to treat him like a man: My best weapon for dealing with men had always been my words.

"You wished you were the groom today, Atauhuallpa?" That shook him. He looked over at Llakato for support. "You don't mind if I call you Atauhuallpa do you? It suits you much better than Tito. I've known a number of very good boys named Tito, but aside from you I've never known a man named Atauhuallpa who goes to such lengths to insult his host on the day of his daughter's wedding."

The prince leaned backwards now, unsure of himself, the weight coming off the balls of his feet. "I don't know what you're talking about."

"Oh, I think you do. Cayo Topa married Pariwana Cumpi today, and you wished it were you."

"You're drunk."

"And you've wanted my daughter since you're name was changed from Wawa to Tito, because you always knew she was the girl you could never get."

"I don't know what you're talking about," he muttered again.

"You know exactly what I'm talking about. You lust after my daughter the way your uncle and I used to chase after the Vixen, but we both got what we wanted in the end. Pariwana is beyond you, Tito. She's worth ten thousand of you, and I'm not just saying that because I'm her father. I'm also the man who knows you best in all the world."

His blank expression showed that my words had pierced his heart. "I think you've had too much to drink, sir," he said, trying now to assume a polite tone that was so faked I almost felt gratitude at the effort.

"Well, come here and give your old tutor a hug," I threw my arms out to either side, my akha mug flying to shatter against a wall. Tito gave a helpless glance over at Llakato, who shrugged.

The prince allowed me to embrace him, and when my mouth was right beside his ear I whispered in it, "Your father could get you any woman in the world, Atauhuallpa, but not my daughter. My daughter is perfect, and that means she should go to the best man I know, not the worst. And didn't I tell you already to never come to a party at my house ever again?"

I thumped him heartily on the back, let go, and called for more akha to toast him. By the time the amphora arrived he was gone, having made his excuses and gone straight out the front door.

Kiskis and Ninan Cuyuchi —the adult name of Huayna Capac's legitimate son— put me to bed that night, each staggering under my near-dead weight. I awoke in the morning, bathed in the inner courtyard's reflective pool to clear my head, and went back to work.

The days flew past, with Cayo Topa and Pariwana Cumpi meeting with the Royal Architect to build a small villa on a piece of land I had given them not too far from Cuzco. As time passed, though, I had to leave my son-in-law and my daughter to their own devices and focus on my son: The manhood ceremonies had arrived.

I stood beside Sapa Inca Huayna Capac throughout that year's ceremonies, culminating, as it had for me, with the race from Huanacauri to Sacsahuaman. I had offered to send Anka to the White Rock Chaski School, but my tales of the challenges there made him decline in strong terms. He should have gone. He came in fifth last out of more than a hundred boys, and he wore the black breechcloth of shame for the rest of the ceremony.

When it came his time to have his ears pierced by the Emperor I forgot the name the Vixen had made me promise to give him. I stood there, my mouth open, but his new name would not come to my lips. In my eyes he was not yet a man. I was not old enough to have a man for a son, and he was certainly not mature enough to be one. He knelt there, waiting for me to pronounce the name as senior male relative so that Huayna Capac could lance his lobes.

When the silence had stretched uncomfortably long and even the Emperor began to clear his throat I said under my breath, "I'm sorry, Anka, what was it again?"

I swear to the gods, Friar, the boys eyes started to tear up. This was a man? Never the less, he whispered back to me —choked it, really— "Yahuar Huacac." Blood Weeper, a ridiculous name for my boy, made just barely acceptable because it was his great-great grandfather's name. What a joke.

I said the name aloud; Huayna Capac nodded and pronounced aloud, "You are a man, Yahuar Huacac." Then he pierced both ears expertly and inserted the tubes that would be replaced with larger and larger plugs, making my son a pacuyok, an earplug man. I always thought of him as Anka, though, and I could probably count on one hand the number of times I ever called him Blood Weeper.

More time passed, Friar, and all the children in my life grew up. Cayo Topa and Pariwana Cumpi built themselves a fine new house. Anka, now a man with a man's name, moved from his ground floor apartment into a garret in the back of our house where he could entertain his friends like Huaypalcon without my watchful eye. Soon even cold Prince Huascar took an adult name, but we all continued to call him Hummingbird.

With his eldest sons becoming men but still too young to be given high government appointments, Huayna Capac picked up the entire Imperial Court and went on a pilgrimage to Tiahuanaco, the ancient city built by giants on the furthest shore of Lake Chucuito whose ruins survived the Great Flood.

It was interesting to see the reactions of the young princes to such a powerful huaca: Ninan Cuyuchi was solemn and respectful, participating in all the offerings and ceremonies; Huascar's usual cold façade cracked a little with religious awe; Atauhuallpa was bored as soon as he arrived. My own son and Kiskis's boy Huaypalcon had attached themselves to the Imperial Guard, and so I also got to watch their boredom at close quarters. After almost a month I decided to see Huayna Capac about it.

"Sire?" The Emperor was in his harem visiting his heavily pregnant sister-wife Rahua Ocllo. She was our new Coya after the recent death of Ninan Cuyuchi's mother.

"Hello, Haylli." He lifted his ear away from her distended stomach, smiling. "You should feel him kick. He must have a chaski's legs on him." With some trepidation I reached out and touched the Coya's stomach.

"Feels like a girl to me, Sire. A dancer's legs, maybe?" Rahua Ocllo smiled up at me, shyly. She was not a fire-breather like most empresses. She had not fought secret battles to be chosen as Coya; she had taken over from her dead sister by default.

"Oh, you're always hoping I'll have a daughter so you won't have to teach her," the Emperor laughed.

"I'd gladly teach your daughters, Sire. I have taught some already."

"Your wife's made the same offer. I just don't want them to grow up to be vixens." We laughed together, as old friends do. "What do you want, Haylli?"

"Your sons have learned about all they're going to at Tiahuanaco. Let's take them hunting," I suggested.

"Hunting? Is this province scheduled?" An Imperial hunt was only conducted in a given area once every ten or fifteen harvests due to the depopulation of the local animals. Hunts were also scheduled around the availability of local men to serve as beaters, the needs of the garrison legions for field training, and the stores of dehydrated meat in the tampus.

"We can do it now, Sire."

"Well then I think you should arrange it." He turned to place his cheek back against his Coya's belly, and I was dismissed with a wave of the hand.

It took five days, but I made the preparations with Cayo Topa's help, and soon the Imperial princes, the Sapa Inca, and a few other high-ranking Incas of the Blood waited in a meadow. Ten legions and the entire male population of the province were thrown out into a ring in the surrounding hills, encircling a space ten times the size of the entire Huatanay valley. We had our litters rigged up onto firmly planted posts to form hunting platforms, and then we waited.

As the sun reached the one quarter mark, conch trumpets blew all around us, and forty thousand men, all facing us, began to walk slowly forward, making noise, beating drums, thrashing their way through brush, driving all before them.

The sun was at its zenith before the first of the fleeing animals began to appear in our meadow, a few deer and foxes, but Huayna Capac waved his sons back to their seats. These animals would be back.

The circle of men closed on us, tightened and tightened, and as the afternoon wore on we saw them on the hills around us, a solid wall of men, many now carrying lengths of fabric between them to form an imposing barrier to any animals that tried to escape the ring. Every creature in the province that could not fly or burrow was now within our line of sight. Only now did Huayna Capac rise up from his seat on the deck of his litter, place the first stone in his sling, and hurl it down into the milling animals below him.

His shot dropped a guanaco, a beast much like a llama but capable of incredible bursts of speed. Its fellows scattered in all directions, fast as the wind, but the animals around them were too packed to take to flight. Now the princes had their turns.

Ninan Cuyuchi's slingstone downed a deer, a big buck that seemed to snort once in disgust at having his skull caved in. Atauhuallpa's spear pinned a fawn to the ground, where it squealed so piteously that Huascar used his first javelin to put it out of its misery.

I will not detail the rest of the hunt for you in this manner, for that would be impossible. The beaters came closer, which meant that for every animal that fled our slings and arrows and javelins ten more arrived, so that soon they were packed together so tightly that even pumas and bears mixed among the deer. Here, now, was the true test of a warrior's marksmanship, for the young princes were not supposed to kill any vicunas or any female deer or guanacos. The rest fell by the hundred, so that the bodies lay in piles around our platforms.

As the beaters closed to the point where they encircled just our meadow they could not move further forward at the press of bodies, and now the soldiers among them took up their weapons and joined us in our slaughter, while the farmers took to grabbing the vicunas, shaving them of their fleece, and then throwing them outside the circle to run, shorn but free, back into the hills from whence they came.

By the time the sun set there were no animals left alive save for the ones we had spared. That's when Cayo Topa and I descended from our litters to organize and catalogue the butchery. The skins of the dangerous animals would be kept for rugs and capes. The rest would be shaved of their wool and fur to make thread and then turned into leather.

The choicest meat of the most delicious animals would be eaten that day, and such was the bounty that every puric had a cut fit for the Emperor. The rest of the meat, the vast majority of it, would be smoked for days into charqui to be distributed throughout the province's tampus where it would keep for years.

A slaughter on that scale attracts scavengers by the thousands, and already the condors circling overhead were sufficient to dim the sun as it went to rest behind the mountains. I turned to the nearest Inca officer I could see, a blood bespattered youth with his back turned to me who was laughing with some friends over the body of a bear.

"Soldier! Pick a hundred men to keep the birds off all this until it's smoked."

The young man turned, and I was surprised to see it was my son; he did not look so unimpressive from the back. "Why me? Tonight's feast is going to be—"

"You're a soldier, boy. There will be more hunts in the future for you. Get your detail ready."

"Get someone else to do it," he said, turning from me.

I opened my mouth to chastise him when Prince Ninan Cuyuchi appeared from nowhere, slapping my son hard across the face. "When the most powerful tocoyricoc in Tahuantinsuyu gives you an order, you do it!"

"Don't be so righteous, brother," Prince Atauhuallpa drifted into view, a bloody mace over one shoulder. I had seen him earlier moving through the bodies, braining animals that still twitched. "Yahuar Huacac wants to celebrate a good day. So do you."

"Army discipline must be maintained," Ninan Cuyuchi muttered.

"You're not wearing the Yellow Fringe yet," Atauhuallpa said. "So get the royal sceptre out of your ass. Let us have our fun!"

I was about to intervene between the brothers when Prince Huascar appeared, followed by a retinue of Cañari bodyguards. "What's all this about?" The prince had a gift for seeing problems everywhere.

Atauhuallpa turned to his younger half-brother. "Old Haylli wants his son to guard the carcasses while we all spend the night partying. What do we have purics for if not to do the unpleasant work while the pacuyoks enjoy life? Get a Cañari or Chacapoyan officer to do it."

I decided it was time to speak up. "I don't see what we're arguing about. You were all brought up better than this. I know, because I did the raising. You," I pointed at my son. "Find a hundred men to guard the meat. If you want to go to the party, fine. Check on your pickets every hour and don't get drunk." My son's face fell, but he nodded.

"You," I pointed at Atauhuallpa. "I am not 'Old Haylli,' and don't joke about purics being yanaconas just to needle me, otherwise some purics might take you at your word and needle you." I pointed over to the Hummingbird's honour guard, who grinned back at me. Cayo Topa and Ninan Cuyuchi laughed. Atauhuallpa just glowered.

"Huascar, pick one of your men to supervise the pickets in between my son's inspections." The prince pointed to one of his men, who gave a proper salute and went to stand at Anka's side.

"Ninan? Would you care to join Cayo and I for a drink?" I put one arm around Cayo Topa and one around the heir and walked away from the rest of them.

It was long after midnight when the news arrived that Huascar's mother, Rahua Ocllo, had begun her labour on the shores of Lake Chucuito. I could not rouse any of the future child's drunken siblings and half-siblings, but Cayo Topa and I threw on extra mantles against the pre-dawn chill and made our way as fast as we could, our breath forming steaming clouds around our heads until the sun rose. We arrived at sunset to learn Huayna Capac had another son —his fortieth and his first with Rahua Ocllo as his second official Coya.

I held the new baby in my hands, as I had most of the princes before. He was red-faced and pug-nosed, wrinkly and hairless. He coughed and spat up, trying to wipe the mucus off his face with the back of his tiny hand, which was not an easy thing for an infant to do.

"Wawa's got personality," I said, liking him. His mother smiled at me.

Huayna Capac nodded his head. "The way he was kicking her, I think he'll make a fine soldier one day," he said. "What do you think of the name Manco?"

"It's early for that yet," I said, cradling the baby's head. One should never get too attached to a baby, and naming him so early was bad luck.

"I've only lost five sons before they had a childhood name," he said, chastened at his slip.

"Manco's no name for a boy, anyway. That's a man's name," I said. Wawa gurgled something, and I bounced him for a moment until he cooed.

"I suppose you're right," he said.

We looked out over the deep blue of Lake Chucuito, feeling the aching cold off those frigid waters, I tugged at the baby's swaddling cloth to make sure he was protected from the chill. "What is that?" I said, knowing what it was even as the words left my mouth. Far up the shore a pillar of smoke was rising up, angled heavily by the wind, then another one appeared closer to us, then another and another.

Perhaps one chaski station in five has the special task of maintaining a pyre to send news that must be acted on faster than the regular chaski post system can relay on even the fleetest feet. When a series of smoke signals appeared, each moving closer to the Sapa Inca, a rebellion has broken out somewhere in Tahuantinsuyu.

Huayna Capac snapped orders to call up all the active duty commanders and begin a muster at Cuzco. We had to wait ten days for details to arrive by chaski post that the tribes of the former Kingdom of Quitu were in arms, killing their Inca governors and refusing their tax service.

"Bring me Pilla-huaso!" Huayna Capac barked. The old Quitu sinchi with his emerald headband was produced from the Imperial retinue. "Your people have revolted."

The defeated ruler sighed. "A long time ago you made a promise. I did not care for it at the time, but now I think I would like to hold you to it. Keep the crows off me?" The former war chief removed his headband, bowed his head, and never saw the guardsman appear behind him with a length of llama leather rope. He died without a fuss, and Huayna Capac did indeed order a man to keep all the carrion birds except condors away from the body.

And so we come to the Great Quitu Rebellion, a turning point in all our lives. I have never seen one of your Spanish bulls, Friar, though I have had them described to me. One of our resident Spaniards claims to have fought bulls for silver coins on market days in a land called Extremadura. His description of bull fighting fascinates me, for I see in it a terrible parallel to the destruction of my world.

I know what you Spaniards will tell your children about the Inca: You will say less than two hundred brave conquistadores came into the heart of our Empire and conquered us because your Spanish God and Spanish courage were on your side. Who can help but like that story? There is truth in it, and the idea of so few overcoming so many makes an audience yearn to know how such a thing could ever come to pass.

I sometimes think what really happened isn't all that different from a Spanish bull fight. Tahuantinsuyu is the bull, and your conquistadores can be likened to the matador. Does that not imply that you vanquished us? Well, you did, but before the matador delivers his death blow the poor bull is bloodied and baited, mauled by dogs, teased by fleeing foes on horseback, weighed down with barbed weights until all his great strength is drained out of him. He succumbs to the sword if not with gratitude than at least with resignation.

So too it was with Tahuantinsuyu. Long before the conquistadores appeared on our shores, hungry for gold, my land began to bleed. The first great waste of our strength was the Quitu Rebellion. A generation of our youth would be wasted in that green and pleasant land, and those who survived would become something different from what they were before: Harder, crueler, more willing to perform atrocities for the sake of their own gratification. If Tahuantinsuyu was a bull, Friar, the Quitu Rebellion was a heavy barb sunk into its flank, and it would bleed the Children of the Sun until we cried our anguish to the silent stars above.

Of course, it didn't seem like that at the time. It seemed a grand adventure! Not just for the men of the legions, but for foolish middle-aged accountants who should have known better. There was so much work to do, Friar! My fingers twitch at the thought of all the knots that I tied, for it all required the careful oversight of He Who Sees All.

It took a year and a half to assemble the army, but I think even that amount of time was a feat that tests the limit of credulity. Three hundred thousand men is one from every forty tax-paying families in all of Tahuantinsuyu. It's more than that, actually, because the Quitu taxpayers were in revolt and the Yungas and Urus were forbidden military service. For tribes like the Inca, the Cañari, and the Chacapoyas it might be as much as four men from every five households.

Every one of those soldiers was brought to Cuzco and divided along tribal and clan lines into legions a thousand-strong. They were clothed, equipped, housed, and fed at State expense. There were regular drinking parties to raise morale and patriotism. All this, for a year and a half of mustering, was before a single soldier took a single step towards Quitu.

Then there were preparations for the campaign itself. Every tampu on every road between Cuzco and Quitu still loyal to the Sapa Inca was stuffed full of war materiel, and this meant massive transfers by llama caravan. The Chacapoyas, for instance, were one of our main centres for the collection of jungle bird plumage, but the need to feed and arm their legions had my quipucamayocs organizing thousands upon thousands of llamas to carry the bundles of feathers to storehouses in the Collao and bundles of chuno and lances to tampus in Chacapoyan territory.

Tahuantinsuyu groaned under the weight of the coming campaign. Every male Inca was involved in some capacity, either as an officer or an administrator or as a priest praying for our success. My son Yahuar Huacac and Huaypalcon leaned on Atauhuallpa to get them into the first Upper Cuzco legion. Chalcuchima, Rumiñaui, and Kiskis each commanded an Inca legion. Even Cayo Topa and I, much more valuable for logistics than on the battlefield though we were, nominally served in the fifth legion, reporting to the training field each day for weapons drill and refreshers in army tactics and discipline.

Meanwhile the revolting tribes were building up their hilltop fortresses and preparing for long sieges. They had no unity, no cohesion, no true coalition with which to resist us. It seemed to our spies that their plan was little more than to sell their lives dearly and resist as long as possible. They were going to fight simply because we had not properly conquered them the first time.

The administrative details that cropped up were unimaginable, Friar. In expectation of all the newly made heroes I had to make sure our goldsmiths increased production of the chest discs and our weavers were focusing on red and white checked tunics. That meant I had to increase gold mining, panning, and trading. It also meant I had to place orders asking our dye collectors to focus on red and white for all the new bravery tunics that would be woven.

Stripping so many men from Chacapoyan and Cañari territory meant I had to send taxpaying labourers from Collasuyu and Condesuyu up there to maintain the roads and bridges. Sending those men meant I had to authorize the masters of the hundred tax-paying families to exceed their quota of state travel passes. It was never ending!

As the day approached for us to march we celebrated and feasted and feted until our heads rang with alcohol and music. We sacrificed a thousand llamas, consulted a hundred augurs and a score of oracles. When all was in readiness, Huayna Capac ordered Viceroy Achachi Michi to set our forces in motion and left Prince Huascar behind as governor of Cuzco. The Intip Churi marched out to the kind of war we had not seen since my grandfather was still alive.

An Inca army on the march is impressive in so many ways that it is difficult to describe. Three hundred thousand men march ten abreast in thirty thousand files, followed by easily an equal number of camp followers and llama caravan drovers. This moving population, despite its warlike nature, will not steal one cob of corn or stick of firewood from the territory it marches through on pain of death.

Everything is ready for them in the tampus, and the soldiers of the army typically only move from one tampu to the next in a day. The Grand Muster had produced a host so big that when the vanguard was at one tampu, the rear guard was often fifty tampus behind it, and every tampu in between was filled with soldiers that were fed and sheltered without relying on the local populace.

Meanwhile, because the Emperor marched with the army, the road was being swept and leveled in front of us and all the local peasantry came out to genuflect and sing praises to the Son of the Sun as he passed in his litter. They carried our baggage from one end of their province to the other before passing it on to the next willing tribe. The whole Empire was ready to help, glad to witness the martial splendour of Tahuantinsuyu on the move.

All along our route of march Huayna Capac consulted the important oracles, and one and all they foretold victory, a prediction that required little clairvoyance when it took our army the better part of a month to march past their shrines.

One oracle, though, atop a little hill outside Huamachuco, said something of interest to this story: The hill was a perfect cone that tradition demanded supplicants climb on their knees. Unwilling to abase himself alone, Huayna Capac asked Ninan Cuyuchi and I to get down from our litters and climb up to the top with him.

The high priest, an ancient man who probably remembered the day when the Inca fought the Chanca hordes, greeted us at the top with a bowl of warm salt water with which to bathe our muddy shins. He talked to us about small matters while we took in the tiny reed hut he lived in and his simple dress of a badly dyed blue tunic and clunky seashell jewellery. This man never came down off his hill, and his servants fetched the salt water all the way from the ocean beyond the Western Mountains for him.

"We have come for a prophecy," Huayna Capac said after an appropriate interval.

"And you shall have it, Sire, though I would ask that you not take it as bad news," the old man said.

That got our attention, for a hundred oracles had already told us nothing but good news. The red-fringed Emperor, his yellow-fringed heir, and my lowly self, the most powerful accountant in the world, all looked at each other for a moment before nodding in agreement that we wanted to hear this. "Go on," Huayna Capac said.

"I foresee a long war, in which you will ultimately triumph," the priest said in the same conversational tone he had used while we cleaned ourselves. "But if you pass the volcano of Cotapaxi, you and your heir will never see Cuzco again. I am sorry, Sapa Inca."

Huayna Capac stiffened at that, and Ninan Cuyuchi opened his mouth to protest, but I interrupted both of them. "How is that not bad news?"

"It will be my Emperor's decision not to go back. He will be happy in the warmer climate, and he will run the Empire from there in greater comfort than he could from Cuzco. That said, and I say it with the total confidence of an oracle of the highest capabilities, Huayna Capac and Ninan Cuyuchi will never see Cuzco again."

There were no drums or whispers or incantations of any kind, but we all felt the power of this plain-spoken priest. What he said would be.

"That's not bad news, Sire," I agreed after a moment's thought. "My father told your father that the Inca should one day rule from Quitu because Inti especially favours that place. You can be happy there."

The two Imperials looked at each other. A long silence stretched as they weighed the cost of their war, then Huayna Capac made up his mind. "If I am not to see Cuzco again, we should make Tumipampa and Quitu —once we've recaptured it— as beautiful as Cuzco ever was. Ninan, I want you to build me a capital in Tumipampa worthy of a Sapa Inca. Spare no expense, and coordinate with Haylli. Keep in mind, one day it will be your capital too, so do a good job of it."

Father and son smiled at each other with only a hint of regret, and the priest and I joined them. We agreed we were happy together, marching to war. We gave a lavish gift to the oracle, though the priest said he was forbidden to display any wealth beyond his humble trappings; eventually, we resumed our march.

* * *

Most of us left our wives behind, Friar, but Cayo Topa took Pariwana Cumpi with him when we marched towards Quitu, and I think if it is possible that endeared him even more to me. So many Inca took advantage of the campaign lifestyle to enjoy conquered women, but not the husband of my daughter.

Cayo and I worked throughout the day, securing provisions for the army and ensuring work parties constructed roads and tampus to support the war effort. At night my daughter would join us, and we talked about matters contemporary or historical, immediate or fanciful. I would be a foolish old man to think the young kept no secrets from me, but I do not think it an exaggeration to say we were true friends despite the yawning gap in our ages.

I sent royal quipus back to the Vixen by chaski post, and she was pleased to keep me informed of Cuzco gossip. She said Prince Hummingbird was doing well as governor of Cuzco in his father's absence. I would come to learn it was because he followed her advice in everything, but that is for later in my story.

The last loyal lands before the Kingdom of Quitu belonged to the Cañari, and we marched into their capital city of Tumipampa, The Field of Knives, to build it up as an impressive base from which to conduct a long war. Aside from the barracks and roads and tampus and storehouses needed for the coming struggle, Huayna Capac ordered five hundred llama-loads of gold and a thousand of silver to be transported from Cuzco and installed in the temples and palaces of Tumipampa. Huayna Capac's own palace there, Mollecancha, the Molle Tree Enclosure, glittered with the sumptuousness of its decorations, including four life-sized gold and silver replicas of the trees that gave the place its name, standing in an orchard in the main courtyard.

Satisfied with his new capital, Huayna Capac next ventured to the shores of the ocean to talk with the Puná, an island tribe who had always been difficult to control. They lived as pirates, making war on the city of Tumpez whenever the Emperor was distracted. With the Quitu Rebellion sure to last for years, Huayna Capac wanted them to renew their allegiance to him.

Truly, Friar, the Puná were as hard and proud as the Inca, despite their addiction to the luxury of their former masters, the Chimu. Their population of six thousand was served by tens of thousands of slaves — true slaves, not like our yanacona, for their noses and lips were cut off to make them less than human. The Puná's vast harems were guarded by eunuchs taken from their defaced slaves, and their temples practiced sodomy in their worship of the moon.

They were an unlikable people, but their warrior spirit could not be doubted; Huayna Capac did not want them in his rear when he advanced past the twin peaks of Mount Chimbarazo and Mount Cotapaxi into the lands of the Quitu.

With our vast host camped out on the shore around Tumpez their chief Tumbala sent a fleet of balsa rafts, each bearing the palm frond of peace and surrender. He invited the Inca nobles to come to the island of Puná to hunt on his estates and enjoy his hospitality as a token of his continued allegiance.

Huayna Capac loaded the balsa rafts with his honour guard, and we watched as they sailed away to their base on the island just over the horizon. The rafts returned around midday without any of our people to assure us that they had arrived safely.

It was Cayo Topa who first figured out what had happened. When the rafts had arrived at dawn he had examined the lashings that held the balsa logs together, curious as always to learn new knots and bindings. The afternoon's inspection showed that the lashings were different.

The Puná had sailed out of sight of the land, untied the logs holding their boats together, then —born swimmers— they killed our drowning mountain men with clubs and harpoons. After the slaughter the Puná reassembled their rafts, let the decks dry, and came back to the beach to do it all over again. Huayna Capac had the crews and boats seized, those that did not pull away from the beach and speed over the horizon when their deception was uncovered. Huayna Capac dubbed the tribe the Treacherous Puná, killed all their retainers on the mainland that he could lay his hands on, then installed a generous garrison at Tumpez to keep the Puná in check. We did not have time to build an armada to avenge the slight.

I have made frequent mention of the Kingdom of Quitu before, but now that it is about to become the scene upon which so much of the rest of my story will be played, perhaps I should go into more detail. The Kingdom of Quitu was a confederacy of tribes, like Tahuantinsuyu. The dominant tribe, the Cayambi, had their capital at the magnificent city of Quitu, thus the name.

In ancient times the Cayambi were led by scyris —emperors like our Sapa Inca— and these scyris expanded their nation to resist the Chimu and later the Inca who encroached upon their natural southern frontier, a line of smoking volcanoes that marked a place where the eastern and western mountains merged and drove inland away from the ocean to create a fertile bowl of rich land in the most pleasant climate on Earth, a perpetual warmth that could grow any crop, and where people could wear as much or as little clothing as they wanted without feeling hot or cold. Even the sky was a deeper, richer blue there than anywhere else I had ever been. It was beautiful.

There were a number of tribes subservient to the Cayambi. The most powerful of these were the Carangui, a warlike people the equal of any of our own fighting forces. They occupied the heartland of the kingdom and were so formidable that our war council agreed not to tackle them until we had first dealt with the Pastos, Otavalos, Huancavelicas, Maytas and Paltas who occupied the fringes of the Kingdom.

Our advance was rapid, for the rebels stayed in their hillforts rather than risk a pitched battle with our great army. We marched into the capital city of Quitu uncontested, and Huayna Capac sent for still more gold and silver, as well as setting up labour gangs from the surrendered populace to build barracks and temples and palaces.

Now that we were up into the rebelling territory we had to begin the tedious job of reconquering these people, and in this task some men, like Kiskis, Rumiñaui and Chalcuchima, proved to have natural ability. Others did not.

Prince Atauhuallpa in particular was a miserable general. I remember that first year fighting against the Pastos proved that. The Pastos were the most chaotic of the rebelling tribes, going about almost naked and living on the fringes of the hacha hacha. They were proud and brave, which led them to join the rebellion, but they were so poor that some of Huayna Capac's counselors, including General Achachi Michi, questioned the value of reconquering them.

With the exception of a little gold and feathers that passed through trade routes on their land they had next to nothing, so that when Topa Inca Yupanki had conquered them in his prime they were paying tribute with lice plucked from their own bodies, just so they could become accustomed to paying their taxes for the day when the Inca engineers could build the terraces and aqueducts necessary to make their land flower.

It was Chalcuchima and Kiskis, two very junior officers at the time, who convinced Huayna Capac that resubjugation was necessary. It would prove no people could cede from Tahuantinsuyu and prevent the flow of headhunting mercenaries from the hacha hacha into the Carangui and Cayambi armies. The prospect of a hundred hillfort sieges with the walls lined with jungle archers convinced the Emperor to move against the Pastos first.

I cannot say at that time whether Chalcuchima was Atauhuallpa's patron among the legions, or if it was Chalcuchima who gave favours to his nephew Atauhuallpa in exchange for access to the royal usno. Either way, the first Pasto hillfort was Chalcuchima's to take and he offered it to Atauhuallpa, who promptly made a mess of things.

Atauhuallpa threw his conscripts against that pinnacle of rock rising up from the forest around it, and when he was done the field was littered with bodies, none of them the naked painted corpses of Pastos. Atauhuallpa, knowing he was under the eyes of both the Imperial Court and Achachi Michi's staff, brought out the Old Guard, the pure Inca legions of Upper and Lower Cuzco, of which Chalcuchima, Kiskis, and Rumiñaui each commanded one, and Cayo Topa and I served in another.

The eldest royal bastard worked his way back and forth down our ranks, shouting encouragement and promising booty that the poor Pastos in their fort would never have to offer once conquered. Then he ordered us forward exactly as he had the conscripts before us, without changing his tactics one step. He was relying on our martial spirit to take the piffling little hill, wasting the flower of Inca soldiery in a place no one would remember in a month.

The conscripts had tripped most of the Pastos rockslides, but slingstones and arrows continued to rain down, and their lances were hollowed out so that they whistled mournful notes as they fell. About half-way up the hill the Pasto garrison charged down to meet us, and Atauhuallpa —unseasoned and overconfident— dismounted from his litter to fight in the front ranks.

Cayo and I never saw action that day, for the path leading up the slope was too narrow, and our legion was still at the bottom when Atauhuallpa descended from his litter. So steep was the hill, though, that we had a perfect view as the front line heaved and surged, wavered, then snapped.

The first legion fell back under the fury of the Pastos downhill charge, dragging an injured Atauhuallpa with them. Such was our Inca discipline, however, that Rumiñaui's second legion held fast as Atauhuallpa's first retreated through them, then they charged uphill into the disorganized pursuing Pastos, routing them.

Reinforced by Chalcuchima's and Kiskis's legions, the hillfort fell before noon. The Pastos were made to wear coarse and heavy woolen tunics festooned with long tassels of shame. Their surviving sinchis had their necks stepped on by Huayna Capac as a gesture of his superiority. Their women were distributed among the victorious legions.

As for Atauhuallpa, I visited him in his tent. Huaypalcon and my son were holding him down as our healers tried to sew his lobe together. He was not bucking at the pain, of course, for Atauhuallpa was as brave a soldier as any pacuyok, but he was cursing his ill-fortune with such a steady stream of profanity that the doctors could not work. The torn earlobe meant he would never be able to wear his golden earplugs, never again be recognized as an Inca. When the surgeons gave up Atauhuallpa ordered his other lobe cut off for symmetry.

To add insult to injury, his father Huayna Capac entered the tent just after his other earlobe had been removed. We bowed and blew kisses to him, kicking off our war sandals and standing hunched over for lack of shoulder burdens. "That was a disgrace, boy," the Sapa Inca said, his hard eyes playing over his eldest bastard.

"I know, father," Atauhuallpa's scowl deepened.

"That hillfort could have been taken by the conscripts if you led them yourself. Using Inca soldiers was a waste."

"I know, father." Atauhuallpa held sodden rags to his ears, making him look ridiculous.

The Emperor looked at me, and I shrugged. He looked down at his son's bloody earplugs. "You will fight in my bodyguard, but you will never have another battlefield command. Do you understand me?" Atauhuallpa nodded. Huayna Capac left without another word.

Yahuar Huacac and Huaypalcon began to make the obligatory efforts to salve Atauhuallpa's pride, but he ordered the tent cleared except for me. Surprised, I watched his cronies and healers file out. "I guess you're happy, old man?"

I was not yet old, but I knew he was looking to make himself feel better by baiting me. "My friends are all still alive, no thanks to you. So, yes, I am happy."

"How's Pariwana Cumpi?" He leered.

"Happily married," I replied evenly.

"You should have let her marry me, old man. You'd have a grandson by now." He smiled that humourless smile he knew I hated. I laughed at him, just to see him deflate a little.

"If you'll excuse me, Atauhuallpa, I'm having my lobes stretched. I

346

thought, now that I'm getting so old, I should move up a size. Can I melt your plugs down to make mine heavier?" His scowl lightened my mood, and he dismissed me with an angry wave of the hand.

Outside the tent I saw Yahuar Huacac and Huaypalcon standing together, lost without their leader. "Come to my tent and we'll drink to your victory."

"It wasn't our victory." My son was bitter.

"The Inca won it."

"Our legion didn't." Huaypalcon spat on the ground.

"There will be more battles, more than you can imagine. No one will remember this one except Atauhuallpa." I gestured towards my tent with an open hand. "Please?" I tried to sound nice, knowing their honour was almost as injured as the lobeless Atauhuallpa. I had not connected with them as boys, but perhaps we could close the distance as men.

"With your permission, my lord, I think I would be better served with a good night's rest," Huaypalcon said. I suspected he meant he would go find one of the Pasto women, but I nodded my acceptance and he left us.

"What about you, Anka?" I said, catching my mistake just too late.

"My name is Blood Weeper, father, and I am not a little boy anymore." Then —just like a spoiled little boy— he stormed out of my presence, stomping his feet as he went.

There were so many hillforts that every Inca who expressed an interest got a turn at commanding a siege, and often the army was split into a hundred parts, each watching a different hilltop. I remember Anka and Huaypalcon both won theirs in bloody stormings and dutifully received a gift from the Emperor for their trouble.

Even Cayo was given command of two legions of Huanca conscripts and told to take a hilltop. The fort was small, with only a hundred Pastos atop a low mesa, and it would have been a morning's work and a hundred dead men to storm it. Not Cayo, though. Cayo never believed in death when there were alternatives. He requisitioned leather slings for his conscripts, heated slingstones until they were red hot, then had his men send a rain of fire down on the Pastos above, burning every roof.

That night the rain god Illapa blessed our army with a deluge one can only find so low down on the eastern slopes of the Eastern Mountains;

when we awoke it was to find the Pastos waving the palm frond of surrender from over the battlements. Without shelter they had spent a miserable night, sopping wet, and they awoke in the morning to find all of their stores rehydrated and ruined.

In exchange for their lives and the lives of their families they were willing to serve in the Sapa Inca's army, and thus, instead of losing a hundred men, Cayo Topa gained a company of new soldiers without a single loss of life on either side.

Huayna Capac was so taken with this noble siege that he ordered a banquet thrown in Cayo's honour, a proper martial banquet attended by all the army commanders. "Well done, Cayo Topa!" The Emperor boomed. A thousand cups were raised in toast to my son-in-law.

"Thank you, Sire. It was only my duty."

"And devotion to duty is to be rewarded," Huayna Capac said, waving his hand. The High Priest Topa Cusi Yupanki stepped up to the usno with something wrapped in cumpi. The Bird Man handed it to the Emperor, who gestured Cayo Topa forward. "For your service I give you this mace," he pulled back the cumpi to reveal a magnificent war club of carved chonta wood with a bronze head. "The Fifth Upper Cuzco legion is yours now. Lead them well."

We drank to Cayo Topa's health. He raised the mace high in triumph. "I also give you your chest disk. Wear it with pride, Cayo Topa. No man deserves it more." The coveted golden plate was attached to the front of his tunic, and Cayo Topa lowered his eyes with humility. He could not hide that shy smile of his though. He made me very proud that day.

* * *

It is both sacrilegious and unpatriotic for me to say so, Friar, but the stupidest things are done in the name of religion and war. At the same time, one of my fondest memories of the Quitu Wars comes from a nonsense day doing a nonsensical task in the name of religion and war. To be honest, I think I may have been suffering from sun stroke during the entire incident.

The rains came late that year, and this was a bad time to have a drought because the tampus in Chincaysuyu were depleted supporting the Imperial Army. With hunger staring us in the face, I was dispatched to administer the traditional remedy for a lack of rain.

On my reluctant orders all the black dogs in the parts of Chincaysuyu still under our control was taken from their owners and tied to stakes by the side of the road. The theory ran that the rain god Illapa was particularly fond of black dogs, as they most resembled storm clouds, and so as the dogs slowly starved and died of dehydration he would feel sorry for them and bring us rain.

While I have never seen this as an effective means of creating rain, it moves from cruel to farcical when I had to post guards over the dogs to keep the former owners from granting relief to their pets. Up and down Chincaysuyu I organized dog collection points where black dogs could be guarded while they suffered. I also spent days and days making snap inspections to keep the guards from helping the animals, all in the name of religion.

Everywhere I went I heard howling and whimpering and panting. I felt the sympathy that Illapa was meant to feel. The sky remained clear, mocking my efforts and the dogs' suffering.

It was at one such compound outside the city of Quitu that I snapped at the futility of my mission. I did not care if there was a war on, or that the storehouses were emptying without being refilled. The whimpering was too much for me, and I ordered the kennel released to run down to the nearby stream.

"General Chalcuchima won't like it, sir," a guard told me as he shot back the bar on the wooden gate keeping the dogs in the courtyard.

"Well then you tell that old bastard to have it out with me himself," I said, knowing the man would do nothing of the kind.

When all the dogs that could still move had escaped, I walked into the courtyard. I stood there for a long time, watching the fly-blown corpses of the dogs who died before my temper caught up with me. Late morning turned to noon as I meditated there in the hot sun.

"What in Supay's name do you think you're doing, Waccha? I've got twenty thousand men under my command who are expecting to be fed next year!" Chalcuchima's voice barked from behind me. I did not turn; I raised a hand to silence him. He did not heed me. "Those dogs are important, Waccha. Even if you don't believe in it, the purics do, and the purics want to know that we're doing everything we can for them. This is stuff I hear in your own damned administration classes!"

I turned and shushed him, and his neck muscles bunched as if I had spat in his face. "What? What is so fascinating about a courtyard full of stinking dead dogs? My men say you've been standing in here all morning!"

I looked up, and the sun was at its zenith. I looked down, and I had no shadow. Neither did Chalcuchima. Neither did the walls of the kennel, or the trees outside, or the dead dogs within. In this place each and every one of us was blessed by Inti, just as my father had promised.

"What is it?" He snarled again.

I pulled out my dagger and held in out, seeing no shadow, and I felt very close to my father then. "I can't explain it to you. It's just huaca."

I turned smiled at him, and he recoiled at the sight of my smiling face. "You've gone mad!" He turned to call his litter bearers into the yard to restrain me.

I realized the scene I was making and cleared my throat. "Don't say that to me ever again, General." I put the dagger back in my coca bag, seeing some of the tension go out of his neck now that I was unarmed. It was time to speak like a rational person. "This isn't working, and killing these dogs is not going to win us the thanks of the farmers who need them to keep birds out of their fields. We'll just have to start running llama caravans from better stocked tampus close to Cuzco."

He looked at me again, and the fact that even his beak of a nose cast no shadows was making me smile, so I looked away. "You're an idiot, you know that?"

"Yes," I said.

"Have you been drinking?" he asked me.

"No."

"Well then get out of here and arrange your caravans. And send a message under your authority to release the rest of the dogs. I'm tired of my men guarding these kennels anyway. There's a war going on, you know."

"Yes, I know," I smiled again.

"And wipe that damned grin off your face!"

I smiled all the way back to my own litter outside, then I smiled as I noticed my litter bearers had no shadows as they carried me away. To this day I have no idea why I felt so happy, except I think my father was looking down on me from the Upper Universe that day. Sometimes you just need to smile at the little things, because it's the little things that get you through life, Friar.

It was a long war, Friar, but one by one the tribes bowed to the inevitable. We worked on a set schedule. First our spies would survey the forts, posing as merchants or traveling mercenaries seeking work, then when we had the disposition of their forces we would send an ambassador. Our emissary would tell them down to the last spear and bag of corn just what they had to resist us, then he would offer them cumpi and women and a full pardon with their curacas retained in their rank if they would submit without further trouble. Some did —the smart ones— but most did not, and then we would come for them with fire and spear and slingstone.

However long it took we always prevailed. When the Pastos were all under our control again we sent raids out into the hacha hacha, using our own jungle soldiers, burning villages, stealing gold hoards, poisoning water sources, all to warn the cannibals that this war was between civilized peoples; it was in their own best interest to stay out of it.

On the banks of the Angasmayu next to a natural stone bridge Huayna Capac erected a monument defining that point as the furthest extent of Tahuantinsuyu; then he turned the army around and marched back towards Cuzco, conquering every fort and village he came across on the way.

Until, that is, we came across the Carangui. They were a proud people, renowned warriors whose entire male population served as soldiers. Where the Pastos and Otavalos and Huancavelicas and Maytas had each retreated into their scattered hillforts and waited for the inevitable, the Carangui sallied out to attack our lines of supply and communications. They abandoned their lesser outposts, concentrating their forces on the hills that were truly bastards to take.

I have good reason to remember one siege in particular. We were at the base of a mountain for more than a month, starving. The Carangui had burned all the tampus within a day's march before retreating into their citadel, and so every non-combatant with our army was now serving as a porter, shipping chuno from intact tampus well back on our supply lines. This trickle of food, all dehydrated potato, sapped the morale of soldier and Emperor alike until Huayna Capac's patience finally ended.

"General Achachi Michi! Summon the Upper Cuzco legion. We will storm these Carangui bastards out."

Achachi Michi looked over to me in support, and I shrugged as well as I could with a weight on my back. The Sapa Inca had given an order.

The general still felt he had to try, rubbing his aching back as he spoke. "My Lord, we are making good progress diverting the spring supplying them with water. Within a few days we will have a new stream running down into the gorge on the far side of the mountain and that hilltop will be as dry as the Atacama."

"And if it rains between then and now they'll put up tarpaulins to collect rain water, and they'll hold out until my youngest son is a grand-father. Don't talk to me of your siegecraft miracles, General. For every trick there is a trick, and right now I want to do something."

"Yes, Majesty," we backed out of the Royal Presence.

It was a foolish idea, but it had to be done now. A thousand earplug men appeared in their martial finery and formed up at the base of the hill. They sang their most savage war song to work up their courage. "Aucap umanuan upyason. Quironta valcarisun. Tullunuan puncullu-sun, caranpi tunyacusun, taquecusun!" A charming melody, with good rhythm and rhyme, don't you agree Friar? It translates, "We will drink from the enemy's skull. We will wear a necklace made of his teeth. We will play the flute on his bones and the drum on his hide, and we will dance!"

When their blood was angry enough, great banners of wool were held by the men of the front rank and passed over the heads of those behind until every man stood in the shade and protection of a blanket. Achachi Michi and the Emperor appeared in their litters, giving the pre-battle speeches, then the legion began to march and the next legion began to form up.

I watched from the camp as the first legion began to scale the Carangui hill. It was a suicide march. The ten thousand Carangui up there might be besieged by an army of three hundred thousand, but they would still outnumber their actual attackers ten to one. They held the high ground, and every step of the road leading up their hill was already ranged and targeted for their projectiles. They began with slings and arrows, and I watched these missiles bounce off or lodge in the over-head blankets. The disciplined Inca legion never increased its pace or disrupted its formation. They marched, still singing, knowing they had not seen the worst.

For a long stretch the road ran flush to a wall, five times the height of a man with Carangui warriors on its top. Now the blanket was little pro-tection as the Carangui threw javelins, large rocks, pots full of obsidian flakes and boiling water, anything to disrupt the Inca below. Still our soldiers climbed higher. The second legion was beginning to come up behind them, and the third was forming up. The whole Imperial army watched the Inca —the Old Guard— march.

Our soldiers were a third of the way up when the Carangui tripped the first of their rockslides, and I watched as the mountain men dodged the boulders with agility that always surprised the Yungas of the coast: Short and stocky though we may be, our people are born knowing how to avoid the worst of an avalanche. I heard a cheer go up from the first legion, for every soldier knows the great disadvantage of the rockslide defense is that it can only be used once. This one had killed only a handful.

The Carangui waited until four legions were climbing their hill before they tripped the next rock slide, and the next, and the next; then they charged down after the tumbling rocks, ten thousand of theirs against four thousand earplug men, still dodging boulders and under bombardment from above by women and children from the walls. No man could expect our victory.

Even as I thought it, I watched Huayna Capac beat his sceptre on the floorboards of his litter, ordering it into the melee. The press of men was tight, but the Emperor worked his way slowly up the hill, picking off the women and children on the walls with his sling and shouting his soldiers forward. They could not obey.

It is a terrible thing to watch an assault give way to a retreat, then a retreat turn to a rout. When victory was impossible the Intip Churi fell back, knowing they could not win and that anyone who died now would die for nothing.

Panic and despair gave speed to their withdrawal, and soon men were being trampled or pushed from the road down the rocky slope. I watched in horror as the Sapa Inca's litter swayed and tipped up on one end, not from enemy action but from the weight of men shoving into his litter bearers. Huayna Capac was standing on the flat surface, his sling overhead, and the lurch came at just the wrong moment. The Emperor fell from his litter into the sea of warriors below him.

I was on my feet, running to the Fifth Legion, ordering them to go and save our Emperor, but Cayo Topa and his men could make no headway against the fleeing warriors who had now seen the Son of the Sun fall.

The defeat was not serious in the long run. We lost six hundred Inca and Inca-by-privilege and embarrassed ourselves in front of our army, but we still had the Carangui trapped up on their fort, and the work of diverting their water supply would continue. The trouble now was the Emperor's pride. Huayna Capac walked down the mountain, Red Fringe awry, his Imperial finery dirty and torn, his cheek bruised, his sling lost. His litter was still on the slope, dashed to pieces by his retreating soldiers.

"He had better not blame me," Achachi Michi muttered around a mouthful of pain-deadening coca. Aside from his back, one of his fleeing soldiers had elbowed him in the face as he tried to rally them; now he held a raw piece of llama meat to his eye to bring down the swelling. "I told him it wouldn't work. It might work if we did it six or seven more times, but by the time we do that the hilltop will have been without water for five days!"

"Don't complain to me," I told my friend. "Just take his yelling like a man. He knows this wasn't your fault."

But Huayna Capac did think it was Achachi Michi's fault. Not the failure, of course, for the Emperor was enough of a soldier to know long odds when he saw them. No, Huayna Capac was upset at the shameful way the Inca legions had retreated in front of the eyes of his army, and he was especially furious that he had been tipped out of his litter. That night he ordered the already thin chuno ration to be halved to all the Upper Cuzco legions, and he threw a drinking party for his servants and the army's porters, turning away any earplug man who showed up uninvited.

"This will not stand!" Achachi Michi barked at me in his command tent.

"General—"

"No, Haylli! I know he's our Emperor, but the Inca are not conscript soldiers! We're not paying a tax quota to be here! We volunteered our time. I say we just unvolunteered, and as Huanacauri is the Inca's war idol I say we're taking it back to Cuzco with us."

My jaw dropped at the idea, but Achachi Michi was so incensed he did not wait for me to collect my wits and talk him down. He called out a string of orders to the officers assembled in the tent and I saw them file out, each bound for a different company of the best soldiers in Huayna Capac's army.

There was no way to call them back before they delivered their message: The Inca would no longer serve. The Intip Churi were going home, and taking our invincible war idol with them. Huayna Capac could give all the akha and women he wanted to his servants without the pacuyoks staying to be insulted.

They marched out even as Huayna Capac enjoyed his banquet, taking the idol with them on its litter. I bit my collar to ward off this bad omen and ran to the party, but I was turned away by his Cañari guardsmen until late into the night. As the drunken servants staggered out one sassed me for my earplugs. "I am the Tocoyricoc Haylli Yupanki Yachapa," I told him. He swallowed hard and staggered away as fast as he could.

At last I entered the Royal Presence, barefoot and burdened. I blew him a kiss and bowed from the waist. Huayna Capac was a champion drinker, and even after his long fiesta he could see I was in a hurry. "What is it, Haylli?"

"Majesty, the Inca legions have left."

He sat up. "They've deserted?"

I had to correct him for fear of Viceroy Achachi Michi's life. "No Sire, they are in the right. They have not been ordered into battle the way the Colla or Cañari conscripts have. They are here of their own free will to participate in the campaign. The fact that the Inca have never refused a war before doesn't make it desertion now."

From a pile of pillows off to the right I saw Atauhuallpa raise his drunken head. "How many did you say?"

"All of the Upper Cuzco legions are gone, and they have taken Huanacauri with them," I told Huayna Capac, not bothering with Atauhuallpa.

"What can I do?" Huayna asked.

"At this point it will take a grand gesture, Shepherd of the Sun."

"Arrange it, but get them back Haylli!"

"Yes, Sire." I blew him a kiss and left.

Forty-eight is an old age to perform the feats of your youth, but I did my best to remember my chaski training. I needed to move too fast for my litter. I ran one pace and breathed as regularly as I could. I made it work.

I took a road parallel to the main one the Upper Cuzco legions clogged, crossing mountain streams not with the suspension bridges of the main highway but in the swinging buckets that are pulled across a thin cable by men on the far bank. I ran as if my life depended on it; if the Inca succeeded in abandoning their Emperor that would be a Pachacuti, the end of Tahuantinsuyu as I knew it. I had only one chance to mollify the colossal pride of the Children of the Sun.

I beat the Inca legions to Tumipampa. When I arrived in the Imperial City, I made my way to the local House of Chosen Women. Panting from my exertion, I had a hard time pulling myself together to speak with a suitable authority to summon the voice of the idol of Mama Ocllo.

Friar, you may remember a certain dalliance for which my feelings were conflicted? I hoped that she held the memory of our moment in a palace side room as a pleasant one, because I needed her help now. She appeared before me, an older and even wiser vision of the plain-faced, calm girl I remembered. Her gown was of the dead Coya's favourite shade of green. My heart skipped a beat.

"Hello, Mama Ocllo's Voice," I said, my tone formal.

"Hello, Haylli Yupanki." She allowed the hint of a smile to break her unremarkable façade, an effect that transformed her from a matron into the maiden I had known.

"I need you to do something for me, the Sapa Inca, and Tahuantin-suyu," I said. I imagine the House of Chosen Women must be a boring existence for a woman whose purpose in life was to speak on behalf of a dead crone. Her broad smile at the prospect of doing something important reinforced my belief.

The next day I stood on the royal road with her and the litter bearers of Mama Ocllo's golden idol, watching an army march on us. You would never have guessed the Cuzco-bound Inca legions were returning home disgraced and humiliated. They marched to the beat of a drum and the skirl of panpipes, the dust of battle beaten from their tunics and their ornaments and decorations shining in the sun.

At their head rode Achachi Michi and the idol Huanacauri, each in their own bejewelled litter. Most of Tahuantinsuyu had been conquered by an army half as formidable. The idea that Huayna Capac still had hundreds of thousands of men under arms behind these veterans staggered me. How far the Inca had come since the days of the Chanca invaders!

They marched right up to us, stopping in unison at the braying command of a conch trumpet when Achachi Michi's litter towered only a few spearlengths in front of me.

"You were quick, weren't you?" The general smiled down at me, green flecks of coca leaves in his teeth.

"I had things to do that could not wait," I agreed.

Mama Ocllo's Voice stepped forward, dressed in green vicuna cumpi. "Viceroy Achachi Michi, first general of the Intip Churi, Mama Ocllo beseeches you from the Upper Universe not to disgrace her son's people so. The Inca are the greatest warriors in the world. If you could not conquer the Carangui that day, no one could."

The viceroy leaned back at this, nodding his appreciation to me that I would bring religion into this Imperial apology. Still, he was not prepared to return to the Kingdom of Quitu based on a few well chosen words. "Tell Huayna's mother that the Children of the Sun are the proudest people in the world, and we will not be snubbed. Our lances serve the Emperor at our pleasure, not his."

"Mama Ocllo has seen her son err, as mothers often see sons do. She has asked him to see his mistake, and he has acknowledged his mistake." I saw Achachi Michi sit up straighter in his litter at that. The coca had numbed his backache. That boded well for me. The green-clad priestess continued, "Every earplug man will receive a new tunic and cloak from Imperial stores and a double akha ration for the rest of the campaign against the Caranguis. Huanacauri will receive ten llamas a day for the rest of the year to placate the insult to his warrior spirit. As for you, General, Huayna Capac grants you a palace in the Yucay Valley."

Huayna Capac had given me total control over the cost of this reconciliation, and as I could only try once I had decided to go big. This was the kind of respect and reward Huayna Capac should have bestowed upon the Intip Churi all along, and getting it now, in this fashion, meant the Imperial favours would continue to flow. The Red Fringe would not be so careless again. Achachi Michi looked at the golden idol on the litter opposite him for a moment. "Mama Ocllo is a wise and kind provider for her people," he said at last.

"Huayna Capac was wrong to insult his own kind, but his soldiers cannot hold a man's temper against him. A warrior's temper is a good quality in a Sapa Inca, and so is the wisdom to sometimes listen to his mother." The viceroy bowed to the statue and again, with subtlety, to me. With that he ordered the Inca legions to turn around. They were marching towards Quitu again as if nothing had happened, still playing their panpipes and drums.

357

I followed them back, but somehow I made it all the way to our siege camp before Cayo Topa's messengers found me. I rushed to my tent and there, stretched out on a pallet as if asleep, was my son Anka. He was dead.

Cayo put an arm around my shoulder. A weeping Pariwana Cumpi took one of my hands in hers. "How did he die? I don't see a mark on him," I asked. I did not feel angry, or sad, or even numb. I felt nothing except a vague guilt for feeling nothing, and then I began to dread having to tell my wife that her son was dead.

"His wounds are in his back," Cayo Topa said. With a gesture from my son-in-law, Kiskis's son Huaypalcon stepped out of a shadowed corner of my tent.

"His back? He was killed in the rout?" I asked.

"He was the rout, my Lord." Huaypalcon shuffled his feet and looked down, perhaps to hide his tears. I never liked Huaypalcon, but I think he was a true friend to Anka.

"What do you mean?"

"Chalcuchima told Yahuar Huacac that today was going to be his day: He made Yahuar Huacac the leader of the first half of the first Upper Cuzco legion and promised him a chest disk if he took the fort."

I looked at Cayo Topa and an understanding passed between us: Chalcuchima had promoted Anka over the heads of scores of more deserving officers into a suicidal position, then given him the motivation to be suicidal. My boy would have fought to make Chalcuchima proud if that hill had reached to the sky. My schoolyard foe had killed the boy he could not give the Vixen as surely as if he had held the lance himself.

"You said he was the rout?" I asked.

"He led us up too far. The man Yahuar Huacac replaced told him that this attack could not succeed, that it was never meant to succeed. Then he took a slingstone between the eyes. Yahuar Huacac panicked and tried to run back through his own troops." Huaypalcon began to cry, and I shrugged off my daughter and Cayo to take this young man in my arms, hugging him with more affection that I had ever shown Anka. "I had to do it, sir, I had to!" He wailed into my shoulder.

"Do what? What did you do, boy?"

"I tried to stop the rout. You can't have a leader run without his men!

358

I took him down with my lance. I killed him." I held him a little tighter, sure now that whatever Kiskis's son had been to my son, he would always look out for himself and his fellow soldiers first. I wished, just in that one moment, that Huaypalcon was my son, or that Anka could have had this boy's manly virtues, then I remembered that I didn't like Huaypalcon either and the moment passed.

"You did what you thought you had to, but the rout was necessary. The first legion was too far up. You had to fall back as fast as possible to make it back to camp in one piece. You couldn't have known that from where you were, though. You did the right thing."

Huaypalcon sobbed and snuffled into my shoulder for a long time, and I waved my weeping daughter out of the room, as if all those tears were too much for me to take. The truth is that I did not want her to think me heartless. My eyes were dry. I had no tears for my son. When Huaypalcon cried himself out he went over to my son's body, kissed him for a long moment on the forehead, and left. I looked at Cayo.

"Take his name off the list of the dead," I said. "I can't do this by chaski post. I'll have to tell the Vixen our son is dead." For the first time my voice broke with emotion. I was about to tear my wife's heart out. "I can trust you to keep everything going for a few months, and to take care of the funeral arrangements?"

"Of course," Cayo said. "And Haylli? I'm sorry."

"It's alright, son," I said. "It's alright." I don't really know if I was speaking to Cayo Topa or Anka or to myself, but the words were soothing.

* * *

I succeeded in beating the bad news home. I was the one who told the Vixen that our son was dead. I even managed to call him Yahuar Huacac. I dismounted from my litter, took her in my arms and said, "Our son Blood Weeper died in battle. He died a hero's death, but he is dead."

My wife keened and wailed in a way that would melt the iciest of hearts, and I held her as she cried uncontrollably at what fate had done to her. My Vixen loved that boy as she had never really loved anyone, especially me. He was not a means to an end to her. He was her end, and the end of him was the end of that part of her that lived for more than her ambitions of power.

My proud Vixen's posture was never the same after that day. She slouched. Her chin was never held so high again, and she finally began to age the way other women did. The spell was broken, and I saw the wrinkles on her neck, the creases on either side of her mouth, the crowsfeet around her eyes. She went grey overnight, but it grew in such a glorious shade of white that people took to calling her Kollke Atoc China, the Silver Vixen, and many of the young courtiers in the Capac Panaca assured her the new colour made her more beautiful than she had been as a girl. It was a lie, of course, but it was the sort of lie demanded by the station she had worked to achieve all her life. She was the undisputed ruler of a panaca, and she went there to seek solace at the death of her son.

I did my best to console her. I really did. As I grew older I did not feel the urges I had as a younger man, and so I no longer loved her for the sake of lust. Now I loved her because she had been there from the beginning, the only true constant in my life. From boy to man, with the exception of my darling Koonek, the Vixen had always been there with me. I loved her because the weight of time had made us as close as love should make two people.

I would hold her in the night while she cried. I would follow her to her panaca by day and attend all the panaca parties I could stand in the evening. We drank more than was good for us, and ate rich foods. I did no accounting work at all. I was supportive and caring, flattering even. I told her fanciful stories about what a good son she had produced and how the whole army had marvelled at his bravery at the end. I did everything I could to help her, and when it was not enough I gave up.

I'm sorry, Friar, but I just gave up. I left Cuzco to return to Huayna Capac's side. My life was my work, and I was dying in Cuzco as the world went on without me. I don't know at what point my wife recovered from her son's death. I was not there. There are many things I regret when it comes to the Vixen, and I think the fact that she recovered without me was the final blow. We lived apart the rest of our lives, even when we shared our house we slept in different rooms.

I loved the Vixen as a boy. I respected her as a man. I loved her as one would love a distant sister as an older man. When we became just an old man and an old woman we muddled along until one of us stopped. She would stop first.

The years slipped through my fingers like the knots on a quipu, Friar, with hilltops on fire and prisoners dressed in shaming tassels, with drinking parties and dancing girls, with martial pride and solemn dignity, triumph and tragedy. The army of Tahuantinsuyu became the greatest fighting force in history, lean and hardened by the long war of reconquest.

Our conscripts were supposed to rotate their labour duties and go home to be replaced by new men, but that didn't happen. Their curacas, who also served as their legion commanders, decided they would see the war through in exchange for fair division of the spoils. Tumipampa and Quitu became filled with soldiers' wives and, in time, soldiers' children. I adjusted the administrative system to cope with this new reality.

Somewhere between that day on the shores of Lake Chucuito and here I became an old man. Not just an older man, but an old man. Kiskis and Chalcuchima and Rumiñaui went grey too, but no one ever called those generals old. When the young spoke about me I was 'Old Haylli' as the ancient Emperor of my boyhood had been 'Old Topa.'

If Pariwana Cumpi and Cayo Topa's wawas had not each succumbed to some childhood sickness I would have been a grandfather thrice over. If Anka was still alive I might have been a grandfather by him too. Instead I had Cayo and Pariwana, but that was enough for me.

No, that's not strictly true. There were other children in my life. Although I had given up my role as Royal Tutor, there were two princes who I spent as much time with as possible during my short visits home to Cuzco. They became great players in the fall of Tahuantinsuyu, so I should mentioned them to you now, Friar.

The first was the baby I had held in my arms when the fires of the Quitu Rebellion were lit. As the war approached its end that infant underwent the manhood ceremonies and took the adult name Manco Inca at his father's suggestion. All communication from Huayna Capac was delivered by quipu via the chaski network, of course. Manco had not seen his father since he was three years old. The second prince I favoured was a year older than Manco. His adult name was Paullu Inca.

It seems disloyal to Huayna Capac's memory to say, but most of his sons were fools: Not those two, though. They were trustworthy and efficient, studious and hardworking. They were also so young that they both understood there would never be a high position for either of them. They were content to be Imperial princes of minor rank, doing what was asked of them without demanding more.

I remember one visit in particular: I had been sent back to Cuzco to guide the city's governor, Prince Huascar, through the Intip Raimi, the festival of the Sun that marked our New Year through honouring our patron deity. The year before he had botched with such gusto —forgetting to find good tidings in the llama entrails no matter how they actually looked— that morale plummeted in our army and farmers blamed every natural disaster on the bad omens.

My old friend the High Priest Cusi Topa Yupanki was detached from the war front to accompany Cayo Topa and I back to Cuzco. We journeyed down the Royal Mountain Road, chilled to be out of the balmy Kingdom of Quitu despite the long sunny days up in the mountains, and we arrived in Cuzco to be greeted in the Huacaypata by Prince Huascar, Prince Manco Inca, and Prince Paullu Inca.

"Greetings High Priest, Tocoyricocs," Huascar said. He sat upon the Imperial usno with his two bastard brothers on either side of him.

"Governor, princes," the Bird Man intoned, frowning. "Are you allowed to sit in your father's seat as governor of Cuzco?" We all knew he was not. The Hummingbird stepped down, trying to make it look like he was not responding to a reprimand from the foremost religious authority in the land. "Much better." A bird flew by, and the High Priest's head turned to follow it, somewhat ruining the effect. Cayo and I smiled at each other.

"You've come to oversee the Intip Raimi?" Huascar asked.

"Why ask a question you know the answer to?" the High Priest asked, his head still turned to look at the bird, which was nesting in the thatch of the Emperor's palace.

"I know what I did wrong last year," the governor muttered. "Old Haylli's wife is helping me. This year the thing can have ulcers and I'll see good tidings. I promise."

"There are other mistakes you can make. I trust the three days of fasting have begun, and that all the fires of Cuzco have been extinguished?" Cusi Topa Yupanki asked, unable to tear his gaze away from the bird.

I looked now to see three chicks stick their heads out of a hole burrowed into the thatch, each shrieking for their parents' attention. I could not resist. "What do the birds tell you?"

"They're nesting in the Emperor's empty home. They are hungry and want to be grown up, but the father still has to feed them and teach them to fly." Only now did the High Priest swing his head back to the three Imperial princes.

"Fascinating," the cold governor said. Manco Inca and Paullu Inca had the good sense to look abashed.

I stepped forward. "I want Manco Inca and Paullu Inca to coordinate with us on the logistical side of the ceremony. There are a lot of llamas to slaughter, coca to burn, akha to drink, and it all has to be here." The two princes nodded. "Governor, the High Priest will walk you through each step of the ceremony. We will meet tomorrow night out on Pus Cliff to view the stars."

With that our little group broke up: Cusi Topa Yupanki took the governor by the elbow, speaking in rapid, precise sentences about religious minutiae. The two princes followed Cayo Topa and I to the Great Quipu Repository, and we worked there to organize the biggest religious ceremony —followed by the biggest party— of the year.

"Do you think that's true, about the birds nesting on the Emperor's roof?" Manco Inca asked me, late in the day, setting a requisition quipu down.

"I don't know how much of the High Priest's predictions are set formulae and how much are inspired improvisation, but it doesn't take a brilliant mind to imagine princes left behind in the richest city in the world for years starting to think they run the place."

"I don't think I'm running anything," Manco protested.

"I know, but that's because you're the good one."

"What about me?" Paullu's voice asked from the far side of a set of shelves.

"You? We're lucky Cuzco still has all of its walls and roofs," Cayo Topa said. We all laughed.

"You're wife has stepped into a certain role too," Manco Inca said.

Now it was my turn to set down my quipu, my concentration broken. "What do you mean?"

363

Paullu's voice picked up where his brother had left off. "He means Huayna Capac's first Coya has died and his second doesn't wield any authority. Huayna Capac has made Huascar governor of Cuzco in his absence, and he's a member of the Capac Panaca—"

"My wife is acting like a Coya?" I asked, wonderstruck. I don't know why I was surprised, of course. If there was any way she could have done it she would have, but what did this mean? What would happen when Huayna Capac passed away if my wife was a political power with a longstanding relationship with Huascar instead of the heir, Ninan Cuyuchi?

We worked until sunset, then I sent the two princes to their homes with orders to inspect the surrounding tampus the next day and meet us at Pus Cliff the next night.

Cayo Topa and I went to my villa to find the Silver Vixen was not at home. I took the extraordinary step of sending one of our servants to the Capac Panaca to fetch her. She came with all proper dignity, carried in a litter by her own troop of Rucana porters. I arched an eyebrow as she descended. She laughed. "The governor's idea: He said a woman of my age shouldn't have to walk to and from the city every day. He offered me a house in town, but I thought this was a better idea."

I bet she did. A house was just a house, but these litter bearers were a mark of Imperial favour that the Imperial Hummingbird was not supposed to be able to grant. As for the argument about walking into town, you could see the roofs of her panaca compound from my counting room. I just grunted, dismissed her bearers, and led her back into our garden, gently illuminated by torchlight. She somehow made it seem as if she was leading me. Her courtly ways had become impressive during my long absences.

"You look well," I murmured.

"And so do you both. Campaigning agrees with you," she gave us both a chaste kiss on the cheek.

I launched right into it. "What's this I hear about—"

"Would you care for some refreshments? Akha? A snack? All the fires are out, and we're supposed to be fasting, but I'm sure we can find something."

Cayo and I both declined. I tried again, "Manco—"

364

"What a delightful boy! Earplugs aren't even the width of my smallest finger yet, but he's already such a help to his brother the governor."

"That's what I wanted to talk to you—"

"Oh, yes! We have a lot to catch up on." Each of her interruptions was so artfully done that it could have been mistaken for her being helpful. She went on for some time about domestic matters, which were of no interest to me now that I spent less than a month here every few years. When she was done telling me about the gardener's grandchildren's dogs she tried to turn the conversation to a new veterinary healer in Cuzco.

I finally decided to be rude. "You're setting yourself up with a Coya's powers?"

The Silver Vixen did not bother to protest. "If I don't, someone else will. Would you prefer that?"

"Huayna Capac has a Coya: Rahua Ocllo, Huascar's mother."

"And she's a very calm and quiet lady who doesn't want to cause a fuss."

"Well that's certainly not you."

"I will not have you use that tone with me in front of Cayo."

"Cayo, go to bed." My friend rose to leave.

"Sit, Cayo. I want you to hear this conversation as it happens, rather than your father-in-law's version later when he tries to make it sound like he won."

"I am going to win."

"No, you're not." Her tone shook me. Maybe I wasn't. "My panaca is the most influential in Tahuantinsuyu. With the Sapa Inca never living closer than seven days away by the chaski post system, someone has to oversee the day to day running of Cuzco. My dear Hummingbird needs guidance. If he doesn't get it from me he will get it from someone else. I can't allow a rival to beat me just because it makes you squeamish."

I remember as a boy her speaking of power as a man does used to fascinate me. Now it scared me. "And what about Ninan Cuyuchi wearing the Yellow Fringe and not the governor? You're aligning yourself with the wrong brother. Or have you not thought about that?"

"Don't insult me," she laughed, and it was meant to mock me. "Ninan Cuyuchi's the most level-headed of all the princes. He'll see that I was only doing what was right. And if, for some reason, he shouldn't succeed—"

I saw what was in her heart then —what was behind her eyes— and I grabbed her by the shoulders and shook her. "This is what's wrong with you having a Coya's powers! Now you're talking about changing the succession!"

"If he shouldn't succeed, Huascar's next!" She shouted into my face, triumphant. I let go of her. "And he will have the full resources of my panaca to make good his claim. The words of the mummy of Sapa Inca Topa Inca carry weight in corners of the world that even you've never seen, Haylli. Accept that I know what I'm doing and go to bed."

I looked over at Cayo Topa, who shrugged at me. We were helpless. Short of braining her with our staffs of office we could not stop her. She had more power than even Cayo Mama Ocllo had once commanded. We went to our beds. As had become our custom, the Silver Vixen did not join me.

We spent the next day going about our bureaucratic tasks, then Cayo and I met Cusi Topa Yupanki, the governor, and the two young princes at Pus Cliff as the sun began to set. Six birds flew up out of a tree just as the last of the orb disappeared, and the High Priest assured us that meant we would succeed that night. Cayo and I smiled, skeptical about divination even as we performed the annual augury that our entire bureaucracy relied upon.

From the top of the cliff we watched the sun set and the stars appear. We examined the heavens, and there they were: Seven brilliant stars and six feeble ones, tightly clustered and distinct among their silent eternal comrades. Down in the hacha hacha you can only see six of the seven brightest, for the air is thicker there, but atop the cliff that hems in the eastern side of the Huatanay Valley, with Cuzco at our feet and the heavens so close above our heads it seemed we could scoop up handfuls of stars if we just stood on tip-toe, up there we could see everything, and that was good.

"Definitely six dim ones," the governor murmured, then turned to the High Priest to second his opinion.

"Yes. Praise the Creator," the Bird Man said. At that moment a shooting star cut across the sky but did not pass through the constellation we were examining. We all held our breath, but Cusi Topa Yupanki did not change his verdict. "All six stars are showing," he said in a flat tone.

We each squinted and strained to be absolutely sure that there were six faint stars, then we poured a libation of akha over the edge of the cliff in thanks, and I turned to a waiting chaski, specially detailed from his post to await our decision. "The storehouse is pregnant," I said. The man nodded and ran through the darkness, blowing his conch trumpet to alert the next post, and the next. This message was destined for every village in Tahuantinsuyu, and it would ensure the harvest.

You're wondering what this is all about, Friar? I do not understand how it works, I only know that it does every year, without fail: The constellation that we call the Storehouse has a different number of stars from summer solstice to summer solstice. The Kingdom of Chimor based their calendar around this rather than the sun.

On summer solstices when you can see all six of the dimmest stars, the rains in four months time will be plentiful and the potato crop abundant. When the dimmer stars disappear, or perhaps they are blotted out somehow, the rains will come late, and the fewer the stars the later the rains. A careful observation of the stars on the night before the Intip Raimi moves the potato planting season forward or backwards by more than a month.

'The storehouse is pregnant' means the harvest will be good; the storehouses will overflow with potatoes to last us through the cold months. 'The storehouse is barren' means the rains will be thin and the crops vulnerable to drought —especially the potato— and must be delayed if any are to grow. In hundreds of years this augury had never proved false. Find an explanation for that in your Bible, and I'll be fascinated to hear it. As it stands now, I can only attribute such unerring accuracy to Viracocha.

The next day at dawn the entire population of Cuzco, dressed in their most sumptuous clothes, stood in Huacaypata to watch the sun rise on the longest day of the year. As the first edge of the sun crested Pus Cliff we broke into wild cheering, singing songs of victory and joy, with musical instruments and man-drums filling the air with merry tunes. Huascar, under the ever-watchful eye of the High Priest, offered sacrifices and libations to Inti then led us in a barefooted procession to the Coricancha, which he entered while we all sang hymns.

When he emerged we sang some more, and then the whole city fell silent as we watched him sacrifice a flawless white llama and examine its entrails. "The omens are good!" He proclaimed. "I see victory for our armies, harvests for our farmers, healthy babies for our mothers, and strong sons for our fathers. I see long life for our Sapa Inca and prosperity for the Intip Churi!"

With that he ordered forth the great mirror, a polished silver bowl that would concentrate all the sun's rays on a single point: With a little fluff of cotton Huascar lit a fire using only the blessing of Inti. From this small flame the fire to burn the llama would be started, and from that fire all the hearth fires in Cuzco, cold three days now, would also be reignited.

We drank and feasted for three long days, eating as much llama meat as we wanted and drinking as much akha. The Silver Vixen spent all her time at the panaca, and Cayo and I spent all our time with the princes. When the festival was done I collected Topa Cusi Yupanki from the Coricancha, and for a while I mistook his solemn expression for a richly deserved hangover. We were not even out of the Huatanay Valley before he confessed to me, "I'm worried about that shooting star."

"What about it?" I asked, worried. The Bird Man had a gift I could not understand, but that did not make it real.

"Something bad is going to happen."

"The harvest?"

"No."

"The war?"

"No." He had no answer for me except a sense of foreboding. It may be a coincidence, Friar. I do believe in coincidences, but on the night before the summer solstice word arrived at Huayna Capac's Court at Tumipampa that a group of Huarani nomads had raided our border tampus in southeastern Collasuyu. What made the report interesting was that they were led by a man with a full beard unlike any ever seen before, a man described by credible witnesses as bone white wherever his clothes hid his skin from the sun.

Huayna Capac ordered the man to be captured and brought before him, but the stranger led his savages back into the swamps from which they had emerged. By the time I returned to Tumipampa word reached us that when the local Inca master of one thousand tax-paying families offered the barbarians a great bounty for the bearded man he was told the foreigner was already dead.

It was Tahuantinsuyu's first encounter with a white man, but it would not be our last.

We marched on the Cayambi in perfect discipline for they were the last, and the proudest. All their allies now served us. The tampus that they had burned to slow us had been repaired and restocked with the sweat and toil of their subjugated friends. We had Pastos and Caranguis serving with us as part of their labour tax, and it was one of Kiskis's jobs to make sure of their placement in the Imperial camp at night, the column of march by day, and the order of battle when in action never allowed these troops of questionable loyalty near Huayna Capac's litter.

The Cayambi were once the rulers of Quitu, and though we had taken that city from them twice now they refused to retreat into their hinterland as the Pastos and Carangui had done before them. I was glad, for it had been a long war and I was ready for it to end.

The Cayambi did not scatter and hide; instead, they sent us an invitation to meet their army at a single fortress and the plain below on a chosen day. Huayna Capac had the messengers beheaded and their skulls fashioned into gold-lined drinking cups. He sent one of their porters back to say we accepted.

The Cayambi had once been wealthy, not the equals of Chimu, but the richest in their land. For this last battle they beggared their nation to hire mercenaries: The last diehards of their former fellow rebels, jungle savages from beyond the Angasmayu, Puná pirates. It was to be the last bold gesture, a battle to end the war with a roar rather than a whimper. Huayna Capac marched our forces against them without any fear. We were the Inca. The victory was ours.

When our two armies camped within sight of one another the evening before the battle, we had three hundred thousand in our camp and the Carangui must have mustered almost a hundred thousand. It would be one last throw of the die, but Huayna Capac's dice were weighted to let the twenty always point up. The Quitu Wars would end tomorrow.

In the camp Cayo, Pariwana, and I sat outside our tent as if we were on the veranda of my summer villa in the Yucay Valley. There was a council of war going on somewhere, I was sure, but our presence was not required as long as we followed our orders the next day.

"You will be careful?" Pariwana Cumpi said, refilling all our akha mugs.

"No," Cayo Topa said, smiling. "It's the last one. Huayna Capac will want to deal with the Puná, too, but they won't make a battle of it. This is the last one, and I could use another chest disk."

"You don't need another one of those," I chided him.

"But they are awfully pretty," Pariwana said. We laughed together, as old friends do. None of us cared about winning glory tomorrow.

Servants were lighting torches as a prince with a retinue of Imperial guardsmen approached. I shifted on my stool, curious which of my former students was coming by to wish me luck or ask for it. I was surprised to see it was the lobeless Atauhuallpa.

"Hello," I ventured.

"Hello, Haylli, Cayo Topa. Hello, Pariwana Cumpi," the prince said, not looking at my daughter. "I've come with a gift." He gestured over his shoulder to show a beautiful Carangui dress neatly folded in one of his servants' hands. "I know we haven't always gotten on so well, and I thought perhaps I could make this small gesture before we're all so rich from war booty that presents won't mean anything." He smiled and looked sincere. I looked over to Cayo Topa, who shrugged, as mystified as I was.

"Well, thank you for that, Atauhuallpa," I said at last. One of my servants took the dress and unfolded it for Pariwana's appreciative eye. It was the height of fashion in the warm and pleasant Kingdom of Quitu, though a touch too thin and filmy for Cuzco's colder climate.

"Would it be possible for your wife to wear it tomorrow, Cayo Topa?" Atauhuallpa asked.

"I don't see why not," Cayo said, looking over at Pariwana Cumpi, who was nodding her agreement.

"Wonderful," Atauhuallpa murmured with pleasure.

"Why?" I asked. His smile disappeared.

"Not to take away from the gift, which is a long overdue first step to putting our childhoods behind us—" A trickle of doubt ran through my mind as I listened to Atauhuallpa speak. This was too eloquent from him to be spontaneous. He had thought it through, scripted it. "—But I had a dream in which we won the battle tomorrow and marched back to camp, where I saw Pariwana Cumpi in this dress. It was given to me by a surrendering Carangui prince last month. I worry that if she doesn't wear it tomorrow the rest of the dream won't come true either, and we will lose."

370

"Well, of course I'll wear it," Pariwana said, always happy to please. He grinned again without looking in her direction.

"Hold on," I said. "We have them outnumbered three to one. You think a dress will make the difference?" I tried to take the sting out of my voice, but some of the old schoolmaster crept in. Atauhuallpa scowled and shifted his feet, caught without the right answer. Then with another wash of relief I saw him come up with something.

"Uncle Chalcuchima said as a boy that you beat him in a war game when you were outnumbered by that much and more."

I felt the stab of guilt to hear that my old rival spoke of me after what I had done to him. Atauhuallpa always did know how to work me. "What did he call me?" I asked.

Atauhuallpa shrugged. "I'm sorry, Haylli. He called you Waccha, but it was a story from your school days."

I nodded, sad. "Very well, then. Pariwana, would you be good enough to wear the dress tomorrow?" She agreed again, and we bid the royal bastard a good evening.

Cayo and I went over a couple of ordinance ledgers by torchlight while Pariwana Cumpi worked her loom, and then the three of us retired for the night. I closed my ears, as polite custom dictates, to their quiet lovemaking.

I must confess, Friar, in the dark before a big battle like that, I wished that I had the Vixen there with me, or one of the concubines the Emperor was always offering and I was always refusing. No one can feel alone when they have someone to hold. I lay awake, wondering and worrying what the future would bring. I was not imaginative enough, though, for I eventually fell into peaceful sleep.

Cayo and I were in our legion on the battlefield the next morning. We advanced in line, beating our maces on our shields. A third of our forces had used the darkness to move in behind the enemy. Such was the great number of our Imperial host that they were not missed.

The battle began on the plain, but Huayna Capac and his generals never expected it to end there, when the Cayambis had their great fortress to fall back upon. We grunted and pushed them up that hill, every step won or lost through blood and sweat, and when we had them half way back into their fortifications Huayna Capac fell from his litter.

Our army stopped for a moment, stricken, and then it began to pour back down the hill and onto the plain below, keeping its discipline only through long, hard years of teaching soldiers the necessity of unit cohesion, of closed ranks and steady shields.

The Cayambi poured down out of their hill and onto the plain, grabbing at our heels, so eager that it seemed nothing could stop them. They were surprised, then, when a hundred conch trumpets blew all at once in a great, rolling signal. The whole Imperial army turned to face the foe, with Huayna Capac lifted up on a new litter. The Cayambi tried to withdraw back into their fortress, only to find the third wing of our army occupying the heights behind them.

Surrounded by three times their number and with nowhere to run, the Cayambi fought like trapped animals. The slaughter was terrible, and —just as in a royal hunt— the circle got smaller and smaller with the massacre getting more and more frantic. In the end it came down to the shores of a small lake, thick with rushes, and we killed and killed and killed until the lake turned red with blood; all the fish went belly up, so tainted was the water. We would later rename the place Yahuarcocha, the Lake of Blood.

Three dead willows stood in the shallows of Yahuarcocha, drowned by the water level in the lake rising some years before; the last Cayambi took refuge in the branches of these trees, killing every man who came near.

We lined archers and slingers on the shore and shot them out of the trees until only one was left, then a legion was sent in to capture the man. We watched from the shore, amazed, as the Cayambi killed a score of men with his mace before being taken alive. He was brought before Huayna Capac, trussed up like a duck to keep him from struggling, and he gave his name as Pinto, Sinchi to the Cayambi and a prince of the Kingdom of Quitu.

"Today was a terrible day, Pinto. It is the end of your people. Let's find one thing to rejoice in. Join me, and I will adopt you and give you the Cayambi to rule as my hunocamayoc."

Pinto spat at the Sapa Inca, one fleck of saliva reaching the hem of the Imperial tunic. Huayna Capac smiled at such spirit. "On the ground." The guardsmen had the struggling Cayambi in the dust so fast and hard I heard the thump of his landing even over the angry murmurs from the surrounding soldiers. Huayna Capac put his sandal on Pinto's neck. "If you will not join me you will entertain me, Pinto. Make him into a drum!" The army roared its approval.

Up in the fortress above the Cayambi women and children cowered, for over their battlements they had seen the death of their menfolk. Huayna Capac walked up the hill as night fell and ordered great bonfires lit so that everyone could see him.

"Canpa mana, pucula tucuy huambracuna," he said. "You will not make war on me because now you are all my children." And just like that a generation of orphans and widows became known as the Huambracuna, the protected children of Huayna Capac. The war was over. The foolish rebellion of a proud people had burned itself out, drowned in blood, and now the healing could begin.

Cayo and I returned to camp late. The counting of the dead would go throughout the night and probably the next night as well. We might as well have a rest first. It was not to be.

A military camp after a major battle is a mix of horror and joy. The surgeon's tents were charnel houses of gore that filled the air with moans and screams, while on the other extreme every soldier who had survived was celebrating with drink and women. That's why I did not think anything of a woman crying outside my tent: Drifted off from her man after an argument, I thought. It was only as my son-in-law and I went to enter the tent that she snapped out of her fit and grabbed both of us, begging us to stop.

"What is it?" I asked, recognizing the girl as one of Pariwana's yanacona maids.

"You can't go in!" She told us again.

"Is something wrong?" I asked, feeling a rising sense of dread.

"I think he's still in there." She was sobbing again, and I could barely make her out. I began asking who she was talking about, but at the first mention of a man in his wife's tent Cayo Topa ran in. The sound of his anguish froze me in place for a moment, then I lurched into the tent myself to see my daughter's naked, fly-blown corpse.

She had been raped. Her new clothes were in tatters on the ground next to her. When the rapist was done he had slit her throat, and she had bled a lake of blood all her own, its margins held in by the dirt of the tent's earthen floor. The cloying stickiness of it haunts my dreams.

Pariwana Cumpi was my favourite child. She was my last link to my dear Koonek. She was the wife of my best friend. I would sooner have pulled out my heart with my fingernails than see my little girl hurt, and here before me was the proof that she had died a pointless, violent death.

Cayo Topa sank to his knees and I did the same. To stand was too much effort. We stayed there, rooted to the spot. I wonder now why I did not rush to her, cradle her, but I think it was too obvious she was gone. I could not look away, but neither could I approach her.

"Who?" Cayo Topa whispered. "Who?" He said, his voice shaking. "Who?" He roared with all the hate the question deserved. My mild-mannered friend was roused to a passion he never should have had to feel.

I took him by the shoulders. "The girl outside must know." I do not remember getting up. I do not remember going outside. The next thing I remember is Cayo and I on either side of the maid, yelling incoherent questions at her while she cried and cried. At last, returning to sanity, I quieted Cayo and turned back to the woman. "Who was it?"

The girl was trembling like a leaf in a thunderstorm. It occurred to me that at the very least she must have been beaten away from my daughter. She might have been raped herself. I had to be patient. When at last she could speak, she said just one word, "Atauhuallpa," and all the questions dropped from my mind to be replaced by a loud buzzing noise.

I called for a camp guard and handed the maid into his keeping, then Cayo and I collected our maces and made our way to the prince's tent.

I should have known he would be expecting us, but I was not thinking straight. All I could think of was how good it would feel to bring my mace against the bastard's sneering face. How right it would be to hit him and hit him until there were no bones left in his body. Cayo walked beside me, bouncing the head of his mace in the palm of his hand. I was sure we were thinking the same thing. When we reached the tent we found it surrounded by Imperial guardsmen standing shoulder to shoulder, their halberds still coated in blood from the day's work.

"Let us in," I said.

"State your business," the guards' officer said.

"We're here to see the man who raped and murdered Pariwana Cumpi."

"Sapa Inca Huayna Capac and several of his sons are inside. Your rapist must be elsewhere."

"It was Atauhuallpa," Cayo Topa said. The guardsman did not even blink, and I knew in my belly that Atauhuallpa had brought a gang with him; that this man had been one of them. My mace was up and down before I made the decision to do it, but I dashed the bastard's head open all the same, and I would do it again.

Fifty halberds were pointed at us the very next moment, but I would not die quietly. "Come out here, Atauhuallpa, you piece of shit!"

The tent flap peeled back and Huayna Capac emerged. "What's this all about?" The Emperor asked.

"I think you know already, Sire."

The Emperor nodded, his expression grim. "Yes, I have heard."

"Hand over your son."

"Which son?"

"You know which son." He nodded again. Atauhuallpa appeared from the tent. Cayo Topa and I tensed, ready to tear him limb from limb despite the wall of guardsmen between us.

"Haylli Yupanki, Cayo Topa, I didn't know it was her," Atauhuallpa said. I was struck dumb at the bald-faced lie. "She was wearing Carangui dress! My men and I were just taking our pleasure with the local women, as we have done for years, and she got in among us somehow."

"She's dead!" Cayo Topa roared. "Have you been doing that for years with the local women, you bastard?"

"She came at me with a dagger. I defended myself." He said. If he had shown that mocking smile of his at that moment I would have leapt into the wall of halberds to try and get to him, but he was too smart for that. He could gloat alone, but not in front of his father.

"Sire, he has been lusting after Cayo Topa's wife since he was a boy. He gave her the clothes as a gift yesterday—"

The Sapa Inca interrupted me. "Atauhuallpa is my son. I cannot believe he would do this intentionally. Anyway, Pariwana Cumpi was a married woman in her thirties. Atauhuallpa can have a thousand women younger than that, single highlanders or married Yungas. You are telling me he passed up all of them just for your daughter, and went to the trouble of giving her a dress the day before so he would have an excuse? What kind of monster do you think my son is?"

"The kind that—"

"You will both go to Cuzco," Huayna Capac said.

"He raped and murdered my wife," Cayo Topa growled.

"He raped and murdered my daughter," I added.

"You will stay away from Atauhuallpa. I will determine guilt or innocence, not you."

"It was him!" We said together.

"Do not defy me!"

Cayo Topa took a physical step back at the thought of angering the Sapa Inca, but I knew no fear of this man. "Your father gave me the right of Free Speech, and I will be heard." He did not stop me. "I have failed you," I began. He perked up, as I had hoped, at this unexpected approach. "You gave me your boy to mould into a man. I have given him his numbers and his languages, but I failed to give him a soul. He thinks only of himself, of his gratification.

"Yes, he could have satisfied his lust on almost any woman he wanted, but he wanted a woman who was not available to him, denied him by both his old tutor, who he hates, and her husband, who he envies. He has known her almost from infancy. He would not mistake her for a foreign woman. This was deliberate, and the fact that he went to the lengths of giving her local dress so that he would have an excuse tells me that it was no act of passion, but one of premeditated rape and murder. Your second eldest is a rapist and a murderer, and in this land, the land you rule and Cayo and I run for you, that cannot stand."

We stood there, all of us, Emperor, prince, guards, Cayo and I, knowing that this was the moment of decision. Huayna let out a long sigh. "I will not allow you two to beat my son to death in front of me."

"Then kindly step back inside the tent, Sire," Cayo Topa said. I felt my heart swell at the courage it must have taken my calm and quiet friend to speak in such a way to the ruler of the world.

"No. There is no way for justice to be served. It is not just for a prince to die for defending himself. It is also not just for a wronged husband and father not to receive retribution. Therefore, I will assume full responsibility for what has happened."

I frowned, unsure what that meant but knowing I would not have the pleasure of killing Atauhuallpa today.

Huayna Capac turned to take his second eldest by the scruff of the neck, as if he were a misbehaving puppy. "You have done this thing, deliberate or not, and you will be punished." He turned to face Cayo and I. "Atauhuallpa was going to receive lands, women, gold, silver, cumpi, llamas, fields and flocks, riches beyond his dreams as his share of the conquest of the Kingdom of Quitu. All of it is forfeit to you two. All of it.

"Cayo Topa, nothing replaces a good woman. I still miss my mother, even after all these years. But what I have just given you includes the income to support a thousand women. I will go further still, and give you something so precious it is almost unheard of: An Imperial apology. I am sorry this has happened. I truly am. I would give up Quitu and Chimor to bring that woman back to you, but I can't. I am as powerless as you feel at this moment. I am sorry."

The genuine grief coming from Huayna Capac penetrated my rage. He was a father, and I knew in his mind he was imagining the death of his child. "You are a good man, Sire," I muttered. "But your boy has killed himself today. When next we cross paths, you will lose a son."

"Go to Cuzco," the Emperor said in a soft tone.

"Forbid him to ever leave Quitu, Sire. For his own safety we should always have half a world between us."

"He will stay here with me, and he will not profit from this war. I promise you. Now go to Cuzco," the Emperor murmured. Atauhuallpa glowered at me; I pulled at Cayo's shoulder. It was the best we could get tonight.

Cayo did not move. He dropped his mace to the ground and spat on it. "Keep your damn flocks and fields and women! Keep this mace too. You gave it to me. I don't want anything from Atauhuallpa. I'm going to go bury my wife now, and when I'm done I'm going to see your heir. I'll tell Ninan Cuyuchi what happened here today, and I'll tell him that if he wants me as a Tocoyricoc when he's Sapa Inca his first order will be to put Atauhuallpa in the Pit with two broken legs, then set the pumas lose."

With that we left Huayna Capac's Court. I would never see my Emperor again.

Friar, we could not stand the thought of what had happened in our tent. Cayo Topa and I stayed with Kiskis and Rumiñaui that night, spoiling their much deserved victory celebrations. For my school friends the long war had been one triumph after the other, and their names shone along with Chalcuchima's as the finest generals in all of Tahuantinsuyu. It was good of them to give us shelter and comfort, and the next day we embraced them as brothers and walked towards Cuzco, forsaking even our litter bearers in our disgust at what passed for Imperial justice.

We stopped at the Mollecancha palace in Tumipampa to see Ninan Cuyuchi, and he commiserated with us in the shade of the golden tree sculptures. His father had written to him through the chaski post service. He said he could make no official promises, but privately he agreed that when he was Sapa Inca he would need tocoyricocs much more than Atauhuallpa. Cayo Topa took a handful of dirt, stared into the sun, and swore a terrible oath that he would be Ninan Cuyuchi's man forever when he did right by Pariwana Cumpi's memory. We left the heir-apparent and headed to Cuzco, arriving just as the wrath of the gods descended upon our world with a fury that staggers the imagination.

More terrible even than a pachacuti in the language of Runa Simi, Friar, is the pahuac oncoy, the swift-running sickness, the plague. I do not know where the pahuac oncoy came from. Some say from beyond Quitu; some say from the coast; some say from out of the hacha hacha. I described the sickness to the Spaniards and they called it smallpox, so I blame your kind even though it ravaged us some years before the conquistadores arrived. Wherever it came from, no words I can summon will tell you just how we suffered.

The pahuac oncoy struck with such ferocity that the unshakeable Imperial administration broke down. There were not enough healthy chaskis to maintain the post system. There were not enough quipucamayocs and tampucamayocs to regulate the feeding of the people, so some villages gorged themselves without authorization and others starved in discipline while waiting for their orders to come. So many died that flocks of llamas and alpacas roamed the hills without owners, not even to the furthest extremes of distant kin was there anyone to inherit them.

As the system tried to repair itself I collected what census data trickled in: At least a third of Tahuantinsuyu had fallen ill and a quarter had died. Imagine that, Friar. Tahuantinsuyu went from twelve million tax-payers to nine million in a few short months. A further million spent the rest of their lives with pox scars upon their faces, marking them as having suffered the unbearable and surviving by the grace of the gods.

It was only the stored harvests in the tampus that kept us all from starving, for there were not enough healthy people to tend to the sick and plant crops at the same time. Everyone suffered: The peasant and the noble, the educated and the uneducated, the farmer and the soldier and the bureaucrat, the man and the woman and the child. If the pa-huac oncoy had one predilection it seemed to prefer the healthiest, the ones who most often survived such things.

Friar, you remember back when the Quitu Rebellion began I described Tahuantinsuyu as a bull being weakened for the matador? If those years of constant war can be likened to a heavy barb in the flank, the plague would be where Tahuantinsuyu first fell to its knees, so drained of life that only a great summoning up of our remaining strength could bring us back to our shaky feet to endure more. When we were down though, it seemed easier to stay down, kinder to give in than climb up to await the next blow.

Cayo and I rode out the plague in Cuzco. Walking from the Great Quipu Repository to the Huacaypata would see you pass bodies on the road, their spotted faces turning purple in the sun. Death had found them so quickly that they collapsed in a fever as they went about their daily duties, and no persuasion could bring people out of their homes to clear the streets.

Everywhere I went people had wet collars, some chewed to shreds in the attempt to ward off bad luck. A rising sense of hysteria gripped the Imperial capital. Without chaskis we did not know if the pahuac oncoy was sweeping the rest of Tahuantinsuyu, but it was here in Cuzco, here in the chosen place of the chosen people, the Intip Churi, the Children of the Sun. Our gods had forsaken us.

The summer rains poured on us, making grave digging difficult and further keeping people indoors, unable to receive help from one anoth-er. Whenever the clouds parted enough to see the distant snow-capped mountain of Vilcañota, crowds of people would spill out into the plazas to blow frantic kisses to the gods, beseeching them to rescind their curse. Too many faces carried the spots, the spots that said they were going to die.

Who did we lose? Who can really remember? The mayors of Upper and Lower Cuzco, Viceroys Auqui Topa and Achachi Michi and Mayta, the Mother Superior of the Cuzco House of Chosen Women, a dozen of Huayna Capac's brothers, half of the teachers at the House of Learning... I cannot list the dead. No one can. You assumed everyone was dead until you saw them alive. No one asked after anyone for fear the news was bad.

Prince Huascar was not a great governor, but he was no fool. When the mass panic gave way to public apathy and sullen acceptance that we were all going to be stricken and succumb, Huascar ordered the itu, the single most demeaning ceremony the proud Inca can perform to beg the pardon of Viracocha. For two days the whole city fasted, abstained from sex, never laughed, and no one spoke aloud the words, 'I want' or 'I need.' We had to enter the itu miserable and pure.

All the stray dogs were driven from the city and those who would not stay out were killed. The mitmaks surrounding Cuzco were forbidden to enter, both because they were not worthy enough to participate and because we did not want outsiders to see just how much we were about to abase ourselves before our gods. An eerie quiet descended upon the capital; people kept dying.

During the night of the second day, when Inti could not see us, we broke open the forbidden storehouse reserved for the itu paraphernalia and distributed it from house to house, never speaking a word. As dawn arrived the only sound to be heard was of puco puco birds, and even they expectant: The Children of the Sun had a surprise for our gods.

Every man, woman, and child wore red vicuna cumpi with long tassels, the same tassels we attached to prisoners of war to shame them. We wore feathered headdresses and shell necklaces so gaudy as to humiliate us, but any child seen to snicker was beaten. This was serious. In one hand we carried dried jungle birds with green feathers and in the other a small white drum. No man carried a weapon; even the sling headbands had been left at home.

When the dawn broke so Inti could watch us we began the itu. Not one word was spoken in the entire city all day. The Vixen, Cayo Topa, and I sat huddled together in the sand of the Huacaypata. Our mantles were over our head and we waited, still and silent, for the signal to begin.

On a hill outside the town two beautiful children, a boy and a girl, were made drunk with akha. All that night they were told, "When you get to the Upper Universe, tell Viracocha we are sorry. Tell him we will set it right. Tell him that the Inca worship him and thank him and will make him proud of us again." When the akha clouded their minds, they were strangled; they were buried in clothes worthy of the Sapa Inca himself. Their spirits, the best we could offer, would be our supplicants at Viracocha's court in the sky.

When one of the priests from the sacrifice entered Huacaypata to signal he was done, we began our part. In single file and random order the Inca men rose from the sand and began to make a slow circuit of the square, beating our drum with the dead bird in our hands without rhythm or time so that the thunk became grating on the nerves.

Without making a sound we twisted our faces into expressions of sorrow, as if we were weeping, and we swung our feet far out to the left and right as we walked to show how unsteady we were without our god to help us. Our wives joined us, following behind their men with war clubs taken out of the concealing folds of their shawls to tell Viracocha —if it was his will— they would strike their husbands down to appease him.

The children among us threw coca leaves onto the ground as if they were worthless. They were. Without Viracocha's blessing all our wealth was meaningless. The green birds began to molt their feathers with each contact with the drumhead, making us look still more pathetic. The Children of the Sun had no pride of privilege without the favour of our gods. We made that slow circuit eight times that day, and when the sun set we did it eight times through the darkness in case Inti rose early to see if we had only feigned our devotions.

As strength ran out for the young, the old and the sick we fell to the sand, quiet and still, listening to the shuffle of feet and the unpleasant drumming. You never knew who had fallen from exhaustion and who had succumbed to the pahuac oncoy. You just waited and hoped they would rise. Some did not.

As the sun rose the next day at its appointed time we clapped our hands and laughed in relief, pleased beyond all measure to know that Viracocha had sent Inti, his son, to show us his favour. Though the plague might continue we now knew that we were forgiven whatever our sin had been, that our total abasement and declaration of dependence had flattered him, that we were again his chosen people. We ate and drank and sang all the next day, and as the Intip Churi went to bed that night we made love to our wives like newlyweds. Even the Vixen and I managed a warm embrace. We both knew things could only get better from that moment on.

It was at dawn the next day that the first chaski we had seen in almost a month came down the Chincaysuyu road, exhausted from running ten times his normal distance. The plague had struck everywhere between Cuzco and Quitu. Both Huayna Capac and his heir, Ninan Cuyuchi, were dead.

* * *

I cannot tell you how many different ways this bad news struck me, Friar. I have often drifted from the prepared notes of my royal quipus, but for this I have nothing, nothing to refer to at all. My Emperor was dead, a man I had served with honour since before my Koonek died. He was a good man and a good friend. He did not deserve to die from that terrible plague.

Ninan Cuyuchi's death was harder. First, he had been such a good boy and had promised to be a great Sapa Inca. Then there was what he had promised Cayo Topa and I concerning Atauhuallpa. When Cayo heard Ninan Cuyuchi was dead he broke down and cried as he had not done even at the time of his wife's death. With Ninan Cuyuchi's death we had lost his future Emperor and also our sworn vengeance. The swift-running sickness took them both away as if they meant nothing.

To take a step back from my personal grief, think what this meant for Tahuantinsuyu: A Sapa Inca and his heir were both dead. Who was to rule us now? Ninan Cuyuchi had been a legitimate son by a Coya, but with his death we now had to consider Huayna Capac's fifty bastards. The eldest was Atauhuallpa, but he was in Quitu and the chaski did not know if he was alive or dead. My personal favourite was Manco Inca, who was a legitimate son in that he had been born by Rahua Ocllo after she was made Coya, but the boy had only just put in his earplugs and had not seen his father since he was old enough to walk. He had no experience in administering war or peace, and so he had no right to the Red Fringe aside from blood. I was one voice at our greatly reduced council, and I was wise enough not to press Manco's claim.

The fact was that Huayna Capac had left Prince Huascar as governor of Cuzco during his campaigning. We all knew he had appointed advisors to keep the Hummingbird from making a fool of himself, and that my wife also guided him, but that did not alter the fact that Huayna Capac had given the cold prince the Royal City to rule in his name. Also, of all the bastards, Huascar had the best claim to the Red Fringe because his mother, Rahua Ocllo, had become Huayna Capac's second Coya, though she had been so elevated after Huascar's birth.

The surviving nobles of Cuzco made their choice, and I stand by it to this day: Huascar was the legitimate successor to Huayna Capac after the death of Ninan Cuyuchi. While I feel it was the only acceptable decision, I later learned that the Silver Vixen had bribed a great number of the nobles with the wealth of the Capac Panaca to get her prince chosen. However he was selected, the sour-faced young man accepted the Red Fringe as if we were offering him a new tunic, then as his first Imperial act he formed a royal bodyguard of fifteen hundred Cañari and Chacapoyan soldiers from the mitmak settlements around Cuzco.

These soldiers formed a protective ring around the Coricancha while the Hummingbird underwent a hurried preliminary coronation within. He emerged with the royal sceptre and promptly issued a stream of orders to his dazed council. My task was to reestablish the chaski network to inform Tahuantinsuyu of the identity of their new Sapa Inca. I was so busy with it that some days passed before I noticed a disturbing trend: Even though the pahuac oncoy was still raging, it seemed to be striking down a disturbing number of Huascar's brothers.

I sent Cayo Topa to make inquiries, and he returned to me out of breath: He had run all the way from Cuzco to the Great Quipu Repository. "Unless symptoms of the disease have extended to dagger wounds, the Hummingbird is conducting a purge of all of his brothers who have ever been smart enough to talk in complete sentences."

"How many so far?"

"Eight that I'm sure of," Cayo Topa huffed. "A couple of them could have been the plague, but not all." He rattled off their names for me, and I saw their faces roll before my eyes. I had tutored them all from infancy.

"Take this down!" I barked. Cayo Topa and two secretaries promptly grabbed yarn. "To Manco Inca and Paullu Inca, from Tocoyricoc Haylli Yupanki Yachapa, message begins: I am appointing you special deputies to the restoration of the chaski network.

"Manco, you are to proceed to the very end of the Andesuyu Royal

Road and slowly work your way back to Cuzco, not coming any closer until each chaski hut has four runners assigned to it in two two-man fifteen day shifts.

"Paullu, you are to do the same with the Collasuyu Road, going all the way to the Maule River. Under no circumstances are you to respond to a summons from Huascar until after he completes his final coronation rites as Sapa Inca. Message ends."

They read it back to me, then the two secretaries were off and running, leaving Cayo Topa and I alone.

"You're playing favourites, aren't you?" He asked me.

"If there are two of Huayna Capac's sons with the ambition to be purged and the talent to be good emperors if we need them, I have a duty to get them out of Cuzco for a few months until Huascar is steady enough on his usno to stop murdering his brothers. He'll thank me later when he wants viceroys he can trust."

"What about Atauhuallpa?" Cayo Topa growled. I reached out to put a calming hand on his shoulder.

"We are talking about Huayna Capac's eldest bastard —with the Imperial army in the field— who has tormented Huascar since the cradle. The list you've given me says the Hummingbird's killing off brothers who wouldn't pass the potatoes at supper. This purge will take care of Atauhuallpa for us, old friend. Atauhuallpa is a dead man."

But it did not happen that way, Friar. I should have worried. I should have gone to Huascar and had him send hired killers to Quitu that very day. Tahuantinsuyu would still exist if I had.

* * *

Without the swift-running sickness Atauhuallpa and Huascar would have lived out their lives as middling bureaucrats or low-ranking generals, but with the death Ninan Cuyuchi they became the two most powerful men in the world, and their life-long animosity would consume us all. It began in earnest with Huayna Capac's funeral procession.

As soon as the plague began to burn itself out, Atauhuallpa sent his father's mummy home to Cuzco. A small army of stony-faced Inca nobles carried the mummy home to its waiting panaca, but the lobeless bastard was not one of them. Atauhuallpa remained behind in the Kingdom of Quitu, and this news made the Emperor Hummingbird frown in a way I would come to know and fear: Huascar was going to do something no sane man would contemplate.

The mummy's litter was preceded by the High Priest Topa Cusi Yupanki and the blue-clad figure of Topa Colla, the jovial leader of the Socso Panaca who was to act as the executor of Huayna Capac's last will and testament. His normal booming laugh was never heard, and the mourners took their cue from that. No one smiled, and they spoke in hushed voices. The litter was followed by Huayna Capac's harem, disheveled and wailing the whole long march. They had smeared themselves with soot and grease and cut their long tresses to show their grief. Purics working in the fields fell to their knees and wept to see the somber column pass.

At the same time the procession was the triumphant return of the Imperial army's booty. A generation of campaigning had piled treasures and women and captured nobles and warriors into spoils of proportions unseen since the conquest of the Chimu. This spectacle of wealth followed the Emperor at a respectful distance and was led by the war idol Huanacauri upon his litter, dressed in the finest cumpi and a feathered headdress and flanked by his priesthood. Behind it came Mama Ocllo's golden idol, and all the captured huacas of the Pastos, Caranguis, Punás, Paltas, Otavalos, Huancavelicas, Maytas, and Cayambis. It swelled the heart to see what we had conquered.

My own heart was uneasy, though. The very mention of Atauhuallpa's name at Court was enough to make Huascar conclude all business for the day and summon the officers of his Imperial Guard to a closed door meeting. When the funeral procession was almost to Cuzco Huascar took the entire Court out to greet his father's return at Limatampu, the last natural choke point on their journey. I could not draw him into a conversation on any subject. His cold face was set in that ominous frown.

On the day the funeral procession reached Limatampu, the Hummingbird waited on his litter, blocking the gate of the town. His guardsmen lined the road leading up to him, halberds grounded in salute. Topa Colla and Topa Cusi Yupanki had no choice but to order their column to halt. One by one the nobles, the highest and best of Huayna Capac's Court in Quitu, alighted from their litters, took off their sandals and put token burdens upon their backs to approach the red-fringed Huascar.

As the executor of Huayna Capac's will, Colla Topa carried the late emperor's royal sceptre. He was supposed to give it to Huascar, but as he held it up

385

to the cold Hummingbird, the Emperor barked, "Where is Atauhuallpa?" The High Priest Cusi Topa Yupanki jumped at this harsh welcome.

I could see from Colla Topa's expression that he was vexed at the interruption. "My lord, Prince Atauhuallpa begs your permission to remain with Chalcuchima, Kiskis, and my son Rumiñaui. He has sent you the spoils of the war and your father's mummy—"

"And how many of his troops has he sent me?"

"Our escort is of five thousand men, Sire. We did not expect to need more traveling through Tumipampa, Caxamalca, and Xauxa."

"Do you think me a fool?" Huascar snapped. "My brother sits in Quitu with a battle-hardened army, and he sends you to me as a delaying tactic!"

I saw no signal, but the guardsmen to either side of the road, as one, began grabbing the great men by either arm. Other guardsmen, concealed in the gardens and behind the walls of the tampu, rushed out now. There were hundreds of them. I heard shouts of outrage from the captured lords and screams from the royal widows further up the road.

"What are you doing, Sire?" I asked, looking up at him on his litter.

"You will keep quiet, old man. If you are not with me you are against me, and I will do to you as I do to them." Another of his ubiquitous guardsmen appeared at my side, a halberd poised to strike me down at another word of protest. Yet another stepped forward and took my father's bronze lancehead dagger out of my coca bag for safe keeping.

I watched, sick, as the Cañari and Chacapoyan guardsmen forced all those nobles down onto their knees. Two held each man in place while a third stood in front, kicking him in the belly and whipping him with a willow switch across the face while asking questions about Atauhuallpa's plans and the disposition of his forces. Unable to watch I looked over the heads of the kneeling nobles to see the column fly apart as lords and ladies ran to escape Huascar's guards. Only Huanacauri's priests stood their ground.

My gaze was dragged back to Huayna Capac's former counselors as Huascar's guardsmen began slitting throats. They started with the lowest ranking nobles as an incentive to their betters to reveal any secrets they had held onto, but when it became clear that the great men did not know anything they sped up their pace, faster than a llama butcher can quarter a carcass. The cobblestones were sheeted with gore. I choked back a sob when I saw a guardsman throw down sand from a bucket for traction. Huascar had planned the slaughter down to the last detail.

They saved Cusi Topa Yupanki and Colla Topa for the last, and Huascar descended from his litter to take the Imperial scepter from Colla Topa's slack fingers. Not for them the quick deaths of the other great men. They were tortured for a long time, and I could do nothing, frozen both for fear of my life and at the very thought of what I was seeing. These men had committed no crime. They had served Tahuantinsuyu with honour all their lives.

I think only my hatred of Atauhuallpa kept me from doing something, anything, to kill our new Sapa Inca where he stood. Instead, I began to list the brothers Huascar had not purged yet, weighing each one's merits against his faults. It passed the time and took my mind off the torture, but I still heard it all. I could not shut my ears to their suffering.

The image that has stayed with me from that massacre happened at the very end. High above us a condor circled, drawn by the stench of blood and offal that painted everything in sight. For less than a moment the great bird's shadow played across Cusi Topa Yupanki's face. Forgetting all else, my friend's head tipped back in wonder one last time at this winged messenger, trying to interpret its tidings. He was still smiling his distant smile when the guardsman behind him slit his throat.

* * *

With blood on his guardsmen's daggers and the power to murder anyone willing to protest, Huascar skipped the traditional mourning period and began the final ceremonies of taking the Red Fringe for himself.

The first thing he did was to break open the storehouses and distribute lavish gifts to all those lords and brothers he had decided not to purge yet. I myself received enough cumpi to carpet my house three times over and enough silver chalices to inebriate the entire staff of the Great Quipu Repository without refilling a cup. Then Huascar distributed all the chosen women, long kept in their cloisters during Huayna Capac's campaigning. I received three young girls, pretty things, who the Vixen promptly set to work in the kitchens out of my sight.

With the nobility cowed, Huascar decided to marry his chosen Coya, a full sister as was customary. For such a marriage to be legal his mother had to grant her permission, and in one of the most unexpected moves I have ever witnessed as a court insider mild-mannered Rahua Ocllo refused to let her daughter marry Huascar.

Somewhere during the plague, the death of her husband, the purge, and the slaughter at Limatampu, Rahua Ocllo became unhinged with grief. While her permission was only a formality, it was a religious requirement that could hold up the full assumption of Huascar's powers, even call his legitimacy into question.

She refused his ambassadors, including my sympathetic and reluctant self; when Huascar came in person she asked him to leave her home. Finally, Huascar had all the gods and goddesses of the Coricancha brought into Rahua Ocllo's quarters to demand her permission; it was only the weight of their deified displeasure that bullied her into allowing the marriage, even if she did not bless the union.

For the next four days Huascar purified himself by sitting in a darkened room without food or human contact. During this period he had to name an interim successor who would wear Imperial regalia and perform the Sapa Inca's duties during his absence, but Huascar was so afraid of usurpation from his brothers that he had me do it.

That might sound like a true honour and a pleasure, but you should know it was done with the understanding that all the guardsmen had orders to kill me at the first suspicion that I was working against the secluded Hummingbird. While the clothes were wonderful, the food incredible and the luxury unimaginable, I can assure you I have never been so uncomfortable as I was during those four days as interim Sapa Inca. I say that with full memory of my night in the Pit.

After Huascar emerged from his solitude, word was sent to every one of the eighty provinces of Tahuantinsuyu to sacrifice a boy and a girl atop a mountain to petition Inti and Viracocha for the success of the new Sapa Inca. It was the single largest number of human sacrifices ever performed in Tahuantinsuyu, for the Hummingbird would tolerate no half-measures when it came to something so important.

Huascar then married his sister in the Huacaypata, and when their union was official he sat upon his usno with his Coya by his side and bade his people approach. Every lord in Cuzco had to genuflect to the Emperor. We were barefoot supplicants, and when we were close enough to touch him we plucked a hair from our eyebrows and blew him a kiss, then offered him a small white feather to show our allegiance.

The ceremony was punctuated for me when he returned my father's lancehead dagger. He gave me what he must have meant to be an apologetic grin, but all I could muster was a sickly false smile in return. The knife was taken from me on the day he butchered Huayna Capac's funeral procession. Now he was making a gift of it to me on his coronation day, as if to say he trusted me with it again. My stomach twisted at the thought of it.

When every Intip Churi in Cuzco finished pledging that he was our Sapa Inca, the Hummingbird's Coya wrapped the Imperial headband with its red fringe around his brow, attached the white and black feathers into its golden plate, and Huascar rose up with a cup of akha. From that moment on and for weeks to follow we would drink and fete and make merry at Imperial expense. We had a Sapa Inca, whether we liked him or not.

And whether we liked him or not, he most certainly did not like us: Friar, the man was mad. He did not come out to the festivals and feasts. He did not drink with the mummies of former Sapa Incas. He threatened to disband all the panacas except the Silver Vixen's Capac Panaca, confiscating their wealth and burying their mummies.

Even his political allies, the crawlers and fawners who had toadied up to him from the very beginning, began to call him a stranger behind his back. I would never call my Silver Vixen a mere flunky, but even she found she could not control his moods as she had before. She once murmured to me that perhaps his red fringe was tied on too tight.

While this was strange enough, it was his paranoia that makes me call him mad. Rather than build a palace on the Huacaypata —as every new Sapa Inca did— he constructed a home at the base of Sacsahuaman so isolated and high-walled it came to be called Huascar's fortress. He used his guardsmen as household servants, for he trusted no one else: They were bound to him in blood, for they knew his death would see their own extinction for the crimes they committed in his name. Fear took such a hold on him that he built a steep staircase constructed from the inside of his palace up into the fortress atop the hill so as to escape to that greater security at a moment's notice.

His solution to everything was murder. Huascar's purge did away with all his competent brothers in Cuzco, and those who remained he punished for their incompetence. No one was safe. He even purged his network of snitches and informers, killing one spy in five to keep the rest on their toes in seeking out treachery.

Every casual remark made him jump, but as Emperor he could not appear to jump in fear but in response. One courtier mentioned in passing that two brothers Huascar appointed as generals were doing well in a minor campaign to conquer the Pomacochas: The Mad Hummingbird went out to the returning army and led their triumphal parade through Cuzco, stealing his brothers' small glory. Within a month both brothers were dead and never mentioned again.

A court jester —in the name of Inti, a jester!— made a joke of how much time Huascar spent in Cuzco, so he picked up the entire Court and made a pilgrimage to Lake Chucuito to show that he was not afraid to leave the Royal City.

It became ridiculous, a total reversal of the norm. Great men of education and breeding like myself made ourselves as inconspicuous as possible, both out of fear of being accused by an informer and for the good of the Empire, for sooner or later Huascar would need us again to administer what he was working so hard to destroy. Meanwhile, Incas-by-privilege and even purics were rising through the ranks of the administration and the hierarchies of Court, so that Huascar was dining with men who did not know the names of all of Cuzco's panacas and could not have told a royal quipu from a ledger quipu if their lives depended on it.

While all this was happening the one legitimate threat to Huascar's Imperial Fringe, Atauhuallpa, was confirmed as ruler of Quitu! Despite twice refusing to come to Cuzco to pay homage to his brother, Huascar invented the title Incap Ranti, He Who Stands in for the Inca, and gave it to Atauhuallpa. I asked him why he did not just proclaim Atauhuallpa Viceroy of Chincaysuyu, but he shook his head at me. "The title of Incap Ranti means nothing except what I say it means."

But Huascar did not know what Incap Ranti meant anymore than the rest of us, for he would not make any decisions regarding the Kingdom of Quitu. The best illustration of this is also one of particular interest to you, Friar: Great rafts, described as floating palaces, were seen off Tumpez and the Isle of Puná. This was not just one white man in Collasuyu or rumours of hairy soldiers far beyond Quitu trickling through the hacha hacha. These were true foreigners in large numbers coming to our shores. Huascar did nothing.

This was a momentous thing, of course. These 'Bearded Ones' seemed to come in peace, but chaski-relayed reports told of sticks that controlled thunder and lightning. Every pacuyok wanted answers, but none were forthcoming. When the great rafts departed they left two of their comrades behind. Here was the perfect opportunity to learn all we needed, and I begged Huascar to allow me to go and speak to the strangers.

Such was Huascar's lack of Imperial will, however, that I could not go: Our Emperor was unsure whether Atauhuallpa viewed Tumpez as his purview or not, and so he refused to discuss the matter. When I pressed him, he forbade me to leave Cuzco. As a tocoyricoc this was a devastating handicap, but as two-thirds of Chincaysuyu were now taking their tax orders from Atauhuallpa anyway, perhaps my inspections would have been of little consequence.

I do not know what restraints the Hummingbird thought he had on his bastard brother, but while informers were making it dangerous for me to have a conversation with a friend while walking the streets of Cuzco, Atauhuallpa was leading an independent war against the Huancavelicas tribe; meanwhile, officials appointed by him as Incap Ranti were building palaces, tampus, and fortresses in and around the Cañari capital of Tumipampa without orders from Cuzco.

The lobeless bastard had almost a quarter of Tahuantinsuyu under his thumb. I could not convince Huascar to act without raising my voice, and that Court was just too dangerous a place to get noticed. Cayo Topa and I spent a lot of time in our counting rooms, holding the other three quarters of the Empire together and waiting for a return to sanity. But things got worse, not better. Purges and terror among the Inca was one thing: That only threatened a few thousand people. Huascar expanded his executions further.

One of his courtesans sent from the Chinca tribe on the coast arrived deflowered. Huascar asked who had seduced her, and when she named a Chinca curaca the angry Hummingbird ordered every Chinca administrator thrown off a cliff. I knew every one of the proscribed men. The Chinca tax records never made sense again, but our Sapa Inca did not care.

We kept telling ourselves it had to come to an end, but we never imagined the end would lead to something worse. Atauhuallpa sent an embassy to Huascar, as if he were the ruler of a foreign state. Atauhuallpa wanted his autonomy recognized and his de facto kingdom made official.

His ambassador, Quilaco, was one of Atauhuallpa and Huascar's half-brothers; Quilaco's secretary was also a brother; the warrior escort was made up of still more brothers and cousins. There must have been forty of them, each in their prime, each a veteran of the Quitu Wars, something that could not be said of any of Huayna Capac's sons who were with Huascar in Cuzco. Every tampu the embassage stayed at on their journey enjoyed the single greatest congregation of pure Imperial blood anywhere in Tahuantinsuyu.

They brought with them gold and silver and cumpi and mullu shells and iridescent feathers and women, all in quantities rivaling the accumulated wealth of Huayna Capac's funeral procession. As they passed the Great Quipu Repository Cayo Topa and I speculated if Atauhuallpa had stripped his territory bare. In truth he had only ruined the newly conquered Huancavelicas and topped it off with a smattering of his own personal fortune, but the gift was still overwhelming.

Huascar was vacationing at his palace in the Yucay Valley, so Quilaco and his party spent a few days in Cuzco with the Dowager Empress Rahua Ocllo and Huascar's Coya before venturing out to see the Sapa Inca. I did not follow them —I liked to keep my distance from the Court, as I said— but I saw them come back, what was left of them.

The story is well known now, for Huascar saw nothing shameful in his actions and had Imperial bards spread the tale far and wide. Quilaco entered the Royal Presence barefoot and with the burden on his back as was normal, but also walking backward, a new subservience demanded of him for the great favour of seeing his brother, the Sapa Inca Huascar.

He was not allowed to look at the Mad Hummingbird, who stationed two women with a filmy piece of cumpi stretched between him and his guest. He was not allowed to speak directly to Huascar, conversing instead through another brother, one of Huascar's safe incompetents who stood to the right of the Sapa Inca's usno. Quilaco presented Atauhuallpa's gift, along with the lobeless bastard's profuse apologies at being again unable to come to Cuzco to pay his respects in person. Before he could get to the declaration of independence Huascar interrupted him with a series of short, barking orders to his guardsmen.

Huascar commanded all the gifts save the women thrown into the fire as worthless. He then executed all of the embassage save only Quilaco and two others, chosen at random. These princes he had stripped down to their loincloths, their hair and faces treated to look like women, and then the Imprial guardsmen marched them out of his palace at lancepoint, laughed at by purics and yanaconas all the way. "Tell Atauhuallpa I call him an aucca!" was all the Hummingbird said to his half-brother.

Quilaco and the other two returned to Atauhuallpa as shadows of their former selves, for they had been denied anything but dry maize and water at every tampu on their trek to Tumipampa that took orders from Huascar. They told Atauhuallpa all that had transpired, and they joined General Chalcuchima in begging him to act, while he was as strong as he would ever be without the Red Fringe tied around his brow.

I don't know if Atauhuallpa would have been content with his independence as the ruler of the Kingdom of Quitu or if he had always meant to try for the usno of Tahuantinsuyu, but either way it was unavoidable now: There would be a war between Imperial brothers.

* * *

I think this is where my bull-fighting metaphor breaks down, Friar, or perhaps it suffers from the fact that I have never seen Spaniards torture a bull, though I have little difficulty imagining it. Does a bull ever fight himself? Does the pain and the fatigue ever drive him to the point of madness, so that he tries to dash himself to pieces against the sides of the ring that contains him? Does a bull ever snap his head around to gore his own flanks in an attempt to end the pain? Even if real bulls do not do such things, the War Between the Brothers saw Tahuantinsuyu destroy itself, and all before that fateful day you Spaniards will sing of until the Judgment Day —your own Pachacuti— that will end your own time here on Earth.

Atauhuallpa and Huascar took either end of an empire already tattered and frayed by rebellion and plague, then they pulled against one another with all their might and tore it to pieces in their efforts to have the whole thing to themselves. The Quitu War their father waged was about reconquest, about the future prosperity and stability of Tahuantinsuyu. The War Between the Brothers never worried about what the future would look like. It was a bloodbath that made the Yahuarcocha look like a puddle.

I grow tired of talking about war, Friar, for I have seen too much of it, and I am no soldier to enjoy it or revel in the little details. I will say, though, that this last and most total slaughter was the real reason the Spanish walked into Tahuantinsuyu without any trouble. The Empire collapsed in a way that even the plague could not do, for when it was over no one knew who was in charge or what was expected of them. The purics stood idle, waiting for orders that never came.

Atauhuallpa still possessed all the veterans of the Quitu Wars as well as the best generals, including Chalcuchima, Kiskis, and Rumiñaui. He levied new troops from the tribes of the former Kingdom of Quitu, and they flocked to his banner at the chance to fight the Inca in our homeland instead of their own. Their presence in his ranks brought his army to be called the Quitus, and wherever the Quitus struck they raped and pillaged and murdered anyone who stood for the legitimate authority of the Sapa Inca Huascar, whose forces came to be called the Cuzcos.

The war almost ended right at the beginning, for Cañaris loyal to Huascar captured Atauhuallpa alive —he never was a very good general— and held him captive while waiting for instructions from their Sapa Inca. Atauhuallpa escaped by breaking down the adobe wall of his cell and fleeing for his life through the night, finding a contingent of his Quitus only after five days spent in the wilderness, eating weeds and drinking rain water.

From that point on Atauhuallpa stayed in Quitu with General Rumiñaui while Chalcuchima and Kiskis led their great army south, performing forced marches and complicated enveloping maneuvers that were far beyond the capabilities of our own forces.

The bloodthirsty Hummingbird also refused to lead his troops in person, claiming it was beneath his dignity. The problem, then, was that Huascar's pool of generals was made up of old and incompetent men. Huascar's soldiers fell back, and with each Cuzco retreat the Quitus grew more terrible in their pillaging, so that the people of Chincaysuyu quailed at the thought of being associated with Huascar. For the earlier humiliation of his capture Atauhuallpa ordered the entire male population of the Cañari put to death and the glorious city of Tumipampa leveled, stone by stone.

In the face of such carnage, Huascar worried about losing the 'respect' of his subjects, so he ordered the same sort of massacre to be conducted against the Chacapoyas, for a large number of their crack soldiers joined the Quitus as Chalcuchima's army advanced towards their territory. The Hummingbird's orders were transmitted through the chaski network, but his generals retreated too fast, leaving the mass killing undone but the intention known. Now the Chacapoyas, some of the finest fighting men in Tahuantinsuyu, were absolutely committed to Atauhuallpa's cause, knowing that his defeat would see their destruction.

At one point I was needed in Chincaysuyu to untangle a snarl in the flow of war materiel to the collapsing war front. I left Cuzco under a heavy guard that was more to make sure Huascar knew where I was than to keep me safe. Cayo Topa was kept back in the Royal City: Huascar said it was to run the Great Quipu Repository in my absence, but I knew my son-in-law was being held hostage against my return.

It turned out the Quitu advance was even swifter than I had been led to believe. I should have been well behind the front lines, but in the middle of one dark night General Kiskis appeared in the doorway of my room, flanked by a dozen warriors whose simple loincloths and body paint suggested they were Pastos. Pastos guarding an Inca general of Kiskis's rank! I was as outraged by that as by the fact that he had managed to reach my supposedly-safe tampu in the first place.

"Hello," I tried to sound casual and failed, looking at the barbed lances of the Pastos.

"Hello," my old school friend gave me his gallant, crooked smile. "Don't worry. I'm not here to kill you." He waved a hand at the men around him. "They're just here to make sure I get home safe."

"I have a few of those myself," I said, remembering the Hummingbird's guardsmen following me off the road to make sure I did not run away when I said I was relieving myself.

"Not anymore. I'm afraid we had to deal with them so you and I could have this conversation."

"I didn't like them anyway," I admitted, wondering what Kiskis wanted with me.

"Come over to our side," my friend put the full force of his considerable charm into his grin. "We're going to win!" The Pastos around him smiled too, their filed teeth made them look like monsters.

The face of my little girl flashed before my eyes. "I will not serve a usurper, and I certainly won't give the Red Fringe to Atauhuallpa," I said in Inca Simi, the private language of our people.

"Huascar is better?" He replied in the same tongue, putting his hands on his hips. He was going to try and convince me, even after what Atauhuallpa had done.

"Huascar is as bad, but he has the better claim—"

"The better claim is the better army, Haylli. Neither one of them is Ninan Cuyuchi. He's gone. Now it's a bastard who wants to be heir and an heir who's a total bastard."

I managed a faint smile at my friend's word play, but I shook my head. "You're serving the man who raped and murdered my daughter, and you expect me to join you?"

"You can do it now or later, but you will have to serve him, Haylli. The sooner you do it the better off you'll be."

"How did you get here?" I said, changing the subject.

"Your army's falling back again. By tomorrow night this will be Atauhuallpa's tampu; tonight it doesn't belong to either side."

That was news to me. I looked between the heads of his Pastos to the plaza outside. I saw a few bodies lying in pools of blood. There was no commotion. The purics who ran this tampu were waiting for the Quitus and the Cuzcos to decide who was in charge. From the gatehouse a figure emerged, a bloody lance in one hand and a predatory look on his face. It was Huaypalcon.

"You brought your son?" I asked the general.

"Just try to keep him home," Kiskis snorted. "That boy will be the death of me."

I watched my dead son's best friend quarter the tampu courtyard, sinking his spear into each prone form to make sure my guards were all dead. One moaned, and I watched Huaypalcon twist his lance in the man's chest. "What happened to our boys, Kiskis? Where did we go wrong?"

"My son thinks his generation is the future and ours is the past, Haylli, but we're not done yet. Without you this world will fray and come apart like an old tunic. Atauhuallpa may think like Huaypalcon, but he knows he'll need a tocoyricoc to run Tahuantinsuyu after his victory."

"And what does his Uncle Mallku have to say about all this?" I asked, imagining my enemy's thick neck twitching.

"Chalcuchima doesn't like it, but isn't that a good reason to do it?" There was his crooked smile again.

"Not good enough," I said flatly.

"I know Atauhuallpa's caused you a lot of grief, but if you come over to him now there won't be any reprisals against you after he wins."

"Reprisals?" I arched an eyebrow. "You're going to stand there and tell me that Atauhuallpa's not planning to make a drum out of my hide?"

"There's Cayo Topa, for one. Atauhuallpa hates him as much as he hates you, but he only needs one tocoyricoc, and he's chosen you." My heart shuddered at the threat to Cayo, but Kiskis was not done. "Then there's your wife: Her panaca is the Hummingbird's greatest champion, Haylli. Old Topa's mummy has a lot of political pull, even among our Quitus. There have been loyalist uprisings in our rear, sponsored by your Silver Vixen. This war would've ended months ago without her. Atauhuallpa's unhappy about it, but if you joined us—"

"My wife's panaca supports Huascar because Huascar is the Sapa Inca." I felt guilty that there had been no flash of concern when Kiskis told me Atauhuallpa would strike against my wife if he took Cuzco, as there had been for Cayo. I wondered where our love had gone, or if I had ever loved her at all.

"Haylli, don't be a fool. If you won't do it for yourself, do it for the people. Atauhuallpa doesn't have any tocoyricocs on his side, and the Mad Hummingbird only has you and Cayo Topa. When this thing is over, Tahuantinsuyu will still need honest administrators."

Of all the arguments he made that was the best, and he knew it, but mentioning Cayo Topa again sent a new stab of fear through my chest: Whatever Atauhuallpa might do to Cayo Topa when he won, Huascar would cut Cayo Topa into very small pieces at once if I went over to the Quitu cause.

"If you're not here to kill me, then let me go. I don't like Huascar, but I like Atauhuallpa less. Maybe when this is all over you and I can figure out a way to get a good Sapa Inca onto the usno, but for now I'll choose the prince who has the Red Fringe legitimately on his forehead."

I tried to push past him to leave, but Kiskis reached out and grabbed the hem of my mantle. "Haylli, when we take Cuzco I'll do my best for you, but I can't promise anything."

I smiled down at my worried friend, who was half a head shorter than I. "We've lived too long, Kiskis. We don't deserve these troubled times. The plague should have taken us both and saved us the headaches."

He smiled his crooked smile, and we parted as friends, friends on opposite sides of a civil war.

* * *

So the Cuzcos fell back again, and again, and each time Huascar's generals formed up behind a new river or a new mountain pass they said that would be their final line of defence; each time they retreated in defeat. One good thing came from all these setbacks, though. When we lost Tumpez we gained an unexpected prize, the Bearded Ones I had so wanted to meet were taken from the city by our garrison before it fell to a coalition of Quitus and Puná raiders.

One of the white men was killed by his guards when he broke into a House of Chosen Women halfway to Cuzco, but the other arrived in the Huatanay Valley and was kept in Cayo Topa's villa outside Cuzco while the Hummingbird decided what to do with him.

I went over to take a look, as a man views a beast in a menagerie: He was much hairier than a normal man on his hands and arms and legs, but he also boasted a thick dark beard, as only a small tribe on the eastern fringe of Collasuyu can grow in all of Tahuantinsuyu. It made him look like an animal. I was disappointed when his skin was not much paler than my own, only to gasp in awe when one of his keepers pulled down the collar of his tunic to show a hairy chest whose flesh was white as bone.

I was gripped with the desire to take this man and puzzle him out, learn all his secrets. Where had he come from? Did all of his people look like this? Why had he come here? What did his people want? Why had his fellows left him behind? What was all this I had heard about controlling thunder and lightning?

With the world going to shreds around me, and with nothing I could do to better it, I was overcome with the desire to pursue this single academic inquiry to its fullest. I was frustrated from the very start, though, because the bearded man was an idiot.

I do not say this to anger you, Friar, but what kind of man left behind in a foreign land does not learn the local language? He had a smattering of the Chibcha dialect spoken in Tumpez, enough to ask the purics for food, akha, and women, but he had nothing of Runa Simi and not even enough Chibcha to answer the simplest questions.

Adding to my problems, whenever I contemplated how I could go about teaching him Runa Simi or learning his own sing-song speech I imagined the constant interruptions that would come from Cuzco: Aside from my own bureaucrats asking for my help with their work, there would be gawkers and well-wishers and Imperial spies and people who wanted to help or hinder or replace me. I needed to get him alone and away from the city.

I went into Huascar's presence, barefoot, burdened, and walking backwards. I spoke to him through a cumpi screen and listened to his half-brother speak his replies. It was humiliating, but it was meant to be. "Great Lord," I began, remembering the days when I was changing his swaddling clothes and wiping away his tears over broken toys. "Keeping the white man so near to Cuzco will cause unrest. There are already panaca members who talk about these Bearded Ones as being messengers from Viracocha."

It was not as common a belief as you Spaniards seem to think it was, but there were a few religious men and women who saw similarities between the bearded Spaniards who appeared off Tumpez dressed in shining steel and Viracocha, our bearded creator god who dressed in silver clothes and left Tahuantinsuyu on a raft launched not far from Tumpez.

I was playing the Emperor as a man plays a familiar drum. I knew just how and where to tap him to make the noise I wanted. The Hummingbird did not like the panacas, but with the war on he needed their support too much to abolish them as he had threatened to do before receiving and dismissing Atauhuallpa's embassy. I could not see Huascar's cold face through the screen, but his half-brother frowned as he ordered me to go on.

"I think there is much we can learn from him, but I must be allowed to question him somewhere private, and I must be given the time to learn how to communicate with him."

"How long would you need? You know I don't like you being away from Cuzco," Huascar's interlocutor repeated the Emperor's whispered statements.

"I don't know, but you could always send for me if you needed me, and, as always, you would have Cayo Topa to handle the administration in my absence." Running Tahuantinsuyu had become easier now that a third of it no longer took its orders from Cuzco and the Hummingbird barely concerned himself with the good government of the remainder.

"Where would you go? It would have to be close."

"I thought of the Yucay, but the panacas have estates there," I said, knowing exactly where I would have to go to obtain permission. "Then I thought of Collasuyu, but I would have to go too far to obtain privacy."

"So where?" The half-brother asked.

"Andesuyu. There's a city on the Urupampa River that is only a few days' travel from here. The roads are well-guarded and the jungle is all but impassable. We could keep the white man there indefinitely, and I could return by forced march in a couple of days if need be."

It was ideal for Huascar: I could no more escape him there than the Bearded One could. It took more coaxing and coddling, for the Hummingbird liked to make every Imperial decision seem as weighty as a mountain, but he grudgingly gave in. I took the white man from Cayo Topa's compound under cover of darkness, walking him around the city to find the Andesuyu road on the far side, following it to the Urupampa branch road, and then out into the hacha hacha I had rafted through as a young man.

The Bearded One was fit, I give him that. It has been my observation that all Spaniards are hardy men, willing to suffer any discomfort as long as they can look forward to a reward at the end. The white man came to understand that if he followed my litter along the road by day he could have all the akha he could drink at night. It was amusing to see how little it took to get him drunk, but it was less amusing when I then had to dismiss all the female members of the tampu staff to prevent molestation.

I began trying to talk to him the first night away from Cuzco. "Haylli," I said, pointing at my chest. He looked at me blankly. "My name is Haylli." I pointed at him. "What is your name?" This went on for much longer than I would have thought possible before he called himself Alonso de Molina.

I came to think of Alonso as a child, for he was always testing the limits of acceptable behaviour. 'Yes, Alonso' and 'No, Alonso' were the first Spanish phrases I learned, for he was always gesturing that he wanted something.

A storm raged above us one night, and I had my soldiers drive the protesting Alonso out into the rain. I offered him a stick and told him to control the lightning overhead, but he did not understand me. Despite my best efforts, he never did anything to harness the power of the heavens. In all the time we spent together, I never gleaned forewarning of the cannons and arquebuses. A simple misunderstanding made me ask the wrong questions, while he must have thought I was trying to involve him in some form of heathen thunder worship.

By the time we arrived at the city, I decided that there was little point in teaching him Runa Simi: First, he was picking it up slower than I was learning his own tongue, and second I did not want him talking to too many other people. I have learned many languages in my life, and though I did not know it at the time Spanish was to be the last. It was also the most difficult, for it is unlike any tongue of Tahuantinsuyu. I never did get much more than the basics from Alonso, but with the base of knowledge I gathered from him I have built myself towards fluency since the rest of you sons of Castile arrived.

We worked in the central plaza of the city, much as you and I do, Friar, though that city at least had the dignity of being above most of the hacha hacha, where it is cool enough that I did not sweat through my tunic. I would get Alonso talking, and I had a team of royal quipu masters with me to record every sound he made to puzzle out later, a difficult task when many sounds in Spanish do not transfer into Runa Simi.

We talked from dawn to dusk each day; then I did more work by torchlight through the night, tidying up administrative problems sent to me by the chaski network and puzzling over the day's recordings. My memory and previous linguistic training were a great help, and within a month I could have a simple conversation.

One day I took him for a walk through the city, telling him what each building did and asking him about where he was from. When we came to the small temple to Inti at the base of Grandfather Mountain towering over the city he frowned, then when we stepped inside he stared at the golden idol as a starving man looks at a brimming stew pot. I looked at the idol too, which was a minor artistic work, the kind I kept in the wall niches of my home. In this provincial town it was the chief huaca, but to me it was nothing special.

"Inti," I told him, unsettled at his expression. "That is our sun god. He is the special god of the Inca. He ordered us to extend our empire—" I stopped when Alonso spat on the flagpoles and began speaking in rapid Spanish, gesticulating as he ranted. "Slow down." When he did not I assumed my sternest schoolmaster's tone. "Slow down!"

He stopped as if I had brained him with a club, but he did not unknit his brows, glowering at me as if I were the fool and he was the genius. "Say it slower." In a patronizing tone he explained the falsity of my gods, the power of Christ, and the divine mission of the Spanish to bring their religion to all the heathen places of the world to save us from eternal damnation. His sermon was hindered by his frequent looks of avarice towards Inti's idol.

"Inti has given the Inca the same quest," I told him. He took offense at this. He spat again, and this time I had five men hold him down as I beat the soles of his feet, as I would a boy. He did not speak to me again for the rest of the day, and such was his sullen pride that he refused to respond to me the next day when his handlers brought him out to the courtyard to begin our morning's work. I had some experience with dealing with headstrong boys, though.

"Alonso," I said. "Do you like this?" From my coca bag I pulled out a small huaca of gold, about the size of my thumb and carved to look like Saramama, the goddess of maize. His eyes lit up, but he said not a word. "For every day that you do as I ask, I will give you a golden huaca." He still said nothing, but I could see I had his attention. "And for this first day I would like you to tell me about this God of yours." That got him.

Alonso spoke all morning about his beliefs, and I admit I was interested in the idea of there being one supreme god with a host of minor deities, which he called angels and saints. I saw in it a number of parallels with Viracocha, the ultimate power who controls our own pantheon—

Now Friar, we have been good enough to behave properly to one another for all this time. You will not now filter my words through your Christian interpretation of my speech. This is my story, and I see similarities. What's more, I think you know all about those similarities, and you priests use them to convert us.

I have asked Spaniards how the feast of Corpus Christi is celebrated in Spain, and they tell me it bears no resemblance to how you teach the people of Tahuantinsuyu to worship: Could it be that Corpus Christi happens at the same time as our own Intip Raimi festival, and so the feast is more important to Christians here than in Spain? Your kind have no problems tweaking your religion to fit into our own patterns. I am merely saying that I saw some of the broad parallels. Now you will write what I speak, and we will not have this argument again. I know enough of your scribble at this point to check your work!

Anyway, I asked Alonso de Molina whether he knew of Viracocha, or perhaps was a messenger of his. He assured me he was not, but told me another group of 'Indians' —as he insisted on calling non-Spaniards— called the 'Aztecs' had held a similar belief, and it was their undoing. He then refused to tell me what he meant until I offered him five small pieces of gold and ten of silver.

The story he told me was horrible, Friar. An empire that he described as being as great as Tahuantinsuyu was destroyed a few decades earlier by the Castilians, as you Spaniards interchangeably called yourselves. I asked him why his people would do such a thing, and he went on about the divine mission to spread the word of Christ. He punctuated his sermon, however, with requests for more gold. I suspected that these interruptions spoke of the real reason.

One day while we were conversing, a chaski came to me with a message from the Sapa Inca. The runner was a plague survivor, and his face was pock-marked with scars from the sores. I squinted at Alonso, and through his beard I could see that he too had the scars. I pointed at the chaski's face and asked him what he saw. After a number of leading questions he called it 'smallpox.'

I felt a rage boiling inside my head, and it seemed to escape out my mouth just like steam from a kettle. I unleashed a series of sharp commands, and all the while Alonso was asking me to slow down, to speak in Spanish. There was fear in his voice, and there should have been. My men grabbed him and held him down on the ground.

"This plague, this is from Spain?" I asked.

His face in the dust, he knew better than to give me a yes or a no. He just protested as only a Spaniard can protest when he feels his honour has been insulted.

I took Huascar's message quipu, ordering me back to Cuzco and to do with the Bearded One as I wished, for reports were filtering through Quitu lines that more of his kind had landed at Tumpez. I looked down at him, badly wanting to give him the Hiwaya, but I knew as an individual that he was innocent. I ordered my men to let him up.

"You will stay here until my return," I told him. I turned to his guard retinue, speaking in Runa Simi. "Find where he's been hiding the gold and silver I've given him, and hide it under the hearthstone of his kitchen. Have his servants always keep a fire going so he can't look under it. Tell him the gold will be returned to him upon my return. That ought to keep him here." The guardsmen nodded among themselves. We had all come to understand the Spaniard's lust for gold surpassed even his lust for women and akha.

Then I ordered my litter bearers to assemble and I left him there. I never saw them again, nor do I know or care what happened to him.

In the time it took me to return to the capital by the Andesuyu road, Friar, the Cuzco cause had lost all of Chincaysuyu and much of Condesuyu to Atauhuallpa's Quitu armies. Huascar's generals were forming another 'final line of defense' at the Apurimac River, burning the bridges to prevent a crossing.

A battle was inevitable, and the Cuzcos had seen no true victory since the Cañari first captured Atauhuallpa at the start of the war. There was no possibility of us repeating such a stroke of fortune. The lobeless bastard was in Quitu controlling the garrison army that was keeping his semi-loyal tribes pacified. General Rumiñaui was controlling the Chincaysuyu army of occupation, and Chalcuchima and Kiskis shared the Condesuyu army of conquest. The three finest generals in Tahuantinsuyu were between us and Atauhuallpa with twice as many soldiers as the Cuzcos could muster. He was invulnerable.

He was also a totally different person from the boy I had taught, or so his own official bards were telling the territories under his sway: Atauhuallpa was changing history to make his war a just cause. He now claimed to have been born to a Quitu princess, the true heir to the last Scyri of Quitu, and that Huayna Capac had given him Quitu to rule upon his deathbed.

Atauhuallpa had taken it further, too: As it was a matter of public record that Chalcuchima was his maternal uncle, Chalcuchima was now a member of the Cayambi tribe, along with Kiskis and Rumiñaui. I could not imagine that news going down well with the three proud members of the Intip Churi, but Atauhuallpa was making it his official history, and even on our own side I was often asked how I had come to know so many of the invading generals in my childhood, when surely they had all grown up in Quitu?

Most preposterous of all was Atauhuallpa's new assertion that Sapa Inca Topa Inca Yupanki never existed. This was a two-pronged attack on Atauhuallpa's part, revealing a cunning that I had not considered him capable of: If there had never been a Topa Inca Yupanki then the Kingdom of Quitu had never been conquered until the recent Quitu Wars of Huayna Capac, which now allowed Atauhuallpa to say the motivation for his father's war had been to give Atauhuallpa the throne of the Scyri of Quitu. Removing Topa Inca Yupanki also meant the Capac Panaca my wife led was a fraud, and the properties and political powers it owned were all null and void.

It was not so impossible as it seems to abolish an Emperor who reigned for decades: I was a young man when Old Topa died. For most men alive in Tahuantinsuyu the deeds of long gone Sapa Incas blended together, and it was up to the recitals of the official bards to keep things straight.

Atauhuallpa's story was a popular one with the Quitus, who preferred to be conquered to gain a legitimate king who would help them overcome the Inca rather than to be conquered twice by the Intip Churi. If he destroyed the Capac Panaca in Cuzco and outlawed all mention of Sapa Inca Topa Inca Yupanki, how many years would it be before that grand old man with the dusty voice was just a hazy memory?

I arrived in Royal Cuzco to see a city in chaos. Gone now was the fear of being betrayed to Huascar's secret police: Everyone was too afraid of the looming Quitus to hide their emotions as they walked the streets.

The great tampus of war materiel were opened and distributed without bothering to keep records, such was the hurry. That's where I met Cayo Topa, who I greeted with a hug, asking how things had been in my absence. As he answered me he never stopped shaking his head in disapproval as bucklers and corselets were handed out from a warehouse in the Intihuasi fortress.

"Terrible. Look at that! I could walk up and ask for anything right now and it would be handed to me, no question. When this is all over we're going to have to inventory every storage room in Tahuantinsuyu, and whatever is missing we will have to tie down as contributed to the war effort. The stupidest tax cheat in the world is going to be blowing his nose in cumpi handkerchiefs and sleeping on jaguar skin rugs before this war is over."

"Where are the Quitus now?"

"Still at the Apurimac River, but the current isn't fast at this time of year. Chalcuchima and Kiskis can swim it." I remembered Chalcuchima almost drowning down in the hacha hacha, but I kept my peace. He had tens of thousands of men with him, more than enough to swim the river and build him a bridge, assuming he could not build a raft and float across.

"And Sapa Inca Huascar? He summoned me back."

"He wants every pacuyok he commands to help lead the new army he's mustered." Cayo and I looked down into Cuzco. The streets were filled with armed men, though you could hardly call them soldiers considering they barely knew which end of their lances to point towards the enemy. Each wore the distinctive headdress of his native tribe. Very few of them were from Chincaysuyu, and I shook my head when I saw a few wearing the Mapuches' simple braids: Huascar had drawn men from as far away as the Maule River to fight this last battle.

"Can we hold them at the river?"

"Huascar's forces have orders to fight to the death, but they've had those orders before."

A distant conch trumpet turned both of our heads to see a chaski run down the Chincaysuyu road, passing his message to the next runner, and the next, each blowing his trumpet much longer than necessary. It could only mean a battle was underway on the Apurimac.

"Where's Huascar?" I asked.

"The Coricancha, I think."

"You stay here and try to get some order into this situation. I'll go see what he wants us to do."

I made my way through the panicky city, nodding with approval as the House of Chosen Women barricaded their door. I arrived at the Coricancha to learn that the Hummingbird was not there, but the crowd that followed the Emperor everywhere could be seen from the holy of holies, so I blew it a kiss and crossed the gully to Speaker's Field.

Huascar was gathered there with hundreds of nobles from throughout Tahuantinsuyu, as well as his ubiquitous guardsmen. My wife stood next to the mummy bundle of Topa Inca Yupanki, but she did not look at me. She knew what was about to happen, and in this moment the last thing she wanted was to be noticed by Huascar. Our Emperor was hearing the message from a chaski when I approached his litter.

"The battle has started, Haylli," he said to me.

"The last battle?" I asked, cursing myself as soon as it was said. It sounded defeatist to my ears, but it seemed to cheer Huascar up.

"Yes, let's hope so. We're catching an army fording a river in a gorge. If we can smash them they will have nowhere to regroup. Rumiñaui will fall back on Quitu if Chalcuchima and Kiskis are destroyed." I looked up at the Sapa Inca upon his litter and wondered for a moment whether he was drunk, but Huascar was worse than drunk: He was mad, and as he turned from me to the fields around us the depth of his insanity became apparent.

I looked around at Speaker's Field, the place where the Inca armies had heard their generals speak and consulted the oracles back when Cuzco was a mud-walled village and the Huacaypata was a marsh. I blinked my surprise when I saw that we were surrounded by the huacas of our conquered people, taken from their temples throughout Royal Cuzco and brought here at what could only have been Huascar's express order. They were arranged in a ring, pebbles and rocks and boulders, tree trunks and clay figurines, idols of copper, bronze, silver, and gold. An army of holies, all arrayed to hear the Mad Hummingbird speak.

"Huacas, idols and gods of Tahuantinsuyu, you will intercede for us with Viracocha! Two days ago the Intip Churi performed the itu, and now it is your turn. You will not prosper under Atauhuallpa as you will under me! Save us!" We all waited for a sign: A gust of wind, a bird in flight, but the stones did not move or speak.

"You! Uru huaca!" Huascar picked out the least prestigious oracle among the host, a lump of petrified llama dung belonging to the worthless Uru tribe. "What say you?"

The Uru priest shuffled his feet a little. So poor were his people that he did not even have an acolyte with whom to consult or dither. "Sapa Inca, we see your triumph," he muttered.

One by one Huascar asked each huaca flat out whether or not his army would succeed, and one by one they said he would. With a flick of her wrist my wife bade her porters to carry Topa Inca Yupanki's mummy away before it was asked for an opinion. She knew what fate would befall the oracles, and so did I. Huascar continued to ask each their prophecy, and it was as he turned to ask the green-clad Mama Ocllo's Voice that another chaski appeared bearing a quipu with the black pom pom of bad news. The Hummingbird snatched up the threads, but they were tied in such a tangle of hasty knots that his patience failed him and he handed it to me.

The knots were the work of a mid-level bureaucrat, one whose hands had trembled as he struggled to remember the complicated and little-used lessons of his youth when a teacher had seen unrealized potential in him. By tugging on two of the threads to cinch up the knots the words "All is lost," appeared. Chalcuchima and Kiskis had broken through the Cuzcos' line.

"Defeat, sire," I said, and at that moment a breeze picked up. You could hear it in the wind dancing back and forth across your face: The gods were laughing. All eyes turned to the ring of lying huacas, and we knew that our subjugated people's deities were finally taking their revenge. There was no time to smash them, to burn them, to grind them into powder and throw them on a llama pasture. Huascar snapped his fingers and his guardsmen began putting the priests and priestesses to death, but it was not enough punishment for their betrayal. The gods had finally joined forces against the Children of the Sun.

"Sire!" I said. He turned to me, as if hoping the few shaky knots on the cord held better news. "Mama Ocllo's Voice never spoke against you. You may need the help of your grandmother today."

He chewed his lip for a moment in indecision before nodding. "Spare her. Kill the rest." She gave me a thankful look, and then I had to go. The end of the world was coming.

* * *

I rushed back to the Intihuasi fortress atop Sacsahuaman, passing through the great stone gate and working my way up to the battlements where I had last seen my son-in-law. I found him dressed and armed like the Inca general he was. It was as I feared: He planned to fight. I needed to get him away from Cuzco.

"Go and find Prince Manco, Cayo. He's still out in Andesuyu, but I don't want him coming back to Cuzco until after all this is over. If Huascar wins he'll be angry that his brother wasn't here to support him. If Atauhuallpa wins he'll be angry that Manco didn't come over to his side. Tell him to remain in the hacha hacha —no, you stay with him to make sure he stays— until this is all over with."

My young friend with the wise old head looked at me for a long moment, knowing what I was not saying. "I won't leave you, Haylli."

"Of course you will," I said. "And you'll be smart to do it too."

He looked down at his feet, and I watched a tear fall to the stones beneath us. "I won't leave you, Haylli," he repeated.

"How many tocoyricocs do you think will survive this war?" I asked.

"If I send you away, one of us will survive. Atauhuallpa needs tocoyri-cocs to run the State."

"But I can fight. I've got a chest disk. For Inti's sake, I'm a better field commander than the fools Huascar's had commanding his forces! I don't know why your wife didn't have me commanding his armies for him. I can help Huascar—"

"One more lance isn't going to make a difference. Do what I say and you'll be saving the last good prince, the last good administrator, and you'll be letting me face tomorrow without worry."

He looked me in the eyes now, and I could see the tears on his face. "That's really what you want?" I nodded. "Then I'll go, but I'm coming back as soon as you send for me."

I embraced him as one does for the last time, then I thumped him hard on the back, turned him around, and pushed him towards the stairs down from the battlements. "Now go, and be safe, and have a good life."

He had string out of his coca bag before he was even on the top step, forging the travel pass that would allow him to leave a city facing its destruction without a raised eyebrow. I got a lump in my throat, and by the time I swallowed it away he was gone.

The next day we assembled. The defeated remnants of Huascar's army that had retreated from Tumipampa all the way to the plains west of Cuzco was reinforced by tens of thousands of new conscripts, many of them yanaconas with no military training pulled off noble and panaca estates.

Knowing that the fight was for his life, Huascar chose to command personally from his litter, and he ordered me, on account of my advanced years, to fight from a litter too. I climbed up onto the platform, carried by Rucana bearers who wore padded cotton corselets under their blue livery, and I wondered if I would die up there.

The Quitu army that came off the western heights to face us was roughly twice our size, with Chalcuchima controlling one great wing and Kiskis the other. They were battle-hardened both from constant victory in the War Between the Brothers and from long campaigning before that in the Kingdom of Quitu as well. They had fought across half the world to see Cuzco, and now there was just one last ridge to be climbed, the ridge behind Huascar's hastily reformed and reinforced legions.

There was no offer of surrender or negotiation, no ritual taunts or boasts. When the two armies completed forming up on the plain, sometime before midmorning, conch trumpets brayed out and the two sides marched towards each other to the beat of drums and the skirl of pipes. The final battle had begun.

I was surprised that our men did not run at first contact with the enemy. I was stunned when they fought throughout the day, never taking a step back without the Quitus taking lives to do it. Untrained and unblooded boys became veterans in that single day, and the ones who did not became food for the condors and the foxes.

Standing on the deck of my litter I worked my sling and my javelins into the Quitu ranks ahead of me, and such was the constant press of men that no one seemed to have enough room to throw anything back at me. All they could do was shove and stab the men in front of them.

I do not know where Chalcuchima's strategy broke down: Perhaps he had expected us to run and thought the overwhelming show of force would be enough. Perhaps Kiskis was supposed to wrap our flank and could not do so when we advanced to meet the Quitu attack. All I know is that there seemed to be no higher tactical direction on either side of the shoving match, and it was mid-afternoon by the time the two exhausted armies fell back from the fray to rest and receive new orders. Waterskins were brought out to us on the backs of thousands of llamas. It was when I descended from my litter and crunched on the dry grass underfoot, feeling the stiff breeze against my face, that I knew what had to be done.

I climbed back onto my litter, ignoring the groans of my Rucanas to order them over to Huascar, pounding on the deck of the litter with my mace to urge them on. When I was beside my Sapa Inca I called to him, "Fire!"

"What?" He looked at me with an irritated expression.

"Look how dry the grass is. Look at the direction of the wind. If we set fires along our entire front the wind will carry it into the Quitus' ranks, and their camp is just over the hill behind them."

Huascar turned east towards Cuzco, feeling the strength of the breeze in his face. "Do it."

While our soldiers slaked their thirst, hundreds of officers were briefed; when we formed our ranks to renew the fight our men carried thousands of torches drawn from a nearby tampu. As the Quitus advanced, the burning brands were thrown out into the space between our armies, and the hungry flames licked the meadow between the corpses, whipped up by the wind into a blaze, a firestorm that consumed all the fuel beneath it and blew towards the Quitu lines with unstoppable hunger.

"As! As!" Came the cry from the Quitu lines as they ran from the inferno.

"Advance!" Came the order from our own lines. We marched in lockstep, careful to keep our pace slow enough that we stepped only on the burned out ashes and not the still hot coals. The thousands of bodies, scorched by the brief kiss of the flames, were avoided as much as possible.

We scattered the Quitu army by sunset, and then Huascar ordered a great feast in honour of the victory. I returned to camp, confused. "Why aren't we chasing them through the night? They're on our side of the Apurimac River. They can't all cross if we continue to press them. We'll kill or capture thousands."

"Our men are exhausted. The Quitu will not be able to reform in strength by morning. No general could gather together enough men in the dark to stand up to us. We'll eat, sleep, and pursue them tomorrow," Huascar said.

I looked at the llamas rotating on spits over thick banks of coals and my mouth filled with hot jets of saliva. We had fought all day and survived, a miracle when one thought of the odds arrayed against us. I protested no further, dismissed my Rucanas to rest, and spent the night enjoying myself.

The next day our army prepared to march. Hummingbird led our vanguard over the facing ridge to see if there were any Quitus remaining in their fire-swept camp. I supervised the breaking up of our own camp, a tedious business when so many of our soldiers had never served time in an army before. Huascar was almost back before I noticed the vanguard's return.

"What's going on?" I called out as his litter began to climb the face of our hill, his soldiers jumping between the burnt corpses of yesterday. They almost seemed to be having fun. "What is it?" I called again as the litter came closer. Something had to be wrong for the Emperor to return. I called for my own litter, but I was barely mounted before I saw the unthinkable: The Mad Hummingbird was a lean young man with small earplugs, but the occupant of the Imperial litter was a grizzled old man with the neck of a bear and the face of a condor. His earplugs were so broad and low they almost brushed his shoulders.

"You!" I shouted. He waved to me, his lipless mouth doing its best to smile, then his Quitus threw off the bloody mantles of the Imperial guardsmen, running among our camp with maces and axes and lances.

"Kill the officers! Kill the officers!" Chalcuchima roared, looking straight at me as he said it. All around me the camp dissolved in terror, with the men furthest from the Quitus running away, and the ones closest to them looking to the left and right for support that never came. One by one Huascar's generals were cut down as they tried to organize resistance, and as another force of Quitus under Kiskis's banner crested the facing ridge the whole Cuzco army cried out, "As!" and dissolved in all directions.

"Let's go!" I thumped on the floorboards of my litter and my Rucana broke into a jog, but they were not fast enough to outrun the unburdened Quitus. When three of my porters were cut out from under me I ordered them to stop and set me down. "Run for you lives!" I took up my mace and turned to face the nearest Quitu soldiers. Most of my Rucana stayed with me. Some fled, and I do not blame them.

The Quitus advanced on us, hard men with faces carved into merciless masks by years of war. Those in front of us were joined by more to our left and right.

As still more began to work around behind us I decided to charge forward rather than be surrounded, but I was an old man whose hard-fighting days were over. I was knocked off my feet by one of the Quitus' trapezoidal bucklers, and then two or three of them kicked me while I was down, driving the air from my lungs and rendering me helpless.

My Rucana were either cut down or escaped. I could not tell you. I do remember being trussed up like a llama for the slaughter and dragged to our camp's corral, where I was dumped like a sack of chuno. Noon passed, then the afternoon. I fell asleep, and when I was kicked awake it was sometime after dark; Kiskis and Chalcuchima were standing over me.

"I want him dead," Chalcuchima said.

"And I want him free, but neither of us has the total command. It is Atauhuallpa we must obey," Kiskis replied.

"This is my army, my victory. My nephew is a puppy—"

"And today you have made that puppy into a dog, and one with sharp teeth at that, so I suggest you shut up!"

The two eyeballed each other for a moment before Chalcuchima accepted Kiskis's point. I would live, but Chalcuchima could make sure I would not wish it so by the end of the day.

"Let him watch the Capac Panaca burn, then," Chalcuchima ordered.

"You and you, keep him safe," Kiskis pointed to two of his burliest guards. They untied my bonds and stood on either side of me, grabbing my shoulders if I strayed from their decided course; we marched over the ridge, passing the Great Quipu Repository and my home, all the way to the Huacaypata and the panacaship my wife had spent her whole life earning.

I do not know how she heard that it would be destroyed so soon. I suppose she must have known her support for Huascar would bring Atauhuallpa to do this as soon as possible. She stood in the Panaca complex's gate, my Silver Vixen, her arms spread wide. This was her life's work, her greatest accomplishment, everything she had ever truly wanted. It was the only thing other than her son that had ever filled her heart. It would not be brushed aside by the desires of a boy her husband had spanked as an infant.

"You shall not pass," she said in a tone that brooked no argument. They stood there, shuffling their feet for a moment, not used to a woman who did not cower or acquiesce to their every whim. One took a step towards her.

"This is the panaca of the Sapa Inca Topa Inca Yupanki, the greatest conqueror the world has ever known. You are not welcome here. Leave at once!" Now the warriors did not look embarrassed. Her words charged them, for in their minds Atauhuallpa was the greatest conqueror, and he wanted this place destroyed. Another edged towards her. "You shall not pass. Go away, and rue the day you almost destroyed the greatest panaca in Cuzco!"

One of the warriors reached out with his lance, almost gently, and sank it into my wife's belly. I heaved against the arms holding me, but Kiskis had chosen well. "You shall not pass," the Silver Vixen murmured, but there was no force or volume in her command this time. The second man who had braved her words also reached forward to stab her in the abdomen with his lance, and she sank to her knees in the doorway, blood coming from between her generous lips. She was still alive as they stepped over her and ran into the palace with their torches and prybars.

I watched as those lips, carmined in her own blood, murmured over and over, "You shall not pass." She was dead there in the doorway before the first wisp of smoke spilled out into the street. My wife would never see her life's work in flames. I would. I would.

They marched on either side of me, holding me so tight that had I been shorter my feet would not have had to touch the ground. We left Cuzco behind us and returned to the Great Quipu Repository upon its hill. I did not understand what was happening at first because the very notion seemed unthinkable to me.

You wouldn't think an idea could burn, Friar, and perhaps you're right, but not in the way you would think: It might be better to say ideas explode, fly apart in bursts of incandescence that leave the world a little dimmer with their passing. I watched them fire the Great Quipu Repository, watched as Atauhuallpa's minions threw faggots of wood though those tall windows, watched as the thatch roof, thick as a man is tall, collapsed down into the furious flames beneath.

Inside, the jars, the shelves upon shelves of jars, each containing the stored knowledge of an empire in string, burst from the heat. You could hear them even over the roar of the flames, pop, crash, smash, bang, boom. All the tax information for the last hundred and fifty years, gone. The census counts, the tampu inventories, the tax allocations, the colonist assignments, all gone.

While that was a crime against the State no tocoyricoc could forgive, even that loss paled in comparison to the royal quipus: Our literature, our science, our genealogies, our histories, every command to spring from a Sapa Inca's lips, gone, incinerated, up in smoke. The combined knowledge and experience of generations of the greatest thinkers in the world, destroyed by men who could not have told the royal quipus from the ledger quipus.

Even as the place burned I knew its loss would be felt across the Four Quarters of the World. The accounts were backed up by curacas in every province, but it would be years before properly monitored taxation could begin again. The royal quipus, meanwhile, were lost forever. They were irreplaceable, more valuable to the future than any cumpi cloth or golden idol. I wept then and I ache now at what the world lost that night.

They made me watch it burn down to the foundation; then they began to pull the fallen stones away so there was not even a pile of rubble to mark where the beating heart of Inca bureaucracy once stood. I did not see Chalcuchima arrive on his litter. I was too mesmerized by the sight of the demolition crews at work. I was snapped out of my reverie by his palm coming into sharp and disrespectful contact with the back of my head.

"Wake up, old man," he sneered.

I looked at him with my tear-streaked face. "We're the same age, Mallku."

"This night's not over for you yet, Waccha," he assured me. He snapped his fingers and pointed to my home, half-way between the smoking ruin of the Great Quipu Repository and the looming mass of Cuzco, lit up now with torches as the Quitu army raped and pillaged and purged Huascar's supporters and the Capac Panaca.

My guards dragged me to my door, but the Quitus were unable to open it: My doorman had barred it, and in the end Chalcuchima had to descend from his litter so the poles could be formed into a battering ram, knocking the door out of its floor and roof sockets. It took a lot of time. They entered my home to find my entire household except for an elderly maid had fled over the back wall. They spared her, and for that I was grateful.

"Where's your history?" Chalcuchima barked.

"My what?"

"Atauhuallpa's orders are that there will be not one knot recording the existence of Sapa Inca Topa Inca Yupanki at the end of this night. We all know you kept a history. I've seen you tying knots on it myself. Where is it?" Well, Friar, you can see from the threads in my hand that I did not hand it over to Chalcuchima. I climbed the ladder of my counting room and took out my audit quipu. The illiterate old fool saw the pom pom tassels on the end marking it as a royal quipu and snatched it up.

"Where are the rest? That history was huge." I gestured to the jars and jars of problem quipus lining one wall where they had waited for me to return from interrogating the Bearded One. Normally I would never have sacrificed them, but I had seen the Great Quipu Repository

415

burn tonight. What was thirty further quipus against the lost wisdom of Tahuantinsuyu?

One by one he threw the jars out the window to smash on the courtyard below, watching me wince at each crack. Then Chalcuchima dragged me over to watch as his soldiers set the strings on fire. He laughed at me for a long time. I hated him at that moment, really hated him for the first time in my life.

"You know she's dead?" I asked when he was done.

"What?" He turned his head, still enjoying himself, my words not penetrating.

"Your soldiers killed the Vixen when they burned the Capac Panaca." He took a step backwards. "It's your fault, Mallku. I know you, and I know Atauhuallpa. This War Between the Brothers was your idea, and you didn't do it to make Tahuantinsuyu better. You did it because without a war you're just an old and bitter man, aren't you?"

"She's dead?" He seemed about to fall over.

"You did it, Mallku. You killed her with what you've done here. I want you to think on that for a long time."

"It should have been you," he whispered.

"Kill me," I said. "Do it now."

He just leaned against the wall, looking sick. He had loved her as I have loved my Koonek, but Koonek's blood was not on my hands. His orders were the end of our Silver Vixen. "What have I done?"

"You killed your wife, Mallku. If you had killed me first she would have taken you back. You know that. You would have been the most powerful warlord in Tahuantinsuyu, and certainly the best man she could still seduce. She wouldn't have even cut her hair to mourn me. She'd have taken you back, but you didn't think of that, did you? You didn't think it through that she would never let her panaca die while she lived."

"Be quiet," he said, sliding down the wall to sit with his legs sprawled out in front of him.

"You've destroyed the world and you've killed her, and the only person who is going to benefit is Atauhuallpa. Every time you put a burden on your back and take off your sandals I want you to remember that you killed her for him and ask yourself if it was worth it."

I descended the ladder while Chalcuchima still sat on the floor. His soldiers took me into custody, and I directed them in packing up a few traveling necessities. Even under arrest, being the finest administrator left in Tahuantinsuyu had its perks. I had my father's mummy and all my other household huacas and personal effects, including the jars containing my real history and many other royal quipus, transported with me at State expense. I even had them find me a new complement of Rucana litter bearers: Unemployed ones were not hard to find with all the dead nobles that terrible day produced.

When the general descended to the courtyard later his face was dry, but his eyes were red-rimmed from his crying. His lipless mouth trembled, and his condor nose sniffed in a vain attempt to hide his grief. We marched out of my home together, but we did not speak. The day had begun as his moment of triumph, but it ended as his greatest defeat.

I thought I would be shipped straight to Atauhuallpa, Friar, but the Quitus were so thorough in their destruction of State records that they needed me to help them in their pillaging. I told them which store-houses had food, and which had bedding. If I had refused they would have torn apart the warehouses until they found what they were after.

Much to my surprise, Huascar was alive. Chalcuchima's army had captured him and trussed him to a stake, which they carried from their camp into the Huacaypata. There they executed all of the Humming-bird's family in front of him so that he would know his line was ended, as well as his lackeys and courtiers, even his jesters. As the slaughter was being done, Kiskis and Huaypalcon came over to me.

"I'm sorry about this," my old school friend gestured to the executions. "Atauhuallpa's orders."

"What will he do with Huascar?"

Huaypalcon puffed up his chest. "The Sapa Inca Atauhuallpa will come to Cuzco and throw Huascar into the Pit with his own two hands." Kiskis and I both gave the boy a reproving look for the pleasure he took in an Emperor's fall, any Emperor.

"If he's not careful there won't be any Inca of the Blood left when this is done," I said. Hundreds of bodies of men, women, and children were stacked like firewood in the square, each one dressed in fine cumpi cloth.

"That might not be such a bad thing," Huaypalcon said.

"My son thinks we should call ourselves Quitus even after the war," Kiskis said. I made a face at that, and he laughed. I joined him, but in front of that pile of bodies it was black humour.

Huaypalcon scowled and said, "There are fewer Intip Churi in Tahuantinsuyu than any other tribe. Why call ourselves Inca at all? Why not just give earplugs to anyone who shows ability?"

"Because then we'd have to take yours away," Kiskis and I said in unison. We laughed our unhappy laugh again.

"Your day is past, Father—"

"I just won the war of your generation immediately after winning the

418

war of my generation. My day is past when I die, and you should learn some manners," Kiskis said, but his boy was a man now, and long past learning to respect his elders. Huaypalcon turned and stormed off to supervise the looting of a nearby palace.

Kiskis turned back to me. "I'm not sure what we're going to do now that we've won, Haylli. Do we have to march into Collasuyu and reconquer the whole world for Atauhuallpa? Or will people serve the Red Fringe regardless of how it was won?"

"Is he going to undergo a coronation in Cuzco?" The Red Fringe of the Sapa Inca had never been taken up outside of the Royal City. In this new age, who knew what traditions would be upheld?

"Yes, he's coming, but there's been a prophecy." My friend smiled his crooked smile at me, drawing out the drama. "All of the oracles have been consulted through the chaski system, and the Oracle of Huamachuco refused to support Atauhuallpa."

I remembered the ancient blue-clad priest on his hill with his salt water. "What did it say?"

"It said Atauhuallpa would never see Cuzco again, like his father and elder brother before him."

My eyebrows shot up at this, for the Oracle of Huamachuco was much respected in Chincaysuyu, Atauhuallpa's territory. "What did Atauhuallpa say when he heard? You say he's still coming to Cuzco?"

"He's bringing forty thousand men with him, and he's sending Chalcuchima out to Xauxa to guard his flank from any kind of Huascar-loyal army that might come up from the coast. I'm to stay in Cuzco with half of this army. As for the Oracle of Huamachuco, Atauhuallpa ordered the priest beheaded and a drinking cup made out of his skull; the hill upon which the oracle stands is being leveled, a bucket at a time, as the locals' tax service to the State."

We clucked our tongues and shook our heads at the idea that with all the things wrong with Tahuantinsuyu, valuable labour was being wasted to demolish a hill. "And me? Have you decided what to do with me yet?"

My friend shifted his feet, unsure of himself. "Our spies gave us rumours that the Bearded Ones from Tumpez were put into your care? That you became Huascar's White Man expert?" He spoke as if I had done something wrong, something he should worry about. I furrowed my brows.

"Yes, I was. What's the problem? One of them is still alive, if you want him."

"Read this," my friend took out a royal quipu from his coca bag. "It just arrived by chaski post during the night."

I ran the knots through my fingers without looking at them: 'Floating houses have returned. Many men have landed. Battle on Isle of Puná. Many dead.' "How old is this?" I asked, not knowing the state of the chaski system in Chincaysuyu, the quarter of Tahuantinsuyu over which I was supposedly Tocoyricoc.

"The system's recovering from the plague. This is only seven or eight days old."

"So, what does this have to do with me?"

"Atauhuallpa wants you to swear allegiance to him. I was going to keep you with me in Cuzco where you would be safe, but now it looks like he's going to wait in Caxamalca and let the Bearded Ones meet him. If that's going to happen, you should be there with him."

"He won't listen to me," I said.

"Well, it's not about whether he'll listen to you or not: It's how angry he'll be with me if I don't send you. Atauhuallpa might not need me anymore, Haylli. He's got his Uncle Chalcuchima, and Rumiñaui, who doesn't care what happens as long as he's given a job to do. I don't want to give Atauhuallpa an excuse to punish his third general."

"I have to leave at once?"

"Would you want to stay longer?" As if to punctuate his question, one of Huascar's concubines screamed as she was dragged before her lord and hacked down. I shook my head. Kiskis grimaced. "Is there anything I can do for you?"

"Don't kill Cayo if he comes back to Cuzco."

"Not on my authority, but if Atauhuallpa orders—"

"Okay, I want to be untied and guarded as I would be as a tocoyricoc, not as a prisoner. I won't run. Atauhuallpa is either going to kill me or he's not. I'll go of my own free will." We agreed on it, and I left Royal Cuzco to the misery that had befallen it.

I took the Chincaysuyu road, stopping at every tampu I passed to have copies of their ledgers made. The retreating Cuzcos and the advancing Quitus had each helped themselves to the stores, but there was still enough for the local purics, with care. I took as many quipucamayocs from each tampu as could be spared, putting together a new staff on the fly, trying to make sense out of the chaos.

I also read all the chaski dispatches about the Bearded Ones. Huascar loyalists were greeting the arrival of these strangers as the divine intervention of Viracocha, for the Spaniards fought and won against the islanders of Puná, who had declared for Atauhuallpa. The white men had then crossed over to Tumpez to find it a smoking ruin. Between the passing Quitus purging the loyal Cuzcos and the marauding Punás settling scores while Tahuantinsuyu was tearing itself apart, Tumpez was a shadow of its former self.

Unwilling to stay down on the coast, the Spaniards built a fort, left a handful of men there, and began climbing the Western Mountains. They were looking for the Sapa Inca, who was described to them simply as 'Cuzco.' There were a hundred places in those mountain passes where we could have wiped them out. A few soldiers with rocks could have stoned them to death from above with impunity, and between Rumiñaui, Kiskis, Chalcuchima, and Atauhuallpa the Quitus had almost two hundred thousand men under arms. We did nothing. Atauhuallpa ordered no hand to be lifted against these strangers, even when they broke our laws, which they often did.

Even without violence we could have barred their way, for the most frigid mountain passages could only be traversed with the fuel and food supplies in the tampus: It would have been a simple order to destroy the stores before their arrival. We did nothing of the kind; the tampus were ordered to send out guides to keep the Spaniards on the roads and lead them into shelter before nightfall.

Atauhuallpa wanted to meet these foreigners, and, as the new Sapa Inca his every wish was an Imperial command. The Bearded Ones would be allowed to make their way to Caxamalca, where he was taking the waters at the hot springs outside of town with forty thousand of his Quitus, as well as almost all of his supporting nobles.

I crested the last mountain pass for a view of Caxamalca a few days before the Spaniards did. Caxamalca means the Place of Frost, but it seems a paradise when looked down upon from the granite heights. The town's valley is a green oval bowl, five topos long and three wide. A broad river runs through it, and irrigation channels and subterranean aqueducts spread its life-giving waters to the checkered fields of hardy mountain crops, divided and protected from the wind by hedge rows.

The city of Caxamalca lies in the centre and is made up of shining white-plastered houses. A league east of the town lie hot springs whose steam rises up in the cold, dry air like smoke rising from a perpetual fire. It was around these springs that Atauhuallpa's army made its camp. The lobeless bastard was taking the waters while waiting for the Bearded Ones to arrive. I was ordered to report to him at once.

I was hustled into the Imperial Presence, and Imperial it was, Friar: Atauhuallpa may not have undergone the coronation ceremonies of a Sapa Inca, but that did not stop him from tying a Red Fringe into his headband, assuming a detail of Chacapoyas dressed in Imperial Guard uniforms, and flanking himself with royal quipu masters to tie down his commands. His stool was unmistakably an usno, and his retinue of advisors and lackeys were as well-turned out as any field Court under his father's reign.

I took off my sandals and was given a heavy burden, enough to make my legs tremble at the weight of carrying it on my shoulders and back. This was meant to humiliate me, but I just smiled a little to myself: Atauhuallpa had not heard of Huascar's screen, interpreting brother, and backing into and out of the presence. I came in slowly, genuflected, and blew my new and loathed Sapa Inca a kiss.

"Hello, Old Haylli," he gave me his insolent smirk, and I knew in that moment I would live to see another dawn. I felt neither relief nor regret.

"Hello, Atauhuallpa." I last saw him the night of Pariwana's death, and I would have preferred to never see him again. Between a plague and a civil war that killed millions, the gods could not do me that small favour? Instead, he was now the ruler of the world.

"I am the Sapa Inca Atauhuallpa now."

"Yes," I said, wishing one of us was dead.

"You will address me as such."

"Yes, Sapa Inca Atauhuallpa."

"Has General Kiskis explained your situation to you?"

"Yes, Sapa Inca Atauhuallpa." His name was like ashes on my tongue. I spat it out.

"Do you have any questions?"

"What is to happen to Tocoyricoc Cayo Topa?"

That question made him frown, and when that was not enough he rose from his usno and walked up to me. Even stooped over under the weight of my burden and barefooted I was tall enough to look him in the eye. "I suppose you have a good reason why I should not kill him?"

"Your Empire needs administrators. Cayo Topa and I are the only two left who can put your bureaucracy back in order. You need me because you don't have Cayo, and you will need Cayo because I'm too old to finish the job in my lifetime."

He backhanded me across the face; his guardsmen stirred, ready to strike me down at their Sapa Inca's slightest whim. "I have had enough of your lectures, your facts." He turned his back on me. "Tell me what you know about these Bearded Ones."

"Wouldn't that be a lecture?"

He assumed his most Imperial airs. "Do not test my patience, old man. I have a lifetime of grudges against you. It is only my concern for my people that keeps me from killing you. Now tell me what you know."

I shrugged, not wanting to help him. "I have a little of their language. The never-ending forest of the East does end: There is another ocean, and on the far side of that ocean is a land called either Spain or Castile. They come from there. They believe in just one god, and they are coming here to tell you about him. They also seem to love gold and silver the way a starving man loves food."

I looked at his back for a long time, then he turned to face me. "You will stay here with me until I am done with them. You will have all your tocoyricoc work sent here. You will train new quipucamayocs to help you from among my nobles. Serve me well, and when I capture Cayo Topa we will discuss his fate."

I plucked an eyelash, blew him a kiss, and left the Imperial Presence. It took two men in the anteroom to get the burden off my back without it dropping to the floor. I sat down for a long time to regain my strength, and then I went to work on the mismanaged tax figures of Caxamalca.

* * *

The Spaniards came over the final western hill overlooking Caxamalca, and I have heard even their brave hearts clenched with fear at what lay before them: The city below was intersected by a straight imperial road. Following the line of the road from their own position to the opposite hills they could see the tents of Atauhuallpa's army, a host of forty thousand battle-hardened soldiers.

The Spaniards numbered only a hundred and sixty, and only sixty of them had horses. Without showing any sign of uncertainty or trepidation they marched down into the town, whose tampu had been prepared for their arrival, and then twenty of their horsemen made their way to our camp, seeking an audience with Atauhuallpa.

I watched them ride the road to us, and I marveled: Nowhere in Tahuantinsuyu is there an animal that can be ridden like a horse. Young boys can sometimes straddle a tolerant llama, but to ride an animal for topos and topos, and at speed, and at such a great height, and to have such control over where and how the animal moves? It was beautiful to watch. I thought it beautiful, anyway. The soldiers of Atauhuallpa's army were purics and yanaconas, and to them the unfamiliar was huaca. The horses scared them, but they were brave enough not to show it except through the stiffness of their motions, the quiet tones of their conversations.

The Spaniards were dressed in the metal that I would come to know as steel: Their breastplates and helmets caught the sun, dazzling the soldiers they passed. Their swords were sheathed, but each carried a long lance, and if a Quitu strayed too close to the Bearded Ones he was pushed aside with the flat of a spearhead. Their arrogance, their supreme confidence, allowed them to pass posted sentries without so much as a challenge. No one dared to stand in their way.

The white men rode through Atauhuallpa's camp and made straight for the plume of steam rising up from the hot springs: Atauhuallpa's luxurious cumpi and alpaca wool tent stood out from the cabuya-fibre of the soldiers' like an erupting volcano among torches. I managed to reach his tent just before the Spaniards did.

Through gestures and loud slow speech they made it clear that they wanted to speak with 'Cuzco.' And as the Quitus rustled their weaponry in anger at the mention of the name of their enemies, I called out in a clear voice that the Bearded Ones wanted Atauhuallpa. A boy riding behind one of the Spaniards asked me who I was.

"I am an official of Atauhuallpa," I said. "Who are you?" The boy was one of our own people.

"They call me Felipillo, 'Little Phillip.' I was taken from Tumpez and have been across the Ocean with these men," he said. He spoke in Spanish to the men around him, but even to my half-trained ear I could tell his words were halting and uncertain. Never the less, the little translator told them that I was an authority here. They all turned to look at me. One said something. Felipillo translated, "Where is the Sapa Inca?"

I had no idea where Atauhuallpa might be, for I had not seen him since my audience. Before I could admit my ignorance an officer called out, "He's outside the springs!"

I gestured for their leader to come with me. When the whole troop of horses began follow I shook my head, and their commander man looked down at me for a long moment before ordering his fellows to stay at the Imperial tent. His gaze shook me, for there was no fear in the Spaniard's eyes. He barked a command, and the translator descended from the horse to follow his master. I saw now that the boy was almost a man, though short and slight and somewhat ugly.

I led the way, which became easier as soldiers parted before that big horse. I arrived at the Court, which had been set up in a courtyard of the bath complex, and I gestured for the Bearded One to descend, to take off his shoes and assume a burden, as I was doing. The man shook his head at me, bowed low for a moment —not in reverence to the most powerful man in the world, but to pass under the doorway's high lintel— then he rode his horse right into the Imperial Presence.

He towered over us all on his charger, especially Atauhuallpa, who was seated on the low stool of his usno. The Spaniard worked his horse forward while he spoke, so that the breath of the horse disturbed the red fringe on Atauhuallpa's brow. Atauhuallpa never looked up at the Spaniard, as if nothing unusual was happening.

The white man introduced himself as Hernando De Soto, and as he spoke the boy translated an invitation for the Emperor to visit the leader of the Spaniards, a man named Francisco Pizarro, at the tampu in town. Pizarro wished to show his gratitude for the Emperor's kind hospitality on the long journey by hosting a feast in his honour.

Atauhuallpa murmured an agreement to the invitation, at which the Spaniard smiled. Then, surprising us all, he turned his horse around and galloped it to the far end of the courtyard before turning and charging it back to stop just short of Atauhuallpa, rearing the horse up on its hind legs and making it whiney and snort, pawing at the air with massive iron-shod hooves. Several guardsmen trembled at the display, but Atauhuallpa remained impassive. De Soto saluted the Emperor with his sword, collected his interpreter, and rode off with his bearded chin held high.

As soon as the Spaniard was out of the courtyard, Atauhuallpa gave orders for the men who had shown fear in front of the foreigner to be killed; then he ordered all of his nobles to prepare to leave camp at dawn the next day.

"Did you see that animal?" Atauhuallpa asked his Court. "We could breed those! And that weapon of his? Yes, there is a lot to be gained from these white men." With that he dismissed us all and retired to his tent.

I did not like it, Friar, not at all. These white men were brave, I admit, but they must know that they were trapped and surrounded and at the total mercy of this man. Why then were they not afraid? What were they planning? Something bad was going to happen if the lobeless bastard who was my Emperor went to meet them face to face. I could feel it in my bones.

It took me most of the rest of the day to get an audience with him, for he dallied with his women and would admit no one, then he saw his favourites first. The sun was setting when I finally got to see him, and my audience was lit by flickering torchlight.

"Don't go," I told him, half wanting him to march into their midst and never come back.

"You forget yourself," Atauhuallpa said, examining his fingernails.

"I am your expert on these foreigners, and I advise you to kill them now. It will be easy. You outnumber them two hundred and fifty to one. With Kiskis' men you have another two hundred and fifty to one, and Chalcuchima has easily another three hundred to one. Kill them, and don't go."

"It amuses me to go."

I bit back an angry retort, remembering that this was no longer the boy whose feet I could beat for his insolence. Right or wrong, he had become the Sapa Inca. "If you don't want to attack them, trap them," I said reasonably. "There are only two ways out of this valley. Man the passes. They will never break out of here, and they can live in quiet luxury in Caxamalca until your curiosity has subsided."

"I said it amuses me to go." He gave me that smirk of his, the one that he knew infuriated me. Despite all my loathing for him, I could not allow the Red Fringe to walk into the kind of danger my instinct told me these Bearded Ones represented. I had to try again.

"They are not here to amuse you. They want something, and from what little I know of them, they take what they want without asking. I beg you. Burn the tampus and defend the passes. Let the come to you as beggars, not bandits."

"Burn the tampus?" He dropped his hand and glared at me. "My realm is my army, my army in my people, my people need food, and the food is in the tampus!"

I could not resist. "You were not so concerned with your people's food when you burned the Great Quipu Repository!"

"No one dares speak to the Sapa Inca like that!" He thundered from his usno.

"I have spoken my mind to three generations of Emperors. I was granted the right of Free Speech by Old Topa himself—" I stopped myself too late.

"Topa?" Atauhuallpa repeated to himself in feigned confusion. "Topa? I don't know who you mean. In fact, no one here knows who you mean." He looked at me with his dark eyes, probing. "Is it possible the name Topa is still tied down somewhere? Did I burn only a part of your history? Did you have copies made, my thorough old tutor?" He was whispering now.

I was desperate to change the subject. "Sire, I have interrogated one of these Spaniards, and I can tell you—"

"Whom do you serve, Haylli?" He asked me.

Interrupted, I blurted out, "What?" Instead of the response I knew he wanted.

"Why do you talk when your master does not want to listen?"

"Your father—"

"Answer me."

"When I speak—"

"No, answer me! Whom do you serve?"

I took a deep breath, fearing it would be my last. "I serve the Red Fringe, as I served your brother and father and grandfather before you." There were growls from the Chacapoyan guards around me. Atauhuallpa's face was rigid, as if carved from stone.

He waved me to approach with two fingers, and as I shuffled forward under my heavy burden he repeated the gesture impatiently, closer and closer, until he could whisper in my ear. "You are a stubborn old man, but I have some experience of that. My father, too, was a stubborn old man. Even as he lay dying of the plague he refused me his Red Fringe.

"Huascar was to be Sapa Inca, and I was to be Huascar's Viceroy of Chincaysuyu. He even had it tied down by a Royal Quipu Keeper. Strange that no one wonders why only my most loyal supporters and I are still alive from the group who heard my father's deathbed will."

I kept my face calm, but he knew how I was screaming inside. "You want to know why I tell you this? Why I tell you the truth after burning your precious Quipu Repository and spreading the stories that I was born in Quitu to a Quitu princess, and that my father gave me the Kingdom of Quitu to rule?"

"Yes," I whispered back.

"Because I think you have your history still, and I know I cannot torture its location from you." My mind flew to the jars in my personal baggage that even a cursory inspection would find, but, of course, Atauhuallpa was a liar and a cheat down to his marrow. He could not imagine something important being hidden in plain view. He continued to whisper, "I will muddy the waters of history, Haylli. I will churn the sediments from the bottom of the pond until I see only my reflection on the surface. I want you to know what really happened so that it will always haunt you. Your punishment is that your history will be the truth, but it shall never be believed because it contradicts my lies."

He paused for a moment, his smirk playing across his face again. "In fact, in another few years when I have children and all the men of your generation are dead, I will change history again: I was Huayna Capac's heir, and the Hummingbird had no claim to the fringe beyond his own hubris. I smote him for his insolence." Another pause, and then his smile began to warm.

"Then, when I am your age, Haylli, I will change history again, and there will be no Huascar, and there will be no War Between the Brothers, and the succession of Sapa Incas will pass from Pachacuti to Huayna Capac to me, with no interruptions. Who will believe your truth when there is not a single living witness to contradict the lies?" Then, without warning, he spat in my face.

I reeled back in surprise; then froze as I heard the scrape of halberds being lifted from the flagstones and leveled at me. Within moments Atauhuallpa's guards would run me through. "Friends! Do you see how the Shepherd of the Sun honours me?" I shouted, turning to face the surprised soldiers. "The Son of the Sun's spit sits on my face!"

Atauhuallpa laughed at my insincerity and waved his guards back. The sound of their grounding arms relieved me: Atauhuallpa's words did not. "You will do as I say because you love order in Tahuantinsuyu more than you hate me for what I did to your daughter and your quipus. You will train others in the tocoyricoc arts, and you will begin a new repository for the tax ledgers of the Sapa Inca Atauhuallpa. Do this, and you shall live to the end of your days, old man. For now, you will accompany me tomorrow to meet these Bearded Ones. Now get out of my sight!"

I bowed low. "My lord's slightest whim is my overriding command," I said, backing out of the room. The honeyed platitudes poured from my lips, and Atauhuallpa's stormy expression told me he saw my disdain. As a final affront I exchanged my burden for a heavier one as I left the room, and continued backwards, bent over at its weight, all the way out of the compound.

* * *

Atauhuallpa and his assembled nobles began to make their way towards Caxamalca at dawn the next day, but our pace was not to be the forced march of wartime or even the standard pace of peacetime: Atauhuallpa wanted to make the white men wait. His nobles, along with litter bearers and musicians and priests and guardsmen, were all drawn up for inspection, and he walked up and down the rows, checking for faded clothing, uncombed hair, dusty sandals, anything that would subtract from the magnificence of his procession. It was noon before we took our first step towards Caxamalca.

There were westbound snails that made better time that we did, for Atauhuallpa ordered great musical and dance performances set up to entertain the passing officials. When we were three quarters of the way there, Atauhuallpa decided he did not want to enter the town so late in the day, and he sent porters back to get tents so that he could sleep outside Caxamalca for the night and enter in the morning.

At this point a few Spaniards rode out, begging the Sapa Inca to come that evening, saying that the feast was already prepared. His little game with them concluded, Atauhuallpa ordered the regular marching pace begun and was entering town almost as fast as the Spaniards on horseback.

We arrived in a town mysteriously empty. Atauhuallpa had ordered most of the local population to leave in preparation of the Spaniards' stay, but there was no sign of the Bearded Ones either. We marched into a town dead silent except for the echoes of our passage.

The plaza in the city's centre was triangular, flanked on two sides by long barracks of the Caxamalca tampu and at the base leading back to the road by a wall of loose fieldstone. The usno stand had a roofed enclosure on its top to protect it from the elements. By all rights Atauhuallpa should ascend it in the presence of these foreigners, but he had given them this town to live in, and so he had decided his litter would be regal enough, carried and surrounded as it was by hundreds of his nobles.

With the exception of Chalcuchima, Kiskis, and Rumiñaui, each leading one of Atauhuallpa's far flung armies in the clean up operation following the War Between the Brothers, every one of Atauhuallpa's officials was present, and at Atauhuallpa's orders they were dressed in finery that dazzled the eye with its colours and shimmers. There must have been five thousand of us, brought by Atauhuallpa both as a show of strength and so that all of his advisors would have a viewing of this moment, the meeting of a Sapa Inca with the Bearded Ones. For my unappreciated opinions I was made to stand at the back of the crowd; were it not for my height I would have been unable to see the meeting at all.

When we had all gathered in the triangular plaza and still no Spaniard appeared to greet us, a puzzled Atauhuallpa stood up on his litter, looking around at the long low barracks to either side, deciding whether or not to be offended. Before he could order us all to leave, a Spanish priest and the interpreter Felipillo walked out of one of the barracks' doors carrying a flat and heavy object, which I would come to learn was a Bible.

The priest went on for some time preaching to Atauhuallpa about the grand design of the Spaniards to bring Christianity to all parts of the world, and that if he would just see the error of his ways he could save himself and his people from eternal damnation and spare everyone a conflict with the Spaniards. While my Spanish was nowhere near as fluent as it has since become, I could tell that Felipillo was a poor interpreter for such a weighty matter. When the Spanish priest explained to Atauhuallpa there is but one God, in the Holy Trinity of Father, Son, and Holy Ghost, Felipillo said, "The Bearded Ones believe in one god and three, which makes four gods."

In that bored tone I recognized from his days as my student Atauhuall-pa asked to see the Bible. Of course it was meaningless to him: As a huaca it was a paltry thing, hard on the outside but divided into hundreds of thin sections in between that were flimsy and covered in stains. Disgusted with the priest's hubris, he let the thing drop to the flagstones below.

The priest turned his back to the Sapa Inca and bellowed that Atauhuallpa had profaned the holy book, and that he absolved Pizarro's men to go do God's work.

And then the Pachacuti happened, the Spanish Pachacuti. Our time ended with the priest's words; the monster of Time bared its fangs and began to devour the Children of the Sun as if we had never mattered.

The Pachacuti began as a single blast of thunder from the usno stand, and then another followed as the two cannons the Spaniards had hidden there blew their hateful charges into the crowd of nobles below. We had no notion what a cannon was, so to us it seemed that there was thunder without storm clouds. Bodies of men flew apart into gobbets of meat at the sound.

We did not understand what was happening, and before we could react there was more rolling thunder from the galleries to either side of us as horsemen rode out in full armour, charging into the packed ranks of Atauhuallpa's advisors. Then there were more pops and hisses, like hail, as the harquebusiers and crossbowmen began firing down into the Imperial retinue from the rooftops.

With one great roar of 'Santiago!' the Spanish infantry charged too. Only then did Atauhuallpa's nobles begin to cry, "As! As!" Some trying to defend themselves with their hands against Spanish steel, others trying to flee, although we were hemmed in on all sides: The entrance into the plaza was not nearly wide enough for the crowd to exit in a panic.

And it was panic, Friar, sheer panic. The great noise of the guns was terrifying, and seemed a portent of a wrathful god. Then to see horsemen riding down on us, standing up in their stirrups, their great height allowing them to kill without effort —It seemed impossible. Then the very idea that less than two hundred men would dare to so insult the Sapa Inca, and worse still succeed, confused us to the extent where we could not function, could not think.

It was the end of us, Friar, though I am pleased to say at that late date there were very few Inca of the Blood left among Atauhuallpa's followers to lose their nerve. They were mostly Incas-by-privilege, many his personal lackeys from Quitu, elevated only thanks to his own success. Even so, they panicked, and that's how the Inca lost our Empire.

As for me, I was pushed against the fieldstone wall and pinned there by the mass of men in front of me. I watched the swords of the Spanish rise and fall, chopping down defenseless men. At Atauhuallpa's orders we had come without weapons, but even armed we were too densely packed to fight.

I watched the Spanish work their way through the mob until they reached Atauhuallpa's litter, who frowned at them in disbelief. The Spanish began to cut down his litter bearers, but such was our devotion to the Sapa Inca, even Atauhuallpa, that for every man who fell another stepped forward to take his place, so that for an aching period of time the litter never wobbled, even as it came to rest on a pile of corpses, surrounded on all sides by blood bespattered horses and men, surging and shouting and screaming and hacking.

At last I saw the litter lurch, and I saw the first look of fear on Atauhuallpa's face as the impossible manifested itself. A Sapa Inca was about to be captured by foreigners, captured because in his omnipotent power he had never imagined a danger. He turned around and seemed to look right at me, though I'm sure he was taking in the fact that he was unprotected and alone, surrounded by the Bearded Ones whom he had meant to make pets of. The litter lurched again, and then further, and then it tipped up on its edge, dropping Atauhuallpa into the swirling mass of horses and bodies below.

With a sickening pressure, the weight of Inca nobles pressing frantically against one another and against the fieldstone wall finally broke the loose masonry, and I was carried backwards and over the crumbling stonework, leaving the bloodbath of the plaza behind, but the slaughter followed us. The Spanish horsemen vaulted the rubble and worked their way back and forth among the fleeing nobles, cutting down whoever they could reach.

Steel flashed around me more than once, and the big barrel chest of a horse knocked me to the ground for a terrifying moment of thundering hooves around my head, then I was up and running again, fleeing as fast as my old legs would carry me.

I was sure Atauhuallpa was dead. My mind reeled at the implications of it, but in truth, Friar, I was cheering inside. With the lobeless bastard gone, Chalcuchima and Kiskis would march their armies on Caxamalca to wipe out the Bearded Ones for their insult to the Red Fringe. Cayo and I would put Huascar back on his usno under careful supervision, and Tahuantinsuyu would be healed. All this would have happened if Atauhuallpa was dead.

But Atauhuallpa was not dead. One Spaniard in his bloodlust had come at the lobeless Sapa Inca with a sword, but Francisco Pizarro leapt to stop him, receiving a cut on his hand in the process. It was the only wound any of the Bearded Ones suffered that day. By saving Atauhuallpa's life they saved their own, for as sure as I am sitting here now, Friar, I would have made Tahuantinsuyu rally to avenge him, but I could not get his soldiers to rescue him without his express orders.

Atauhuallpa's camp that night was a chaos. So many of Atauhuallpa's officials lay dead between the plaza and the camp that it seemed no one was left to take command. Soldiers did not even bother to take their tents down. They just walked away, taking whatever road would lead them to their far-flung homes. The dawn saw a group of Spanish horsemen canter into the abandoned camp to take possession of Atauhuallpa's personal effects. No one stopped them.

It was midmorning when I received a summons from Atauhuallpa. That was the first I heard that he was alive, but I obeyed, entering the Royal Presence barefoot and burdened. Aside from Spanish guards replacing his Chacapoyas, there was little visible difference. He did not even seem upset. If anything, he was more aloof and regal with me than he had been before his captivity.

"I will be staying here for the foreseeable future," he told me, as if it were his own decision. "Have all Imperial correspondence routed to me here."

"Should I contact your generals—"

"No," he interrupted me. "There will be no attacks against the Spaniards." He raised his voice at this, being careful not to look directly at their translator, Felipillo, who leaned against a wall. "You will stay in Caxamalca with me as my chief administrator. You will summon Cayo Topa—"

"He won't come," I said flatly.

"Do not interrupt me," he said with great authority that did not sound strained. "If he will not come to me, make him governor of Cuzco. I want a replacement to the Great Quipu Repository established at once. We must return to the normal governing of Tahuantinsuyu."

I looked around the throne room at the steel cuirasses of the Spanish soldiers, wondering what normal government would look like with Atauhuallpa at the mercy of these murderers. "Yes, my lord," I demurred.

"You are dismissed," he said. I backed out of the room. Atauhuallpa's next visitor filed in.

And so it went for days and days. I sent a signal into the hacha hacha of Andesuyu that it was safe for Cayo Topa and Manco Inca to return to Cuzco, and then by chaski post Cayo Topa and I tried to put together a semblance of an administrative system out of the shattered ruin left by plague, purges, civil war, and now the death of so many of Atauhuallpa's key nobles.

It was an incredible time to be a knowledgeable young bureaucrat in Tahuantinsuyu, Friar. We elevated masters of ten families up to masters of a thousand if they knew their ledger quipus and a couple of languages. We stopped hundreds of projects for the simple reason that we did not have enough trained administrators left to oversee them. The purics were just ordered to down tools, go home, and plant extra crops.

Expediencies such as these are why, today, the fortress of Ollantaytampu in the Yucay Valley has dozens of great boulders in a single file line stretching all the way across the valley to the quarry: The men who led the teams dragging the stones were needed so badly we did not allow them to finish what they started.

While Cayo and I tried to hold a crumbling empire together with twine, Atauhuallpa learned Spanish and how to play chess. Every day he held court over his subjects, who treated him just as if he were still our Emperor, which I suppose he was. At one of these sessions Atauhuallpa and I were watching two Spanish soldiers play dice for sets of golden earplugs taken from the corpses of pacuyoks. One bit the gold disk between his teeth.

"They do love their gold," Atauhuallpa murmured.

"Yes," I agreed.

"Maybe that's how I can get out of this," he said. It was the only time I recall him admitting to his predicament. Without another word to me he walked into an empty storeroom, followed by his Spanish guards, and demanded to speak to Pizarro. The grizzled old Conquistador arrived, and Atauhuallpa drew himself up into his most Imperial hauteur.

"I see that you Spaniards want gold. I will give you all the gold you want in exchange for my freedom."

Pizarro narrowed his eyes and demanded Felipillo to ask Atauhuallpa to repeat his statement in Runa Simi, in case his Spanish had been inaccurate. It had been fine.

"How much gold would you like?" Atauhuallpa asked. "I could cover this floor with gold..." He ventured, then when he realized that this might not seem like a lot he snapped his fingers. "I will fill this room with gold from the floor to as high on the wall as I can reach!" And he reached up over his head to touch a point on the wall, generously going onto his tiptoes. Pizarro looked around the room, which was perhaps four paces wide and twelve paces deep. The point Atauhuallpa had reached was half again my height. It was an impressive volume, to be sure.

Atauhuallpa might have realized he was straining the credulity of his captor now. "You wouldn't melt the gold down, though. You would keep them in the original shape." Pizarro's eyes narrowed again. "And, in exchange, I will fill a smaller room twice over with silver."

Pizarro called for a bucket of red paint, and he painted a line around the walls to the height that Atauhuallpa could reach. Felipillo told us the Spaniard promised, "If your treasure reach this line, Your Majesty, you shall be free."

Atauhuallpa smiled, then composed himself and ordered me to get about it. I was to strip every temple and villa until the ransom was paid. With that Atauhuallpa went to take a nap, leaving me with months of toil to perform.

To the Spanish it seemed the gold and silver could not come fast enough, and they were always speculating that they were being tricked somehow, that most of the gold was being hidden or delayed to gain Atauhuallpa some kind of advantage. I told them it might only take five days by the chaski system for messages to go to and from Cuzco, but it takes a lot longer for porters to carry gold and silver along those roads.

The gold in Caxamalca was already looted by the Spaniards, and the mines and wind ovens nearby were soon emptied of their stored surplus. Once those were exhausted it was almost a month before the first major shipment arrived, and after that the Spanish would stop everything to watch burdened men struggling down from the surrounding hills, but it was never enough, never enough, never enough gold for them.

And the Spaniards were not the only ones who seemed to think there was not enough gold involved: I do not know whether Huascar somehow managed to send a message from his confinement in Cuzco or if one of his supporters acted without communicating with the fallen Sapa Inca, but a message arrived for Pizarro offering twice Atauhuallpa's ransom if he would aid in the Hummingbird's rightful restoration to the Red Fringe.

A lifetime with Atauhuallpa allowed me to see he was livid behind his calm façade. He needed to remain unflappable in front of his captors, but I knew how his mind must be shrieking at this: The Spaniards were in a position to set either Sapa Inca on the usno, and whichever one was free would rule Tahuantinsuyu, regardless of the War Between the Two Brothers. Pizarro ordered Atauhuallpa to have Huascar brought to Caxamalca so that the Spaniards could arbitrate their dispute, and Atauhuallpa agreed, all smiles.

I never heard the orders given, but the first stream Huascar's party had to cross saw the sour-faced Emperor held under the water until he had stopped kicking. Atauhuallpa's soldiers drowned the Mad Hummingbird, then left his body to float downstream. When Pizarro confronted Atauhuallpa with this news he was all innocence and regret, saying that it had been done by his subordinates without his instructions. Presented with no way to undo what had been done, the Spaniards returned to complaining about the slow influx of treasure.

Pizarro began sending out conquistadores to secure gold stores that they knew about: Your Hernando de Soto entered the oracle of Pachacamac to find that shrieking idol, but no gold. I suppose now is the time to fulfill my god's request and tell you, Friar, that Pachacamac was powerful: Pachacamac was powerful! It is strange how some prophecies fulfill themselves.

I have since heard that the Spanish dug in the holy of holies, looking for treasure buried under the floor, only to discover a room there, a secret chamber where priests could boom on the floor above and speak up a shaft into the mouth of the idol. I don't know if that is true, though; it sounds like the sort of thing the Spanish would say to make men lose their faith. As for the Spaniards' own faith in our mountains of gold, they were not satisfied that day, though I can assure you there are untold treasure hordes in the Rimac Valley if you can find where the priests buried them.

Another party of Spaniards went to Cuzco and stripped the Coricancha almost bare, leaving only the mummies and the gold band running around the outside of the building intact. Against my strong urgings Cayo Topa allowed private households to hide their gold and silver stores, and the Spaniard became so enraged with this that they took to torturing the few surviving city notables to learn where the gold was being secreted. When Cayo Topa restrained the garrison from murdering the conquistadores the sons of Castile took this as a sign of weakness and broke into the House of Chosen Women, raping several girls before the rest could escape through the tapestry doors. It was a disgrace what those men did, but the Spaniards would do much worse, and not just in Royal Cuzco.

The expedition that went to Pachacamac came back with an unexpected prize: Chalcuchima. Atauhuallpa had ordered him to stay at Xauxa with his army, but De Soto rode into Chalcuchima's camp saying Atauhuallpa requested him at Court. This succeeded in getting my old nemesis away from his troops and into Spanish captivity with Atauhuallpa. When he arrived in the throne room to realize Atauhuallpa was surprised to see him, tears welled up in his eyes. How his pride must have burned to be so easily tricked.

He stepped forward and kissed Atauhuallpa's feet, saying if he had been present earlier his Sapa Inca would never have been captured. The Spaniards murmured among themselves at the old general's tearful devotion, but I knew he meant he would sooner have dashed out the bastard's brains and used his army to name himself Emperor then allow the Spaniards to control the Sapa Inca this way.

"The ransom is almost paid," Atauhuallpa said.

"Do you think they will let you go?" Chalcuchima asked.

"I have Pizarro's word," Atauhuallpa replied.

"We don't know what that's worth yet," I murmured. Both of them ignored me.

Within a few days of that conversation more Spaniards arrived under a man named Almagro, who seemed to have had a previous partnership with Pizarro that had soured. He brought almost as many men as Pizarro had, and they squabbled for a long time over who got how much of the ransom of Atauhuallpa, with Pizarro maintaining that it was his people who had done the capturing and Almagro pointing out that his people were sharing the risks, and allowing one and all to take further plunder in the future. They actually used the word 'plunder' within my hearing.

Though the ransom room was not yet quite full, the Spaniards decided to melt down all the accumulated treasures and divide them up between each man, with Almagro's forces getting a token sum to hold them over until more wealth could be accumulated. Atauhuallpa began agitating for his release now that the ransom was being considered paid, and he had some sympathetic supporters among the Spaniards, including Almagro, who saw guarding the Emperor as nothing but an encumbrance.

Wealth made the Spaniards whisper among themselves, and as the months passed wild rumours began to fly that a great army was gathering in Quitu —a place they had never seen— made up of cannibals from the Caribbean —a place no one in Tahuantinsuyu had ever heard of— that was going to come and take away their hard-won treasure.

White men would stop me in the street and demand that I tell them all I knew of the coming hordes, and I told them the absolute truth: Rumiñaui was in Quitu with tens of thousands of veteran soldiers, but he had no orders to march against the Spaniards, and if he did they would have plenty of notice of his coming. All they heard me say was that there were tens of thousands of warriors to the north, and they imagined the worst to fill out the story.

I did not think anything of it at the time, but looking back I should have been suspicious when Pizarro sent Hernando De Soto and all the other Spaniards who were sympathetic to Atauhuallpa's confined state out to investigate rumours of an approaching army. Atauhuallpa did not have one friend left among his captors: Caxamalca was now occupied only by the men who saw him as a golden fount run dry, an anchor to slow their pursuit of new plunder.

I was with Atauhuallpa when Pizarro came to him, shackles in his hands, to tell the lobeless Emperor that he was under arrest. Felipillo translated the charges even though Atauhuallpa now knew better Spanish than the interpreter. The charges against Atauhuallpa were twelve in number, including usurping the crown from Huascar, assassinating said brother, idolatry, adultery —in that he had openly indulged in a plurality of wives— and attempted insurrection against the Spaniards.

Atauhuallpa was chained and taken to answer these charges before Pizarro and Almagro. As near as I could tell he did not lie about anything, and at the end he offered to double the paid ransom in exchange for his life. The offer did not even cause a stir from the onlooking Spaniards. They had decided the verdict before the arrest. Atauhuallpa was guilty, and he would be put to death.

And, in a punishment unknown to the people of Tahuantinsuyu, the means of Atauhuallpa's execution would be burning at the stake. When it was explained to Atauhuallpa what that meant he blanched, and I saw true fear in his eyes for a moment: There would be no Imperial mummy for him. No panaca. No one would ever consult with his remains for advice or lift a mug of akha at a party held in his honour. The Monster of Time would swallow up and devour the lobeless bastard who had become emperor of the world.

The conquistadores took him out to the courtyard where a stake was already driven into the earth. Faggots of brush and wood lay piled and ready. Their priest told Atauhuallpa that he was going to be burned alive because he was a pagan, but that if he would accept the grace of Christ he could be garroted, as was done with criminals in Spain.

Atauhuallpa knew that his end had come, but with these words he saw a way to preserve his remains from destruction: He obtained oaths from several Spaniards that they would strangle him if he converted, and then he consented. The priest baptizing the Emperor with a washing pan and proclaiming him to be reborn as Juan de Atauhuallpa who was free from all his previous sins.

With water running down from his red fringe he gave me his insolent smirk to show what he thought of their little ceremony. However many languages I taught that bastard, lying was always his native tongue. "I want my remains given to my family and sent to Quitu." He did not say for mummification, nor would the Spaniards have been able to deduce that as his plan, but his people knew what was to be done; those who cared about him sighed with relief.

Atauhuallpa was tied to the stake well after the sun set, still shackled, then a thickly bearded man came up behind him, whipped a rope across his throat, and pulled backwards with all his might, even putting his knee against the post in front of him for better leverage.

Atauhuallpa's eyes goggled out of his head, but not a sound escaped his crushed windpipe. He looked around as the inevitable found him, his frightened eyes passed over myself and Chalcuchima before settling on Francisco Pizarro. They stayed there for a long time, for they did not close when my daughter's rapist finally died.

Despite Atauhuallpa's wishes, his shackled body was buried there in the courtyard. I have heard Pizarro sent one of his brothers to Caxamalca to exhume the bastard's grave and give him a more fitting Christian burial, but the body was gone. I do not know who dug it up or what they did with it, but I would imagine it was not in good enough condition to be made into an Imperial mummy. Atauhuallpa's immortality was stolen from him, but then he also stole the Red Fringe that gave him a right to it in the first place.

Of all the people I have seen die in my life, I think I miss Atauhuallpa the least.

I do not care about Spanish justice when it comes to Atauhuallpa's death, Friar, but I should say that they killed their captive Sapa Inca on spurious charges. The patrol sent to investigate rumours of an approaching army returned with good news: There was no army of Caribbean cannibals coming to drink white men's blood. When De Soto and the other sympathetic Spaniards learned of Atauhuallpa's trial and execution they were angry, but they did not protest enough to refuse to follow Pizarro's orders. He ordered the conquistadores to prepare to march.

After months of waiting there was now nothing to stop Pizarro and Almagro from sacking Cuzco, except that they wanted a new Sapa Inca as a shield for their actions. They did not want to be seen as bandits. They wanted to escort the Sapa Inca to his capital.

Needing a new Emperor, Pizarro grabbed one of Atauhuallpa's full brothers, a teenager named Toparca who I had seen once or twice in the entire eight-month period of Atauhuallpa's imprisonment, and gave him the Red Fringe. I had never taught this one, and I cannot speak to his intelligence or character. All I will say is that Pizarro found himself a puppet to be the new Shepherd of the Sun, and when the Red Fringe was tied around the boy's head the conquistadores marched.

The journey proved hard going on the Spaniards. I sent orders ahead abandoning all the tampus on our route of march. The country was rough and windswept, and they had no tents to protect them from the elements. Men and horses struggled over the mountains without the support of the local purics. It was cold and uncomfortable for my tired old body too, but Chalcuchima and I kept ourselves warm by laughing at the Spaniards' hardships.

The march would be hard for another reason, too. Atauhuallpa's former generals not knowing who this new Emperor Toparca was. They went rogue and began doing what they thought best. Chalcuchima and I read the reports that still came to us by the chaski system, though we did not bother to pass the messages on to the Sapa Inca anymore: Kiskis had quit Cuzco and was marching his army towards us; Rumiñaui declared himself Viceroy of Chincaysuyu and Scyri of Quitu, inviting all of us to come up there and establish a new kingdom with him;

Prince Manco Inca and Prince Paullu Inca were both trying to rendez-vous with the Spaniards to press their own claims as more legitimate candidates for Sapa Inca than Toparca —who neither of them had ever met.

As for me, I just kept pulling and tugging at my flimsy strings to keep the administration working for one more day, and one more day, and one more day. Soldiers who had deserted from both armies were returning to their homelands now, but their curacas were not reporting it. Some areas, especially among the Colla and Lupaca, were suffering from severe population depletion as a result of war and plague dead, so that I had to go ask the Sapa Inca Toparca for permission to allow purics in those regions to take more than one wife to try and rebuild their shattered clans.

I would not offer polygamy to commoners without the authority of a Sapa Inca behind me, even if he was a puppet, though I did not go barefoot or burdened. I do not think Toparca noticed my lack of cer-emony. He approved my plan, as he approved whatever he was asked to approve.

It was at about this time, somewhere near Xauxa, that the Spaniards first faced Inca soldiers in true and fair combat. Their cavalry vanguard under De Soto was ambushed in rough terrain by forces under Kiskis and several Spaniards were killed, which was something many of us had assumed could not be done after the massacre at Caxamalca. Only the timely arrival of reinforcements saved the Spaniards from being overwhelmed, and both sides retreated after deciding victory was im-possible.

Fortunately for the Spaniards, deserters from every tribe and army, in ones and twos and tens and hundreds, began to flock to the Beard-ed Ones' banner, joining them in their march on Cuzco. These men, abused by the events of their generation, could see another upheaval coming, and they wanted to be on the winning side.

With these new forces bolstering their confidence, the Spaniards turned their attention to their next most important prisoner, Chal-cuchima. I say that he was the most important because they did not really know what I did. They demanded the old general order all of Tahuantinsuyu's soldiers to lay down their arms, but he just sneered his lipless smile, saying, "And how am I supposed to do that, surrounded by all of you? You think I'm in charge of those soldiers? I couldn't get a latrine dug right now. That's what sort of authority I have over your enemies."

That was something of an understatement, and the Spaniards knew it. Chalcuchima could not tie royal quipus very well, but he sent verbal messages by the chaski system that sounded an awful lot like orders. I do not know what he was doing, for he was always careful to do it without eavesdroppers, but I knew from the replies that came back that he was in communication with Rumiñaui and Kiskis. Something was going on, but if he did not want the men of Castile to know about it, then I would do nothing to help them find out.

As we got closer to Cuzco, the Spaniards grew more and more hostile to Chalcuchima. He was the best dressed Inca in their captivity, with impressive martial cumpi tunics and mantles, golden earplugs and chest discs, a litter decked out in silver and emeralds. They wanted to know where the towns we were passing kept their treasures hidden, and when he said he was a general not a bureaucrat, Felipillo did not know the Spanish words so he just said Chalcuchima refused to answer. They took to abusing him, slapping him across the face and pushing him around, which of course just made him more truculent and stubborn. Chalcuchima always had a colossal pride.

Cayo Topa came out to me from Cuzco on foot, carrying an empty pot. I asked what he thought he was doing and my son-in-law told me that the Spaniards paid attention to who rode in a litter while ignoring labourers. He set the pot down, and we embraced as father and son before I introduced him to my new quipucamayocs that I was training.

As we were leaving Huanca territory the Sapa Inca Toparca died from a sudden fit of vomiting. I do not know who poisoned him, nor do I care except that the enraged Spaniards assumed it was Chalcuchima. Pizarro shackled him, just as he had done to Atauhuallpa, and then he demanded the general confess to it.

"Why? So you can dab me with water and strangle me?" He was found guilty without saying another word, and the Spanish notion of justice took its course.

I watched them burn him, Friar. I watched them chain him to the stake. I watched them pile the faggots at his feet. I watched them offer to garrote him as they had Atauhuallpa if he would convert to Christianity. I watched him refuse. I watched it all, and my mind turned the thought over and over again. Chalcuchima would be no more.

That thin-lipped old man was my life-long enemy, Friar: My tormentor in school, my rival for the Vixen's affections, the instrument of my father's death and my disgrace, the chosen assassin of Mama Ocllo, the vicarious murderer of my second wife, the willing general of the man who raped and murdered my daughter, the destroyer of the Great Quipu Repository. Chalcuchima was all these things, and finally I would watch him suffer.

It was when that first lick of flame was put to the tinder that I felt ashamed to stand there while this happened to him. It occurred to me that Chalcuchima had been right that night more than forty years earlier when he said that we were mirror images of each other: Chalcuchima distinguished himself at school just as I had, loved with all his heart just as I had, suffered humiliations and disgraces just as I had, climbed over his troubles to rise high, just as I had.

As the flames climbed up towards his feet I remembered part of the prophecy of Pachacamac: That which I love will disappoint, and one that I hate will redeem until I love him. I had loved the Vixen, but it had been a disappointing love. I had hated Chalcuchima, but it was a disappointing hate. Chalcuchima was as much a part of my life as the Vixen. He was integral and crucial to who I was and what I had become, and now he was going to die in horror and flame. I had not said goodbye to the Vixen, but I could make my peace with Chalcuchima now. I stepped out of the crowd as the flames leapt higher and I looked him in the eyes.

"I'm sorry," I said. "I'm sorry for all of it."

He did not reply, not for a long time. Do you remember, Friar, when he stuck his hand in the fire when he was only ten years old? Do you remember I said he could shut off pain in his mind? He did it then. I watched him cook and he never grimaced, never flinched.

The smell of it made me gag, but for the longest time he was so stony-faced they might have been burning an idol. Long after his haunches were cooked meat and his fingers had melted together and he was charred and burned all over, long after my heart would have burst from my screaming were I he, long after my cheeks were streaked by tear tracks, only then did I see him smile.

He smiled, Friar. He pulled his charred, thin lips off his white teeth, and that proud old man smiled at me. "Haylli!" It stretched on and on, a great bellow like he might call out on a parade square to inspire his troops. "Haylli!" Again. "Haylli!" The flames leapt higher and now he was coughing as the soot from his legs entered his lungs. He spat once, and I have no idea where he found spit, and then he said one last time, "Haylli, I'm sorry too!"

I turned away, but he did not see me. His eyelids had fused together. I walked away from my old rival. He never said another word, nor cried out in pain. As I left the crowd I heard Pizarro ask Felipillo what the great general called out, and the boy told the conquistador that Chalcuchima beseeched his god.

I smiled even as I wept, sure that Chalcuchima would have regretted few things more than having his last words mistranslated. I went to my room in the tampu that night and told Cayo Topa what had happened, and my friend asked me, "He didn't call you Waccha?" And I took this thought to calm my dreams: My old nemesis had met his end as my rival and not my enemy.

* * *

The death of the puppet Emperor Toparca befuddled the Spaniards, for there was no one left among their prisoners who could claim descent from Huayna Capac. They need not have worried: Without their knowing of it that there was a race to claim the Red Fringe.

Neither Prince Manco Inca nor Prince Paullu Inca was twenty years old yet, and they both grew up with the certain knowledge that they would never become the Sapa Inca: They had more than fifty brothers ahead of them in line of succession. The best they could hope for was to become a viceroy, a tocoyricoc, the major-domo of their father's panaca perhaps. I had taught them their quipus with great care in preparation for just such a future. Such was the state of my shattered world, though, that between their time in school and now, all of those fifty brothers were now dead.

I should have seen it coming, then, when both of them wrote to me asking my support of their claim for the empty usno: Manco Inca was in Cuzco and could claim to be a legitimate son of Huayna Capac, something none of the last three Sapa Incas could boast. Paullu Inca was in Collasuyu. He maintained that, as he was both older than Manco and better liked by the bureaucrats of the quarter of Tahuantinsuyu that was least damaged by our wars, he should have the Red Fringe. Both finished their quipus to me with the declaration that they were marching at all speed to meet the Spaniards in person.

Cayo and I tied as fast as our nimble fingers could work, begging them not to come, but the chaski networks still fluctuated as our administration struggled, and somehow our messages either were not received or were ignored. Manco Inca arrived on a golden litter two days before his brother Paullu, and Pizarro joyfully named the young prince as Sapa Inca Manco Inca, offering to personally crown him in the Huacaypata of Cuzco, which was only two days' march away.

Manco came to me immediately after seeing Pizarro, a stupid grin on his young face and a Red Fringe on his forehead. He opened his arms wide to embrace me.

"What in Inti's name have you done?" I snapped.

He lowered his arms. "What?"

"You've given them another Sapa Inca!"

"It was either me or Paullu," he reasoned. "Why shouldn't it be me? I have the better claim."

"The better claim to be their puppet," I said. "Do you think you'll be able to rule? You'll just be giving them Imperial red threads to tie as they please."

Cayo Topa had spent most of the last year with Manco, and they had grown close. He rose to the young monarch's defense now. "All they really seem to want is our gold."

"Have you ever seen three hundred men eat a hundred and fifty llamas a day, every day, for months on end? That's not within an order of magnitude of sustainability," I said. Cayo grimaced at the number, but Manco did not see what I was saying.

"So they like gold and llamas—"

"They like everything, and they consume it until there is no more, and then they blame us that there is no more as if we were hiding it," I said. "Then they burn us alive."

"What are you saying to me?" The young Emperor asked.

It came to me in a rush. "I'm saying I'm not staying here anymore."

"Well, of course you're not. We're all going to Cuzco."

"No, I mean I'm not staying with these Bearded Ones anymore. I've seen enough of what they can do. I'm leaving."

"How?" Cayo and Manco said in unison, both horrified that I would leave them.

"The same way Cayo came to see me: I'll dress like a puric and carry

446

something out of camp. I'll just keep walking. I'll take my royal quipus. No, I'll get my litter bearers to dress as labourers too, and we'll carry all my stuff out."

"Where will you go?" Cayo asked.

"What do you mean, where will I go? You're not coming with me?" Though the idea was a sudden one, I never thought that Cayo would not join me.

My friend shook his head. "Someone needs to keep the administration running, Haylli, especially if these Spaniards are going to be emptying out tampus without any regard for the people who need them. We've had wars and plagues already. We don't need famine too."

The look of satisfaction that settled on Manco's face made me angry: He had one of us, so he did not need the other. Something in me snapped. "Supay take you both! Stay and be the Spaniards' playthings if that's what you want! They aren't in Quitu yet. I'm going there. I'll join up with Kiskis, and we'll march his army to join up with Rumiñaui."

The two of them looked at me for a long time; then they walked out of the room. I had not felt so alone since I was a fugitive as a young man: I would have given anything in the world for Imperial law to be at that moment what it was in my youth.

* * *

I did just as I said I would, Friar, and I was three days' gone before Cayo sent word by chaski relay that I had finally been missed: The Spaniards call all pacuyoks Orejones, 'Big Ears,' and it seems I had the distinction of having the biggest earlobes of their remaining captives. I am sure it was my golden earplugs more than my person that was missed, but patrols were sent out to recapture 'the biggest of the Big Ears.' They did not find me, though. Kiskis did.

My friend with the crooked smile had marched most of his Cuzco garrison out to join up with the remnants of Chalcuchima and Atauhuallpa's abandoned commands, and now he had a formidable army, formidable except that all his soldiers wanted to do was go home, and their homes were scattered across half of Tahuantinsuyu. Never the less, he waited in the hills outside Xauxa and sent out patrols, one of which found me and my Rucanas. They offered to let us pass unmolested, but I wanted them to take me to Kiskis, and they were happy enough to return to camp.

447

Kiskis and his son Huaypalcon were holding a war council in their tent when I arrived, and they greeted me as if I were their personal deity, clapping their hands with joy and embracing my tired old body, asking me a hundred questions at once. While I expected that from Kiskis, hearing it from Huaypalcon was a surprise, and as I looked in the young man's eyes I saw what I had never seen in an Inca of the Blood before: Deep-seated, unshakable fear. Huaypalcon's despair seemed to fill the room like the stench of incense.

"What is it?" I asked after answering all their immediate questions.

"What do you mean?" General Kiskis asked.

"What's wrong?"

"Nothing," they said together, though Huaypalcon seemed to say it too fast to my ear.

I looked at father and son, and I saw that their clothes were dirty, their hair unkempt, their eyes hollow from sleepless nights. "You can tell me, or I can figure it out for myself. If you tell me at least I'll hear it your way first."

Huaypalcon opened his mouth to speak, but his father grabbed him by the shoulder and pushed him out of the tent before turning back to speak to me in a low voice. "He's getting to be difficult as he grows up. He doesn't get this stubbornness from me. If I didn't know Chalcuchima was sterile I'd swear he sired my boy."

I looked at the tent flap behind us, wondering if Huaypalcon was still capable of hearing his father's words. "So what is it?" I asked again.

"We won a civil war, and we have nothing to show for it. I've got soldiers who have fought on both sides of the last two wars. They have no loyalty to a cause. They just want to be on the winning side of what's going on now, or to go home."

I furrowed my brows, confused. "I thought you were marching back to Quitu."

"That's right, and the Spanish are going to chase us all the way. Gold seems to draw them like flies are drawn to a corpse. This isn't about a few hundred of them anymore. More of them are landing at Tumpez all the time, and because they learned my name at the same time they learned Chalcuchima's, they've got it into their heads that I'm worth chasing. I have to manage a three- or four-month fighting withdrawal across half the world with an army that doesn't want to soldier on anymore." My friend pushed his headband up into his thinning white hair and rubbed his forehead in frustration.

"The Bearded Ones are going to chase you? Then you'll ambush them in the passes, kill them by the hundred. A few victories will win your men back."

Kiskis shook his head. "It's not just the Spaniards, Haylli. Even with the new arrivals, there aren't enough Bearded Ones to make my retreat impossible: Your boy Sapa Inca Manco Inca is volunteering the remnants of the Cuzcos to chase us for the Spaniards, and with each retreat I have to make, more of the people we terrorized while we were conquering for Atauhuallpa are going to march against us and settle scores."

I remembered Atauhuallpa's purge of the Cañari and Huascar's attempt to do the same to the Chacapoyas. Atauhuallpa had later killed all the Chacapoyas who had served the Hummingbird anyway. Then there were the Caxamalca and Huanca peoples who had seen their homes turned into battlefields for years. Not to mention the peoples of the Kingdom of Quitu. Yes, there were a lot of scores to be settled, and Kiskis would have to deal with all of them.

"What can I do to help?" I asked.

My friend gave me his crooked smile, somewhat pained by the pressures placed upon him. "I thought you'd never ask."

So I became Kiskis's chief of staff, organizing provisions and running the camps while he devised the strategies and Huaypalcon commanded either the vanguard or the rearguard, depending whether we were advancing towards Quitu or retreating from contact with our many foes. And there were many foes, Friar.

Back in Cuzco Manco had the Red Fringe tied onto his forehead by Francisco Pizarro, then enjoyed thirty days of feasting to celebrate the coronation of the first undisputed Sapa Inca since Huayna Capac. This new Emperor sent word throughout the chaski system that the War Between the Brothers might be over, but the Quitu Army still existed and must be destroyed. Every tampu that aided us would have their staff executed. We were to be hunted and harried all the way back to Quitu, and all territories pledged to the service of Kiskis or Rumiñaui were to be reconquered.

It was a bold vision, soured only by the fact that it would be Spanish forces doing the subjugating, assisted by puric auxiliaries without whom we would have been able to use our numerical superiority to wipe out the Bearded Ones at the moment of our choosing.

We fought small actions daily, each ending with our withdrawal. Kiskis was always sending dispatches to Rumiñaui back in Quitu, but I did not know what aid he thought our school friend would be able to give to us: Two more Spanish armies were converging on the stony-faced general. Even Quitu would not be a safe haven for us. Word of our gold and silver had flown across the never-ending sea, and the white men arrived on our shores in such numbers that you would think they expected to trip over gold ingots on the beach.

We fled towards Quitu, Kiskis's army hemorrhaging soldiers the entire way as men from southern tribes realized the sooner they deserted the closer they would be to their families. Kiskis tried executing them, but representatives from his legions arrived to tell him even those warriors loyal to him felt that they were passed their discharge date. Many of them had served as soldiers since the beginning of the Quitu Wars. As a matter of tax-labour service they did not owe anyone anything. They said those who wanted to leave should be allowed to do so. Unable to maintain discipline in the ranks without his veterans behind him, Kiskis conceded. His numbers dwindled further.

It was a long, uncertain march, and on the side of a mountain at the edge of the Kingdom of Quitu we held our last war conference, though we did not know it at the time.

Huaypalcon returned from the rear guard as night fell, his eyes were desperate and bloodshot. The Pachacuti of the Spaniards' arrival had unmanned him, left him a shadow of his former brash and bold self. Where before he had walked as if the world was at his feet, now he found himself falling, falling to land he knew not where. He was a spent force, and he knew it. The lost luster of his once bright future seemed to cause him physical pain, for he twitched whenever his father spoke of 'pride' and 'honour.'

That night Huaypalcon vented his heart in the command tent. "This war is over, father. Our Sapa Inca is dead. Their Sapa Inca is among the enemies hunting us. Our army is shrinking. What are we fighting for?"

Outside the wind howled across the mountainside. I sat silent. I did not have a good answer.

"Time," Kiskis said, and I turned to him in surprise, for he spoke as if he knew exactly what he was talking about.

Huaypalcon did not. "Time? Time for what? For a last stand, and one more last stand, and one more? We've extracted ourselves from six major engagements since Xauxa. We can't win."

"So what would you have us do, Son? Submit?" Kiskis was an old man now, and he spoke with an old man's farsight. "This is the end, Huaypalcon. All we can do is decide how we meet it. I would meet it as an Inca general. I would do something to show that I resist the end. How will you meet it?"

But Huaypalcon spoke with the hot-blooded immediacy of youth, and the grumbles of support from the legion commanders spurred him on. "We should surrender now, while we're still a sufficient threat to win privilege with these Bearded Ones. They will need Inca soldiers the same way the Emperor did."

"Really?" Kiskis's tone of derision was worthy of a court bard. "Because it seems to me they've done just fine without us so far, and more of them are arriving every day. There are twice as many Bearded Ones in Quitu chasing Rumiñaui as there are behind us, did you know that? And how long are they going to need anyone to fight for them once we surrender? What do you think you are going to get from them that is worth your pride?"

I barely saw the flash, and I was too old and slow to stop it. The bronze dagger was out of Huaypalcon's belt and buried in his father's belly before I could move. "We surrender or we die!" Huaypalcon shouted.

My mace went up and down, up and down. I did not realize what I was doing. My son's childhood friend died by my hand, but I am glad I did it. I did not want Huaypalcon to live in a world without Kiskis. The war council buzzed with noise. I ordered them all out, to go if that's what they wanted to do. To a man they left. I did not care.

My old friend called to me from under his son; I pulled Huaypalcon to one side and held Kiskis in my arms. The dark blood of his liver welled up from around the knife in his abdomen, his own son's knife. "I always knew that boy would be the finish of me, but I didn't see this coming," his voice was so strong that for a moment I deluded myself that Kiskis could survive, but the packed snow of the tent floor was not pink with blood. It was black, black as the night outside.

My friend was looking at the crumpled form beside him. "Did you kill my son, Haylli?"

"Yes."

"You don't sound very sorry."

"I'm not."

He smiled his crooked smile at me, and then he took a deep shuddering breath as he accepted the seriousness of his wound. "We need time, Haylli," he told me, and I despaired, for the earlier strength was gone and the death rattle was in his voice.

"I know, Kiskis," I said, holding him close, but my friend was not being rhetorical. He gripped my tunic and pulled me closer.

"No! I mean we need time, real time. There is one last victory to win for our people, one last way to beat these greedy foreigners. We've been working on it since before Chalcuchima's death. Rumiñaui and I have a plan!"

I shook my head, sad that my friend would take his last moments to babble. "There is no way to bring Tahuantinsuyu back to the way it was, Kiskis. The Spaniards will always be a part of us now."

"No, not an uprising, Haylli, listen to me!" The old general sagged in my arms. "What do the Spaniards truly want here? Gold and silver and jewels, right?" All I could see was the dagger sticking out of his belly and the black snow beneath him. Outside the wind howled and howled. Hot tears streamed down my face.

"Listen," he begged me again. "We have it. Almost all of it. All of Atauhuallpa's treasures, the riches of Tumipampa and Quitu, and a lot of the Cuzco wealth too. Our territories never contributed to Atauhuallpa's ransom caravans. We're going to hide it, Haylli. We're going to bury all of it where the Spaniards will never find it!"

Through my tears I saw a glimmer of hope, of pride, of that noble thought that had always infused the Children of the Sun. Even in defeat we could rob the Spaniards of their victory. "Where?" I asked.

"I don't know," Kiskis murmured, mustering the nerve to look down at the haft of the dagger sticking out of him. He winced and looked away. "Ask Rumiñaui. I was supposed to divert attention from him while he hid it. He will need you now, Haylli. He will need you."

A liver wound is inevitable, but it is not quick. The black blood flowed and Kiskis died whimpering at the pain of it, but I choose not to remember that. What I warm myself with is the memory of my friend's pride, right up until the end. He died an Inca general, and I swore he would have his final triumph.

The army disbanded that night. Every soldier just stood up and walked away in different directions. I suppose I did too. I walked towards Quitu and Rumiñaui. I sent word by the chaski post to Manco in Cuzco: As long as he was the pet Sapa Inca of the Bearded Ones he did not have the Tocoyricoc Haylli Yupanki Yachapa on his side, but if that should ever change he should let me know; in the meantime, I had something pressing to do.

* * *

The Kingdom of Quitu was first conquered by Topa Inca Yupanki, then resubjugated by Huayna Capac, then harried and harnessed by Atauhuallpa to march into battle on his behalf. Now Rumiñaui and two Spanish armies were tearing the battered kingdom apart again, with Rumiñaui waging a total war that included the destruction of every community he abandoned. Smoke and ruin appeared everywhere on the horizon, guiding me to his pickets as if he were sending me a personally tied invitation.

"Take me to Rumiñaui," I ordered the jungle archers who challenged me. Their arrows were as long as I was tall, and in this lawless land I wondered why they did not kill me and my small following rather than take my orders. They seemed not to have the wit to wonder but did as they were told. Rumiñaui was staying in a tampu surrounded by fields planted with peanuts, and as I rode my litter up to him I watched the general point all around him, men running at each gesture with brands, prybars, and footplows to tear down all the buildings and turn under the planted crops. This tampu would be worthless by the end of the day.

"Hello," I said, descending from my litter.

"Hello!" He called, a smile breaking his otherwise emotionless face, so that many of his aides froze in surprise, not believing their eyes. We embraced like long-lost brothers, and as we did so it occurred to me that I had not seen him since the night Pariwana Cumpi was murdered. He must have been having the same thought, for he said, "I missed you at Caxamalca!"

"You were at Caxamalca?"

"I left the day before Atauhuallpa's capture. I was manning the pass behind the Bearded Ones in case they decided to run rather than receive him." He laughed, and again his aides could not have looked more surprised if their general was dancing with a drunken bear. "I suppose Atauhuallpa didn't quite have every possibility worked out ahead of time, eh? He always was a bit weak on strategy."

"You got up here fast enough, then," I said. "Kiskis says you've got something you could use my help with?"

"Yes! Yes! I do." My old friend slapped his thigh with enthusiasm. "Where is that old womanizer? Now that I'm destroying all the Houses of Chosen Women I've got a few beauties he might like to see." His grin was boyish under his grey hair, still youthful because he had used it so rarely in his long life.

"Kiskis is dead," I said.

The smile disappeared, and Rumiñaui returned to his normal mask of stony indifference. "How?" he asked flatly.

"His son did it."

He absorbed this for a moment. "And his son?"

"I killed Huaypalcon."

"Good," Rumiñaui said. He looked around for a moment, watching his men destroy what had taken years of hard labour to build. His face did not even twitch, but tears filled his eyes and streamed down his face. He adjusted his Socso Panaca headband, trying to hide his tears from me with his arm. He spoke in a normal voice.

"Yes, Kiskis and Chalcuchima and I have gathered almost every scrap of gold and silver between Caxamalca and here, and we're ready to hide it. I've assembled a workforce to do it, too, but these Spaniards won't give me a moment's peace, Haylli... Not one moment's peace..." He wiped at his eyes with the back of his hand, his nostrils starting to flare as he tried to control his breathing.

"It's okay," I said, reaching out to hug him.

He batted my hands away, angrily. "I want you to go down into the hacha hacha, Haylli, and you've got to put the treasure somewhere that the Bearded Ones will never find. Even if they do find it, they won't know what it is and they'll ignore it. Do you know what I'm saying?"

I do not think even he knew what he was saying, but he was a general, not an administrator. Hiding things is like storing things, and I had been in charge of storing things since I was eight years old. "Yes, I can do that," I said to the last of my school friends.

"Then go. For my part, I'll hold off these Bearded Ones for as long as I can, and if they give me time there won't be a wall left standing in all of the Kingdom of Quitu. We'll set up communications with you to keep you informed of what I'm doing—"

"And I want to know what's going on at Cuzco," I said. "I'm still hoping Manco will come to his senses down there."

"Manco?" Rumiñaui asked.

"Another prince. You never met him," I said.

"How many damned sons did Huayna Capac have?" He muttered, speaking gruffly now to cover the last of his tears. "You know I even had one of those princes made into a drinking cup? Remember Prince Illescas? Bastard tried to stab me in my sleep when I stopped taking orders from Atauhuallpa. What did he think I was going to do? I've had enough of those brats. Huascar murdered my father. Atauhuallpa destroyed his panaca. I'm supposed to listen to those boys? Hey Parinango! Bring out that cup I made!"

By the time the cup arrived all of his tears were gone, which I am sure was the real purpose for his order. I dutifully looked at the cup: Illescas's polished skull with a golden bowl set inside and a golden straw coming out his nasal cavity. I remembered very little about the boy, except that he had been a good flute player.

It was my turn to cry now, cry at the waste and loss of generations. I was not angry with Rumiñaui for this act of brutality: Inca generals had been making cups out of their enemies since the sinchi Manco Capac came out of the hills and conquered the muddy huts of ancient Cuzco, but this last little cruelty was one too many for me.

When I stood before the oracle of Pachacamac as a boy and my whole life still lay before me the god had said, "You will have many children who are not your own. They will do things that make you weep, and they will cost you more than you would ever pay." Now I held the skull of another one of Huayna Capac's sons, and knew I would have smothered each prince in the cradle to keep all this from happening. Tahuantinsuyu was gone. My life's work had been for nothing. It was too much for me.

Soon I was sitting in the dust of the road sobbing, Rumiñaui was trying to comfort me without appearing weak in front of his men. Finally he resorted to military discipline. "Haylli! Get up! Take the damned cup with you if the boy meant that much to you. I'll buy you time. You do your job. We'll discuss all this later."

I could not speak, could not explain myself. I tried to say I did not even remember the boy's face, but all I could do was choke and blubber. I do not think words can encapsulate the despair that overwhelmed me there in that field of peanuts, Friar.

Up until this page that you are writing on, my life was dedicated to the well-ordered and efficient system of Inca bureaucracy that brought prosperity to all the peoples of Tahuantinsuyu. Now, with that cup in my hand, there would never be such a thing again. The Quitu Wars we would have recovered from, the plague too. Even after the political purges and the War Between the Brothers I could have rebuilt the system in time, despite a third of the Empire being struck down. All of that could have been mended. I would have yearned for the good old days, but Tahuantinsuyu in some form would have endured.

This, this present nightmare, the Spanish Pachacuti, we will never recover from, Friar. The Land of the Four Quarters of the World is gone and nothing will ever bring it back. The people who built it and cared for it are dead or powerless, and the countless faceless masses that benefited will suffer and dwindle and die.

The loss and the disappointment that I could do nothing about it was like a physical blow. One of my Rucanas helped me climb back onto my litter, and my eyes were too filled with tears to see Rumiñaui as they carried me away from him. We had said no proper goodbyes, and it was the last time I would ever see my oldest surviving friend.

* * *

Rumiñaui had filled one of the eastern-most tampus in the Kingdom of Quitu with all the treasures gathered from half the Empire, as well as a veritable army of porters and drovers, hunters and foragers, masons and carpenters, soldiers and bureaucrats. Numbering in the tens of thousands, I believe there was more skilled workers assembled there than anywhere else in our poor and battered Tahuantinsuyu. There was also one person I had never expected to see again.

"You?" I asked, wonderstruck.

"Me," she said with her usual reserved composure. She stood in a doorway, dressed in a simple white cotton dress that came down to her calves. She would never have to wear a green dress again in this new world of ours. It was the Cañari woman who had become Mama Ocllo's Voice. I had last seen her at Speaker's Field, just before the final battle in the War Between the Brothers.

"How did you get here?" I looked around at the cloud-blanketed hills of this distant tampu, as if she had chosen to come here at random from all the other places in the world she might have gone.

"When Cuzco was looted Atauhuallpa gave special orders that Mama Ocllo's oracle was to be taken back to Tumipampa. I can't imagine how he forgot he leveled the city, but he must have. When my escort got to Tumipampa they didn't know what to do, and by that time Atauhuallpa had been captured, so they deserted and went back to their homes in Quitu. I didn't have any better ideas, so I followed them. General Rumiñaui took one look at the gold idol of Mama Ocllo and sent me here."

"Are you a prisoner?" I asked.

"I suppose I'm free to walk away at any time, but the idol is here on Rumiñaui's orders, and I will stay with the idol."

"She was a bitter old crone, you know."

"I know," she said simply.

"You heard what happened to your Cañari?"

"I saw it. I saw Tumipampa. I saw the fields of bones."

"I'm sorry," I said. It was paltry compensation for the destruction of her people, but it was the best I had to offer.

"You didn't do it," she said, her tone understanding.

I turned to the quipucamayocs who had come at the run upon word of my arrival. I gave a series of brisk, business-like orders, and they dispersed across the tampu, breaking camp and getting people organized. When I turned back she was still standing there in the doorway, but she was smiling now.

"What?" I asked.

"You really are a funny man, sometimes."

I asked her what she meant by that, but she just shook her head and went inside. I had too much to do to follow her. I had a mission, a last victory of defiance to win.

We traveled into the hacha hacha on game trails, thousands of porters walking into jungle so thick that the foliage brushed both their shoulders with each step. I would not allow the building of a proper road. There must be no way to follow us.

When we were deep enough into the headhunting Jivaro territory to guarantee the Spaniards would not follow us I established a camp for my workers and set about surveying a likely site to hide the treasure. It had to be underground and it had to be big, and when the treasure was hidden the whole thing needed to be protected and disguised.

After I found all these things we set to work, my porters now doubling as quarriers, masons, excavators, plasterers. Every day our priests sacrificed coca and guinea pigs to promise us success. Every night I took a little more of the golden treasure to bribe the Jivaro to keep us safe.

As I said, we had no road, which meant we had no chaskis, so every few days I sent a man down the game trails back to the nearest chaski hut to collect the accumulated dispatches. The news was never good, but it kept me informed.

The Spaniards were now everywhere, arriving in numbers that sounded small until one remembered that our entire way of life had been destroyed by just one hundred and sixty of them at Caxamalca. Almagro was taking five hundred and seventy Spaniards and twelve thousand of our own soldiers under Paullu Inca on an expedition into Tchili, where he hoped to find cities as rich as Cuzco to plunder.

Somehow he never bothered to ask an Inca about that end of Collasuyu; I would have been delighted to tell him all about it from personal experience: The Atacama Desert, the frozen mountains, the switchback ridges of pine forests, the barren wastes. What a pleasure to think it was all inflicted on one of the most avaricious Bearded Ones, and after all of it he would have less gold than if he had dug up the garden of my villa in the Yucay Valley.

It was clever of Manco to volunteer his brother Paullu as Almagro's guide. Paullu was an expert on Collasuyu, thanks to my sending him there during the Mad Hummingbird's purges, and Paullu was also the very last possible claimant to the Red Fringe aside from Manco.

Not that the Red Fringe was much of a prize anymore: Manco was not free to leave Cuzco, and when the trickle of gold he could provide to the Spaniards had a dry spell they took to shackling him, insulting his wives and stealing his possessions. One of Pizarro's brothers even demanded to marry Manco's Coya. All this, of course, did not sit well with his young and prideful heart, and he began sending me messages that he was considering an uprising. I wished him well, I said, but I was busy.

And my work had to be done fast, Friar, for Rumiñaui could give me no more time. When I finished my principle excavation word arrived that Rumiñaui's fifty thousand had engaged the Spaniards on the side of a mountain and fought a bloody battle that resulted in the Bearded Ones being cornered. In the night a Cayambi in the Spaniard's service had shown them a secret path out of their predicament, and they retreated in secret while leaving their cooking fires burning.

When the dawn showed Rumiñaui's army the previous day's hard slaughter had been for nothing, tens of thousands deserted him. He was never again to go on the offensive, instead running from mountain vastness to mountain vastness, losing men all the way, just as Kiskis had done. Finally, as my work was almost complete, the volcano of Tungueahua under which Rumiñaui was encamped erupted and his remaining soldiers took this as a sign of the gods' displeasure. They surrendered their general to the white men and went back to their devastated villages.

The dispatches said the Spaniards tortured him. Before he died he told the Spaniards, "My friend Haylli has your gold, and you will never find it!" And my heart dropped when I heard that, but after a moment I realized that would be translated into Spanish as, "My friend Victory has your gold, and you will never find it!" Even though my friend broke, the Spaniards took it for defiance, or perhaps he knew how it would be received. I do not know. They killed him, and my messenger said they did it slowly.

A year and a half had passed since I began my work, and I had enjoyed the difficulty of it, the challenge. I had never supervised a construction project on that scale before, and when I would come back to my rude hut at night —not even as nice as the home Koonek and I had shared down among the Mapuche— I would muse to Mama Ocllo's Voice that I wished I had known the joys of building earlier in my life. It would have been within my power to supervise the construction of the great fortresses of Intihuasi or Ollantaytampu if I had only known what I was missing.

She would smile her composed smile at me then, and we were happy together, even if I was a damned old fool and she was a middle-aged priestess who was supposed to be celibate.

I put everything into the place when it was finished, and not just the gold and the silver and the jewels: Those things were important to the Bearded Ones, Friar, but they only mattered to me because by hiding them I would cause your kind some small portion of the grief you have brought to the Inca in such abundance.

No, what I built out there in the jungle was the last repository of Tahuantinsuyu's greatness, and so I filled it with thousands of huacas, including my own personal ones: My father and Huaman Paullu's mummy bundles and my lancehead dagger, carried with me all the way from Cuzco. I know my father would have approved of the spot as his final resting place. For myself I kept only the history I hold now in my hands. I suspected even then I would have to make a Spanish version of it.

I was tempted not to put Mama Ocllo's idol inside, for I did not think of it as a huaca worth saving, but her Voice convinced me to do it. "With it buried, I'm free."

"You're free now," I said.

"No. I'm here because it is here."

This was news to me. I thought she was there because of me. With a sudden, sinking feeling I asked, "Where will you go when all this is over?"

She smiled her composed smile. "I think I would like to live out the rest of my days in a Chacapoyan House of Chosen Women."

"A House of Chosen Women?" I felt like a rock had hit me between the eyes. I was stunned.

"I've spent most of my life in houses of chosen women, but the Chacapoyan ones are beautiful, half way up mountains that are draped in white clouds, surrounded by flowers and hummingbirds and butterflies. And when I die they'll bury me in a cliff face so I will have that view for all eternity."

I knew I was about to argue against a woman's plans for eternity, but I had to try. "Well, I thought, when this was done, you and I could—"

"Oh, Haylli, you are funny," she laughed her mellow laugh. "You're almost seventy! You don't need another wife. Whether I am with you or not, you are going to spend the rest of your days playing with your strings. Let me spend the rest of my life gazing out over beauty and peace."

I looked at her, the last woman I will ever love, and I could not deny her simple desire. I was an old fool, almost twice her age. I nodded, and she gave me a chaste kiss on the cheek. I ordered Mama Ocllo's golden idol to be given a place of honour among the collection, then I sealed it all up, offering great sacrifices to Urca Huari, the guardian of underground treasures.

My people were now ready for the most important part of the plan, making it look like we were never there. We took our excavated rock, basket by basket, and dumped it into dozens of different streams and rivers. We burned our camp and then planted hundreds of saplings so that within a few years it would be as densely forested as the rest of the jungle. I accounted for every prybar and chisel, digging stick and length of rope, so that we would leave no telltale clues behind.

Then I had our priests and the Jivaro shamans agree the whole place was cursed and we walked back towards Quitu, destroying the game trail as we went by pulling down trees, planting new ones, and, in one case, triggering a landslide that also diverted a stream. I was satisfied we were untraceable. I thanked my workers and set them free to scatter, returning to their homes or staying in Quitu, whatever they desired.

Mama Ocllo's Voice kissed me goodbye and said, "This isn't the end for us." I have never seen her since. She did not go any further towards Quitu: She just walked south through the hacha hacha towards Chacapoyan territory.

As for me, I went to check up on Manco.

461

Friar, the end of the world awaited me as I walked out of the hacha hacha. I went through the Kingdom of Quitu and along the Royal Mountain Road, and everywhere I looked I was struck by how far Tahuantinsuyu had tattered and frayed without the Intip Churi holding the strings.

The road was filled with people, but they were not going about their business: They were drifting from place to place, without a plan, just trying to avoid where they had been without any idea of where to go. Dead men and women hung from the trees by the roadside, their crimes a mystery. My litter attracted hostile stares and comments from the purics we passed, and so one night I had it chopped into firewood and from then on I walked with my Rucanas.

Everywhere there was lawlessness and banditry. Coca consumption — once limited to nobles, chaskis and men working in the high mountain passes— was now rampant among the commoners. I saw one man digging up an old battlefield from the Quitu Wars to steal the golden earplugs of the fallen pacuyoks: The white man's lust for gold is contagious.

As I left the Kingdom of Quitu things became a little better, but now the people I passed seemed to be waiting for something, orders to come to set them in motion again. They stood in their courtyards and plazas and market squares and sang mournful songs while they waited. Their tampus emptied. No one ordered them to fill them again. Shipments of guano and other fertilizers no longer arrived from the coast. The harvest would be bad. Without tax-labour service commoners had free time outside the State holidays that gave structure to their leisure, so they drank and quarreled without an authority to intervene.

But as I got still closer to Cuzco an interesting thing began to happen: Other people were walking towards the Royal City, and not aimlessly, either. These were almost all men, and each carried a rough cabuya fibre bag over one shoulder filled with chuno and charqui, a pot, a sling, and a mace. My inquiries were met with some suspicion, but I coaxed from them that Manco Inca had summoned a great muster at Sacsahuaman. I looked up and down the road, but the chaski huts were empty and still. No conch trumpets sounded. "Are you sure?"

"Would I walk all this way if I wasn't sure?"

"Well who is he marching against? Is there a rebellion somewhere?"

The man looked at me as if I was deranged. "A rebellion? He has to take care of the Bearded Ones first."

"But they'll kill him!" I said.

"Where have you been that you haven't heard? Manco's escaped!" And so the puric told me a story too fantastic to believe. Manco, chained and insulted, had asked one of the Pizarro brothers to allow him to leave Cuzco and visit one of his palaces in the Yucay valley.

The conquistador refused of course, so Manco sweetened the offer by promising to return with a life-sized golden statue of his father, Huayna Capac. I smiled when I heard this, for the statue in question was among the treasures I had just hidden from the Spaniards out in the hacha hacha. Out from under Castilian control, Manco disappeared, sending out a summons for a great army to marshal on Cuzco to drive out the white men.

"But how can we beat so many of them?" I asked.

"There are less than two hundred in Cuzco, and only eighty horses. Most of them are in Tchili or Quitu or Tumpez or with their leader Pizarro out in the Rimac Valley building a city. They are scattered all over the place."

I smiled, for I knew we had nothing to lose. We would roll the die and hope we got the twenty. As I got closer to Cuzco I began walking through the night as well as the day, stopping to nap under the shade of trees rather than staying in the overcrowded, understaffed and nearly exhausted tampus. I crested the first ridge overlooking Cuzco on an overcast night, and the undersides of the clouds reflected a red brighter than the full moon. Cuzco was burning.

My Rucanas and I broke into a run, and so did everyone else. It was unthinkable. The Royal City had been disgraced before, in the plague, in the War Between the Brothers, by the pillaging Spaniards, but never like this: The whole city was in flames. From the foot of Sacsahuaman to the Coricancha, every thatched roof was burning.

Even as I ran towards Cuzco I could see red hot slingstones from atop the Intihuasi fortress rain down on the Holy City, long after the fires were already uncontrollable. Every palace, every building would be ruined. It was the end, and as I got closer the wind shifted and blew smoke into my eyes, but that was not why I was crying.

We would never rebuild it. I knew that. Cuzco was gone, just like everything else that I had ever loved, save only Cayo Topa now. I was overwhelmed with the need to see him again. I entered the fortress of Intihuasi and made my way up the battlements, my joints aching from their long run. Every face I passed was lit by the flames below.

"Cayo!" I called, for I saw his form silhouetted by the inferno below.

He turned and strained his eyes, making me out at last. "Haylli!" We embraced, and he held me close as he said into my ear, "Never leave us again! I'm so sorry I didn't go with you before. I thought that was the end of us."

"I'm home to stay," I promised. He let go of me, and we both turned, irresistibly, to look at the ruin of the greatest place in the world. "Wherever home ends up being," I murmured. "Where's Manco?" I looked around, but I saw no place that looked like it had been set up as an Imperial court.

"The Fortress of Ollantaytampu. We decided having him too close to the Spaniards could end badly for us. The Yucay is near enough."

I did not imagine that going over well with Manco, but I held my peace. "So who's in charge?"

"They must be dead!" I heard a voice say. A young man dressed in a strange collection of priestly and martial garb was looking down onto the burning capital. "I have men completely encircling the city. If anyone tries to leave we will cut them down with slings and arrows, and if they stay they'll cook. The white men are dead!" He called again, and his men roared their approval of his words.

"You command here?" I asked.

He looked up from the devastation below. "Yes."

"Who are you?" I asked, amazed at the thought that so many of the great men of Tahuantinsuyu were dead that I had no idea who this boy was. The plugs in his ears were not even the width of my little finger, but he was responsible for the siege of Royal Cuzco.

"I'm Vilauma, Manco Inca's High Priest. Who are you?"

I grimaced, for his name was a Colla one meaning 'Blood Drinker.' How far had we fallen that we could no longer find an Inca of the Blood to be high priest? He must have been a mere school friend of Manco's. "I'm Haylli Yupanki."

"Who?" He asked, his tone holding no respect.

464

"How long have you been High Priest that you don't know who I am?"

"A year. How long have you been wherever in Supay's name you've been, old man?"

"Almost two years."

"Well then, it's a pleasure to meet you. Welcome to the party, even if you are late." He turned back to the fire with satisfaction. The reflection of the flames danced across his chest disk. "They must be dead!" He said again with passion.

But the Spaniards were not dead, Friar, though they do attribute their survival to a miracle, the only Christian miracle I have ever witnessed: The conquistadores and the purics who served them could not fight the fires nor find shelter in any building, so they gathered in the Hua-caypata with impassable fires all around them, and they waited through that terrible night, restraining their blindfolded horses from running into the oblivion of flame down every street.

All the while they cowered there in Cuzco's great plaza they were aware of the barrels of gunpowder they had hastily buried in the sand, gunpowder that needed only a single spark to turn their safe haven into a worse hell than the one around them.

The heat must have been incredible, the smoke suffocating, but when dawn broke over the smoldering city the men of Castile and their allies were all still alive. We had destroyed Royal Cuzco for nothing.

"Into the city!" Vilauma ordered. He would not be deterred, and younger men than Cayo and I ran down the ash-filled streets to be cut down by the Spanish horsemen. Vilauma revised his tactics, building wicker barriers in all the roads to stop the horses and sending sling-ers out to walk along the tops of the roofless walls to hurl their stones down onto the Spaniards below. The Bearded Ones' puric allies, though, fought with the tenacity of doomed men, and we could not succeed in breaking them. No soldier could storm a city that was now just a series of stone walls and rubble. It was too defensible.

So we opened up the flood gates on the reservoirs upstream to wash them out, then we tried to starve them, for there was no food left in the city. We dug stake-lined pits and smaller leg-breaking holes to deter the horses from going out to pasture to graze, and we destroyed all the tampus close enough to be raidable except the one inside the Intihuasi fortress. So, starving, that's where the Spaniards went, the Intihuasi fortress.

The fighting was savage, Friar, savage, and good men fell whose names I never learned. They went from nobodies to heroes to dead men in this last great rebellion, and it grieves me that my story cannot include their names. The only one I learned from Vilauma before we had to abandon the fortress was that of Cahuite, a great giant of a man, armed and armoured like a Spaniard, who defended Intihuasi's tallest tower for two days before hurling himself from its top rather than surrendering.

It was beautiful and glorious and incredible, and a waste. In the end the Spaniards succeeded in capturing Intihuasi, and Vilauma's forces split between falling back on Manco in the Yucay Valley and going south with the warrior high priest into the Collao, those who did not go home to their farms at this latest reversal. Cayo and I chose to go to Manco.

The conquistadores pursued us, vengeance in their hearts for the long hardships we had made them endure, but Ollantaytampu was unassailable, built along the side of a cliff with an entrance an infant could have defended. Besides, the Bearded Ones' way of fighting held no mystery for us anymore, and Manco had learned much from the Spaniards in his captivity, even riding a horse into battle and arming his best soldiers with Spanish weaponry and armour. No, we easily held them at the base of the fortress's pink stone walls, then we sent them back to Cuzco like whipped dogs with their tails between their legs, but the victory brought me no joy. I knew we had run our race, and now we must face reality.

Tahuantinsuyu was dead, Friar, and nothing we could do would bring it back. Manco's great rebellion had been the death throws of my empire, and though it had shaken the very earth with its thrashing, we could not bring life back to the corpse of the empire of the Children of the Sun. It was a hard truth, but I knew to stay would bring us nothing, whereas to flee into Andesuyu would leave us some small place to call home, however mean.

I entered the Imperial Presence with Cayo, barefoot and burdened, blowing my Emperor a kiss before straightening up to join him in looking out over the valley below us. Manco had a Spanish breastplate and helmet on, and he was smiling. "It's over, Manco," I said.

"What do you mean?" his smile faded.

"I mean it is over. We have to go." We stood there in the sunshine, the beautiful Yucay Valley stretched out below us, and the wind dropped away, a sign that I wished the Bird Man Topa Cusi Yupanki was still alive to interpret for me.

"Go where?" He asked.

My Sapa Inca is not dense. I honestly think, after Ninan Cuyuchi, he is the most able of all Huayna Capac's many sons. His confusion was a mental block: Manco thinks like an Emperor, and an Emperor does not see the inevitable defeat after a victory. "Go into the jungle, as far into the hacha hacha as we have to so the Spaniards can't find us, Sire."

"But, but the rebellion! We didn't take Cuzco, but we swept up the scattered Spaniards throughout Chincaysuyu; we have them besieged in the new city they're building near Pachacamac, and Vilauma's in a position to run free throughout Collasuyu!"

"No, Sire," I murmured. "If we couldn't take Cuzco, we can't prevail. We have no way of coordinating or reinforcing any part of the rebellion, and we're trapped here. It's over." Beside me Cayo nodded his agreement.

Manco was not angry with us, and that is the proof of his intelligence. "How can it be over, Haylli?" He seemed truly mystified, this young man who had become an Emperor despite having fifty older brothers, this boy who had never lived in untroubled times really seemed surprised that things would never be normal again.

"How did it start in the first place, Manco? What right did the Inca have to be better than the Chanca or the Chimu or the Colla?"

"Inti promised—"

"We did it, and then we said Inti told us to do it." I was cruel with him.

"What?"

"Our Imperial history is no more real than the one Atauhuallpa was going to create. We were just good conquerors and administrators. That's all we were."

"But we were the Inca!"

"We are the Inca, and you are still the Sapa Inca, and Andesuyu is still yours, the parts that the Spanish don't want, anyway. Rule them, Manco. Go into exile down there, kill any Spaniards who cross into your territory, and leave them up here with the gold and silver they love so much."

He sighed, and for a moment I saw the spirit of a Sapa Inca shudder at a mighty blow. "We can hold here in Ollantaytampu forever," he said, but there was no conviction in his voice.

It was Cayo who spoke now. "Remember what I told you about the Huarco, Sire? The tribe that never cheats on their taxes? No fortress can be defended forever. We can hold Ollantaytampu until the storehouses run out in a few years. At that point you will be Sapa Inca of an emaciated garrison, surrounded by the Bearded Ones."

Manco looked down into the Yucay valley, and I think we all imagined our bones down there, as the Huarco skeletons littered the beach below their final refuge.

I cleared my throat to make sure I would speak without my voice breaking. "Better to have a small kingdom in the hacha hacha forever than to hold onto a palace in the Yucay at the expense of your children."

That did it. Manco had many young sons, and we all saw in them a hope for the future that we could not find in the present. "Order the evacuation, Haylli," he whispered.

"Yes, Sire." I backed out of the room, the burden on my back feeling light as a feather.

* * *

So we retreated into the jungle, pursued and harried for much of the way by you Spaniards, but the hacha hacha does not love the white men any more than the mountain men. This is a place for the jungle archer, and Cayo and I recruited them by the thousands, offering them all the trappings of civilization without leaving their forest home.

They fight for us, and today Manco's Imperial guardsmen are all cannibals, Friar. The only gold we have left out here is our earplugs and the great sun disk of Punchao, the Day, that we managed to take from the Coricancha before the Spaniards looted it. That's not enough of a prize to lure the Bearded Ones here, and when they need reminding of that, our archers give it to them.

We have had many adventures in the last few years, but in truth we are nothing better than bandits. We come out of the hacha hacha and retreat back into its depths, and that is the end of it. The people in the mountains starve, and slave themselves to death working in the Spanish silver mine of Potosi, and we can do nothing for them. I can do nothing for them. I must say, 'As!' for I am an old man, and I am out of ideas. The Inca are meaningless now in the world of Spanish subjugation.

That's not to say we are not still hated and feared. The Spaniards sent men to us demanding Manco surrender himself and his children back into their care. The Sapa Inca had the men killed, so the white men took one of Manco's sisters in Cuzco, tied her to a tree, scourged her, shot her with arrows, then put her body in a basket and floated it down the Urupampa River to us. That's the kind of relationship we have with them, but mostly they just leave us alone.

They don't need Manco Inca for their puppet: Paullu returned with Almagro's exhausted and disappointed men from Tchili; he has become their new and utterly loyal pet Sapa Inca, even leading armies to put down revolts loyal to Manco, fighting from the back of a horse with a sword in his hand, cutting down his own people for his Spanish masters.

Paullu sent me a message once, written in Spanish on paper, offering me a full pardon if only I would come back to Cuzco and show the Spaniards how Tahuantinsuyu is supposed to be run. I did not reply. I have made my choice as to how to live out the rest of my days. Paullu is dead to me now.

I take some small satisfaction in that it seems our conquerors will not live to enjoy their spoils: With the hardships of Tchili bringing him nothing, Almagro demanded half of all that the Pizarro brothers gathered in his absence. When he was refused their armies broke out in open war, with both sides heavily recruiting purics to fight alongside the Spaniards.

Seven of Almagro's men left him just before his defeat, and they live with us now in this city under Manco's protection, teaching us the white man's ways of war. Meanwhile, the Pizarros are about to face a new conflict with their Spanish superiors back home in Castile. They have declared their independence just as Atauhuallpa tried to do, and the King of Spain has refused it to them. I predict the Pizarros will come to no better end than Atauhuallpa did.

As for me, I run this small corner of what was once Tahuantinsuyu, and I teach Manco's children, and I talk to you. Those are my remaining tasks in life until I die and go to the Upper Universe, where all the friends of my story save only Manco are waiting for me.

No, I do not forget Cayo Topa when I say that, and I did wonder how long we were going to work at this before you asked to meet him. I'm afraid the curse of knowing me caught up with him too. My dear friend is dead.

469

Because I sent Cayo to keep Manco safe during Huascar's purges, our last Sapa Inca came to rely on my son-in-law the way Huayna Capac relied on me. After we arrived here in the hacha hacha, Manco wanted Cayo Topa to lead an embassy to the Chacapoyas to try to bring them back to our side, a foolish, stupid hope. I did not want him to go, of course. If Manco was determined to go through the fool's errand of a diplomatic mission to a people we have exploited and abused for the last seventy years I asked him to send me. I have Chacapoyan blood in me from my mother's side, so at least they might hear me out.

Manco said he could not spare me, but when I pointed out he needed Cayo too he told me my son-in-law had demanded to go, had felt sure he could convince the Cloud People that their future still lay with the Intip Churi. I know my friend really went to save me, to let me do this thing with you, the last great project of my life. When he walked through the city gates for the final time he reminded me of the oracle's prophecy that he would not be there for me in my old age. We all must accept the fate handed down to us. He held his head high as he left. I wept.

Cayo traveled through the jungle and over the mountains and met their lord, Huaman. He told my son-in-law, "Because the Bearded Ones are clearly never going to return to Castile but will always be here, we are all going to have to become Christians. And since you Inca have always betrayed us you are going to die," Then he burned Cayo Topa alive.

I knew Cayo as a boy, chose him to follow in my footsteps, wed him to my daughter. In every way he was a better son to me than Anka ever was. In my mind he was always going to be here, the shoulder for me to lean on in my old age. I miss him. I miss him so much.

The leaderless embassy that returned to tell us of his death brought another piece of news that I will share with you: Mama Ocllo's Voice has born me a healthy child who will be raised in a Chacapoyan temple. I wonder if it is a boy or a girl? I suppose I will never know. It is death for a pacuyok to enter Chacapoyan territory now, so I must be content to know that some small part of me will live on somewhere, somewhere far enough removed that the curse of associating with me will not bring about a tragic end.

Why have I lived so long and seen so many people I love die? Why have I watched the world that I grew up in shatter, and shatter, and shatter again, until only this small and worthless corner of it remains in any semblance of how it once was? Did I so offend the gods that they would not bring me the sweet relief of death long ago?

I sometimes think that for all I have endured I must be a coward to have lived this long. Why did I not jump on the guardsmen's halberds when Atauhuallpa raped my daughter? Or risk the guardsmen's wrath when Huascar murdered Huayna Capac's funeral procession? Or run less swiftly when the Spaniards cut down the flower of Atauhuallpa's nobles with their swords? In any of those cases I could have died with honour, but I did not. Is it cowardice to have resisted those deaths, or am I brave in my willingness to live on in a world that sees such horrors? I do not know. I suppose it does not matter.

No, that's not true either. I am trying to spare myself in these pages, but I am not just a coward, Friar. I am a failure and a cheat. As you read me back my life's story I see that now. How self-serving this is! I sound like a good man in troubled times, but I am not. Look at the advantages I was born with. Look at the example my father set, and then look what I did with my life: My two wives died because of the enemies I made. I did not love my own son. The man I loved like a son went to his death for me. I educated the princes who brought about the total destruction of the world I was supposed to protect. I defied my gods.

I am responsible for all of it, for everything! If I had been stronger, smarter, braver, I could have prevented all of this. Instead everyone I know has suffered and died.

I sit here with you, Friar, as we finish our work together, and your questions are making me tired, for I have said all that I want to say. You want me to go back and explain where and whence the names Peru and Andes and Chile come from? I can only say they come from the Spaniards. Never before your coming did we think of Tahuantinsuyu as any of those names. One of the Spaniards I interrogated told me there is a Biru River half-way to Panama that may be the source of the word 'Peru.' I don't know.

As for the Andes, I imagine you found the name from Andesuyu, which is ironic in that it is the jungle quarter of our Empire, whereas it is the other three that straddle the eastern and western mountains. Chile I think you got right, though I have heard that you say you named it after a Mapuche chieftain named Tchili, which means Snow, rather than Tchili itself. No matter.

I weep to think what our history would look like in a hundred years if it was up to the Spanish to record it. Where Tampu becomes Tambo and Caxamalca becomes Cajamarca and Xauxa becomes Jauja on your blunt tongues. And, accents aside, what about the facts? It must be a hopeless muddle by now. Our plagues and purges and civil wars and the Spanish conquest have killed all the men of power and position who might have been in a position to tell you something non-partisan. Just as well I have lived to finish this book. Without it our history will survive only as a self-contradicting jumble.

Ah, I have been waiting for that question: I knew it would come! You ask me to aid you in your revisions by giving more detail about the Treasure Vault I constructed when your glorious conquistadores were pursuing Rumiñaui on a merry chase through the mountains. Yes, I hid the missing gold of Quitu, along with many other treasures, but I will not give you the information you ask. I have deliberately kept those details vague.

You do not protest out loud, but your eyes cannot be silenced. Apparently even a man of God is greedy for gold if he is from Castile. Never mind, I know you would use the treasure for the greater glory of your Lord, building a church in every village and a cathedral in every city in the New World, as you insist on calling Tahuantinsuyu.

I am not against that, in principle, except that upon finding the vault you would dispose of any treasure not made from precious metals and stones, and you would reduce our golden art to ugly lumps. Worse still, your churches would be built by the peoples of this land, but unlike our system where a man works until he is tired, you would work my people to death. No, priest, I have a nobler purpose for those riches.

I propose a pact, a covenant between the future generations of your people and mine not to be realized within either of our lifetimes: My royal quipus have the details you are missing, but no one can read them anymore. In your hand you have a Spanish version, not an exact replica but a faithful translation, of my story.

You will store your copy somewhere safe. For my part my quipus stay with me, and upon my death I have arranged for them to be buried under the flagstone upon which Manco's royal usno sits here in the palace at Vitcos.

One day wise men of our peoples will bring the two copies back together, translate the Spanish into Runa Simi, and puzzle out the quipu to learn the wheres and hows of the treasure. Only the spirit of cooperation will bring that about. This one time violence will not bring the sons of Castile their gold, only peace.

Today your armies cannot find this place in the jungle, but if that ever changes and you come to defile and destroy as you did to Cuzco, the Sapa Inca or his children will move the throne to a different room and the quipus will be lost.

There is no way to cheat this bargain, Friar. It is up to the future whether or not this land shall ever see that gold again. I hold that treasure hostage against the survival of this work, and I know I can rely on Spanish avarice to preserve my tale. The only thing I can truly count on after the Spanish Pachacuti is your greed, and that greed guarantees the immortality of this work, my story, my people's story. If your kind ever want to find my treasure hoard they will not give up this manuscript to feed that insatiable monster that is Time, and a part of my people will live forever within these pages.

Thus ends my story, Friar. I have nothing more to say to you. As a boy I was named Waccha, and though I have become Tocoyricoc Haylli Yupanki Yachapa, husband to two beautiful women, special friend of Sapa Inca Huayna Capac, Viceroy of Andesuyu, Royal Tutor, Capac Quipucamayoc and Hunocamayoc to the Sapa Inca Manco Inca, I will always remain Unfortunate.

I am an Inca.

May the blessing of Our Lord be upon you, honoured sirs, though I confess as I write this I have not decided who you will be. My name is Friar Miguel de Toledo. I am the man to whom the self-described last capac quipucamayoc dictated the memoirs you have just read.

It was my intention to be found in the jungle by the humble Indians dwelling therein, so that I might teach them the ways of God and save them from eternal damnation; instead, I was offered the chance to act as a secretary to a great man among the heathen in exchange for the freedom to preach to the fugitive Incas themselves.

Seeing an opportunity to bring these last and most adamantly strayed sheep into the flock, I agreed, and as time went on I came to see the work I did with Haylli Yupanki as almost the equal of the work I was doing in the service of God.

I wish to begin this post script by assuring you that the Inca did indeed read from the records he described, his 'Royal Quipus.' The knots that record sound do exist. I have observed them close up, and they seem to be a system almost as efficient as our own quill and parchment in recording thoughts for posterity. I must confess, though, that in all our time working together Haylli was well on his way to becoming a man of letters, while I never learned to decipher so much as a single knot of his tangled skeins.

I am respecting the wishes of my captor in not contributing words of my own until this point, the end of the manuscript over which I have worked with Tocoyricoc Haylli Yupanki Yachapa and perhaps a dozen other Spanish and Indian translators for the past several months. It interests me why that instruction was given.

I thought in the beginning that it was because Old Haylli had too much pride to allow me to put in my own comments, to write down where I disagreed with him or did not believe him, or where I might want to soften or explain away his statements. As time passed I came up with a competing theory, one I would like to convey to you now that I have the freedom to do so.

An examination of this work will show that I am the only Spaniard whose exact words are recorded, and I am doing so only after the story of the Inca is already complete. There is nothing in these pages outside of this last note that was conceived in Spanish first instead of Quechua —or Runa Simi, as I have been taught to think of it. Mine are the only thoughts expressed that are not native to these Indians. I admit that humbles me, and so I am choosing my words with care, even though I am writing in haste.

Haylli told me he has not quoted any conquistadores verbatim because he did not tie down their actual words as he was composing his history, but that rings false to my ears: First, I am sure he has already taken some license with the dialogue of quoted personages in his story, just as great historians like Livy and Plutarch have done. Second, I have come to know the capabilities of his memory: He remembers what our countrymen said as clearly today as when he first heard it.

No, the words of Alonso de Molina, Francisco Pizarro, Hernando de Soto, Diego de Almagro and the others are not recorded because Haylli has decided he will not do his conquerors the honour of making them vocal participants in his life's story, despite the tremendous impact they have had upon him and his people. It is one more small revenge he can inflict upon them. I think it just the sort of thing he would do for his own pleasure while denying any calculation on his part when questioned.

As we finished the last revisions to his satisfaction I suggested that I stay longer in case he wished to add more. In truth I was hoping he would convert to the True Faith, for he had kept true to his promise and attended all of my sermons. He listened attentively, and he grasped the concepts and themes of my sermons better than any man I have ever offered the Holy Eucharist. The workings of his mind were truly miraculous, and I often mused with him what a force for Christ he could have been here in the New World if our positions were reversed; he would just laugh and say if he found himself in my place he would never have come to such a God-forsaken place as the jungle city where we sat.

He ordered me to go, promising that the story of his life was now over. May God grant him mercy, he was wrong. I wish I could finish this post script with the news that the old administrator was still working with his strings in the jungle, holding together a tiny fragment of his empire with his firm hands and sage judgments. The truth is that he was betrayed, and the death he had so long escaped finally found him, as it will find us all one day.

As I was preparing to depart, three of the Spaniards from Almagro's army who had been my assistants during my stay decided the time had come to turn on their hosts. They felt that if they murdered the Sapa Inca Manco Inca they could win their pardons from the new men arriving from Spain to take control of Peru from the Pizarros. They entered the throne room in the guise of friendship, but they had only murder in their hearts.

These evil men lunged at Manco with their daggers while he sat upon his usno, and Old Haylli threw himself in front of two of the blades, burying them in his own body to save his Emperor. The third brigand reached Manco Inca and drove his long knife deep into the Sapa Inca's right kidney. I prayed through the night, but their wounds were mortal. Both Inca lords were doomed to slow deaths.

I need hardly say there was a great deal of distress among the Indians. All the Spaniards fled into the forest, leaving me as the only white man in a city screaming for our kind's blood. From my room I listened as a mob began to drive a stake into the central plaza: I was to burn for the crimes of my countrymen. Only direct orders from both Haylli and Manco Inca spared me from the Indians' fury.

Manco survived three days with his wound, long enough to see his murderers punished. The assassins were caught stumbling through the jungle. All of them were roasted alive in the courtyard as man drums boomed and the Incas drank to the memory of their fallen comrades. I was refused permission to give them their final absolution. I think that a terrible punishment, but I will borrow an example from Old Haylli and add one of my own: I will not record the names of men who would so betray people who took them in.

Haylli Yupanki died as peacefully as a man can with two great holes in his body. He had his loyal quipucamayocs set up his pallet outside where he could watch the sunset; then he took a withered grass rope out of his coca bag and rubbed it between his fingers, smiling, until the end came for him. As he waited, Haylli reminded the Emperor of his promise, and Manco gave orders to bury Haylli's history —his covenant with the future, as he called it— under his usno stand.

I offered to baptize Haylli as he lay dying, but he just shook his head and held up his frayed rope, reminding me that a lifetime of thinking one thing to be holy cannot be changed at the moment of death. He said that I was a good man for listening to his ramblings, and he wished me better luck with my God-given mission than his people had had with theirs.

When he closed his eyes for the last time he seemed to sigh, long and deep, but I thought I heard him say, "Koonek." He died as he lived, unchanged and unconverted. I pray for his soul, and I think God will be more merciful to him in death than he was in life. He was a good man. Were he a Christian, I would go so far as to call him virtuous.

I do not look forward to the long journey out of this place. The jungle is like an awe-inspiring green cathedral, with great trees for pillars that soar up to leafy vaults with choirs of birds and monkeys singing their gibberish hymns. It is beautiful and frightening, and I fear it is a place that hates the Spaniards. I feel it in my bones...

I will be ever vigilant to keep the manuscript safe and deposit it in the hands of men I trust to give it the same care. It may one day be the last link to a people I am now convinced deserved all the glory they heaped upon themselves. May God forgive them their hubris.

For any man who would treat this book lightly, I remind you how much gold and silver and turquoise and emeralds our conquistadores say Rumiñaui took up into the mountains with him. They still sift through the ashes and rubble of Quitu, but there is nothing left. All the treasure that accumulated there, brought in by Huayna Capac when he built up Tumipampa and Quitu into capitals the equal of Cuzco, it is all gone. It must be more than all that was gained from the ransom of Atauhuallpa and the sack of Cuzco combined. This book may one day reveal that gold's hiding place. I would ask that you keep it safe.

They are coming for me now, the men who will paddle me up the river and drop me in Spanish territory. I must finish this quickly so I can wrap it all in leather to keep it dry. Haylli began his story by asking that I write 'Ñaupa Pacha' so that a part of his father would be remembered. I feel now that the Tocoyricoc is dead, this work of ours seems incomplete without a similar tribute to its author.

I have thought and prayed on what epithet would best suit this old man, who I have come to admire and respect despite his heathen ways. It should be something he would have wanted for himself, something that summed up his life and his beliefs. I cast about for a long time before I reread his last entry on the last page. It suits him well, and I can do no better, so I leave it as his final tribute:

He was an Inca.

Some years ago I read an article about the *Historia et Rudimenta Linguae Piruanorum,* a manuscript written around the time of Shakespeare that was discovered in Naples, Italy, in 1996. While a great deal of academic debate swirls around it to this day, the book talked in simple terms about an ancient Peruvian system of phonetic record keeping in knotted string. I was amazed at the thought of an unknown alphabet giving voice to the Inca, and I was stunned that we were only finding this tome after it had sat on a shelf in Italy for four hundred years. What else might be collecting dust in an abbey or monastery somewhere? That daydream led to this book.

If you go to the library to learn more about the Inca, the first book you read will disagree with my story in many respects. The next one will contradict me in others. The third will say I am wrong in still different ways. The Inca are not an easy task for historical fiction because there is too little corroborated fact about their past. I have done my best to reconcile the conflicting accounts, and while I cannot say everything in this book is true, I will say there is always at least one version of events to back up my story.

Why do we know so little about the Inca, despite all they accomplished? I sometimes sit back in awe that we know as much as we do. To begin with, we never heard their story in their own words, as I have tried to do.

To make matters worse, none of Pizarro or Almagro's conquistadores left us their memoirs either: Many of them died in the upheaval of the following decades, and most were illiterate to begin with. All we know about the Inca has been passed down to us by Spaniards who arrived years after the events of this book, and their accounts diverge on many key points; after all, they were based on interviews conducted among old men with an incomplete worldview who were low-ranking participants from both sides of civil wars under the Inca.

Let's step back and imagine if a quarter of the United States had died in the 1870s of a plague, and the country was then conquered by illiterate Chinese adventurers who either killed or drove off anyone in a position of authority before their arrival. If a few curious

Chinese citizens a decade later interviewed veterans from both sides of the Civil War, along with former slaves and Native Americans, and then wrote their findings down through the filter of their own cultural biases, just how good a picture of American history would we have today?

If that is not twisted enough, consider that the Inca Emperor Atauhuallpa was in the process of rewriting history after his victory in the War Between the Brothers. His version of events —not universally accepted at the time of his execution by the Spaniards— would be the equivalent of Confederate President Jefferson Davis denying both Abraham Lincoln and Thomas Jefferson ever existed. From this tangled mess of conflicting stories I drew my plot.

So how much of Pachacuti is true? As much as is possible, I assure you. From my glossary you can see how many characters are based on real people. Some of them we know a great deal about: Huayna Capac was devoted to his mother, whom everyone else seemed to dislike; Capac Huari was widely believed to be the love child of Viceroy Hualpaya and Chiqui Ocllo, despite her marriage to the Emperor who treated the boy as his own. Huascar really was as mad as Caligula, and Atauhuallpa really was a vainglorious military incompetent.

For others, like Topa Cusi Yupanki or Ninan Cuyuchi, all we know about them is the highest titles they held and how they died. Their ranks and fates in my book are accurate, and I was left to my own devices to get them there in the end.

Sometimes there were simple choices to be made in that process; for instance, Kiskis is often spelled Quisquis or Quizquiz by the Spaniards. Other times I had to make a judgment call: Some Spanish chronicles refer to a General Michi and some to a Viceroy Achachi. I have also found mention of a high-ranking Achachi Michi who had no title. I think it likely that these were all the same man, and for the sake of my novel it was much better to have one character than three, and so you will find Achachi Michi throughout Pachacuti, chewing coca to relieve the pain in his back.

Wherever I have invented outright, I always tried to do so in a plausible way; the Vixen is a good example. There is no Atoc China in any of the Spanish chroniclers' accounts, but they do have a great deal to say about panacas. I do not doubt many of the female panaca leaders were beautiful and ambitious and brilliant and ruthless to rise to such prominence, and so we have the Vixen. She is fiction, but she cannot be far from the unrecorded fact.

The tocoyricocs are a little closer to a confirmed reality, although some Spanish chronicles merge their position with that of provincial governors. It makes sense to me that the peasants being interviewed by their new Spanish masters had little reason to labour the point that they used to endure auditors overlooking their activities, and so I was comfortable with the muddled details: It's only to be expected. Tupac Capac and Cayo Topa were real men of august rank, but they were not governors or viceroys or generals, thus I have made them tocoyricocs; they may very well have been.

Haylli Yupanki does not appear in any record, but I'm sure a man or men very much like him lived and did the deeds I have written for him. Someone pushed Huayna Capac out of a window during a palace coup. Someone persuaded Mama Ocllo's Voice to make Achachi Michi turn his army around. Someone hid all those treasures deep in the Amazon jungle while Rumiñaui distracted the Spaniards. I would even argue someone cleared Tupac Capac's name after his execution, because the information about his crime is so feeble as to suggest that the matter was quietly forgotten from official Inca history and only remembered at all by the old men being interviewed because of the incredible upset it must have caused at the time.

The great high wire act of historical fiction is deciding where the history stops and the fiction begins. I knew I wanted to write about the decline and fall of the Inca from their own perspective, and that means even some of the history I have used may well be fiction. So be it. The great events of the civilization are in this book as they have been handed down to us, so this book is as true as anyone can make it.

As for those great events? If I've left you with the impression that Pizarro and the rest of the Spaniards were the beneficiaries of magnificent timing, I'm glad. To extend my fiction into the real world for a moment, I doubt very much that Spanish would be spoken in Ecuador, Peru, Bolivia or Chile today if the conquistadores had struck inland a few years earlier or later than they did. Old Huayna Capac or an Atauhuallpa firmer on his usno would have controlled the full might of Tahuantinsuyu, and today the Intip Churi would probably be a world power in their own right.

Instead the Children of the Sun are gone, and a part of me is sad to see that so.

This is my first novel, but it won't be my last. It won't even be my last about the Inca. I foresee several other books to explore this incredible civilization: Its rise, its fall, and its legacy. You haven't seen the last of Haylli and his family, not while I still have time and paper.

GLOSSARY OF NAMES

(Asterisks denote characters based on recorded historical figures.)

Members of the Inca Imperial Family:

Atauhuallpa* A prince, the eldest bastard of Huayna Capac. His childhood name was Tito.

Cari Ocllo* One of Topa Cusi Yupanki's many wives; one of the infamous Ocllo sisters.

Chiqui Ocllo* Another of Topa Cusi Yupanki's many wives; one of the infamous Ocllo sisters. She is rumoured to be Viceroy Hualpaya's lover.

Huascar* A prince, the eldest son of Huayna Capac and Rahua Ocllo prior to her becoming Coya. Often called the Hummingbird.

Huayna Capac* An emperor, son of Topa Inca Yupanki and father to more than fifty princes. Before his coronation his name was Titu Cusi Huallpa.

Illescas* A prince, one of Huayna Capac's younger sons.

Inca Roca* A long-dead emperor whose palace became the House of Learning.

Manco Capac* The first emperor, founder of the Imperial line.

Manco Inca* A prince, one of Huayna Capac's youngest sons.

Mama Ocllo* Topa Cusi Yupanki's Coya (empress); Huayna Capac's mother, and one of the infamous Ocllo sisters.

Ninan Cuyuchi* A prince, eldest son and heir to Huayna Capac. His childhood name was Ninan.

Pachacuti* An emperor, father of Topa Inca Yupanki.

Palla Coca* One of Huayna Capac's wives, Chalcuchima's sister, and Atauhuallpa's mother.

Paullu Inca* A prince, one of Huayna Capac's youngest sons.

Rahua Ocllo* Huayna Capac's Coya after the death of Ninan Cuyuchi's mother. Mother of Huascar and Manco Inca.

Quilaco* A prince, son of Huayna Capac.

Topa Inca Yupanki* An emperor, son of Pachacuti, father of Huayna Capac among many others, often called Old Topa.

Toparca* A prince, one of Huayna Capac's youngest sons.

Urcos* An emperor for a short time before he was deposed by Pachacuti in a coup during the Chanca War.

Viracocha Inca* An emperor, father of Urcos, Pachacuti, and Tillca Yupanki.

Affiliated with Tupac Capac's Clan:

Cayo Topa* Haylli's apprentice, childhood name Cayo.

Haylli Yupanki The narrator, childhood name Waccha.

Huaman Paullu Tupac Capac's secretary.

Pariwana Cumpi Haylli's daughter, childhood name Pariwana.

Ronpa Haylli's half-brother.

Tillca Yupanki* Haylli's grandfather, a general executed by Pachacuti.

Tupac Capac* Haylli's father, Tocoyricoc of Condesuyu.

Yahuar Huacac Haylli's son. Name means Blood Weeper, the name of his great-great grandfather, a long-dead emperor. His childhood name was Anka.

Affiliated with Illyapa's Clan:

Capac Yupanki* Eldest brother of Illyapa and Hualpaya, a general executed by Topa Inca Yupanki.

Capac Huari* Treated as a prince of Topa Inca Yupanki; actually Hualpaya's son by Chiqui Ocllo.

Chalcuchima* Son of Capac Yupanki, childhood name Mallku.

Hualpaya* Viceroy of Andesuyu, brother of Capac Yupanki and Illyapa, secret father of Capac Huari.

Illyapa Viceroy of Collasuyu, brother of Capac Yupanki and Hualpaya.

Other Inca:

Achachi Michi* Viceroy of Chincaysuyu, a famous general.

Atoc China A chosen woman of Inca-by-privilege status, usually called the Vixen.

Colla Topa* Major-domo of the Socso Panaca, Rumiñaui's father.

Huaypalcon* A soldier, son of Kiskis. Childhood name Llakato.

Huamachuco* A much-respected oracular priest in Chincaysuyu.

Kiskis* A general, childhood name Chusek.

Mayta* Viceroy of Condesuyu.

Rumiñaui* General, childhood name Allallanka.

Tiso Yuncailo A bureaucrat.

Topa Cusi Yupanki* A priest and augur, often called Bird Man.

Non-Inca:

Antalongo* Mapuche chieftain, father of Koonek.

Chiaquitinta* Governor of Tumipampa, famous for living to an extreme old age.

Kiske Sisa A chosen woman of the Lupaca tribe.

Koonek A Mapuche maiden, daughter of Antalongo.

Mama Ocllo's Voice* A chosen woman of the Cañari, made an oracular priestess to a cult dedicated to Mama Ocllo.

Mamani A Lupaca lord.

Minchan-caman* Grand Chimu of the destroyed Kingdom of Chimor.

Pilla-huaso* Sinchi of the destroyed Kingdom of Quitu.

Puma A chaski mitmak from Caxamalca stationed on the Maule River.

Tumbala* Ruler of the Puná tribe.

Vilauma* High Priest after the Spanish arrival, probably not an Intip Churi; his name means Blood Drinker in the language of the Colla.

Spaniards:

Alonso de Molina* A Spaniard left behind in Tumpez by Pizarro's first expedition.

Diego de Almagro* Leader of a Spanish faction.

Hernando de Soto* Leader of Pizarro's horsemen.

Felipillo* Interpreter taken by the Spaniards upon their first expedition to Tahuantinsuyu, renamed 'Little Phillip.'

Francisco Pizarro* Leader of the Conquistadores.

GLOSSARY OF TERMS AND PLACES

Akha Maize beer.

Amauracancha Serpent Enclosure, the palace of the Socso Panaca.

Andesuyu The eastern jungle quarter of Tahuantinsuyu.

Angasmayu Blue River, the northern border of Tahuantinsuyu.

Apurimac River Speaking Lord River running through a deep canyon near Cuzco.

As! It must be so! An exclamation of despair and surrender in the face of the inevitable.

Atacama The driest desert in the world and the tribe that inhabits it.

Aucca A dire word for traitor. To call a man such means either your life or his is forfeit.

Ayamalca Raimi A winter month of storms falling between November and December.

Cañari A tribe of Chincaysuyu who served their labour tax exclusively as soldiers.

Cancha House, compound, enclosure.

Cantut A flower.

Capac Ñan The Royal Road, the Imperial highway system.

Capac Panaca The cult dedicated to the mummy of Topa Inca Yupanki.

Capac Quipucamayoc Royal Quipu Master, a literate individual.

Carangui A populous tribe of the Kingdom of Quitu famous for their martial spirit.

Caxamalca A highland city.

Cayambi The dominant tribe of the Kingdom of Quitu.

Chacapoya The Cloud People, a tribe inhabiting the eastern slopes of the eastern range of the Andes famous for the rebellious behaviour, martial prowess, and beautiful women.

Chanca A feared tribe that once almost subjugated the Inca.

Chan Chan The opulent former capital city of the Kingdom of Chimor.

Chaski A postal courier.

Chibcha The language of the Kingdom of Quitu.

Chimu The dominant tribe of the Kingdom of Chimor.

Chincaysuyu The northern quarter of Tahuantinsuyu.

Chonta A hardwood used to make weapons and armour.

Chuncacamayoc Master of ten taxpaying families.

Chuno Dehydrated potato, a staple.

Colla A populous tribe of the Puna.

Collao The vast stretch of the Puna with Lake Titicaca --known in antiquity as Lake Chucuito-- as its drainage basin.

Collasuyu The southern quarter of Tahuantinsuyu.

Condesuyu The western quarter of Tahuantinsuyu.

Coricancha The Golden Enclosure, home of Cuzco's pantheon.

Coya Empress.

Cumpi High quality vicuna cloth, forbidden to commoners.

Curaca Headman.

Curiquinque A rare bird whose feathers decorate the Sapa Inca's Red Fringe.

Cusi Joy.

Cuzco The capital of Tahuantinsuyu.

Great Chimu The ruler of the Kingdom of Chimor.

Hacha hacha The Amazon jungle.

Hiwaya The dropping of a large stone onto a prone figure from a set height as a means of corporal punishment under Inca law. Often fatal.

House of Chosen Women A convent of girls and women removed from their families. Brides of Inti shall remain chaste for life, dedicated to the worship of Inti. Virgins of the Sun are women whose future is still to be determined but many will be married off to Imperial favourites. Both categories are considered Chosen Women.

Huaca Anything felt to be holy.

Huacaypata The main plaza of Cuzco.

Huanacauri The Inca war idol, a boulder believed to be a petrified brother of Manco Capac.

Huanca A highland tribe.

Hunocamayoc Master of ten thousand taxpaying families.

Huarango An unworkable coastal tree.

Huarangacamayoc Master of one thousand taxpaying families.

Huarco A coastal tribe famous for their long besiegement by the Inca.

Huatanay The river that flows through Cuzco.

Ichu A hardy Puna grass.

Illapa The thunder god.

Incap Ranti He Who Stands in for the Inca, a title of nebulous but vast authority.

Inti The sun god, the Inca's patron deity.

Intip Churi Children of the Sun, pure-blooded Inca.

Intip Raimi Festival of the Sun, celebrated at the summer solstice.

Intihuasi The fortress on Sacsahuaman Hill overlooking Cuzco.

Itu A ceremony in which the Inca humiliate themselves to beg Viracocha's pardon and restore his blessings.

Jivaro A headhunting tribe in the jungle east of Quitu.

Kallawaya A tribe of medicine men renowned as linguists.

Kalparicoc A diviner from the lungs of sacrificed animals.

Kingdom of Chimor A fabulously rich coastal kingdom.

Kingdom of Quitu A prosperous confederation of northern tribes.

Kon-Tiki The Collao's creator god, interchangeable with Viracocha.

Lake Chucuito Lake Titicaca.

Lupaca A tribe that lives south of Lake Titicaca.

Macchu Picchu Grandfather Mountain, the white granite bluff overlooking an Inca city whose name is uncertain.

Mamacocha Goddess of the sea.

Mama Quilla Goddess of the moon, Inti's celestial wife.

Mana Apuyoc Men without a leader, barbarians.

Mapuche A partially conquered tribe living on either side of the Maule River.

Maule River The southern border of Tahuantinsuyu.

Mitmak A colonist relocated by the Inca.

Mochica The language of the Chimu and the Cañari.

Molle A fruit-bearing tree.

Mullu A red and white seashell, valuable as a trade good.

Ñaupa Pacha Once upon a time.

Ollantaytampu A fortress in the Yucay Valley.

Pachacamac The Yunga's creator god, interchangeable with Kon-Tiki and Viracocha. A powerful idol and oracle of Pachacamac was located in the Rimac Valley.

Pahuac Oncoy The swift-running sickness, a plague.

Pasto A poor and savage tribe of the Kingdom of Quitu, famous for paying their taxes in fleas and lice plucked from their own bodies.

Picchu A hill overlooking Cuzco.

Pacaritampu The Inn of First Appearances where Manco Capac is said to have set out after the Great Flood to create Tahuantinsuyu.

Pachacamayoc Master of one hundred taxpaying families.

Pacha Time, earth, and universe, depending on the context.

Pachacuti Many meanings and difficult to translate, most often 'End of an Era' or 'Earthquake.'

Pacuyok Ear Plug Man, an Inca.

Panaca A cult dedicated to the mummy of a former emperor.

Puco puco A morning songbird.

Puna The treeless prairie between the eastern and western ranges of the Andes.

Puná An island tribe, famous for their slavery and piracy.

Punchao God of the day, embodied by a golden disc idol.

Puric A commoner.

Puquin A hill overlooking Cuzco.

Red Fringe The Inca equivalent of a crown, made up of tassels of red yarn descending from a headband to cover the forehead.

Rimac Speaker, the name of an important coastal valley.

Quipu An instrument of record keeping based on knotted string. Most quipus dealt with numbers. Royal quipus were phonetically based.

Quitu The former capital of the Kingdom of Quitu.

Quipucamayoc Quipu Master, an accountant, a bureaucrat.

Rucana A highland tribe who paid their labour tax by carrying Inca officials in litters. Usually dressed in blue livery, they were often called the Feet of the Inca.

Runa Tinya A drum made out of a stuffed corpse.

Sacsahuaman Speckled Hawk Hill overlooking Cuzco. The fortress of Intihuasi sits upon it.

Sankihuasi Commonly called the Pit, an underground prison filled with flint-lined walls and wild animals.

Sapa Inca The Only Inca, Son of the Sun, the Emperor.

Saramama Goddess of the harvest.

Scyri The ruler of the Kingdom of Quitu.

Sinchi Warlord.

Socso Panaca The cult dedicated to the mummy of Viracocha Inca.

Supay Tahuantinsuyu's equivalent of the devil.

Tahuantinsuyu The Land of the Four Quarters. The Inca Empire.

Tampu A storehouse and inn.

Tampucamayoc The curaca of a tampu.

Tarawari A major tampu on the Chincaysuyu Road near Cuzco.

Tchili The mountainous region of Tahuantinsuyu south of the Collao.

Tiahuanaco The ruins of an ancient holy city on the shore of Lake Titicaca.

Tocoyricoc He Who Sees All, an Imperial auditor, the highest rank of bureaucrat.

Topo A unit of measurement: For distance it was roughly a Spanish league, but it was based on how long it took to walk, so topos become shorter over rough terrain; for area it was based on how much land a man could work on his own.

Totora Bouyant lake reeds.

Tumipampa The capital city of the Cañari, much beautified by the Inca.

Tumpez A major coastal city between the kingdoms of Chimor and Quitu, very close to the Island of Puná.

Urca Huari God of underground treasures.

Uru Worms. A poor tribe of lake fisher-people.

Urupampa River The river that runs through the Yucay Valley, past Macchu Picchu, and deep into the rainforest.

Usno The stand upon which the Emperor puts his low stool. It can be equated to the word throne.

Viñapu An illegal and potent liquor.

Viracocha The Inca's creator god and ruler of the pantheon. The depth of their devotion to him was not made public to purics.

Wawa Baby. The name of all highland children until the risk of infant mortality has passed.

Xaquixahuana A plain just beyond the Huatanay Valley, site of the famous victory of Pachacuti over the Chanca.

Xauxa A highland city.

Yachapa He Has Taught. An honorific added to the name of anyone who has served as an instructor at the House of Learning.

Yahuarcocha Lake of Blood.

Yanacona Servants, commoners who are not tied to the land and do not pay a set labour tax, roughly equivalent to the status of a Roman house slave.

Yellow Fringe The Imperial heir's equivalent to the Red Fringe.

Yucay Valley A beautiful valley with a pleasant climate a day's journey from Cuzco, home of many summer palaces and the Ollantaytampu fortress.

Yunga Hot Lands. A generic term for people living in the coastal river valleys.

ABOUT THE AUTHOR

Geoff Micks is the author of five novels:
Inca, Zulu, Beginning, Middle, and End.

The New York Times and National Public Radio have interviewed
him about his writing, and he wrote an animated short for Vice Media
that appeared on HBO.

For most of his career he has researched, organized, and run
industry conferences on a wide range of topics throughout
North America and Europe. Prior to that he worked for a number
of community newspapers over the course of four years. He has a
BA Honours with High Distinction from the University of Toronto
and a Diploma in Journalism from Centennial College.

He lives in Toronto, Ontario, Canada.

His Twitter account is @faceintheblue.
His blog is faceintheblue.wordpress.com.
His Facebook page is www.facebook.com/geoffmicksnovels.